TRIPLE ZECK

TRIPLE
ZECK

A Nero Wolfe Omnibus

REX STOUT

The Viking Press/New York

CONTENTS

And Be a Villain   1

The Second Confession   161

In the Best Families   331

and be a villain

Meet it is I set it down,

That one may smile, and smile, and be a villain. . . .

—HAMLET, ACT I

1

For the third time I went over the final additions and subtractions on the first page of Form 1040, to make good and sure. Then I swiveled my chair to face Nero Wolfe, who was seated behind his desk to the right of mine reading a book of poems by a guy named Van Doren, Mark Van Doren. So I thought I might as well use a poetry word.

"It's bleak," I said.

There was no sign that he heard.

"Bleak," I repeated. "If it means what I think it does. Bleak!"

His eyes didn't lift from the page, but he murmured, "What's bleak?"

"Figures." I leaned to slide the Form 1040 across the waxed grain of his desk. "This is March thirteenth. Four thousand three hundred and twelve dollars and sixty-eight cents, in addition to the four quarterly installments already paid. Then we have to send in 1040-ES for 1948, and a check for ten thousand bucks goes with it." I clasped my fingers at the back of my head and asked grimly, "Bleak or not?"

He asked what the bank balance was and I told him. "Of course," I conceded, "that will take care of the two wallops from our rich uncle just mentioned, also a loaf of bread and a sliver of shad roe, but weeks pass and bills arrive, not to be so crude as to speak of paying Fritz and Theodore and me."

Wolfe had put down the poetry and was scowling at the Form 1040, pretending he could add. I raised my voice:

"But you own this house and furniture, except the chair and other items in my room which I bought myself, and you're the boss and you know best. Sure. That electric company bird would have been good for at least a grand over and above expenses on his

forgery problem, but you couldn't be bothered. Mrs. What's-her-
name would have paid twice that, plenty, for the lowdown on that
so-called musician, but you were too busy reading. That lawyer by
the name of Clifford was in a bad hole and had to buy help, but he
had dandruff. That actress and her gentleman protector—"

"Archie. Shut up."

"Yes, sir. Also what do you do? You come down from your beautiful orchids day before yesterday and breeze in here and tell me
merrily to draw another man-size check for that World Government outfit. When I meekly mention that the science of bookkeep-
ing has two main branches, first addition and second subtraction—"

"Leave the room!"

I snarled in his direction, swiveled back to my desk position, got
the typewriter in place, inserted paper with carbon, and started to
tap out, from my work sheet, Schedule G for line 6 of Schedule C.
Time passed and I went on with the job, now and then darting a
glance to the right to see if he had had the brass to resume on the
book. He hadn't. He was leaning back in his chair, which was big
enough for two but not two of him, motionless, with his eyes closed.
The tempest was raging. I had a private grin and went on with my
work. Somewhat later, when I was finishing Schedule F for line 16
of Schedule C, a growl came from him:

"Archie."

"Yes, sir." I swiveled.

"A man condemning the income tax because of the annoyance
it gives him or the expense it puts him to is merely a dog baring its
teeth, and he forfeits the privileges of civilized discourse. But it is
permissible to criticize it on other and impersonal grounds. A
government, like an individual, spends money for any or all of three
reasons: because it needs to, because it wants to, or simply because
it has it to spend. The last is much the shabbiest. It is arguable, if not
manifest, that a substantial proportion of this great spring flood of
billions pouring into the Treasury will in effect get spent for that last
shabby reason."

"Yeah. So we deduct something? How do I word it?"

Wolfe half opened his eyes. "You are sure of your figures?"

"Only too sure."

"Did you cheat much?"

"Average. Nothing indecent."

"I have to pay the amounts you named?"

"Either that or forfeit some privileges."

"Very well." Wolfe sighed clear down, sat a minute, and straightened in his chair. "Confound it. There was a time when a thousand dinars a year was ample for me. Get Mr. Richards of the Federal Broadcasting Company."

I frowned at him, trying to guess; then, because I knew he was using up a lot of energy sitting up straight, I gave up, found the number in the book, dialed, and, by using Wolfe's name, got through to Richards three minutes under par for a vice-president. Wolfe took his phone, exchanged greetings, and went on:

"In my office two years ago, Mr. Richards, when you handed me a check, you said that you felt you were still in my debt—in spite of the size of the check. So I'm presuming to ask a favor of you. I want some confidential information. What amount of money is involved, weekly let us say, in the radio program of Miss Madeline Fraser?"

"Oh." There was a pause. Richards's voice had been friendly and even warm. Now it backed off a little: "How did you get connected with that?"

"I'm not connected with it, not in any way. But I would appreciate the information—confidentially. Is it too much for me?"

"It's an extremely unfortunate situation, for Miss Fraser, for the network, for the sponsors—everyone concerned. You wouldn't care to tell me why you're interested?"

"I'd rather not." Wolfe was brusque. "I'm sorry I bothered you—"

"You're not bothering me, or if you are you're welcome. The information you want isn't published, but everyone in radio knows it. Everyone in radio knows everything. Exactly what do you want?"

"The total sum involved."

"Well . . . let's see . . . counting air time, it's on nearly two hundred stations . . . production, talent, scripts, everything . . . roughly, thirty thousand dollars a week."

"Nonsense," Wolfe said curtly.

"Why nonsense?"

"It's monstrous. That's over a million and a half a year."

"No, around a million and a quarter, on account of the summer vacation."

"Even so. I suppose Miss Fraser gets a material segment of it?"

"Quite material. Everyone knows that too. Her take is around five thousand a week, but the way she splits it with her manager, Miss Koppel, is one thing everyone doesn't know—at least I don't."

Richards's voice had warmed up again. "You know, Mr. Wolfe, if you felt like doing me a little favor right back you could tell me confidentially what you want with this."

But all he got from Wolfe was thanks, and he was gentleman enough to take them without insisting on the return favor. After Wolfe had pushed the phone away he remarked to me:

"Good heavens. Twelve hundred thousand dollars!"

I, feeling better because it was obvious what he was up to, grinned at him. "Yes, sir. You would go over big on the air. You could read poetry. By the way, if you want to hear her earn her segment, she's on every Tuesday and Friday morning from eleven to twelve. You'd get pointers. Was that your idea?"

"No." He was gruff. "My idea is to land a job I know how to do. Take your notebook. These instructions will be a little complicated on account of the contingencies to be provided for."

I got my notebook from a drawer.

2

After three tries that Saturday at the listed Manhattan number of Madeline Fraser, with don't answer as the only result, I finally resorted to Lon Cohen of the *Gazette* and he dug it out for me that both Miss Fraser and her manager, Miss Deborah Koppel, were week-ending up in Connecticut.

As a citizen in good standing—anyway pretty good—my tendency was to wish the New York Police Department good luck in its contacts with crime, but I frankly hoped that Inspector Cramer and his homicide scientists wouldn't get Scotch tape on the Orchard case before we had a chance to inspect the contents. Judging from the newspaper accounts I had read, it didn't seem likely that Cramer was getting set to toot a trumpet, but you can never tell how much is being held back, so I was all for driving to Connecticut and horning in on the week end, but Wolfe vetoed it and told me to wait until Monday.

By noon Sunday he had finished the book of poems and was drawing pictures of horses on sheets from his memo pad, testing a theory he had run across somewhere that you can analyze a man's character from the way he draws a horse. I had completed Forms

1040 and 1040-ES and, with checks enclosed, they had been mailed. After lunch I hung around the kitchen a while, listening to Wolfe and Fritz Brenner, the chef and household jewel, arguing whether horse mackerel is as good as Mediterranean tunny fish for *vitello tonnato*— which, as prepared by Fritz, is the finest thing on earth to do with tender young veal. When the argument began to bore me because there was no Mediterranean tunny fish to be had anyhow, I went up to the top floor, to the plant rooms that had been built on the roof, and spent a couple hours with Theodore Horstmann on the germination records. Then, remembering that on account of a date with a lady I wouldn't have the evening for it, I went down three flights to the office, took the newspapers for five days to my desk, and read everything they had on the Orchard case.

When I had finished I wasn't a bit worried that Monday morning's paper would confront me with a headline that the cops had wrapped it up.

3

The best I was able to get on the phone was an appointment for 3:00 P.M., so at that hour Monday afternoon I entered the lobby of an apartment house in the upper Seventies between Madison and Park. It was the palace type, with rugs bought by the acre, but with the effect somewhat spoiled, as it so often is, by a rubber runner on the main traffic lane merely because the sidewalk was wet with rain. That's no way to run a palace. If a rug gets a damp dirty footprint, what the hell, toss it out and roll out another one, that's the palace spirit.

I told the distinguished-looking hallman that my name was Archie Goodwin and I was bound for Miss Fraser's apartment. He got a slip of paper from his pocket, consulted it, nodded, and inquired:

"And? Anything else?"

I stretched my neck to bring my mouth within a foot of his ear, and whispered to him:

"Oatmeal."

He nodded again, signaled with his hand to the elevator man, who was standing outside the door of his car fifteen paces away, and said in a cultivated voice, "Ten B."

"Tell me," I requested, "about this password gag, is it just since the murder trouble or has it always been so?"

He gave me an icy look and turned his back. I told the back: "That costs you a nickel. I fully intended to give you a nickel."

With the elevator man I decided not to speak at all. He agreed. Out at the tenth floor, I found myself in a box no bigger than the elevator, another palace trick, with a door to the left marked 10A and one to the right marked 10B. The elevator man stayed there until I had pushed the button on the latter, and the door had opened and I had entered.

The woman who had let me in, who might easily have been a female wrestling champion twenty years back, said, "Excuse me, I'm in a hurry," and beat it on a trot. I called after her, "My name's Goodwin!" but got no reaction.

I advanced four steps, took off my hat and coat and dropped them on a chair, and made a survey. I was in a big square sort of a hall, with doors off to the left and in the wall ahead. To the right, instead of a wall and doors, it just spread out into an enormous living room which contained at least twenty different kinds of furniture. My eye was professionally trained to take in anything from a complicated street scene to a speck on a man's collar, and really get it, but for the job of accurately describing that room I would have charged double. Two of the outstanding items were a chrome-and-red-leather bar with stools to match and a massive old black walnut table with carved legs and edges. That should convey the tone of the place.

There was nobody in sight, but I could hear voices. I advanced to pick out a chair to sit on, saw none that I thought much of, and settled on a divan ten feet long and four feet wide, covered with green burlap. A near-by chair had pink embroidered silk. I was trying to decide what kind of a horse the person who furnished that room would draw, when company entered the square hall sector from one of the doors in the far wall—two men, one young and handsome, the other middle-aged and bald, both loaded down with photographic equipment, including a tripod.

"She's showing her age," the young man said.

"Age hell," the bald man retorted, "she's had a murder, hasn't she? Have you ever had a murder?" He caught sight of me and asked his companion, "Who's that?"

"I don't know, never saw him before." The young man was trying to open the entrance door without dropping anything. He succeeded, and they passed through, and the door closed behind them.

In a minute another of the doors in the square hall opened and the female wrestler appeared. She came in my direction, but, reaching me, trotted on by, made for a door near a corner off to the left, opened it, and was gone.

I was beginning to feel neglected.

Ten minutes more and I decided to take the offensive. I was on my feet and had taken a couple of steps when there was another entrance, again from an inside door at the far side of the square hall, and I halted. The newcomer headed for me, not at a jerky trot but with a smooth easy flow, saying as she approached:

"Mr. Goodwin?"

I admitted it.

"I'm Deborah Koppel." She offered a hand. "We never really catch up with ourselves around here."

She had already given me two surprises. At first glance I had thought her eyes were small and insignificant, but when she faced me and talked I saw they were quite large, very dark, and certainly shrewd. Also, because she was short and fat, I had expected the hand I took to be pudgy and moist, but it was firm and strong though small. Her complexion was dark and her dress was black. Everything about her was either black or dark, except the gray, almost white by comparison, showing in her night-black hair.

"You told Miss Fraser on the phone," she was saying in her high thin voice, "that you have a suggestion for her from Mr. Nero Wolfe."

"That's right."

"She's very busy. Of course she always is. I'm her manager. Would you care to tell me about it?"

"I'd tell you anything," I declared. "But I work for Mr. Wolfe. His instructions are to tell Miss Fraser, but now, having met you, I'd like to tell her *and* you."

She smiled. The smile was friendly, but it made her eyes look even shrewder. "Very good ad libbing," she said approvingly. "I wouldn't want you to disobey your instructions. Will it take long?"

"That depends. Somewhere between five minutes and five hours."

"By no means five hours. Please be as brief as you can. Come this way."

She turned and started for the square hall and I followed. We went through a door, crossed a room that had a piano, a bed, and an electric refrigerator in it, which left it anybody's guess how to name it, and on through another door into a corner room big enough to have six windows, three on one side and three on another. Every object in it, and it was anything but empty, was either pale yellow or pale blue. The wood, both the trim and the furniture, was painted blue, but other things—rugs, upholstery, curtains, bed coverlet—were divided indiscriminately between the two colors. Among the few exceptions were the bindings of the books on the shelves and the clothes of the blond young man who was seated on a chair. The woman lying on the bed kept to the scheme, with her lemon-colored house gown and her light blue slippers.

The blond young man rose and came to meet us, changing expression on the way. My first glimpse of his face had shown me a gloomy frown, but now his eyes beamed with welcome and his mouth was arranged into a smile that would have done a brush salesman proud. I suppose he did it from force of habit, but it was uncalled for because I was the one who was going to sell something.

"Mr. Goodwin," Deborah Koppel said. "Mr. Meadows."

"Bill Meadows. Just make it Bill, everyone does." His handshake was out of stock but he had the muscle for it. "So you're Archie Goodwin? This is a real pleasure! The next best thing to meeting the great Nero Wolfe himself!"

A rich contralto voice broke in:

"This is my rest period, Mr. Goodwin, and they won't let me get up. I'm not even supposed to talk, but when the time comes that I don't talk—!"

I stepped across to the bed, and as I took the hand Madeline Fraser offered she smiled. It wasn't a shrewd smile like Deborah Koppel's or a synthetic one like Bill Meadows's, but just a smile from her to me. Her gray-green eyes didn't give the impression that she was measuring me, though she probably was, and I sure was measuring her. She was slender but not skinny and she looked quite long, stretched out on the bed. With no makeup on it at all it was quite possible to look at her face without having to resist an impulse to look somewhere else, which was darned good for a woman certainly close to forty and probably a little past it, especially since I personally can see no point in spending eyesight on females over thirty.

"You know," she said, "I have often been tempted—bring chairs up, Bill—to ask Nero Wolfe to be a guest on my program."

She said it like a trained broadcaster, breaking it up so it would sound natural but arranging the inflections so that listeners of any mental age whatever would get it.

"I'm afraid," I told her with a grin, "that he wouldn't accept unless you ran wires to his office and broadcast from there. He never leaves home on business, and rarely for anything at all." I lowered myself onto one of the chairs Bill had brought up, and he and Deborah Koppel took the other two.

Madeline Fraser nodded. "Yes, I know." She had turned on her side to see me without twisting her neck, and the hip curving up under the thin yellow gown made her seem not quite so slender. "Is that just a publicity trick or does he really like it?"

"I guess both. He's very lazy, and he's scared to death of moving objects, especially things on wheels."

"Wonderful! Tell me all about him."

"Some other time, Lina," Deborah Koppel put in. "Mr. Goodwin has a suggestion for you, and you have a broadcast tomorrow and haven't even looked at the script."

"My God, is it Monday already?"

"Monday and half past three," Deborah said patiently.

The radio prima donna's torso popped up to perpendicular as if someone had given her a violent jerk. "What's the suggestion?" she demanded, and flopped back again.

"What made him think of it," I said, "was something that happened to him Saturday. This great nation took him for a ride. Two rides. The Rides of March."

"Income tax? Me too. But what—"

"That's good!" Bill Meadows exclaimed. "Where did you get it? Has it been on the air?"

"Not that I know of. I created it yesterday morning while I was brushing my teeth."

"We'll give you ten bucks for it—no, wait a minute." He turned to Deborah. "What percentage of our audience ever heard of the Ides of March?"

"One-half of one," she said as if she were quoting a published statistic. "Cut."

"You can have it for a dollar," I offered generously. "Mr. Wolfe's suggestion will cost you a lot more. Like everyone in the upper brackets, he's broke." My eyes were meeting the gray-green gaze of Madeline Fraser. "He suggests that you hire him to investigate the murder of Cyril Orchard."

"Oh, Lord," Bill Meadows protested, and brought his hands up to press the heels of his palms against his eyes. Deborah Koppel looked at him, then at Madeline Fraser, and took in air for a deep sigh. Miss Fraser shook her head, and suddenly looked older and more in need of makeup.

"We have decided," she said, "that the only thing we can do about that is forget it as soon as possible. We have ruled it out of conversation."

"That would be fine and sensible," I conceded, "if you could make everyone, including the cops and the papers, obey the rule. But aside from the difficulty of shutting people up about any old kind of a murder, even a dull one, it was simply too good a show. Maybe you don't realize how good. Your program has an eight million audience, twice a week. Your guests were a horse-race tipster and a professor of mathematics from a big university. And smack in the middle of the program one of them makes terrible noises right into the microphone, and keels over, and pretty soon he's dead, and he got the poison right there on the broadcast, in the product of one of your sponsors."

I darted glances at the other two and then back to the woman on the bed. "I knew I might meet any one of a dozen attitudes here, but I sure didn't expect this one. If you don't know, you ought to, that one like that doesn't get ruled out of conversation, not only not in a week, but not in twenty years—not when the question is still open who provided the poison. Twenty years from now people would still be arguing about who was it, Madeline Fraser or Deborah Koppel or Bill Meadows or Nathan Traub or F. O. Savarese or Elinor Vance or Nancylee Shepherd or Tully Strong—"

The door came open and the female wrestler entered and announced in a hasty breath:

"Mr. Strong is here."

"Send him in, Cora," Miss Fraser told her.

I suppose I would have been struck by the contrast between Tully Strong and his name if I hadn't known what to expect from his pictures in the papers. He looked like them in the obvious points —the rimless spectacles, the thin lips, the long neck, the hair brushed flat—but somehow in the flesh he didn't look as dumb and vacant as the pictures. I got that much noted while he was being greeted, by the time he turned to me for the introduction.

"Mr. Strong," Deborah Koppel told me, "is the secretary of our Sponsors' Council."

"Yes, I know."

"Mr. Goodwin," she told him, "has called with a suggestion from Nero Wolfe. Mr. Wolfe is a private detective."

"Yes, I know." Tully Strong smiled at me. With lips as thin as his it is often difficult to tell whether it's a smile or a grimace, but I would have called it a smile, especially when he added, "We are both famous, aren't we? Of course you are accustomed to the glare of the spotlight, but it is quite new to me." He sat down. "What does Mr. Wolfe suggest?"

"He thinks Miss Fraser ought to hire him to look into the murder of Cyril Orchard."

"Damn Cyril Orchard." Yes, it had been a smile, for now it was a grimace, and it was quite different. "Damn him to hell!"

"That's pretty tough," Bill Meadows objected, "since he may be there right now."

Strong ignored him to ask me, "Aren't the police giving us enough trouble without deliberately hiring someone to give us more?"

"Sure they are," I agreed, "but that's a shortsighted view of it. The person who is really giving you trouble is the one who put the poison in the Hi-Spot. As I was explaining when you came, the trouble will go on for years unless and until he gets tapped on the shoulder. Of course the police may get him, but they've had it for six days now and you know how far they've got. The one that stops the trouble will be the one that puts it where it belongs. Do you know that Mr. Wolfe is smart or shall I go into that?"

"I had hoped," Deborah Koppel put in, "that Mr. Wolfe's suggestion would be something concrete. That he had a . . . an idea."

"Nope." I made it definite. "His only idea is to get paid twenty thousand dollars for ending the trouble."

Bill Meadows let out a whistle. Deborah Koppel smiled at me. Tully Strong protested indignantly:

"Twenty thousand!"

"Not from me," said Madeline Fraser, fully as definite as I had been. "I really must get to work on my broadcast, Mr. Goodwin."

"Now wait a minute." I concentrated on her. "That's only one of my points, getting the trouble over, and not the best one. Look at it this way. You and your program have had a lot of publicity out of this, haven't you?"

She groaned. "Publicity, my God! The man calls it publicity!"

"So it is," I maintained, "but out of the wrong barrel. And it's going to keep coming, still out of the wrong barrel, whether you like it or not. Again tomorrow every paper in town will have your name in a front-page headline. You can't help that, but you can decide what the headline will say. As it stands now you know darned well what it will say. What if, instead of that, it announces that you have engaged Nero Wolfe to investigate the murder of the guest on your program because of your passionate desire to see justice done? The piece would explain the terms of the arrangement: you are to pay the expenses of the investigation—unpadded, we don't pad expenses—and that's all you are to pay unless Mr. Wolfe gets the murderer with evidence to convict. If he comes through you pay him a fee of twenty thousand dollars. Would that get the headline or not? What kind of publicity would it be, still out of the wrong barrel? What percentage of your audience and the general public would it persuade, not only that you and yours are innocent, but that you are a hero to sacrifice a fortune for the sake of justice? Ninety-nine and one-half per cent. Very few of them would stop to consider that both the expenses and the fee will be deductible on your income tax and, in your bracket, the actual cost to you would be around four thousand dollars, no more. In the public mind you would no longer be one of the suspects in a sensational murder case, being hunted—you would be a champion of the people, *hunting* a murderer."

I spread out my hands. "And you would get all that, Miss Fraser, even if Mr. Wolfe had the worst flop of his career and all it cost you was expenses. Nobody could say you hadn't tried. It's a big bargain for you. Mr. Wolfe almost never takes a case on a contingent basis, but when he needs money he breaks rules, especially his own."

Madeline Fraser had closed her eyes. Now she opened them again, and again her smile was just from her to me. "The way you tell it," she said, "it certainly is a bargain. —What do you think, Debby?"

"I think I like it," Miss Koppel said cautiously. "It would have to be discussed with the network and agencies and sponsors."

"Mr. Goodwin."

I turned my head. "Yes, Mr. Strong?"

Tully Strong had removed his spectacles and was blinking at me. "You understand that I am only the secretary of the Council of the sponsors of Miss Fraser's program, and I have no real authority. But I know how they feel about this, two of them in particular, and of course it is my duty to report this conversation to them without delay, and I can tell you off the record that it is extremely probable they would prefer to accept Mr. Wolfe's offer on their own account. For the impression on the public I think they would consider it desirable that Mr. Wolfe should be paid by them—on the terms stated by you. Still off the record, I believe this would apply especially to the makers of Hi-Spot. That's the bottled drink the poison was put into."

"Yeah, I know it is." I looked around at the four faces. "I'm sort of in a hole. I hoped to close a deal with Miss Fraser before I left here, but Miss Koppel says it has to be discussed with others, and now Mr. Strong thinks the sponsors may want to take it over. The trouble is the delay. It's already six days old, and Mr. Wolfe should get to work at once. Tonight if possible, tomorrow at the latest."

"Not to mention," Bill Meadows said, smiling at me, "that he has to get ahead of the cops and keep ahead if he wants to collect. It seems to me— Hello, Elinor!" He left his chair in a hurry. "How about it?"

The girl who had entered without announcement tossed him a nod and a word and came toward the bed with rapid steps. I say girl because, although according to the newspapers Elinor Vance already had under her belt a Smith diploma, a play written and nearly produced, and two years as script writer for the Madeline Fraser program, she looked as if she had at least eight years to go to reach my deadline. As she crossed to us the thought struck me how few there are who still look attractive even when they're obviously way behind on sleep and played out to the point where they're about ready to drop.

"I'm sorry to be so late, Lina," she said all in a breath, "but they kept me down there all day, at the District Attorney's office . . . I couldn't make them understand . . . they're terrible, those men are . . ."

She stopped, and her body started to shake all over.

"Goddam it," Bill Meadows said savagely. "I'll get you a drink."

"I'm already getting it, Bill," Tully Strong called from a side of the room.

"Flop here on the bed," Miss Fraser said, getting her feet out of the way.

"It's nearly five o'clock." It was Miss Koppel's quiet determined voice. "We're going to start to work right now or I'll phone and cancel tomorrow's broadcast."

I stood up, facing Madeline Fraser, looking down at her. "What about it? Can this be settled tonight?"

"I don't see how." She was stroking Elinor Vance's shoulder. "With a broadcast to get up, and people to consult . . ."

"Then tomorrow morning?"

Tully Strong, approaching with the drink for Elinor Vance, handed it to her and then spoke to me:

"I'll phone you tomorrow, before noon if possible."

"Good for you," I told him, and beat it.

4

Without at all intending to, I certainly had turned it into a seller's market.

The only development that Monday evening came not from the prospective customers, but from Inspector Cramer of Homicide, in the form of a phone call just before Fritz summoned Wolfe and me to dinner. It was nothing shattering. Cramer merely asked to speak to Wolfe, and asked him:

"Who's paying you on the Orchard case?"

"No one," Wolfe said curtly.

"No? Then Goodwin drives your car up to Seventy-eighth Street just to test the tires?"

"It's my car, Mr. Cramer, and I help to pay for the streets."

It ended in a stalemate, and Wolfe and I moved across the hall to the dining room, to eat fried shrimps and Cape Cod clam cakes. With those items Fritz serves a sour sauce thick with mushrooms which is habit-forming.

Tuesday morning the fun began, with the first phone call arriving before Wolfe got down to the office. Of course that didn't mean sunup, since his morning hours upstairs with Theodore and the orchids are always and forever from nine to eleven. First was Richards of the Federal Broadcasting Company. It is left to my discretion whether to buzz the plant rooms or not, and this seemed to call for it, since Richards had done us a favor the day before. When I got him through to Wolfe it appeared that what he wanted was to introduce another FBC vice-president, a Mr. Beech. What Mr. Beech wanted was to ask why the hell Wolfe hadn't gone straight to the FBC with his suggestion about murder, though he didn't put it that way. He was very affable. The impression I got, listening in as instructed, was that the network had had its tongue hanging out for years, waiting and hoping for an excuse to hand Wolfe a hunk of dough. Wolfe was polite to him but didn't actually apologize.

Second was Tully Strong, the secretary of the Sponsors' Council, and I conversed with him myself. He strongly hoped that we had made no commitment with Miss Fraser or the network or anyone else because, as he had surmised, some of the sponsors were interested and one of them was excited. That one, he told me off the record, was the Hi-Spot Company, which, since the poison had been served to the victim in a bottle of Hi-Spot, The Drink You Dream Of, would fight for its exclusive right to take Wolfe up. I told him I would refer it to Wolfe without prejudice when he came down at eleven o'clock.

Third was Lon Cohen of the *Gazette*, who said talk was going around and would I kindly remember that on Saturday he had moved heaven and earth for me to find out where Madeline Fraser was, and how did it stand right now? I bandied words with him.

Fourth was a man with a smooth low-pitched voice who gave his name as Nathan Traub, which was one of the names that had been made familiar to the public by the newspaper stories. I knew, naturally, that he was an executive of the advertising agency which handled the accounts of three of the Fraser sponsors, since I had read the papers. He seemed to be a little confused as to just what he wanted, but I gathered that the agency felt that it would be immoral for Wolfe to close any deal with anyone concerned without getting an okay from the agency. Having met a few agency men in my travels, I thought it was nice of them not to extend it to cover any deal with anyone about anything. I told him he might hear from us later.

Fifth was Deborah Koppel. She said that Miss Fraser was going on the air in twenty minutes and had been too busy to talk with the people who must be consulted, but that she was favorably inclined toward Wolfe's suggestion and would give us something definite before the day ended.

So by eleven o'clock, when two things happened simultaneously—Wolfe's entering the office and my turning on the radio and tuning it to the FBC station, WPIT—it was unquestionably a seller's market.

Throughout Madeline Fraser's broadcast Wolfe leaned back in his chair behind his desk with his eyes shut. I sat until I got restless and then moved around, with the only interruptions a couple of phone calls. Bill Meadows was of course on with her, as her stooge and feeder, since that was his job, and the guests for the day were an eminent fashion designer and one of the Ten Best-Dressed Women. The guests were eminently lousy and Bill was nothing to write home about, but there was no getting away from it that Fraser was good. Her voice was good, her timing was good, and even when she was talking about White Birch Soap you would almost as soon leave it on as turn it off. I had listened in on her the preceding Friday for the first time, no doubt along with several million others, and again I had to hand it to her for sitting on a very hot spot without a twitch or a wriggle.

It must have been sizzling hot when she got to that place in the program where bottles of Hi-Spot were opened and poured into glasses—drinks for the two guests and Bill Meadows and herself. I don't know who had made the decision the preceding Friday, her first broadcast after Orchard's death, to leave that in, but if she did she had her nerve. Whoever had made the decision, it had been up to her to carry the ball, and she had sailed right through as if no bottle of Hi-Spot had ever been known even to make anyone belch, let alone utter a shrill cry, claw at the air, have convulsions, and die. Today she delivered again. There was no false note, no quiver, no slack or speedup, nothing; and I must admit that Bill handled it well too. The guests were terrible, but that was the style to which they had accustomed us.

When it was over and I had turned the radio off Wolfe muttered: "That's an extremely dangerous woman."

I would have been more impressed if I hadn't known so well his conviction that all women alive are either extremely dangerous or extremely dumb. So I merely said:

"If you mean she's damn clever I agree. She's awful good."

He shook his head. "I mean the purpose she allows her cleverness

to serve. That unspeakable prepared biscuit flour! Fritz and I have
tried it. Those things she calls Sweeties! Pfui! And that salad dressing abomination—we have tried that too, in an emergency. What
they do to stomachs heaven knows, but that woman is ingeniously
and deliberately conspiring in the corruption of millions of palates.
She should be stopped!"

"Okay, stop her. Pin a murder on her. Though I must admit, having seen—"

The phone rang. It was Mr. Beech of FBC, wanting to know if
we had made any promises to Tully Strong or to anyone else connected with any of the sponsors, and if so whom and what? When
he had been attended to I remarked to Wolfe:

"I think it would be a good plan to line up Saul and Orrie and
Fred—"

The phone rang. It was a man who gave his name as Owen, saying he was in charge of public relations for the Hi-Spot Company,
asking if he could come down to West Thirty-fifth Street on the run
for a talk with Nero Wolfe. I stalled him with some difficulty and
hung up. Wolfe observed, removing the cap from a bottle of beer
which Fritz had brought:

"I must first find out what's going on. If it appears that the police
are as stumped as—"

The phone rang. It was Nathan Traub, the agency man, wanting
to know everything.

Up till lunch, and during lunch, and after lunch, the phone rang.
They were having one hell of a time trying to get it decided how
they would split the honor. Wolfe began to get really irritated and
so did I. His afternoon hours upstairs with the plants are from four
to six, and it was just as he was leaving the office, headed for his
elevator in the hall, that word came that a big conference was on
in Beech's office in the FBC building on Forty-sixth Street.

At that, when they once got together apparently they dealt the
cards and played the hands without any more horsing around, for
it was still short of five o'clock when the phone rang once more. I
answered it and heard a voice I had heard before that day:

"Mr. Goodwin? This is Deborah Koppel. It's all arranged."

"Good. How?"

"I'm talking on behalf of Miss Fraser. They thought you should
be told by her, through me, since you first made the suggestion to
her and therefore you would want to know that the arrangement is

satisfactory to her. An FBC lawyer is drafting an agreement to be signed by Mr. Wolfe and the other parties."

"Mr. Wolfe hates to sign anything written by a lawyer. Ten to one he won't sign it. He'll insist on dictating it to me, so you might as well give me the details."

She objected. "Then someone else may refuse to sign it."

"Not a chance," I assured her. "The people who have been phoning here all day would sign anything. What's the arrangement?"

"Well, just as you suggested. As you proposed it to Miss Fraser. No one objected to that. What they've been discussing was how to divide it up, and this is what they've agreed on . . ."

As she told it to me I scribbled it in my notebook, and this is how it looked:

	Per cent of expenses	Share of fee
Hi-Spot	50	$10,000
FBC	28	5,500
M. Fraser	15	3,000
White Birch Soap	5	1,000
Sweeties	2	500
	100	$20,000

I called it back to check and then stated, "It suits us if it suits Miss Fraser. Is she satisfied?"

"She agrees to it," Deborah said. "She would have preferred to do it alone, all herself, but under the circumstances that wasn't possible. Yes, she's satisfied."

"Okay. Mr. Wolfe will dictate it, probably in the form of a letter, with copies for all. But that's just a formality and he wants to get started. All we know is what we've read in the papers. According to them there are eight people that the police regard as—uh, possibilities. Their names—"

"I know their names. Including mine."

"Sure you do. Can you have them all here at this office at half past eight this evening?"

"All of them?"

"Yes, ma'am."

"But is that necessary?"

"Mr. Wolfe thinks so. This is him talking through me, to Miss Fraser through you. I ought to warn you, he can be an awful nui-

sance when a good fee depends on it. Usually when you hire a man
to do something he thinks you're the boss. When you hire Wolfe he
thinks he's the boss. He's a genius and that's merely one of the ways
it shows. You can either take it or fight it. What do you want, just
the publicity, or do you want the job done?"

"Don't bully me, Mr. Goodwin. We want the job done. I don't
know if I can get Professor Savarese. And that Shepherd girl—she's
a bigger nuisance than Mr. Wolfe could ever possibly be."

"Will you get all you can? Half past eight. And keep me informed?"

She said she would. After I had hung up I buzzed Wolfe on the
house phone to tell him we had made a sale.

It soon became apparent that we had also bought something. It
was only twenty-five to six, less than three-quarters of an hour
since I had finished with Deborah Koppel, when the doorbell rang.
Sometimes Fritz answers it and sometimes me—usually me, when
I'm home and not engaged on something that shouldn't be interrupted. So I marched to the hall and to the front door and pulled
it open.

On the stoop was a surprise party. In front was a man-about-
town in a topcoat the Duke of Windsor would have worn any day.
To his left and rear was a red-faced plump gentleman. Back of them
were three more, miscellaneous, carrying an assortment of cases
and bags. When I saw what I had to contend with I brought the
door with me and held it, leaving only enough of an opening for
room for my shoulders.

"We'd like to see Mr. Nero Wolfe," the topcoat said like an old
friend.

"He's engaged. I'm Archie Goodwin. Can I help?"

"You certainly can! I'm Fred Owen, in charge of public relations
for the Hi-Spot Company." He was pushing a hand at me and I took
it. "And this is Mr. Walter B. Anderson, the president of the Hi-
Spot Company. May we come in?"

I reached to take the president's hand and still keep my door
block intact. "If you don't mind," I said, "it would be a help if you'd
give me a rough idea."

"Certainly, glad to! I would have phoned, only this has to be
rushed if we're going to make the morning papers. So I just persuaded Mr. Anderson, and collected the photographers, and came.
It shouldn't take ten minutes—say a shot of Mr. Anderson looking

at Mr. Wolfe as he signs the agreement, or vice versa, and one of them shaking hands, and one of them side by side, bending over in a huddle inspecting some object that can be captioned as a clue—how about that one?"

"Wonderful!" I grinned at him. "But damn it, not today. Mr. Wolfe cut himself shaving, and he's wearing a patch, and vain as he is it would be very risky to aim a camera at him."

That goes to show how a man will degrade himself on account of money. Meaning me. The proper and natural thing to do would have been to kick them off the stoop down the seven steps to the sidewalk, especially the topcoat, and why didn't I do it? Ten grand. Maybe even twenty, for if Hi-Spot had been insulted they might have soured the whole deal.

The effort, including sacrifice of principle, that it took to get them on their way without making them too sore put me in a frame of mind that accounted for my reaction somewhat later, after Wolfe had come down to the office, when I had explained the agreement our clients had come to, and he said:

"No. I will not." He was emphatic. "I will not draft or sign an agreement one of the parties to which is that Sweeties."

I knew perfectly well that was reasonable and even noble. But what pinched me was that I had sacrificed principle without hesitation, and here he was refusing to. I glared at him:

"Very well." I stood up. "I resign as of now. You are simply too conceited, too eccentric, and too fat to work for."

"Archie. Sit down."

"No."

"Yes. I am no fatter than I was five years ago. I am considerably more conceited, but so are you, and why the devil shouldn't we be? Some day there will be a crisis. Either you'll get insufferable and I'll fire you, or I'll get insufferable and you'll quit. But this isn't the day and you know it. You also know I would rather become a policeman and take orders from Mr. Cramer than work for anything or anyone called Sweeties. Your performance yesterday and today has been highly satisfactory."

"Don't try to butter me."

"Bosh. I repeat that I am no fatter than I was five years ago. Sit down and get your notebook. We'll put it in the form of a letter, to all of them jointly, and they can initial our copy. We shall ignore Sweeties"—he made a face—"and add that two per cent and that five hundred dollars to the share of the Federal Broadcasting Company."

That was what we did.

By the time Fritz called us to dinner there had been phone calls from Deborah Koppel and others, and the party for the evening was set.

5

There are four rooms on the ground floor of Wolfe's old brownstone house on West Thirty-fifth Street not far from the Hudson River. As you enter from the stoop, on your right are an enormous old oak clothes rack with a mirror, the elevator, the stairs, and the door to the dining room. On your left are the doors to the front room, which doesn't get used much, and to the office. The door to the kitchen is at the rear, the far end of the hall.

The office is twice as big as any of the other rooms. It is actually our living room too, and since Wolfe spends most of his time there you have to allow him his rule regarding furniture and accessories: nothing enters it or stays in it that he doesn't enjoy looking at. He enjoys the contrast between the cherry of his desk and the cardato of his chair, made by Meyer. The bright yellow couch cover has to be cleaned every two months, but he likes bright yellow. The three-foot globe over by the bookshelves is too big for a room that size, but he likes to look at it. He loves a comfortable chair so much that he won't have any other kind in the place, though he never sits on any but his own.

So that evening at least our guests' fannies were at ease, however the rest of them may have felt. There were nine of them present, six invited and three gate-crashers. Of the eight I had wanted Deborah Koppel to get, Nancylee Shepherd hadn't been asked, and Professor F. O. Savarese couldn't make it. The three gate-crashers were Hi-Spot's president and public relations man, Anderson and Owen, who had previously only got as far as the stoop, and Beech, the FBC vice-president.

At nine o'clock they were all there, all sitting, and all looking at Wolfe. There had been no friction at all except a little brush I had with Anderson. The best chair in the room, not counting Wolfe's, is one of red leather which is kept not far from one end of Wolfe's desk. Soon after entering Anderson had spotted it and squat-claimed it. When I asked him courteously to move to the other side of the room he went rude on me. He said he liked it there.

"But," I said, "this chair, and those, are reserved for the candidates."

"Candidates for what?"

"For top billing in a murder trial. Mr. Wolfe would like them sort of together, so they'll all be under his eye."

"Then arrange them that way."

He wasn't moving. "I can't ask you to show me your stub," I said pointedly, "because this is merely a private house, and you weren't invited, and my only argument is the convenience and pleasure of your host."

He gave me a dirty look but no more words, got up, and went across to the couch. I moved Madeline Fraser to the red leather chair, which gave the other five candidates more elbow room in their semicircle fronting Wolfe's desk. Beech, who had been standing talking to Wolfe, went and took a chair near the end of the couch. Owen had joined his boss, so I had the three gate-crashers off to themselves, which was as it should be.

Wolfe's eyes swept the semicircle, starting at Miss Fraser's end. "You are going to find this tiresome," he said conversationally, "because I'm just starting on this and so shall have to cover details that you're sick of hearing and talking about. All the information I have has come from newspapers, and therefore much of it is doubtless inaccurate and some of it false. How much you'll have to correct me on I don't know."

"It depends a lot," said Nathan Traub with a smile, "on which paper you read."

Traub, the agency man, was the only one of the six I hadn't seen before, having only heard his smooth low-pitched voice on the phone, when he had practically told me that everything had to be cleared through him. He was much younger than I had expected, around my age, but otherwise he was no great surprise. The chief difference between any two advertising executives is that one goes to buy a suit at Brooks Brothers in the morning and the other one goes in the afternoon. It depends on the conference schedule. The suit this Traub had bought was a double-breasted gray which went very well with his dark hair and the healthy color of his cheeks.

"I have read them all." Wolfe's eyes went from left to right again. "I did so when I decided I wanted a job on this case. By the way, I assume you all know who has hired me, and for what?"

There were nods. "We know all about it," Bill Meadows said.

"Good. Then you know why the presence of Mr. Anderson, Mr. Owen, and Mr. Beech is being tolerated. With them here, and of course Miss Fraser, ninety-five per cent of the clients' interest is represented. The only one absent is White Birch Soap."

"They're not absent." Nathan Traub was politely indignant. "I can speak for them."

"I'd rather you'd speak for yourself," Wolfe retorted. "The clients are here to listen, not to speak." He rested his elbows on the arms of his chair and put the tips of his thumbs together. With the gate-crashers put in their places, he went on, "As for you, ladies and gentlemen, this would be much more interesting and stimulating for you if I could begin by saying that my job is to learn which one of you is guilty of murder—and to prove it. Unfortunately we can't have that fillip, since two of the eight—Miss Shepherd and Mr. Savarese—didn't come. I am told that Mr. Savarese had an engagement, and there is a certain reluctance about Miss Shepherd that I would like to know more about."

"She's a nosy little chatterbox." From Tully Strong, who had removed his spectacles and was gazing at Wolfe with an intent frown.

"She's a pain in the neck." From Bill Meadows.

Everybody smiled, some nervously, some apparently meaning it.

"I didn't try to get her," Deborah Koppel said. "She wouldn't have come unless Miss Fraser herself had asked her, and I didn't think that was necessary. She hates all the rest of us."

"Why?"

"Because she thinks we keep her away from Miss Fraser."

"Do you?"

"Yes. We try to."

"Not from me too, I hope." Wolfe sighed down to where a strip of his yellow shirt divided his vest from his trousers, and curled his palms and fingers over the ends of his chair arms. "Now. Let's get at this. Usually when I talk I dislike interruptions, but this is an exception. If you disagree with anything I say, or think me in error, say so at once. With that understood:

"Frequently, twice a week or oftener, you consider the problem of guests for Miss Fraser's program. It is in fact a problem, because you want interesting people, famous ones if possible, but they must be willing to submit to the indignity of lending their presence, and their assent by silence, if nothing more, to the preposterous statements made by Miss Fraser and Mr. Meadows regarding the products they advertise. Recently—"

"What's undignified about it?"

"There are no preposterous statements!"

"What's this got to do with what we're paying you for?"

"You disagree." Wolfe was unruffled. "I asked for it. Archie, include it in your notes that Mr. Traub and Mr. Strong disagree. You may ignore Mr. Owen's protest, since my invitation to interrupt did not extend to him."

He took in the semicircle again. "Recently a suggestion was made that you corral, as a guest, a man who sells tips on horse races. I understand that your memories differ as to when that suggestion was first made."

Madeline Fraser said, "It's been discussed off and on for over a year."

"I've always been dead against it," Tully Strong asserted.

Deborah Koppel smiled. "Mr. Strong thought it would be improper. He thinks the program should never offend anybody, which is impossible. Anything and everything offends somebody."

"What changed your mind, Mr. Strong?"

"Two things," said the secretary of the Sponsors' Council. "First, we got the idea of having the audience vote on it—the air audience— and out of over fourteen thousand letters ninety-two point six per cent were in favor. Second, one of the letters was from an assistant professor of mathematics at Columbia University, suggesting that the second guest on the program should be him, or some other professor, who could speak as an expert on the law of averages. That gave it a different slant entirely, and I was for it. Nat Traub, for the agency, was still against it."

"And I still am," Traub declared. "Can you blame me?"

"So," Wolfe asked Strong, "Mr. Traub was a minority of one?"

"That's right. We went ahead. Miss Vance, who does research for the program in addition to writing scripts, got up a list of prospects. I was surprised to find, and the others were too, that more than thirty tip sheets of various kinds are published in New York alone. We boiled it down to five and they were contacted."

I should have warned them that the use of contact as a verb was not permitted in that office. Now Wolfe would have it in for him.

Wolfe frowned. "All five were invited?"

"Oh, no. Appointments were made for them to see Miss Fraser—the publishers of them. She had to find out which one was most likely to go over on the air and not pull something that would hurt the program. The final choice was left to her."

"How were the five selected?"

"Scientifically. The length of time they had been in business, the quality of paper and printing of the sheets, the opinions of sports writers, things like that."

"Who was the scientist? You?"

"No . . . I don't know . . ."

"I was," a firm quiet voice stated. It was Elinor Vance. I had put her in the chair nearest mine because Wolfe isn't the only one who likes to have things around that he enjoys looking at. Obviously she hadn't caught up on sleep yet, and every so often she had to clamp her teeth to keep her chin from quivering, but she was the only one there who could conceivably have made me remember that I was not primarily a detective, but a man. I was curious how her brown eyes would look if and when they got fun in them again some day. She was going on:

"First I took out those that were plainly impossible, more than half of them, and then I talked it over with Miss Koppel and Mr. Meadows, and I think one or two others—I guess Mr. Strong—yes, I'm sure I did—but it was me more than them. I picked the five names."

"And they all came to see Miss Fraser?"

"Four of them did. One of them was out of town—in Florida."

Wolfe's gaze went to the left. "And you, Miss Fraser, chose Mr. Cyril Orchard from those four?"

She nodded. "Yes."

"How did you do that? Scientifically?"

"No." She smiled. "There's nothing scientific about me. He seemed fairly intelligent, and he had much the best voice of the four and was the best talker, and I liked the name of his sheet, *Track Almanac*—and then I guess I was a little snobbish about it too. His sheet was the most expensive—ten dollars a week."

"Those were the considerations that led you to select him?"

"Yes."

"You had never seen or heard of him before he came to see you as one of the four?"

"I hadn't seen him, but I had heard of him, and I had seen his sheet."

"Oh?" Wolfe's eyes went half shut. "You had?"

"Yes, about a month before that, maybe longer, when the question of having a tipster on the program had come up again, I had subscribed to some of the sheets—three or four of them—to see what they were like. Not in my name, of course. Things like that are done in my manager's name—Miss Koppel. One of them was this *Track Almanac.*"

"How did you happen to choose that one?"

"My God, I don't know!" Madeline Fraser's eyes flashed momentarily with irritation. "Do you remember, Debby?"

Deborah shook her head. "I think we phoned somebody."

"The New York State Racing Commission," Bill Meadows offered sarcastically.

"Well." Wolfe leaned forward to push a button on his desk. "I'm going to have some beer. Aren't some of you thirsty?"

That called for an intermission. No one had accepted a previous offer of liquids I had made, but now they made it unanimous in the affirmative, and I got busy at the table at the far wall, already equipped. Two of them joined Wolfe with the beer, brought by Fritz from the kitchen, and the others suited their fancy. I had suggested to Wolfe that it would be fitting to have a case of Hi-Spot in a prominent place on the table, but he had merely snorted. On such occasions he always insisted that a red wine and a chilled white wine must be among those present. Usually they had no takers, but this time there were two, Miss Koppel and Traub, who went for the Montrachet; and, being strongly in favor of the way its taste insists on sneaking all over the inside of your head, I helped out with it. There is only one trouble about serving assorted drinks to a bunch of people in the office on business. I maintain that it is a legitimate item for the expense account for the clients, and Wolfe says no, that what anyone eats or drinks in his house is on him. Another eccentricity. Also he insists that they must all have stands or tables at their elbows for their drinks.

So they did.

6

Wolfe, for whom the first bottle of beer is merely a preamble, filled his glass from the second bottle, put the bottle down, and leaned back.

"What I've been after," he said in his conversational tone again, "is how that particular individual, Mr. Cyril Orchard, became a guest on that program. The conclusion from the newspaper accounts is that none of you, including Miss Shepherd and Mr. Savarese, knew him from Adam. But he was murdered. Later I'll discuss this with you severally, but for now I'll just put it to all of you: had you had any dealings with, or connection with, or knowledge of, Cyril Orchard prior to his appearance on that program? Other than what I have just been told?"

Starting with Madeline Fraser, he got either a no or a shake of the head from each of the six.

He grunted. "I assume," he said, "that the police have unearthed no contradiction to any of your negatives, since if they had you would hardly be foolish enough to try to hold to them with me. My whole approach to this matter is quite different from what it would be if I didn't know that the police have spent seven days and nights working on it. They have been after you, and they have their training and talents; also they have authority and a thousand men—twenty thousand. The question is whether their methods and abilities are up to this job; all I can do is use my own."

Wolfe came forward to drink beer, used his handkerchief on his lips, and leaned back again.

"But I need to know what happened—from you, not the newspapers. We now have you in the broadcasting studio Tuesday morning, a week ago today. The two guests—Mr. Cyril Orchard and Professor Savarese—have arrived. It is a quarter to eleven. The rest of you are there, at or near the table which holds the microphones. Seated at one side of the narrow table are Miss Fraser and Professor Savarese; across from them, facing them, are Mr. Orchard and Mr. Meadows. Voice levels are being taken. About twenty feet from the table is the first row of chairs provided for the studio audience. That audience consists of some two hundred people, nearly all women, many of whom, devoted followers of Miss Fraser, frequently attend the broadcasts. Is that picture correct—not approximately correct, but correct?"

They nodded. "Nothing wrong with it," Bill Meadows said.

"Many of them," Miss Fraser stated, "would come much oftener if they could get tickets. There are always twice as many applications for tickets as we can supply."

"No doubt," Wolfe growled. He had shown great restraint, not telling her how dangerous she was. "But the applicants who didn't get tickets, not being there, do not concern us. An essential element of the picture which I haven't mentioned is not yet visible. Behind the closed door of an electric refrigerator over against the wall are eight bottles of Hi-Spot. How did they get there?"

An answer came from the couch, from Fred Owen. "We always have three or four cases in the studio, in a locked cab——"

"If you please, Mr. Owen." Wolfe wiggled a finger at him. "I want to hear as much as I can of the voices of these six people."

"They were there in the studio," Tully Strong said. "In a cabinet. It's kept locked because if it wasn't they wouldn't be there long."

"Who had taken the eight bottles from the cabinet and put them in the refrigerator?"

"I had." It was Elinor Vance, and I looked up from my notebook for another glance at her. "That's one of my chores every broadcast."

One trouble with her, I thought, is overwork. Script writer, researcher, bartender—what else?

"You can't carry eight bottles," Wolfe remarked, "at one time."

"I know I can't, so I took four and then went back for four more."

"Leaving the cabinet unlocked—no." Wolfe stopped himself. "Those refinements will have to wait." His eyes passed along the line again. "So there they are, in the refrigerator. —By the way, I understand that the presence at the broadcast of all but one of you was routine and customary. The exception was you, Mr. Traub. You very rarely attend. What were you there for?"

"Because I was jittery, Mr. Wolfe." Traub's advertising smile and smooth low-pitched voice showed no resentment at being singled out. "I still thought having a race tout on the program was a mistake, and I wanted to be on hand."

"You thought there was no telling what Mr. Orchard might say?"

"I knew nothing about Orchard. I thought the whole idea was a stinker."

"If you mean the whole idea of the program, I agree—but that's not what we're trying to decide. We'll go on with the broadcast. First, one more piece of the picture. Where are the glasses they're going to drink from?"

"On a tray at the end of the table," Deborah Koppel said.

"The broadcasting table? Where they're seated at the microphones?"

"Yes."

"Who put them there?"

"That girl, Nancylee Shepherd. The only way to keep her back of the line would be to tie her up. Or of course not let her in, and Miss Fraser will not permit that. She organized the biggest Fraser Girls' Club in the country. So we—"

The phone rang. I reached for it and muttered into it.

"Mr. Bluff," I told Wolfe, using one of my fifteen aliases for the caller. Wolfe got his receiver to his ear, giving me a signal to stay on.

"Yes, Mr. Cramer?"

Cramer's sarcastic voice sounded as if he had a cigar stuck in his mouth, as he probably had. "How are you coming up there?"

"Slowly. Not really started yet."

"That's too bad, since no one's paying you on the Orchard case. So you told me yesterday."

"This is today. Tomorrow's paper will tell you all about it. I'm sorry, Mr. Cramer, but I'm busy."

"You certainly are, from the reports I've got here. Which one is your client?"

"You'll see it in the paper."

"Then there's no reason—"

"Yes. There is. That I'm extremely busy and exactly a week behind you. Good-by, sir."

Wolfe's tone and his manner of hanging up got a reaction from the gate-crashers. Mr. Walter B. Anderson, the Hi-Spot president, demanded to know if the caller had been Police Inspector Cramer, and, told that it was, got critical. His position was that Wolfe should not have been rude to the Inspector. It was bad tactics and bad manners. Wolfe, not bothering to draw his sword, brushed him aside with a couple of words, but Anderson leaped for his throat. He had not yet, he said, signed any agreement, and if that was going to be Wolfe's attitude maybe he wouldn't.

"Indeed." Wolfe's brows went up a sixteenth of an inch. "Then you'd better notify the press immediately. Do you want to use the phone?"

"By God, I wish I could. I have a right to—"

"You have no right whatever, Mr. Anderson, except to pay your share of my fee if I earn it. You are here in my office on sufferance. Confound it, I am undertaking to solve a problem that has Mr. Cramer so nonplused that he desperately wants a hint from me before I've even begun. He doesn't mind my rudeness; he's so accustomed to it that if I were affable he'd haul me in as a material witness. Are you going to use the phone?"

"You know damn well I'm not."

"I wish you were. The better I see this picture the less I like it." Wolfe went back to the line of candidates. "You say, Miss Koppel, that this adolescent busybody, Miss Shepherd, put the tray of glasses on the table?"

"Yes, she—"

"She took them from me," Elinor Vance put in, "when I got them from the cabinet. She was right there with her hand out and I let her take them."

"The locked cabinet that the Hi-Spot is kept in?"

"Yes."

"And the glasses are heavy and dark blue, quite opaque, so that anything in them is invisible?"

"Yes."

"You didn't look into them from the top?"

"No."

"If one of them had something inside you wouldn't have seen it?"

"No." Elinor went on, "If you think my answers are short and quick, that's because I've already answered these questions, and many others, hundreds of times. I could answer them in my sleep."

Wolfe nodded. "Of course. So now we have the bottles in the refrigerator and the glasses on the table, and the program is on the air. For forty minutes it went smoothly. The two guests did well. None of Mr. Traub's fears were realized."

"It was one of the best broadcasts of the year," Miss Fraser said.

"Exceptional," Tully Strong declared. "There were thirty-two studio laughs in the first half hour."

"How did you like the second half?" Traub asked pointedly.

"We're coming to it." Wolfe sighed. "Well, here we are. The moment arrives when Hi-Spot is to be poured, drunk, and eulogized. Who brought it from the refrigerator? You again, Miss Vance?"

"No, me," Bill Meadows said. "It's part of the show for the mikes, me pushing back my chair, walking, opening the refrigerator door and closing it, and coming back with the bottles. Then someone—"

"There were eight bottles in the refrigerator. How many did you get?"

"Four."

"How did you decide which ones?"

"I didn't decide. I always just take the four in front. You realize that all Hi-Spot bottles are exactly alike. There wouldn't be any way to tell them apart, so how would I decide?"

"I couldn't say. Anyway, you didn't?"

"No. As I said, I simply took the four bottles that were nearest to me. That's natural."

"So it is. And carried them to the table and removed the caps?"

"I took them to the table, but about removing the caps, that's something we don't quite agree on. We agree that I didn't do it, because I put them on the table as usual and then got back into my chair, quick, to get on the mike. Someone else always takes the caps from the bottles, not always the same one, and that day Debby—Miss Koppel was right there, and Miss Vance, and Strong, and Traub. I was on the mike and didn't see who removed the caps. The action there is a little tight and needs help, with taking off the caps, pouring into the glasses, and getting the glasses passed around—and the bottles have to be passed around too."

"Who does the passing?"

"Oh, someone—or, rather, more than one. You know, they just get passed—the glasses and bottles both. After pouring into the glasses the bottles are still about half full, so the bottles are passed too."

"Who did the pouring and passing that day?"

Bill Meadows hesitated. "That's what we don't agree about." He was not at ease. "As I said, they were all right there—Miss Koppel and Miss Vance, and Strong and Traub. That's why it was confusing."

"Confusing or not," Wolfe said testily, "it should be possible to remember what happened, so simple a thing as that. This is the detail where, above all others, clarity is essential. We know that Mr. Orchard got the bottle and glass which contained the cyanide, because he drank enough of it to kill him. But we do not know, at least I don't, whether he got it by a whim of circumstance or by the deliberate maneuver of one or more of those present. Obviously that's a vital point. That glass and bottle were placed in front of Mr. Orchard by somebody—not this one, or this one, but that one. Who put it there?"

Wolfe's gaze went along the line. They all met it. No one had anything to say, but neither was anyone impelled to look somewhere else. Finally Tully Strong, who had his spectacles back on, spoke:

"We simply don't remember, Mr. Wolfe."

"Pfui." Wolfe was disgusted. "Certainly you remember. No wonder Mr. Cramer has got nowhere. You're lying, every one of you."

"No," Miss Fraser objected. "They're not lying really."

"The wrong pronoun," Wolfe snapped at her. "My comment included you, Miss Fraser."

She smiled at him. "You may include me if you like, but I don't. It's like this. These people are not only associated with one another in connection with my program, they are friends. Of course they have arguments—there's always bound to be some friction when two people are often together, let alone five or six—but they are friends and they like one another." Her timing and inflections were as good as if she had been on the air. "This is a terrible thing, a horrible thing, and we all knew it was the minute the doctor came and looked at him, and then looked up and said nothing should be touched and no one should leave. So could you really expect one of them to say —or, since you include me, could you expect one of us to say—*yes, I gave him the glass with poison in it?*"

"What was left in the bottle was also poisoned."

"All right, the bottle too. Or could you expect one of us to say, *yes, I saw my friend give him the glass and bottle?* And name the friend?"

"Then you're agreeing with me. That you're all lying."

"Not at all." Miss Fraser was too earnest to smile now. "The pouring and passing the glasses and bottles was commonplace routine, and there was no reason for us to notice details enough to keep them in our minds at all. Then came that overwhelming shock, and the confusion, and later came the police, and the strain and tension of it, and we just didn't remember. That isn't the least bit surprising. What would surprise me would be if someone did remember, for instance if Mr. Traub said positively that Mr. Strong put that glass and bottle in front of Mr. Orchard, it would merely prove that Mr.

Traub hates Mr. Strong, and that would surprise me because I don't believe that any one of us hates another one."

"Nor," Wolfe murmured dryly, "that any of you hated Mr. Orchard—or wanted to kill him."

"Who on earth could have wanted to kill that man?"

"I don't know. That's what I've been hired to find out—provided the poison reached its intended destination. You say you're not surprised, but I am. I'm surprised the police haven't locked you all up."

"They damn near did," Traub said grimly.

"I certainly thought they would arrest me," Madeline Fraser declared. "That was what was in my mind—it was all that was in my mind—as soon as I heard the doctor say cyanide. Not who had given him that glass and bottle, not even what the effect would be on my program, but the death of my husband. He died of cyanide poisoning six years ago."

Wolfe nodded. "The papers haven't neglected that. It was what leaped first to your mind?"

"Yes, when I heard the doctor say cyanide. I suppose you wouldn't understand—or perhaps you would—anyway it did."

"It did to mine too," Deborah Koppel interposed, in a tone that implied that someone had been accused of something. "Miss Fraser's husband was my brother. I saw him just after he died. Then that day I saw Cyril Orchard, and—" She stopped. Having her in profile, I couldn't see her eyes, but I saw her clasped hands. In a moment she went on, "Yes, it came to my mind."

Wolfe stirred impatiently. "Well. I won't pretend that I'm exasperated that you're such good friends that you haven't been able to remember what happened. If you had, and had told the police, I might not have this job." He glanced at the clock on the wall. "It's after eleven. I had thought it barely possible that I might get a wedge into a crack by getting you here together, but it seems hopeless. You're much too fond of one another. Our time has been completely wasted. I haven't got a thing, not a microscopic morsel, that I hadn't already got from the papers. I may never get anything, but I intend to try. Which of you will spend the night here with me? Not all the night; probably four or five hours. I shall need that long, more or less, with each of you, and I would like to start now. Which of you will stay?"

There were no eager volunteers.

"My Lord!" Elinor Vance protested. "Over and over and over again."

"My clients," Wolfe said, "are your employer, your network, and your sponsors. Mr. Meadows?"

"I've got to take Miss Fraser home," Bill objected. "I could come back."

"I'll take her," Tully Strong offered.

"That's foolish." Deborah Koppel was annoyed. "I live only a block away and we'll take a taxi together."

"I'll go with you," Elinor Vance suggested. "I'll drop you and keep the taxi on uptown."

"I'll ride with you," Tully Strong insisted.

"But you live in the Village!"

"Count me in," Bill Meadows said stubbornly. "I can be back here in twenty minutes. Thank God tomorrow's Wednesday."

"This is all unnecessary," the president of Hi-Spot broke in with authority. He had left the couch and was among the candidates, who were also on their feet. "My car is outside and I can take all of you who are going uptown. You can stay here with Wolfe, Meadows." He turned and stepped to the desk. "Mr. Wolfe, I haven't been greatly impressed this evening. Hardly at all impressed."

"Neither have I," Wolfe agreed. "It's a dreary outlook. I would prefer to abandon it, but you and I are both committed by that press release." Seeing that some of them were heading for the hall, he raised his voice. "If you please? A moment. I would like to make appointments. One of you tomorrow from eleven to one, another from two to four, another in the evening from eight-thirty to twelve, and another from midnight on. Will you decide on that before you go?"

They did so, with me helping them and making notes of the decisions. It took a little discussion, but they were such good friends that there was no argument. The only thing that soured the leave-taking at all was when Owen made an opportunity to pass me a crack about no patch or cut being visible on Wolfe's face. He might at least have had the decency to let it lay.

"I said nothing about his face," I told him coldly. "I said he cut himself shaving. He shaves his legs. I understood you wanted him in kilts for the pictures."

Owen was too offended to speak. Utterly devoid of a sense of humor.

When the others had gone Bill Meadows was honored with the red leather chair. On a low table at his elbow I put a replenished glass, and Fritz put a tray holding three sandwiches made with his own bread, one of minced rabbit meat, one of corned beef, and one of Georgia country ham. I arranged myself at my desk with my note-book, a plate of sandwiches to match Bill's, a pitcher of milk and a glass. Wolfe had only beer. He never eats between dinner and break-fast. If he did he never would be able to say he is no fatter than he was five years ago, which isn't true anyhow.

In a way it's a pleasure to watch Wolfe doing a complete over-haul on a man, or a woman either, and in another way it's enough to make you grit your teeth. When you know exactly what he's after and he's sneaking up on it without the slightest sound to alarm the victim, it's a joy to be there. But when he's after nothing in particular, or if he is you don't know what, and he pokes in this hole a while and then tries another one, and then goes back to the first one, and as far as you can see is getting absolutely nowhere, and the hours go by, and your sandwiches and milk are all gone long ago, sooner or later the time comes when you don't even bother to get a hand in front of your yawns, let alone swallow them.

If, at four o'clock that Wednesday morning, Wolfe had once more started in on Bill Meadows about his connections with people who bet on horse races, or about the favorite topics of conversation among the people we were interested in when they weren't talking shop, or about how he got into broadcasting and did he like it much, I would either have thrown my notebook at him or gone to the kitchen for more milk. But he didn't. He pushed back his chair and manipulated himself to his feet. If anyone wants to know what I had in the notebook he can come to the office any time I'm not busy and I'll read it to him for a dollar a page, but he would be throwing his money away at any price.

I ushered Bill out. When I returned to the office Fritz was there tidying up. He never goes to bed until after Wolfe does. He asked me:

"Was the corned beef juicy, Archie?"

"Good God," I demanded, "do you expect me to remember that far back? That was days ago." I went to spin the knob on the safe and jiggle the handle, remarking to Wolfe:

"It seems we're still in the paddock, not even at the starting post.

Who do you want in the morning? Saul and Orrie and Fred and Johnny? For what? Why not have them tail Mr. Anderson?"

"I do not intend," Wolfe said glumly, "to start spending money until I know what I want to buy—not even our clients' money. If this poisoner is going to be exposed by such activities as investigation of sales of potassium cyanide or of sources of it available to these people, it is up to Mr. Cramer and his twenty thousand men. Doubtless they have already done about all they can in those directions, and many others, or he wouldn't have phoned me squealing for help. The only person I want to see in the morning is—who is it? Who's coming at eleven?"

"Debby. Miss Koppel."

"You might have taken the men first, on the off chance that we'd have it before we got to the women." He was at the door to the hall. "Good night."

7

If, thirty-three hours later, at lunch time on Thursday, anyone had wanted to know how things were shaping up, he could have satisfied his curiosity by looking in the dining room and observing Wolfe's behavior at the midday meal, which consisted of corn fritters with autumn honey, sausages, and a bowl of salad. At meals he is always expansive, talkative, and good-humored, but throughout that one he was grim, sullen, and peevish. Fritz was worried stiff.

Wednesday we had entertained Miss Koppel from eleven to one, Miss Fraser from two to four, Miss Vance from eight-thirty in the evening until after eleven, and Nathan Traub from midnight on; and Tully Strong Thursday morning from eleven until lunch time.

We had got hundreds of notebook pages of nothing.

Gaps had of course been filled in, but with what? We even had confessions, but of what? Bill Meadows and Nat Traub both confessed that they frequently bet on horse races. Elinor Vance confessed that her brother was an electroplater, and that she was aware that he constantly used materials which contained cyanide. Madeline Fraser confessed that it was hard to believe that anyone would have put poison into one of the bottles without caring a damn which one of the four broadcasters it got served to. Tully Strong

confessed that the police had found his fingerprints on all four of
the bottles, and accounted for them by explaining that while the
doctor had been kneeling to examine Cyril Orchard, he, Strong, had
been horrified by the possibility that there had been something
wrong with a bottle of Hi-Spot, the product of the most important
sponsor on the Council. In a panic he had seized the four bottles,
with the idiotic notion of caching them somewhere, and Miss Fraser
and Traub had taken them from him and replaced them on the table.
That was a particularly neat confession, since it explained why the
cops had got nowhere from prints on the bottles.

Deborah Koppel confessed that she knew a good deal about
cyanides, their uses, effects, symptoms, doses, and accessibility, because she had read up on them after the death of her brother
six years ago. In all the sessions those were the only two times Wolfe
got really disagreeable, when he was asking about the death of
Lawrence Koppel—first with Deborah, the sister, and then with
Madeline Fraser, the widow. The details had of course been pie
for the newspapers during the past week, on account of the coincidence of the cyanide, and one of the tabloids had even gone so far
as to run a piece by an expert, discussing whether it had really been
suicide, though there hadn't been the slightest question about it
at the time or at any time since.

But that wasn't the aspect that Wolfe was disagreeable about.
Lawrence Koppel's death had occurred at his home in a little town
in Michigan called Fleetville, and what Wolfe wanted to know was
whether there had been anyone in or near Fleetville who was named
Orchard, or who had relatives named Orchard, or who had later
changed his name to Orchard. I don't know how it had entered
his head that that was a hot idea, but he certainly wrung it dry and
kept going back to it for another squeeze. He spent so much time
on it with Madeline Fraser that four o'clock, the hour of his afternoon date with the orchids, came before he had asked her anything at all about horse races.

The interviews with those five were not all that happened that
day and night and morning. Wolfe and I had discussions, of the
numerous ways in which a determined and intelligent person can
get his hands on a supply of cyanide, of the easy access to the bottles in the refrigerator in the broadcasting studio, of the advisability
of trying to get Inspector Cramer or Sergeant Purley Stebbins to
cough up some data on things like fingerprints. That got us exactly

as far as the interviews did. Then there were two more phone calls from Cramer, and some from Lon Cohen and various others; and there was the little detail of arranging for Professor F. O. Savarese to pay us a visit.

Also the matter of arranging for Nancylee Shepherd to come and be processed, but on that we were temporarily stymied. We knew all about her: she was sixteen, she lived with her parents at 829 Wixley Avenue in the Bronx, she had light yellow hair and gray eyes, and her father worked in a storage warehouse. They had no phone, so at four Wednesday, when Miss Fraser had left and Wolfe had gone up to the plants, I got the car from the garage and drove to the Bronx.

829 Wixley Avenue was the kind of apartment house where people live not because they want to, but because they have to. It should have been ashamed of itself and probably was. There was no click when I pushed the button marked Shepherd, so I went to the basement and dug up the janitor. He harmonized well with the building. He said I was way behind time if I expected to get any effective results—that's what he said—pushing the Shepherd button. They had been gone three days now. No, not the whole family, Mrs. Shepherd and the girl. He didn't know where they had gone, and neither did anyone else around there. Some thought they had skipped, and some thought the cops had 'em. He personally thought they might be dead. No, not Mr. Shepherd too. He came home from work every afternoon a little after five, and left every morning at half past six.

A glance at my wrist showing me ten to five, I offered the animal a buck to stick around the front and give me a sign when Shepherd showed up, and the look in his eye told me that I had wasted at least four bits of the clients' money.

It wasn't a long wait. When Shepherd appeared I saw that it wouldn't have been necessary to keep the janitor away from his work, for from the line of the eyebrows it was about as far up to the beginning of his hair as it was down to the point of his chin, and a sketchy description would have been enough. Whoever designs the faces had lost all sense of proportion. As he was about to enter the vestibule I got in front of him and asked without the faintest touch of condescension:

"Mr. Shepherd?"

"Get out," he snarled.

"My name's Goodwin and I'm working for Miss Madeline Fraser. I understand your wife and daughter—"

"Get out!"

"But I only want—"

"Get out!"

He didn't put a hand on me or shoulder me, and I can't understand yet how he got past me to the vestibule without friction, but he did, and got his key in the door. There were of course a dozen possible courses for me, anything from grabbing his coat and holding on to plugging him in the jaw, but while that would have given me emotional release it wouldn't have got what I wanted. It was plain that as long as he was conscious he wasn't going to tell me where Nancylee was, and unconscious he couldn't. I passed.

I drove back down to Thirty-fifth Street, left the car at the curb, went in to the office, and dialed Madeline Fraser's number. Deborah Koppel answered, and I asked her:

"Did you folks know that Nancylee has left home? With her mother?"

Yes, she said, they knew that.

"You didn't mention it when you were here this morning. Neither did Miss Fraser this afternoon."

"There was no reason to mention it, was there? We weren't asked."

"You were asked about Nancylee, both of you."

"But not if she had left home or where she is."

"Then may I ask you now? Where is she?"

"I don't know."

"Does Miss Fraser?"

"No. None of us knows."

"How did you know she was gone?"

"She phoned Miss Fraser and told her she was going."

"When was that?"

"That was . . . that was Sunday."

"She didn't say where she was going?"

"No."

That was the best I could get. When I was through trying and had hung up, I sat and considered. There was a chance that Purley Stebbins of Homicide would be in the mood for tossing me a bone, since Cramer had been spending nickels on us, but if I asked him for it he would want to make it a trade, and I had nothing to offer.

So when I reached for the phone again it wasn't that number, but the *Gazette's,* that I dialed.

Lon Cohen immediately got personal. Where, he wanted to know, had I got the idea that an open press release made an entry in my credit column?

I poohed him. "Some day, chum, you'll get a lulu. Say in about six months, the way we're going. A newspaper is supposed to render public service, and I want some. Did you know that Nancylee Shepherd and her mother have blown?"

"Certainly. The father got sore because she was mixed up in a murder case. He damn near killed two photographers. Father has character."

"Yeah, I've met Father. What did he do with his wife and daughter, bury them?"

"Shipped 'em out of town. With Cramer's permission, as we got it here, and of course Cramer knew where but wasn't giving out. Naturally we thought it an outrage. Is the great public, are the American people, to be deceived and kept in ignorance? No. You must have had a hunch, because we just got it here—it came in less than an hour ago. Nancylee and her mother are at the Ambassador in Atlantic City, sitting room, bedroom, and bath."

"You don't say. Paid for by?"

He didn't know. He agreed that it was intolerable that the American people, of whom I was one, should be uninformed on so vital a point, and before he hung up he said he would certainly do something about it.

When Wolfe came down to the office I reported developments. At that time we still had three more to overhaul, but it was already apparent that we were going to need all we could get, so Wolfe told me to get Saul Panzer on the phone. Saul wasn't in, but an hour later he called back.

Saul Panzer free-lances. He has no office and doesn't need one. He is so good that he demands, and gets, double the market, and any day of the week he gets so many offers that he can pick as he pleases. I have never known him to turn Wolfe down except when he was so tied up he couldn't shake loose.

He took this on. He would take a train to Atlantic City that evening, sleep there, and in the morning persuade Mrs. Shepherd to let Nancylee come to New York for a talk with Wolfe. He would bring her, with Mother if necessary.

As Wolfe was finishing with Saul, Fritz entered with a tray. I looked at him with surprise, since Wolfe seldom takes on beer during the hour preceding dinner, but then, as he put the tray on the desk, I saw it wasn't beer. It was a bottle of Hi-Spot, with three glasses. Instead of turning to leave, Fritz stood by.

"It may be too cold," Fritz suggested.

With a glance of supercilious distaste at the bottle, Wolfe got the opener from his top drawer, removed the cap, and started pouring.

"It seems to me," I remarked, "like a useless sacrifice. Why suffer? If Orchard had never drunk Hi-Spot before he wouldn't know whether it tasted right or not, and even if he didn't like it they were on the air and just for politeness he would have gulped some down." I took the glass that Fritz handed me, a third full. "Anyway he drank enough to kill him, so what does it matter what we think?"

"He may have drunk it before." Wolfe held the glass to his nose, sniffed, and made a face. "At any rate, the murderer had to assume that he might have. Would the difference in taste be too great a hazard?"

"I see." I sipped. "Not so bad." I sipped again. "The only way we can really tell is to drink this and then drink some cyanide. Have you got some?"

"Don't bubble, Archie." Wolfe put his glass down after two little tastes. "Good heavens. What the devil is in it, Fritz?"

Fritz shook his head. "Ipecac?" he guessed. "Horehound? Would you like some sherry?"

"No. Water. I'll get it." Wolfe got up, marched to the hall, and turned toward the kitchen. He believes in some good healthy exercise before dinner.

That evening, Wednesday, our victims were first Elinor Vance and then Nathan Traub. It was more than three hours after midnight when Wolfe finally let Traub go, which made two nights in a row.

Thursday morning at eleven we started on Tully Strong. In the middle of it, right at noon, there was a phone call from Saul Panzer. Wolfe took it, giving me the sign to stay on. I knew from the tone of Saul's voice, just pronouncing my name, that he had no bacon.

"I'm at the Atlantic City railroad station," Saul said, "and I can either catch a train to New York in twenty minutes or go jump in the ocean, whichever you advise. I couldn't get to Mrs. Shepherd just by asking, so I tried a trick but it didn't work. Finally she and the daughter came down to the hotel lobby, but I thought it would be better to wait until they came outside, if they came, and they did. My approach was one that has worked a thousand times, but it didn't with her. She called a cop and wanted him to arrest me for annoying her. I made another try later, on the phone again, but four words was as far as I got. Now it's no use. This is the third time I've flopped on you in ten years, and that's too often. I don't want you to pay me, not even expenses."

"Nonsense." Wolfe never gets riled with Saul. "You can give me the details later, if there are any I should have. Will you reach New York in time to come to the office at six o'clock?"

"Yes."

"Good. Do that."

Wolfe resumed with Traub. As I have already mentioned, the climax of that two hours' hard work was when Traub confessed that he frequently bet on horse races. As soon as he had gone Wolfe and I went to the dining room for the lunch previously described, corn fritters with autumn honey, sausages, and a bowl of salad. Of course what added to his misery was the fact that Savarese was expected at two o'clock, because he likes to have the duration of a meal determined solely by the inclination of him and the meal, not by some extraneous phenomenon like the sound of a doorbell.

But the bell rang right on the dot.

8

You have heard of the exception that proves the rule. Professor F. O. Savarese was it.

The accepted rule is that an Italian is dark and, if not actually a runt, at least not tall; that a professor is dry and pedantic, with eye trouble; and that a mathematician really lives in the stratosphere and is here just visiting relatives. Well, Savarese was an Italian-American professor of mathematics, but he was big and blond and buoyant, two inches taller than me, and he came breezing in like a March morning wind.

He spent the first twenty minutes telling Wolfe and me how fascinating and practical it would be to work out a set of mathe-

matical formulas that could be used in the detective business. His
favorite branch of mathematics, he said, was the one that dealt
with the objective numerical measurement of probability. Very well.
What was any detective work, any kind at all, but the objective
measurement of probability? All he proposed to do was to add the
word *numerical,* not as a substitute or replacement, but as an ally
and reinforcement.

"I'll show you what I mean," he offered. "May I have paper and
pencil?"

He had bounded over to me before I could even uncross my legs,
took the pad and pencil I handed him, and bounded back to the
red leather chair. When the pencil had jitterbugged on the pad for
half a minute he tore off the top sheet and slid it across the desk to
Wolfe, then went to work on the next sheet and in a moment tore
that off and leaped to me with it.

"You should each have one," he said, "so you can follow me."

I wouldn't try to pretend I could put it down from memory, but
I still have both of those sheets, in the folder marked ORCHARD, and
this is what is on them:

$$u = \frac{1}{V_2\pi \cdot D}\left\{1 - \tfrac{1}{2}k\left(\frac{X}{D} - \tfrac{1}{3}\frac{X^3}{D^3}\right)\right\}e^{-\frac{1}{4}X^2/D^2}$$

"That," Savarese said, his whole face smiling with eager interest
and friendliness and desire to help, "is the second approximation of
the normal law of error, sometimes called the generalized law of
error. Let's apply it to the simplest kind of detective problem, say
the question which one of three servants in a house stole a
diamond ring from a locked drawer. I should explain that X is the
deviation from the mean, D is the standard deviation, k is—"

"Please!" Wolfe had to make it next door to a bellow, and did.
"What are you trying to do, change the subject?"

"No." Savarese looked surprised and a little hurt. "Am I? What
was the subject?"

"The death of Mr. Cyril Orchard and your connection with it."

"Oh. Of course." He smiled apologetically and spread his hands,
palms up. "Perhaps later? It is one of my favorite ideas, the application of the mathematical laws of probability and error to detective
problems, and a chance to discuss it with you is a golden opportunity."

"Another time. Meanwhile"—Wolfe tapped the generalized law

of error with a finger tip—"I'll keep this. Which one of the people at that broadcast placed that glass and bottle in front of Mr. Orchard?"

"I don't know. I'm going to find it very interesting to compare your handling of me with the way the police did it. What you're trying to do, of course, is to proceed from probability toward certainty, as close as you can get. Say you start, as you see it, with one chance in five that I poisoned Orchard. Assuming that you have no subjective bias, your purpose is to move as rapidly as possible from that position, and you don't care which direction. Anything I say or do will move you one way or the other. If one way, the one-in-five will become one-in-four, one-in-three, and so on until it becomes one-in-one and a minute fraction, which will be close enough to affirmative certainty so that you will say you know that I killed Orchard. If it goes the other way, your one-in-five will become one-in-ten, one-in-one-hundred, one-in-one-thousand; and when it gets to one-in-ten-billion you will be close enough to negative certainty so that you will say you know that I did not kill Orchard. There is a formula—"

"No doubt." Wolfe was controlling himself very well. "If you want to compare me with the police you'll have to let me get a word in now and then. Had you ever seen Mr. Orchard before the day of the broadcast?"

"Oh, yes, six times. The first time was thirteen months earlier, in February 1947. You're going to find me remarkably exact, since the police have had me over all this, back and forth. I might as well give you everything I can that will move you toward affirmative certainty, since subjectively you would prefer that direction. Shall I do that?"

"By all means."

"I thought that would appeal to you. As a mathematician I have always been interested in the application of the calculation of probabilities to the various forms of gambling. The genesis of normal distributions—"

"Not now," Wolfe said sharply.

"Oh—of course not. There are reasons why it is exceptionally difficult to calculate probabilities in the case of horse races, and yet people bet hundreds of millions of dollars on them. A little over a year ago, studying the possibilities of some formulas, I decided to look at some tip sheets, and subscribed to three. One of them was the *Track Almanac,* published by Cyril Orchard. Asked by the police why I chose that one, I could only say that I didn't know. I forget. That is suspicious, for them and you; for me, it is simply a fact that I don't remember. One day in February last year a daily double featured by Orchard came through, and I went to see him. He had some intelligence, and if he had been interested in the mathematical problems involved I could have made good use of him, but he wasn't. In spite of that I saw him occasionally, and he once spent a week end with me at the home of a friend in New Jersey. Altogether, previous to that broadcast, I had seen him, been with him, six times. That's suspicious, isn't it?"

"Moderately," Wolfe conceded.

Savarese nodded. "I'm glad to see you keep as objective as possible. But what about this? When I learned that a popular radio program on a national network had asked for opinions on the advisability of having a horse race tipster as a guest, I wrote a letter strongly urging it, asked for the privilege of being myself the second guest on the program, and suggested that Cyril Orchard should be the tipster invited." Savarese smiled all over, beaming. "What about your one-in-five now?"

Wolfe grunted. "I didn't take that position. You assumed it for me. I suppose the police have that letter you wrote?"

"No, they haven't. No one has it. It seems that Miss Fraser's staff doesn't keep correspondence more than two or three weeks, and my letter has presumably been destroyed. If I had known that in time I might have been less candid in describing the letter's contents to the police, but on the other hand I might not have been. Obviously my treatment of that problem had an effect on my calculations of the probability of my being arrested for murder. But for a free decision I would have had to know, first, that the letter had been destroyed, and, second, that the memories of Miss Fraser's staff were vague about its contents. I learned both of those facts too late."

Wolfe stirred in his chair. "What else on the road to affirmative certainty?"

"Let's see." Savarese considered. "I think that's all, unless we go into observation of distributions, and that should be left for a secondary formula. For instance, my character, a study of which, *a posteriori*, would show it to be probable that I would commit murder for the sake of a sound but revolutionary formula. One detail of that would be my personal finances. My salary as an assistant professor is barely enough to live on endurably, but I paid ten dollars a week for that *Track Almanac*."

"Do you gamble? Do you bet on horse races?"

"No. I never have. I know too much—or rather, I know too little. More than ninety-nine per cent of the bets placed on horse races are outbursts of emotion, not exercises of reason. I restrict my emotions to the activities for which they are qualified." Savarese waved a hand. "That starts us in the other direction, toward a negative certainty, with its conclusion that I did not kill Orchard, and we might as well go on with it. Items:

"I could not have managed that Orchard got the poison. I was seated diagonally across from him, and I did not help pass the bottles. It cannot be shown that I have ever purchased, stolen, borrowed, or possessed any cyanide. It cannot be established that I would, did, or shall profit in any way from Orchard's death. When I arrived at the broadcasting studio, at twenty minutes to eleven, everyone else was already there and I would certainly have been observed if I had gone to the refrigerator and opened its door. There is no evidence that my association with Orchard was other than as I have described it, with no element of animus or of any subjective attitude."

Savarese beamed. "How far have we gone? One-in-one-thousand?"

"I'm not with you," Wolfe said with no element of animus. "I'm not on that road at all, nor on any road. I'm wandering around poking at things. Have you ever been in Michigan?"

For the hour that was left before orchid time Wolfe fired questions at him, and Savarese answered him briefly and to the point. Evidently the professor really did want to compare Wolfe's technique with that of the police, for, as he gave close attention to each question as it was asked, he had more the air of a judge or referee sizing something up than of a murder suspect, guilty or innocent, going through an ordeal. The objective attitude.

He maintained it right up to four o'clock, when the session ended, and I escorted the objective attitude to the front door, and Wolfe went to his elevator.

A little after five Saul Panzer arrived. Coming only up to the middle of my ear, and of slight build, Saul doesn't even begin to fill the red leather chair, but he likes to sit in it, and did so. He is pretty objective too, and I have rarely seen him either elated or upset about anything that had happened to him, or that he had caused to happen to someone else, but that day he was really riled.

"It was bad judgment," he told me, frowning and glum. "Rotten judgment. I'm ashamed to face Mr. Wolfe. I had a good story ready, one that I fully expected to work, and all I needed was ten minutes with the mother to put it over. But I misjudged her. I had discussed her with a couple of the bellhops, and had talked with her on the phone, and had a good chance to size her up in the hotel lobby and when she came outside, and I utterly misjudged her. I can't tell you anything about her brains or character, I didn't get that far, but she certainly knows how to keep the dogs off. I came mighty close to spending the day in the pound."

He told me all about it, and I had to admit it was a gloomy tale. No operative likes to come away empty from as simple a job as that, and Saul Panzer sure doesn't. To get his mind off of it, I mixed him a highball and got out a deck of cards for a little congenial gin. When six o'clock came and brought Wolfe down from the plant rooms, ending the game, I had won something better than three bucks.

Saul made his report. Wolfe sat behind his desk and listened, without interruption or comment. At the end he told Saul he had nothing to apologize for, asked him to phone after dinner for instructions, and let him go. Left alone with me, Wolfe leaned back and shut his eyes and was not visibly even breathing. I got at my typewriter and tapped out a summary of Saul's report, and was on my way to the cabinet to file it when Wolfe's voice came:

"Archie."

"Yes, sir."

"I am stripped. This is no better than a treadmill."

"Yes, sir."

"I have to talk with that girl. Get Miss Fraser."

I did so, but we might as well have saved the nickel. Listening in on my phone, I swallowed it along with Wolfe. Miss Fraser was sorry that we had made little or no progress. She would do anything she could to help, but she was afraid, in fact she was certain, that it would be useless for her to call Mrs. Shepherd at Atlantic City and ask her to bring her daughter to New York to see Wolfe. There was no doubt that Mrs. Shepherd would flatly refuse. Miss Fraser admitted that she had influence with the child, Nancylee, but asserted that she had none at all with the mother. As for phoning Nancylee and persuading her to scoot and come on her own, she wouldn't consider it. She couldn't very well, since she had supplied the money for the mother and daughter to go away.

"You did?" Wolfe allowed himself to sound surprised. "Miss Koppel told Mr. Goodwin that none of you knew where they had gone."

"We didn't, until we saw it in the paper today. Nancylee's father was provoked, and that's putting it mildly, by all the photographers and reporters and everything else, and he blamed it on me, and I offered to pay the expense of a trip for them, but I didn't know where they decided to go."

We hung up, and discussed the outlook. I ventured to suggest two or three other possible lines of action, but Wolfe had his heart set on Nancylee, and I must admit I couldn't blame him for not wanting to start another round of conferences with the individuals he had been working on. Finally he said, in a tone that announced he was no longer discussing but telling me:

"I have to talk with that girl. Go and bring her."

I had known it was coming. "Conscious?" I asked casually.

"I said with her, not to her. She must be able to talk. You could revive her after you get her here. I should have sent you in the first place, knowing how you are with young women."

"Thank you very much. She's not a young woman, she's a minor. She wears socks."

"Archie."

"Yes, sir."

"Get her."

9

I had a bad break. An idea that came to me at the dinner table, while I was pretending to listen to Wolfe telling how men with mustaches a foot long used to teach mathematics in schools in Montenegro, required, if it was to bear fruit, some information from the janitor at 829 Wixley Avenue. But when, immediately after dinner, I drove up there, he had gone to the movies and I had to wait over an hour for him. I got what I hoped would be all I needed, generously ladled out another buck of Hi-Spot money, drove back downtown and put the car in the garage, and went home and up to my room. Wolfe, of course, was in the office, and the door was standing open, but I didn't even stop to nod as I went by.

In my room I gave my teeth an extra good brush, being uncertain how long they would have to wait for the next one, and then did my packing for the trip by putting a comb and hairbrush in my topcoat pocket. I didn't want to have a bag to take care of. Also I made a phone call. I made it there instead of in the office because Wolfe had put it off on me without a trace of a hint regarding ways and means, and if he wanted it like that okay. In that case there was no reason why he should listen to me giving careful and explicit instructions to Saul Panzer. Downstairs again, I did pause at the office door to tell him good night, but that was all I had for him.

Tuesday night I had had a little over three hours' sleep, and Wednesday night about the same. That night, Thursday, I had less than three, and only in snatches. At six-thirty Friday morning, when I emerged to the cab platform at the Atlantic City railroad station, it was still half dark, murky, chilly, and generally unattractive. I had me a good yawn, shivered from head to foot, told a taxi driver I was his customer but he would please wait for me a minute, and then stepped to the taxi just behind him and spoke to the driver of it:

"This time of day one taxi isn't enough for me, I always need two. I'll take the one in front and you follow, and when we stop we'll have a conference."

"Where you going?"

"Not far." I pushed a dollar bill at him. "You won't get lost."

He nodded without enthusiasm and kicked his starter. I climbed into the front cab and told the driver to pull up somewhere in the vicinity of the Ambassador Hotel. It wasn't much of a haul, and a few minutes later he rolled to the curb, which at that time of day had space to spare. When the other driver stopped right behind us I signaled to him, and he came and joined us.

"I have enemies," I told them.

They exchanged a glance and one of them said, "Work it out yourself, bud, we're just hackies. My meter says sixty cents."

"I don't mean that kind of enemies. It's wife and daughter. They're ruining my life. How many ways are there for people to leave the Ambassador Hotel? I don't mean dodges like fire escapes and coal chutes, just normal ways."

"Two," one said.

"Three," the other said.

"Make up your minds."

They agreed on three, and gave me the layout.

"Then there's enough of us," I decided. "Here." I shelled out two finifs, with an extra single for the one who had carried me to even them up. "The final payment will depend on how long it takes, but you won't have to sue me. Now listen."

They did so.

Ten minutes later, a little before seven, I was standing by some kind of a bush with no leaves on it, keeping an eye on the ocean-front entrance of the Ambassador. Gobs of dirty gray mist being batted around by icy gusts made it seem more like a last resort than a resort. Also I was realizing that I had made a serious mistake when I had postponed breakfast until there would be time to do it right. My stomach had decided that since it wasn't going to be needed any more it might as well try shriveling into a ball and see how I liked that. I tried to kid it along by swallowing, but because I hadn't brushed my teeth it didn't taste like me at all, so I tried spitting instead, but that only made my stomach shrivel faster. After less than half an hour of it, when my watch said a quarter past seven, I was wishing to God I had done my planning better when one of my taxis came dashing around a corner to a stop, and the driver called to me and opened the door.

"They're off, bud."

"The station?"

"I guess so. That way." He made a U turn and stepped on the gas. "They came out the cab entrance and took one there. Tony's on their tail."

I didn't have to spur him on because he was already taking it hop, skip, and jump. My wrist watch told me nineteen past—eleven minutes before the seven-thirty for New York would leave. Only four of them had been used up when we did a fancy swerve and jerked to a stop in front of the railroad station. I hopped out. Just ahead of us a woman was paying her driver while a girl stood at her elbow.

"Duck, you damn fool," my driver growled at me. "They ain't blind, are they?"

"That's all right," I assured him. "They know I'm after them. It's a war of nerves."

Tony appeared from somewhere, and I separated myself from another pair of fives and then entered the station. There was only one ticket window working, and mother and child were at it, buying. I moseyed on to the train shed, still with three minutes to go, and was about to glance over my shoulder to see what was keeping them when they passed me on the run, holding hands, daughter in front and pulling Mom along. From the rear I saw them climb on board the train, but I stayed on the platform until the signal had been given and the wheels had started to turn, and then got on.

The diner wasn't crowded. I had a double orange juice, griddle cakes with broiled ham, coffee, French toast with sausage cakes, grape jelly, and more coffee. My stomach and I made up, and we agreed to forget it ever happened.

I decided to go have a look at the family, and here is something I'm not proud of. I had been so damn hungry that no thought of other stomachs had entered my head. But when, three cars back, I saw them and the look on their faces, the thought did come. Of course they were under other strains too, one in particular, but part of that pale, tight, anguished expression unquestionably came from hunger. They had had no time to grab anything on the way, and their manner of life was such that the idea of buying a meal on a train might not even occur to them.

I went back to the end of the car, stood facing the occupants, and called out:

"Get your breakfast in the dining car, three cars ahead! Moderate prices!"

Then I passed down the aisle, repeating it at suitable intervals, once right at their seat. It worked. They exchanged some words and then got up and staggered forward. Not only that, I had made other sales too: a woman, a man, and a couple.

By the time the family returned we were less than an hour from New York. I looked them over as they came down the aisle. Mother was small and round-shouldered and her hair was going gray. Her nose still looked thin and sharp-pointed, but not as much so as it had when she was starving. Nancylee was better-looking, and much more intelligent-looking, than I would have expected from her pictures in the papers or from Saul's description. She had lots of medium-brown hair coming below her shoulders, and blue eyes, so dark that you had to be fairly close to see the blue, that were always on the go. She showed no trace either of Mom's pointed nose or of Pop's acreage of brow. If I had been in high school I would gladly have bought her a Coke or even a sundae.

Danger would begin, I well knew, the minute they stepped off the train at Pennsylvania Station and mounted the stairs. I had decided what to do if they headed for a taxi or bus or the subway, or if Mom started to enter a phone booth. So I was right on their heels when the moment for action came, but the only action called for was a pleasant walk. They took the escalator to the street level, left the station by the north exit, and turned left. I trailed. At Ninth Avenue they turned uptown, and at Thirty-fifth Street left again. That cinched it that they were aiming straight for Wolfe's house, non-stop, and naturally I was anything but crestfallen, but what really did my heart good was the timing. It was exactly eleven o'clock, and Wolfe would get down from the plant rooms and settled in his chair just in time to welcome them.

So it was. West of Tenth Avenue they began looking at the numbers, and I began to close up. At our stoop they halted, took another look, and mounted the steps. By the time they were pushing the button I was at the bottom of the stoop, but they had taken no notice of me. It would have been more triumphant if I could have done it another way, but the trouble was that Fritz wouldn't let them in until he had checked with Wolfe. So I took the steps two at a time, used my key and flung the door open, and invited them:

"Mrs. Shepherd? Go right in."

She crossed the threshold. But Nancylee snapped at me:

"You were on the train. There's something funny about this."

"Mr. Wolfe's expecting you," I said, "if you want to call that funny. Anyway, come inside to laugh, so I can shut the door."

She entered, not taking her eyes off of me. I asked them if they wanted to leave their things in the hall, and they didn't, so I escorted them to the office. Wolfe, in his chair behind his desk, looked undecided for an instant and then got to his feet. I really appreciated that. He never rises when men enter, and his customary routine when a woman enters is to explain, if he feels like taking the trouble, that he keeps his chair because getting out of it and back in again is a more serious undertaking for him than for most men. I knew why he was breaking his rule. It was a salute to me, not just for producing them, but for getting them there exactly at the first minute of the day that he would be ready for them.

"Mrs. Shepherd," I said, "this is Mr. Nero Wolfe. Miss Nancylee Shepherd."

Wolfe bowed. "How do you do, ladies."

"My husband," Mom said in a scared but determined voice. "Where's my husband?"

"He'll be here soon," Wolfe assured her. "He was detained. Sit down, madam."

I grinned at him and shook my head. "Much obliged for trying to help, but that's not the line." I shifted the grin to the family. "I'll have to explain not only to you but to Mr. Wolfe too. Have you got the telegram with you? Let me have it a minute?"

Mom would have opened her handbag, but Nancylee stopped her. "Don't give it to him!" She snapped at me, "You let us out of here right now!"

"No," I said, "not right now, but I will in about five minutes if you still want to go. What are you afraid of? Didn't I see to it that you got some breakfast? First I would like to explain to Mr. Wolfe, and then I'll explain to you." I turned to Wolfe. "The telegram Mrs. Shepherd has in her bag reads as follows: *Take first train to New York and go to office of Nero Wolfe at 918 West Thirty-fifth Street. He is paying for this telegram. Bring Nan with you. Meet me there. Leave your things in your hotel room. Shake a leg. Al.* Saul sent it from a telegraph office in the Bronx at six-thirty this morning. You will understand why I had to go up there again to see the janitor. The *shake a leg* made it absolutely authentic, along with other things."

"Then Father didn't send it!" Nancylee was glaring at me. "I thought there was something funny about it!" She took her mother's arm. "Come on, we're going!"

"Where, Nan?"

"We're leaving here!"

"But where are we going?" Near-panic was in Mom's eyes and voice. "Home?"

"That's the point," I said emphatically. "That's just it. Where? You have three choices. First, you can go home, and when the head of the family comes from work you can tell him how you were taken in by a fake telegram. Your faces show how much that appeals to you. Second, you can take the next train back to Atlantic City, but in that case I phone immediately, before you leave, to Mr. Shepherd at the warehouse where he works, and tell him that you're here with a wild tale about a telegram, and of course he'll want to speak to you. So again you would have to tell him about being fooled by a fake telegram."

Mom looked as if she needed some support, so I moved a chair up behind her and she sat.

"You're utterly awful," Nancylee said. "Just utterly!"

I ignored her and continued to her mother. "Or, third, you can stay here and Mr. Wolfe will discuss some matters with Nancylee, and ask her some questions. It may take two hours, or three, or four, so the sooner he gets started the better. You'll get an extra good lunch. As soon as Mr. Wolfe is through I'll take you to the station and put you on a train for Atlantic City. We'll pay your fare both ways and all expenses, such as taxi fare, and your breakfast, and dinner on the train going back. Mr. Shepherd, whom I have met, will never know anything about it." I screwed my lips. "Those are the only choices I can think of, those three."

Nancylee sat down and—another indication of her intelligence—in the red leather chair.

"This is terrible," Mom said hopelessly. "This is the worst thing . . . you don't look like a man that would do a thing like this. Are you absolutely sure my husband didn't send that telegram? Honestly?"

"Positively not," I assured her. "He doesn't know a thing about it and never will. There's nothing terrible about it. Long before bedtime you'll be back in that wonderful hotel room."

She shook her head as if all was lost.

"It's not so wonderful," Nancylee asserted. "The shower squirts sideways and they won't fix it." Suddenly she clapped a hand to her mouth, went pop-eyed, and sprang from the chair.

"Jumping cats!" she squealed. "Where's your radio? It's Friday! She's broadcasting!"

"No radio," I said firmly. "It's out of order. Here, let me take your coat and hat."

10

During the entire performance, except when we knocked off for lunch, Mrs. Shepherd sat with sagging shoulders on one of the yellow chairs. Wolfe didn't like her there and at various points gave her suggestions, such as going up to the south room for a nap or up to the top to look at the orchids, but she wasn't moving. She was of course protecting her young, but I swear I think her main concern was that if she let us out of her sight we might pull another telegram on her signed Al.

I intend to be fair and just to Nancylee. It is quite true that this is on record, on a page of my notebook:

W: You have a high regard for Miss Fraser, haven't you, Miss Shepherd?

N: Oh, yes! She's simply utterly!

On another page:

W: Why did you leave high school without graduating, if you were doing so well?

N: I was offered a modeling job. Just small time, two dollars an hour not very often and mostly legs, but the cash was simply sweet!

W: You're looking forward to a life of that—modeling?

N: Oh, no! I'm really very serious-minded. *Am* I! I'm going into radio. I'm going to have a program like Miss Fraser—you know, human and get the laughs, but worthwhile and *good*. How often have you been on the air, Mr. Wolfe?

On still another page:

W: How have you been passing your time at Atlantic City?

N: Rotting away. That place is as dead as last week's date. Simply stagnating. Utterly!

Those are verbatim, and there are plenty more where they came from, but there are other pages to balance them. She could talk to the point when she felt like it, as for instance when she explained that she would have been suspicious of the telegram, and would have insisted that her mother call her father at the warehouse by long distance, if she hadn't learned from the papers that Miss Fraser had engaged Nero Wolfe to work on the case. And when he got her going on the subject of Miss Fraser's staff, she not only showed that she had done a neat little job of sizing them up, but also conveyed it to us without including anything that she might be called upon either to prove or to eat.

It was easy to see how desperate Wolfe was from the way he confined himself, up to lunch time, to skating around the edges, getting her used to his voice and manner and to hearing him ask any and every kind of question. By the time Fritz summoned us to the dining room I couldn't see that he had got the faintest flicker of light from any direction.

When we were back in the office and settled again, with Mom in her same chair and Nancylee dragging on a cigarette as if she had been at it for years, Wolfe resumed as before, but soon I noticed that he was circling in toward the scene of the crime. After getting himself up to date on the East Bronx Fraser Girls' Club and how Nancylee had organized it and put it at the top, he went right on into the studio and began on the Fraser broadcasts. He learned that Nancylee was always there on Tuesday, and sometimes on Friday too. Miss Fraser had promised her that she could get on a live mike some day, at least for a line or two. On the network! Most of the time she sat with the audience, front row, but she was always ready to help with anything, and frequently she was allowed to, but only on account of Miss Fraser. The others thought she was a nuisance.

"Are you?" Wolfe asked.

"You bet I am! But Miss Fraser doesn't think so because she knows I think she's the very hottest thing on the air, simply super, and then there's my club, so you see how that is. The old ego mego."

You can see why I'd like to be fair and just to her.

Wolfe nodded as man to man. "What sort of things do you help with?"

"Oh." She waved a hand. "Somebody drops a page of script, I pick it up. One of the chairs squeaks, I hear it first and bring another one. The day it happened, I got the tray of glasses from the cabinet and took them to the table."

"You did? The day Mr. Orchard was a guest?"

"Sure, I often did that."

"Do you have a key to the cabinet?"

"No, Miss Vance has. She opened it and got the tray of glasses out." Nancylee smiled. "I broke one once, and did Miss Fraser throw a fit? No definitely. She just told me to bring a paper cup, that's how super she is."

"Marvelous. When did that happen?"

"Oh, a long while ago, when they were using the plain glasses, before they changed to the dark blue ones."

"How long ago was it?"

"Nearly a year, it must be." Nancylee nodded. "Yes, because it was when they first started to drink Hi-Spot on the program, and the first few times they used plain clear glasses and then they had to change—"

She stopped short.

"Why did they have to change?"

"I don't know."

I expected Wolfe to pounce, or at least to push. There was no doubt about it. Nancylee had stopped herself because she was saying, or starting to say, something that she didn't intend to let out, and when she said she didn't know she was lying. But Wolfe whirled and skated off:

"I suspect to get them so heavy they wouldn't break." He chuckled as if that were utterly amusing. "Have you ever drunk Hi-Spot, Miss Shepherd?"

"Me? Are you kidding? When my club got to the top they sent me ten cases. Truckloads!"

"I don't like it much. Do you?"

"Oh . . . I guess so. I guess I adore it, but not too much at a time. When I get my program and have Shepherd Clubs I'm going to work it a different way." She frowned. "Do you think Nancylee Shepherd is a good radio name, or is Nan Shepherd better, or should I make one up? Miss Fraser's name was Oxhall, and she married a man named Koppel but he died, and when she got into radio she didn't want to use either of them and made one up."

"Either of yours," Wolfe said judiciously, "would be excellent. You must tell me some time how you're going to handle your clubs. Do you think Hi-Spot has pepper in it?"

"I don't know, I never thought. It's a lot of junk mixed together. Not at all frizoo."

"No," Wolfe agreed, "not frizoo. What other things do you do to help out at the broadcasts?"

"Oh, just like I said."

"Do you ever help pass the glasses and bottles around—to Miss Fraser and Mr. Meadows and the guests?"

"No, I tried to once, but they wouldn't let me."

"Where were you—the day we're talking about—while that was being done?"

"Sitting on the piano bench. They want me to stay in the audience while they're on the air, but sometimes I don't."

"Did you see who did the passing—to Mr. Orchard, for instance?"

Nancylee smiled in good-fellowship. "Now you'd like to know that, wouldn't you? But I didn't. The police asked me that about twenty million times."

"No doubt. I ask you once. Do you ever take the bottles from the cabinet and put them in the refrigerator?"

"Sure, I often do that—or I should say I help. That's Miss Vance's job, and she can't carry them all at once, so she has to make two trips, so quite often she takes four bottles and I take three."

"I see. I shouldn't think she would consider you a nuisance. Did you help with the bottles that Tuesday?"

"No, because I was looking at the new hat Miss Fraser had on, and I didn't see Miss Vance starting to get the bottles."

"Then Miss Vance had to make two trips, first four bottles and then three?"

"Yes, because Miss Fraser's hat was really something for the preview. Utterly first run! It had—"

"I believe you." Wolfe's voice sharpened a little, though perhaps only to my experienced ear. "That's right, isn't it, first four bottles and then three?"

"Yes, that's right."

"Making a total of seven?"

"Oh, you can add!" Nancylee exclaimed delightedly. She raised her right hand with four fingers extended, then her left hand with three, and looked from one to the other. "Correct. Seven!"

"Seven," Wolfe agreed. "I can add, and you can, but Miss Vance and Mr. Meadows can't. I understand that only four bottles are required for the program, but that they like to have extra ones in the refrigerator to provide for possible contingencies. But Miss Vance and Mr. Meadows say that the total is eight bottles. You say seven. Miss Vance says that they are taken from the cabinet to the refrigerator in two lots, four and four. You say four and three."

Wolfe leaned forward. "Miss Shepherd." His voice cut. "You will explain to me immediately, and satisfactorily, why they say eight and you say seven. Why?"

She didn't look delighted at all. She said nothing.

"Why?" It was the crack of a whip.

"I don't know!" she blurted.

I had both eyes on her, and even from a corner of one, with the other one shut, it would have been as plain as daylight that she did know, and furthermore that she had clammed and intended to stay clammed.

"Pfui." Wolfe wiggled a finger at her. "Apparently, Miss Shepherd, you have the crackbrained notion that whenever the fancy strikes you you can say you don't know, and I'll let it pass. You tried it about the glasses, and now this. I'll give you one minute to start telling me why the others said the customary number of bottles taken to the refrigerator is eight, and you say seven. —Archie, time it."

I looked at my wrist, and then back at Nancylee. But she merely stayed a clam. Her face showed no sign that she was trying to make one up, or even figuring what would happen if she didn't. She was simply utterly not saying anything. I let her have an extra ten seconds, and then announced:

"It's up."

Wolfe sighed. "I'm afraid, Miss Shepherd, that you and your mother will not return to Atlantic City. Not today. It is—"

A sound of pain came from Mom—not a word, just a sound. Nancy cried:

"But you promised—"

"No. I did not. Mr. Goodwin did. You can have that out with him, but not until after I have given him some instructions." Wolfe turned to me. "Archie, you will escort Miss Shepherd to the office of Inspector Cramer. Her mother may accompany you or go home, as she prefers. But first take this down, type it, and take it with you. Two carbons. A letter to Inspector Cramer."

Wolfe leaned back, closed his eyes, pursed his lips, and in a moment began:

"Regarding the murder of Cyril Orchard, I send you this information by Mr. Goodwin, who is taking Miss Nancylee Shepherd to you. He will explain how Miss Shepherd was brought to New York from Atlantic City. Paragraph.

"I suggest that Miss Madeline Fraser should be arrested without delay, charged with the murder of Cyril Orchard. It is obvious that the members of her staff are joined in a conspiracy. At first I assumed that their purpose was to protect her, but I am now convinced that I was wrong. At my office Tuesday evening it was ludicrously transparent that they were all deeply concerned about Miss Fraser's getting home safely, or so I then thought. I now believe that their concern was of a very different kind. Paragraph.

"That evening, here, Mr. Meadows was unnecessarily explicit and explanatory when I asked him how he decided which bottles to take from the refrigerator. There were various other matters which aroused my suspicion, plainly pointing to Miss Fraser, among them their pretense that they cannot remember who placed the glass and bottle in front of Mr. Orchard, which is of course ridiculous. Certainly they remember; and it is not conceivable that they would conspire unanimously to defend one of their number from exposure, unless that one were Miss Fraser. They are moved, doubtless, by varying considerations—loyalty, affection, or merely the desire to keep their jobs, which they will no longer have after Miss Fraser is arrested and disgraced—and, I hope, punished as the law provides. Paragraph.

"All this was already in my mind, but not with enough conviction to put it to you thus strongly, so I waited until I could have a talk with Miss Shepherd. I have now done that. It is plain that she too is in the conspiracy, and that leaves no doubt that it is Miss Fraser who is being shielded from exposure, since Miss Shepherd would do anything for her but nothing for any of the others. Miss Shepherd has lied to me twice that I am sure of, once when she said that she didn't know why the glasses that they drank from were changed, and once when she would give no explanation of her contradiction of the others regarding the number of bottles put in the refrigerator. Mr. Goodwin will give you the details of that. Paragraph.

"When you have got Miss Fraser safely locked in a cell, I would suggest that in questioning her you concentrate on the changing of the glasses. That happened nearly a year ago, and therefore it seems likely that the murder of Mr. Orchard was planned far in advance. This should make it easier for you, not harder, especially if you are able to persuade Miss Shepherd, by methods available to you, to tell all she knows about it. I do not—*Archie!*"

If Nancylee had had a split personality and it had been the gun-girl half of her that suddenly sprang into action, I certainly would have been caught with my fountain pen down. But she didn't pull a gat. All she did was come out of her chair like a hurricane, get to me before I could even point the pen at her, snatch the notebook and hurl it across the room, and turn to blaze away at Wolfe:

"That's a lie! It's all a lie!"

"Now, Nan," came from Mrs. Shepherd, in a kind of shaky hopeless moan.

I was on my feet at the hurricane's elbow, feeling silly. Wolfe snapped at me:

"Get the notebook and we'll finish. She's hysterical. If she does it again put her in the bathroom."

Nancylee was gripping my coat sleeve. "No!" she cried. "You're a stinker, you know you are! Changing the glasses had nothing to do with it! And I don't know why they changed them, either—you're just a stinker—"

"Stop it!" Wolfe commanded her. "Stop screaming. If you have anything to say, sit down and say it. Why did they change the glasses?"

"I don't know!"

In crossing the room for it I had to detour around Mom, and, doing so, I gave her a pat on the shoulder, but I doubt if she was aware of it. From her standpoint there was nothing left. When I got turned around again Nancylee was still standing there, and from the stiffness of her back she looked put for the day. But as I reached my desk suddenly she spoke, no screaming:

"I honestly don't know why they changed the glasses, because I was just guessing, but if I tell you what I was guessing I'll have to tell you something I promised Miss Fraser I would never tell anybody."

Wolfe nodded. "As I said. Shielding Miss Fraser."

"I'm not shielding her! She doesn't have to be shielded!"

"Don't get hysterical again. What was it you guessed?"

"I want to phone her."

"Of course you do. To warn her. So she can get away."

Nancylee slapped a palm on his desk.

"Don't do that!" he thundered.

"You're such a stinker!"

"Very well. Archie, lock her in the bathroom and phone Mr. Cramer to send for her."

I stood up, but she paid no attention to me. "All right," she said, "then I'll tell her how you made me tell, and my mother can tell her too. When they got the new glasses I didn't know why, but I noticed right away, the broadcast that day, about the bottles too. That day Miss Vance didn't take eight bottles, she only took seven. If it hadn't been for that I might not have noticed, but I did, and when they were broadcasting I saw that the bottle they gave Miss Fraser had a piece of tape on it. And every time after that it has always been seven bottles, and they always give Miss Fraser the one with tape on it. So I thought there was some connection, the new glasses and the tape on the bottle, but I was just guessing."

"I wish you'd sit down, Miss Shepherd. I don't like tipping my head back."

"I wouldn't care if you broke your old neck!"

"Now, Nan," her mother moaned.

Nancylee went to the red leather chair and lowered herself onto the edge of it.

"You said," Wolfe murmured, "that you promised Miss Fraser not to tell about this. When did you promise, recently?"

"No, a long time ago. Months ago. I was curious about the tape on the bottle, and one day I asked Miss Vance about it, and afterward Miss Fraser told me it was something very personal to her and she made me promise never to tell. Twice since then she has asked me if I was keeping the promise and I told her I was and I always would. And now here I am! But you saying she should be arrested for murder . . . just because I said I didn't know . . ."

"I gave other reasons."

"But she won't be arrested now, will she? The way I've explained?"

"We'll see. Probably not." Wolfe sounded comforting. "No one has ever told you what the tape is on the bottle for?"

"No."

"Haven't you guessed?"

"No, I haven't, and I'm not going to guess now. I don't know what it's for or who puts it on or when they put it on, or anything about it except what I've said, that the bottle they give Miss Fraser has a piece of tape on it. And that's been going on a long time, nearly a year, so it couldn't have anything to do with that man getting murdered just last week. So I hope you're satisfied."

"Fairly well," Wolfe conceded.

"Then may I phone her now?"

"I'd rather you didn't. You see, she has hired me to investigate this murder, and I'd prefer to tell her about this myself—and apologize for suspecting her. By the way, the day Mr. Orchard was poisoned—did Miss Fraser's bottle have tape on it that day as usual?"

"I didn't notice it that day, but I suppose so, it always did."

"You're sure you didn't notice it?"

"What do you think? Am I lying again?"

Wolfe shook his head. "I doubt it. You don't sound like it. But one thing you can tell me, about the tape. What was it like and where was it on the bottle?"

"Just a piece of Scotch tape, that's all, around the neck of the bottle, down nearly to where the bottle starts to get bigger."

"Always in the same place?"

"Yes."

"How wide is it?"

"You know, Scotch tape, about that wide." She held a thumb and fingertip about half an inch apart.

"What color?"

"Brown—or maybe it looks brown because the bottle is."

"Always the same color?"

"Yes."

"Then it couldn't have been very conspicuous."

"I didn't say it was conspicuous. It wasn't."

"You have good eyesight, of course, at your age." Wolfe glanced at the clock and turned to me. "When is the next train for Atlantic City?"

"Four-thirty," I told him.

"Then you have plenty of time. Give Mrs. Shepherd enough to cover all expenses. You will take her and her daughter to the station. Since they do not wish it to be known that they have made this trip, it would be unwise for them to do any telephoning, and of course you will make sure that they board the right train, and that the train actually starts. As you know, I do not trust trains either to start or, once started, to stop."

"We're going back," Mom said, unbelieving but daring to hope.

11

There was one little incident I shouldn't skip, on the train when I had found their seats for them and was turning to go. I had made no effort to be sociable, since their manner, especially Nancylee's, had made it plain that if I had stepped into a manhole they wouldn't even have halted to glance down in. But as I turned to go Mom suddenly reached up to pat me on the shoulder. Apparently the pat I had given her at one of her darkest moments had been noticed after all, or maybe it was because I had got them Pullman seats. I grinned at her, but didn't risk offering to shake hands in farewell. I ride my luck only so far.

Naturally another party was indicated, but I didn't realize how urgent it was until I got back to the office and found a note, on a sheet from Wolfe's memo pad, waiting for me under a paperweight on my desk—he being, as per schedule, up in the plant rooms. The note said:

AG—

Have all seven of them here
at six o'clock.

NW

Just like snapping your fingers. I scowled at the note. Why couldn't it be after dinner, allowing more time both to get them and to work on them? Not to mention that I already had a fairly good production record for the day, with the 11:00 A.M. delivery I had made. My watch said ten to five. I swallowed an impulse to mount to the plant rooms and give him an argument, and reached for the phone.

I ran into various difficulties, including resistance to a summons on such short notice, with which I was in complete sympathy. Bill Meadows balked good, saying that he had already told Wolfe everything he knew, including the time he had thrown a baseball through a windowpane, and I had to put pressure on him with menacing hints. Madeline Fraser and Deborah Koppel were reluctant but had to admit that Wolfe should either be fired or given all possible help. They agreed to bring Elinor Vance. Nathan Traub, whom I got first, at his office, was the only one who offered no objection, though he commented that he would have to call off an important appointment. The only two I fell down on were Savarese and Strong. The professor had left town for the week end, I supposed to hunt formulas, and Tully Strong just couldn't be found, though I tried everywhere, including all the sponsors.

Shortly before six I phoned up to Wolfe to report. The best he had for me was a grunt. I remarked that five out of seven, at that hour on a Friday, was nothing to be sneezed at. He replied that seven would have been better.

"Yeah," I agreed. "I've sent Savarese and Strong telegrams signed Al, but what if they don't get them on time?"

So there were five. Wolfe doesn't like to be seen, by anyone but Fritz or me, sitting around waiting for people, I imagine on the theory that it's bad for his prestige, and therefore he didn't come down to the office until I passed him the word that all five were there. Then he favored us by appearing. He entered, bowed to them, crossed to his chair, and got himself comfortable. It was cozier and more intimate than it had been three days earlier, with the gate-crashers absent.

There was a little conversation. Traub offered some pointed remarks about Wolfe's refusal to admit reporters for an interview. Ordinarily, with an opening like that, Wolfe counters with a nasty crusher, but now he couldn't be bothered. He merely waved it away.

"I got you people down here," he said, perfectly friendly, "for a single purpose, and if you're not to be late for your dinners we'd better get at it. Tuesday evening I told you that you were all lying to me, but I didn't know then how barefaced you were about it. Why the devil didn't you tell me about the piece of tape on Miss Fraser's bottle?"

They all muffed it badly, even Miss Fraser, with the sole exception of Traub. He alone looked just bewildered.

"Tape?" he asked. "What tape?"

It took the other four an average of three seconds even to begin deciding what to do about their faces.

"Who is going to tell me about it?" Wolfe inquired. "Not all of you at once. Which one?"

"But," Bill Meadows stammered, "we don't know what you're talking about."

"Nonsense." Wolfe was less friendly. "Don't waste time on that. Miss Shepherd spent most of the day here and I know all about it." His eyes stopped on Miss Fraser. "She couldn't help it, madam. She did quite well for a child, and she surrendered only under the threat of imminent peril to you."

"What's this all about?" Traub demanded.

"It's nothing, Nat," Miss Fraser assured him. "Nothing of any importance. Just a little . . . a sort of joke . . . among us . . . that you don't know about . . ."

"Nothing to it!" Bill Meadows said, a little too loud. "There's a perfectly simple—"

"Wait, Bill." Deborah Koppel's voice held quiet authority. Her gaze was at Wolfe. "Will you tell us exactly what Nancylee said?"

"Certainly," Wolfe assented. "The bottle served to Miss Fraser on the broadcast is always identified with a strip of Scotch tape. That has been going on for months, nearly a year. The tape is either brown, the color of the bottle, or transparent, is half an inch wide, and encircles the neck of the bottle near the shoulder."

"Is that all she told you?"

"That's the main thing. Let's get that explained. What's the tape for?"

"Didn't Nancylee tell you?"

"She said she didn't know."

Deborah was frowning. "Why, she must know! It's quite simple. As we told you, when we get to the studio the day of a broadcast Miss Vance takes the bottles from the cabinet and puts them in the refrigerator. But that gives them only half an hour or a little longer to get cold, and Miss Fraser likes hers as cold as possible, so a bottle for her is put in earlier and the tape put on to tell it from the others."

"Who puts it there and when?"

"Well—that depends. Sometimes one of us puts it there the day before . . . sometimes it's one left over from the preceding broadcast . . ."

"Good heavens," Wolfe murmured. "I didn't know you were an imbecile, Miss Koppel."

"I am not an imbecile, Mr. Wolfe."

"I'll have to have more than your word for it. I presume the explanation you have given me was concocted to satisfy the casual curiosity of anyone who might notice the tape on the bottle—and, incidentally, I wouldn't be surprised if it was offered to Miss Shepherd and after further observation she rejected it. That's one thing she didn't tell me. For that purpose the explanation would be adequate—except with Miss Shepherd—but to try it on me! I'll withdraw the 'imbecile,' since I blurted it at you without warning, but I do think you might have managed something a little less flimsy."

"It may be flimsy," Bill Meadows put in aggressively, "but it happens to be true."

"My dear sir." Wolfe was disgusted. "You too? Then why didn't it satisfy Miss Shepherd, if it was tried on her, and why was she sworn to secrecy? Why weren't all the bottles put in the refrigerator in advance, to get them all cold, instead of just the one for Miss Fraser? There are—"

"Because someone—" Bill stopped short.

"Precisely," Wolfe agreed with what he had cut off. "Because hundreds of people use that studio between Miss Fraser's broadcasts, and someone would have taken them from the refrigerator, which isn't locked. That's what you were about to say, but didn't, because you realized there would be the same hazard for one bottle as for eight." Wolfe shook his head. "No, it's no good. I'm tired of your lies; I want the truth; and I'll get it because nothing else can meet the tests I am now equipped to apply. Why is the tape put on the bottle?"

They looked at one another.

"No," Deborah Koppel said to anybody and everybody.

"What *is* all this?" Traub demanded peevishly.

No one paid any attention to him.

"Why not," Wolfe inquired, "try me with the same answer you have given the police?"

No reply.

Elinor Vance spoke, not to Wolfe. "It's up to you, Miss Fraser. I think we have to tell him."

"No," Miss Koppel insisted.

"I don't see any other way out of it, Debby," Madeline Fraser declared. "You shouldn't have told him that silly lie. It wasn't good enough for him and you know it." Her gray-green eyes went to Wolfe. "It would be fatal for me, for all of us, if this became known. I don't suppose you would give me your word to keep it secret?"

"How could I, madam?" Wolfe turned a palm up. "Under the circumstances? But I'll share it as reluctantly, and as narrowly, as the circumstances will permit."

"All right. Damn that Cyril Orchard, for making this necessary. The tape on the bottle shows that it is for me. My bottle doesn't contain Hi-Spot. I can't drink Hi-Spot."

"Why not?"

"It gives me indigestion."

"Good God!" Nathan Traub cried, his smooth low-pitched voice transformed into a squeak.

"I can't help it, Nat," Miss Fraser told him firmly, "but it does."

"And that," Wolfe demanded, "is your desperate and fatal secret?"

She nodded. "My Lord, could anything be worse? If that got around? If Leonard Lyons got it, for instance? I stuck to it the first few times, but it was no use. I wanted to cut that from the program, serving it, but by that time the Hi-Spot people were crazy about it, especially Anderson and Owen, and of course I couldn't tell them the truth. I tried faking it, not drinking much, but even a few sips made me sick. It must be an allergy."

"I congratulate you," Wolfe said emphatically.

"Good God," Traub muttered. He pointed a finger at Wolfe. "It is absolutely essential that this get to no one. No one whatever!"

"It's out now," Miss Koppel said quietly but tensely. "It's gone now."

"So," Wolfe asked, "you used a substitute?"

"Yes." Miss Fraser went on: "It was the only way out. We used black coffee. I drink gallons of it anyhow, and I like it either hot or cold. With sugar in it. It looks enough like Hi-Spot, which is dark brown, and of course in the bottle it can't be seen anyway, and we changed to dark blue glasses so it couldn't be seen that it didn't fizz."

"Who makes the coffee?"

"My cook, in my apartment."

"Who bottles it?"

"She does—my cook—she puts it in a Hi-Spot bottle, and puts the cap on."

"When, the day of the broadcast?"

"No, because it would still be hot, or at least warm, so she does it the day before and puts it in the refrigerator."

"Not at the broadcasting studio?"

"Oh, no, in my kitchen."

"Does she put the tape on it?"

"No, Miss Vance does that. In the morning she gets it—she always comes to my apartment to go downtown with me—and she puts the tape on it, and takes it to the studio in her bag, and puts it in the refrigerator there. She has to be careful not to let anyone see her do that."

"I feel better," Bill Meadows announced abruptly. He had his handkerchief out and was wiping his forehead.

"Why?" Wolfe asked him.

"Because I knew this had to come sooner or later, and I'm glad it was you that got it instead of the cops. It's been a cockeyed farce, all this digging to find out who had it in for this guy Orchard. Nobody wanted to poison Orchard. The poison was in the coffee and Orchard got it by mistake."

That finished Traub. A groan came from him, his chin went down, and he sat shaking his head in despair.

Wolfe was frowning. "Are you trying to tell me that the police don't know that the poisoned bottle held coffee?"

"Oh, sure, they know that." Bill wanted to help now. "But they've kept it under their hats. You notice it hasn't been in the papers. And none of us has spilled it, you can see why we wouldn't. They know it was coffee all right, but they think it was meant for Orchard, and it wasn't, it was meant for Miss Fraser."

Bill leaned forward and was very earnest. "Damn it, don't you see what we're up against? If we tell it and it gets known, God help the program! We'd get hooted off the air. But as long as we don't tell it, everybody thinks the poison was meant for Orchard, and that's why I said it was a farce. Well, we didn't tell, and as far as I'm concerned we never would."

"How have you explained the coffee to the police?"

"We haven't explained it. We didn't know how the poison got in the bottle, did we? Well, we didn't know how the coffee got there either. What else could we say?"

"Nothing, I suppose, since you blackballed the truth. How have you explained the tape?"

"We haven't explained it."

"Why not?"

"We haven't been asked to."

"Nonsense. Certainly you have."

"I haven't."

"Thanks, Bill." It was Madeline Fraser, smiling at him. "But there's no use trying to save any pieces." She turned to Wolfe. "He's trying to protect me from—don't they call it tampering with evidence? You remember that after the doctor came Mr. Strong took the four bottles from the table and started off with them, just a foolish impulse he had, and Mr. Traub and I took them from him and put them back on the table."

Wolfe nodded.

"Well, that was when I removed the tape from the bottle."

"I see. Good heavens! It's a wonder all of you didn't collectively gather them up, and the glasses, and march to the nearest sink to wash up." Wolfe went back to Bill. "You said Mr. Orchard got the poisoned coffee by mistake. How did that happen?"

"Traub gave it to him. Traub didn't—"

Protests came at him from both directions, all of them joining in. Traub even left his chair to make it emphatic.

Bill got a little flushed, but he was stubborn and heedless. "Since we're telling it," he insisted, "we'd better tell it all."

"You're not sure it was Nat," Miss Koppel said firmly.

"Certainly I'm sure! You know damn well it was! You know

damn well we all saw—all except Lina—that Orchard had her bottle, and of course it was Traub that gave it to him, because Traub was the only one that didn't know about the tape. Anyhow I saw him! —That's the way it was, Mr. Wolfe. But when the cops started on us apparently we all had the same idea—I forget who started it—that it would be best not to remember who put the bottle in front of Orchard. So we didn't. Now that you know about the tape, I do remember, and if the others don't they ought to."

"Quit trying to protect me, Bill," Miss Fraser scolded him. "It was my idea, about not remembering. I started it."

Again several of them spoke at once. Wolfe showed them a palm:

"Please! —Mr. Traub. Manifestly it doesn't matter whether you give me a yes or a no, since you alone were not aware that one of the bottles had a distinction; but I ask you pro forma, did you place that bottle before Mr. Orchard?"

"I don't know," Traub said belligerently, "and I don't care. Meadows doesn't know either."

"But you did help pass the glasses and bottles around?"

"I've told you I did. I thought it was fun." He threw up both hands. "Fun!"

"There's one thing," Madeline Fraser put in, for Wolfe. "Mr. Meadows said that they all saw that Mr. Orchard had my bottle, except me. That's only partly true. I didn't notice it at first, but when I lifted the glass to drink and smelled the Hi-Spot I knew someone else had my glass. I went ahead and faked the drinking, and as I went on with the script I saw that the bottle with the tape on it was a little nearer to him than to me—as you know, he sat across from me. I had to decide quick what to do—not me with the Hi-Spot, but him with the coffee. I was afraid he would blurt out that it tasted like coffee, especially since he had taken two big gulps. I was feeling relieved that apparently he wasn't going to, when he sprang up with that terrible cry . . . so what Mr. Meadows said was only partly true. I suppose he was protecting me some more, but I'm tired of being protected by everybody."

"He isn't listening, Lina," Miss Koppel remarked.

It was a permissible conclusion, but not necessarily sound. Wolfe had leaned back in his chair and closed his eyes, and even to me it might have seemed that he was settling for a snooze but for two details: first, dinner time was getting close, and second, the tip of his right forefinger was doing a little circle on the arm of his chair, around and around. The silence held for seconds, made a minute, and started on another one.

Someone said something.

Wolfe's eyes came half open and he straightened up.

"I could," he said, either to himself or to them, "ask you to stay to dinner. Or to return after dinner. But if Miss Fraser is tired of being protected, I am tired of being humbugged. There are things I need to know, but I don't intend to try to pry them out of you without a lever. If you are ready to let me have them, I'm ready to take them. You know what they are as well as I do. It now seems obvious that this was an attempt to kill Miss Fraser. What further evidence is there to support that assumption, and what evidence is there, if any, to contradict it? Who wants Miss Fraser to die, and why? Particularly, who of those who had access to the bottle of coffee, at any time from the moment it was bottled at her apartment to the moment when it was served at the broadcast? And so on. I won't put all the questions; you know what I want. Will any of you give it to me—any of it?"

His gaze passed along the line. No one said a word.

"One or more of you," he said, "might prefer not to speak in the presence of the others. If so, do you want to come back later? This evening?"

"If I had anything to tell you," Bill Meadows asserted, "I'd tell you now."

"You sure would," Traub agreed.

"I thought not," Wolfe said grimly. "To get anything out of you another Miss Shepherd would be necessary. One other chance: if you prefer not even to make an appointment in the presence of the others, we are always here to answer the phone. But I would advise you not to delay." He pushed his chair back and got erect. "That's all I have for you now, and you have nothing for me."

They didn't like that much. They wanted to know what he was going to do. Especially and unanimously, they wanted to know what about their secret. Was the world going to hear of what a sip of Hi-Spot did to Madeline Fraser? On that Wolfe refused to commit himself. The stubbornest of the bunch was Traub. When the others finally left he stayed behind, refusing to give up the fight, even trying to follow Wolfe into the kitchen. I had to get rude to get rid of him.

When Wolfe emerged from the kitchen, instead of bearing left toward the dining room he returned to the office, although dinner was ready.

I followed. "What's the idea? Not hungry?"

"Get Mr. Cramer."

I went to my desk and obeyed.

Wolfe got on.

"How do you do, sir." He was polite but far from servile. "Yes. No. No, indeed. If you will come to my office after dinner, say at nine o'clock, I'll tell you why you haven't got anywhere on that Orchard case. No, not only that, I think you'll find it helpful. No, nine o'clock would be better."

He hung up, scowled at me, and headed for the dining room. By the time he had seated himself, tucked his napkin in the V of his vest, and removed the lid from the onion soup, letting the beautiful strong steam sail out, his face had completely cleared and he was ready to purr.

12

Inspector Cramer, adjusted to ease in the red leather chair, with beer on the little table at his elbow, manipulated his jaw so that the unlighted cigar made a cocky upward angle from the left side of his mouth.

"Yes," he admitted. "You can have it all for a nickel. That's where I am. Either I'm getting older or murderers are getting smarter."

He was in fact getting fairly gray and his middle, though it would never get into Wolfe's class, was beginning to make pretensions, but his eyes were as sharp as ever and his heavy broad shoulders showed no inclination to sink under the load.

"But," he went on, sounding more truculent than he actually was because keeping the cigar where he wanted it made him talk through his teeth, "I'm not expecting any nickel from you. You don't look as if you needed anything. You look as pleased as if someone had just given you a geranium."

"I don't like geraniums."

"Then what's all the happiness about? Have you got to the point where you're ready to tell Archie to mail out the bills?"

He not only wasn't truculent; he was positively mushy. Usually he called me Goodwin. He called me Archie only when he wanted to peddle the impression that he regarded himself as one of the family, which he wasn't.

Wolfe shook his head. "No, I'm far short of that. But I am indeed pleased. I like the position I'm in. It seems likely that you and your trained men—up to a thousand of them, I assume, on a case as blazoned as this one—are about to work like the devil to help me earn a fee. Isn't that enough to give me a smirk?"

"The hell you say." Cramer wasn't so sugary. "According to the papers your fee is contingent."

"So it is."

"On what you do. Not on what we do."

"Of course," Wolfe agreed. He leaned back and sighed comfortably. "You're much too clearsighted not to appraise the situation, which is a little peculiar, as I do. Would you like me to describe it?"

"I'd love it. You're a good describer."

"Yes, I think I am. You have made no progress, and after ten days you are sunk in a morass, because there is a cardinal fact which you have not discovered. I have. I have discovered it by talking with the very persons who have been questioned by you and your men many times, and it was not given to me willingly. Only by intense and sustained effort did I dig it out. Then why should I pass it on to you? Why don't I use it myself, and go on to triumph?"

Cramer put his beer glass down. "You're telling me."

"That was rhetoric. The trouble is that, while without this fact you can't even get started, with it there is still a job to be done; that job will require further extended dealing with these same people, their histories and relationships; and I have gone as far as I can with them unless I hire an army. You already have an army. The job will probably need an enormous amount of the sort of work for which your men are passably equipped, some of them even adequately, so why shouldn't they do it? Isn't it the responsibility of the police to catch a murderer?"

Cramer was now wary and watchful. "From you," he said, "that's one hell of a question. More rhetoric?"

"Oh, no. That one deserves an answer. Yours, I feel sure, is yes, and the newspapers agree. So I submit a proposal: I'll give you the fact, and you'll proceed to catch the murderer. When that has been done, you and I will discuss whether the fact was essential to your success; whether you could possibly have got the truth and the evidence without it. If we agree that you couldn't, you will so inform my clients, and I shall collect my fee. No document will be required; an oral statement will do; and of course only to my clients. I don't care what you say to journalists or to your superior officers."

Cramer grunted. He removed the cigar from his mouth, gazed at the mangled end suspiciously as if he expected to see a bug crawling, and put it back where it belonged. Then he squinted at Wolfe:

"Would you repeat that?"

Wolfe did so, as if he were reading it off, without changing a word.

Cramer grunted again. "You say if we agree. You mean if you agree with me, or if I agree with you?"

"Bah. It couldn't be plainer."

"Yeah. When you're plainest you need looking at closest. What if I've already got this wonderful fact?"

"You didn't have it two hours ago. If you have it now, I have nothing to give and shall get nothing. If when I divulge it you claim to have had it, you'll tell me when and from whom you got it." Wolfe stirred impatiently. "It is, of course, connected with facts in your possession—for instance, that the bottle contained sugared coffee instead of Hi-Spot."

"Sure, they've told you that."

"Or that your laboratory has found traces of a certain substance, in a band half an inch wide, encircling the neck of the bottle."

"They haven't told you *that*." Cramer's eyes got narrower. "There are only six or seven people who could have told you that, and they all get paid by the City of New York, and by God you can name him before we go any farther."

"Pfui." Wolfe was disgusted. "I have better use for my clients' money than buying information from policemen. Why don't you like my proposal? What's wrong with it? Frankly, I hope to heaven you accept it, and immediately. If you don't I'll have to hire two dozen men and begin all over again on those people, and I'd rather eat baker's bread—almost."

"All right." Cramer did not relax. "Hell, I'd do anything to save you from that. I'm on. Your proposal, as you have twice stated it, provided I get the fact, and all of it, here and now."

"You do. Here it is, and Mr. Goodwin will have a typed copy for you. But first—a little detail—I owe it to one of my clients to request that one item of it be kept confidential, if it can possibly be managed."

"I can't keep murder evidence confidential."

"I know you can't. I said if it can possibly be managed."

"I'll see, but I'm not promising, and if I did promise I probably wouldn't keep it. What's the item? Give it to me first."

"Certainly. Miss Fraser can't drink Hi-Spot because it gives her indigestion."

"What the hell." Cramer goggled at him. "Orchard didn't drink Hi-Spot, he drank coffee, and it didn't give him indigestion, it killed him."

Wolfe nodded. "I know. But that's the item, and on behalf of my clients I ask that it be kept undisclosed if possible. This is going to take some time, perhaps an hour, and your glass and bottle are empty. Archie?"

I got up and bartended without any boyish enthusiasm because I wasn't very crazy about the shape things were taking. I was keeping my fingers crossed. If Wolfe was starting some tricky maneuver and only fed him a couple of crumbs, with the idea of getting a full-sized loaf, not baker's bread, in exchange, that would be one thing, and I was ready to applaud if he got away with it. If he really opened the bag and dumped it out, letting Cramer help himself, that would be something quite different. In that case he was playing it straight, and that could only mean that he had got fed up with them, and really intended to sit and read poetry or draw horses and let the cops earn his fee for him. That did not appeal to me. Money may be everything, but it makes a difference how you get it.

He opened the bag and dumped it. He gave Cramer all we had. He even quoted, from memory, the telegram that had been sent to Mom Shepherd, and as he did so I had to clamp my jaw to keep from making one of four or five remarks that would have fitted the occasion. I had composed that telegram, not him. But I kept my trap shut. I do sometimes ride him in the presence of outsiders, but rarely for Cramer to hear, and not when my feelings are as strong as they were then.

Also Cramer had a lot of questions to ask, and Wolfe answered them like a lamb. And I had to leave my chair so Cramer could rest his broad bottom on it while he phoned his office.

"Rowcliff? Take this down, but don't broadcast it." He was very crisp and executive, every inch an inspector. "I'm at Wolfe's office, and he did have something, and for once I think he's dealing off the top of the deck. We've got to start all over. It's one of those goddam babies where the wrong person got killed. It was intended for the Fraser woman. I'll tell you when I get there, in half an hour, maybe a little more. Call in everybody that's on the case. Find out where the Commissioner is, and the D.A. Get that Elinor Vance and that Nathan Traub, and get the cook at the Fraser apartment. Have those three there by the time I come. We'll take the others in the morning. Who was it went to Michigan—oh, I remember, Darst. Be sure you don't miss him, I want to see him . . ."

And so forth. After another dozen or so executive orders Cramer hung up and returned to the red leather chair.

"What else?" he demanded.

"That's all," Wolfe declared. "I wish you luck."

Having dropped his chewed-up cigar in my wastebasket when he usurped my chair, Cramer got out another one and stuck it in his mouth without looking at it. "I'll tell you," he said. "You gave me a fact, no doubt about that, but this is the first time I ever saw you turn out all your pockets, so I sit down again. Before I leave I'd like to sit here a couple of minutes and ask myself, what for?"

Wolfe chuckled. "Didn't I just hear you telling your men to start to work for me?"

"Yeah, I guess so." The cigar slanted up. "It seems plausible, but I've known you to seem plausible before. And I swear to God if there's a gag in this it's buried too deep for me. You don't even make any suggestions."

"I have none."

And he didn't. I saw that. And there wasn't any gag. I didn't wonder that Cramer suspected him, considering what his experiences with him had been in the past years, but to me it was only too evident that Wolfe had really done a strip act, to avoid overworking his brain. I have sat in that office with him too many hours, and watched him put on his acts for too many audiences, not to know when he is getting up a charade. I certainly don't always know what he is up to, but I do know when he is up to nothing at all. He was simply utterly going to let the city employees do it.

"Would you suggest, for instance," Cramer inquired, "to haul Miss Fraser in on a charge of tampering with evidence? Or the others for obstructing justice?"

Wolfe shook his head. "My dear sir, you are after a murderer, not tamperers or obstructers. Anyway you can't get convictions on charges like that, except in very special cases, and you know it. You are hinting that it isn't like me to expose a client to such a charge, but will you arrest her? No. What you will do, I hope, is find out who it is that wants to kill her. How could I have suggestions for you? You know vastly more about it than I do. There are a thousand lines of investigation, in a case like this, on which I haven't moved a finger; and doubtless you have explored all of them. I won't insult you by offering a list of them. I'll be here, though, I'm always here, should you want a word with me."

Cramer got up and went.

13

I can't deny that from a purely practical point of view the deal that Wolfe made with Cramer that Friday evening was slick, even fancy, and well designed to save wear and tear on Wolfe's energy and the contents of his skull. No matter how it added up at the end it didn't need one of Professor Savarese's formulas to show how probable it was that the fact Wolfe had furnished Cramer would turn out to be an essential item. That was a good bet at almost any odds.

But.

There was one fatal flaw in the deal. The city scientists, in order to earn Wolfe's fee for him while he played around with his toys, had to crack the case. That was the joker. I have never seen a more completely uncracked case than that one was, a full week after Wolfe had made his cute little arrangement to have his detective work done by proxy. I kept up to date on it both by reading the newspapers and by making jaunts down to Homicide headquarters on Twentieth Street, for chats with Sergeant Purley Stebbins or other acquaintances, and twice with Cramer himself. That was humiliating, but I did want to keep myself informed somehow about the case Wolfe and I were working on. For the first time in history I was perfectly welcome at Homicide, especially after three or four days had passed. It got to be pathetic, the way they would greet me like a treasured pal, no doubt thinking it was just possible I had come to contribute another fact. God knows they needed one. For of course they were reading the papers too, and the press was living up to one of its oldest traditions by bawling hell out of the cops for bungling a case which, by prompt and competent—you know how it goes.

So far the public had not been informed that Hi-Spot gave Miss Fraser indigestion. If the papers had known that!

Wolfe wasn't lifting a finger. It was not, properly speaking, a relapse. Relapse is my word for it when he gets so offended or disgusted by something about a case, or so appalled by the kind or amount of work it is going to take to solve it, that he decides to pretend he has never heard of it, and rejects it as a topic of conversation. This wasn't like that. He just didn't intend to work unless he had to. He was perfectly willing to read the pieces in the papers, or to put down his book and listen when I returned from one of my visits to Homicide. But if I tried to badger him into some mild exertion like hiring Saul and Fred and Orrie to look under some stones, or even thinking up a little errand for me, he merely picked up his book again.

If any of the developments, such as they were, meant anything to him, he gave no sign of it. Elinor Vance was arrested, held as a material witness, and after two days released on bail. The word I brought from Homicide was that there was nothing to it except that she had by far the best opportunity to put something in the coffee, with the exception of the cook. Not that there weren't plenty of others; the list had been considerably lengthened by the discovery that the coffee had been made, bottled, and kept overnight in Miss Fraser's apartment, with all the coming and going there.

Then there was the motive-collecting operation. In a murder case you can always get some motives together, but the trouble is you can never be sure which ones are sunfast for the people concerned. It all depends. There was the guy in Brooklyn a few years ago who stabbed a dentist in and around the heart eleven times because he had pulled the wrong tooth. In this case the motive assortment was about average, nothing outstanding but fairly good specimens. Six months ago Miss Fraser and Bill Meadows had had a first-class row, and she had fired him and he had been off the program for three weeks. They both claimed that they now dearly loved each other.

Not long ago Nat Traub had tried to persuade a soup manufacturer, one of the Fraser sponsors, to leave her and sign up for an evening comedy show, and Miss Fraser had retaliated by talking the sponsor into switching to another agency. Not only that, there were vague hints that Miss Fraser had started a campaign for a similar switch by other sponsors, including Hi-Spot, but they couldn't be nailed down. Again, she and Traub insisted that they were awful good friends.

The Radio Writers Guild should have been delighted to poison Miss Fraser on account of her tough attitude toward demands of the Guild for changes in contracts, and Elinor Vance was a member of the Guild in good standing. As for Tully Strong, Miss Fraser had opposed the formation of a Sponsors' Council, and still didn't like it, and of course if there were no Council there would be no secretary.

And so on. As motives go, worth tacking up but not spectacular. The one that would probably have got the popular vote was Deborah Koppel's. Somebody in the D.A.'s office had induced Miss Fraser to reveal the contents of her will. It left ten grand each to a niece and nephew, children of her sister who lived in Michigan, and all the rest to Deborah. It would be a very decent chunk, somewhere in six figures, with the first figure either a 2 or a 3, certainly worth a little investment in poison for anyone whose mind ran in that direction. There was, however, not the slightest indication that Deborah's mind did. She and Miss Fraser, then Miss Oxhall, had been girlhood friends in Michigan, had taught at the same school, and had become sisters-in-law when Madeline had married Deborah's brother Lawrence.

Speaking of Lawrence, his death had of course been looked into again, chiefly on account of the coincidence of the cyanide. He had been a photographer and therefore, when needing cyanide, all he had to do was reach to a shelf for it. What if he hadn't killed himself after all? Or what if, even if he had, someone thought he hadn't, believed it was his wife who had needed the cyanide in order to collect five thousand dollars in insurance money, and had now arranged, after six years, to even up by giving Miss Fraser a dose of it herself?

Naturally the best candidate for that was Deborah Koppel. But they couldn't find one measly scrap to start a foundation with. There wasn't the slightest evidence, ancient or recent, that Deborah and Madeline had ever been anything but devoted friends, bound together by mutual interest, respect, and affection. Not only that, the Michigan people refused to bat an eye at the suggestion that Lawrence Koppel's death had not been suicide. He had been a neurotic hypochondriac, and the letter he had sent to his best friend, a local lawyer, had cinched it. Michigan had been perfectly willing to answer New York's questions, but for themselves they weren't interested.

Another of the thousand lines that petered out into nothing was the effort to link up one of the staff, especially Elinor Vance, with Michigan. They had tried it before with Cyril Orchard, and now they tried it with the others. No soap. None of them had ever been there.

Wolfe, as I say, read some of this in the papers, and courteously listened to the rest of it, and much more, from me. He was not, however, permitted to limit himself strictly to the role of spectator. Cramer came to our office twice during that week, and Anderson, the Hi-Spot president, once; and there were others.

There was Tully Strong, who arrived Saturday afternoon, after a six-hour session with Cramer and an assortment of his trained men. He had probably been pecked at a good deal, as all of them had, since they had told the cops a string of barefaced lies, and he was not in good humor. He was so sore that when he put his hands on Wolfe's desk and leaned over at him to make some remarks about treachery, and his spectacles slipped forward nearly to the tip of his nose, he didn't bother to push them back in place.

His theory was that the agreement with Wolfe was null and void because Wolfe had violated it. Whatever happened, Wolfe not only would not collect his fee, he would not even be reimbursed for expenses. Moreover, he would be sued for damages. His disclosure of a fact which, if made public, would inflict great injury on Miss Fraser and her program, the network, and Hi-Spot, was irresponsible and inexcusable, and certainly actionable.

Wolfe told him bosh, he had not violated the agreement.

"No?" Strong straightened up. His necktie was to one side and his hair needed a comb and brush. His hand went up to his spectacles, which were barely hanging on, but instead of pushing them back he removed them. "You think not? You'll see. And, besides, you have put Miss Fraser's life in danger! I was trying to protect her! We all were!"

"All?" Wolfe objected. "Not all. All but one."

"Yes, all!" Strong had come there to be mad and would have no interference. "No one knew, no one but us, that it was meant for her! Now everybody knows it! Who can protect her now? I'll try, we all will, but what chance have we got?"

It seemed to me he was getting illogical. The only threat to Miss Fraser, as far as we knew, came from the guy who had performed on the coffee, and surely we hadn't told him anything he didn't already know.

I had to usher Tully Strong to the door and out. If he had been capable of calming down enough to be seated for a talk I would have been all for it, but he was really upset. When Wolfe told me to put him out I couldn't conscientiously object. At that he had spunk. Anybody could have told from one glance at us that if I was forced to deal with him physically I would have had to decide what to do with my other hand, in case I wanted to be fully occupied, but when I took hold of his arm he jerked loose and then turned on me as if stretching me out would be pie. He had his specs in one hand, too. I succeeded in herding him out without either of us getting hurt.

As was to be expected, Tully Strong wasn't the only one who had the notion that Wolfe had committed treason by giving their fatal secret to the cops. They all let us know it, too, either by phone or in person. Nat Traub's attitude was specially bitter, probably because of the item that had been volunteered by Bill Meadows, that Traub had served the bottle and glass to Orchard. Cramer's crew must have really liked that one, and I could imagine the different keys they used playing it for Traub to hear. One thing I preferred not to imagine was what we would have got from Mr. Walter B. Anderson, the Hi-Spot president, and Fred Owen, the director of public relations, if anyone had told them the full extent of Wolfe's treachery. Apparently they were still ignorant about the true and horrible reason why one of the bottles had contained coffee instead of The Drink You Dream Of.

Another caller, this one Monday afternoon, was the formula hound, Professor Savarese. He too came to the office straight from a long conference with the cops, and he too was good and mad, but for a different reason. The cops had no longer been interested in his association with Cyril Orchard, or in anything about Orchard at all, and he wanted to know why. They had refused to tell him. They had reviewed his whole life, from birth to date, all over again, but with an entirely different approach. It was plain that what they were after now was a link between him and Miss Fraser. Why? What new factor had entered? The intrusion of a hitherto unknown and unsuspected factor would raise hell with his calculation of probabilities, but if there was one he had to have it, and quick. This was the first good chance he had ever had to test his formulas on the most dramatic of all problems, a murder case, from the inside, and he wasn't going to tolerate any blank spaces without a fight.

What was the new factor? Why was it now a vital question whether he had had any previous association, direct or indirect, with Miss Fraser?

Up to a point Wolfe listened to him without coming to a boil, but he finally got annoyed enough to call on me again to do some more ushering. I obeyed in a halfhearted way. For one thing, Wolfe was passing up another chance to do a dime's worth of work himself, with Savarese right there and more than ready to talk, and for another, I was resisting a temptation. The question had popped into my head, how would this figure wizard go about getting Miss Fraser's indigestion into a mathematical equation? It might not be instructive to get him to answer it, but at least it would pass the time, and it would help as much in solving the case as anything Wolfe was doing. But, not wanting to get us any more deeply involved in treachery than we already were, I skipped it.

I ushered him out.

Anyhow, that was only Monday. By the time four more days had passed and another Friday arrived, finishing a full week since we had supplied Cramer with a fact, I was a promising prospect for a strait jacket. That evening, as I returned to the office with Wolfe after an unusually good dinner which I had not enjoyed, the outlook for the next three or four hours revolted me. As he got himself adjusted comfortably in his chair and reached for his book, I announced:

"I'm going to my club."

He nodded, and got his book open.

"You do not even," I said cuttingly, "ask me which club, though you know damn well I don't belong to any. I am thoroughly fed up with sitting here day after day and night after night, waiting for the moment when the idea will somehow seep into you that a detective is supposed to detect. You are simply too goddam lazy to live. You think you're a genius. Say you are. If in order to be a genius myself I had to be as self-satisfied, as overweight, and as inert as you are, I like me better this way."

Apparently he was reading.

"This," I said, "is the climax I've been leading up to for a week—or rather, that you've been leading me up to. Sure, I know your alibi, and I'm good and sick of it—that there is nothing we can do that the cops aren't already doing. Of all the sausage." I kept my voice dry, factual, and cultured. "If this case is too much for you why don't you try another one? The papers are full of them. How about the gang that stole a truckload of cheese yesterday right here on Eleventh Avenue? How about the fifth-grade boy that hit his teacher in the eye with a jelly bean? Page fifty-eight in the *Times*. Or, if everything but murder is beneath you, what's wrong with the political and economic fortuneteller, a lady named Beula Poole, who got shot in the back of her head last evening? Page one of any paper. You could probably sew that one up before bedtime."

He turned over a page.

"Tomorrow," I said, "is Saturday. I shall draw my pay as usual. I'm going to a fight at the Garden. Talk about contrasts—you in that chair and a couple of good middleweights in a ring."

I blew.

But I didn't go to the Garden. My first stop was the corner drugstore, where I went to a phone booth and called Lon Cohen of the *Gazette*. He was in, and about through, and saw no reason why I shouldn't buy him eight or ten drinks, provided he could have a two-inch steak for a chaser.

So an hour later Lon and I were at a corner table at Pietro's. He had done well with the drinks and had made a good start on the steak. I was having highballs, to be sociable, and was on my third, along with my second pound of peanuts. I hadn't realized how much I had short-changed myself on dinner, sitting opposite Wolfe, until I got into the spirit of it with the peanuts.

We had discussed the state of things from politics to prizefights, by no means excluding murder. Lon had had his glass filled often enough, and had enough of the steak in him, to have reached a state of mind where he might reasonably be expected to be open to suggestion. So I made an approach by telling him, deadpan, that in my opinion the papers were riding the cops too hard on the Orchard case.

He leered at me. "For God's sake, has Cramer threatened to take your license or something?"

"No, honest," I insisted, reaching for peanuts, "this one is really tough and you know it. They're doing as well as they can with what they've got. Besides that, it's so damn commonplace. Every paper always does it—after a week start crabbing and after two weeks start screaming. It's got so everybody always expects it and nobody ever reads it. You know what I'd do if I ran a newspaper? I'd start running stuff that people would read."

"Jesus!" Lon gawked at me. "What an idea! Give me a column on it. Who would teach 'em to read?"

"A column," I said, "would only get me started. I need at least a page. But in this particular case, where it's at now, it's a question of an editorial. This is Friday night. For Sunday you ought to have an editorial on the Orchard case. It's still hot and the public still loves it. But—"

"I'm no editor, I'm a news man."

"I know, I'm just talking. Five will get you ten that your sheet will have an editorial on the Orchard case Sunday, and what will it say? It will be called OUR PUBLIC GUARDIANS, and it will be the same old crap, and not one in a thousand will read beyond the first line. Phooey. If it was me I would call it TOO OLD OR TOO FAT, and I wouldn't mention the cops once. Nor would I mention Nero Wolfe, not by name. I would refer to the blaze of publicity with which a certain celebrated private investigator entered the Orchard case, and to the expectations it aroused. That his record seemed to justify it. That we see now how goofy it was, because in ten days he hasn't taken a trick. That the reason may be that he is getting too old, or too fat, or merely that he hasn't got what it takes when a case is really tough, but no matter what the reason is, this shows us that for our protection from vicious criminals we must rely on our efficient and well-trained police force, and not on any so-called brilliant geniuses. I said I wouldn't mention the cops, but I think I'd better, right at the last. I could add a sentence that while they may have got stuck in the mud on the Orchard case, they are the brave men who keep the structure of our society from you know."

Lon, having swallowed a hunk of steak, would have spoken, but I stopped him:

"They would read that, don't think they wouldn't. I know you're not an editor, but you're the best man they've got and you're allowed to talk to editors, aren't you? I would love to see an editorial like that tried, just as an experiment. So much so that if a paper ran it I would want to show my appreciation the first opportunity I get, by stretching a point a hell of a ways to give it first crack at some interesting little item."

Lon had his eyebrows up. "If you don't want to bore me, turn it the other side up so the interesting little item will be on top."

"Nuts. Do you want to talk about it or not?"

"Sure, I'll talk about anything."

I signaled the waiter for refills.

14

I would give anything in the world, anyway up to four bits, to know whether Wolfe saw or read that editorial before I showed it to him late Sunday afternoon. I think he did. He always glances over the editorials in three papers, of which the *Gazette* is one, and if his eye caught it at all he must have read it. It was entitled THE FALSE ALARM, and it carried out the idea I had given Lon to a T.

I knew of course that Wolfe wouldn't do any spluttering, and I should have realized that he probably wouldn't make any sign or offer any comment. But I didn't, and therefore by late afternoon I was in a hole. If he hadn't read it I had to see that he did, and that was risky. It had to be done right or he would smell an elephant. So I thought it over: what would be the natural thing? How would I naturally do it if I suddenly ran across it?

What I did do was turn in my chair to grin at him and ask casually:

"Did you see this editorial in the *Gazette* called THE FALSE ALARM?"

He grunted. "What's it about?"

"You'd better read it." I got up, crossed over, and put it on his desk. "A funny thing, it gave me the feeling I had written it myself. It's the only editorial I've seen in weeks that I completely agree with."

He picked it up. I sat down facing him, but he held the paper so that it cut off my view. He isn't a fast reader, and he held the pose long enough to read it through twice, but that's exactly what he would have done if he already knew it by heart and wanted me to think otherwise.

"Bah!" The paper was lowered. "Some little scrivener who doubtless has ulcers and is on a diet."

"Yeah, I guess so. The rat. The contemptible louse. If only he knew how you've been sweating and stewing, going without sleep—"

"Archie. Shut up."

"Yes, sir."

I hoped to God I was being natural.

That was all for then, but I was not licked. I had never supposed that he would tear his hair or pace up and down. A little later an old friend of his, Marko Vukcic, dropped in for a Sunday evening snack—five kinds of cheese, guava jelly, freshly roasted chestnuts, and almond tarts. I was anxious to see if he would show the editorial to Marko, which would have been a bad sign. He didn't. After Marko had left, to return to Rusterman's Restaurant, which was the best in New York because he managed it, Wolfe settled down with his book again, but hadn't turned more than ten pages before he dogeared and closed it and tossed it to a far corner of his desk. He then got up, crossed the room to the big globe, and stood and studied geography. That didn't seem to satisfy him any better than the book, so he went and turned on the radio. After dialing to eight different stations, he muttered to himself, stalked back to his chair behind his desk, and sat and scowled. I took all this in only from a corner of one eye, since I was buried so deep in a magazine that I didn't even know he was in the room.

He spoke. "Archie."

"Yes, sir?"

"It has been nine days."

"Yes, sir."

"Since that tour de force of yours. Getting that Miss Shepherd here."

"Yes, sir."

He was being tactful. What he meant was that it had been nine days since he had passed a miracle by uncovering the tape on the bottle and Miss Fraser's indigestion, but he figured that if he tossed me a bone I would be less likely either to snarl or to gloat. He went on:

"It was not then flighty to assume that a good routine job was all that was needed. But the events of those nine days have not supported that assumption."

"No, sir."

"Get Mr. Cramer."

"As soon as I finish this paragraph."

I allowed a reasonable number of seconds to go by, but I admit I wasn't seeing a word. Then, getting on the phone, I was prepared to settle for less than the inspector himself, since it was Sunday evening, and hoped that Wolfe was too, but it wasn't necessary. Cramer was there, and Wolfe got on and invited him to pay us a call.

"I'm busy." Cramer sounded harassed. "Why, have you got something?"

"Yes."

"What?"

"I don't know. I won't know until I've talked with you. After we've talked your busyness may be more productive than it has been."

"The hell you say. I'll be there in half an hour."

That didn't elate me at all. I hadn't cooked up a neat little scheme, and devoted a whole evening to it, and bought Lon Cohen twenty bucks' worth of liquids and solids, just to prod Wolfe into getting Cramer in to talk things over. As for his saying he had something, that was a plain lie. All he had was a muleheaded determination not to let his ease and comfort be interfered with.

So when Cramer arrived I didn't bubble over. Neither did he, for that matter. He marched into the office, nodded a greeting, dropped into the red leather chair, and growled:

"I wish to God you'd forget you're eccentric and start moving around more. Busy as I am, here I am. What is it?"

"My remark on the phone," Wolfe said placidly, "may have been blunt, but it was justified."

"What remark?"

"That your busyness could be more productive. Have you made any progress?"

"No."

"You're no further along than you were a week ago?"

"Further along to the day I retire, yes. Otherwise no."

"Then I'd like to ask some questions about that woman, Beula Poole, who was found dead in her office Friday morning. The papers say that you say it was murder. Was it?"

I gawked at him. This was clear away from me. When he jumped completely off the track like that I never knew whether he was stalling, being subtle, or trying to show me how much of a clod I was.

Then I saw a gleam in Cramer's eye which indicated that even he had left me far behind, and all I could do was gawk some more.

Cramer nodded. "Yeah, it was murder. Why, looking for another client so I can earn another fee for you?"

"Do you know who did it?"

"No."

"No glimmer? No good start?"

"No start at all, good or bad."

"Tell me about it."

Cramer grunted. "Most of it has been in the papers, all but a detail or two we've saved up." He moved further back in the chair, as if he might stay longer than he had thought. "First you might tell me what got you interested, don't you think?"

"Certainly. Mr. Cyril Orchard, who got killed, was the publisher of a horse race tip sheet for which subscribers paid ten dollars a week, an unheard-of price. Miss Beula Poole, who also got killed, was the publisher of a sheet which purported to give inside advance information on political and economic affairs, for which subscribers paid the same unheard-of price of ten dollars a week."

"Is that all?"

"I think it's enough to warrant a question or two. It is true that Mr. Orchard was poisoned and Miss Poole was shot, a big variation in method. Also that it is now assumed that Mr. Orchard was killed by misadventure, the poison having been intended for another, whereas the bullet that killed Miss Poole must have been intended for her. But even so, it's a remarkable coincidence—sufficiently so to justify some curiosity, at least. For example, it might be worth the trouble to compare the lists of subscribers of the two publications."

"Yeah, I thought so too."

"You did?" Wolfe was a little annoyed, as he always was at any implication that someone else could be as smart as him. "Then you've compared them. And?"

Cramer shook his head. "I didn't say I'd compared them, I said I'd thought of it. What made me think of it was the fact that it couldn't be done, because there weren't any lists to compare."

"Nonsense. There must have been. Did you look for them?"

"Sure we did, but too late. In Orchard's case there was a little bad management. His office, a little one-room hole in a building on Forty-second Street, was locked, and there was some fiddling around looking for an employee or a relative to let us in. When we finally entered by having the superintendent admit us, the next day, the place had been cleaned out—not a piece of paper or an address plate or anything else. It was different with the woman, Poole, because it was in her office that she was shot—another one-room hole, on the third floor of an old building on Nineteenth Street, only four blocks from my place. But her body wasn't found until nearly noon the next day, and by the time we got there that had been cleaned out too. The same way. Nothing."

Wolfe was no longer annoyed. Cramer had had two coincidences and he had had only one. "Well." He was purring. "That settles it. In spite of variations, it is now more than curiosity. Of course you have inquired?"

"Plenty. The sheets were printed at different shops, and neither of them had a list of subscribers or anything else that helps. Neither Orchard nor the woman employed any help. Orchard left a widow and two children, but they don't seem to know a damn thing about his business, let alone who his subscribers were. Beula Poole's nearest relatives live out West, in Colorado, and they don't know anything, apparently not even how she was earning a living. And so on. As for the routine, all covered and all useless. No one seen entering or leaving—it's only two flights up—no weapon, no fingerprints that help any, nobody heard the shot—"

Wolfe nodded impatiently. "You said you hadn't made any start, and naturally routine has been followed. Any discoverable association of Miss Poole with Mr. Orchard?"

"If there was we can't discover it."

"Where were Miss Fraser and the others at the time Miss Poole was shot?"

Cramer squinted at him. "You think it might even develop that way?"

"I would like to put the question. Wouldn't you?"

"Yeah. I have. You see, the two offices being cleaned out is a detail we've saved up." Cramer looked at me. "And you'll kindly not peddle it to your pal Cohen of the *Gazette*." He went on to Wolfe: "It's not so easy because there's a leeway of four or five hours on when she was shot. We've asked all that bunch about it, and no one can be checked off."

"Mr. Savarese? Miss Shepherd? Mr. Shepherd?"

"What?" Cramer's eyes widened. "Where the hell does Shepherd come in?"

"I don't know. Archie doesn't like him, and I have learned that it is always quite possible that anyone he doesn't like may be a murderer."

"Oh, comic relief. The Shepherd girl was in Atlantic City with her mother, and still is. On Savarese I'd have to look at the reports, but I know he's not checked off because nobody is. By the way, we've dug up two subscribers to Orchard's tip sheet, bes'des Savarese and the Fraser woman. With no result. They bet on the races and they subscribed, that's all, according to them."

"I'd like to talk with them," Wolfe declared.

"You can. At my office any time."

"Pfui. As you know, I never leave this house on business. If you'll give Archie their names and addresses he'll attend to it."

Cramer said he'd have Stebbins phone and give them to me. I never saw him more cooperative, which meant that he had never been more frustrated.

They kept at it a while longer, but Cramer had nothing more of any importance to give Wolfe, and Wolfe hadn't had anything to give Cramer to begin with. I listened with part of my brain, and with the other part tried to do a little offhand sorting and arranging. I had to admit that it would take quite a formula to have room for the two coincidences as such, and therefore they would probably have to be joined together somehow, but it was no part-brain job for me. Whenever dough passes without visible value received the first thing you think of is blackmail, so I thought of it, but that didn't get me anywhere because there were too many other things in the way. It was obvious that the various aspects were not yet in a condition that called for the application of my particular kind of talent.

After Cramer had gone Wolfe sat and gazed at a distant corner of the ceiling with his eyes open about a thirty-second of an inch. I sat and waited, not wanting to disturb him, for when I saw his lips pushing out, and in again, and out and in, I knew he was exerting himself to the limit, and I was perfectly satisfied. There had been a good chance that he would figure that he had helped all he could for a while, and go back to his reading until Cramer made a progress report or somebody else got killed. But the editorial had stung him good. Finally he transferred the gaze to me and pronounced my name.

"Yes, sir," I said brightly.

"Your notebook. Take this."

I got ready.

"Former subscribers to the publication of Cyril Orchard, or to that of Beula Poole, should communicate with me immediately. Put it in three papers, the *Gazette,* the *News,* and the *Herald-Tribune.* A modest display, say two inches. Reply to a box number. A good page if possible."

"And I'll call for the replies? It saves time."

"Then do so."

I put paper in the typewriter. The phone rang. It was Sergeant Purley Stebbins, to give me the names and addresses of the two Orchard subscribers they had dug up.

15

So beginning Monday morning we were again a going concern, instead of a sitting-and-waiting one, but I was not in my element. I like a case you can make a diagram of. I don't object to complications, that's all right, but if you're out for bear it seems silly to concentrate on hunting for moose tracks. Our fee depended on our finding out how and why Orchard got cyanided by drinking Madeline Fraser's sugared coffee, and here we were spending our time and energy on the shooting of a female named Beula Poole. Even granting it was one and the same guy who pinched the lead pencils and spilled ink on the rug, if you've been hired to nail him for pencil stealing that's what you should work at.

I admit that isn't exactly fair, because most of our Monday activities had to do with Orchard. Wolfe seemed to think it was important for him to have a talk with those two subscribers, so instead of using the phone I went out after them. I had one of them in the office waiting for him at 11:00 A.M.—an assistant office manager for a big tile company. Wolfe spent less than a quarter of an hour on him, knowing, of course, that the cops had spent more and had checked him. He had bet on the races for years. In February a year ago he had learned that a Hialeah daily double featured in a sheet called *Track Almanac* had come through for a killing, and he had subscribed, though the ten bucks a week was a sixth of his salary. He had stayed with it for nine weeks and then quit. So much for him.

The other one was a little different. Her name was Marie Leconne, and she owned a snooty beauty parlor on Madison Avenue. She wouldn't have accepted my invitation if she hadn't been under the illusion that Wolfe was connected with the police, though I didn't precisely tell her so. That Monday evening she was with us a good two hours, but left nothing of any value behind. She had subscribed to *Track Almanac* in August, seven months ago, and had remained a subscriber up to the time of Orchard's death. Prior to subscribing she had done little or no betting on the races; she was hazy about whether it was little, or no. Since subscribing she had bet frequently, but she firmly refused to tell where, through whom, or in what amounts. Wolfe, knowing that I occasionally risk a finif, passed me a hint to have some conversation with her about pertinent matters like horses and jockeys, but she declined to cooperate. All in all she kept herself nicely under control, and flew off the handle only once, when Wolfe pressed her hard for a plausible reason why she had subscribed to a tip sheet at such a price. That aggravated her terribly, and since the one thing that scares Wolfe out of his senses is a woman in a tantrum, he backed away fast.

He did keep on trying, from other angles, but when she finally left all we knew for sure was that she had not subscribed to *Track Almanac* in order to get guesses on the ponies. She was slippery, and nobody's fool, and Wolfe had got no further than the cops in opening her up.

I suggested to Wolfe: "We might start Saul asking around in her circle."

He snorted. "Mr. Cramer is presumably attending to that, and, anyway, it would have to be dragged out of her inch by inch. The advertisement should be quicker."

It was quicker, all right, in getting results, but not the results we were after. There had not been time to make the Monday papers, so the ad's first appearance was Tuesday morning. Appraising it, I thought it caught the eye effectively for so small a space. After breakfast, which I always eat in the kitchen with Fritz while Wolfe has his in his room on a tray, and after dealing with the morning mail and other chores in the office, I went out to stretch my legs and thought I might as well head in the direction of the Herald-Tribune Building. Expecting nothing so soon but thinking it wouldn't hurt to drop in, I did so. There was a telegram. I tore it open and read:

CALL MIDLAND FIVE THREE SEVEN
EIGHT FOUR LEAVE MESSAGE FOR
DUNCAN GIVING APPOINTMENT

I went to a phone booth and put a nickel in the slot, with the idea of calling Cramer's office to ask who Midland 5-3784 belonged to, but changed my mind. If it happened that this led to a hot trail we didn't want to be hampered by city interference, at least I didn't. However, I thought I might as well get something for my nickel and dialed another number. Fritz answered, and I asked him to switch it to the plant rooms.

"Yes, Archie?" Wolfe's voice came, peevish. He was at the bench, repotting, as I knew from his schedule, and he hates to be interrupted at that job. I told him about the telegram.

"Very well, call the number. Make an appointment for eleven o'clock or later."

I walked back home, went to my desk, dialed the Midland number, and asked for Mr. Duncan. Of course it could have been Mrs. or Miss, but I preferred to deal with a man after our experience with Marie Leconne. A gruff voice with an accent said that Mr. Duncan wasn't there and was there a message.

"Will he be back soon?"

"I don't know. All I know is that I can take a message."

I thereupon delivered one, that Mr. Duncan would be expected at Nero Wolfe's office at eleven o'clock, or as soon thereafter as possible.

He didn't come. Wolfe descended in his elevator sharp at eleven as usual, got himself enthroned, rang for beer, and began sorting plant cards he had brought down with him. I had him sign a couple of checks and then started to help with the cards. At half past eleven I asked if I should ring the Midland number to see if Duncan had got the message, and he said no, we would wait until noon.

The phone rang. I went to my desk and told it:

"Nero Wolfe's office, Goodwin speaking."

"I got your message for Duncan. Let me speak to Mr. Wolfe, please."

I covered the transmitter and told Wolfe: "He says Duncan, but it's a voice I've heard. It's not a familiar voice, but by God I've heard it. See if you have."

Wolfe lifted his instrument.

"Yes, Mr. Duncan? This is Nero Wolfe."

"How are you?" the voice asked.

"I'm well, thank you. Do I know you, sir?"

"I really don't know. I mean I don't know if you would recognize me, seeing me, because I don't know how foolishly inquisitive you may have been. But we have talked before, on the phone."

"We have?"

"Yes. Twice. On June ninth, nineteen forty-three, I called to give you some advice regarding a job you were doing for General Carpenter. On January sixteenth, nineteen forty-six, I called to speak about the advisability of limiting your efforts in behalf of a Mrs. Tremont."

"Yes. I remember."

I remembered too. I chalked it against me that I hadn't recognized the voice with the first six words, though it had been over two years since I had heard it—hard, slow, precise, and cold as last week's corpse. It was continuing:

"I was pleased to see that you did limit your efforts as I suggested. That showed—"

"I limited them because no extension of them was required to finish the job I was hired for. I did not limit them because you suggested it, Mr. Zeck." Wolfe was being fairly icy himself.

"So you know my name." The voice never changed.

"Certainly. I went to some trouble and expense to ascertain it. I don't pay much attention to threats, I get too many of them, but at least I like to know who the threatener is. Yes, I know your name, sir. Is that temerarious? Many people know Mr. Arnold Zeck."

"You have had no occasion to. This, Mr. Wolfe, does *not* please me."

"I didn't expect it to."

"No. But I am much easier to get along with when I am pleased. That's why I sent you that telegram and am talking with you now. I have strong admiration for you, as I've said before. I wouldn't want to lose it. It would please me better to keep it. Your advertisement in the papers has given me some concern. I realize that you didn't know that, you couldn't have known it, so I'm telling you. The advertisement disturbs me. It can't be recalled; it has appeared. But it is extremely important that you should not permit it to lead you into difficulties that will be too much for you. The wisest course for you will be to drop the matter. You understand me, don't you, Mr. Wolfe?"

"Oh yes, I understand you. You put things quite clearly, Mr. Zeck, and so do I. I have engaged to do something, and I intend to do it. I haven't the slightest desire either to please you or to displease you, and unless one or the other is inherent in my job you have no reason to be concerned. You understand me, don't you?"

"Yes. I do. But now you know."

The line went dead.

Wolfe cradled the phone and leaned back in his chair, with his eyes closed to a slit. I pushed my phone away, swiveled, and gazed at him through a minute's silence.

"So," I said. "That sonofabitch. Shall I find out about the Midland number?"

Wolfe shook his head. "Useless. It would be some little store that merely took a message. Anyway, he has a number of his own."

"Yeah. He didn't know you knew his name. Neither did I. How did that happen?"

"Two years ago I engaged some of Mr. Bascom's men without telling you. He had sounded as if he were a man of resource and resolution, and I didn't want to get you involved."

"It's the Zeck with the place in Westchester, of course?"

"Yes. I should have signaled you off as soon as I recognized his voice. I tell you nothing because it is better for you to know nothing. You are to forget that you know his name."

"Like that." I snapped my fingers, and grinned at him. "What the hell? Does he eat human flesh, preferably handsome young men?"

"No. He does worse." Wolfe's eyes came half open. "I'll tell you this. If ever, in the course of my business, I find that I am committed against him and must destroy him, I shall leave this house, find a place where I can work—and sleep and eat if there is time for it—and stay there until I have finished. I don't want to do that, and therefore I hope I'll never have to."

"I see. I'd like to meet this bozo. I think I'll make his acquaintance."

"You will not. You'll stay away from him." He made a face. "If this job leads me to that extremity—well, it will or it won't." He glanced at the clock. "It's nearly noon. You'd better go and see if any more answers have arrived. Can't you telephone?"

16

There were no more answers. That goes not only for Tuesday noon, but for the rest of the day and evening, and Wednesday morning, and Wednesday after lunch. Nothing doing.

It didn't surprise me. The nature of the phone call from the man whose name I had been ordered to forget made it seem likely that there was something peculiar about the subscribers to *Track Almanac* and *What to Expect,* which was the name of the political and economic dope sheet published by the late Beula Poole. But even granting that there wasn't, that as far as they were concerned it was all clean and straight, the two publishers had just been murdered, and who would be goop enough to answer such an ad just to get asked a lot of impertinent questions? In the office after lunch Wednesday I made a remark to that effect to Wolfe, and got only a growl for reply.

"We might at least," I insisted, "have hinted that they would get their money back or something."

No reply.

"We could insert it again and add that. Or we could offer a reward for anyone who would give us the name of an Orchard or Poole subscriber."

No reply.

"Or I could go up to the Fraser apartment and get into conversation with the bunch, and who knows?"

"Yes. Do so."

I looked at him suspiciously. He meant it.

"Now?"

"Yes."

"You sure are hard up when you start taking suggestions from me."

I pulled the phone to me and dialed the number. It was Bill Meadows who answered, and he sounded anything but gay, even when he learned it was me. After a brief talk, however, I was willing to forgive him. I hung up and informed Wolfe:

"I guess I'll have to postpone it. Miss Fraser and Miss Koppel are both out. Bill was a little vague, but I gather that the latter has been tagged by the city authorities for some reason or other, and the former is engaged in trying to remove the tag. Maybe she needs help. Why don't I find out?"

"I don't know. You might try."

I turned and dialed Watkins 9-8241. Inspector Cramer wasn't available, but I got someone just as good, or sometimes I think even better, Sergeant Stebbins.

"I need some information," I told him, "in connection with this fee you folks are earning for Mr. Wolfe."

"So do we," he said frankly. "Got any?"

"Not right now. Mr. Wolfe and I are in conference. How did Miss Koppel hurt your feelings, and where is she, and if you see Miss Fraser give her my love."

He let out a roar of delight. Purley doesn't laugh often, at least when he's on duty, and I resented it. I waited until I thought he might hear me and then demanded:

"What the hell is so funny?"

"I never expected the day to come," he declared. "You calling me to ask where your client is. What's the matter, is Wolfe off his feed?"

"I know another one even better. Call me back when you're through laughing."

"I'm through. Haven't you heard what the Koppel dame did?"

"No. I only know what you tell me."

"Well, this isn't loose yet. We may want to keep it a while if we can, I don't know."

"I'll help you keep it. So will Mr. Wolfe."

"That's understood?"

"Yes."

"Okay. Of course they've all been told not to leave the jurisdiction. This morning Miss Koppel took a cab to La Guardia. She was nabbed as she was boarding the nine o'clock plane for Detroit. She says she wanted to visit her sick mother in Fleetville, which is eighty miles from Detroit. But she didn't ask permission to go, and the word we get is that her mother is no sicker than she has been for a year. So we charged her as a material witness. Does that strike you as highhanded? Do you think it calls for a shakeup?"

"Get set for another laugh. Where's Miss Fraser?"

"With her lawyer at the D.A.'s office discussing bail."

"What kind of reasons have you got for Miss Koppel taking a trip that are any better than hers?"

"I wouldn't know. Now you're out of my class. If you want to go into details like that, Wolfe had better ask the Inspector."

I tried another approach or two, but either Purley had given me all there was or the rest was in another drawer which he didn't feel like opening. I hung up and relayed the news to Wolfe.

He nodded as if it were no concern of his. I glared at him:

"It wouldn't interest you to have one or both of them stop in for a chat on their way home? To ask why Miss Koppel simply had to go to Michigan would be vulgar curiosity?"

"Bah. The police are asking, aren't they?" Wolfe was bitter. "I've spent countless hours with those people, and got something for it only when I had a whip to snap. Why compound futility? I need another whip. Call those newspapers again."

"Am I still to go up there? After the ladies get home?"

"You might as well."

"Yeah." I was savage. "At least I can compound some futility."

I phoned all three papers. Nothing. Being in no mood to sit and concentrate on germination records, I announced that I was going out for a walk, and Wolfe nodded absently. When I got back it was after four o'clock and he had gone up to the plant rooms. I fiddled around, finally decided that I might as well concentrate on something and the germination records were all I had, and got Theodore's reports from the drawer, but then I thought why not throw away three more nickels? So I started dialing again.

Herald-Tribune, nothing. *News*, nothing. But the *Gazette* girl said yes, they had one. The way I went for my hat and headed for Tenth Avenue to grab a taxi, you might have thought I was on my way to a murder.

The driver was a philosopher. "You don't see many eager happy faces like yours nowadays," he told me.

"I'm on my way to my wedding."

He opened his mouth to speak again, then clamped it shut. He shook his head resolutely. "No. Why should I spoil it?"

I paid him off outside the *Gazette* building and went in and got my prize. It was a square pale-blue envelope, and the printed return on the flap said:

                    Mrs. W. T. Michaels
                    890 East End Avenue
                    New York City 28

Inside was a single sheet matching the envelope, with small neat
handwriting on it:

> Box P304:
>   Regarding your advertisement, I am not a former subscriber
> to either of the publications, but I may be able to tell you some-
> thing. You may write me, or call Lincoln 3-4808, but do not
> phone before ten in the morning or after five-thirty in the after-
> noon. That is important.
>
>   Hilda Michaels

It was still forty minutes this side of her deadline, so I went
straight to a booth and dialed the number. A female voice answered.
I asked to speak to Mrs. Michaels.

"This is Mrs. Michaels."

"This is the *Gazette* advertiser you wrote to, Box P304. I've just
read—"

"What's your name?" She had a tendency to snap.

"My name is Goodwin, Archie Goodwin. I can be up there in
fifteen minutes or less—"

"No, you can't. Anyway, you'd better not. Are you connected
with the Police Department?"

"No. I work for Nero Wolfe. You may have heard of Nero Wolfe,
the detective?"

"Of course. This isn't a convent. Was that his advertisement?"

"Yes. He—"

"Then why didn't he phone me?"

"Because I just got your note. I'm phoning from a booth in the
Gazette building. You said not—"

"Well, Mr. Goodman, I doubt if I can tell Mr. Wolfe anything
he would be interested in. I really doubt it."

"Maybe not," I conceded. "But he would be the best judge of
that. If you don't want me to come up there, how would it be if you
called on Mr. Wolfe at his office? West Thirty-fifth Street—it's in
the phone book. Or I could run up now in a taxi and—"

"Oh, not now. Not today. I might be able to make it tomorrow—
or Friday—"

I was annoyed. For one thing, I would just as soon be permitted to finish a sentence once in a while, and for another, apparently she had read the piece about Wolfe being hired to work on the Orchard case, and my name had been in it, and it had been spelled correctly. So I took on weight:

"You don't seem to realize what you've done, Mrs. Michaels. You—"

"Why, what have I done?"

"You have landed smack in the middle of a murder case. Mr. Wolfe and the police are more or less collaborating on it. He would like to see you about the matter mentioned in his advertisement, not tomorrow or next week, but quick. I think you ought to see him. If you try to put it off because you've begun to regret sending this note he'll be compelled to consult the police, and then what? Then you'll—"

"I didn't say I regret sending the note."

"No, but the way you—"

"I'll be at Mr. Wolfe's office by six o'clock."

"Good! Shall I come—"

I might have known better than to give her another chance to chop me off. She said that she was quite capable of getting herself transported, and I could well believe it.

17

There was nothing snappy about her appearance. The mink coat, and the dark red woolen dress made visible when the coat had been spread over the back of the red leather chair, unquestionably meant well, but she was not built to cooperate with clothes. There was too much of her and the distribution was all wrong. Her face was so well padded that there was no telling whether there were any bones underneath, and the creases were considerably more than skin deep. I didn't like her. From Wolfe's expression it was plain, to me, that he didn't like her. As for her, it was a safe bet that she didn't like anybody.

Wolfe rustled the sheet of pale-blue paper, glanced at it again, and looked at her. "You say here, madam, that you may be able to tell me something. Your caution is understandable and even commendable. You wanted to find out who had placed the advertisement before committing yourself. Now you know. There is no need—"

"That man threatened me," she snapped. "That's not the way to get me to tell something—if I have something to tell."

"I agree. Mr. Goodwin is headstrong. —Archie, withdraw the threat."

I did my best to grin at her as man to woman. "I take it back, Mrs. Michaels. I was so anxious—"

"If I tell you anything," she said to Wolfe, ignoring me, "it will be because I want to, and it will be completely confidential. Whatever you do about it, of course I have nothing to say about that, but you will give me your solemn word of honor that my name will not be mentioned to anyone. No one is to know I wrote you or came to see you or had anything to do with it."

Wolfe shook his head. "Impossible. Manifestly impossible. You are not a fool, madam, and I won't try to treat you as if you were. It is even conceivable that you might have to take the witness stand in a murder trial. I know nothing about it, because I don't know what you have to tell. Then how could I—"

"All right," she said, surrendering. "I see I made a mistake. I must be home by seven o'clock. Here's what I have to tell you: somebody I know was a subscriber to that *What to Expect* that was published by that woman, Beula Poole. I distinctly remember, one day two or three months ago, I saw a little stack of them somewhere—in some house or apartment or office. I've been trying to remember where it was, and I simply can't. I wrote you because I thought you might tell me something that would make me remember, and I'm quite willing to try, but I doubt if it will do any good."

"Indeed." Wolfe's expression was fully as sour as hers. "I said you're not a fool. I suppose you're prepared to stick to that under any circum——"

"Yes, I am."

"Even if Mr. Goodwin gets headstrong again and renews his threat?"

"That!" She was contemptuous.

"It's very thin, Mrs. Michaels. Even ridiculous. That you would go to the bother of answering that advertisement, and coming down here—"

"I don't mind being ridiculous."

"Then I have no alternative." Wolfe's lips tightened. He released them. "I accept your conditions. I agree, for myself and for Mr. Goodwin, who is my agent, that we will not disclose the source of our information, and that we will do our utmost to keep anyone from learning it. Should anyone ascertain it, it will be against our will and in spite of our precautions in good faith. We cannot guarantee; we can only promise; and we do so."

Her eyes had narrowed. "On your solemn word of honor."

"Good heavens. That ragged old patch? Very well. My solemn word of honor. Archie?"

"My solemn word of honor," I said gravely.

Her head made an odd ducking movement, reminding me of a fat-cheeked owl I had seen at the zoo getting ready to swoop on a mouse.

"My husband," she said, "has been a subscriber to that publication, *What to Expect*, for eight months."

But the owl had swooped because it was hungry, whereas she was swooping just to hurt. It was in her voice, which was still hers but quite different when she said the word husband.

"And that's ridiculous," she went on, "if you want something ridiculous. He hasn't the slightest interest in politics or industry or the stock market or anything like that. He is a successful doctor and all he ever thinks about is his work and his patients, especially his women patients. What would he want with a thing like that *What to Expect?* Why should he pay that Beula Poole money every week, month after month? I have my own money, and for the first few years after we married we lived on my income, but then he began to be successful, and now he doesn't need my money any more. And he doesn't—"

Abruptly she stood up. Apparently the habit had got so strong that sometimes she even interrupted herself. She was turning to pick up her coat.

"If you please," Wolfe said brusquely. "You have my word of honor and I want some details. What has your husband—"

"That's all," she snapped. "I don't intend to answer any silly questions. If I did you'd be sure to give me away, you wouldn't be smart enough not to, and the details don't matter. I've told you the one thing you need to know, and I only hope—"

She was proceeding with the coat, and I had gone to her to help.

"Yes, madam, what do you hope?"

She looked straight at him. "I hope you've got some brains. You don't look it."

She turned and made for the hall, and I followed. Over the years I have opened that front door to let many people out of that house, among them thieves, swindlers, murderers, and assorted crooks, but it has never been a greater pleasure than on that occasion. Added to everything else, I had noticed when helping her with her coat that her neck needed washing.

It had not been news to us that her husband was a successful doctor. Between my return to the office and her arrival there had been time for a look at the phone book, which had him as an M.D. with an office address in the Sixties just off Park Avenue, and for a call to Doc Vollmer. Vollmer had never met him, but knew his standing and reputation, which were up around the top. He had a good high-bracket practice, with the emphasis on gynecology.

Back in the office I remarked to Wolfe, "There goes my pendulum again. Lately I've been swinging toward the notion of getting myself a little woman, but good Godalmighty. Brother!"

He nodded, and shivered a little. "Yes. However, we can't reject it merely because it's soiled. Unquestionably her fact is a fact; otherwise she would have contrived an elaborate support for it." He glanced at the clock. "She said she had to be home by seven, so he may still be in his office. Try it."

I found the number and dialed it. The woman who answered firmly intended to protect her employer from harassment by a stranger, but I finally sold her.

Wolfe took it. "Dr. Michaels? This is Nero Wolfe, a detective. Yes, sir, so far as I know there is only one of that name. I'm in a little difficulty and would appreciate some help from you."

"I'm just leaving for the day, Mr. Wolfe. I'm afraid I couldn't undertake to give you medical advice on the phone." His voice was low, pleasant, and tired.

"It isn't medical advice I need, doctor. I want to have a talk with you about a publication called *What to Expect*, to which you subscribed. The difficulty is that I find it impractical to leave my house. I could send my assistant or a policeman to see you, or both, but I would prefer to discuss it with you myself, confidentially. I wonder if you could call on me this evening after dinner?"

Evidently the interrupting mania in the Michaels family was

confined to the wife. Not only did he not interrupt, he didn't even take a cue. Wolfe tried again:

"Would that be convenient, sir?"

"If I could have another moment, Mr. Wolfe. I've had a hard day and am trying to think."

"By all means."

He took ten seconds. His voice came, even tireder:

"I suppose it would be useless to tell you to go to hell. I would prefer not to discuss it on the phone. I'll be at your office around nine o'clock."

"Good. Have you a dinner engagement, doctor?"

"An engagement? No. I'm dining at home. Why?"

"It just occurred to me—could I prevail on you to dine with me? You said you were just leaving for the day. I have a good cook. We are having fresh pork tenderloin, with all fiber removed, done in a casserole, with a sharp brown sauce moderately spiced. There will not be time to chambrer a claret properly, but we can have the chill off. We shall of course not approach our little matter until afterward, with the coffee—or even after that. Do you happen to know the brandy labeled Remisier? It is not common. I hope this won't shock you, but the way to do it is to sip it with bites of Fritz's apple pie. Fritz is my cook."

"I'll be damned. I'll be there—what's the address?"

Wolfe gave it to him, and hung up.

"I'll be damned too," I declared. "A perfect stranger? He may put horseradish on oysters."

Wolfe grunted. "If he had gone home to eat with that creature things might have been said. Even to the point of repudiation by her and defiance by him. I thought it prudent to avoid that risk."

"Nuts. There's no such risk and you know it. What you're trying to avoid is to give anyone an excuse to think you're human. You were being kind to your fellow man and you'd rather be caught dead. The idea of the poor devil going home to dine with that female hyena was simply too much for your great big warm heart, and you were so damn impetuous you even committed yourself to letting him have some of that brandy of which there are only nineteen bottles in the United States and they're all in your cellar."

"Bosh." He arose. "You would sentimentalize the multiplication table." He started for the kitchen, to tell Fritz about the guest, and to smell around.

18

After dinner Fritz brought us a second pot of coffee in the office, and also the brandy bottle and big-bellied glasses. Most of the two hours had been spent, not on West Thirty-fifth Street in New York, but in Egypt. Wolfe and the guest had both spent some time there in days gone by, and they had settled on that for discussion and a few arguments.

Dr. Michaels, informally comfortable in the red leather chair, put down his coffee cup, ditched a cigarette, and gently patted his midriff. He looked exactly like a successful Park Avenue doctor, middle-aged, well-built and well-dressed, worried but self-assured. After the first hour at the table the tired and worried look had gone, but now, as he cocked an eye at Wolfe after disposing of the cigarette, his forehead was wrinkled again.

"This has been a delightful recess," he declared. "It has done me a world of good. I have dozens of patients for whom I would like to prescribe a dinner with you, but I'm afraid I'd have to advise you not to fill the prescription." He belched, and was well-mannered enough not to try to cheat on it. "Well. Now I'll stop masquerading as a guest and take my proper role. The human sacrifice."

Wolfe disallowed it. "I have no desire or intention to gut you, sir."

Michaels smiled. "A surgeon might say that too, as he slits the skin. No, let's get it done. Did my wife phone you, or write you, or come to see you?"

"Your wife?" Wolfe's eyes opened innocently. "Has there been any mention of your wife?"

"Only by me, this moment. Let it pass. I suppose your solemn word of honor has been invoked—a fine old phrase, really, solemn word of honor—" He shrugged. "I wasn't actually surprised when you asked me about that blackmail business on the phone, merely momentarily confused. I had been expecting something of the sort, because it didn't seem likely that such an opportunity to cause me embarrassment—or perhaps worse—would be missed. Only I would have guessed it would be the police. This is much better, much."

Wolfe's head dipped forward, visibly, to acknowledge the compliment. "It may eventually reach the police, doctor. There may be no help for it."

"Of course, I realize that. I can only hope not. Did she give you the anonymous letters, or just show them to you?"

"Neither. But that 'she' is your pronoun, not mine. With that understood—I have no documentary evidence, and have seen none. If there is some, no doubt I could get it." Wolfe sighed, leaned back, and half closed his eyes. "Wouldn't it be simpler if you assume that I know nothing at all, and tell me about it?"

"I suppose so, damn it." Michaels sipped some brandy, used his tongue to give all the membranes a chance at it, swallowed, and put the glass down. "From the beginning?"

"If you please."

"Well . . . it was last summer, nine months ago, that I first learned about the anonymous letters. One of my colleagues showed me one that he had received by mail. It strongly hinted that I was chronically guilty of—uh, unethical conduct—with women patients. Not long after that I became aware of a decided change in the attitude of one of my oldest and most valued patients. I appealed to her to tell me frankly what had caused it. She had received two similar letters. It was the next day—naturally my memory is quite vivid on this—that my wife showed me two letters, again similar, that had come to her."

The wrinkles on his forehead had taken command again. "I don't have to explain what that sort of thing could do to a doctor if it kept up. Of course I thought of the police, but the risk of possible publicity, or even spreading of rumor, through a police inquiry, was too great. There was the same objection, or at least I thought there was, to hiring a private investigator. Then, the day after my wife showed me the letters—no, two days after—I had a phone call at my home in the evening. I presume my wife listened to it on the extension in her room—but you're not interested in that. I wish to God you were—" Michaels abruptly jerked his head up as if he had heard a noise somewhere. "Now what did I mean by that?"

"I have no idea," Wolfe murmured. "The phone call?"

"It was a woman's voice. She didn't waste any words. She said she understood that people had been getting letters about me, and if it annoyed me and I wanted to stop it I could easily do so. If I would subscribe for one year to a publication called *What to Expect*—she gave me the address—there would be no more letters. The cost would be ten dollars a week, and I could pay as I pleased, weekly, monthly, or the year in advance. She assured me emphatically that there would be no request for renewal, that nothing beyond the one year's subscription would be required, that the letters would stop as soon as I subscribed, and that there would be no more."

Michaels turned a hand to show a palm. "That's all. I subscribed. I sent ten dollars a week for a while—eight weeks—and then I sent a check for four hundred and forty dollars. So far as I know there have been no more letters—and I think I would know."

"Interesting," Wolfe murmured. "Extremely."

"Yes," Michaels agreed. "I can understand your saying that. It's what a doctor says when he runs across something rare like a lung grown to a rib. But if he's tactful he doesn't say it in the hearing of the patient."

"You're quite right, sir. I apologize. But this is indeed a rarity—truly remarkable! If the execution graded as high as the conception . . . what were the letters like, typed?"

"Yes. Plain envelopes and plain cheap paper, but the typing was perfect."

"You said you sent a check. That was acceptable?"

Michaels nodded. "She made that clear. Either check or money order. Cash would be accepted, but was thought inadvisable on account of the risk in the mails."

"You see? Admirable. What about her voice?"

"It was medium in pitch, clear and precise, educated—I mean good diction and grammar—and matter-of-fact. One day I called the number of the publication—as you probably know, it's listed—and asked for Miss Poole. It was Miss Poole talking, she said. I discussed a paragraph in the latest issue, and she was intelligent and informed about it. But her voice was soprano, jerky and nervous, nothing like the voice that had told me how to get the letters stopped."

"It wouldn't be. That was what you phoned for?"

"Yes. I thought I'd have that much satisfaction at least, since there was no risk in it."

"You might have saved your nickel." Wolfe grimaced. "Dr. Michaels, I'm going to ask you a question."

"Go ahead."

"I don't want to, but though the question is intrusive it is also important. And it will do no good to ask it unless I can be assured of a completely candid reply or a refusal to answer at all. You would be capable of a fairly good job of evasion if you were moved to try, and I don't want that. Will you give me either candor or silence?"

Michaels smiled. "Silence is so awkward. I'll give you a straight answer or I'll say 'no comment.'"

"Good. How much substance was there in the hints in those letters about your conduct?"

The doctor looked at him, considered, and finally nodded his head. "It's intrusive, all right, but I'll take your word for it that it's important. You want a full answer?"

"As full as possible."

"Then it must be confidential."

"It will be."

"I accept that. I don't ask for your solemn word of honor. There was not even a shadow of substance. I have never, with any patient, even approached the boundaries of professional decorum. But I'm not like you; I have a deep and intense need for the companionship of a woman. I suppose that's why I married so early—and so disastrously. Possibly her money attracted me too, though I would vigorously deny it; there are bad streaks in me. Anyway, I do have the companionship of a woman, but not the one I married. She has never been my patient. When she needs medical advice she goes to some other doctor. No doctor should assume responsibility for the health of one he loves or one he hates."

"This companionship you enjoy—it could not have been the stimulus for the hints in the letters?"

"I don't see how. All the letters spoke of women patients—in the plural, and patients."

"Giving their names?"

"No, no names."

Wolfe nodded with satisfaction. "That would have taken too much research for a wholesale operation, and it wasn't necessary." He came forward in his chair to reach for the push button. "I am greatly obliged to you, Dr. Michaels. This has been highly distasteful for you, and you have been most indulgent. I don't need to prolong it, and I won't. I foresee no necessity to give the police your name, and I'll even engage not to do so, though heaven only knows what my informant will do. Now we'll have some beer. We didn't get it settled about the pointed arches in the Tulun mosque."

"If you don't mind," the guest said, "I've been wondering if it would be seemly to tip this brandy bottle again."

So he stayed with the brandy while Wolfe had beer. I excused myself and went out for a breath of air, for while they were perfectly welcome to do some more settling about the pointed arches in the Tulun mosque, as far as I was concerned it had been attended to long ago.

It was past eleven when I returned, and soon afterward Michaels arose to go. He was far from being pickled, but he was much more relaxed and rosy than he had been when I let him in. Wolfe was so mellow that he even stood up to say good-by, and I didn't see his usual flicker of hesitation when Michaels extended a hand. He doesn't care about shaking hands indiscriminately.

Michaels said impulsively, "I want to ask you something."

"Then do so."

"I want to consult you professionally—your profession. I need help, I want to pay for it."

"You will, sir, if it's worth anything."

"It will be, I'm sure. I want to know, if you are being shadowed, if a man is following you, how many ways are there of eluding him, and what are they, and how are they executed?"

"Good heavens." Wolfe shuddered. "How long has this been going on?"

"For months."

"Well. —Archie?"

"Sure," I said. "Glad to."

"I don't want to impose on you," Michaels lied. He did. "It's late."

"That's okay. Sit down."

I really didn't mind, having met his wife.

19

That, I thought to myself as I was brushing my hair Thursday morning, covered some ground. That was a real step forward.

Then, as I dropped the brush into the drawer, I asked aloud, "Yeah? Toward what?"

In a murder case you expect to spend at least half your time barking up wrong trees. Sometimes that gets you irritated, but what the hell, if you belong in the detective business at all you just skip it and take another look. That wasn't the trouble with this one. We hadn't gone dashing around investigating a funny sound only to learn it was just a cat on a fence. Far from it. We had left all that to the cops. Every move we had made had been strictly pertinent. Our two chief discoveries—the tape on the bottle of coffee and the way the circulation department of *What to Expect* operated —were unquestionably essential parts of the picture of the death of Cyril Orchard, which was what we were working on.

So it was a step forward. Fine. When you have taken a step forward, the next thing on the program is another step in the same direction. And that was the pebble in the griddle cake I broke a tooth on that morning. Bathing and dressing and eating breakfast, I went over the situation from every angle and viewpoint, and I had to admit this: if Wolfe had called me up to his room and asked for a suggestion on how I should spend the day, I would have been tongue-tied.

What I'm doing, if you're following me, is to justify what I did do. When he did call me up to his room, and wished me a good morning, and asked how I had slept, and told me to phone Inspector Cramer and invite him to pay us a visit at eleven o'clock, all I said was:

"Yes, sir."

There was another phone call which I had decided to make on my own. Since it involved a violation of a law Wolfe had passed I didn't want to make it from the office, so when I went out for a stroll to the bank to deposit a check from a former client who was paying in installments, I patronized a booth. When I got Lon Cohen I told him I wanted to ask him something that had no connection with the detective business, but was strictly private. I said I had been offered a job at a figure ten times what he was worth, and fully half what I was, and, while I had no intention of leaving Wolfe, I was curious. Had he ever heard of a guy named Arnold Zeck, and what about him?

"Nothing for you," Lon said.

"What do you mean, nothing for me?"

"I mean you don't want a Sunday feature, you want the lowdown, and I haven't got it. Zeck is a question mark. I've heard that he owns twenty Assemblymen and six district leaders, and I've also heard that he is merely a dried fish. There's a rumor that if you

print something about him that he resents your body is washed
ashore at Montauk Point, mangled by sharks, but you know how
the boys talk. One little detail—this is between us?"

"Forever."

"There's not a word on him in our morgue. I had occasion to look
once, several years ago—when he gave his yacht to the Navy. Not
a thing, which is peculiar for a guy that gives away yachts and
owns the highest hill in Westchester. What's the job?"

"Skip it. I wouldn't consider it. I thought he still had his yacht."

I decided to let it lay. If the time should come when Wolfe had
to sneak outdoors and look for a place to hide, I didn't want it
blamed on me.

Cramer arrived shortly after eleven. He wasn't jovial, and neither
was I. When he came, as I had known him to, to tear Wolfe to pieces,
or at least to threaten to haul him downtown or send a squad with a
paper signed by a judge, he had fire in his eye and springs in his
calves. This time he was so forlorn he even let me hang up his hat
and coat for him. But as he entered the office I saw him squaring
his shoulders. He was so used to going into that room to be belligerent that it was automatic. He growled a greeting, sat, and demanded:

"What have you got this time?"

Wolfe, lips compressed, regarded him a moment and then
pointed a finger at him. "You know, Mr. Cramer, I begin to suspect
I'm a jackass. Three weeks ago yesterday, when I read in the paper
of Mr. Orchard's death, I should have guessed immediately why
people paid him ten dollars a week. I don't mean merely the general idea of blackmail; that was an obvious possibility; I mean the
whole operation, the way it was done."

"Why, have you guessed it now?"

"No. I've had it described to me."

"By whom?"

"It doesn't matter. An innocent victim. Would you like to have
me describe it to you?"

"Sure. Or the other way around."

Wolfe frowned. "What? You know about it?"

"Yeah, I know about it. I do now." Cramer wasn't doing any bragging. He stayed glum. "Understand I'm saying nothing against the
New York Police Department. It's the best on earth. But it's a large
organization, and you can't expect everyone to know what every-

body else did or is doing. My part of it is Homicide. Well. In September nineteen forty-six, nineteen months ago, a citizen lodged a complaint with a precinct detective sergeant. People had received anonymous letters about him, and he had got a phone call from a man that if he subscribed to a thing called *Track Almanac* for one year there would be no more letters. He said the stuff in the letters was lies, and he wasn't going to be swindled, and he wanted justice. Because it looked as if it might be a real job the sergeant consulted his captain. They went together to the *Track Almanac* office, found Orchard there, and jumped him. He denied it, said it must have been someone trying to queer him. The citizen listened to Orchard's voice, both direct and on the phone, and said it hadn't been his voice on the phone, it must have been a confederate. But no lead to a confederate could be found. Nothing could be found. Orchard stood pat. He refused to let them see his subscription list, on the ground that he didn't want his customers pestered, which was within his rights in the absence of a charge. The citizen's lawyer wouldn't let him swear a warrant. There were no more anonymous letters."

"Beautiful," Wolfe murmured.

"What the hell is so beautiful?"

"Excuse me. And?"

"And nothing. The captain is now retired, living on a farm in Rhode Island. The sergeant is still a sergeant, as he should be, since apparently he doesn't read the papers. He's up in a Bronx precinct, specializing on kids that throw stones at trains. Just day before yesterday the name Orchard reminded him of something! So I've got that. I've put men onto the other Orchard subscribers that we know about, except the one that was just a sucker—plenty of men to cover anybody at all close to them, to ask about anonymous letters. There have been no results on Savarese or Madeline Fraser, but we've uncovered it on the Leconne woman, the one that runs a beauty parlor. It was the same routine—the letters and the phone call, and she fell for it. She says the letters were lies, and it looks like they were, but she paid up to get them stopped, and she pushed us off, and you too, because she didn't want a stink."

Cramer made a gesture. "Does that describe it?"

"Perfectly," Wolfe granted.

"Okay. You called me, and I came because I swear to God I don't see what it gets me. It was you who got brilliant and made it that the poison was for the Fraser woman, not Orchard. Now that looks crazy, but what don't? If it was for Orchard after all, who and why in that bunch? And what about Beula Poole? Were she and Orchard teaming it? Or was she horning in on his list? By God, I never saw anything like it! Have you been giving me a runaround? I want to know!"

Cramer pulled a cigar from his pocket and got his teeth closed on it.

Wolfe shook his head. "Not I," he declared. "I'm a little dizzy myself. Your description was sketchy, and it might help to fill it in. Are you in a hurry?"

"Hell no."

"Then look at this. It is important, if we are to see clearly the connection of the two events, to know exactly what the roles of Mr. Orchard and Miss Poole were. Let us say that I am an ingenious and ruthless man, and I decide to make some money by blackmailing wholesale, with little or no risk to myself."

"Orchard got poisoned," Cramer growled, "and she got shot."

"Yes," Wolfe agreed, "but I didn't. I either know people I can use or I know how to find them. I am a patient and resourceful man. I supply Orchard with funds to begin publication of *Track Almanac*. I have lists prepared, with the greatest care, of persons with ample incomes from a business or profession or job that would make them sensitive to my attack. Then I start operating. The phone calls are made neither by Orchard nor by me. Of course Orchard, who is in an exposed position, has never met me, doesn't know who I am, and probably isn't even aware that I exist. Indeed, of those engaged in the operation, very few know that I exist, possibly only one."

Wolfe rubbed his palms together. "All this is passably clever. I am taking from my victims only a small fraction of their income, and I am not threatening them with exposure of a fearful secret. Even if I knew their secrets, which I don't, I would prefer not to use them in the anonymous letters; that would not merely harass them, it would fill them with terror, and I don't want terror, I only want money. Therefore, while my lists are carefully compiled, no great amount of research is required, just enough to get only the kind of people who would be least likely to put up a fight, either by going to the police or by any other method. Even should one resort to the police, what will happen? You have already answered that, Mr. Cramer, by telling what did happen."

"That sergeant was dumb as hell," Cramer grumbled.

"Oh, no. There was the captain too. Take an hour sometime to consider what you would have done and see where you come out. What if one or two more citizens have made the same complaint? Mr. Orchard would have insisted that he was being persecuted by an enemy. In the extreme case of an avalanche of complaints, most improbable, or of an exposure by an exceptionally capable policeman, what then? Mr. Orchard would be done for, but I wouldn't. Even if he wanted to squeal, he couldn't, not on me, for he doesn't know me."

"He has been getting money to you," Cramer objected.

"Not to me. He never gets within ten miles of me. The handling of the money is an important detail and you may be sure it has been well organized. Only one man ever gets close enough to me to bring me money. It shouldn't take me long to build up a fine list of subscribers to *Track Almanac*—certainly a hundred, possibly five hundred. Let us be moderate and say two hundred. That's two thousand dollars a week. If Mr. Orchard keeps half, he can pay all expenses and have well over thirty thousand a year for his net. If he has any sense, and he has been carefully chosen and is under surveillance, that will satisfy him. For me, it's a question of my total volume. How many units do I have? New York is big enough for four or five, Chicago for two or three, Detroit, Philadelphia, and Los Angeles for two each, at least a dozen cities for one. If I wanted to stretch it I could easily get twenty units working. But we'll be moderate again and stop at twelve. That would bring me in six hundred thousand dollars a year for my share. My operating costs shouldn't be more than half that; and when you consider that my net is really net, with no income tax to pay, I am doing very well indeed."

Cramer started to say something, but Wolfe put up a hand:

"Please. As I said, all that is fairly clever, especially the avoidance of real threats about real secrets, but what makes it a masterpiece is the limitation of the tribute. All blackmailers will promise that this time is the last, but I not only make the promise, I keep it. I have an inviolable rule never to ask for a subscription renewal."

"You can't prove it."

"No, I can't. But I confidently assume it, because it is the essence, the great beauty, of the plan. A man can put up with a pain—and this was not really a pain, merely a discomfort, for people with good incomes—if he thinks he knows when it will stop, and if it stops when the time comes. But if I make them pay year after year, with no end in sight, I invite sure disaster. I'm too good a businessman for that. It is much cheaper and safer to get four new subscribers a week for each unit; that's all that is needed to keep it at a constant two hundred subscribers."

Wolfe nodded emphatically. "By all means, then, if I am to stay in business indefinitely, and I intend to, I must make that rule and rigidly adhere to it; and I do so. There will of course be many little difficulties, as there are in any enterprise, and I must also be prepared for an unforeseen contingency. For example, Mr. Orchard may get killed. If so I must know of it at once, and I must have a man in readiness to remove all papers from his office, even though there is nothing there that could possibly lead to me. I would prefer to have no inkling of the nature and extent of my operations reach unfriendly parties. But I am not panicky; why should I be? Within two weeks one of my associates—the one who makes the phone calls for my units that are managed by females—begins phoning the *Track Almanac* subscribers to tell them that their remaining payments should be made to another publication called *What to Expect*. It would have been better to discard my *Track Almanac* list and take my loss, but I don't know that. I only find it out when Miss Poole also gets killed. Luckily my surveillance is excellent. Again an office must be cleaned out, and this time under hazardous conditions and with dispatch. Quite likely my man has seen the murderer, and can even name him; but I'm not interested in catching a murderer; what I want is to save my business from these confounded interruptions. I discard both those cursed lists, destroy them, burn them, and start plans for two entirely new units. How about a weekly sheet giving the latest shopping information? Or a course in languages, any language? There are numberless possibilities."

Wolfe leaned back. "There's your connection, Mr. Cramer."

"The hell it is," Cramer mumbled. He was rubbing the side of his nose with his forefinger. He was sorting things out. After a moment he went on, "I thought maybe you were going to end up by killing both of them yourself. That would be a connection too, wouldn't it?"

"Not a very plausible one. Why would I choose that time and

place and method for killing Mr. Orchard? Or even Miss Poole—why there in her office? It wouldn't be like me. If they had to be disposed of surely I would have made better arrangements than that."

"Then you're saying it was a subscriber."

"I make the suggestion. Not necessarily a subscriber, but one who looked at things from the subscriber's viewpoint."

"Then the poison was intended for Orchard after all."

"I suppose so, confound it. I admit that's hard to swallow. It's sticking in my throat."

"Mine too." Cramer was skeptical. "One thing you overlooked. You were so interested in pretending it was you, you didn't mention who it really is. This patient ruthless bird that's pulling down over half a million a year. Could I have his name and address?"

"Not from me," Wolfe said positively. "I strongly doubt if you could finish him, and if you tried he would know who had named him. Then I would have to undertake it, and I don't want to tackle him. I work for money, to make a living, not just to keep myself alive. I don't want to be reduced to that primitive extremity."

"Nuts. You've been telling me a dream you had. You can't stand it for anyone to think you don't know everything, so you even have the brass to tell me to my face that you know his name. You don't even know he exists, any more than Orchard did."

"Oh yes I do. I'm much more intelligent than Mr. Orchard."

"Have it your way," Cramer conceded generously. "You trade orchids with him. So what? He's not in my department. If he wasn't behind these murders I don't want him. My job is homicide. Say you didn't dream it, say it's just as you said, what comes next? How have I gained an inch or you either? Is that what you got me here for, to tell me about your goddam units in twelve different cities?"

"Partly. I didn't know your precinct sergeant had been reminded of something. But that wasn't all. Do you feel like telling me why Miss Koppel tried to get on an airplane?"

"Sure I feel like it, but I can't because I don't know. She says to see her sick mother. We've tried to find another reason that we like better, but no luck. She's under bond not to leave the state."

Wolfe nodded. "Nothing seems to fructify, does it? What I really wanted was to offer a suggestion. Would you like one?"

"Let me hear it."

"I hope it will appeal to you. You said that you have had men working in the circles of the Orchard subscribers you know about, and that there have been no results on Professor Savarese or Miss Fraser. You might have expected that, and probably did, since those two have given credible reasons for having subscribed. Why not shift your aim to another target? How many men are available for that sort of work?"

"As many as I want."

"Then put a dozen or more onto Miss Vance—or, rather, onto her associates. Make it thorough. Tell the men that the object is not to learn whether anonymous letters regarding Miss Vance have been received. Tell them that that much has been confidently assumed, and that their job is to find out what the letters said, and who got them and when. It will require pertinacity to the farthest limit of permissible police conduct. The man good enough actually to secure one of the letters will be immediately promoted."

Cramer sat scowling. Probably he was doing the same as me, straining for a quick but comprehensive flashback of all the things that Elinor Vance had seen or done, either in our presence or to our knowledge. Finally he inquired:

"Why her?"

Wolfe shook his head. "If I explained you would say I was telling you another dream. I assure you that in my opinion the reason is good."

"How many letters to how many people?"

Wolfe's brows went up. "My dear sir! If I knew that would I let you get a finger in it? I would have her here ready for delivery, with evidence. What the deuce is wrong with it? I am merely suggesting a specific line of inquiry on a specific person whom you have already been tormenting for over three weeks."

"You're letting my finger in now. If it's any good why don't you hire men with your clients' money and sail on through?"

Wolfe snorted. He was disgusted. "Very well," he said. "I'll do that. Don't bother about it. Doubtless your own contrivances are far superior. Another sergeant may be reminded of something that happened at the turn of the century."

Cramer stood up. I thought he was going to leave without a word, but he spoke. "That's pretty damn cheap, Wolfe. You would never have heard of that sergeant if I hadn't told you about him. Freely."

He turned and marched out. I made allowances for both of them because their nerves were on edge. After three weeks for Cramer, and more than two for Wolfe, they were no closer to the killer of Cyril Orchard than when they started.

20

I have to admit that for me the toss to Elinor Vance was a passed ball. It went by me away out of reach. I halfway expected that now at last we would get some hired help, but when I asked Wolfe if I should line up Saul and Fred and Orrie he merely grunted. I wasn't much surprised, since it was in accordance with our new policy of letting the cops do it. It was a cinch that Cramer's first move on returning to his headquarters would be to start a pack sniffing for anonymous letters about Elinor Vance.

After lunch I disposed of a minor personal problem by getting Wolfe's permission to pay a debt, though that wasn't the way I put it. I told him that I would like to call Lon Cohen and give him the dope on how subscriptions to *Track Almanac* and *What to Expect* had been procured, of course without any hint of a patient ruthless master mind who didn't exist, and naming no names. My arguments were (a) that Wolfe had fished it up himself and therefore Cramer had no copyright, (b) that it was desirable to have a newspaper under an obligation, (c) that it would serve them right for the vicious editorial they had run, and (d) that it might possibly start a fire somewhere that would give us a smoke signal. Wolfe nodded, but I waited until he had gone up to the plant rooms to phone Lon to pay up. If I had done it in his hearing he's so damn suspicious that some word, or a shade of a tone, might have started him asking questions.

Another proposal I made later on didn't do so well. He turned it down flat. Since it was to be assumed that I had forgotten the name Arnold Zeck, I used Duncan instead. I reminded Wolfe that he had told Cramer that it was likely that an employee of Duncan's had seen the killer of Beula Poole, and could even name him. What I proposed was to call the Midland number and leave a message for Duncan to phone Wolfe. If and when he did so Wolfe would make an offer: if Duncan would come through on the killer, not for quotation of course, Wolfe would agree to forget that he had ever heard tell of anyone whose name began with Z—pardon me, D.

All I got was my head snapped off. First, Wolfe would make no such bargain with a criminal, especially a dysgenic one; and second, there would be no further communication between him and that nameless buzzard unless the buzzard started it. That seemed short-sighted to me. If he didn't intend to square off with the bird unless he had to, why not take what he could get? After dinner that evening I tried to bring it up again, but he wouldn't discuss it.

The following morning, Friday, we had a pair of visitors that we hadn't seen for quite a while: Walter B. Anderson, the Hi-Spot president, and Fred Owen, the director of public relations. When the doorbell rang a little before noon and I went to the front and saw them on the stoop, my attitude was quite different from what it had been the first time. They had no photographers along, and they were clients in good standing entitled to one hell of a beef if they only knew it, and there was a faint chance that they had a concealed weapon, maybe a hatpin, to stick into Wolfe. So without going to the office to check I welcomed them across the threshold.

Wolfe greeted them without any visible signs of rapture, but at least he didn't grump. He even asked them how they did. While they were getting seated he shifted in his chair so he could give his eyes to either one without excessive exertion for his neck muscles. He actually apologized:

"It isn't astonishing if you gentlemen are getting a little impatient. But if you are exasperated, so am I. I had no idea it would drag on like this. No murderer likes to be caught, naturally; but this one seems to have an extraordinary aversion to it. Would you like me to describe what has been accomplished?"

"We know pretty well," Owen stated. He was wearing a dark brown double-breasted pin-stripe that must have taken at least five fittings to get it the way it looked.

"We know too well," the president corrected him. Usually I am tolerant of the red-faced plump type, but every time that geezer opened his mouth I wanted to shut it and not by talking.

Wolfe frowned. "I've admitted your right to exasperation. You needn't insist on it."

"We're not exasperated with you, Mr. Wolfe," Owen declared.

"I am," the president corrected him again. "With the whole damn thing and everything and everyone connected with it. For a while I've been willing to string along with the idea that there can't be any argument against a Hooper in the high twenties, but I've thought

I might be wrong and now I know I was. My God, blackmail! Were you responsible for that piece in the *Gazette* this morning?"

"Well . . ." Wolfe was being judicious. "I would say that the responsibility rests with the man who conceived the scheme. I discovered and disclosed it—"

"It doesn't matter." Anderson waved it aside. "What does matter is that my company and my product cannot and will not be connected in the public mind with blackmail. That's dirty. That makes people gag."

"I absolutely agree," Owen asserted.

"Murder is moderately dirty too," Wolfe objected.

"No," Anderson said flatly. "Murder is sensational and exciting, but it's not like blackmail and anonymous letters. I'm through. I've had enough of it."

He got a hand in his breast pocket and pulled out an envelope, from which he extracted an oblong strip of blue paper. "Here's a check for your fee, the total amount. I can collect from the others— or not. I'll see. Send me a bill for expenses to date. You understand, I'm calling it off."

Owen had got up to take the check and hand it to Wolfe. Wolfe took a squint at it and let it drop to the desk.

"Indeed." Wolfe picked up the check, gave it another look, and dropped it again. "Have you consulted the other parties to our arrangement?"

"No, and I don't intend to. What do you care? That's the full amount, isn't it?"

"Yes, the amount's all right. But why this headlong retreat? What has suddenly scared you so?"

"Nothing has scared me." Anderson came forward in his chair. "Look, Wolfe. I came down here myself to make sure there's no slip-up on this. The deal is off, beginning right now. If you listened to the Fraser program this morning you didn't hear my product mentioned. I'm paying that off too, and clearing out. If you think I'm scared you don't know me. I don't scare. But I know how to take action when the circumstances require it, and that's what I'm doing."

He left his chair, leaned over Wolfe's desk, stretched a short fat arm, and tapped the check with a short stubby forefinger. "I'm no welcher! I'll pay your expenses just like I'm paying this! I'm not blaming you, to hell with that, but from this minute—you—are—not —working—for—me!"

With the last six words the finger jabbed the desk, at the rate of about three jabs to a word.

"Come on, Fred," the president commanded, and the pair tramped out to the hall.

I moseyed over as far as the office door to see that they didn't make off with my new twenty-dollar gray spring hat, and, when they were definitely gone, returned to my desk, sat, and commented to Wolfe:

"He seems to be upset."

"Take a letter to him."

I got my notebook and pen. Wolfe cleared his throat.

"Not dear Mr. Anderson, dear sir. Regarding our conversation at my office this morning, I am engaged with others as well as you, and, since my fee is contingent upon a performance, I am obliged to continue until the performance is completed. The check you gave me will be held in my safe until that time."

I looked up. "Sincerely?"

"I suppose so. There's nothing insincere about it. When you go out to mail it go first to the bank and have the check certified."

"That shifts the contingency," I remarked, opening the drawer where I kept letterheads, "to whether the bank stays solvent or not."

It was at that moment, the moment when I was putting the paper in the typewriter, that Wolfe really settled down to work on the Orchard case. He leaned back, shut his eyes, and began exercising his lips. He was like that when I left on my errand, and still like that when I got back. At such times I don't have to tiptoe or keep from rustling papers; I can bang the typewriter or make phone calls or use the vacuum cleaner and he doesn't hear it.

All the rest of that day and evening, up till bedtime, except for intermissions for meals and the afternoon conclave in the plant rooms, he kept at it, with no word or sign to give me a hint what kind of trail he had found, if any. In a way it was perfectly jake with me, for at least it showed that he had decided we would do our own cooking, but in another way it wasn't so hot. When it goes on hour after hour, as it did that Friday, the chances are that he's finding himself just about cornered, and there's no telling how desperate he'll be when he picks a hole to bust out through. A couple of years ago, after spending most of a day figuring one out, he ended up with a charade that damn near got nine human beings asphyxiated with ciphogene, including him and me, not to mention Inspector Cramer.

When both the clock and my wrist watch said it was close to midnight, and there he still was, I inquired politely:

"Shall we have some coffee to keep awake?"

His mutter barely reached me: "Go to bed."

I did so.

21

I needn't have worried. He did give birth, but not to one of his fantastic freaks. The next morning, Saturday, when Fritz returned to the kitchen after taking up the breakfast tray he told me I was wanted.

Since Wolfe likes plenty of air at night but a good warm room at breakfast time it had been necessary, long ago, to install a contraption that would automatically close his window at 6:00 A.M. As a result the eight o'clock temperature permits him to have his tray on a table near the window without bothering to put on a dressing gown. Seated there, his hair not yet combed, his feet bare, and all the yardage of his yellow pajamas dazzling in the morning sun, he is something to blink at, and it's too bad that Fritz and I are the only ones who ever have the privilege.

I told him it was a nice morning, and he grunted. He will not admit that a morning is bearable, let alone nice, until, having had his second cup of coffee, he has got himself fully dressed.

"Instructions," he growled.

I sat down, opened my notebook, and uncapped my pen. He instructed:

"Get some ordinary plain white paper of a cheap grade; I doubt if any of ours will do. Say five by eight. Type this on it, single-spaced, no date or salutation."

He shut his eyes. "Since you are a friend of Elinor Vance, this is something you should know. During her last year at college the death of a certain person was ascribed to natural causes and was never properly investigated. Another incident that was never investigated was the disappearance of a jar of cyanide from the electroplating shop of Miss Vance's brother. It would be interesting to know if there was any connection between those two incidents. Possibly an inquiry into both of them would suggest such a connection."

"That all?"

"Yes. No signature. No envelope. Fold the paper and soil it a little; give it the appearance of having been handled. This is Saturday, but an item in the morning paper tells of the withdrawal of Hi-Spot from sponsorship of Miss Fraser's program, so I doubt if those people will have gone off for week ends. You may even find that they are together, conferring; that would suit our purpose best. But either together or singly, see them; show them the anonymous letter; ask if they have ever seen it or one similar to it; be insistent and as pestiferous as possible."

"Including Miss Vance herself?"

"Let circumstances decide. If they are together and she is with them, yes. Presumably she has already been alerted by Mr. Cramer's men."

"The professor? Savarese?"

"No, don't bother with him." Wolfe drank coffee. "That's all."

I stood up. "I might get more or better results if I knew what we're after. Are we expecting Elinor Vance to break down and confess? Or am I nagging one of them into pulling a gun on me, or what?"

I should have known better, with him still in his pajamas and his hair tousled.

"You're following instructions," he said peevishly. "If I knew what you're going to get I wouldn't have had to resort to this shabby stratagem."

"Shabby is right," I agreed, and left him.

I would of course obey orders, for the same reason that a good soldier does, namely he'd better, but I was not filled with enough zeal to make me hurry my breakfast. My attitude as I set about the preliminaries of the operation was that if this was the best he could do he might as well have stayed dormant. I did not believe that he had anything on Elinor Vance. He does sometimes hire Saul or Orrie or Fred without letting me know what they're up to or, more rarely, even that they're working for him, but I can always tell by seeing if money has been taken from the safe. The money was all present or accounted for. You can judge my frame of mind when I state that I halfway suspected that he had picked on Elinor merely because I had gone to a little trouble to have her seated nearest to me the night of the party.

He was, however, right about the week ends. I didn't start on the phone calls until nine-thirty, not wanting to get them out of bed for something which I regarded as about as useful as throwing rocks at the moon. The first one I tried, Bill Meadows, said he hadn't had breakfast yet and he didn't know when he would have some free time, because he was due at Miss Fraser's apartment at eleven for a conference and there was no telling how long it would last. That indicated that I would have a chance to throw at two or more moons with one stone, and another couple of phone calls verified it. There was a meeting on. I did the morning chores, buzzed the plant rooms to inform Wolfe, and left a little before eleven and headed uptown.

To show you what a murder case will do to people's lives, the password routine had been abandoned. But it by no means followed that it was easier than it had been to get up to apartment 10B. Quite the contrary. Evidently journalists and others had been trying all kinds of dodges to get a ride in the elevator, for the distinguished-looking hallman wasn't a particle interested in what I said my name was, and he steeled himself to betray no sign of recognition. He simply used the phone, and in a few minutes Bill Meadows emerged from the elevator and walked over to us. We said hello.

"Strong said you'd probably show up," he said. Neither his tone nor his expression indicated that they had been pacing up and down waiting for me. "Miss Fraser wants to know if it's something urgent."

"Mr. Wolfe thinks it is."

"All right, come on."

He was so preoccupied that he went into the elevator first.

I decided that if he tried leaving me alone in the enormous living room with the assorted furniture, to wait until I was summoned, I would just stick to his heels, but that proved to be unnecessary. He couldn't have left me alone there because that was where they were.

Madeline Fraser was on the green burlap divan, propped against a dozen cushions. Deborah Koppel was seated on the piano bench. Elinor Vance perched on a corner of the massive old black walnut table. Tully Strong had the edge of his sitter on the edge of the pink silk chair, and Nat Traub was standing. That was all as billed, but there was an added attraction. Also standing, at the far end of the long divan, was Nancylee Shepherd.

"It was Goodwin," Bill Meadows told them, but they would probably have deduced it anyhow, since I had dropped my hat and coat in the hall and was practically at his elbow. He spoke to Miss Fraser:

"He says it's something urgent."

Miss Fraser asked me briskly, "Will it take long, Mr. Goodwin?" She looked clean and competent, as if she had had a good night's sleep, a shower, a healthy vigorous rub, and a thorough breakfast.

I told her I was afraid it might.

"Then I'll have to ask you to wait." She was asking a favor. She certainly had the knack of being personal without making you want to back off. "Mr. Traub has to leave soon for an appointment, and we have to make an important decision. You know, of course, that we have lost a sponsor. I suppose I ought to feel low about it, but I really don't. Do you know how many firms we have had offers from, to take the Hi-Spot place? Sixteen!"

"Wonderful!" I admired. "Sure, I'll wait." I crossed to occupy a chair outside the conference zone.

They forgot, immediately and completely, that I was there. All but one: Nancylee. She changed position so she could keep her eyes on me, and her expression showed plainly that she considered me tricky, ratty, and unworthy of trust.

"We've got to start eliminating," Tully Strong declared. He had his spectacles off, holding them in his hand. "As I understand it there are just five serious contenders."

"Four," Elinor Vance said, glancing at a paper she held. "I've crossed off Fluff, the biscuit dough. You said to, didn't you, Lina?"

"It's a good company," Traub said regretfully. "One of the best. Their radio budget is over three million."

"You're just making it harder, Nat," Deborah Koppel told him. "We can't take all of them. I thought your favorite was Meltettes."

"It is," Traub agreed, "but these are all very fine accounts. What do you think of Meltettes, Miss Fraser?" He was the only one of the bunch who didn't call her Lina.

"I haven't tried them." She glanced around. "Where are they?"

Nancylee, apparently not so concentrated on me as to miss any word or gesture of her idol, spoke up: "There on the piano, Miss Fraser. Do you want them?"

"We have got to eliminate," Strong insisted, stabbing the air with his spectacles for emphasis. "I must repeat, as representative of the other sponsors, that they are firmly and unanimously opposed to

Sparkle, if it is to be served on the program as Hi-Spot was. They never liked the idea and they don't want it resumed."

"It's already crossed off," Elinor Vance stated. "With Fluff and Sparkle out, that leaves four."

"Not on account of the sponsors," Miss Fraser put in. "We just happen to agree with them. They aren't going to decide this. We are."

"You mean you are, Lina." Bill Meadows sounded a little irritated. "What the hell, we all know that. You don't want Fluff because Cora made some biscuits and you didn't like 'em. You don't want Sparkle because they want it served on the program, and God knows I don't blame you."

Elinor Vance repeated, "That leaves four."

"All right, eliminate!" Strong persisted.

"We're right where we were before," Deborah Koppel told them. "The trouble is, there's no real objection to any of the four, and I think Bill's right, I think we have to put it up to Lina."

"I am prepared," Nat Traub announced, in the tone of a man burning bridges, "to say that I will vote for Meltettes."

For my part, I was prepared to say that I would vote for nobody. Sitting there taking them in, as far as I could tell the only strain they were under was the pressure of picking the right sponsor. If, combined with that, one of them was contending with the nervous wear and tear of a couple of murders, he was too good for me. As the argument got warmer it began to appear that, though they were agreed that the final word was up to Miss Fraser, each of them had a favorite among the four entries left. That was what complicated the elimination.

Naturally, on account of the slip of paper I had in my pocket, I was especially interested in Elinor Vance, but the sponsor problem seemed to be monopolizing her attention as completely as that of the others. I would of course have to follow instructions and proceed with my errand as soon as they gave me a chance, but I was beginning to feel silly. While Wolfe had left it pretty vague, one thing was plain, that I was supposed to give them a severe jolt, and I doubted if I had what it would take. When they got worked up to the point of naming the winner—settling on the lucky product that would be cast for the role sixteen had applied for—bringing up the subject of an anonymous letter, even one implying that one of them was a chronic murderer, would be an anticlimax. With a serious problem like that just triumphantly solved, what would they care about a little thing like murder?

But I was dead wrong. I found that out incidentally, as a by-product of their argument. It appeared that two of the contenders were deadly rivals, both clawing for children's dimes: a candy bar called Happy Andy and a little box of tasty delights called Meltettes. It was the latter that Traub had decided to back unequivocally, and he, when the question came to a head which of those two to eliminate, again asked Miss Fraser if she had tried Meltettes. She told him no. He asked if she had tried Happy Andy. She said yes. Then, he insisted, it was only fair for her to try Meltettes.

"All right," she agreed. "There on the piano, Debby, that little red box. Toss it over."

"No!" a shrill voice cried. It was Nancylee. Everyone looked at her. Deborah Koppel, who had picked up the little red cardboard box, asked her:

"What's the matter?"

"It's dangerous!" Nancylee was there, a hand outstretched. "Give it to me. I'll eat one first!"

It was only a romantic kid being dramatic, and all she rated from that bunch, if I had read their pulses right, was a laugh and a brush-off, but that was what showed me I had been dead wrong. There wasn't even a snicker. No one said a word. They all froze, staring at Nancylee, with only one exception. That was Deborah Koppel. She held the box away from Nancylee's reaching hand and told her contemptuously:

"Don't be silly."

"I mean it!" the girl cried. "Let me—"

"Nonsense." Deborah pushed her back, opened the flap of the box, took out an object, popped it into her mouth, chewed once or twice, swallowed, and then spat explosively, ejecting a spray of little particles.

I was the first, by maybe a tenth of a second, to realize that there was something doing. It wasn't so much the spitting, for that could conceivably have been merely her way of voting against Meltettes, as it was the swift terrible contortion of her features. As I bounded across to her she left the piano bench with a spasmodic jerk, got erect with her hands flung high, and screamed:

"Lina! Don't! Don't let—"

I was at her, with a hand on her arm, and Bill Meadows was

there too, but her muscles all in convulsion took us along as she fought toward the divan, and Madeline Fraser was there to meet her and get supporting arms around her. But somehow the three of us together failed to hold her up or get her onto the divan. She went down until her knees were on the floor, with one arm stretched rigid across the burlap of the divan, and would have gone the rest of the way but for Miss Fraser, also on her knees.

I straightened, wheeled, and told Nat Traub: "Get a doctor quick." I saw Nancylee reaching to pick up the little red cardboard box and snapped at her: "Let that alone and behave yourself." Then to the rest of them: "Let everything alone, hear me?"

22

Around four o'clock I could have got permission to go home if I had insisted, but it seemed better to stay as long as there was a chance of picking up another item for my report. I had already phoned Wolfe to explain why I wasn't following his instructions.

All of those who had been present at the conference were still there, very much so, except Deborah Koppel, who had been removed in a basket when several gangs of city scientists had finished their part of it. She had been dead when the doctor arrived. The others were still alive but not in a mood to brag about it.

At four o'clock Lieutenant Rowcliff and an assistant D.A. were sitting on the green burlap divan, arguing whether the taste of cyanide should warn people in time to refrain from swallowing. That seemed pointless, since whether it should or not it usually doesn't, and anyway the only ones who could qualify as experts are those who have tried it, and none of them is available. I moved on. At the big oak table another lieutenant was conversing with Bill Meadows, meanwhile referring to notes on loose sheets of paper. I went on by. In the dining room a sergeant and a private were pecking away at Elinor Vance. I passed through. In the kitchen a dick with a pug nose was holding a sheet of paper, one of a series, flat on the table while Cora, the female wrestler, put her initials on it.

Turning and going back the way I had come, I continued on to the square hall, opened a door at its far end, and went through. This, the room without a name, was more densely populated than the others. Tully Strong and Nat Traub were on chairs against opposite walls. Nancylee was standing by a window. A dick was seated in the center of the room, another was leaning against a wall, and Sergeant Purley Stebbins was sort of strolling around.

That called the roll, for I knew that Madeline Fraser was in the room beyond, her bedroom, where I had first met the bunch of them, having a talk with Inspector Cramer. The way I knew that, I had just been ordered out by Deputy Commissioner O'Hara, who was in there with them.

The first series of quickies, taking them one at a time on a gallop, had been staged in the dining room by Cramer himself. Cramer and an assistant D.A. had sat at one side of the table, with the subject across from them, and me seated a little to the rear of the subject's elbow. The theory of that arrangement was that if the subject's memory showed a tendency to conflict with mine, I could tip Cramer off by sticking out my tongue or some other signal without being seen by the subject. The dick-stenographer had been at one end of the table, and other units of the personnel had hung around.

Since they were by no means strangers to Cramer and he was already intimately acquainted with their biographies, he could keep it brief and concentrate chiefly on two points: their positions and movements during the conference, and the box of Meltettes. On the former there were some contradictions on minor details, but only what you might expect under the circumstances; and I, who had been there, saw no indication that anyone was trying to fancy it up.

On the latter, the box of Meltettes, there was no contradiction at all. By noon Friday, the preceding day, the news had begun to spread that Hi-Spot was bowing out, though it had not yet been published. For some time Meltettes had been on the Fraser waiting list, to grab a vacancy if one occurred. Friday morning Nat Traub, whose agency had the Meltettes account, had phoned his client the news, and the client had rushed him a carton of its product by messenger. A carton held forty-eight of the little red cardboard boxes. Traub, wishing to lose no time on a matter of such urgency and importance, and not wanting to lug the whole carton, had taken one little box from it and dropped it in his pocket, and hotfooted it to the FBC building, arriving at the studio just before the conclusion of the Fraser broadcast. He had spoken to Miss Fraser and Miss Koppel on behalf of Meltettes and handed the box to Miss Koppel.

Miss Koppel had passed the box on to Elinor Vance, who had put it in her bag—the same bag that had been used to transport sugared coffee in a Hi-Spot bottle. The three women had lunched in a near-by restaurant and then gone to Miss Fraser's apartment, where they had been joined later by Bill Meadows and Tully Strong for an exploratory discussion of the sponsor problem. Soon after their arrival at the apartment Elinor had taken the box of Meltettes from her bag and given it to Miss Fraser, who had put it on the big oak table in the living room.

That had been between two-thirty and three o'clock Friday afternoon, and that was as far as it went. No one knew how or when the box had been moved from the oak table to the piano. There was a blank space, completely blank, of about eighteen hours, ending around nine o'clock Saturday morning, when Cora, on a dusting mission, had seen it on the piano. She had picked it up for a swipe of the dustcloth on the piano top and put it down again. Its next appearance was two hours later, when Nancylee, soon after her arrival at the apartment, had spotted it and been tempted to help herself, even going so far as to get her clutches on it, but had been scared off when she saw that Miss Koppel's eye was on her. That, Nancylee explained, was how she had known where the box was when Miss Fraser had asked.

As you can see, it left plenty of room for inch-by-inch digging and sifting, which was lucky for everybody from privates to inspectors who are supposed to earn their pay, for there was no other place to dig at all. Relationships and motives and suspicions had already had all the juice squeezed out of them. So by four o'clock Saturday afternoon a hundred grown men, if not more, were scattered around the city, doing their damnedest to uncover another little splinter of a fact, any old fact, about that box of Meltettes. Some of them, of course, were getting results. For instance, word had come from the laboratory that the box, as it came to them, had held eleven Meltettes; that one of them, which had obviously been operated on rather skillfully, had about twelve grains of cyanide mixed into its insides; and that the other ten were quite harmless, with no sign of having been tampered with. Meltettes, they said, fitted snugly into the box in pairs, and the cyanided one had been on top, at the end of the box which opened.

And other reports, including of course fingerprints. Most of them had been relayed to Cramer in my presence. Whatever he may have thought they added up to, it looked to me very much like a repeat performance by the artist who had painted the sugared coffee picture: so many crossing lines and overlapping colors that no resemblance to any known animal or other object was discernible.

Returning to the densely populated room with no name after my tour of inspection, I made some witty remark to Purley Stebbins and lowered myself into a chair. As I said, I could probably have bulled my way out and gone home, but I didn't want to. What prospect did it offer? I would have fiddled around until Wolfe came down to the office, made my report, and then what? He would either have grunted in disgust, found something to criticize, and lowered his iron curtain again, or he would have gone into another trance and popped out around midnight with some bright idea like typing an anonymous letter about Bill Meadows flunking in algebra his last year in high school. I preferred to stick around in the faint hope that something would turn up.

And something did. I had abandoned the idea of making some sense out of the crossing lines and overlapping colors, given up trying to get a rise out of Purley, and was exchanging hostile glares with Nancylee, when the door from the square hall opened and a lady entered. She darted a glance around and told Purley Inspector Cramer had sent for her. He crossed to the far door which led to Miss Fraser's bedroom, opened it, and closed it after she had passed through.

I knew her by sight but not her name, and even had an opinion of her, namely that she was the most presentable of all the female dicks I had seen. With nothing else to do, I figured out what Cramer wanted with her, and had just come to the correct conclusion when the door opened again and I got it verified. Cramer appeared first, then Deputy Commissioner O'Hara. Cramer spoke to Purley:

"Get 'em all in here."

Purley flew to obey. Nat Traub asked wistfully, "Have you made any progress, Inspector?"

Cramer didn't even have the decency to growl at him, let alone reply. That seemed unnecessarily rude, so I told Traub:

"Yeah, they've reached an important decision. You're all going to be frisked."

It was ill-advised, especially with O'Hara there, since he has never forgiven me for being clever once, but I was frustrated and edgy. O'Hara gave me an evil look and Cramer told me to close my trap.

The others came straggling in with their escorts. I surveyed the lot and would have felt genuinely sorry for them if I had known which one to leave out. There was no question now about the kind of strain they were under, and it had nothing to do with picking a sponsor.

Cramer addressed them:

"I want to say to you people that as long as you cooperate with us we have no desire to make it any harder for you than we have to. You can't blame us for feeling we have to bear down on you, in view of the fact that all of you lied, and kept on lying, about the bottle that the stuff came out of that killed Orchard. I called you in here to tell you that we're going to search your persons. The position is this, we would be justified in taking you all down and booking you as material witnesses, and that's what we'll do if any of you object to the search. Miss Fraser made no objection. A policewoman is in there with her now. The women will be taken in there one at a time. The men will be taken by Lieutenant Rowcliff and Sergeant Stebbins, also one at a time, to another room. Does anyone object?"

It was pitiful. They were in no condition to object, even if he had announced his intention of having clusters of Meltettes tattooed on their chests. Nobody made a sound except Nancylee, who merely shrilled:

"Oh, I never!"

I crossed my legs and prepared to sit it out. And so I did, up to a point. Purley and Rowcliff took Tully Strong first. Soon the female dick appeared and got Elinor Vance. Evidently they were being thorough, for it was a good eight minutes before Purley came back with Strong and took Bill Meadows, and the lady took just as long with Elinor Vance. The last two on the list were Nancylee in one direction and Nat Traub in the other.

That is, they were the last two as I had it. But when Rowcliff and Purley returned with Traub and handed Cramer some slips of paper, O'Hara barked at them:

"What about Goodwin?"

"Oh, him?" Rowcliff asked.

"Certainly him! He was here, wasn't he?"

Rowcliff looked at Cramer. Cramer looked at me.

I grinned at O'Hara. "What if I object, Commissioner?"

"Try it! That won't help you any!"

"The hell it won't. It will either preserve my dignity or start a string of firecrackers. What do you want to bet my big brother can't lick your big brother?"

He took a step toward me. "You resist, do you?"

"You're damn right I do." My hand did a half circle. "Before twenty witnesses."

He wheeled. "Send him down, Inspector. To my office. Charge him. Then have him searched."

"Yes, sir." Cramer was frowning. "First, would you mind stepping into another room with me? Perhaps I haven't fully explained the situation—"

"I understand it perfectly! Wolfe has cooperated, so you say—to what purpose? What has happened? Another murder! Wolfe has got you all buffaloed, and I'm sick and tired of it! Take him to my office!"

"No one has got me buffaloed," Cramer rasped. "Take him, Purley. I'll phone about a charge."

23

There were two things I liked about Deputy Commissioner O'Hara's office. First, it was there that I had been clever on a previous occasion, and therefore it aroused agreeable memories, and second, I like nice surroundings and it was the most attractive room at Centre Street, being on a corner with six large windows, and furnished with chairs and rugs and other items which had been paid for by O'Hara's rich wife.

I sat at ease in one of the comfortable chairs. The contents of my pockets were stacked in a neat pile on a corner of O'Hara's big shiny mahogany desk, except for one item which Purley Stebbins had in his paw. Purley was so mad his face was a red sunset, and he was stuttering.

"Don't be a g-goddam fool," he exhorted me. "If you clam it with O'Hara when he gets here he'll jug you sure as hell, and it's after six o'clock so where'll you spend the night?" He shook his paw at me, the one holding the item taken from my pocket. "Tell me about this!"

I shook my head firmly. "You know, Purley," I said without rancor, "this is pretty damn ironic. You frisked that bunch of suspects and got nothing at all—I could tell that from the way you and Rowcliff looked. But on me, absolutely innocent of wrongdoing, you find what you think is an incriminating document. So here I am, sunk, facing God knows what kind of doom. I try to catch a glimpse of the future, and what do I see?"

"Oh, shut up!"

"No, I've got to talk to someone." I glanced at my wrist. "As you say, it's after six o'clock. Mr. Wolfe has come down from the plant rooms, expecting to find me awaiting him in the office, ready for my report of the day's events. He'll be disappointed. You know how he'll feel. Better still, you know what he'll do. He'll be so frantic he'll start looking up numbers and dialing them himself. I am offering ten to one that he has already called the Fraser apartment and spoken to Cramer. How much of it do you want? A dime? A buck?"

"Can it, you goddam ape." Purley was resigning. "Save it for O'Hara, he'll be here pretty soon. I hope they give you a cell with bedbugs."

"I would prefer," I said courteously, "to chat."

"Then chat about this."

"No. For the hundredth time, no. I detest anonymous letters and I don't like to talk about them."

He went to a chair and sat facing me. I got up, crossed to bookshelves, selected CRIME AND CRIMINALS, by Mercier, and returned to my seat with it.

Purley had been wrong. O'Hara was not there pretty soon. When I glanced at my wrist every ten minutes or so I did it on the sly because I didn't want Purley to think I was getting impatient. It was a little past seven when I looked up from my book at the sound of a buzzer. Purley went to a phone on the desk and had a talk with it. He hung up, returned to his chair, sat, and after a moment spoke:

"That was the Deputy Commissioner. He is going to have his dinner. I'm to keep you here till he comes."

"Good," I said approvingly. "This is a fascinating book."

"He thinks you're boiling. You bastard."

I shrugged.

I kept my temper perfectly for another hour or more, and then, still there with my book, I became aware that I was starting to lose control. The trouble was that I had begun to feel hungry, and that was making me sore. Then there was another factor: what the hell was Wolfe doing? That, I admit, was unreasonable. Any phoning he did would be to Cramer or O'Hara, or possibly someone at the

D.A.'s office, and with me cooped up as I was I wouldn't hear even an echo. If he had learned where I was and tried to get me, they wouldn't have put him through, since Purley had orders from O'Hara that I was to make no calls. But what with feeling hungry and getting no word from the outside world, I became aware that I was beginning to be offended, and that would not do. I forced my mind away from food and other aggravating aspects, including the number of revolutions the minute hand of my watch had made, and turned another page.

It was ten minutes to nine when the door opened and O'Hara and Cramer walked in. Purley stood up. I was in the middle of a paragraph and so merely flicked one eye enough to see who it was. O'Hara hung his hat and coat on a rack, and Cramer dropped his on a chair. O'Hara strode to his desk, crossing my bow so close that I could easily have tripped him by stretching a leg.

Cramer looked tired. Without spending a glance on me he nodded at Purley.

"Has he opened up?"

"No, sir. Here it is." Purley handed him the item.

They had both had it read to them on the phone, but they wanted to see it. Cramer read it through twice and then handed it to O'Hara. While that was going on I went to the shelves and replaced the book, had a good stretch and yawn, and returned to my chair.

Cramer glared down at me. "What have you got to say?"

"More of the same," I told him. "I've explained to the sergeant, who has had nothing to eat by the way, that that thing has no connection whatever with any murder or any other crime, and therefore questions about it are out of order."

"You've been charged as a material witness."

"Yeah, I know, Purley showed it to me. Why don't you ask Mr. Wolfe? He might be feeling generous."

"The hell he might. We have. Look, Goodwin—"

"I'll handle him, Inspector." O'Hara speaking. He was an energetic cuss. He had gone clear around his desk to sit down, but now he arose and came clear around it again to confront me. I looked up at him inquiringly, not a bit angry.

He was trying to control himself. "You can't possibly get away with it," he stated. "It's incredible that you have the gall to try it, both you and Wolfe. Anonymous letters are a central factor in this case, a vital factor. You went up to that apartment today to see those people, and you had in your pocket an anonymous letter about one of them, practically accusing her of murder. Do you mean to tell me that you take the position that that letter has no connection with the crimes under investigation?"

"I sure do. Evidently Mr. Wolfe does too." I made a gesture. "Corroboration."

"You take and maintain that position while aware of the penalty that may be imposed upon conviction for an obstruction of justice?"

"I do."

O'Hara turned and blurted at Cramer, "Get Wolfe down here! Damn it, we should have hauled him in hours ago!"

This, I thought to myself, is something like. Now we ought to see some fur fly.

But we didn't, at least not as O'Hara had it programed. What interfered was a phone call. The buzzer sounded, and Purley, seeing that his superiors were too worked up to hear it, went to the desk and answered. After a word he told Cramer, "For you, Inspector," and Cramer crossed and got it. O'Hara stood glaring down at me, but, having his attention called by a certain tone taken by Cramer's voice, turned to look that way. Finally Cramer hung up. The expression on his face was that of a man trying to decide what it was he just swallowed.

"Well?" O'Hara demanded.

"The desk just had a call," Cramer said, "from the WPIT newsroom. WPIT is doing the script for the ten o'clock newscast, and they're including an announcement received a few minutes ago from Nero Wolfe. Wolfe announces that he has solved the murder cases, all three of them, with no assistance from the police, and that very soon, probably sometime tomorrow, he will be ready to tell the District Attorney the name of the murderer and to furnish all necessary information. WPIT wants to know if we have any comment."

Of course it was vulgar, but I couldn't help it. I threw back my head and let out a roar. It wasn't so much the news itself as it was the look on O'Hara's face as the full beauty of it seeped through to him.

"The fat bum!" Purley whimpered.

I told O'Hara distinctly: "The next time Cramer asks you to step into another room with him I'd advise you to step."

He didn't hear me.

"It wasn't a question," Cramer said, "of Wolfe having me buffaloed. With him the only question is what has he got and how and when will he use it. If that goes on the air I would just as soon quit."

"What—" O'Hara stopped to wet his lips. "What would you suggest?"

Cramer didn't answer. He pulled a cigar from his pocket, slow motion, got it between his teeth, took it out again and hurled it for the wastebasket, missing by two feet, walked to a chair, sat down, and breathed.

"There are only two things," he said. "Just let it land is one. The other is to ask Goodwin to call him and request him to recall the announcement—and tell him he'll be home right away to report." Cramer breathed again. "I won't ask Goodwin that. Do you want to?"

"No! It's blackmail!" O'Hara yelled in pain.

"Yeah," Cramer agreed. "Only when Wolfe does it there's nothing anonymous about it. The newscast will be on in thirty-five minutes."

O'Hara would rather have eaten soap. "It may be a bluff," he pleaded. "Pure bluff!"

"Certainly it may. And it may not. It's easy enough to call it—just sit down and wait. If you're not going to call on Goodwin I guess I'll have to see if I can get hold of the Commissioner." Cramer stood up.

O'Hara turned to me. I have to hand it to him, he looked me in the eye as he asked:

"Will you do it?"

I grinned at him. "That warrant Purley showed me is around somewhere. It will be vacated?"

"Yes."

"Okay, I've got witnesses." I crossed to the desk and began returning my belongings to the proper pockets. The anonymous letter was there where O'Hara had left it when he had advanced to overwhelm me, and I picked it up and displayed it. "I'm taking this," I said, "but I'll let you look at it again if you want to. May I use the phone?"

I circled the desk, dropped into O'Hara's personal chair, pulled the instrument to me, and asked the male switchboard voice to get Mr. Nero Wolfe. The voice asked who I was and I told it. Then we had some comedy. After I had waited a good two minutes there was a knock on the door and O'Hara called come in. The door swung wide open and two individuals entered with guns in their hands, stern and alert. When they saw the arrangements they stopped dead and looked foolish.

"What do you want?" O'Hara barked.

"The phone," one said. "Goodwin. We didn't know . . ."

"For Christ's sake!" Purley exploded. "Ain't I here?" It was a breach of discipline, with his superiors present.

They bumped at the threshold, getting out, pulling the door after them. I couldn't possibly have been blamed for helping myself to another hearty laugh, but there's a limit to what even a Deputy Commissioner will take, so I choked it off and sat tight until there was a voice in my ear that I knew better than any other voice on earth.

"Archie," I said.

"Where are you?" The voice was icy with rage, but not at me.

"I'm in O'Hara's office, at his desk, using his phone. I am half starved. O'Hara, Cramer, and Sergeant Stebbins are present. To be perfectly fair, Cramer and Purley are innocent. This boneheaded play was a solo by O'Hara. He fully realizes his mistake and sincerely apologizes. The warrant for my arrest is a thing of the past. The letter about Miss Vance is in my pocket. I have conceded nothing. I'm free to go where I please, including home. O'Hara requests, as a personal favor, that you kill the announcement you gave WPIT. Can that be done?"

"It can if I choose. It was arranged through Mr. Richards."

"So I suspected. You should have seen O'Hara's face when the tidings reached him. If you choose, and all of us here hope you do, go ahead and kill it and I'll be there in twenty minutes or less. Tell Fritz I'm hungry."

"Mr. O'Hara is a nincompoop. Tell him I said so. I'll have the announcement suspended temporarily, but there will be conditions. Stay there. I'll phone you shortly."

I cradled the phone, leaned back, and grinned at the three inquiring faces. "He'll call back. He thinks he can head it off temporarily, but he's got some idea about conditions." I focused on O'Hara. "He said to tell you that he says you're a nincompoop, but I think it would be more tactful not to mention it, so I won't."

"Someday," O'Hara said through his teeth, "he'll land on his nose."

They all sat down and began exchanging comments. I didn't

listen because my mind was occupied. I was willing to chalk up for Wolfe a neat and well-timed swagger, and to admit that it got the desired results, but now what? Did he really have anything at all, and if so how much? It had better be fairly good. Cramer and Stebbins were not exactly ready to clasp our hands across the corpses, and as for O'Hara, I only hoped to God that when Wolfe called back he wouldn't tell me to slap the Deputy Commissioner on the back and tell him it had been just a prank and wasn't it fun? All in all, it was such a gloomy outlook that when the buzzer sounded and I reached for the phone I would just as soon have been somewhere else.

Wolfe's voice asked if they were still there and I said yes. He said to tell them that the announcement had been postponed and would not be broadcast at ten o'clock, and I did so. Then he asked for my report of the day's events.

"Now?" I demanded. "On the phone?"

"Yes," he said. "Concisely, but including all essentials. If there is a contradiction to demolish I must know it."

Even with the suspicion gnawing at me that I had got roped in for a supporting role in an enormous bluff, I did enjoy it. It was a situation anyone would appreciate. There I was, in O'Hara's chair at his desk in his office, giving a detailed report to Wolfe of a murder I had witnessed and a police operation I had helped with, and for over half an hour those three bozos simply utterly had to sit and listen. Whatever position they might be in all too soon, all they could do now was take it and like it. I did enjoy it. Now and then Wolfe interrupted with a question, and when I had finished he took me back to fill in a few gaps. Then he proceeded to give me instructions, and as I listened it became apparent that if it was a bluff at least he wasn't going to leave me behind the enemy lines to fight my way out. I asked him to repeat it to make sure I had it straight. He did so.

"Okay," I said. "Tell Fritz I'm hungry." I hung up and faced the three on chairs:

"I'm sorry it took so long, but he pays my salary and what could I do? As I told you, the announcement has been postponed. He is willing to kill it, but that sort of depends. He thinks it would be appropriate for Inspector Cramer and Sergeant Stebbins to help with the windup. He would appreciate it if you will start by delivering eight people at his office as soon as possible. He wants the five who were at the Fraser apartment today, not including the girl, Nancylee, or Cora the cook. Also Savarese. Also Anderson, president of the Hi-Spot Company, and Owen, the public relations man. All he wants you to do is to get them there, and to be present yourselves, but with the understanding that he will run the show. With that provision, he states that when you leave you will be prepared to make an arrest and take the murderer with you, and the announcement he gave WPIT will not be made. You can do the announcing." I arose and moved, crossing to a chair over by the wall near the door to reclaim my hat and coat. Then I turned:

"It's after ten o'clock, and if this thing is on I'm not going to start it on an empty stomach. In my opinion, even if all he has in mind is a game of blind man's buff, which I doubt, it's well worth it. Orchard died twenty-five days ago. Beula Poole nine days. Miss Koppel ten hours. You could put your inventory on a postage stamp." I had my hand on the doorknob. "How about it? Feel like helping?"

Cramer growled at me, "Why Anderson and Owen? What does he want them for?"

"Search me. Of course he likes a good audience."

"Maybe we can't get them."

"You can try. You're an inspector and murder is a very bad crime."

"It may take hours."

"Yeah, it looks like an all-night party. If I can stand it you can, not to mention Mr. Wolfe. All right, then we'll be seeing you." I opened the door and took a step, but turned:

"Oh, I forgot, he told me to tell you, this anonymous letter about Elinor Vance is just some homemade bait that didn't get used. I typed it myself this morning. If you get a chance tonight you can do a sample on my machine and compare."

O'Hara barked ferociously, "Why the hell didn't you say so?"

"I didn't like the way I was asked, Commissioner. The only man I know of more sensitive than me is Nero Wolfe."

24

It was not surprising that Cramer delivered the whole order. Certainly none of those people could have been compelled to go out into the night, and let themselves be conveyed to Nero Wolfe's office, or any place else, without slapping a charge on them, but it doesn't take much compelling when you're in that kind of a fix. They were all there well before midnight.

Wolfe stayed up in his room until they all arrived. I had supposed that while I ate my warmed-over cutlets he would have some questions or instructions for me, and probably both, but no. If he had anything he already had it and needed no contributions from me. He saw to it that my food was hot and my salad crisp and then beat it upstairs.

The atmosphere, as they gathered, was naturally not very genial, but it wasn't so much tense as it was glum. They were simply sunk. As soon as Elinor Vance got onto a chair she rested her elbows on her knees and buried her face in her hands, and stayed that way. Tully Strong folded his arms, let his head sag until his chin met his chest, and shut his eyes. Madeline Fraser sat in the red leather chair, which I got her into before President Anderson arrived, looking first at one of her fellow beings and then at another, but she gave the impression that she merely felt she ought to be conscious of something and they would do as well as anything else.

Bill Meadows, seated near Elinor Vance, was leaning back with his hands clasped behind his head, glaring at the ceiling. Nat Traub was a sight, with his necktie off center, his hair mussed, and his eyes bloodshot. His facial growth was the kind that needs shaving twice a day, and it hadn't had it. He was so restless he couldn't stay in his chair, but when he left it there was no place he wanted to go, so all he could do was sit down again. I did not, on that account, tag him for it, since he had a right to be haggard. A Meltette taken from a box delivered by him had poisoned and killed someone, and it wasn't hard to imagine how his client had reacted to that.

Two conversations were going on. Professor Savarese was telling Purley Stebbins something at length, presumably the latest in formulas, and Purley was making himself an accessory by nodding now and then. Anderson and Owen, the Hi-Spot delegates, were standing by the couch talking with Cramer, and, judging from the snatches I caught, they might finally decide to sit down and they might not. They had been the last to arrive. I, having passed the word to Wolfe that the delivery had been completed, was wondering what was keeping him when I heard the sound of his elevator.

They were so busy with their internal affairs that Traub and I were the only ones who were aware that our host had joined us until he reached the corner of his desk and turned to make a survey. The conversations stopped. Savarese bounded across to shake hands. Elinor Vance lifted her head, showing such a woebegone face that I had to restrain an impulse to take the anonymous letter from my pocket and tear it up then and there. Traub sat down for the twentieth time. Bill Meadows unclasped his hands and pressed his finger tips against his eyes. President Anderson sputtered:

"Since when have you been running the Police Department?"

That's what a big executive is supposed to do, go straight to the point.

Wolfe, getting loose from Savarese, moved to his chair and got himself arranged in it. I guess it's partly his size, unquestionably impressive, which holds people's attention when he is in motion, but his manner and style have a lot to do with it. You get both suspense and surprise. You know he's going to be clumsy and wait to see it, but by gum you never do. First thing you know there he is, in his chair or wherever he was bound for, and there was nothing clumsy about it at all. It was smooth and balanced and efficient.

He looked up at the clock, which said twenty to twelve, and re-marked to the audience, "It's late, isn't it?" He regarded the Hi-Spot president:

"Let's not start bickering, Mr. Anderson. You weren't dragged here by force, were you? You were impelled either by concern or curiosity. In either case you won't leave until you hear what I have to say, so why not sit down and listen? If you want to be contentious wait until you learn what you have to contend with. It works better that way."

He took in the others. "Perhaps, though, I should answer Mr. Anderson's question, though it was obviously rhetorical. I am not running the Police Department, far from it. I don't know what you were told when you were asked to come here, but I assume you know that nothing I say is backed by any official authority, for I have none. Mr. Cramer and Mr. Stebbins are present as observers. That is correct, Mr. Cramer?"

The Inspector, seated on the corner of the couch, nodded. "They understand that."

"Good. Then Mr. Anderson's question was not only rhetorical, it was gibberish. I shall—"

"I have a question!" a voice said, harsh and strained.

"Yes, Mr. Meadows, what is it?"

"If this isn't official, what happens to the notes Goodwin is making?"

"That depends on what we accomplish. They may never leave this house, and end up by being added to the stack in the cellar. Or a transcription of them may be accepted as evidence in a courtroom. —I wish you'd sit down, Mr. Savarese. It's more tranquil if everyone is seated."

Wolfe shifted his center of gravity. During his first ten minutes in a chair minor adjustments were always required.

"I should begin," he said with just a trace of peevishness, "by admitting that I am in a highly vulnerable position. I have told Mr. Cramer that when he leaves here he will take a murderer with him; but though I know who the murderer is, I haven't a morsel of evidence against him, and neither has anyone else. Still—"

"Wait a minute," Cramer growled.

Wolfe shook his head. "It's important, Mr. Cramer, to keep this unofficial—until I reach a certain point, if I ever do—so it would be best for you to say nothing whatever." His eyes moved. "I think the best approach is to explain how I learned the identity of the murderer—and by the way, here's an interesting point: though I was already close to certitude, it was clinched for me only two hours ago, when Mr. Goodwin told me that there were sixteen eager candidates for the sponsorship just abandoned by Hi-Spot. That removed my shred of doubt."

"For God's sake," Nat Traub blurted, "let the fine points go! Let's have it!"

"You'll have to be patient, sir," Wolfe reproved him. "I'm not merely reporting, I'm doing a job. Whether a murderer gets arrested, and tried, and convicted, depends entirely on how I handle this. There is no evidence, and if I don't squeeze it out of you people now, tonight, there may never be any. The trouble all along, both for the police and for me, has been that no finger pointed without wavering. In going for a murderer as well concealed as this one it is always necessary to trample down improbabilities to get a path started, but it is foolhardy to do so until a direction is plainly indicated. This time there was no such plain indication, and, frankly, I had begun to doubt if there would be one—until yesterday morning, when Mr. Anderson and Mr. Owen visited this office. They gave it to me."

"You're a liar!" Anderson stated.

"You see?" Wolfe upturned a palm. "Some day, sir, you're going to get on the wrong train by trying to board yours before it arrives. How do you know whether I'm a liar or not until you know what I'm saying? You did come here. You gave me a check for the full amount of my fee, told me that I was no longer in your hire, and said that you had withdrawn as a sponsor of Miss Fraser's program. You gave as your reason for withdrawal that the practice of blackmail had been injected into the case, and you didn't want your product connected in the public mind with blackmail because it is dirty and makes people gag. Isn't that so?"

"Yes. But—"

"I'll do the butting. After you left I sat in this chair twelve straight hours, with intermissions only for meals, using my brain on you. If I had known then that before the day was out sixteen other products were scrambling to take your Hi-Spot's place, I would have reached my conclusion in much less than twelve hours, but I didn't. What I was exploring was the question, what had happened to you? You had been so greedy for publicity that you had even made a trip down here to get into a photograph with me. Now, suddenly, you were fleeing like a comely maiden from a smallpox scare. Why?"

"I told you—"

"I know. But that wasn't good enough. Examined with care, it was actually flimsy. I don't propose to recite all my twistings and windings for those twelve hours, but first of all I rejected the reason you gave. What, then? I considered every possible circumstance and all conceivable combinations. That you were yourself the murderer and feared I might sniff you out; that you were not the murderer, but the blackmailer; that, yourself innocent, you knew the identity of one of the culprits, or both, and did not wish to be associated with the disclosure; and a thousand others. Upon each and all of my conjectures I brought to bear what I knew of you—your position, your record, your temperament, and your character. At the end only one supposition wholly satisfied me. I concluded that you had somehow become convinced that someone closely connected with that program, which you were sponsoring, had committed the murders, and that there was a possibility that that fact would be discovered. More: I concluded that it was not Miss Koppel or Miss Vance or Mr. Meadows or Mr. Strong, and certainly not Mr. Savarese. It is the public mind that you are anxious about, and in the public mind those people are quite insignificant.

Miss Fraser is that program, and that program is Miss Fraser. It could only be her. You knew, or thought you knew, that Miss Fraser herself had killed Mr. Orchard, and possibly Miss Poole too, and you were getting as far away from her as you could as quickly as you could. Your face tells me you don't like that."

"No," Anderson said coldly, "and you won't either before you hear the last of it. You through?"

"Good heavens, no. I've barely started. As I say, I reached that conclusion, but it was nothing to crow about. What was I to do with it? I had a screw I could put on you, but it seemed unwise to be hasty about it, and I considered a trial of other expedients. I confess that the one I chose to begin with was feeble and even sleazy, but it was at breakfast this morning, before I had finished my coffee and got dressed, and Mr. Goodwin was fidgety and I wanted to give him something to do. Also, I had already made a suggestion to Mr. Cramer which was designed to give everyone the impression that there was evidence that Miss Vance had been blackmailed, that she was under acute suspicion, and that she might be charged with murder at any moment. There was a chance, I thought, that an imminent threat to Miss Vance, who is a personable young woman, might impel somebody to talk."

"So you started that," Elinor Vance said dully.

Wolfe nodded. "I'm not boasting about it. I've confessed it was worse than second-rate, but I thought Mr. Cramer might as well try it; and this morning, before I was dressed, I could devise nothing better than for Mr. Goodwin to type an anonymous letter about you and take it up there—a letter which implied that you had committed murder at least twice."

"Goddam pretty," Bill Meadows said.

"He didn't do it," Elinor said.

"Yes, he did," Wolfe disillusioned her. "He had it with him, but didn't get to use it. The death of Miss Koppel was responsible not only for that, but for other things as well—for instance, for this gathering. If I had acted swiftly and energetically on the conclusion I reached twenty-four hours ago, Miss Koppel might be alive now. I owe her an apology but I can't get it to her. What I can do is what I'm doing."

Wolfe's eyes darted to Anderson and fastened there. "I'm going to put that screw on you, sir. I won't waste time appealing to you, in the name of justice or anything else, to tell me why you abruptly turned tail and scuttled. That would be futile. Instead, I'll tell you a homely little fact: Miss Fraser drank Hi-Spot only the first few times it was served on her program, and then had to quit and substitute coffee. She had to quit because your product upset her stomach. It gave her a violent indigestion."

"That's a lie," Anderson said. "Another lie."

"If it is it won't last long. —Miss Vance. Some things aren't as important as they once were. You heard what I said. Is it true?"

"Yes."

"Mr. Strong?"

"I don't think this—"

"Confound it, you're in the same room and the same chair! Is it true or not?"

"Yes."

"Mr. Meadows?"

"Yes."

"That should be enough. —So, Mr. Anderson—"

"A put-up job," the president sneered. "I left their damn program."

Wolfe shook his head. "They're not missing you. They had their choice of sixteen offers. No, Mr. Anderson, you're in a pickle. Blackmail revolts you, and you're being blackmailed. It is true that newspapers are reluctant to offend advertisers, but some of them couldn't possibly resist so picturesque an item as this, that the product Miss Fraser puffed so effectively to ten million people made her so ill that she didn't dare swallow a spoonful of it. Indeed yes, the papers will print it; and they'll get it in time for Monday morning."

"You sonofabitch." Anderson was holding. "They won't touch it. Will they, Fred?"

But the director of public relations was frozen, speechless with horror.

"I think they will," Wolfe persisted. "One will, I know. And open publication might be better than the sort of talk that would get around when once it's started. You know how rumors get distorted; fools would even say that it wasn't necessary to add anything to Hi-Spot to poison Mr. Orchard. Really, the blackmail potential of this is very high. And what do you have to do to stop it? Something hideous and insupportable? Not at all. Merely tell me why you suddenly decided to scoot."

Anderson looked at Owen, but Owen was gazing fixedly at Wolfe as at the embodiment of evil.

"It will be useless," Wolfe said, "to try any dodge. I'm ready for you. I spent all day yesterday on this, and I doubt very much if I'll accept anything except what I have already specified: that someone or something had persuaded you that Miss Fraser herself was in danger of being exposed as a murderer or a blackmailer. However, you can try."

"I don't have to try." He was a stubborn devil. "I told you yesterday. That was my reason then, and it's my reason now."

"Oh, for God's sake!" Fred Owen wailed. "Oh, my God!"

"Goddam it," Anderson blurted at him, "I gave my word! I'm sewed up! I promised!"

"To whom?" Wolfe snapped.

"All right," Owen said bitterly, "keep your word and lose your shirt. This is ruin! This is dynamite!"

"To whom?" Wolfe persisted.

"I can't tell you, and I won't. That was part of the promise."

"Indeed. Then that makes it simple." Wolfe's eyes darted left. "Mr. Meadows, a hypothetical question. If it was you to whom Mr. Anderson gave the pledge that keeps him from speaking, do you now release him from it?"

"It wasn't me," Bill said.

"I didn't ask you that. You know what a hypothetical question is. Please answer to the if. If it was you, do you release him?"

"Yes. I do."

"Mr. Traub, the same question. With that if, do you release him?"

"Yes."

"Miss Vance? Do you?"

"Yes."

"Mr. Strong. Do you?"

Of course Tully Strong had had time, a full minute, to make up his mind what to say. He said it:

"No!"

25

Eleven pairs of eyes fastened on Tully Strong.

"Aha," Wolfe muttered. He leaned back, sighed deep, and looked pleased.

"Remarkable!" a voice boomed. It was Professor Savarese. "So simple!"

If he expected to pull some of the eyes his way, he got cheated. They stayed on Strong.

"That was a piece of luck," Wolfe said, "and I'm grateful for it. If I had started with you, Mr. Strong, and got your no, the others might have made it not so simple."

"I answered a hypothetical question," Tully asserted, "and that's all. It doesn't mean anything."

"Correct," Wolfe agreed. "In logic, it doesn't. But I saw your face when you realized what was coming, the dilemma you would be confronted with in a matter of seconds, and that was enough. Do you now hope to retreat into logic?"

Tully just wasn't up to it. Not only had his face been enough when he saw it coming; it was still enough. The muscles around his thin tight lips quivered as he issued the command to let words through.

"I merely answered a hypothetical question," was the best he could do. It was pathetic.

Wolfe sighed again. "Well. I suppose I'll have to light it for you. I don't blame you, sir, for being obstinate about it, since it may be assumed that you have behaved badly. I don't mean your withholding information from the police; most people do that, and often for reasons much shoddier than yours. I mean your behavior to your employers. Since you are paid by the eight sponsors jointly your loyalty to them is indivisible; but you did not warn all of them that Miss Fraser was, or might be, headed for disgrace and disaster, and that therefore they had better clear out; apparently you confined it to Mr. Anderson. For value received or to be received, I presume —a good job?"

Wolfe shrugged. "But now it's all up." His eyes moved. "By the way, Archie, since Mr. Strong will soon be telling us how he knew

it was Miss Fraser, you'd better take a look. She's capable of anything, and she's as deft as a bear's tongue. Look in her bag."

Cramer was on his feet. "I'm not going—"

"I didn't ask you," Wolfe snapped. "Confound it, don't you see
how ticklish this is? I'm quite aware I've got no evidence yet, but
I'm not going to have that woman displaying her extraordinary
dexterity in my office. Archie?"

I had left my chair and stepped to the other end of Wolfe's desk,
but I was in a rather embarrassing position. I am not incapable of
using force on a woman, since after all men have never found
anything else to use on them with any great success when it comes
right down to it, but Wolfe had by no means worked up to a point
where the audience was with me. And when I extended a hand
toward the handsome leather bag in Madeline Fraser's lap, she gave
me the full force of her gray-green eyes and told me distinctly:

"Don't touch me."

I brought the hand back. Her eyes went to Wolfe:

"Don't you think it's about time I said something? Wouldn't it
look better?"

"No." Wolfe met her gaze. "I'd advise you to wait, madam. All
you can give us now is a denial, and of course we'll stipulate that.
What else can you say?"

"I wouldn't bother with a denial," she said scornfully. "But it
seems stupid for me to sit here and let this go on indefinitely."

"Not at all." Wolfe leaned toward her. "Let me assure you of one
thing, Miss Fraser, most earnestly. It is highly unlikely, whatever
you say or do from now on, that I shall ever think you stupid. I am
too well convinced of the contrary. Not even if Mr. Goodwin opens
your bag and finds in it the gun with which Miss Poole was shot."

"He isn't going to open it."

She seemed to know what she was talking about. I glanced at
Inspector Cramer, but the big stiff wasn't ready yet to move a finger.
I picked up the little table that was always there by the arm of the
red leather chair, moved it over to the wall, went and brought one
of the small yellow chairs, and sat, so close to Madeline Fraser that
if we had spread elbows they would have touched. That meant no
more notes, but Wolfe couldn't have everything. As I sat down by
her, putting in motion the air that had been there undisturbed, I
got a faint whiff of a spicy perfume, and my imagination must have
been pretty active because I was reminded of the odor that had

reached me that day in her apartment, from the breath of Deborah
Koppel as I tried to get her onto the divan before she collapsed. It
wasn't the same at all except in my fancy. I asked Wolfe:

"This will do, won't it?"

He nodded and went back to Tully Strong. "So you have not one
reason for reluctance, but several. Even so, you can't possibly stick
it. It has been clearly demonstrated to Mr. Cramer that you are
withholding important information directly pertinent to the crimes
he is investigating, and you and others have already pushed his
patience pretty far. He'll get his teeth in you now and he won't let
go. Then there's Mr. Anderson. The promise he gave you is half gone,
now that we know it was you he gave it to, and with the threat I'm
holding over him he can't reasonably be expected to keep the other
half."

Wolfe gestured. "And all I really need is a detail. I am satisfied
that I know pretty well what you told Mr. Anderson. What happened yesterday, just before he took alarm and leaped to action?
The morning papers had the story of the anonymous letters—the
blackmailing device by which people were constrained to make
payments to Mr. Orchard and Miss Poole. Then that story had supplied a missing link for someone. Who and how? Say it was Mr.
Anderson. Say that he received, some weeks ago, an anonymous
letter or letters blackguarding Miss Fraser. He showed them to
her. He received no more letters. That's all he knew about it. A little
later Mr. Orchard was a guest on the Fraser program and got
poisoned, but there was no reason for Mr. Anderson to connect that
event with the anonymous letters he had received. That was what
the story in yesterday's papers did for him; they made that connection. It was now perfectly plain: anonymous letters about Miss
Fraser; Miss Fraser's subscription to *Track Almanac;* the method by
which those subscriptions were obtained; and Mr. Orchard's death
by drinking poisoned coffee ostensibly intended for Miss Fraser.
That did not convict Miss Fraser of murder, but at a minimum it
made it extremely inadvisable to continue in the role of her sponsor.
So Mr. Anderson skedaddled."

"I got no anonymous letters," Anderson declared.

"I believe you." Wolfe didn't look away from Tully Strong. "I
rejected, tentatively, the assumption that Mr. Anderson had himself received the anonymous letters, on various grounds, but chiefly
because it would be out of character for him to show an anonymous

letter to the subject of it. He would be much more likely to have the letter's allegations investigated, and there was good reason to assume that that had not been done. So I postulated that it was not Mr. Anderson, but some other person, who had once received an anonymous letter or letters about Miss Fraser and who was yesterday provided with a missing link. It was a permissible guess that that person was one of those now present, and so I tried the experiment of having the police insinuate an imminent threat to Miss Vance, in the hope that it would loosen a tongue. I was too cautious. It failed lamentably; and Miss Koppel died."

Wolfe was talking only to Strong. "Of course, having no evidence, I have no certainty that the information you gave Mr. Anderson concerned anonymous letters. It is possible that your conviction, or suspicion, about Miss Fraser, had some other basis. But I like my assumption because it is neat and comprehensive; and I shall abandon it only under compulsion. It explains everything, and nothing contradicts it. It will even explain, I confidently expect, why Mr. Orchard and Miss Poole were killed. Two of the finer points of their operation were these, that they demanded only a small fraction of the victim's income, limited to one year, and that the letters did not expose, or threaten to expose, an actual secret in the victim's past. Even if they had known such secrets they would not have used them. But sooner or later—this is a point on which Mr. Saverese could speak with the authority of an expert, but not now, some other time—sooner or later, by the law of averages, they would use such a secret by inadvertence. Sooner or later the bugaboo they invented would be, for the victim, not a mischievous libel, but a real and most dreadful terror."

Wolfe nodded. "Yes. So it happened. The victim was shown the letter or letters by some friend—by you, Mr. Strong—and found herself confronted not merely by the necessity of paying an inconsequential tribute, but by the awful danger of some disclosure that was not to be borne; for she could not know, of course, that the content of the letter had been fabricated and that its agreement with reality was sheer accident. So she acted. Indeed, she acted! She killed Mr. Orchard. Then she learned, from a strange female voice on the phone, that Mr. Orchard had not been the sole possessor of the knowledge she thought he had, and again she acted. She killed Miss Poole."

"My God," Anderson cut in, "you're certainly playing it strong, with no cards."

"I am, sir," Wolfe agreed. "It's time I got dealt to, don't you think? Surely I've earned at least one card. You can give it to me, or Mr. Strong can. What more do you want, for heaven's sake? Rabbits from a hat?"

Anderson got up, moved, and was confronting the secretary of the Sponsors' Council. "Don't be a damn fool, Tully," he said with harsh authority. "He knows it all, you heard him. Go ahead and get rid of it!"

"This is swell for me," Tully said bitterly.

"It would have been swell for Miss Koppel," Wolfe said curtly, "if you had spoken twenty hours ago. How many letters did you get?"

"Two."

"When?"

"February. Around the middle of February."

"Did you show them to anyone besides Miss Fraser?"

"No, just her, but Miss Koppel was there so she saw them too."

"Where are they now?"

"I don't know. I gave them to Miss Fraser."

"What did they say?"

Tully's lips parted, stayed open a moment, and closed again.

"Don't be an ass," Wolfe snapped. "Mr. Anderson is here. What did they say?"

"They said that it was lucky for Miss Fraser that when her husband died no one had been suspicious enough to have the farewell letters he wrote examined by a handwriting expert."

"What else?"

"That was all. The second one said the same thing, only in a different way."

Wolfe's eyes darted to Anderson. "Is that what he told you, sir?"

The president, who had returned to the couch, nodded. "Yes, that's it. Isn't it enough?"

"Plenty, in the context." Wolfe's head jerked around to face the lady at my elbow. "Miss Fraser. I've heard of only one farewell letter your husband wrote, to a friend, a local attorney. Was there another? To you, perhaps?"

"I don't think," she said, "that it would be very sensible for me to try to help you." I couldn't detect the slightest difference in her voice. Wolfe had understated it when he said she was an extremely dangerous woman. "Especially," she went on, "since you are apparently accepting those lies. If Mr. Strong ever got any anonymous letters he never showed them to me—nor to Miss Koppel, I'm sure of that."

"I'll be damned!" Tully Strong cried, and his specs fell off as he gawked at her.

It was marvelous, and it certainly showed how Madeline Fraser got people. Tully had been capable of assuming that she had killed a couple of guys, but when he heard her come out with what he knew to be a downright lie he was flabbergasted.

Wolfe nodded at her. "I suppose," he admitted, "it would be hopeless to expect you to be anything but sensible. You are aware that there is still no evidence, except Mr. Strong's word against yours. Obviously the best chance is the letter your husband wrote to his friend, since the threat that aroused your ferocity concerned it." His face left us, to the right. "Do you happen to know, Mr. Cramer, whether that letter still exists?"

Cramer was right up with him. He had gone to the phone on my desk and was dialing. In a moment he spoke:

"Dixon there? Put him on. Dixon? I'm at Wolfe's office. Yeah, he's got it, but by the end of the tail. Two things quick. Get Darst and have him phone Fleetville, Michigan. He was out there and knows 'em. Before Lawrence Koppel died he wrote a letter to a friend. We want to know if that letter still exists and where it is, and they're to get it if they can and keep it, but for God's sake don't scare the friend into burning it or eating it. Tell Darst it's so important it's the whole case. Then get set with a warrant for an all-day job on the Fraser woman's apartment. What we're looking for is cyanide, and it can be anywhere—the heel of a shoe, for instance. You know the men to get—only the best. Wolfe got it by the tail with one of his crazy dives into a two-foot tank, and now we've got to hang onto it. What? Yes, damn it, of course it's her! Step on it!"

He hung up, crossed to me, thumbed me away, moved the chair aside, and stood by Miss Fraser's chair, gazing down at her. Keeping his gaze where it was, he rumbled:

"You might talk a little more, Wolfe."

"I could talk all night," Wolfe declared. "Miss Fraser is worth it. She had good luck, but most of the bad luck goes to the fumblers, and she is no fumbler. Her husband's death must have been managed with great skill, not so much because she gulled the authorities, which may have been no great feat, but because she completely deceived her husband's sister, Miss Koppel. The whole operation with Mr. Orchard was well conceived and executed, with the finest subtlety in even the lesser details—for instance, having the subscription in Miss Koppel's name. It was simple to phone Mr. Orchard that that money came from her, Miss Fraser. But best of all was the climax—getting the poisoned coffee served to the intended victim. That was one of her pieces of luck, since apparently Mr. Traub, who didn't know about the taped bottle, innocently put it in front of Mr. Orchard, but she would have managed without it. At that narrow table, with Mr. Orchard just across from her, and with the broadcast going on, she could have manipulated it with no difficulty, and probably without anyone becoming aware of any manipulation. Certainly without arousing any suspicion of intent, before or after."

"Okay," Cramer conceded. "That doesn't worry me. And the Poole thing doesn't either, since there's nothing against it. But the Koppel woman?"

Wolfe nodded. "That was the masterpiece. Miss Fraser had in her favor, certainly, years of intimacy during which she had gained Miss Koppel's unquestioning loyalty, affection, and trust. They held steadfast even when Miss Koppel saw the anonymous letters Mr. Strong had received. It is quite possible that she received similar letters herself. We don't know, and never will, I suppose, what finally gave birth to the worm of suspicion in Miss Koppel. It wasn't the newspaper story of the anonymous letters and blackmailing, since that appeared yesterday, Friday, and it was on Wednesday that Miss Koppel tried to take an airplane to Michigan. We may now assume, since we know that she had seen the anonymous letters, that something had made her suspicious enough to want to inspect the farewell letter her brother had sent to his friend, and we may certainly assume that Miss Fraser, when she learned what her dearest and closest friend had tried to do, knew why."

"That's plain enough," Cramer said impatiently. "What I mean—"

"I know. You mean what I meant when I said it was a masterpiece. It took resourcefulness, first-rate improvisation, and ingenuity to make use of the opportunity offered by Mr. Traub's delivery of the box of Meltettes; and only a maniacal stoicism could have left those deadly tidbits there on the piano where anybody might casually have eaten one. Probably inquiry would show that it was not as haphazard as it seems; that it was generally known that the box was there to be sampled by Miss Fraser and therefore no one would loot it. But the actual performance, as Mr. Goodwin described it to me, was faultless. There was then no danger to a bystander, for if anyone but Miss Koppel had started to eat one of the things Miss Fraser could easily have prevented it. If the box had been handed to Miss Fraser, she could either have postponed the sampling or have taken one from the second layer instead of the top. What chance was there that Miss Koppel would eat one of the things? One in five, one in a thousand? Anyway, she played for that chance, and again she had luck; but it was not all luck, and she performed superbly."

"This is incredible," Madeline Fraser said. "I knew I was strong, but I didn't know I could do this. Only a few hours ago my dearest friend Debby died in my arms. I should be with her, sitting with her through the night, but here I am, sitting here, listening to this . . . this nightmare . . ."

"Cut," Bill Meadows said harshly. "Night and nightmare. Cut one."

The gray-green eyes darted at him. "So you're ratting, are you, Bill?"

"Yes, I'm ratting. I saw Debby die. And I think he's got it. I think you killed her."

"Bill!" It was Elinor Vance, breaking. "Bill, I can't stand it!" She was on her feet, shaking all over. "I can't!"

Bill put his arms around her, tight. "All right, kid. I hope to God she gets it. You were there too. What if you had decided to eat one?"

The phone rang and I got it. It was for Cramer. Purley went and replaced him beside Miss Fraser, and he came to the phone. When he hung up he told Wolfe:

"Koppel's friend still has that letter, and it's safe."

"Good," Wolfe said approvingly. "Will you please get her out of here? I've been wanting beer for an hour, and I'm not foolhardy enough to eat or drink anything with her in the house." He looked around. "The rest of you are invited to stay if you care to. You must be thirsty."

But they didn't like it there. They went.

26

The experts were enthusiastic about the letter Lawrence Koppel had written to his friend. They called it one of the cleverest forgeries they had ever seen. But what pleased Wolfe most was the finding of the cyanide. It was in the hollowed-out heel of a house slipper, and was evidently the leavings of the supply Mrs. Lawrence Koppel had snitched six years ago from her husband's shelf.

It was May eighteenth that she was sentenced on her conviction for the first-degree murder of Deborah Koppel. They had decided that was the best one to try her for. The next day, a Wednesday, a little before noon, Wolfe and I were in the office checking over catalogues when the phone rang. I went to my desk for it.

"Nero Wolfe's office, Archie Goodwin speaking."

"May I speak to Mr. Wolfe, please?"

"Who is it?"

"Tell him a personal matter."

I covered the transmitter. "Personal matter," I told Wolfe. "A man whose name I have forgotten."

"What the devil! Ask him."

"A man," I said distinctly, "whose name I have forgotten."

"Oh." He frowned. He finished checking an item and then picked up the phone on his desk, while I stayed with mine. "This is Nero Wolfe."

"I would know the voice anywhere. How are you?"

"Well, thank you. Do I know you?"

"Yes. I am calling to express my appreciation of your handling of the Fraser case, now that it's over. I am pleased and thought you should know it. I have been, and still am, a little annoyed, but I am satisfied that you are not responsible. I have good sources of information. I congratulate you on keeping your investigation within the limits I prescribed. That has increased my admiration of you."

"I like to be admired," Wolfe said curtly. "But when I undertake an investigation I permit prescription of limits only by the requirements of the job. If that job had taken me across your path you would have found me there."

"Then that is either my good fortune—or yours."

The connection went.

I grinned at Wolfe. "He's an abrupt bastard."

Wolfe grunted. I returned to my post at the end of his desk and picked up my pencil.

"One little idea," I suggested. "Why not give Dr. Michaels a ring and ask if anyone has phoned to switch his subscription? No, that won't do, he's paid up. Marie Leconne?"

"No. I invite trouble only when I'm paid for it. And to grapple with him the pay would have to be high."

"Okay." I checked an item. "You'd be a problem in a foxhole, but the day may come."

"It may. I hope not. Have you any Zygopetalum crinitum on that page?"

"Good God no. It begins with a Z!"

the second confession

1

"I didn't mind it at all," our visitor said gruffly but affably. "It's a pleasure." He glanced around. "I like rooms that men work in. This is a good one."

I was still swallowing my surprise that he actually looked like a miner, at least my idea of one, with his big bones and rough weathered skin and hands that would have been right at home around a pick handle. Certainly swinging a pick was not what he got paid for as chairman of the board of the Continental Mines Corporation, which had its own building down on Nassau Street not far from Wall.

I was also surprised at the tone he was using. When, the day before, a masculine voice had given a name on the phone and asked when Nero Wolfe could call at his office, and I had explained why I had to say never, and it had ended by arranging an appointment at Wolfe's office for eleven the next morning, I had followed up with a routine check on a prospective client by calling Lon Cohen at the *Gazette*. Lon had told me that the only reason James U. Sperling didn't bite ears off was because he took whole heads and ate them bones and all. But there he was, slouching in the red leather chair near the end of Wolfe's desk like a big friendly roughneck, and I've just told you what he said when Wolfe started the conversation by explaining that he never left the office on business and expressing a regret that Sperling had had to come all the way to our place on West Thirty-fifth Street nearly to Eleventh Avenue. He said it was a pleasure!

"It will do," Wolfe murmured in a gratified tone. He was behind his desk, leaning back in his custom-made chair, which was warranted safe for a quarter of a ton and which might some day really be put to the test if its owner didn't level off. He added, "If you'll tell me what your problem is perhaps I can make your trip a good investment."

Seated at my own desk, at a right angle to Wolfe's and not far away, I allowed myself a mild private grin. Since the condition of his bank balance did not require the use of sales pressure to snare a client, I knew why he was spreading the sugar. He was merely being sociable because Sperling had said he liked the office. Wolfe didn't like the office, which was on the first floor of the old brownstone house he owned. He didn't like it, he loved it, and it was a good thing he did, since he was spending his life in it—except when he was in the kitchen with Fritz, or in the dining room across the hall at mealtime, or upstairs asleep, or in the plant rooms up on the roof, enjoying the orchids and pretending he was helping Theodore with the work.

My private grin was interrupted by Sperling firing a question at me: "Your name's Goodwin, isn't it? Archie Goodwin?"

I admitted it. He went to Wolfe.

"It's a confidential matter."

Wolfe nodded. "Most matters discussed in this office are. That's commonplace in the detective business. Mr. Goodwin and I are used to it."

"It's a family matter."

Wolfe frowned, and I joined in. With that opening it was a good twenty-to-one shot that we were going to be asked to tail a wife, and that was out of bounds for us. But James U. Sperling went on.

"I tell you that because you'd learn it anyhow." He put a hand to the inside breast pocket of his coat and pulled out a bulky envelope. "These reports will tell you that much. They're from the Bascom Detective Agency. You know them?"

"I know Mr. Bascom." Wolfe was still frowning. "I don't like ground that's been tramped over."

Sperling went right on by. "I had used them on business matters and found them competent, so I went to Bascom with this. I wanted information about a man named Rony, Louis Rony, and they've been at it a full month and they haven't got it, and I need it urgently. Yesterday I decided to call them off and try you. I've looked you up, and if you've earned your reputation I should have come to you first." He smiled like an angel, surprising me again, and convincing me that he would stand watching. "Apparently you have no equal."

Wolfe grunted, trying not to look pleased. "There was a man in Marseille—but he's not available and he doesn't speak English. What information do you want about Mr. Rony?"

"I want proof that he's a Communist. If you get it and get it soon, your bill can be whatever you want to make it."

Wolfe shook his head. "I don't take jobs on those terms. You don't know he's a Communist, or you wouldn't be bidding so high for proof. If he isn't, I can't very well get evidence that he is. As for my bill being whatever I want to make it, my bills always are. But I charge for what I do, and I can do nothing that is excluded by circumstance. What I dig up is of necessity contingent on what has been buried, but the extent of my digging isn't, nor my fee."

"You talk too much," Sperling said impatiently but not impolitely.

"Do I?" Wolfe cocked an eye at him. "Then you talk." He nodded sidewise at me. "Your notebook, Archie."

The miner waited until I had it ready, open at a fresh page, and then spoke crisply, starting with a spelling lesson. "L-o-u-i-s R-o-n-y. He's in the Manhattan phone book, both his law office and his home, his apartment—and anyway, it's all in that." He indicated the bulky envelope, which he had tossed onto Wolfe's desk. "I have two daughters. Madeline is twenty-six and Gwenn is twenty-two. Gwenn was smart enough to graduate with honors at Smith a year ago, and I'm almost sure she's sane, but she's too damn curious and she turns her nose up at rules. She hasn't worked her way out of the notion that you can have independence without earning it. Of course it's all right to be romantic at her age, but she overdoes it, and I think what first attracted her to this man Rony was his reputation as a champion of the weak and downtrodden, which he has got by saving criminals from the punishment they deserve."

"I think I've seen his name," Wolfe murmured. "Haven't I, Archie?"

I nodded. "So have I. It was him that got What's-her-name, that baby peddler, out from under a couple of months ago. He seems to be on his way to the front page."

"Or to jail," Sperling snapped, and there was nothing angelic about his tone. "I think I handled this wrong, and I'm damned sure my wife did. It was the same old mistake, and God only knows why parents go on making it. We even told her, and him too, that he would no longer be admitted into our home, and of course you know what the reaction was to that. The only concession she made, and I doubt if that was to us, was never to come home after daylight."

"Is she pregnant?" Wolfe inquired.

Sperling stiffened. "What did you say?" His voice was suddenly as hard as the hardest ore ever found in any mine. Unquestionably he expected it to crush Wolfe into pretending he hadn't opened his mouth, but it didn't.

"I asked if your daughter is pregnant. If the question is immaterial I withdraw it, but surely it isn't preposterous unless she also turns her nose up at natural laws."

"She is my daughter," Sperling said in the same hard tone. Then suddenly his rigidity gave way. All the stiff muscles loosened, and he was laughing. When he laughed he roared, and he really meant it. In a moment he controlled it enough to speak. "Did you hear what I said?" he demanded.

Wolfe nodded. "If I can believe my ears."

"You can." Sperling smiled like an angel. "I suppose with any man that's one of his tenderest spots, but I might be expected to remember that I am not just any man. To the best of my knowledge my daughter is not pregnant, and she would have a right to be astonished if she were. That's not it. A little over a month ago my wife and I decided to correct the mistake we had made, and she told Gwenn that Rony would be welcome at our home as often as she wanted him there. That same day I put Bascom onto him. You're quite right that I can't prove he's a Communist or I wouldn't have had to come to you, but I'm convinced that he is."

"What convinced you?"

"The way he talks, the way I've sized him up, the way he practices his profession—and there are things in Bascom's reports, you'll see that when you read them—"

"But Mr. Bascom got no proof."

"No. Damn it."

"Whom do you call a Communist? A liberal? A pink intellectual? A member of the party? How far left do you start?"

Sperling smiled. "It depends on where I am and who I'm talking to. There are occasions when it may be expedient to apply the term to anyone left of center. But to you I'm using it realistically. I think Rony is a member of the Communist party."

"If and when you get proof, what are you going to do with it?"

"Show it to my daughter. But it has to be proof. She already knows what I think; I told her long ago. Of course she told Rony, and he looked me in the eye and denied it."

Wolfe grunted. "You may be wasting your time and money. Even if you get proof, what if it turns out that your daughter regards a Communist party card as a credential for romance?"

"She doesn't. Her second year in college she got interested in communism and went into it, but it didn't take her long to pull out. She says it's intellectually contemptible and morally unsound. I told you she's smart enough." Sperling's eyes darted to me and went back to Wolfe. "By the way, what about you and Goodwin? As I said, I looked you up, but is there any chance I'm putting my foot in it?"

"No," Wolfe assured him. "Though of course only the event can certify us. We agree with your daughter." He looked at me. "Don't we?"

I nodded. "Completely. I like the way she put it. The best I can do is 'a Commie is a louse' or something like that."

Sperling looked at me suspiciously, apparently decided that I merely had IQ trouble, and returned to Wolfe, who was talking.

"Exactly what," he was asking, "is the situation? Is there a possibility that your daughter is already married to Mr. Rony?"

"Good God no!"

"How sure are you?"

"I'm sure. That's absurd—but of course you don't know her. There's no sneak in her—and anyhow, if she decides to marry him she'll tell me—or her mother—before she tells him. That's how she'd do it—" Sperling stopped abruptly and set his jaw. In a moment he let it loose and went on, "And that's what I'm afraid of, every day now. If she once commits herself it's all over. I tell you it's urgent. It's damned urgent!"

Wolfe leaned back in his chair and closed his eyes. Sperling regarded him a while, opened his mouth and closed it again, and looked at me inquiringly. I shook my head at him. When, after another couple of minutes, he began making and unmaking fists with his big bony hands, I reassured him.

"It's okay. He never sleeps in the daytime. His mind works better when he can't see me."

Finally Wolfe's lids went up and he spoke. "If you hire me," he told Sperling, "it must be clear what for. I can't engage to get proof that Mr. Rony is a Communist, but only to find out if proof exists, and, if it does, get it if possible. I'm willing to undertake that, but it seems an unnecessary restriction. Can't we define it a little better? As I understand it, you want your daughter to abandon all thought of marrying Mr. Rony and stop inviting him to your home. That's your objective. Right?"

"Yes."

"Then why restrict my strategy? Certainly I can try for proof that he's a Communist, but what if he isn't? Or what if he is but we can't prove it to your daughter's satisfaction? Why limit the operation to that one hope, which must be rather forlorn if Mr. Bascom has spent a month at it and failed? Why not hire me to reach your objective, no matter how—of course within the bounds permitted to civilized man? I would have a much clearer conscience in accepting your retainer, which will be a check for five thousand dollars."

Sperling was considering. "Damn it, he's a Communist!"

"I know. That's your fixed idea and it must be humored. I'll try that first. But do you want to exclude all else?"

"No. No, I don't."

"Good. And I have—yes, Fritz?"

The door to the hall had opened and Fritz was there.

"Mr. Hewitt, sir. He says he has an appointment. I seated him in the front room."

"Yes." Wolfe glanced at the clock on the wall. "Tell him I'll see him in a few minutes." Fritz went, and Wolfe returned to Sperling.

"And I have correctly stated your objective?"

"Perfectly."

"Then after I've read Mr. Bascom's reports I'll communicate with you. Good day, sir. I'm glad you like my office—"

"But this is urgent! You shouldn't waste an hour!"

"I know." Wolfe was trying to stay polite. "That's another characteristic of matters discussed in this office—urgency. I now have an appointment, and shall then eat lunch, and from four to six I shall be working with my plants. But your affair need not wait on that. Mr. Goodwin will read the reports immediately, and after lunch he will go to your office to get all required details—say two o'clock?"

James U. Sperling didn't like it at all. Apparently he was set to devote the day to arranging to save his daughter from a fate worse than death, not even stopping for meals. He was so displeased that he merely grunted an affirmative when, as I let him out the front door, I courteously reminded him that he was to expect me at his office at 2:15 and that he could save himself the trouble of mailing the check by handing it to me then. I took time out for a brief survey of the long black Wethersill limousine waiting for him at the curb before I returned to the office.

The door to the front room was open and Wolfe's and Hewitt's voices came through. Since their mutual interest was up in the plant rooms and they wouldn't be using the office, I got the bulky envelope Sperling had left on Wolfe's desk and made myself comfortable to read Bascom's reports.

2

A couple of hours later, at five to two, Wolfe returned his empty coffee cup to the saucer, pushed his chair back, got all of him upright, walked out of the dining room, and headed down the hall toward his elevator. I, having followed, called to his half an acre of back, "How about three minutes in the office first?"

He turned. "I thought you were going to see that man with a daughter."

"I am, but you won't talk business during meals, and I read Bascom's reports, and I've got questions."

He shot a glance at the door to the office, saw how far away it was, growled, "All right, come on up," and turned and made for the elevator.

If he has his rules so do I, and one of mine is that a three-by-four private elevator with Wolfe in it does not need me too, so I took the stairs. One flight up was Wolfe's bedroom and a spare. Two flights up was my bedroom and another spare. The third flight put me on the roof. There was no dazzling blaze of light, as in winter, since this was June and the shade slats were all rolled down, but there was a blaze of color from the summer bloomers, especially in the middle room. Of course I saw it every day, and I had business on my mind, but even so I slowed up as I passed a bench of white and yellow Dendrobium bensoniae that were just at their peak.

Wolfe was in the potting room, taking his coat off, with a scowl all ready for me.

"Two things," I told him curtly. "First, Bascom not only—"

He was curter. "Did Mr. Bascom get any lead at all to the Communist party?"

"No. But he—"

"Then he got nothing for us." Wolfe was rolling up his shirt sleeves. "We'll discuss his reports after I've read them. Did he have good men on it?"

"He sure did. His best."

"Then why should I hire an army to stalk the same phantom, even with Mr. Sperling's money? You know what that amounts to, trying to track a Communist down, granting that he is one—especially when what is wanted is not presumption, but proof. Bah. A will-o'-the-wisp. I defined the objective and Mr. Sperling agreed. See him and get details, yes. Get invited to his home, socially. Meet Mr. Rony and form an opinion of him. More important, form one of the daughter, as intimately and comprehensively as possible. Make appointments with her. Seize and hold her attention. You should be able to displace Mr. Rony in a week, a fortnight at the most—and that's the objective."

"I'll be damned." I shook my head reproachfully. "You mean make a pass at her."

"Your terms are yours, and I prefer mine. Mr. Sperling said his daughter is excessively curious. Transfer her curiosity from Mr. Rony to you."

"You mean break her heart."

"You can stop this side of tragedy."

"Yeah, and I can stop this side of starting." I looked righteous and outraged. "You've gone a little too far. I like being a detective, and I like being a man, with all that implies, but I refuse to degrade whatever glamour I may—"

"Archie!" He snapped it.

"Yes, sir."

"With how many young women whom you met originally through your association with my business have you established personal relationships?"

"Between five and six thousand. But that's not—"

"I'm merely suggesting that you reverse the process and establish the personal relationship first. What's wrong with that?"

"Everything." I shrugged. "Okay. Maybe nothing. It depends. I'll take a look at her."

"Good. You're going to be late." He started for the supply shelves.

I raised my voice a little. "However, I've still got a question, or two, rather. Bascom's boys had a picnic trying to tail Rony. The first time out, before anything could have happened to make him suspicious, he had his nose up and pulled a fade. From then on not only did they have to use only the best, but often even that wasn't good enough. He knew the whole book and some extra chapters. He may or may not be a Communist, but he didn't learn all that in Sunday school."

"Pfui. He's a lawyer, isn't he?" Wolfe said contemptuously. He took a can of Elgetrol from the shelf and began shaking it. "Confound it, let me alone."

"I will in a minute. The other thing, three different times, times when they didn't lose him, he went into Bischoff's Pet Shop on Third Avenue and stayed over an hour, and he doesn't keep any pets."

Wolfe stopped shaking the can of Elgetrol. He looked at it as if he didn't know what it was, hesitated, put the can back on the shelf, and looked at me.

"Oh," he said, not curtly. "He did?"

"Yes, sir."

Wolfe looked around, saw the oversized chair in its place, and went to it and sat down.

I wasn't gratified at having impressed him. In fact, I would have preferred to pass the chance up, but I hadn't dared. I remembered too well a voice—a hard, slow, precise voice, cold as last week's corpse—which I had heard only three times altogether, on the telephone. The first time had been in January 1946, and the second and third had been more than two years later, while we were looking for the poisoner of Cyril Orchard. Furthermore, I remembered the tone of Wolfe's voice when he said to me, when we had both hung up after the second phone call, "I should have signaled you off, Archie, as soon as I recognized his voice. I tell you nothing because it is better for you to know nothing. You are to forget that you know his name. If ever, in the course of my business, I find that I am committed against him and must destroy him, I shall leave this house, find a place where I can work—and sleep and eat if there is time for it—and stay there until I have finished."

I have seen Wolfe tangle with some tough bozos in the years I've been with him, but none of them has ever had him talking like that.

Now he was sitting glaring at me as if I had put vinegar on his caviar.

"What do you know about Bischoff's Pet Shop?" he demanded.

"Nothing to speak of. I only know that last November, when Bischoff came to ask you to take on a job, you told him you were too busy and you weren't, and when he left and I started beefing you told me that you were no more eager to be committed for Arnold Zeck than against him. You didn't explain how you knew that that pet shop is a branch of Zeck's far-flung shenanigans, and I didn't ask."

"I told you once to forget that you know his name."

"Then you shouldn't have reminded me of it. Okay, I'll forget again. So I'll go down and phone Sperling that you're too busy and call it off. He hasn't—"

"No. Go and see him. You're late."

I was surprised. "But what the hell? What's wrong with my deducting? If Rony went three times in a month to that pet shop, and probably more, and stayed over an hour, and doesn't keep pets, and I deduce that he is presumably an employee or something of the man whose name I forget, what—"

"Your reasoning is quite sound. But this is different. I was aware of Mr. Bischoff's blemish, no matter how, when he came to me, and refused him. I have engaged myself to Mr. Sperling, and how can I scuttle?" He looked up at the clock. "You'd better go." He sighed. "If it could be managed to keep one's self-esteem without paying for it . . ."

He went and got the can of Elgetrol and started shaking it, and I headed out.

3

That was two o'clock Thursday. At two o'clock Saturday, forty-eight hours later, I was standing in the warm sunshine on a slab of white marble as big as my bedroom, flicking a bright blue towel as big as my bathroom, to chase a fly off of one of Gwenn Sperling's bare legs. Not bad for a rake's progress, even though I was under an assumed name. I was now Andrew instead of Archie. When I had told Sperling of Wolfe's suggestion that I should meet the family, not of course displaying Wolfe's blueprint, and he had objected to disclosing me to Rony, I had explained that we would use hired help for tailing and similar routine, and that I would have a try at getting Rony to like me. He bought it without haggling and invited me to spend the week end at Stony Acres, his country place up near Chappaqua, but said I'd have to use another name because he was pretty sure his wife and son and elder daughter, Madeline, knew about Archie Goodwin. I said modestly that I doubted it, and insisted on keeping the Goodwin because it was too much of a strain to keep remembering to answer to something else, and we settled for changing Archie to Andrew. That would fit the A. G. on the bag Wolfe had given me for my birthday, which I naturally wanted to have along because it was caribou hide and people should see it.

The items in Bascom's reports about Louis Rony's visits to Bischoff's Pet Shop had cost Sperling some dough. If it hadn't been for that Wolfe would certainly have let Rony slide until I reported on my week end, since it was a piddling little job and had no interest for him except the fee, and since he had a sneaking idea that women came on a lope from every direction when I snapped my fingers, which was foolish because it often takes more than snapping your fingers. But when I got back from my call on Sperling Thursday afternoon Wolfe had already been busy on the phone, getting Saul Panzer and Fred Durkin and Orrie Cather, and when they came to the office Friday morning for briefing Saul was assigned to a survey of Rony's past, after reading Bascom, and Fred and Orrie were given special instructions for fancy tailing. Obviously what Wolfe was doing was paying for his self-esteem—or letting Sperling pay for it. He had once told Arnold Zeck, during their third and last phone talk, that when he undertook an investigation he permitted prescription of limits only by requirements of the job, and now he was leaning backward. If Rony's Pet Shop visits really meant that he was on one of Zeck's payrolls, and if Zeck was still tacking up his KEEP OFF signs, Nero Wolfe had to make it plain that no one was roping him off. We've got our pride. So Saul and Fred and Orrie were at it.

So was I, the next morning, Saturday, driving north along the winding Westchester parkways, noticing that the trees seemed to have more leaves than they knew what to do with, keeping my temper when some dope of a snail stuck to the left lane as if he' had built it, doing a little snappy passing now and then just to keep my hand in, dipping down off the parkway onto a secondary road, fol-

lowing it a couple of miles as directed, leaving it to turn into a graveled drive between ivy-covered stone pillars, winding through a
park and assorted horticultural exhibits until I broke cover and saw
the big stone mansion, stopping at what looked as if it might be the
right spot, and telling a middle-aged sad-looking guy in a mohair
uniform that I was the photographer they were expecting.

Sperling and I had decided that I was the son of a business associate who was concentrating on photography, and who wanted
pictures of Stony Acres for a corporation portfolio, for two reasons: first, because I had to be something, and second, because I
wanted some good shots of Louis Rony.

Four hours later, having met everybody and had lunch and used
both cameras all over the place in as professional a manner as I
could manage, I was standing at the edge of the swimming pool,
chasing a fly off of Gwenn's leg. We were both dripping, having
just climbed out.

"Hey," she said, "the snap of that towel is worse than a fly bite—
if there was a fly."

I assured her there had been.

"Well, next time show it to me first and maybe I can handle it
myself. Do that dive from the high board again, will you? Where's
the Leica?"

She had been a pleasant surprise. From what her father had said
I had expected an intellectual treat in a plain wrapper, but the
package was attractive enough to take your attention off of the
contents. She was not an eye-stopper, and there was no question
about her freckles, and while there was certainly nothing wrong
with her face it was a little rounder than I would specify if I were
ordering à la carte; but she was not in any way hard to look at, and
those details which had been first disclosed when she appeared in
her swimming rig were completely satisfactory. I would never have
seen the fly if I had not been looking where it lit.

I did the dive again and damn near pancaked. When I was back
on the marble, wiping my hair back, Madeline was there, saying,
"What are you trying to do, Andy, break your back? You darned
fool!"

"I'm making an impression," I told her. "Have you got a trapeze
anywhere? I can hang by my toes."

"Of course you can. I know your repertory better than you think
I do. Come and sit down and I'll mix you a drink."

Madeline was going to be in my way a little, in case I decided to humor Wolfe by trying to work on Gwenn. She was more spectacular than Gwenn, with her slim height and just enough curves not to call anywhere flat, her smooth dark oval face, and her big dark eyes which she liked to keep half shut so she could suddenly open them on you and let you have it. I already knew that her husband was dead, having been shot down in a B-17 over Berlin in 1943, that she thought she had seen all there was but might be persuaded to try another look, that she liked the name Andy, and that she thought there was just a chance that I might know a funny story she hadn't heard. That was why she was going to be in my way a little.

I went and sat with her on a bench in the sun, but she didn't mix me a drink because three men were gathered around the refreshment cart and one of them attended to it—James U. Sperling, Junior. He was probably a year or two older than Madeline and resembled his father hardly at all. There was nothing about his slender straightness or his nice smooth tanned skin or his wide spoiled mouth that would have led anyone to say he looked like a miner. I had never seen him before but had heard a little of him. I couldn't give you a quote, but my vague memory was that he was earnest and serious about learning to make himself useful in the corporation his father headed, and he frequently beat it to Brazil or Nevada or Arizona to see how mining was done, but he got tired easy and had to return to New York to rest, and he knew lots of people in New York willing to help him rest.

The two men with him at the refreshment cart were guests. Since our objective was confined to Rony and Gwenn I hadn't bothered with the others except to be polite, and I wouldn't be dragging them in if it wasn't that later on they called for some attention. Also it was beginning to look as if they could stand a little attention right then, on account of a situation that appeared to be developing, so the field of my interest was spreading out a little. If I ever saw a woman make a pass, Mrs. Paul Emerson, Connie to her friends and enemies, was making one at Louis Rony.

First the two men. One of them was just a super, a guy some older than me named Webster Kane. I had gathered that he was some kind of an economist who had done some kind of a job for Continental Mines Corporation, and he acted like an old friend of the family. He had a big well-shaped head and apparently didn't own a hairbrush, didn't care what his clothes looked like, and was not swimming but was drinking. In another ten years he could pass for a senator.

I had welcomed the opportunity for a close-up of the other man because I had often heard Wolfe slice him up and feed him to the cat. At six-thirty P.M. on WPIT, five days a week, Paul Emerson, sponsored by Continental Mines Corporation, interpreted the news. About once a week Wolfe listened to him, but seldom to the end; and when, after jabbing the button on his desk that cut the circuit, Wolfe tried some new expressions and phrases for conveying his opinion of the performance and the performer, no interpreter was needed to clarify it. The basic idea was that Paul Emerson would have been more at home in Hitler's Germany or Franco's Spain. So I was glad of a chance to take a slant at him, but it didn't get me much because he confused me by looking exactly like my chemistry teacher in high school out in Ohio, who had always given me better marks than I had earned. Also it was a safe bet that he had ulcers— I mean Paul Emerson—and he was drinking plain soda with only one piece of ice. In swimming trunks he was really pitiful, and I had taken some pictures of him from the most effective angles to please Wolfe with.

It was Emerson's wife, Connie, who seemed to be heading for a situation that might possibly have a bearing on our objective as defined by Wolfe. She couldn't have had more than four or five years to dawdle away until her life began at forty, and was therefore past my deadline, but it was by no means silly of her to assume that it was still okay for her to go swimming in mixed company in broad daylight. She was one of those rare blondes that take a good tan, and had better legs and arms, judged objectively, than either Gwenn or Madeline, and even from the other side of the wide pool the blue of her eyes carried clear and strong. That's where she was at the moment, across the pool, sitting with Louis Rony, getting her breath after showing him a double knee lock that had finally put him flat, and he was no matchstick. It was a new technique for making a pass at a man, but it had obvious advantages, and anyway she had plenty of other ideas and wasn't being stingy with them. At lunch she had buttered rolls for him. Now I ask you.

I didn't get it. If Gwenn was stewing about it she was keeping it well hid, though I had noticed her casting a few quick glances. There was a chance that she was counterattacking by pretending she would rather help me take pictures than eat, and that she loved to watch me dive, but who was I to suspect a fine freckled girl of pretending? Madeline had made a couple of cracks about Connie's routine, without any sign that she really cared a damn. As for Paul Emerson, the husband, the sour look on his undistinguished map when his glance took in his wife and her playmate didn't seem to mean much, since it stayed sour no matter where he was glancing.

Louis Rony was the puzzle, though. The assumption was that he was making an all-out play for Gwenn, either because he was in love with her or because he wanted something that went with her; and if so, why the monkeyshines with the mature and beautifully tanned blonde? Was he merely trying to give Gwenn a nudge? I had of course done a survey on him, including the contrast between his square-jawed rugged phiz and the indications that the race of fat and muscle would be a tie in another couple of years, but I wasn't ready for a final vote. From my research on him, which hadn't stopped with Bascom's reports, I knew all about his record as a sensational defender of pickpockets, racketeers, pluggers, fences, and on down the line, but I was holding back on whether he was a candidate for the throne Abe Hummel had once sat on, or a Commie trying out a new formula for raising a stink, or a lieutenant, maybe even better, in one of Arnold Zeck's field divisions, or merely a misguided sucker for guys on hot spots.

However, the immediate puzzle about him was more specific. The question for the moment wasn't what did he expect to accomplish with Connie Emerson, or what kind of fuel did he have in his gas tank, but what was all the fuss about the waterproof wallet, or bag, on the inside of his swimming trunks? I had seen him give it his attention, not ostentatiously, four times altogether; and by now my curiosity had really got acute, for the fourth time, right after the knee-lock episode with Connie, he had gone so far as to pull it out for a look and stuff it back in again. My eyes were still as good as ever, and there was no doubt about what it was.

Naturally I did not approve of it. At a public beach, or even at a private beach or pool where there is a crowd of strangers and he changes with other males in a common room, a man has a right to guard something valuable by putting it into a waterproof container and keeping it next to his hide, and he may even be a sap if he doesn't. But Rony, being a house guest like the rest of us, had changed in his own room, which wasn't far from mine on the second floor. It is not nice to be suspicious of your hosts or fellow guests, and even if you think you ought to be there must have been at least a dozen first-class hiding places in Rony's room for an object small enough to go in that thing he kept worrying about. It was an insult to everybody, including me. It was true that he kept his worry so inconspicuous that apparently no one else noticed it, but he had no right to take such a risk of hurting our feelings, and I resented it and intended to do something about it.

Madeline's fingers touched my arm. I finished a sip of my Tom Collins and turned my head.

"Yeah?"

"Yeah what?" she smiled, opening her eyes.

"You touched me."

"No, did I? Nothing."

It was evidently meant as a teaser, but I was watching Gwenn poise for a back flip, and anyway there was an interruption. Paul Emerson had wandered over and now growled down at me.

"I forgot to mention it, Goodwin, I don't want any pictures unless they have my okay—I mean for publication."

I tilted my head back. "You mean any at all, or just of you?"

"I mean of me. Please don't forget that."

"Sure. I don't blame you."

When he had made it to the edge of the pool and fallen in, presumably on purpose, Madeline spoke.

"Do you think a comparative stranger like you ought to take swipes at a famous character like him?"

"I certainly do. You shouldn't be surprised, if you know my repertory so well. What was that crack, anyhow?"

"Oh—when we go in I guess I'll have to show you something. I should control my tongue better."

On the other side Rony and Connie Emerson had got their breath back and were making a dash for the pool. Jimmy Sperling, whom I preferred to think of as Junior, called to ask if I could use a refill, and Webster Kane said he would attend to it. Gwenn stopped before me, dripping again, to say that the light would soon be right for the west terrace and we ought to put on some clothes, and didn't I agree with her?

It was one of the most congenial jobs of detecting I had had in a long while, and there wouldn't have been a cloud in sight if it hadn't been for that damn waterproof wallet or bag that Rony was so anxious about. That called for a little work, but it would have to wait.

4

Hours later, in my room on the second floor, which had three big windows, two three-quarter beds, and the kind of furniture and rugs I will never own but am perfectly willing to use as a transient without complaining, I got clean and neat for dinner. Then I retrieved my keys from where I had hid them behind a book on a shelf, took my medicine case from the caribou bag, and unlocked it. This was a totally different thing from Rony's exhibition of bad manners, since I was there on business, and the nature of my business required me to carry various unusual items in what I called my medicine case. All I took from it was a tiny, round, soft light brown object, which I placed tenderly in the little inner coin pocket inside the side pocket of my jacket. I handled it with tweezers because it was so quick to dissolve that even the moisture of my fingers might weaken it. I relocked the medicine case and returned it to the bag.

There was a knock on my door and I said come in. It opened and Madeline entered and advanced, enveloped in a thin white film of folds that started at her breasts and stopped only at her ankles. It made her face smaller and her eyes bigger.

"How do you like my dress, Archie?" she asked.

"Yep. You may not call that formal, but it certainly—" I stopped. I looked at her. "I thought you said you liked the name Andy. No?"

"I like Archie even better."

"Then I'd better change over. When did Father confide in you?"

"He didn't." She opened the eyes. "You think I think I'm sophisticated and just simply impenetrable, don't you? Maybe I am, but I wasn't always. Come along, I want to show you something." She turned and started off.

I followed her out and walked beside her along the wide hall, across a landing, and down another hall into another wing. The room she took me into, through a door that was standing open, was twice as big as mine, which I had thought was plenty big enough, and in addition to the outdoor summer smell that came in the open windows it had the fragrance of enormous vases of roses that were placed around. I would just as soon have taken a moment to glance around at details, but she took me across to a table, opened a bulky leather-bound portfolio as big as an atlas to a page where there was a marker, and pointed.

"See? When I was young and gay!"

I recognized it instantly because I had one like it at home. It was a clipping from the *Gazette* of September ninth, 1940. I have not had my picture in the paper as often as Churchill or Rocky Graziano, or even Nero Wolfe, but that time it happened that I had been lucky and shot an automatic out of a man's hand just before he pressed the trigger.

I nodded. "A born hero if I ever saw one."

She nodded back. "I was seventeen. I had a crush on you for nearly a month."

"No wonder. Have you been showing this around?"

"I have not! Damn it, you ought to be touched!"

"Hell, I am touched, but not as much as I was an hour ago. I thought you liked my nose or the hair on my chest or something, and here it was only a childhood memory."

"What if I feel it coming back?"

"Don't try to sweeten it. Anyway, now I have a problem. Who else might possibly remember this picture—and there have been a couple of others—besides you?"

She considered. "Gwenn might, but I doubt it, and I don't think anyone else would. If you have a problem, I have a question. What are you here for? Louis Rony?"

It was my turn to consider, and I let her have a poker smile while I was at it.

"That's it," she said.

"Or it isn't. What if it is?"

She came close enough to take hold of my lapels with both hands, and her eyes were certainly big. "Listen, you born hero," she said earnestly. "No matter what I might feel coming back or what I don't, you be careful where you head in on anything about my sister. She's twenty-two. When I was her age I was already pretty well messed up, and she's still as clean as a rose—my God, I don't mean a rose, you know what I mean. I agree with my dad about Louis Rony, but it all depends on how it's done. Maybe the only way not to hurt her too much is to shoot him. I don't really know what he is to her. I'm just telling you that what matters isn't Dad or

Mother or me or Rony, but it's my sister, and you'd better believe me."

It was the combination of circumstances. She was so close, and the smell of roses was so strong, and she was so damned earnest after dallying around with me all afternoon, that it was really automatic. When, after a minute or two, she pushed at me, I let her go, reached for the portfolio and closed it, and took it to a tier of shelves and put it on the lowest one. When I got back to her she looked a little flushed but not too overcome to speak.

"You darned fool," she said, and had to clear her throat. "Look at my dress now!" She ran her fingers down through the folds. "We'd better go down."

As I went with her down the wide stairs to the reception hall it occurred to me that I was getting my wires crossed. I seemed to have a fair start on establishing a personal relationship, but not with the right person.

We ate on the west terrace, where the setting sun, coming over the tops of the trees beyond the lawn, was hitting the side of the house just above our heads as we sat down. By that time Mrs. Sperling was the only one who was calling me Mr. Goodwin. She had me at her right, probably to emphasize my importance as the son of a business associate of the Chairman of the Board, and I still didn't know whether she knew I was in disguise. It was her that Junior resembled, especially the wide mouth, though she had filled in a little. She seemed to have her department fairly under control, and the looks and manners of the help indicated that they had been around quite a while and intended to stay.

After dinner we loafed around the terrace until it was about dark and then went inside, all but Gwenn and Rony, who wandered off across the lawn. Webster Kane and Mrs. Sperling said they wanted to listen to a broadcast, or maybe it was video. I was invited to partake of bridge, but said I had a date with Sperling to discuss photography plans for tomorrow, which was true. He led me to a part of the house I hadn't seen yet, into a big high-ceilinged room with four thousand books around the walls, a stock ticker, and a desk with five phones on it among other things, gave me a fourth or fifth chance to refuse a cigar, invited me to sit, and asked what I wanted. His tone was not that of a host to a guest, but of a senior executive to one not yet a junior executive by a long shot. I arranged my tone to fit.

"Your daughter Madeline knows who I am. She saw a picture of me once and seems to have a good memory."

He nodded. "She has. Does it matter?"

"Not if she keeps it to herself, and I think she will, but I thought you ought to know. You can decide whether you had better mention it to her."

"I don't think so. I'll see." He was frowning, but not at me. "How is it with Rony?"

"Oh, we're on speaking terms. He's been pretty busy. The reason I asked to see you is something else. I notice there are keys for the guest-room doors, and I approve of it, but I got careless and dropped mine in the swimming pool, and I haven't got an assortment with me. When I go to bed I'll want to lock my door because I'm nervous, so if you have a master key will you kindly lend it to me?"

There was nothing slow about him. He was already smiling before I finished. Then he shook his head. "I don't think so. There are certain standards—oh, to hell with standards. But he is here as my daughter's guest, with my permission, and I think I would prefer not to open his door for you. What reason have you—"

"I was speaking of my door, not someone else's. I resent your insinuation, and I'm going to tell my father, who owns stock in the corporation, and he'll resent it too. Can I help it if I'm nervous?"

He started to smile, then thought it deserved better than that, and his head went back for a roar of laughter. I waited patiently. When he had done me justice he got up and went to the door of a big wall safe, twirled the knob back and forth, and swung the door open, pulled a drawer out and fingered its contents, and crossed to me with a tagged key in his hand.

"You can also shove your bed against the door," he suggested.

I took the key. "Yes, sir, thank you, I will," I told him and departed.

When I returned to the living room, which was about the size of a tennis court, I found that the bridge game had not got started. Gwenn and Rony had rejoined the party. With a radio going, they were dancing in a space by the doors leading to the terrace, and Jimmy Sperling was dancing with Connie Emerson. Madeline was at the piano, concentrating on trying to accompany the radio, and Paul Emerson was standing by, looking down at her flying fingers with his face sourer than ever. At the end of dinner he had taken three kinds of pills, and perhaps had picked the wrong ones. I went and asked Madeline to dance, and it took only a dozen steps to know how good she was. Still more relationship.

A little later Mrs. Sperling came in, and she was soon followed by Sperling and Webster Kane. Before long the dancing stopped, and someone mentioned bed, and it began to look as if there would be no chance to dispose of the little brown capsule I had got from my medicine case. Some of them had patronized the well-furnished bar on wheels which had been placed near a long table back of a couch, but not Rony, and I had about decided that I was out of luck when Webster Kane got enthusiastic about nightcaps and started a selling campaign. I made mine bourbon and water because that was what Rony had shown a preference for during the afternoon, and the prospect brightened when I saw Rony let Jimmy Sperling hand him one. It went as smooth as if I had written the script. Rony took a swallow and then put his glass on the table when Connie Emerson wanted both his hands to show him a rumba step. I took a swallow from mine to make it the same level as his, got the capsule from my pocket and dropped it in, made my way casually to the table, put my glass down by Rony's in order to have my hands for getting out a cigarette and lighting it, and picked the glass up again, but the wrong one—or I should say the right one. There wasn't a chance the maneuver had been observed, and it couldn't have been neater.

But there my luck ended. When Connie let him go Rony went to the table and retrieved his glass, but the damn fool didn't drink. He just held on to it. After a while I tried to prime him by sauntering over to where he was talking with Gwenn and Connie, joining in, taking healthy swallows from my glass, and even making a comment on the bourbon, but he didn't lift it for a sip. The damn camel. I wanted to ask Connie to get a knee lock on him so I could pour it down his throat. Two or three of them were saying good night and leaving, and I turned around to be polite. When I turned back again Rony had stepped to the bar to put his glass down, and when he moved away there were no glasses there but empty ones. Had he suddenly gulped it down? He hadn't. I went to put my glass down, reached across for a pretzel, and lowered my head enough to get a good whiff of the contents of the ice bucket. He had dumped it in there.

I guess I told people good night; anyway I got up to my room. Naturally I was sore at myself for having bungled it, and while I undressed I went back over it carefully. It was a cinch he hadn't seen me switch the glasses, with his back turned and no mirror he could have caught it in. Neither had Connie, for her view had been blocked by him and she only came up to his chin. I went over it again and decided no one could have seen me, but I was glad Nero Wolfe wasn't there to explain it to. In any case, I concluded in the middle of a deep yawn, I wouldn't be using Sperling's master key. Whatever reason Rony might have had for ditching the drink, he sure had ditched it, which meant he was not only undoped but also alerted . . . and therefore . . . therefore something, but what . . . therefore . . . the thought was important and it was petering out on me. . . .

I reached for my pajama top but had to stop to yawn, and that made me furious because I had no right to yawn when I had just fumbled on a simple little thing like doping a guy . . . only I didn't feel furious at all . . . I just felt awful damn sleepy. . . .

I remember saying to myself aloud through gritted teeth, *"You're doped you goddam dope and you get that door locked,"* but I don't remember locking it. I know I did, because it was locked in the morning.

5

All day Sunday was a nightmare. It rained off and on all day. I dragged myself out of bed at ten o'clock with a head as big as a barrel stuffed with wet feathers, and five hours later it was still the size of a keg and the inside was still swampy. Gwenn was keeping after me to take interiors with flashbulbs, and I had to deliver. Strong black coffee didn't seem to help, and food was my worst enemy. Sperling thought I had a hangover, and he certainly didn't smile when I returned the master key and refused to report events if any. Madeline thought there was something funny about it, but the word funny has different meanings at different times. There was one thing, when I got roped in for bridge I seemed to be clairvoyant and there was no stopping me. Jimmy suspected I was a shark but tried to conceal it. About the worst was when Webster Kane decided I was in exactly the right condition to start a course in economics and devoted an hour to the first lesson.

I was certainly in no shape to make any headway in simple fractions, let alone economics or establishing a relationship with a girl like Gwenn. Or Madeline either. Sometime during the afternoon Madeline got me alone and started to open me up for a look at my intentions and plans—or rather, Wolfe's—regarding her sister, and I did my best to keep from snarling under the strain. She was willing to reciprocate, and I collected a few items about the family and guests without really caring a damn. The only one who was dead set against Rony was Sperling himself. Mrs. Sperling and Jimmy, the brother, had liked him at first, then had switched more or less to Sperling's viewpoint, and later, about a month ago, had switched again and taken the attitude that it was up to Gwenn. That was when Rony had been allowed to darken the door again. As for the guests, Connie Emerson had apparently decided to solve the problem by getting Rony's mind off of Gwenn and onto someone else, namely her; Emerson seemed to be neither more nor less sour on Rony than on most of his other fellow creatures; and Webster Kane was judicious. Kane's attitude, of some importance because of his position as a friend of the family, was that he didn't care for Rony personally but that a mere suspicion didn't condemn him. He had had a hot argument with Sperling about it.

Some of the stuff Madeline told me might have been useful in trying to figure who had doped Rony's drink if I had been in any condition to use it, but I wasn't. I would have made myself scarce long before the day was done but for one thing. I intended to get even, or at least make a stab at it.

As for the doping, I had entered a plea of not guilty, held the trial, and acquitted myself. The possibility that I had taken my own dope was ruled out; I had made that switch clean. And Rony had not seen the switch or been told of it; I was standing pat on that. Therefore Rony's drink had been doped by someone else, and he had either known it or suspected it. It would have been interesting to know who had done it, but there were too many nominations. Webster Kane had been mixing, helped by Connie and Madeline, and Jimmy had delivered Rony's drink to him. Not only that, after Rony had put it down on the table I had by no means had my eyes fixed on it while I was making my way across. So while Rony might have a name for the supplier of the dose I had guzzled, to me he was just X.

That, however, was not what had me hanging on. To hell with X, at least for the present. What had me setting my jaw and bidding four spades, or trotting around after Gwenn with two cameras and my pockets bulging with flashbulbs, when I should have been home in bed, was a picture I would never forget: Louis Rony pouring into a bucket the drink I had doped for him, while I stood and gulped the last drop of the drink someone else had doped for him. He would pay for that or I would never look Nero Wolfe in the face again.

Circumstances seemed favorable. I collected the information cautiously and without jostling. Rony had come by train Friday evening and been met at the station by Gwenn, and had to return to town this evening, Sunday; and no one was driving in. Paul and Connie Emerson were house guests at Stony Acres for a week; Webster Kane was there for an indefinite period, preparing some economic something for the corporation; Mom and the girls were there for the summer; and Sperling Senior and Junior would certainly not go to town Sunday evening. But I would, waiting until late to miss the worst of the traffic, and surely Rony would prefer a comfortable roomy car to a crowded train.

I didn't ask him. Instead, I made the suggestion, casually, to Gwenn. Later I made it pointedly to Madeline, and she agreed to drop a word in if the occasion offered. Then I got into the library alone with Sperling, suggested it to him even more pointedly, asked him which phone I could use for a New York call, and told him the call was not for him to hear. He was a little difficult about it, which I admit he had a right to be, but by that time I could make whole sentences again and I managed to sell him. He left and closed the door behind him, and I got Saul Panzer at his home in Brooklyn and talked to him all of twenty minutes. With my head still soggy, I had to go over it twice to be sure not to leave any gaps.

That was around six o'clock, which meant I had four more hours to suffer, since I had picked ten for the time of departure and was now committed to it, but it wasn't so bad. A little later the clouds began to sail around and you could tell them apart, and the sun even took a look at us just before it dropped over the edge; and what was more important, I risked a couple of nibbles at a chicken sandwich and before I was through the sandwich was too, and also a piece of cherry pie and a glass of milk. Mrs. Sperling patted me on the back and Madeline said that now she would be able to get some sleep.

It was six minutes past ten when I slid behind the wheel of the convertible, asked Rony if he had remembered his toothbrush, and rolled along the plaza into the curve of the drive.

"What's this," he asked, "a forty-eight?"

"No," I said, "forty-nine."

He let his head go back to the cushion and shut his eyes.

There were enough openings among the clouds to show some stars but no moon. We wound along the drive, reached the stone pillars, and eased out onto the public road. It was narrow, with an asphalt surface that wouldn't have been hurt by a little dressing, and for the first mile we had it to ourselves, which suited me fine. Just beyond a sharp turn the shoulder widened at a spot where there was an old shed at the edge of thick woods, and there at the roadside, headed the way we were going, a car was parked. I was going slow on account of the turn, and a woman darted out and blinked a flashlight, and I braked to a stop. As I did so the woman called, "Got a jack, mister?" and a man's voice came, "My jack broke, you got one?"

I twisted in the seat to back off the road onto the grass. Rony muttered at me, "What the hell," and I muttered back, "Brotherhood of man." As the man and woman came toward us I got out and told Rony, "Sorry, but I guess you'll have to move; the jack's under the seat." The woman, saying something about what nice people we were, was on his side and opened the door for him, and he climbed out. He went out backwards, facing me, and just as he was clear something slammed against the side of my head and I sank to the ground, but the grass was thick and soft. I stayed down and listened. It was only a few seconds before I heard my name.

"Okay, Archie."

I got to my feet, reached in the car to turn off the engine and lights, and circled around the hood to the other side, away from the road. Louis Rony was stretched out flat on his back. I didn't waste time checking on him, knowing that Ruth Brady could give lectures on the scientific use of a persuader, and anyhow she was kneeling at his head with her flashlight.

"Sorry to break into your Sunday evening, Ruth darling."

"Nuts to you, Archie my pet. Don't stand talking. I don't like this, out here in the wilderness."

"Neither do I. Don't let him possum."

"Don't worry. I've got a blade of grass up his nose."

"Good. If he wiggles tap him again." I turned to Saul Panzer, who had his shirt sleeves rolled up. "How are the wife and children?"

"Wonderful."

"Give 'em my love. You'd better be busy the other side of the car, in case of traffic."

He moved as instructed and I went to my knees beside Ruth. I expected to find it on him, since it wouldn't have been sensible for him to take such pains with it when he went swimming and then carelessly pack it in his bag, which had been brought down by one of the help. And I did find it on him. It was not in a waterproof container but in a cellophane envelope, in the innermost compartment of his alligator-skin wallet. I knew that must be it, because nothing else on him was out of the ordinary, and because its nature was such that I knelt there and goggled, with Ruth's flashlight focused on it.

"The surprise is wasted on me," she said scornfully. "I'm on. It's yours and you had to get it back. Comrade!"

"Shut up." I was a little annoyed. I removed it from the cellophane cover and inspected it some more, but there was nothing tricky about it. It was merely what it was, a membership card in the American Communist party, Number 128-394, and the name on it was William Reynolds. What annoyed me was that it was so darned pat. Our client had insisted that Rony was a Commie, and the minute I do a little personal research on him, here's his membership card! Of course the name meant nothing. I didn't like it. It's an anticlimax to have to tell a client he was dead right in the first place.

"What do they call you, Bill or Willie?" Ruth asked.

"Hold this," I told her, and gave her the card. I got the key and opened up the car trunk, hauled out the big suitcase, and got the big camera and some bulbs. Saul came to help. Ruth was making comments which we ignored. I took three pictures of that card, once held in Saul's hand, once propped up on the suitcase, and once leaning against Rony's ear. Then I slipped it back in the cellophane cover and replaced it in the wallet, and put the wallet where I found it, in Rony's breast pocket.

One operation remained, but it took less time because I had more experience at taking wax impressions of keys than at photography. The wax was in the medicine case, and the keys, eight of them, were in Rony's fold. There was no need to label the impressions, since I

didn't know which key was for what anyway. I took all eight, not
wanting to skimp.

"He can't last much longer," Ruth announced.

"He don't need to." I shoved a roll of bills at Saul, who had put the
suitcase back in the trunk. "This came out of his wallet. I don't
know how much it is and don't care, but I don't want it on me. Buy
Ruth a string of pearls or give it to the Red Cross. You'd better get
going, huh?"

They lost no time. Saul and I understand each other so well that
all he said was, "Phone in?" and I said, "Yeah." The next minute
they were off. As soon as their car was around the next bend I
circled to the other side of the convertible, next the road, stretched
out on the grass, and started groaning. When nothing happened I
quit after a while. Just as my weight was bringing the wet in the
ground through the grass and on through my clothes, and I was
about to shift, a noise came from Rony's side and I let out a groan.
I got onto my knees, muttered an expressive word or two, groaned
again, reached for the handle of the door and pulled myself to my
feet, reached inside and turned on the lights, and saw Rony sitting
on the grass inspecting his wallet.

"Hell, you're alive," I muttered.

He said nothing.

"The bastards," I muttered.

He said nothing. It took him two more minutes to decide to try
to stand up.

I admit that an hour and fifty minutes later, when I drove away
from the curb in front of his apartment on Thirty-seventh Street
after letting him out, I was totally in the dark about his opinion of
me. He hadn't said more than fifty words all the way, leaving it to
me to decide whether we should stop at a State Police barracks to
report our misfortune, which I did, knowing that Saul and Ruth
were safely out of the county; but I couldn't expect the guy to be
very talkative when he was busy recovering after an expert operation by Ruth Brady. I couldn't make up my mind whether he had
been sitting beside me in silent sympathy with a fellow sufferer or
had merely decided that the time for dealing with me would have
to come later, after his brain had got back to something like normal.

The clock on the dash said 1:12 as I turned into the garage on
Eleventh Avenue. Taking the caribou bag, but leaving the other
stuff in the trunk, I didn't feel too bad as I rounded the corner into

Thirty-fifth Street and headed for our stoop. I was a lot better prepared to face Wolfe than I had been all day, and my head was now
clear and comfortable. The week end hadn't been a washout after
all, except that I was coming home hungry, and as I mounted the
stoop I was looking forward to a session in the kitchen, knowing
what to expect in the refrigerator kept stocked by Wolfe and
Fritz Brenner.

I inserted the key and turned the knob, but the door would open
only two inches. That surprised me, since when I am out and expected home it is not customary for Fritz or Wolfe to put on the
chain bolt except on special occasions. I pushed the button, and in
a moment the stoop light went on and Fritz's voice came through
the crack.

"That you, Archie?"

That was odd too, since through the one-way glass panel he had
a good view of me. But I humored him and told him it really was
me, and he let me in. After I crossed the threshold he shut the door
and replaced the bolt, and then I had a third surprise. It was past
Wolfe's bedtime, but there he was in the door to the office, glowering at me.

I told him good evening. "Quite a reception I get," I added. "Why
the barricade? Someone been trying to swipe an orchid?" I turned
to Fritz. "I'm so damn hungry I could even eat your cooking." I
started for the kitchen, but Wolfe's voice stopped me.

"Come in here," he commanded. "Fritz, will you bring in a tray?"

Another oddity. I followed him into the office. As I was soon to
learn, he had news that he would have waited up all night to tell
me, but something I had said had pushed it aside for the moment.
No concern at all, not even life or death, could be permitted to
shove itself ahead of food. As he lowered himself into the chair behind his desk he demanded, "Why are you so hungry? Doesn't Mr.
Sperling feed his guests?"

"Sure." I sat. "There's nothing wrong with the grub, but they put
something in the drinks that takes your appetite. It's a long story.
Want to hear it tonight?"

"No." He looked at the clock. "But I must. Go ahead."

I obliged. I was still getting the characters introduced when Fritz
came with the tray, and I bit into a sturgeon sandwich and went on.
I could tell from Wolfe's expression that for some reason anything
and everything would be welcome, and I let him have it all. By the

time I finished it was after two o'clock, the tray had been cleaned up except for a little milk in the pitcher, and Wolfe knew all that I knew, leaving out a few little personal details.

I emptied the pitcher into the glass. "So I guess Sperling's hunch was good and he really is a Commie. With a picture of the card and the assortment I got of Rony, I should think you could get that lined up by that character who has appeared as Mr. Jones on our expense list now and then. He may not actually be Uncle Joe's nephew, but he seems to be at least a deputy in the Union Square Politburo. Can't you get him to research it?"

Fritz had brought another tray, with beer, and Wolfe poured the last of the second bottle.

"I could, yes." He drank and put the glass down. "But it would be a waste of Mr. Sperling's money. Even if that is Mr. Rony's card and he is a party member, as he well may be, I suspect that it is merely a masquerade." He wiped his lips. "I have no complaint of your performance, Archie, which was in character, and I should know your character; and I can't say you transgressed your instructions, since you had a free hand, but you might have phoned before assuming the risks of banditry."

"Really." I was sarcastic. "Excuse me, but since when have you invited constant contact on a little job like tripping up a would-be bridegroom?"

"I haven't. But you were aware that another factor had entered, or at least been admitted as conjecture. It is no longer conjecture. You didn't phone me, but someone else did. A man—a voice you are acquainted with. So am I."

"You mean Arnold Zeck?"

"No name was pronounced. But it was that voice. As you know, it is unmistakable."

"What did he have to say?"

"Neither was Mr. Rony's name pronounced, nor Mr. Sperling's. But he left no room for dubiety. In effect I was told to cease forthwith any inquiry into the activities or interests of Mr. Rony or suffer penalties."

"What did you have to say?"

"I—demurred." Wolfe tried to pour beer, found the bottle was empty, and set it down. "His tone was more peremptory than it was the last time I heard it, and I didn't fully conceal my resentment. I stated my position in fairly strong terms. He ended with an ultimatum. He gave me twenty-four hours to recall you from your week end."

"He knew I was up there?"

"Yes."

"I'll be damned." I let out a whistle. "This Rony boy is really something. A party member *and* one of Mr. Z's little helpers—which isn't such a surprising combination, at that. And not only have I laid hands on him, but Saul and Ruth have too. Goddam it! I'll have to —when did this phone call come?"

"Yesterday afternoon—" Wolfe glanced up at the clock. "Saturday, at ten minutes past six."

"Then his ultimatum expired eight hours ago and we're still breathing. Even so, it wouldn't have hurt to get time out for changing our signals. Why didn't you phone me and I could—"

"Shut up!"

I lifted the brows. "Why?"

"Because even if we are poltroons cowering in a corner, we might have the grace not to talk like it! I reproach you for not phoning. You reproach me for not phoning. It is only common prudence to keep the door bolted, but there is no possible—"

That may not have been his last syllable, but if he got one more in I didn't hear it. I have heard a lot of different noises here and there, and possibly one or two as loud as the one that interrupted Wolfe and made me jump out of my chair halfway across the room, but nothing much like it. To reproduce it you could take a hundred cops, scatter them along the block you live in, and have them start unanimously shooting windows with forty-fives.

Then complete silence.

Wolfe said something.

I grabbed a gun from a drawer, ran to the hall, flipped the switch for the stoop light, removed the chain bolt, opened the door, and stepped out. Across the street to the left two windows went up, and voices came and heads poked out, but the street was deserted. Then I saw that I wasn't standing on the stone of the stoop but on a piece of glass, and if I didn't like that piece there were plenty of others. They were all over the stoop, the steps, the area-way, and the sidewalk. I looked straight up, and another piece came flying down, missed me by a good inch, and crashed and tinkled at my feet. I backed across the sill, shut the door, and turned to face Wolfe, who was standing in the hall looking bewildered.

"He took it out on the orchids," I stated. "You stay here. I'll go up and look."

As I went up the stairs three at a time I heard the sound of the elevator. He must have moved fast. Fritz was behind me but couldn't keep up. The top landing, which was walled with concrete tile and plastered, was intact. I flipped the light switch and opened the door to the first plant room, the warm room, but I stopped after one step in because there was no light. I stood for five seconds, waiting for my eyes to adjust, and by then Wolfe and Fritz were behind me.

"Let me get by," Wolfe growled like a dog ready to spring.

"No." I pushed back against him. "You'll scalp yourself or cut your throat. Wait here till I get a light."

He bellowed past my shoulder. "Theodore! *Theodore!*"

A voice came from the dim starlit ruins. "Yes, sir! What happened?"

"Are you all right?"

"No, sir! What—"

"Are you hurt?"

"No, I'm not hurt, but what happened?"

I saw movement in the direction of the corner where Theodore's room was, and a sound came of glass falling and breaking.

"You got a light?" I called.

"No, the doggone lights are all—"

"Then stay still, damn it, while I get a light."

"Stand still!" Wolfe roared.

I beat it down to the office. By the time I got back up again there were noises from windows across the street, and also from down below. We ignored them. The sight disclosed by the flashlights was enough to make us ignore anything. Of a thousand panes of glass and ten thousand orchid plants some were in fact still whole, as we learned later, but it certainly didn't look like it that first survey. Even with the lights, moving around through that jungle of jagged glass hanging down and protruding from plants and benches and underfoot wasn't really fun, but Wolfe had to see and so did Theodore, who was okay physically but got so damn mad I thought he was going to choke.

Finally Wolfe got to where a dozen Odontoglossum harryanum, his current pride and joy, were kept. He moved the light back and forth over the gashed and fallen stems and leaves and clusters, with fragments of glass everywhere, turned, and said quietly, "We might as well go downstairs."

"The sun will be up in two hours," Theodore said through his teeth.

"I know. We need men."

When we got to the office we phoned Lewis Hewitt and G. M. Hoag for help before we called the police. Anyway, by that time a prowl car had come.

6

Six hours later I pushed my chair back from the dining table, stretched all the way, and allowed myself a good thorough yawn without any apology, feeling that I had earned it. Ordinarily I have my breakfast in the kitchen with Fritz, and Wolfe has his in his room, but that day wasn't exactly ordinary.

A gang of fourteen men, not counting Theodore, was up on the roof cleaning up and salvaging, and an army of glaziers was due at noon. Andy Krasicki had come in from Long Island and was in charge. The street was roped off because of the danger from falling glass. The cops were still nosing around out in front and across the street, and presumably in other quarters too, but none was left in our house except Captain Murdoch, who, with Wolfe, was seated at the table I was just leaving, eating griddlecakes and honey.

They knew all about it, back to a certain point. The people who lived in the house directly across the street were away for the summer. On its roof they had found a hundred and ninety-two shells from an SM and a tommy gun, and they still had scientists up there collecting clues to support the theory that that was where the assault had come from, in case the lawyer for the defense should claim that the shells had been dropped by pigeons. Not that there was yet any call for a lawyer for the defense, since there were no defendants. So far there was no word as to how they had got to the roof of the unoccupied house. All they knew was that persons unknown had somehow got to that roof and from it, at 2:24 A.M., had shot hell out of our plant rooms, and had made a getaway through a passage into Thirty-sixth Street, and I could have told them that much without ever leaving our premises.

I admit we weren't much help. Wolfe didn't even mention the name of Sperling or Rony, let alone anything beginning with Z. He refused to offer a specific guess at the identity of the perpetrators, and it wasn't too hard to get them to accept that as the best to be had, since it was quite probable that there were several inhabitants of the metropolitan area who would love to make holes not only in Wolfe's plant rooms but in Wolfe himself. Even so, they insisted that some must be more likely to own tommy guns and more willing to use them in such a direct manner, but Wolfe said that was irrelevant because the gunners had almost certainly been hired on a piece-work basis.

I left the breakfast table as soon as I was through because there were a lot of phone calls to make—to slat manufacturers, hardware stores, painters, supply houses, and others. I was at it when Captain Murdoch left and Wolfe took the elevator to the roof, and still at it when Wolfe came down again, trudged into the office, got himself lowered into his chair, leaned back, and heaved a deep sigh.

I glanced at him. "You'd better go up and take a nap. And I'll tell you something. I can be just as stubborn as you can, and courage and valor and spunk are very fine things and I'm all for them, but I'm also a fairly good bookkeeper. If this keeps up, as I suppose it will, the balance sheet will be a lulu. I have met Gwenn socially and therefore might be expected to grit my teeth and stick; but you haven't, and all you need to do is return his retainer. What I want to say is that if you do I promise never to ride you about it. Never. Want me to get the Bible?"

"No." His eyes were half closed. "Is everything arranged for the repairs and replacements?"

"As well as it can be now."

"Then call that place and speak to the elder daughter."

I was startled. "Why her? What reason have you—"

"Pfui. You thought you concealed the direction your interest took —your personal interest—but you didn't. I know you too well. Call her and learn if all the family is there—all except the son, who probably doesn't matter. If they are, tell her we'll be there in two hours and want to see them."

"We?"

"Yes. You and I."

I got at the phone. He was not really smashing a precedent. It was true that he had an unbreakable rule not to stir from his office to see anyone on business, but what had happened that night had taken this out of the category of business and listed it under struggle for survival.

One of the help answered, and I gave my name and asked for Miss Madeline Sperling. Her husband's name had been Pendleton, but she had tossed it in the discard. My idea was to keep to essentials, but she had to make it a conversation. Rony had called Gwenn only half an hour ago and told her about the holdup, and of course Madeline wanted it all over again from me. I had to oblige. She thought she was worried about my head, and I had to assure her there were no bad cracks in it from the bandit's blow. When I finally got her onto the subject at hand, though, and she knew from the way I put it that this was strictly business and deserved attention, she snapped nicely into it and made it straight and simple. I hung up and turned to Wolfe.

"All set. They're there, and she'll see that they stay until we come. We're invited for lunch."

"Including her sister?"

"All of 'em."

He glanced at the clock, which said 11:23. "We should make it by one-thirty."

"Yeah, easy. I think I know where I can borrow an armored car. The route goes within five miles of where a certain man has a palace on a hill."

He made a face. "Get the sedan."

"Okay, if you'll crouch on the floor or let me put you in the trunk. It's you he's interested in, not me. By the way, what about Fred and Orrie? I've phoned Saul and warned him that there are other elements involved besides the law boys, and I should think Fred and Orrie might take a day off. After you have a talk with the family, whatever you're going to say, you can have them pick it up again if that's the program, which I hope to God it isn't."

He made that concession. I couldn't get Fred or Orrie, but they would certainly call in soon and word was left with Fritz to tell them to lay off until further notice. Then Wolfe had to go up to the roof for another look while I went to the garage for the car, so it was nearly noon when we got rolling. Wolfe, in the back seat as always, because that gave him a better chance to come out alive when we crashed, had a firm grip on the strap with his right hand, but that was only routine and didn't mean he was any shakier than usual when risking his neck in a thing on wheels. However, I noticed in the mirror that he didn't shut his eyes once the whole trip, although he hadn't been in bed for thirty hours now.

The day was cloudy and windy, not one of June's best samples, though no rain fell. When we were approaching Stony Acres and reached the spot on the secondary road where Rony and I had been assaulted by highwaymen, I stopped to show Wolfe the terrain, and told him Saul had reported that the take from Rony had been three hundred and twelve bucks, and was awaiting instructions for disposal.

Wolfe wasn't interested in the terrain. "Are we nearly there?"

"Yes, sir. A mile and a half."

"Go ahead."

When we rolled up to the front entrance of the mansion, we were honored. It was not the sad looking guy in a mohair uniform who appeared and came to us, but James U. Sperling himself. He was not smiling. He spoke through the open car window.

"What does this mean?"

He couldn't be blamed for not knowing that Wolfe would never stay in a vehicle any longer than he had to, since their acquaintance was brief. Before replying, Wolfe pushed the door open and manipulated himself out onto the gravel.

Meanwhile Sperling was going on. "I tried to get you on the phone, but by the time I got the number you had left. What are you trying to do? You know damn well I don't want this."

Wolfe met his eye. "You looked me up, Mr. Sperling. You must know that I am not harebrained. I assure you that I can justify this move, but I can do so only by proceeding with it. When I have explained matters to you and your family, we'll see if you can find any alternative to approval. I'll stake my reputation that you can't."

Sperling wanted to argue it then and there, but Wolfe stood pat, and seeing that he had to choose between letting us come on in and ordering us off the place, the Chairman of the Board preferred the former. He and Wolfe headed for the door. Since no help had shown up, I took the car around the house to a graveled plaza in the rear, screened by shrubbery, left it there, and made for the nearest entrance, which was the west terrace. As I was crossing it a door opened and there was Madeline. I told her hello.

She inspected me with her head cocked to one side and the big dark eyes half open. "You don't look so battered."

"No? I am. Internal injuries. But not from the holdup. From—" I waved a hand. "You ought to know."

"I'm disappointed in you." Her eyes went open. "Why didn't you shoot them?"

"My mind was elsewhere. You ought to know that too. We can compare notes on that some other time. Thank you very much for stalling it until it was too late for your father to head us off. Also thank you for taking my word for it that this is the best we can do for Gwenn. How many names have I got here now and where do they fit?"

"Oh, you're Archie everywhere. I explained that much to Webster and Paul and Connie too, because they'll eat lunch with us and it would have been too complicated, and anyway with Nero Wolfe here—they're not halfwits. Incidentally, you've made lunch late; we usually have it at one, so come on. How's your appetite?"

I told her I'd rather show her than tell her, and we went in.

Lunch was served in the big dining room. Wolfe and I were the only ones with neckties on, though the day was too chilly for extremes like shorts. Sperling had a striped jacket over a light blue silk shirt open at the neck. Jimmy and Paul Emerson were sporting dingy old coat sweaters, one brown and one navy. Webster Kane varied it with a wool shirt with loud red and yellow checks. Mrs. Sperling was in a pink rayon dress and a fluffy pink sweater, unbuttoned; Connie Emerson in a dotted blue thing that looked like a dressing gown but maybe I didn't know; Gwenn in a tan shirt and slacks; and Madeline in a soft but smooth wool dress of browns and blacks that looked like a PSI fabric.

So it was anything but a formal gathering, but neither was it free and easy. They ate all right, but they all seemed to have trouble deciding what would be a good thing to talk about. Wolfe, who can't stand a strained atmosphere at meals, tried this and that with one and then another, but the only line that got anywhere at all was a friendly argument with Webster Kane about the mechanism of money and a book by some Englishman which nobody else had ever heard of, except maybe Sperling, who may have known it by heart but wasn't interested.

When that was over and we were on our feet again, there was no loitering around. The Emersons, with Paul as sour as ever and Connie not up to form in her dressing gown if she will excuse me, went in the direction of the living room, and Webster Kane said he had work to do and went the other way. The destination of the rest of us had apparently been arranged. With Sperling in the lead, we marched along halls and across rooms to arrive at the library, the room with books and a stock ticker where I had wangled the master key and had later phoned Saul Panzer. Wolfe's eyes, of course, immediately swept the scene to appraise the chairs, which Sperling and Jimmy began herding into a group; and, knowing he had had a hard night, I took pity on him, grabbed the best and biggest one, and put it in the position I knew he would like. He gave me a nod of appreciation as he got into it, leaned back and closed his eyes, and sighed.

The others got seated, except Sperling, who stood and demanded, "All right, justify this. You said you could."

7

Wolfe stayed motionless for seconds. He raised his hands to press his fingertips against his eyes, and again was motionless. Finally he let his hands fall to the chair arms, opened the eyes, and directed them at Gwenn.

"You look intelligent, Miss Sperling."

"We're all intelligent," Sperling snapped. "Get on."

Wolfe looked at him. "It's going to be long-winded, but I can't help it. You must have it all. If you try prodding me you'll only lengthen it. Since you head a large enterprise, sir, and therefore are commander-in-chief of a huge army, surely you know when to bully-rag and when to listen. Will you do me a favor? Sit down. Talking to people who are standing makes my neck stiff."

"I want to say something," Gwenn declared.

Wolfe nodded at her. "Say it."

She swallowed. "I just want to be sure you know that I know what you're here for. You sent that man"—she flashed a glance at me which gave me a fair idea of how my personal relationship with her stood as of now—"to snoop on Louis Rony, a friend of mine, and that's what this is about." She swallowed again. "I'll listen because my family—my mother and sister asked me to, but I think you're a cheap filthy little worm, and if I had to earn a living the way you do I'd rather starve!"

It was all right, but it would have been better if she had ad libbed it instead of sticking to a script that she had obviously prepared in advance. Calling Wolfe little, which she wouldn't have done if she had worded it while looking at him, weakened it.

Wolfe grunted. "If you had to earn a living the way I do, Miss Sperling, you probably *would* starve. Thank you for being willing to listen, no matter why." He glanced around. "Does anyone else have an irrepressible comment?"

"Get on," said Sperling, who was seated.

"Very well, sir. If at first I seem to wander, bear with me. I want to tell you about a man. I know his name but prefer not to pronounce it, so shall call him X. I assure you he is no figment; I only wish he were. I have little concrete knowledge of the immense properties he owns, though I do know that one of them is a high and commanding hill not a hundred miles from here on which, some years ago, he built a large and luxurious mansion. He has varied and extensive sources of income. All of them are illegal and some of them are morally repulsive. Narcotics, smuggling, industrial and commercial rackets, gambling, waterfront blackguardism, professional larceny, blackmailing, political malfeasance—that by no means exhausts his curriculum, but it sufficiently indicates its character. He has, up to now, triumphantly kept himself invulnerable by having the perspicacity to see that a criminal practicing on a large scale over a wide area and a long period of time can get impunity only by maintaining a gap between his person and his crimes which cannot be bridged; and by having unexcelled talent, a remorseless purpose, and a will that cannot be dented or deflected."

Sperling jerked impatiently in his chair. Wolfe looked at him as a sixth-grade teacher looks at a restless boy, moved his eyes for a roundup of the whole audience, and went on.

"If you think I am describing an extraordinary man, I am indeed. How, for instance, does he maintain the gap? There are two ways to catch a criminal: one, connect him with the crime itself; or two, prove that he knowingly took a share of the spoils. Neither is feasible with X. Take for illustration a typical crime—anything from a triviality like pocket picking or bag snatching up to a major raid on the public treasury. The criminal or gang of criminals nearly always takes full responsibility for the operation itself, but in facing the problem of disposal of the loot, which always appears, and of protection against discovery and prosecution, which is seldom entirely absent, he cannot avoid dealing with others. He may need a fence, a lawyer, a witness for an alibi, a channel to police or political influence—no matter what; he will almost inevitably need someone or something. He goes to one he knows, or knows about, one named A. A, finding a little difficulty, consults B. We are already, observe, somewhat removed from the crime, and B now takes us still further away by enlisting the help of C. C, having trouble with a stubborn knot in the thread, communicates with D. Here we near the terminal. D knows X and how to get to him.

"In and around New York there are many thousands of crimes each month, from mean little thefts to the highest reaches of fraud and thuggery. In a majority of them the difficulties of the criminals are met, or are not met, either by the criminals themselves or by A or B or C. But a large number of them get up to D, and if they reach D they go to X. I don't know how many D's there are, but certainly not many, for they are selected by X after a long and hard scrutiny and the application of severe tests, since he knows that a D once accepted by him must be backed with a fierce loyalty at almost any cost. I would guess that there are very few of them and, even so, I would also guess that if a D were impelled, no matter how, to resort to treachery, he would find that that too had been foreseen and provision had been made."

Wolfe turned a palm up. "You see where X is. Few criminals, or A's or B's or C's, even know he exists. Those few do not know his name. If a fraction of them have guessed his name, it remains a guess. Estimates of the total annual dollar volume involved in criminal operations in the metropolitan area vary from three hundred million to half a billion. X has been in this business more than twenty years now, and the share that finds its way tortuously to him must be considerable, after deducting his payments to appointed and elected persons and their staffs. A million a year? Half that? I don't know. I do know that he doesn't pay for everything he gets. Some years ago a man not far from the top of the New York Police Department did many favors for X, but I doubt if he was ever paid a cent. Blackmailing is one of X's favorite fields, and that man was susceptible."

"Inspector Drake," Jimmy blurted.

Wolfe shook his head. "I am not giving names, and anyway I said not far from the top." His eyes went from right to left and back again. "I am obliged for your forbearance; these details are necessary. I have told you that I know X's name, but I have never seen him. I first got some knowledge of him eleven years ago, when a police officer came to me for an opinion regarding a murder he was working on. I undertook a little inquiry through curiosity, a luxury I no longer indulge in, and found myself on a trail leading onto ground where the footing was treacherous for a private investigator. Since I had no client and was not committed, I reported what I had found to the police officer and dropped it. I then knew there was such a man as X, and something of his activities and methods, but not his name.

"During the following eight years I saw hints here and there that X was active, but I was busy with my own affairs, which did not happen to come into contact with his. Then, early in 1946, while I was engaged on a job for a client, I had a phone call. A voice I had never heard—hard, cold, precise, and finicky with its grammar—advised me to limit my efforts on behalf of my client. I replied that my efforts would be limited only by the requirements of the job I had undertaken to do. The voice insisted, and we talked some, but only to an impasse. The next day I finished the job to my client's satisfaction, and that ended it."

Wolfe closed his fingers into fists and opened them again. "But for my own satisfaction I felt that I needed some information. The character of the job, and a remark the voice had made during our talk, raised the question whether the voice could have been that of X himself. Not wishing to involve the men I often hire to help me, and certainly not Mr. Goodwin, I got men from an agency in another city. Within a month I had all the information I needed for my satisfaction, including of course X's name, and I dismissed the men and destroyed their reports. I hoped that X's affairs and mine would not again touch, but they did. Months later, a little more than a year ago, I was investigating a murder, this time for a client—you may remember it. A man named Orchard poisoned while appearing on a radio program?"

All but Sperling nodded, and Mrs. Sperling said she had been listening to the program the day it happened. Wolfe went on.

"I was in the middle of that investigation when the same voice called me on the phone and told me to drop it. He was not so talkative that second time, perhaps because I informed him that I knew his name, which was of course childish of me. I ignored his fiat. It soon transpired that Mr. Orchard and a woman who had also been killed had both been professional blackmailers, using a method which clearly implied a large organization, ingeniously contrived and ably conducted. I managed to expose the murderer, who had been blackmailed by them. The day after the murderer was sentenced another phone call came from X. He had the cheek to congratulate me on keeping my investigation within the limits he had prescribed! I told him that his prescription had been ignored. What had happened was that I had caught the murderer, which was my job, without stretching the investigation to an attack on X himself, which had been unnecessary and no part of my commitment."

Sperling had been finding it impossible to get properly settled in his chair. Now he broke training and demanded,

"Damn it, can't you cut this short?"

"Not and earn my fee," Wolfe snapped. He resumed.

"That was in May of last year—thirteen months ago. In the interval I have not heard from X, because I haven't happened to do anything with which he had reason to interfere. That good fortune ended—as I suppose it was bound to do soon or late, since we are both associated with crime—day before yesterday, Saturday, at sixten P.M. He phoned again. He was more peremptory than formerly, and gave me an ultimatum with a time limit. I responded to his tone as a man of my temperament naturally would—I am congenitally tart and thorny—and I rejected his ultimatum. I do not pretend that I was unconcerned. When Mr. Goodwin returned from his week end here, after midnight on Sunday, yesterday, and gave me his report, I told him of the phone call and we discussed the situation at length."

Wolfe looked around. "Do any of you happen to know that there are plant rooms on the roof of my house, in which I keep thousands of orchids, all of them good and some of them new and rare and extremely beautiful?"

Yes, they all did, again all but Sperling.

Wolfe nodded. "I won't try to introduce suspense. Mr. Goodwin and I were in my office talking, between two and three o'clock this morning, when we heard an outlandish noise. Men hired by X had mounted to the roof of a building across the street, armed with submachine guns, and fired hundreds of rounds at my plant rooms, with what effect you can guess. I shall not describe it. Thirty men are there now, salvaging and repairing. That my gardener was not killed was fortuitous. The cost of repairs and replacements will be around forty thousand dollars, and some of the damaged or destroyed plants are irreplaceable. The gunmen have not been found and probably never will be, and what if they are? It was incorrect to say they were hired by X. They were hired by a D or C or B—most likely a C. Assuredly X is not on speaking terms with anyone as close to crime as a gunman, and I doubt if a D is. In any—"

"You say," Sperling put in, "this just happened? Last night?"

"Yes, sir. I mentioned the approximate amount of the damage because you'll have to pay it. It will be on my bill."

Sperling made a noise. "It may be on your bill, but I won't have to pay it. Why should I?"

"Because you'll owe it. It is an expense incurred on the job you gave me. My plant rooms were destroyed because I ignored X's ultimatum, and his demand was that I recall Mr. Goodwin from here and stop my inquiry into the activities and character of Louis Rony. You wanted me to prove that Mr. Rony is a Communist. I can't do that, but I can prove that he is one of X's men, either a C or a D, and is therefore a dangerous professional criminal."

The quickest reaction was from Madeline. Before Wolfe had finished she said, "My God!" and got up, crossed impolitely in front of people to Gwenn, and put her hand on her sister's shoulder. Then Mrs. Sperling was up too, but she just stood a second and sat down again. Jimmy, who had been frowning at Wolfe, shifted the frown to his father.

The Chairman of the Board sat a moment gazing at Wolfe, then gazed a longer moment at his younger daughter, and then arose and went to her and said, "He says he can prove it, Gwenn."

I am not lightning, but I had caught on quite a while back that Wolfe's real target was Gwenn, so it was her I was interested in. When Wolfe had started in, the line of her pretty lips and the stubbornness in her eyes had made it plain that she simply didn't intend to believe a word he said, but as he went on telling about a mysterious X who couldn't possibly be her Louis she had relaxed a little, and was even beginning to think that maybe it was an interesting story when suddenly Rony's name popped in, and then the shot straight at her. When she felt Madeline's hand on her shoulder she put her own hand up to place it on top of her sister's, and said in a low voice, "It's all right, Mad." Then she spoke louder to Wolfe.

"It's a lot of bunk!"

When Sperling stood in front of her, Wolfe and I couldn't see her. Wolfe stated to Sperling's back, "I've barely started, you know. I've merely given you the background. Now I must explain the situation."

Gwenn was on her feet at once, saying firmly, "You won't need me for that. I know what the situation is well enough."

They all started talking. Madeline had hold of Gwenn's arm. Mrs. Sperling was out of her depth but was flapping. Jimmy was being completely ignored but kept trying. Wolfe allowed them a couple of minutes and then cut in sharply.

"Confound it, are you a bunch of ninnies?"

Sperling wheeled on him. "You shouldn't have done it like this! You should have told me! You should—"

"Nonsense! Utter nonsense. For months you have been telling your daughter that Mr. Rony is a Communist, and she has quite properly challenged you to prove it. If you had tried to tell her this she would have countered with the same challenge, and where would you have been? I am better armed. Will you please get out of the way so I can see her?—Thank you.—Miss Sperling, you were not afraid to challenge your father to show you proof. But now you want to walk out. So you're afraid to challenge me? I don't blame you."

"I'm not afraid of anything!"

"Then sit down and listen. All of you. Please?"

They got back to their chairs. Gwenn wasn't so sure now that all she needed was a simple and steadfast refusal to believe a word. Her lower lip was being held tight by her teeth, and her eyes were no longer straight and stubborn at Wolfe. She even let me have a questioning, unsure glance, as if I might contribute something that would possibly help.

Wolfe focused on her. "I didn't skimp on the background, Miss Sperling, because without it you can't decide intelligently, and, though your father is my client, the decision rests with you. The question that must be answered is this: am I to proceed to assemble proof or not? If I—"

"You said you had proof!"

"No, I didn't. I said I could prove it, and I can—and if I must I will. I would vastly prefer not to. One way out would be for me simply to quit—to return the retainer your father has paid me, shoulder the expense of my outlay on this job and restoration of my damaged property, and let X know that I have scuttled. That would unquestionably be the sensible and practical thing to do, and I do not brag that I'm not up to it. It is a weakness I share with too many of my fellow men, that my self-conceit will not listen to reason. Having undertaken to do a job offered to me by your father in good faith, and with no excuse for withdrawal that my vanity will accept, I do not intend to quit.

"Another way out would be for you to assume that I am not a liar; or that if I am one, at least I am incapable of such squalid trickery as the invention of this rigmarole in order to earn a fee by preventing you from marrying a man who has your affection and is worthy of it. If you make either of those assumptions, it follows that Mr. Rony is a blackguard, and since you are plainly not a fool you will have done with him. But—"

"You said you could prove it!"

Wolfe nodded. "So I can. If my vanity won't let me scuttle, and if you reject both those assumptions, that's what I'll have to do. Now you see why I gave you so full a sketch of X. It will be impossible to brand Mr. Rony without bringing X in, and even if that were feasible X would get in anyway. Proof of that already exists, on the roof of my house. You may come home with me and take a look at it—by the way, I have failed to mention another possibility."

Wolfe looked at our client. "You, sir, could of course pay my bill to date and discharge me. In that event I presume your daughter would consider my indictment of Mr. Rony as unproven as yours, and she would proceed—to do what? I can't say; you know her better than I do. Do you want to send me home?"

Sperling was slumped in his chair, his elbow resting on its arm and his chin propped on his knuckles, with his gaze now on Gwenn and now on Wolfe. "Not now," he said quietly. "Only—a question—how much of that was straight fact?"

"Every word."

"What is X's name?"

"That will have to wait. If we are forced into this, and you still want me to work for you, you will of course have to have it."

"All right, go ahead."

Wolfe went back to Gwenn. "One difficulty in an attempt to expose X, which is what this would amount to, will be the impossibility of knowing when we are rubbing against him. I am acquainted, more or less, with some three thousand people living or working in New York, and there aren't more than ten of them of whom I could say with certainty that they are in no way involved in X's activities. None may be; any may be. If that sounds extreme, Miss Sperling, remember that he has been devising and spreading his nets all your lifetime, and that his talents are great.

"So I can't match him in ubiquity, no matter how many millions your father contributes to the enterprise, but I must match his inaccessibility, and I shall. I shall move to a base of operations which will be known only to Mr. Goodwin and perhaps two others; for it is not a fantasy of trepidation, but a painful fact, that when he perceives my objective, as he soon will, he will start all his machinery after me. He has told me on the telephone how much he admires me, and I was flattered, but now I'll have to pay for it. He will know it is a mortal encounter, and he does not underrate me—I only wish he did."

Wolfe lifted his shoulders and let them down again. "I'm not whimpering—or perhaps I am. I shall expect to win, but there's no telling what the cost will be. It may take a year, or five years, or ten." He gestured impatiently. "Not for finishing your Mr. Rony; that will be the merest detail. It won't be long until you'll have to talk with him through the grill in the visitors' room, if you still want to see him. But X will never let it stop there, though he might want me to think he would. Once started, I'll have to go on to the end. So the cost in time can't be estimated.

"Neither can the cost in money. I certainly haven't got enough, nothing like it, and I won't be earning any, so your father will have to foot the bill, and he will have to commit himself in advance. If I stake my comfort, my freedom, and my life, he may properly be expected to stake his fortune. Whatever his resources may be—"

Wolfe interrupted himself. "Bah!" he said scornfully. "You deserve complete candor. As I said, Mr. Rony is a mere trifle; he'll be disposed of in no time, once I am established where I can be undisturbed. But I hope I have given you a clear idea of what X is like. He will know I can't go on without money and, when he finds he can't get at me, will try to stop the source of supply. He will try many expedients before he resorts to violence, for he is a man of sense and knows that murder should always be the last on the list, and of course the murder of a man in your father's position would be excessively dangerous; but if he thought it necessary he would risk it. I don't—"

"You can leave that out," Sperling cut in. "If she wants to consider the cost in money she can, but I'll not have her saving my life. That's up to me."

Wolfe looked at him. "A while ago you told me to go ahead. What about it now? Do you want to pay me off?"

"No. You spoke about your vanity, but I've got more up than vanity. I'm not quitting and I don't intend to."

"Listen, Jim—" his wife began, but to cut her off he didn't even have to speak. He only looked at her.

"In that case," Wolfe told Gwenn, "there are only two alternatives. I won't drop it, and your father won't discharge me, so the decision rests with you, as I said it would. You may have proof if you insist on it. Do you?"

"You said," Madeline exploded at me, "it would be the best you could do for her!"

"I still say it," I fired back. "You'd better come down and look at the plant rooms too!"

Gwenn sat gazing at Wolfe, not stubbornly—more as if she were trying to see through him to the other side.

"I have spoken," Wolfe told her, "of what the proof, if you insist on it, will cost me and your father and family. I suppose I should mention what it will cost another person: Mr. Rony. It will get him a long term in jail. Perhaps that would enter into your decision. If you have any suspicion that it would be necessary to contrive a frame-up, reject it. He is pure scoundrel. I wouldn't go to the extreme of calling him a cheap filthy little worm, but he is in fact a shabby creature. Your sister thinks I'm putting it brutally, but how else can I put it? Should I hint that he may be not quite worthy of you? I don't know that, for I don't know you. But I do know that I have told you the truth about him, and I'll prove it if you say I must."

Gwenn left her chair. Her eyes left Wolfe for the first time since her unsure glance at me. She looked around at her family.

"I'll let you know before bedtime," she said firmly, and walked out of the room.

8

More than four hours later, at nine o'clock in the evening, Wolfe yawned so wide I thought something was going to give.

We were up in the room where I had slept Saturday night, if it can be called sleep when a dose of dope has knocked you out. Immediately after Gwenn had ended the session in the library by beating it, Wolfe had asked where he could go to take a nap, and Mrs. Sperling had suggested that room. When I steered him there he went straight to one of the three-quarter beds and tested it, pulled the coverlet off, removed his coat and vest and shoes, lay down, and in three minutes was breathing clear to China. I undressed the other bed to get a blanket to put over him, quit trying to fight temptation, and followed his example.

When we were called to dinner at seven o'clock I was conscripted for courier duty, to tell Mrs. Sperling that under the circumstances Mr. Wolfe and I would prefer either to have a sandwich upstairs or go without, and it was a pleasure to see how relieved she was. But even in the middle of that crisis she didn't let her household suffer shame, and instead of a sandwich we got jellied consommé, olives and cucumber rings, hot roast beef, three vegetables, lettuce and tomato salad, cold pudding with nuts in it, and plenty of coffee. It was nothing to put in your scrapbook, but was more than adequate, and except for the jellied consommé, which he hates, and the salad dressing, which he made a face at, Wolfe handled his share without comment.

I wouldn't have been surprised if he had had me take him home as soon as the library party was over, but neither was I surprised that he was staying. The show that he had put on for them hadn't been a show at all. He had meant every word of it, and I had meant it along with him. That being so, it was no wonder that he wanted the answer as soon as it was available, and besides, he would be needed if Gwenn had questions to ask or conditions to offer. Not only that, if Gwenn said nothing doing I don't think he would have gone home at all. There would have been a lot of arranging to do with Sperling, and when we finally got away from Stony Acres we wouldn't have been headed for Thirty-fifth Street but for a foxhole.

At nine o'clock, after admiring Wolfe's yawn, I looked around for an excuse to loosen up my muscles, saw the coffee tray, which had been left behind when the rest of the dinner remains had been called for, and decided that would do. I got it and took it downstairs. When I delivered it to the kitchen there was no one around and, feeling in need of a little social contact, I did a casual reconnoiter. I tried the library first. The door to it was open and Sperling was there, at his desk, looking over some papers. When I entered he honored me with a glance but no words.

After I had stood a moment I informed him, "We're upstairs hanging on."

"I know it," he said without looking up.

He seemed to think that completed the conversation, so I retired. The living room was uninhabited, and when I stepped out to the west terrace no one was to be seen or heard. The game room, which was down a flight, was dark, and the lights I turned on disclosed no fellow beings. So I went back upstairs and reported to Wolfe.

"The joint is deserted, except for Sperling, and I think he's going over his will. You scared 'em so that they all scrammed."

"What time is it?"

"Nine-twenty-two."

"She said before bedtime. Call Fritz."

We had talked with Fritz only an hour ago, but what the hell, it was on the house, so I went to the instrument on the table between the beds and got him. There was nothing new. Andy Krasicki was up on the roof with five men, still working, and had reported that enough glass and slats were in place for the morning's weather, whatever it might be. Theodore was still far from cheerful, but had had a good appetite for dinner, and so on.

I hung up and relayed the report to Wolfe, and added, "It strikes me that all that fixing up may be a waste of our client's money. If Gwenn decides we've got to prove it and we make a dive for a foxhole, what do glass and slats matter? It'll be years before you see the place again, if you ever do. Incidentally, I noticed you gave yourself a chance to call it off, and also Sperling, but not me. You merely said that your base of operations will be known only to Mr. Goodwin, taking Mr. Goodwin for granted. What if he decides he's not as vain as you are?"

Wolfe, who had put down a book by Laura Hobson to listen to my end of the talk with Fritz, and had picked it up again, scowled at me.

"You're twice as vain as I am," he said gruffly.

"Yeah, but it may work different. I may be so vain I won't want me to take such a risk. I may not want to deprive others of what I've got to be vain about."

"Pfui. Do I know you?"

"Yes, sir. As well as I know you."

"Then don't try shaking a bogy at me. How the devil could I contemplate such a plan without you?" He returned to the book.

I knew he thought he was handing me a compliment which should make me beam with pleasure, so I went and flopped on the bed to beam. I didn't like any part of it, and I knew Wolfe didn't either. I had a silly damn feeling that my whole future depended on the verdict of a fine freckled girl, and while I had nothing against fine girls, freckled or unfreckled, that was going too far. But I wasn't blaming Wolfe, for I didn't see how he could have done any better. I had brought a couple of fresh magazines up from the living room, but I never got to look at them, because I was still on the bed trying to decide whether I should hunt up Madeline to see if she couldn't do something that would help on the verdict, when the phone buzzed. I rolled over to reach for it.

It was one of the help saying there was a call for Mr. Goodwin. I thanked her and then heard a voice I knew.

"Hello, Archie?"

"Right. Me."

"This is a friend."

"So you say. Let me guess. The phones here are complicated. I'm in a bedroom with Mr. Wolfe. If I pick up the receiver I get an outside line, but on the other hand your incoming call was answered downstairs."

"I see. Well, I'm sitting here looking at an Indian holding down papers. I went out for a walk, but there was too much of a crowd, so I decided to ride and here I am. I'm sorry you can't keep the date."

"So am I. But I might be able to make it later if you'll sit tight. Okay?"

"Okay."

I hung up, got to my feet, and told Wolfe, "Saul started to go somewhere, found he had a tail on him, shook it off, and went to the office to report. He's there now. Any suggestions?"

Wolfe closed the book on a finger to mark the place. "Who was following him?"

"I doubt if he knows, but he didn't say. You heard what I told him about the phone."

Wolfe nodded and considered a moment. "How far will you have to go?"

"Oh, I guess I can stand it, even in the dark. Chappaqua is seven minutes and Mount Kisco ten. Any special instructions?"

He had none, except that since Saul was in the office he might as well stick there until he heard from us again, so I shoved off.

I left the house by the west terrace because that was the shortest route to the place behind shrubbery where I had parked the car, and found a sign of life. Paul and Connie Emerson were in the living room looking at television, and Webster Kane was on the terrace, apparently just walking back and forth. I exchanged greetings with them on the fly and proceeded.

It was a dark night, with no stars on account of the clouds, but the wind was down. As I drove to Chappaqua I let my mind drift into a useless habit, speculating on who Saul's tail had been—state or city employees, or an A, B, C, or D. After I got to a booth in a drugstore and called Saul at the office and had a talk with him, it was still nothing but a guess. All Saul knew was that it had been a stranger and that it hadn't been too easy to shake him. Since it was Saul Panzer, I knew I didn't have to check any on the shaking part, and since he had no news to report except that he had acquired a tail, I told him to make himself comfortable in one of the spare rooms if he got sleepy, treated myself to a lemon coke, and went back to the car and drove back to Stony Acres.

Madeline had joined the pair in the living room, or maybe I should just put it that she was there when I entered. When she came to intercept me the big dark eyes were wide open, but not for any effect they might have on me. Her mind was obviously too occupied with something else for dallying.

"Where have you been?" she asked.

I told her to Chappaqua to make a phone call. She took my arm and eased me along through the door into the reception hall, and there faced me to ask, "Have you seen Gwenn?"

"No. Why, where is she?"

"I don't know. But I think—"

She stopped. I filled in, "I supposed she was off in a corner making up her mind."

"You didn't go out to meet her?"

"Now I ask you," I objected. "I'm not even a worm, I just work for one. Why would she be meeting me?"

"I suppose not." Madeline hesitated. "After dinner she told Dad she would let him know as soon as she could, and went up to her room. I went in and wanted to talk to her, but she chased me out, and I went to Mother's room. Later I went back to Gwenn's room and she let me talk some, and then she said she was going outdoors. I went downstairs with her. She went out the back way. I went back up to Mother, and when I came down again and found you had gone out I thought maybe you had met her."

"Nope." I shrugged. "She may have had trouble finding the answer in the house and went outdoors for it. After all, she said before bedtime and it's not eleven yet. Give her time. Meanwhile you ought to relax. How about a game of pool?"

She ignored the invitation. "You don't know Gwenn," she stated.

"Not very well, no."

"She has a good level head, but she's as stubborn as a mule. She's a little like Dad. If he had kept off she might have had enough of Louis long ago. But now—I'm scared. I suppose your Nero Wolfe did the best he could, but he left a hole. Dad hired him to find out something about Louis that would keep Gwenn from marrying him. Is that right?"

"Right."

"And the way Nero Wolfe put it, one of four things had to happen. Either he had to quit the job, or Dad had to fire him, or Gwenn had to believe what he said about Louis and drop him, or he had to keep on and get proof. But he left out something else that could happen. What if Gwenn went away with Louis and married him? That would fix it too, wouldn't it? Would Dad want Wolfe to go on, to keep after Louis if he was Gwenn's husband? Gwenn wouldn't think so." Madeline's fingers gripped my arm. "I'm scared! I think she went to meet him!"

"I'll be damned. Did she take a bag?"

"She wouldn't. She'd know I'd try to stop her, and Dad too—all of us. If your Nero Wolfe is so damn smart, why didn't he think of this?"

"He has blind spots, and people running off to get married is one of them. But I should have—my God, am I thick. How long ago did she leave?"

"It must have been an hour—about an hour."

"Did she take a car?"

Madeline shook her head. "I listened for it. No."

"Then she must have—" I stopped to frown and think. "If that wasn't it, if she just went out to have more air while she decided, or possibly to meet him here somewhere and have a talk, where would she go? Has she got a favorite spot?"

"She has several." Madeline was frowning back at me. "An old apple tree in the back field, and a laurel thicket down by the brook, and a—"

"Do you know where there's a flashlight?"

"Yes, we keep—"

"Get it."

She went. In a moment she was back, and we left by the front door. She seemed to think the old apple tree was the best bet, so we circled the house halfway, crossed the lawn, found a path through a shrubbery border, and went through a gate into a pasture. Madeline called her sister's name but no answer came, and when we got to the old apple tree there was no one there. We returned to the vicinity of the house the other way, around back of the barn and kennels and other outbuildings, with a halt at the barn to see if Gwenn had got romantic and saddled a horse to go to meet her man, but the horses were all there. The brook was in the other direction, in the landscape toward the public road, and we headed that way. Occasionally Madeline called Gwenn's name, but not loud enough to carry to the house. We both had flashlights. I used mine only when I needed it, and by that time our eyes had got adjusted. We stuck to the drive until we reached the bridge over the brook and then Madeline turned sharp to the left. I admit she had me beat at cross-country going in the dark. The bushes and lower limbs had formed the habit of reaching out for me from the sides, and while Madeline hardly used her light at all, I shot mine right or left now and then, as well as to the front.

We were about twenty paces from the drive when I flashed my light to the left and caught a glimpse of an object on the ground by a bush that stopped me. The one glimpse was enough to show me what it was—there was no doubt about that—but not who it was. Madeline, ahead of me, was calling Gwenn's name. I stood. Then she called to me, "You coming?" and I called back that I was and started forward. I was opening my mouth to tell her that I was taking time out and would be with her in a minute, when she called Gwenn's name again, and an answer came faintly through the trees in the night. It was Gwenn's voice.

"Yes, Mad, I'm here!"

So I had to postpone a closer inspection of the object behind the bush. Madeline had let out a little cry of relief and was tearing ahead, and I followed. I got tangled in a thicket before I knew it and had to fight my way out, and nearly slid into the brook; then I was in the clear again, headed toward voices, and soon my light picked them up at the far side of an open space. I crossed to them.

"What's all the furor?" Gwenn was asking her sister. "Good Lord, I came outdoors on a summer night, so what? That's been known to happen before, hasn't it? You even brought a detective along!"

"This isn't just a summer night," Madeline said shortly, "and you know darned well it isn't. How did I know—anyway, you haven't even got a jacket on."

"I know I haven't. What time is it?"

I aimed the light at my wrist and told her. "Five past eleven."

"Then he didn't come on that train either."

"Who didn't?" Madeline asked.

"Who do you suppose?" Gwenn was pent up. "That dangerous criminal! Oh, I suppose he is. All right, he is. But I wasn't going to cross him off without telling him first, and not on the phone or in a letter, either. I phoned him to come here."

"Sure," Madeline said, not like a loving sister. "So you could make him tell you who X is and make him reform."

"Not me," Gwenn declared. "Reforming is your department. I was simply going to tell him we're through—and good-by. I merely preferred to do it that way, before telling Dad and the rest of you. He was coming up on the nine-twenty-three and taxi from the station and meet me here. I thought he had missed it—and now I guess he didn't get the next one either—but there's a—what time is it?"

I told her. "Nine minutes after eleven."

"There's a train at eleven-thirty-two, and I'll wait for that and then quit. I don't usually wait around for a man for two hours, but this is different. You admit that, don't you, Mad?"

"If you could use a suggestion from a detective," I offered, "I think you ought to phone him again and find out what happened. Why don't you girls go and do that, and I'll wait here in case he shows up. I promise not to say a word to him except that you'll soon be back. Get a jacket, too."

That appealed to them. The only part that didn't appeal to me was that they might wave flashlights around on their way to the drive, but they went in another direction, a shortcut by way of the rose garden. I waited until they were well started and then headed toward the drive, used the light to spot the object on the ground by the bush, and went to it.

First, was he dead? He was. Second, what killed him? The answer to that wasn't as conclusive, but there weren't many alternatives. Third, how long ago had he died? I had a guess for that one, with some experience to go by. Fourth, what was in his pockets? That took more care and time on account of complications. For instance, when I had frisked him at the roadside Sunday night, after Ruth Brady had prepared him for me, I had used a fair amount of caution, but now fair wasn't good enough. I gave his leather wallet a good rub with my handkerchief, inside and out, put prints from both his hands all over it but kept them haphazard, and returned it to his pocket. It contained a good assortment of bills, so he must have cashed a check since I had cleaned him. I wanted very much to repeat the performance on the Communist party membership card and its cellophane holder, but couldn't because it wasn't there. Naturally that irritated me, and I felt all the seams and linings to make sure. It wasn't on him.

My mind was completely on getting the job done right and in time, before the girls returned, but when I finally gave up on the membership card I felt my stomach suddenly go tight, and I stood up and backed off. It will happen that way sometimes, no matter how thick and hard you think your shell is, when you least expect it. I turned to face the other way, made my chest big, and took some deep breaths. If that doesn't work the only thing to do is lie down. But I didn't have to, and anyhow I would have had to pop right up again, for in between two breaths I heard voices. Then I saw that I had left the flashlight turned on, there on the ground. I got it and turned it off, and made my way back to the clearing beyond the thicket in the dark, trying not to sound like a charging moose.

I was at my post, a patient sentinel, when the girls appeared and crossed the open space to me, with Madeline asking as they approached, "Did he come?"

"Not a sound of him," I told them, preferring the truth when it will serve the purpose. "Then you didn't get him?"

"I got a phone-answering service." That was Gwenn. "They said he would be back after midnight and wanted me to leave a message. I'm going to stay here a little while, in case he came on the eleven-thirty-two, and then quit. Do you think something happened to him?"

"Certainly something happened to him, if he stood you up, but God knows what. Time will tell." The three of us were making a little triangle. "You won't need me, and if he comes you won't want me. I'm going in to Mr. Wolfe. His nerves are on edge with the suspense, and I want to ease his mind. I won't go around the house shouting it, but I want to tell him he'll be going home soon."

They didn't care for that much but had to admit it was reasonable, and I got away. I took the shortcut as they directed, got lost in the woods twice but finally made it to the open, skirted the rose garden and crossed the lawn, and entered the house by the front door. In the room upstairs Wolfe was still reading the book. As I closed the door behind me he started to scorch me with an indignant look for being gone so long, but when he saw my face, which he knows better than I do, he abandoned it.

"Well?" he asked mildly.

"Not well at all," I declared. "Somebody has killed Louis Rony, I think by driving a car over him, but that will take more looking. It's behind a bush about twenty yards from the driveway, at a point about two-thirds of the distance from the house to the public road. It's a rotten break in every way, because Gwenn had decided to toss him out."

Wolfe was growling. "Who found it?"

"I did."

"Who knows about it?"

"No one. Now you."

Wolfe got up, fast. "Where's my hat?" He looked around. "Oh, downstairs. Where are Mr. and Mrs. Sperling? We'll tell them there is nothing more for us to do here and we're going home—but not in a flurry—merely that it's late and we can go now—come on!"

"Flurry hell. You know damn well we're stuck."

He stood and glared at me. When that didn't seem to be improving the situation any he let himself go back onto the chair, felt the book under his fanny, got up and grabbed it—and for a second I thought he was going to throw it at something, maybe even me. For him to throw a book, loving them as he did, would have been a real novelty. He controlled himself in time, tossed the book onto a handy table, got seated again, and rasped at me, "Confound it, sit down! Must I stretch my neck off?"

I didn't blame him a particle. I would have been having a tantrum myself if I hadn't been too busy.

9

"The first thing," I said, "is this: have I seen it or not? If I have, there's the phone, and any arrangements to be made before company comes will have to be snappy. If I haven't, take your time. It's behind the bush on the side away from the drive and might not be noticed for a week, except for dogs. So?"

"I don't know enough about it," Wolfe said peevishly. "What were you doing there?"

I told him. That first question was too urgent, for me personally, to fill in with details such as stopping at the barn to count the horses, but I didn't skip any points that mattered, like Madeline's reason for being upset over Gwenn's trip outdoors, or like my handling of the fingerprint problem on the wallet. I gave it to him compact and fast but left out no essentials. When I finished he had only three questions:

"Have you had the thought, however vaguely, with or without evidence to inspire it, that Miss Sperling took you past that spot intentionally?"

"No."

"Can footprints be identified in the vicinity of the body?"

"I'm not sure, but I doubt it."

"Can your course be traced, no matter how, as you went from the thicket to the body and back again?"

"Same answer. Davy Crockett might do it. I didn't have him in mind at the time, and anyhow it was dark."

Wolfe grunted. "We're away from home. We can't risk it. Get them all up here—the Sperlings. Go for the young women yourself, or the young one may not come. Just get them; leave the news for me. Get the young women first, and the others when you're back in the house. I don't want Mr. Sperling up here ahead of them."

I went, and wasted no time. It was only a simple little chore, compared with other occasions when he had sent me from the office to get people, and this time my heart was in my work. Evidently the answer to the question whether I had seen the body was to be yes, and in that case the sooner the phone got used the better. Wolfe would do his part, that was all right, but actually it was up to me, since I was old enough to vote and knew how to dial a number. On the long list of things that cops don't like, up near the top is acting as if finding a corpse is a purely private matter.

It was simple with the girls. I told Gwenn that Wolfe had just received information which made it certain that Rony would not show up, and he wanted to see her at once to tell her about it, and of course there was no argument. Back at the house, the others were just as simple. Jimmy was downstairs playing ping-pong with Connie, and Madeline went and got him. Mr. and Mrs. Sperling were in the living room with Webster Kane and Paul Emerson, and I told them that Wolfe would like to speak with them for a minute. Just Sperlings.

There weren't enough chairs for all of us in the bedroom, so for once Wolfe had to start a conversation with most of his audience standing, whether he liked it or not. Sperling was obviously completely fed up with his long wait, a full seven hours now, for an important decision about his affairs to be made by someone else, even his own daughter, and he wanted to start in after Gwenn, but Wolfe stopped him quick. He fired a question at them.

"This afternoon we thought we were discussing a serious matter. Didn't we?"

They agreed.

He nodded. "We were. Now it is either more serious or less, I don't know which. It's a question of Mr. Rony alive or Mr. Rony dead. For he is now dead."

There's a theory that it's a swell stunt to announce a man's death to a group of people when you think one of them may have killed him, and watch their faces. In practice I've never seen it get anybody to first base, let alone on around, not even Nero Wolfe, but it's still attractive as a theory, and therefore I was trying to watch all of them at once, and doubtless Wolfe was too.

They all made noises, some of them using words, but nobody screamed or fainted or clutched for support. The prevailing expression was plain bewilderment, all authentic as far as I could tell, but as I say, no matter how popular a theory may be, it's still a theory.

Gwenn demanded, "You mean Louis?"

Wolfe nodded. "Yes, Miss Sperling. Louis Rony is dead. Mr.

Goodwin found his body about an hour ago, when he was out with your sister looking for you. It is on this property, behind a bush not far from where they found you. It seems—"

"Then—then he did come!"

I doubt if it was as heartless as it looks. I would not have called Gwenn heartless. In the traffic jam in her head caused by the shock, it just happened that that little detail got loose first. I saw Madeline dart a sharp glance at her. The others were finding their tongues for questions. Wolfe pushed a palm at them.

"If you please. There is no time—"

"What killed him?" Sperling demanded.

"I was about to tell you. The indications are that a car ran over him, and the body was dragged from the drive for concealment behind the bush, but of course it requires further examination. It hadn't been there long when it was found, not more than two hours. The police must be notified without delay. I thought, Mr. Sperling, you might prefer to do that yourself. It would look better."

Gwenn was starting to tremble. Madeline took her arm and led her to a bed and pushed her onto it, with Jimmy trying to help. Mrs. Sperling was stupefied.

"Are you saying—" Sperling halted. He was either incredulous or doing very well. "Do you mean he was murdered?"

"I don't know. Murder requires premeditation. If after inquiry the police decide it was murder they'll still have to prove it. That, of course, will start the routine hunt for motive, means, opportunity— I don't know whether you're familiar with it, but if not, I'm afraid you soon will be. Whom are you going to notify, the county authorities or the State Police? You have a choice. But you shouldn't postpone it. You will—"

Mrs. Sperling spoke for the first time. "But this is—this will be terrible! Here on our place! Why can't you take it away—away somewhere for miles—and leave it somewhere—"

No one paid any attention to her. Sperling asked Wolfe, "Do you know what he was doing here?"

"I know what brought him. Your daughter phoned him to come." Sperling jerked to the bed. "Did you do that, Gwenn?"

There was no reply from Gwenn. Madeline furnished it. "Yes, Dad, she did. She decided to drop him and wanted to tell him first."

"I hope," Wolfe said, "that your wife's suggestion needs no comment, for a dozen reasons. He took a cab here from the station—"

"My wife's suggestions seldom need comment. There is no way of keeping the police out of it? I know a doctor—"

"None. Dismiss it."

"You're an expert. Will they regard it as murder?"

"An expert requires facts to be expert about. I haven't got enough. If you want a guess, I think they will."

"Shouldn't I have a lawyer here?"

"That will have to come later. You'll probably need one or more." Wolfe wiggled a finger. "It can't be delayed longer, sir. Mr. Goodwin and I are under an obligation, both as citizens and as men holding licenses as private detectives."

"You're under obligation to me too. I'm your client."

"We know that. We haven't ignored it. It was eleven o'clock when Mr. Goodwin found a corpse with marks of violence, and it was his legal duty to inform the authorities immediately. It is now well after midnight. We felt we owed you a chance to get your mind clear. Now I'm afraid I must insist."

"Damn it, I want to think!"

"Call the police and think while they're on the way."

"No!" Sperling yanked a chair around and sat on its edge, close to Wolfe, facing him. "Look here. I hired you on a confidential matter, and I have a right to expect you to keep it confidential. There is no reason why it should be disclosed, and I certainly don't want it to be. It was a privileged—"

"No, sir." Wolfe was crisp. "I am not a member of the bar, and communications to detectives, no matter what you're paying them, are not privileged."

"But you—"

"No, please. You think if I repeat the conversation I had with you and your family this afternoon it will give the impression that all of you, except one, had good reason to wish Mr. Rony dead, and you're quite right. That will make it next to impossible for them to regard his death as something short of murder, and, no matter what your position in this community may be, you and your family will be in a devil of a fix. I'm sorry, but I can't help it. I have withheld information from the police many times, but only when it concerned a case I was myself engaged on and I felt I could make better use of it if I didn't share it. Another—"

"Damn it, you're engaged on this case!"

"I am not. The job you hired me for is ended, and I'm glad of it.

You remember how I defined the objective? It has been reached—though not, I confess, by my—"

"Then I hire you for another job now. To investigate Rony's death."

Wolfe frowned at him. "You'd better not. I advise against it."

"You're hired."

Wolfe shook his head. "You're in a panic and you're being impetuous. If Mr. Rony was murdered, and if I undertake to look into it, I'll get the murderer. It's conceivable that you'll regret you ever saw me."

"But you're hired."

Wolfe shrugged. "I know. Your immediate problem is to keep me from repeating that conversation to the police, and, being pugnacious and self-assured, you solve your problems as they come. But you can't hire me today and fire me tomorrow. You know what I would do if you tried that."

"I know. You won't be fired. You're hired." Sperling arose. "I'll phone the police."

"Wait a minute!" Wolfe was exasperated. "Confound it, are you a dunce? Don't you know how ticklish this is? There were seven of us in that conversation—"

"We'll attend to that after I've phoned."

"No, we won't. I'll attend to it now." Wolfe's eyes darted around. "All of you, please. Miss Sperling?"

Gwenn was face down on the bed and Madeline was seated on the edge.

"Do you have to bark at her now?" Madeline demanded.

"I'll try not to bark. But I do have to speak to her—all of you."

Gwenn was sitting up. "I'm all right," she said. "I heard every word. Dad hired you again, to—oh, my God." She hadn't been crying, which was a blessing since it would have demoralized Wolfe, but she looked fairly ragged. "Go ahead," she said.

"You know," Wolfe told them curtly, "what the situation is. I must first have a straight answer to this: have any of you repeated the conversation we had in the library, or any part of it, to anyone?"

They all said no.

"This is important. You're sure?"

"Connie was—" Jimmy had to clear his throat. "Connie was asking questions. She was curious." He looked unhappy.

"What did you tell her?"

"Oh, just—nothing much."

"Damn it, how much?" Sperling demanded.

"Not anything, Dad, really. I guess I mentioned Louis—but nothing about X and all that crap."

"You should have had more sense." Sperling looked at Wolfe. "Shall I get her?"

Wolfe shook his head. "By no means. We'll have to risk it. That was all? None of you has reported that conversation?"

They said no again.

"Very well. The police will ask questions. They will be especially interested in my presence here—and Mr. Goodwin's. I shall tell them that Mr. Sperling suspected that Mr. Rony, who was courting his daughter, was a Communist, and that—"

"No!" Sperling objected. "You will not! That's—"

"Nonsense." Wolfe was disgusted. "If they check in New York at all, and they surely will, they'll learn that you hired Mr. Bascom, and what for, and then what? No; that much they must have. I shall tell them of your suspicion, and that you engaged me to confirm it or remove it. You were merely taking a natural and proper precaution. I had no sooner started on the job, by sending Mr. Goodwin up here and putting three men to work, than an assault was made on my plant rooms in the middle of the night and great damage was done. I thought it probable that Mr. Rony and his comrades were responsible for the outrage; that they feared I would be able to expose and discredit him, and were trying to intimidate me.

"So today—yesterday now—I came here to discuss the matter with Mr. Sperling. He gathered the family for it because it was a family affair, and we assembled in the library. He then learned that what I was after was reimbursement; I wanted him to pay for the damage to my plant rooms. The whole time was devoted to an argument between Mr. Sperling and me on that point alone. No one else said anything whatever—at least nothing memorable. You stayed because you were there and there was no good reason to get up and go. That was all."

Wolfe's eyes moved to take them in. "Well?"

"It'll do," Sperling agreed.

Madeline was concentrating hard. She had a question. "What did you stay here all evening for?"

"A good question, Miss Sperling, but my conduct can be left to

me. I refused to leave here without the money or a firm commitment on it."

"What about Gwenn's phoning Louis to come up here?"

Wolfe looked at Gwenn. "What did you tell him?"

"This is awful," Gwenn whispered. She was gazing at Wolfe as if
she couldn't believe he was there. She repeated aloud, "This is
awful!"

Wolfe nodded. "No one will contradict you on that. Do you remember what you said to him?"

"Of course I do. I just told him I had to see him, and he said he
had some appointments and the first train he could make was the
one that leaves Grand Central at eight-twenty. It gets to Chappaqua
at nine-twenty-three."

"You told him nothing of what had happened?"

"No, I—I didn't intend to. I was just going to tell him I had decided to call it off."

"Then that's what you'll tell the police." Wolfe returned to Madeline. "You have an orderly mind, Miss Sperling, and you want to
get this all neatly arranged. It can't be done that way; there's too
much of it. The one vital point, for all of you, is that the conversation in the library consisted exclusively of our argument about paying for the damage to my plant rooms. Except for that, you will
all adhere strictly to fact. If you try anything else you're sunk. You
probably are anyway, if a strong suspicion is aroused that one of
you deliberately murdered Mr. Rony, and if one of the questioners
happens to be a first-rate man, but that's unlikely and we'll have to
chance it."

"I've always been a very poor liar," Mrs. Sperling said forlornly.

"Damn it," Sperling said, not offensively. "Go up and go to bed!"

"An excellent idea," Wolfe assented. "Do that, madam." He
turned to Sperling. "Now, if you will—"

The Chairman of the Board went to the telephone.

10

At eleven o'clock the next morning, Tuesday, Cleveland Archer,
District Attorney of Westchester County, said to James U. Sperling,
"This is a very regrettable affair. Very."

It would probably have been not Archer himself, but one of his assistants, sitting there talking like that, but for the extent of Stony Acres, the number of rooms in the house, and the size of Sperling's tax bill. That was only natural. Wolfe and I had had a couple of previous contacts with Cleveland Archer, most recently when we had gone to the Pitcairn place near Katonah to get a replacement for Theodore when his mother was sick. Archer was a little plump and had a round red face, and he could tell a constituent from a tourist at ten miles, but he wasn't a bad guy.

"Very regrettable," he said.

None of the occupants of the house had been kept up all night, not even me, who had found the body. The State cops had arrived first, followed soon by a pair of county dicks from White Plains, and, after some rounds of questions without being too rude, they had told everyone to go to bed—that is, everyone but me. I was singled out not only because I had found the body, which was just a good excuse, but because the man who singled me would have liked to do unto me as I would have liked to do unto him. He was Lieutenant Con Noonan of the State Police, and he would never forget how I had helped Wolfe make a monkey of him in the Pitcairn affair. Add to that the fact that he was fitted out at birth for a career as a guard at a slave-labor camp and somehow got delivered to the wrong country, and you can imagine his attitude when he came and saw Wolfe and me there. He was bitterly disappointed when he learned that Wolfe was on Sperling's payroll and therefore he would have to pretend he knew how to be polite. He was big and tall and in love with his uniform, and he thought he was handsome. At two o'clock one of the county boys, who was really in charge, because the body had not been found on a public highway, told me to go to bed.

I slept five hours, got up and dressed, went downstairs, and had breakfast with Sperling, Jimmy, and Paul Emerson. Emerson looked as sour as ever, but claimed he felt wonderful because of an unusual experience. He said he couldn't remember when he had had a good night's sleep, on account of insomnia, but that last night he had gone off the minute his head hit the pillow, and he had slept like a log. Apparently, he concluded, what he needed was the stimulant of a homicide at bedtime, but he didn't see how he could manage that often enough to help much. Jimmy tried halfheartedly to help along with a bum joke, Sperling wasn't interested, and I was busy eating in order to get through and take Wolfe's breakfast tray up to him.

From the bedroom I phoned Fritz and learned that Andy and the others were back at work on the roof and everything was under control. I told him I couldn't say when we'd be home, and I told Saul to stay on call but to go out for air if he wanted some. I figured that he and Ruth were in the clear, since with Rony gone no one could identify the bandits but me. I also told Saul of the fatal accident that had happened to a friend of the Sperling family, and he felt as Archer did later, that it was very regrettable.

When Wolfe had cleaned the tray I took it back downstairs and had a look around. Madeline was having strawberries and toast and coffee on the west terrace, with a jacket over her shoulders on account of the morning breeze. She didn't look as if homicides stimulated her the way they did Paul Emerson, to sounder sleep. I had wondered how her eyes would be, wide open or half shut, when her mind was too occupied to keep them to a program, and the answer seemed to be wide open, even though the lids were heavy and the whites not too clear.

Madeline told me that things had been happening while I was upstairs. District Attorney Archer and Ben Dykes, head of the county detectives, had arrived and were in the library with Sperling. An Assistant District Attorney was having a talk with Gwenn up in her room. Mrs. Sperling was staying in bed with a bad headache. Jimmy had gone to the garage for a car to drive to Mount Kisco on a personal errand, and had been told nothing doing because the scientific inspection of the Sperlings' five vehicles had not been completed. Paul and Connie Emerson had decided that house guests must be a nuisance in the circumstances, and that they should leave, but Ben Dykes earnestly requested them to stay; and anyhow their car too, with the others in the garage, was not available. A New York newspaper reporter had got as far as the house by climbing a fence and coming through the woods to the lawn, and had been bounced by a State cop.

It looked as if it wouldn't be merely a quick hello and good-by, in spite of the size of the house and grounds, with all the fancy trees and bushes and three thousand roses. I left Madeline to her third cup of coffee on the terrace and strolled to the plaza behind the shrubbery where I had left the sedan. It was still there, and so were two scientists, making themselves familiar with it. I stood and watched them a while without getting as much as a glance from them, and then moved off. Moseying around, it seemed to me that something was missing. How had all the law arrived, on foot or horseback? It needed investigation. I circled the house and struck out down the front drive. In the bright June morning sun the landscape certainly wasn't the same as it had been the night before when I had taken that walk with Madeline. The drive was perfectly smooth, whereas last night it had kept having warts where my feet landed.

As I neared the bridge over the brook I got my question answered. Fifteen paces this side of the brook a car was parked in the middle of the drive, and another car was standing on the bridge. More scientists were at work on the drive, concentrated at its edge, in the space between the two cars. So they had found something there last night that they wanted to preserve for daylight inspection, and no cars had been allowed to pass, including the DA's. I thoroughly approved. Always willing to learn, I approached and watched the operations with deep interest. One who was presumably not a scientist but an executive, since he was just standing looking, inquired, "You doing research?"

"No, sir," I told him. "I smelled blood, and my grandfather was a cannibal."

"Oh, a gag man. You're not needed. Beat it."

Not feeling like arguing, I stood and watched. In about ten minutes, not less, he reminded me, "I said beat it."

"Yeah, I know. I didn't think you were serious, because I have a friend who is a lawyer, and that would be silly." I tilted my head back and sniffed twice. "Chicken blood. From a White Wyandotte rooster with catarrh. I'm a detective."

I had an impulse to go take a look at the bush where I had found Rony, which looked much closer to the drive than it had seemed last night, but decided that might start a real quarrel, and I didn't want to make enemies. The executive was glaring at me. I grinned at him as a friend and headed back up the drive.

As I mounted the three steps to the wide front terrace a State employee in uniform stepped toward me.

"Your name Goodwin?"

I admitted it.

He jerked his head sideways. "You're wanted inside."

I entered and crossed the vestibule to the reception hall. Madeline, passing through, saw me and stopped.

"Your boss wants you."

"The worm. Where, upstairs?"

"No, the library. They sent for him and they want you too."

I went to the library.

Wolfe did not have the best chair this time, probably because it had already been taken by Cleveland Archer when he got there. But the one he had would do, and on a little table at his elbow was a tray with a glass and two bottles of beer. Sperling was standing, but after I had pulled up a chair and joined them he sat down too. Archer, who had a table in front of him with some papers on it, was good enough to remember that he had met me before, since of course there was always a chance that I might buy a plot in Westchester and establish a voting residence there.

Wolfe said Archer had some questions to ask me.

Archer, not at all belligerent, nodded at me. "Yes, I've got to be sure the record is straight. Sunday night you and Rony were waylaid on Hotchkiss Road."

It didn't sound like a question, but I was anxious to co-operate, so I said that was right.

"It's a coincidence, you see," Archer explained. "Sunday night he got blackjacked and robbed, and Monday night he got run over and killed. A sort of epidemic of violence. It makes me want to ask, was there any connection?"

"If you're asking me, none that I know of."

"Maybe not. But there were circumstances—I won't say suspicious, but peculiar. You gave a false name and address when you reported it at the State Police barracks."

"I gave the name Goodwin."

"Don't quibble," Wolfe muttered, pouring beer.

"I suppose you know," I told Archer, "that I was sent up here by Mr. Wolfe, who employs me, and that Mr. Sperling and I arranged what my name and occupation would be to his family and guests. Rony was present while I was reporting at the barracks, and I didn't think I ought to confuse him by changing names on him when he was still dim."

"Dim?"

"As you said, he had just been blackjacked. His head was not clear."

Archer nodded. "Even so, giving a false name and address to the police should be avoided whenever possible. You were held up by a man and a woman."

"That's right."

"You reported the number of the license on their car, but it's no good."

"That doesn't surprise me."

"No. Nor me. Did you recognize either the man or the woman?"

I shook my head. "Aren't you wasting your time, Mr. Archer?" I pointed at the papers on the table. "You must have it all there."

"I have, certainly. But now that the man who was with you has been killed, that might sharpen your memory. You're in the detective business, and you've been around a lot and seen lots of people. Haven't you remembered that you had seen that man or woman before?"

"No, sir. After all, this is—okay. No, sir."

"Why did you and Rony refuse to let the police take your wallets to get fingerprints?"

"Because it was late and we wanted to get home, and anyway it looked to me as if they were just living up to routine and didn't really mean it."

Archer glanced at a paper. "They took around three hundred dollars from Rony, and over two hundred from you. Is that right?"

"For Rony, so he said. For me, right."

"He was wearing valuable jewelry—stickpin, cufflinks, and a ring. It wasn't taken. There was luggage in the car, including two valuable cameras. It wasn't touched. Didn't that strike you as peculiar?"

I turned a hand over. "Now listen, Mr. Archer. You know damn well they have their prejudices. Some of them take everything that's loose, even your belt or suspenders. These babies happened to prefer cash, and they got over five Cs. The only thing that struck me worth mentioning was something on the side of the head."

"It left no mark on you."

"Nor on Rony either. I guess they had had practice."

"Did you go to a doctor?"

"No, sir. I didn't know that Westchester required a doctor's certificate in a holdup case. It must be a very progressive county. I'll remember it next time."

"You don't have to be sarcastic, Goodwin."

"No, sir." I grinned at him. "Nor do you have to be so goddam sympathetic with a guy who got a bat on the head on a public road in your jurisdiction. Thank you just the same."

"All right." He flipped a hand to brush it off. "Why did you feel so bad you couldn't eat anything all day Sunday?"

I admit that surprised me. Wolfe had mentioned the possibility that there would be a first-rate man among the questioners, and while this sudden question was no proof of brilliancy it certainly showed that someone had been good and thorough.

"The boys have been getting around," I said admiringly. "I didn't know any of the servants here had it in for me—maybe they used the third degree. Or could one of my fellow guests have spilled it?" I leaned forward and spoke in a low voice. "I had nine drinks and they were all doped."

"Don't clown," Wolfe muttered, putting down an empty glass.

"What then?" I demanded. "Can I tell him it must have been something I ate with my host sitting here?"

"You didn't have nine drinks," Archer stated. "You had two or three."

"Okay." I surrendered. "Then it must have been the country air. All I know is, I had a headache and my stomach kept warning me not to make any shipments. Now ask me if I went to a doctor. I ought to tell you, Mr. Archer, that I think I may get sore, and if I get sore I'll start making wisecracks, and if I do that you'll get sore. What good will that do us?"

The District Attorney laughed. His laughing routine was quite different from Sperling's, being closer to a giggle than a roar, but it suited him all right. No one joined him, and after a moment he looked around apologetically and spoke to James U. Sperling.

"I hope you don't think I'm taking this lightly. This is a very regrettable affair. Very."

"It certainly is," Sperling agreed.

Archer nodded, puckering his mouth. "Very regrettable. There's no reason why I shouldn't be entirely frank with you, Mr. Sperling—and in Mr. Wolfe's presence, since you have retained him in your interest. It is not the policy of my office to go out of its way to make trouble for men of your standing. That's only common sense. We have considered your suggestion that Rony was killed elsewhere, in a road accident, and the body brought here and concealed on your property, but we can't—that is, it couldn't have happened that way. He got off the train at Chappaqua at nine-twenty-three, and the taxi driver brought him to the entrance to your grounds and saw him start walking up the driveway. Not only that, there is clear evidence that he was killed, run over by a car, on your drive at a point about thirty feet this side of the bridge crossing the brook. That evidence is still being accumulated, but there is already enough to leave no room for doubt. Do you want me to send for a man to give you the details?"

"No," Sperling said.

"You're welcome to them at any time. The evidence indicates that the car was going east, away from the house, toward the entrance, but that is not conclusive. Inspection of the cars belonging here has not been completed. It is possible that it was some other car—any car—which came in from the road, but you will understand why that theory is the least acceptable. It seems improbable, but we haven't rejected it, and frankly, we see no reason for rejecting it unless we have to."

Archer puckered his lips again, evidently considering words that were ready to come, and decided to let them through. "My office cannot afford to be offhand about sudden and violent death, even if it wanted to. In this case we have to answer not only to our own consciences, and to the people of this county whose servants we are, but also to—may I say, to other interests. There have already been inquiries from the New York City authorities, and an offer of co-operation. They mean it well and we welcome it, but I mention it to show that the interest in Rony's death is not confined to my jurisdiction, and that of course increases my responsibility. I hope—do I make my meaning clear?"

"Perfectly," Sperling assented.

"Then you will see that nothing can be casually overlooked—not that it should be or would be, in any event. Anyhow, it can't be. As you know, we have questioned everyone here fairly rigorously—including all of your domestic staff—and we have got not the slightest clue to what happened. No one knows anything about it at all, with the single exception of your younger daughter, who admits—I should say states—that she asked Rony to come here on that train and meet her at a certain spot on this property. No one—"

Wolfe grunted. "Miss Sperling didn't ask him to come on that train. She asked him to come. It was his convenience that determined the train."

"My mistake," Archer conceded. "Anyhow, it was her summons that brought him. He came on that train. It was on time. He got into the taxi at once, and the driving time from the railroad station to the entrance to these grounds is six or seven minutes, therefore he arrived at half past nine—perhaps a minute or so later. He may have headed straight for the place of his rendezvous, or he may have loitered on the drive—we don't know."

Archer fingered among the papers before him, looked at one, and sat up again. "If he loitered, your daughter may have been at the place of rendezvous at the time he was killed. She intended to get there at nine-thirty but was delayed by a conversation with her sister and was a little late—she thinks about ten minutes, possibly fifteen. Her sister, who saw her leave the house, corroborates that. If Rony loitered—"

"Isn't this rather elaborate?" Sperling put in.

Archer nodded. "These things usually are. If Rony loitered on the drive, and if your daughter was at the place of rendezvous at the time he was killed, why didn't she hear the car that killed him? She says she heard no car. That has been thoroughly tested. It is slightly downhill along the drive clear to the entrance. From the place of rendezvous, beyond that thicket, the sound of a car going down the drive is extremely faint. Even with a car going up the drive you have to listen for it, and last night there was some wind from the northeast. So Rony might have been killed while your daughter was there waiting for him, and she might have heard nothing."

"Then damn it, why so much talk about it?"

Archer was patient. "Because that's all there is to talk about. Except for your daughter's statement, nothing whatever has been contributed by anyone. No one saw or heard anything. Mr. Goodwin's contribution is entirely negative. He left here at ten minutes to ten—" Archer looked at me. "I understand that time is definite?"

"Yes, sir. When I get in the car I have a habit of checking the dash clock with my wrist watch. It was nine-fifty."

Archer returned to Sperling. "He left at nine-fifty to drive to Chappaqua to make a phone call, and noticed nothing along the drive. He returned thirty or thirty-five minutes later, and again noticed nothing—so his contribution is entirely negative. By the way, your daughter didn't hear his car either—or doesn't remember hearing it."

Sperling was frowning. "I still would like to know why all the concentration on my daughter."

"I don't concentrate on her," Archer objected. "Circumstances do."

"What circumstances?"

"She was a close friend of Rony's. She says that she was not engaged to marry him, but she—uh, saw a great deal of him. Her association with him had been the subject of—uh, much family discussion. It was that that led to your engaging the services of Nero Wolfe, and he doesn't concern himself with trivialities. It was that that brought him up here yesterday, and his—"

"It was not. He wanted me to pay for the damage to his plant rooms."

"But because he thought it was connected with your employment of him. His aversion to leaving his place for anything at all is well known. There was a long family conference—"

"Not a conference. He did all the talking. He insisted that I must pay the damage."

Archer nodded. "You all agree on that. By the way, how did it come out? Are you paying?"

"Is that relevant?" Wolfe inquired.

"Perhaps not," Archer conceded. "Only, since you have been engaged to investigate this other matter—I'll withdraw the question if it's impertinent."

"Not at all," Sperling declared. "I'm paying the damage, but not because I'm obliged to. There's no evidence that it had any connection with me or my affairs."

"Then it's none of my business," Archer further conceded. "But the fact remains that something happened yesterday to cause your daughter to decide to summon Rony and tell him she was through with him. She says that it was simply that the trouble her friendship with him was causing was at last too much for her, and she made up her mind to end it. That may well be. I can't even say that I'm skeptical about it. But it is extremely unfortunate, *extremely*, that she reached that decision the very day that Rony was to die a violent death, under circumstances which no one can explain and for which no one can be held accountable."

Archer leaned forward and spoke from his heart. "Listen, Mr. Sperling. You know quite well I don't want to make trouble for you. But I have a duty and a responsibility, and, besides that, I'm not functioning in a vacuum. Far from it! I can't say how many people know about the situation here regarding your daughter and

Rony, but certainly some do. There are three guests here in the house right now, and one of them is a prominent broadcaster. Whatever I do or don't do, people are going to believe that that situation and Rony's death are connected, and therefore if I tried to ignore it I would be hooted out of the county. I've got to go the limit on this homicide, and I'm going to. I've got to find out who killed Rony and why. If it was an accident no one will be better pleased than me, but I've got to know who was responsible. It's going to be unpleasant—" Archer stopped because the door had swung open. Our heads turned to see the intruder. It was Ben Dykes, the head of the county detectives, and behind him was the specimen who had been born in the wrong country, Lieutenant Con Noonan of the State Police. I didn't like the look on Noonan's face, but then I never do.

"Yes, Ben?" Archer demanded impatiently. No wonder he was irritated, having been interrupted in the middle of his big speech.

"Something you ought to know," Dykes said, approaching.

"What is it?"

"Maybe you'd rather have it privately."

"Why? We have nothing to conceal from Mr. Sperling, and Wolfe's working for him. What is it?"

Dykes shrugged. "They've finished on the cars and got the one that killed him. It's the one they did last, the one that's parked out back. Nero Wolfe's."

"No question about it!" Noonan crowed.

11

I had a funny mixed feeling. I was surprised, I was even flabbergasted, that is true. But it is also true that the surprise was canceled out by its exact opposite; that I had been expecting this all along. They say that the conscious mind is the upper tenth and everything else is down below. I don't know how they got their percentages, but if they're correct I suppose nine-tenths of me had been doing the expecting, and it broke through into the upper layer when Ben Dykes put it into words.

Wolfe darted a glance at me. I lifted my brows and shook my head. He nodded and lifted his glass for the last of his beer.

"That makes it different," said Sperling, not grief-stricken. "That seems to settle it."

"Look, Mr. Archer," Lieutenant Noonan offered. "It's only a hit-and-run now, and you're a busy man and so is Dykes. This Goodwin thinks he's tough. Why don't I just take him down to the barracks?"

Archer, skipping him, asked Dykes, "How good is it? Enough to bank on?"

"Plenty," Dykes declared. "It all has to go to the laboratory, but there's blood on the under side of the fender, and a button with a piece of his jacket wedged between the axle and the spring, and other things. It's good all right."

Archer looked at me. "Well?"

I smiled at him. "I couldn't put it any better than you did, Mr. Archer. My contribution is entirely negative. If that car killed Rony I was somewhere else at the time. I wish I could be more help, but that's the best I can do."

"I'll take him to the barracks," Noonan offered again.

Again he was ignored. Archer turned to Wolfe. "You own the car, don't you? Have you got anything to say?"

"Only that I don't know how to drive, and that if Mr. Goodwin is taken to a barracks, as this puppy suggests, I shall go with him."

The DA came back to me. "Why don't you come clean with it? We can wind it up in ten minutes and get out of here."

"I'm sorry," I said courteously. "If I tried to fake it at a minute's notice I might botch it up and you'd catch me in a lie."

"You won't tell us how it happened?"

"Not I won't. I can't."

Archer stood up and spoke to Sperling. "Is there another room I can take him to? I have to be in court at two o'clock and I'd like to finish this if possible."

"You can stay here," Sperling said, leaving his chair, eager to co-operate. He looked at Wolfe. "I see you've finished your beer. If you'll come—"

Wolfe put his hands on the chair arms, got himself erect, took three steps, and was facing Archer. "As you say, I own the car. If Mr. Goodwin is taken away without first notifying me, and without a warrant, this affair will be even more regrettable than it is now. I don't blame you for wanting to talk with him; you don't know him as well as I do; but I owe it to you to say that you will be wasting valuable time."

He marched to the door, with Sperling at his heels, and was gone. Dykes asked, "Will you want me?"

"I might," Archer said. "Sit down."

Dykes moved to the chair Wolfe had vacated, sat, took out a notebook and pencil, inspected the pencil point, and settled back. Meanwhile Noonan walked across and deposited himself in the chair Sperling had used. He hadn't been invited and he hadn't asked if he was wanted. Naturally I was pleased, since if he had acted otherwise I would have had to take the trouble to change my opinion of him.

Archer, his lips puckered, was giving me a good look. He spoke. "I don't understand you, Goodwin. I don't know why you don't see that your position is impossible."

"That's easy," I told him. "For exactly the same reason that you don't."

"That I don't see it's impossible? But I do."

"Like hell you do. If you did you'd be on your way by now, leaving me to Ben Dykes or one of your assistants. You've got a busy schedule ahead of you, but here you still are. May I make a statement?"

"By all means. That's just what I want you to do."

"Fine." I clasped my hands behind my head. "There's no use going over what I did and when. I've already told it three times and it's on the record. But with this news, that it was Mr. Wolfe's car that killed him, you don't have to bother any more with what anybody was doing, even me, at eight o'clock or nine or ten. You know exactly when he was killed. It couldn't have been before nine-thirty, because that's when he got out of the cab at the entrance. It couldn't have been after nine-fifty, because that's when I got in the car to drive to Chappaqua. Actually it's even narrower, say between nine-thirty-two and nine-forty-six—only fourteen minutes. During that time I was up in the bedroom with Mr. Wolfe. Where were the others? Because of course it's all in the family now, since our car was used. Someone here did it, and during that fourteen minutes. You'll want to know where the key to the ignition was. In the car. I don't remove it when I'm parking on the private grounds of a friend or a client. I did remove it, however, when I got back from Chappaqua, since it might be there all night. I didn't know how long it would take Sperling to decide to let go of forty grand. You will also want to know if the engine was warm when I got in and started it. I don't know. It starts like a dream, warm or cold. Also it is June. Also, if all it had done was roll down the drive and kill Rony, and turn around at the entrance and come back again, and there wasn't time for much more than that, it wouldn't have got warmed up to speak of."

I considered a moment. "That's the crop."

"You can eat that timetable," Noonan said in his normal voice, which you ought to hear. "Try again, bud. He wasn't killed in that fourteen minutes. He was killed at nine-fifty-two, when you went down the drive on your way to Chappaqua. Do your statement over."

I turned my head to get his eyes. "Oh, you here?"

Archer said to Dykes, "Ask him some questions, Ben."

I had known Ben Dykes sort of off and on for quite a while, and as far as I knew he was neither friend nor enemy. Most of the enforcers of the law, both in and out of uniform, in the suburban districts, have got an inferiority complex about New York detectives, either public or private, but Dykes was an exception. He had been a Westchester dick for more than twenty years, and all he cared about was doing his work well enough to hang onto his job, steering clear of mudholes, and staying as honest as he could.

He kept after me, with Archer cutting in a few times, for over an hour. In the middle of it a colleague brought sandwiches and coffee in to us, and we went ahead between bites. Dykes did as well as he could, and he was an old hand at it, but even if he had been one of the best, which he wasn't, there was only one direction he could get at me from, and from there he always found me looking straight at him. He was committed to one simple concrete fact: that going down the drive on my way to Chappaqua I had killed Rony, and I matched it with the simple concrete fact that I hadn't. That didn't allow much leeway for a fancy grilling, and the only thing that prolonged it to over an hour was their earnest desire to wrap it up quick and cart it away from Stony Acres.

Archer looked at his wrist watch for the tenth time. A glance at mine showed me 1:20.

"The only thing to do," he said, "is get a warrant. Ben, you'd better phone—no, one of the men can ride down with me and bring it back."

"I'll go," Noonan offered.

"We've got plenty of men," Dykes said pointedly, "since it looks like we're through here."

Archer had got up. "You leave us no other course, Goodwin," he told me. "If you try to leave the county before the warrant comes you'll be stopped."

"I've got his car key," Dykes said.

"This is so damned unnecessary!" Archer complained, exasperated. He sat down again and leaned forward at me. "For God's sake, haven't I made it plain enough? There's no possibility of jeopardy for a major crime, and very little of any jeopardy at all. It was night. You didn't see him until you were on top of him. When you got out and went to him he was dead. You were rattled, and you had an urgent confidential phone call to make. You didn't want to leave his body there in the middle of the drive, so you dragged it across the grass to a bush. You drove to Chappaqua, made the phone call, and drove back here. You entered the house, intending to phone a report of the accident, and were met by Miss Sperling, who was concerned about the absence of her sister. You went out with her to look for the sister, and you found her. Naturally you didn't want to tell her, abruptly and brutally, of Rony's death. Within a short time you went to the house and told Wolfe about it, and he told Sperling, and Sperling notified the police. You were understandably reluctant to admit that it was your car that had killed him, and you could not bring yourself to do so until the course of the investigation showed you that it was unavoidable. Then, to me, to the highest law officer of the county, you stated the facts—all of them."

Archer stretched another inch forward. "If those facts are set down in a statement, and you sign it, what will happen? You can't even be charged with leaving the scene of an accident, because you didn't—you're here and haven't left here. I'm the District Attorney. It will be up to me to decide if any charge shall be lodged against you, and if so what charge. What do you think I'll decide? Considering all the circumstances, which you're as familiar with as I am, what would any man of sense decide? Whom have you injured, except one man by an unavoidable accident?"

Archer turned to the table, found a pad of paper, got a pen from his pocket, and offered them to me. "Here. Write it down and sign it, and let's get it over with. You'll never regret it, Goodwin, you have my word for that."

I smiled at him. "Now I *am* sorry, Mr. Archer, I really am."

"Don't be sorry! Just write it down and sign it."

I shook my head. "I guess you'll have to get the warrant, but you'd better count ten. I'm glad you weren't peddling a vacuum cleaner or you'd have sold me. But I won't buy signing such a statement. If all it had to have in it was what you said—hitting him and dragging him off the road, and going on to make the phone call, and coming back and helping Miss Sperling hunt her sister, and getting the cops notified but not mentioning the fact that it was me that ran over him—if that was all there was to it I might possibly oblige you, in spite of the fact that it wouldn't be true, just to save trouble all around. But one detail that you didn't include would be too much for me."

"What? What are you talking about?"

"The car. I'm in the detective business. I'm supposed to know things. I'm certainly supposed to know that if you run over a man and squash him the way Rony was squashed, the car will have so much evidence on it that a blindfolded Boy Scout could get enough to cinch it. Yet I drove the car back here and parked it, and played innocent all night and all morning, so Ben Dykes could walk in on us at noon and announce aha, it was Nero Wolfe's car! That I will not buy. It would get me a horse laugh from the Battery to Spuyten Duyvil. I would never live it down. And speaking of a warrant, I don't think any judge or jury would buy it either."

"We could make it—"

"You couldn't make it anything but what it is. I'll tell you another thing. I don't believe Ben Dykes has bought it, and I doubt very much if you have. Ben may not like me much, I don't know, but he knows damn well I'm not a sap. He went after me as well as he could because you told him to and you're the boss. As for you, I can't say, except that I don't blame you a bit for not liking to start fires under people like the Sperlings. If nothing else, they hire only the best lawyers. As for this bird in uniform named Noonan, you may be a church member and I'd better keep within bounds."

"You see what he's like, sir," Noonan said under restraint. "I told you he thinks he's tough. If you had let me take him to the barracks—"

"Shut up!" Archer squeaked.

It may not be fair to call it a squeak, but it was close to it. He was harassed and I felt sorry for him. In addition to everything else, he was going to be late at court, as he realized when he took another look at his watch. He ignored me and spoke to Dykes.

"I've got to go, Ben. Take care of these papers. If anyone wants to leave the place you can't hold them, the way it stands now, but ask them not to leave the jurisdiction."

"What about Wolfe and Goodwin?"

"I said anyone. We can't hold them without a warrant, and that will have to wait. But the car stays where it is. Immobilize it and keep a guard on it. Have you tried it for prints?"

"No, sir, I thought—"

"Do so. Thoroughly. Keep a man at the car and one at the entrance, and you stay. You might have another try at the servants, especially that assistant gardener. Tell Mr. Sperling that I'll be back some time between five and six—it depends on when court adjourns. Tell him I would appreciate it if they can all find it convenient to be here."

He trotted out without even glancing at me, which I thought was uncalled for.

I grinned at Ben Dykes, strolled insolently out of the room, and went in search of Wolfe, to do a little mild bragging. I found him out at the greenhouse, inspecting some concrete benches with automatic watering.

12

A couple of hours later Wolfe and I were up in the bedroom. He had found that the biggest chair there, while it would do for a short stretch, was no good for a serious distance, and therefore he was on the bed with his book, flat on his back, though he hated to read lying down. His bright yellow shirt was still bright but badly wrinkled, worse than it ever was at home, since he changed every day; and both his yellow socks showed the beginnings of holes at the big toes, which was no wonder, considering that they hadn't been changed either and were taking the push of more than an eighth of a ton for the second day.

I had finally got around to the magazines I had brought upstairs the previous evening. There was a knock at the door and I said come in.

It was the Chairman of the Board. He closed the door and approached. I said hello. Wolfe let his book down to rest on his belly but otherwise stayed put.

"You look comfortable," Sperling said like a host.

Wolfe grunted. I said something gracious.

Sperling moved a chair around to a different angle and sat.

"So you talked yourself out of it?" he asked.

"I doubt if I rate a credit line," I said modestly. "The picture was out of focus, that's all. It would have needed too much retouching, and all I did was point that out."

He nodded. "I understand from Dykes that the District Attorney offered to guarantee immunity if you would sign a statement."

"Not quite. He didn't offer to put it in writing. Not that I think he would have crossed me, but I liked the immunity I already had. As I heard a guy say once, virtue is never left to stand alone."

"Where did you get that?" Wolfe demanded from his pillows. "That's Confucius."

I shrugged. "It must have been him I heard say it."

Our host gave me up and turned to Wolfe. "The District Attorney will be back between five and six. He left word that he would like all of us to be here. What does that mean?"

"Apparently," Wolfe said dryly, "it means that he feels compelled to annoy you some more, much as he would prefer not to. By the way, I wouldn't underrate Mr. Archer. Don't let the defects of his personality mislead you."

"They haven't. But what evidence has he got that this was anything but an accident?"

"I don't know, beyond what he hinted to you. Possibly none. Even if he accepts it as an accident, he needs to find out who was driving the car. Being a man in your position, Mr. Sperling, a man of wealth and note, bestows many advantages and privileges, but it also bestows handicaps. Mr. Archer knows he cannot afford to have it whispered that he winked at this affair because you are such a man. The poor devil."

"I understand that." Sperling was controlling himself admirably, considering that he had stated before witnesses that he would pay for the damage to the plant rooms. "But what about you? You have spent three hours this afternoon questioning my family and guests and servants. You have no intention of running for office, have you?"

"Good heavens, no." From Wolfe's tone you might have thought he had been asked if he intended to take up basketball. "But you have hired me to investigate Mr. Rony's death. I was trying to earn my fee. I admit it doesn't look much like it at this moment, but I had a hard night Sunday, and I'm waiting to learn what line Mr. Archer is going to take. What time is it, Archie?"

"Quarter past four."

"Then he should be here in an hour or so."

Sperling stood up. "Things are piling up at my office," he said, just stating a fact, and strode out of the room.

"On him a crown looks good," I remarked.

"It doesn't chafe him," Wolfe agreed, and went back to his book.

After a while it began to irritate me to see the toes of the yellow socks sticking up with holes started, so I tossed the magazines on a table, wandered out of the room, on downstairs, and outdoors. Sounds came from the direction of the swimming pool, and I went that way. The wind was no longer even a breeze, the sun was warm and friendly, and for anyone who likes grass and flowers and trees better than sidewalks and buildings it would have been a treat.

Connie Emerson and Madeline were in the pool. Paul Emerson, in a cotton shirt and slacks, not too clean, was standing on the marble at the edge, scowling at them. Gwenn, in a dress dark in color but summery in weight, was in a chair under an umbrella, her head leaning back and her eyes closed.

Madeline interrupted an expert crawl to call to me, "Come on in!"

"No trunks!" I called back.

Gwenn, hearing, swiveled her head to give me a long straight look, had nothing to say, turned her head back as before, and shut her eyes.

"You not getting wet?" I asked Emerson.

"I got cramps Saturday," he said in an irritated tone, as if I should have had sense enough to know that. "How does it stand now?"

"What? The cramp situation?"

"The Rony situation."

"Oh. He's still dead."

"That's surprising." The eminent broadcaster flicked a glance at me, but liked the sunlight on the water better. "I bet he rises from the grave. I hear it was your car."

"Mr. Wolfe's car, yeah. So they say."

"Yet here you are without a guardian, no handcuffs. What are they doing, giving you a medal?"

"I'm waiting and hoping. Why, do you think I deserve one?"

Emerson tightened his lips and relaxed them again, a habit he had. "Depends on whether you did it on purpose or not. If it was accidental I don't think you ought to get more than honorable mention. How does it stand? Would it help any if I put in a word for you?"

"I don't—excuse me, I'm being paged."

I stooped to grab the hand Madeline was putting up at me, braced myself, and straightened, bringing her out of the water onto the marble and on up to her feet.

"My, you're big and strong," she said, standing and dripping. "Congratulations!"

"Just for that? Gee, if I wanted to I could pull Elsa Maxwell—"

"No, not that. For keeping out of jail. How did you do it?"

I waved a hand. "I've got something on the DA."

"No, really? Come and sit while I let the sun dry me, and tell me about it."

She went and stretched out on the grassy slope, and I sat beside her. She had been doing some fast swimming but wasn't out of breath, and her breast, with nothing but the essentials covered, rose and fell in easy smooth rhythm. Even with her eyes closed for the sun she seemed to know where I was looking, for she said complacently, "I expand three inches. If that's not your type I'll smoke more and get it down. Is it true that you were driving the car when it ran over Louis?"

"Nope. Not guilty."

"Then who was?"

"I don't know yet. Ask me tomorrow and keep on asking me. Call my secretary and make appointments so you can keep on asking me. She expands four inches."

"Who, your secretary?"

"Yes, ma'am."

"Bring her up here. We'll do a pentathlon and the winner gets you. What would you advise me to do?"

Her eyes, opened from force of habit, blinked in the sun and went shut again. I asked, "You mean to train for the pentathlon?"

"Certainly not. I won't have to. I mean when the District Attorney comes to ask more questions. You know he's coming?"

"Yeah, I heard about it."

"All right, what shall I do? Shall I tell him that I may have a suspicion that I might have an idea about someone using your car?"

"You might take a notion that you might try it. Shall we make it
up together? Who shall we pick on?"

"I don't want to pick on anybody. That's the trouble. Why
should anyone pay a penalty for accidentally killing Louis Rony?"

"Maybe they shouldn't." I patted her round brown soft firm shoulder to see if it was dry yet. "There I'm right with you, ma'am. But
the hell of it—"

"Why do you keep on calling me ma'am?"

"To make you want me to call you something else. Watch and
see if it don't work. It always does. The hell of it is that both the
DA and Nero Wolfe insist on knowing, and the sooner they find
out the sooner we can go on to other things like pentathlons. Knowing how good you are at dare-base, I suppose you do have an idea
about someone using my car. What gave it to you?"

She sat up, said, "I guess my front's dry," turned over onto a fresh
spot, and stretched out again, face down. The temptation to pat
was now stronger than before, but I resisted it.

"What gave it to you?" I asked as if it didn't matter much.

No reply. In a moment her voice came, muffled. "I ought to think
it over some more."

"Yeah, that never does any harm, but you haven't got much time.
The DA may be here any minute. Also you asked my advice, and
I'd be in better shape to make it good if I knew something about
your idea. Go ahead and describe it."

She turned her head enough to let her eyes, now shielded from
the sun, take me in at an angle. "You could be clever if you worked
at it," she said. "It's fun to watch you going after something. Say
I saw or heard something last night and now I tell you about it.
Within thirty seconds, for as you say there isn't much time, you
would have to go in to wash your hands, and as soon as you're in
the house you run upstairs and tell Nero Wolfe. He gets busy immediately, and probably by the time the District Attorney gets here the
answer is all ready for him—or if it doesn't go as fast as that, when
they do get the answer it will be Nero Wolfe that started it, and
so the bill he sends my father can be bigger than it could have been
otherwise. I don't know how much money Dad has spent on me in
my twenty-six years, but it's been plenty, and now for the first time

in my life I can save him some. Isn't that wonderful? If you had a widowed middle-aged daughter whose chest expanded three inches, wouldn't you want her to act as I am acting?"

"No, ma'am," I said emphatically.

"Of course you would. Call me something else, like darling or little cabbage. Here we are, locked in a tussle, you trying to make money for your boss and me trying to save money for my father, and yet we're—"

She sat up abruptly. "Is that a car coming? Yes, it is." She was on her feet. "Here he comes, and I've got to do my hair!" She streaked for the house.

13

I walked into the bedroom and announced to Wolfe, "The law has arrived. Shall I arrange to have the meeting held up here?"

"No," he said testily. "What time is it?"

"Eighteen minutes to six."

He grunted. "I'd have a devil of a time getting anywhere on this from the office, with these people here for the summer. You'd have to do it all, and you don't seem to take to this place very well. You gulp down drinks that have been drugged, plan and execute hold-ups, and leave my car where it can be used to kill people."

"Yep," I agreed cheerfully, "I'm no longer what I used to be. If I were you I'd fire me. Am I fired?"

"No. But if I'm to spend another night here, and possibly more, you'll have to go home to get me some shirts and socks and other things." He was gazing gloomily at his toes. "Have you seen those holes?"

"I have. Our car's immobilized, but I can borrow one. If you want to keep up with developments you'd better shake a leg. The elder daughter thinks she saw or heard something last night that gave her an idea about someone using your car, and she's making up her mind whether to tell the DA about it. I tried to get her to tell me, but she was afraid I might pass it on to you. Still another proof I've seen my best days. At least you can be there when she spills it, if you'll get off that bed and put your shoes on."

He pushed himself up, swung his legs around, and grunted as he reached for his shoes. He had them on and was tying a lace when there was a knock at the door, and before I uttered an invitation it swung open. Jimmy Sperling appeared, said, "Dad wants you in the library," and was gone, without closing the door. Apparently his visits to mines had had a bad effect on his manners.

Wolfe took his time about getting his shirttail in and putting on his tie and vest and jacket. We went along the hall to the stairs, and down, and took the complicated route to the library without seeing a soul, and I supposed they had already assembled for the meeting, but they hadn't. When we entered there were only three people there: the District Attorney, the Chairman of the Board, and Webster Kane. Again Archer had copped the best chair and Wolfe had to take second choice. I was surprised to see Webster Kane and not to see Ben Dykes, and pleased not to see Madeline. Maybe there would still be time for me to finagle a priority on her idea.

Wolfe spoke to Archer. "I congratulate you, sir, on your good judgment. I knew that Mr. Goodwin was incapable of such a shenanigan, but you didn't. You had to use your brain, and you did so."

Archer nodded. "Thanks. I tried to." He looked around. "I had a bad afternoon in court, and I'm tired. I shouldn't be here, but I said I'd come. I'm turning this matter over to Mr. Gurran, one of my assistants, who is a much better investigator than I am. He was tied up today and couldn't come with me, but he would like to come and talk with all of you tomorrow morning. Meanwhile—"

"May I say something?" Sperling put in.

"Certainly. I wish you would."

Sperling spoke easily, with no tension in his voice or manner. "I'd like to tell you exactly what happened. When Dykes came in this morning and said he had evidence that it was Wolfe's car, I thought that settled it. I believe I said so. Naturally I thought it was Goodwin, knowing that he had driven to Chappaqua last evening. Then when I learned that you weren't satisfied that it was Goodwin, I was no longer myself satisfied, because I knew you would have welcomed that solution if it had been acceptable. I put my mind on the problem as it stood then, with the time limit narrowed as it was, and I remembered something. The best way to tell you about it is to read you a statement."

Sperling's hand went to his inside breast pocket and came out with a folded paper. "This is a statement," he said, unfolding it, "dated today and signed by Mr. Kane. Webster Kane."

Archer was frowning. "By Kane?"

"Yes. It reads as follows:

"On Monday evening, June 20, 1949, a little before half past nine, I entered the library and saw on Mr. Sperling's desk some letters which I knew he wanted mailed. I had heard him say so. I knew he was upset about some personal matter and supposed he had forgotten about them. I decided to go to Mount Kisco and mail them in the post office so they would make the early morning train. I left the house by way of the west terrace, intending to go to the garage for a car, but remembered that Nero Wolfe's car was parked near by, much closer than the garage, and decided to take it instead.

"The key was in the car. I started the engine and went down the drive. It was the last few minutes of dusk, not yet completely dark, and, knowing the drive well, I didn't switch the lights on. The drive is a little downhill, and I was probably going between twenty and twenty-five miles an hour. As I was approaching the bridge over the brook I was suddenly aware of an object in the drive, on the left side, immediately in front of the car. There wasn't time for me to realize, in the dim light, that it was a man. One instant I saw there was an object, and the next instant the car had hit it. I jammed my foot on the brake, but not with great urgency, because at that instant there was no flash of realization that I had hit a man. But I had the car stopped within a few feet. I jumped out and ran to the rear, and saw it was Louis Rony. He was lying about five feet back of the car, and he was dead. The middle of him had been completely crushed by the wheels of the car.

"I could offer a long extenuation of what I did then, but it will serve just as well to put it into one sentence and simply say that I lost my head. I won't try to describe how I felt, but will tell what I did. When I had made certain that he was dead, I dragged the body off the drive and across the grass to a shrub about fifty feet away, and left it on the north side of the shrub, the side away from the drive. Then I went back to the car, drove across the bridge and on to the entrance, turned around, drove back up to the house, parked the car where I had found it, and got out.

"I did not enter the house. I paced up and down the terrace, trying to decide what to do, collecting my nerves enough to go in and tell what had happened. While I was there on the terrace

Goodwin came out of the house, crossed the terrace, and went in the direction of the place where the car was parked. I heard him start the engine and drive away. I didn't know where he was going. I thought he might be going to New York and the car might not return. Anyway, his going away in the car seemed somehow to make up my mind for me. I went into the house and up to my room, and tried to compose my mind by working on an economic report I was preparing for Mr. Sperling.

"This afternoon Mr. Sperling told me that he had noticed that the letters on his desk, ready for mailing, were gone. I told him that I had taken them up to my room, which I had, intending to have them taken to Chappaqua early this morning, but that the blocking of the road by the police, and their guarding of all the cars, had made it impossible. But his bringing up the matter of the letters changed the whole aspect of the situation for me, I don't know why. I at once told him, of my own free will, all of the facts as herein stated. When he told me that the District Attorney would be here later this afternoon, I told him that I would set down those facts in a written signed statement, and I have now done so. This is that statement."

Sperling looked up. "Signed by Webster Kane," he said. He stretched forward to hand the paper to the District Attorney. "Witnessed by me. If you want it more detailed I don't think he'll have any objection. Here he is—you can ask him."

Archer took it and ran his eye over it. In a moment he looked up and, with his head to one side, gazed at Kane. Kane met the gaze.

Archer tapped the paper with a finger. "You wrote and signed this, did you, Mr. Kane?"

"I did," Kane said clearly and firmly but without bragging.

"Well—you're a little late with it, aren't you?"

"I certainly am." Kane did not look happy, but he was bearing up. The fact that he let his hair do as it pleased was of some advantage to him, for it made it seem less unlikely that a man with the head and face of a young statesman—that is, young for a statesman—would make such a fool of himself. He hesitated and then went on, "I am keenly aware that my conduct was indefensible. I can't even explain it in terms that make sense to me now. Apparently I'm not as good in a crisis as I would like to think I am."

"But this wasn't much of a crisis, was it? An unavoidable accident? It happens to lots of people."

"I suppose it does—but I had killed a man. It seemed like a hell of a crisis to me." Kane gestured. "Anyhow, you see what it did to me. It threw me completely off balance."

"Not completely." Archer glanced at the paper. "Your mind was working well enough so that when Goodwin went to the car and drove away, down that same drive, only fifteen minutes after the accident, you thought there was a good chance that it would be blamed on him. Didn't you?"

Kane nodded. "I put that in the statement deliberately, even though I knew it could be construed like that. I can only say that if that thought was in my mind I wasn't conscious of it. How did I put it?"

Archer looked at the paper. "Like this: 'His going away in the car seemed somehow to make up my mind for me. I went into the house and up to my room,' and so on."

"That's right." Kane looked and sounded very earnest. "I was simply trying to be thoroughly honest about it, after behavior of which I was ashamed. If I had in me the kind of calculation you have described I didn't know it."

"I see." Archer looked at the paper, folded it, and sat holding it. "How well did you know Rony?"

"Oh—not intimately. I had seen him frequently the past few months, mostly at the Sperling home in New York or here."

"Were you on good terms with him?"

"No."

It was a blunt uncompromising no. Archer snapped, "Why not?"

"I didn't like what I knew of the way he practiced his profession. I didn't like him personally—I just didn't like him. I knew that Mr. Sperling suspected him of being a Communist, and while I had no evidence or knowledge of my own, I thought that the suspicion might easily be well founded."

"Did you know that Miss Gwenn Sperling was quite friendly with him?"

"Certainly. That was the only reason he was allowed to be here."

"You didn't approve of that friendship?"

"I did not, no, sir—not that my approval or disapproval mattered any. Not only am I an employee of Mr. Sperling's corporation, but for more than four years I have had the pleasure and honor of being a friend—a friend of the family, if I may say that?"

He looked at Sperling. Sperling nodded to indicate that he might say that.

Kane went on. "I have deep respect and affection for all of them, including Miss Gwenn Sperling, and I thought Rony wasn't fit to be around her. May I ask a question?"

"Certainly."

"I don't know why you're asking about my personal opinion of Rony unless it's because you suspect me of killing him, not by accident, but intentionally. Is that it?"

"I wouldn't say I suspect that, Mr. Kane. But this statement disposes of the matter with finality, and before I accept it as it stands—" Archer puckered his lips. "Why, do you resent my questions?"

"I do not," Kane said emphatically. "I'm in no position to resent questions, especially not from you. But it—"

"I do," Sperling blurted. He had been restraining himself. "What are you trying to do, Archer, make some mud if you can't find any? You said this morning it wasn't the policy of your office to go out of the way to make trouble for men of my standing. When did you change your policy?"

Archer laughed. It was even closer to a giggle than it had been in the morning, but it lasted longer and it sounded as if he was enjoying it more.

"You're entirely justified," he told Sperling. "I'm tired and I was going on merely through habit. I also said this morning that if it was an accident no one would be better pleased than me but I had to know who was responsible. Well, this certainly should satisfy me on that." He put the folded paper in his pocket. "No, I don't want to make mud. God knows enough gets made without me helping." He got to his feet. "Will you call at my office in White Plains tomorrow morning, Mr. Kane—say around eleven o'clock? If I'm not there ask for Mr. Gurran."

"I'll be there," Kane promised.

"What for?" Sperling demanded.

"For a formality." Archer nodded. "That's all, a formality. I'll commit myself to that now. I can't see that any good purpose would be served by a charge and a prosecution. I'll phone Gurran this evening and ask him to look up the motor vehicle statutes regarding an accident occurring on private property. It's possible there will have to be a fine or suspension of driving license, but under all the circumstances I would prefer to see it wiped off."

He extended a hand to Sperling. "No hard feelings, I hope?"

Sperling said not. Archer shook with Kane, with Wolfe, and even with me. He told us all that he hoped that the next time he saw us it would be on a more cheerful occasion. He departed.

Wolfe was sitting with his head tilted to one side, as if it needed too much energy to keep it straight, and his eyes were shut. Kane and Sperling and I were standing, having been polite enough to arise to tell Archer good-by, unlike Wolfe.

Kane spoke to Sperling. "Thank God that's over. If you don't need me any more I'll go and see if I can get some work done. I'd rather not show up at dinner. Of course they'll have to know about it, but I'd prefer not to face them until tomorrow."

"Go ahead," Sperling agreed. "I'll stop by your room later."

Kane started off. Wolfe opened his eyes, muttered, "Wait a minute," and straightened his head.

Kane halted and asked, "Do you mean me?"

"If you don't mind." Wolfe's tone wasn't as civil as his words. "Can your work wait a little?"

"It can if it has to. Why?"

"I'd like to have a little talk with you."

Kane sent a glance at Sperling, but it didn't reach its destination because the Chairman of the Board had taken another piece of paper from his pocket and was looking at it. This one was unfolded, oblong, and pink in color. As Kane stood hesitating, Sperling stepped to Wolfe and extended his hand with the paper in it.

"You earned it," he said. "I'm glad I hired you."

Wolfe took the paper, lowered his eyes to it, and looked up. "Indeed," he said. "Fifty thousand dollars."

Sperling nodded, as I nod to a bootblack when I tip him a dime. "Added to five makes fifty-five. If it doesn't cover your damage and expenses and fee, send me a bill."

"Thank you, I'll do that. Of course I can't tell what expenses are still to come. I may—"

"Expenses of what?"

"Of my investigation of Mr. Rony's death. I may—"

"What is there to investigate?"

"I don't know." Wolfe put the check in his pocket. "I may be easily satisfied. I'd like to ask Mr. Kane a few questions."

"What for? Why should you?"

"Why shouldn't I?" Wolfe was bland. "Surely I'm entitled to as many as Mr. Archer. Does he object to answering a dozen questions? Do you, Mr. Kane?"

"Certainly not."

"Good. I'll make it brief, but I do wish you'd sit down."

Kane sat, but on the edge of the chair. Sperling did not concede that much. He stood with his hands in his pockets, looking down at Wolfe with no admiration.

"First," Wolfe asked, "how did you determine that Mr. Rony was dead?"

"My God, you should have seen him!"

"But I didn't; and you couldn't have seen him any too well, since it was nearly dark. Did you put your hand inside and feel his heart?"

Kane shook his head. I wasn't surprised he didn't nod it, since I had learned for myself that Rony's upper torso had been in no condition for that test, with his clothes all mixed up with his ribs. That was how I had described it to Wolfe.

"I didn't have to," Kane said. "He was all smashed."

"Could you see how badly he was smashed, in the dark?"

"I could feel it. Anyhow it wasn't pitch dark—I could see some."

"I suppose you could see a bone, since bones are white. I understand that a humerus—the bone of the upper arm—had torn through the flesh and the clothing and was extruding several inches. Which arm was it?"

That was a pure lie. He understood no such thing, and it wasn't true.

"My God, I don't know," Kane protested. "I wasn't making notes of things like that."

"I suppose not," Wolfe admitted. "But you saw, or felt, the bone sticking out?"

"I—perhaps I did—I don't know."

Wolfe gave that up. "When you dragged him across to the shrub, what did you take hold of? What part of him?"

"I don't remember."

"Nonsense. You didn't drag him a yard or two, it was fifty feet or more. You couldn't possibly forget. Did you take him by the feet? The head? The coat collar? An arm?"

"I don't remember."

"I don't see how you could help remembering. Perhaps this will bring it back to you: when you got him behind the shrub was his head pointing toward the house or away from the house?"

Kane was frowning. "I should remember that."

"You should indeed."

"But I don't." Kane shook his head. "I simply don't remember."

"I see." Wolfe leaned back. "That's all, Mr. Kane." He flipped a hand. "Go and get on with your work."

Kane was on his feet before Wolfe had finished. "I did the best I could," he said apologetically. "As I said, I don't seem to measure up very well in a crisis. I must have been so rattled I didn't know what I was doing." He glanced at Sperling, got no instructions one way or another, glanced again at Wolfe, sidled between two chairs, headed for the door, and was gone.

When the door had closed behind him Sperling looked down at Wolfe and demanded, "What good did that do?"

Wolfe grunted. "None at all. It did harm. It made it impossible for me, when I return home, to forget all this and set about restoring my plants." He slanted his head back to get Sperling's face. "He must owe you a great deal—or he would hate to lose his job. How did you get him to sign that statement?"

"I didn't get him to. As it says, he wrote and signed it of his own free will."

"Pfui. I know what it says. But why should I believe that when I don't believe anything in it?"

"You're not serious." Sperling smiled like an angel. "Kane is one of this country's leading economists. Would a man of his reputation and standing sign such a statement if it weren't true?"

"Whether he would or not, he did." Wolfe was getting peevish. "With enough incentive, of course he would; and you have a good supply. You were lucky he was around, since he was ideal for the purpose." Wolfe waved a hand, finishing with Mr. Kane. "You handled it well; that statement is admirably drafted. But I wonder if you fully realize the position you've put me in?"

"Of course I do." Sperling was sympathetic. "You engaged to do a job and you did it well. Your performance here yesterday afternoon was without a flaw. It persuaded my daughter to drop Rony, and that was all I wanted. The accident of his death doesn't detract from the excellence of your job."

"I know it doesn't," Wolfe agreed, "but that job was finished. The trouble is, you hired me for another job, to investigate Mr. Rony's death. I now—"

"That one is finished too."

"Oh, no. By no means. You've hoodwinked Mr. Archer by getting

Mr. Kane to sign that statement, but you haven't gulled me." Wolfe shook his head and sighed. "I only wish you had."

Sperling gazed at him a moment, moved to the chair Archer had used, sat, leaned forward, and demanded, "Listen, Wolfe, who do you think you are, Saint George?"

"I do not." Wolfe repudiated it indignantly. "No matter who killed a wretch like Mr. Rony, and whether by accident or design, I would be quite willing to let that false statement be the last word. But I have committed myself. I have lied to the police. That's nothing, I do it constantly. I warned you last night that I withhold information from the police only when it concerns a case I'm engaged on; and that commits me to stay with the case until I am satisfied that it's solved. I said you couldn't hire me one day and fire me the next, and you agreed. Now you think you can. Now you think you can drop me because I can no longer get you in a pickle by giving Mr. Archer a true account of the conversation in this room yesterday afternoon, and you're right. If I went to him now and confessed, now that he has that statement, he would reproach me politely and forget about it. I wish I could forget about it too, but I can't. It's my self-conceit again. You have diddled me; and I will not be diddled."

"I've paid you fifty-five thousand dollars."

"So you have. And no more?"

"No more. For what?"

"For finishing the job. I'm going to find out who killed Mr. Rony, and I'm going to prove it." Wolfe aimed a finger at him. "If I fail, Mr. Sperling—" He let the finger down and shrugged. "I won't. I won't fail. See if I do."

Suddenly, without the slightest preliminary, Sperling got mad. In a flash his eyes changed, his color changed—he was a different man. Up from the chair, on his feet, he spoke through his teeth.

"Get out! Get out of here!"

Evidently there was only one thing to do, get out. It was nothing much to me, since I had had somewhat similar experiences before, but for Wolfe, who had practically always been in his own office when a conference reached the point of breaking off relations, it was a novelty to be told to get out. He did well, I thought. He neither emphasized dignity nor abandoned it, but moved as if he had taken a notion to go to the bathroom but was in no terrible hurry. I let him precede me, which was only proper.

However, Sperling was a many-sided man. His flare-up couldn't possibly have fizzled out as quick as that, but as I hopped ahead of Wolfe to open the door his voice came.

"I won't stop payment on that check!"

14

The package arrived a little before noon on Wednesday.

We hadn't got back to normal, since there was still a small army busy up in the plant rooms, but in many respects things had settled down. Wolfe had on a clean shirt and socks, meals were regular and up to standard, the street was cleared of broken glass, and we had caught up on sleep. Nothing much had yet been done toward making good on Wolfe's promise to finish the Rony job, but we had only been home fourteen hours and nine of them had been spent in bed.

Then the package came. Wolfe, having been up in the plant rooms since breakfast, was in the office with me, checking invoices and shipping memos of everything from osmundine fiber to steel sash putty. When I went to the front door to answer the bell, and a boy handed me a package about the size of a small suitcase and a receipt to sign, I left the package in the hall because I supposed it was just another item for the operations upstairs, and I was busy. But after I returned to the office it struck me as queer that there was no shipper's name on it, so I went back to the hall for another look. There was no mark of any kind on the heavy wrapping paper but Wolfe's name and address. It was tied securely with thick cord. I lifted it and guessed six pounds. I pressed it against my ear and held my breath for thirty seconds, and heard nothing.

Nuts, I thought, and cut the cord with my knife and slashed the paper. Inside was a fiber carton with the flaps taped down. I got cautious again and severed the flaps from the sides by cutting all the way around, and lifted one corner for a peek. All I saw was newspaper. I inserted the knife point and tore a piece of it off, and what I saw then made me raise my brows. Removing the flaps and the newspaper, and seeing more of the same, I got the carton up under my arm, marched into the office with it, and asked Wolfe, "Do you mind if I unpack this on your desk? I don't want to make a mess in the hall."

Ignoring his protest, I put the package down on his desk and started taking out stacks of twenty-dollar bills. They were used bills, not a new one among them as well as I could tell from the edges, and they were banded in bundles of fifty, which meant a thousand bucks to a bundle.

"What the devil is this?" Wolfe demanded.

"Money," I told him. "Don't touch it, it may be a trap. It may be covered with germs." I was arranging the bundles ten to a pile, and there were five piles. "That's a coincidence," I remarked. "Of course we'll have to check the bundles, but if they're labeled right it's exactly fifty grand. That's interesting."

"Archie." Wolfe was glowering. "What fatuous flummery is this? I told you to deposit that check, not cash it." He pointed. "Wrap that up and take it to the bank."

"Yes, sir. But before I do so—" I went to the safe and got the bank book, opened it to the current page, and displayed it to him. "As you see, the check was deposited. This isn't flummery, it's merely a coincidence. You heard the doorbell and saw me go to answer it. A boy handed me this package and gave me a receipt to sign— General Messenger Service, Twenty-eight West Forty-seventh Street. I thought it might be a clock bomb and opened it in the hall, away from you. There is nothing on the package or in it to show who sent it. The only clue is the newspaper the carton was lined with— from the second section of the *New York Times*. Who do we know that reads the *Times* and has fifty thousand bucks for a practical joke?" I gestured. "Answer that and we've got him."

Wolfe was still glowering, but at the pile of dough, not at me. He reached for one of the bundles, flipped through it, and put it back. "Put it in the safe. The package too."

"Shouldn't we count it first? What if one of the bundles is short a twenty?"

There was no reply. He was leaning back in his chair, pushing his lips out and in, and out and in again. I followed instructions, first returning the stuff to the carton to save space, and then went to the hall for the wrapping paper and cord and put them in the safe also.

I sat at my desk, waited until Wolfe's lips were quiet again, and asked coldly, "How about a raise? I could use twenty bucks a week more. So far this case has brought us one hundred and five thousand, three hundred and twelve dollars. Deduct expenses and the damage—"

"Where did the three hundred and twelve come from?"

"From Rony's wallet. Saul's holding it. I told you."

"You know, of course, who sent that package."

"Not exactly. D, C, B, or A, but which? It wouldn't come straight from X, would it?"

"Straight? No." Wolfe shook his head. "I like money, but I don't like that. I only wish you could answer a question."

"I've answered millions. Try me."

"I've already tried you on this one. Who drugged that drink Saturday evening—the one intended for Mr. Rony which you drank?"

"Yeah. That's *the* question. I myself asked it all day yesterday, off and on, and again this morning, and I don't know."

Wolfe sighed. "That, of course, is what constrains us. That's what forces us to assume that it was not an accident, but murder. But for that I might be able to persuade myself to call it closed, in spite of my deception of Mr. Archer." He sighed again. "As it is, we must either validate the assumption or refute it, and heaven knows how I'm going to manage it. The telephone upstairs has been restored. I wanted to test it, and thought I might as well do so with a call to Mr. Lowenfeld of the police laboratory. He was obliging but didn't help much. He said that if a car is going slightly downhill at twenty-five miles an hour, and its left front hits a man who is standing erect, and its wheels pass over him, it is probable that the impact will leave dents or other visible marks on the front of the car, but not certain. I told him that the problem was to determine whether the man was upright or recumbent when the car hit him, and he said the absence of marks on the front of the car would be suggestive but not conclusive. He also asked why I was still interested in Louis Rony's death. If policemen were women they couldn't be more gossipy. By evening the story will be around that I'm about ready to expose that reptile Paul Emerson as a murderer. I only wish it were true." Wolfe glanced up at the clock. "By the way, I also phoned Doctor Vollmer, and he should be here soon."

So I was wrong in supposing that nothing had been done toward making good on his promise. "Your trip to the country did you good," I declared. "You're full of energy. Did you notice that the *Gazette* printed Kane's statement in full?"

"Yes. And I noticed a defect that escaped me when Mr. Sperling read it. His taking my car, the car of a fellow guest whom he had barely met, was handled too casually. Reading it, it's a false note. I told Mr. Sperling it was well drafted, but that part wasn't. A better explanation could have been devised and put in a brief sentence. I could have—"

The phone ringing stopped him. I reached for my instrument and told the transmitter, "Nero Wolfe's office."

"May I speak to Mr. Wolfe, please?"

There was a faint tingle toward the bottom of my spine. The voice hadn't changed a particle in thirteen months.

"Your name, please?" I asked, hoping my voice was the same too.

"Tell him a personal matter."

I covered the transmitter with a palm and told Wolfe, "X."

He frowned. "What?"

"You heard me. X."

He reached for his phone. Getting no sign to do otherwise, I stayed on.

"Nero Wolfe speaking."

"How do you do, Mr. Wolfe. Goodwin told you who I am? Or my voice does?"

"I know the voice."

"Yes, it's easily recognized, isn't it? You ignored the advice I gave you Saturday. You also ignored the demonstration you received Sunday night. May I say that that didn't surprise me?"

"You may say anything."

"It didn't. I hope there will never be occasion for a more pointed demonstration. It's a more interesting world with you in it. Have you opened the package you received a little while ago?"

"Yes."

"I don't need to explain why I decided to reimburse you for the damage to your property. Do I?"

"Yes."

"Oh, come. Surely not. Not you. If the amount you received exceeds the damage, no matter. I intended that it should. The District Attorney has decided that Rony's death is fully and satisfactorily explained by Kane's statement, and no charge will be made. You have already indicated that you do not concur in that decision by your inquiry to the New York police laboratory, and anyway of course you wouldn't. Not you. Rony was an able young man with a future, and he deserves to have his death investigated by the best brain in New York. Yours. I don't live in New York, as you know. Good-by and good luck."

The connection went. Wolfe cradled his receiver. I did likewise.

"Jesus," I said softly. I whistled. "Now there's a client for you. Money by messenger, snappy phone call, hopes he'll never have to demonstrate by croaking you, keep the change, best brain in New York, go to it, click. As I think I said once before, he's an abrupt bastard."

Wolfe was sitting with his eyes closed to slits. I asked him, "How do I enter it? Under X, or Z for Zeck?"

"Archie."

"Yes, sir."

"I told you once to forget that you know that man's name, and I meant it. The reason is simply that I don't want to hear his name because he is the only man on earth that I'm afraid of. I'm not afraid he'll hurt me; I'm afraid of what he may someday force me to do to keep him from hurting me. You heard what I told Mr. Sperling."

"Okay. But I'm the bookkeeper. What do I put it under, X?"

"Don't put it. First, go through it. As you do so you might as well count it, but the point is to see if there is anything there besides money. Leave ten thousand dollars in the safe. I'll need it soon, tomorrow probably, for something that can't appear in our records. For your information only, it will be for Mr. Jones. Take the remainder to a suburban bank, say somewhere in New Jersey, and put it in a safe deposit box which you will rent under an assumed name. If you need a reference, Mr. Parker will do. After what happened Sunday night—we'll be prepared for contingencies. If we ever meet him head on and have to cut off from here and from everyone we know, we'll need supplies. I hope I never touch it. I hope it's still there when I die, and if so it's yours."

"Thank you very much. I'll be around eighty then and I'll need it."

"You're welcome. Now for this afternoon. First, what about the pictures you took up there?"

"Six o'clock. That was the best they could do."

"And the keys?"

"You said after lunch. They'll be ready at one-thirty."

"Good. Saul will be here at two?"

"Yes, sir."

"Have Fred and Orrie here this evening after dinner. I don't think you'll need them this afternoon; you and Saul can manage. This is what we want. There must—"

But that was postponed by the arrival of Doc Vollmer. Doc's home and office were on our street, toward Tenth Avenue, and over the years we had used his services for everything from stitching up Dora Chapin's head to signing a certificate that Wolfe was batty. When he called he always went to one of the smaller yellow chairs because of his short legs, sat, took off his spectacles and looked at them, put them on again, and asked, "Want some pills?"

Today he added, "I'm afraid I'm in a hurry."

"You always are," Wolfe said, in the tone he uses only to the few people he really likes. "Have you read about the Rony case?"

"Of course. Since you're involved in it—or were."

"I still am. The body is at the morgue in White Plains. Will you go there? You'll have to go to the District Attorney's office first to get yourself accredited. Tell them I sent you, and that I have been engaged by one of Mr. Rony's associates. If they want more than that they can phone me, and I'll try to satisfy them. You want to examine the body—not an autopsy, merely superficially, to determine whether he died instantly or was left to suffer a prolonged agony. What I really want you to inspect is his head, to see if there is any indication that he was knocked out by a blow before the car ran over him. I know the chance of finding anything conclusive is remote, but I wish you'd try, and there'll be no grumbling about your charge for the trip."

Vollmer blinked. "It would have to be done this afternoon?"

"Yes, sir."

"Have you any idea what weapon might have been used?"

"No, sir."

"According to the papers he had no family, no relatives at all. Perhaps I should know whom I'm representing—one of his professional associates?"

"I'll answer that if they ask it. You're representing me."

"I see. Anything to be mysterious." Vollmer stood up. "If one of my patients dies while I'm gone—" He left it hanging and trotted out, making me move fast to get to the front door in time to open it for him. His habit of leaving like that, as soon as he had all he really needed, was one of the reasons Wolfe liked him.

I returned to the office.

Wolfe leaned back. "We have only ten minutes until lunch. Now this afternoon, for you and Saul . . ."

15

The locksmith soaked me $8.80 for eleven keys. That was about double the market, but I didn't bother to squawk because I knew why: he was still collecting for a kind of a lie he had told a homicide dick six years ago at my suggestion. I think he figured that he and I were fellow crooks and therefore should divvy.

Even with keys it might have taken a little maneuvering if Louis Rony had lived in an apartment house with a doorman and elevator man, but as it was there was nothing to it. The address on East Thirty-seventh Street was an old five-story building that had been done over in good style, and in the downstairs vestibule was a row of mailboxes, push buttons, and perforated circles for reception on the speaking tube. Rony's name was at the right end, which meant the top floor. The first key I tried was the right one, and Saul and I entered, went to the self-service elevator, and pushed the button marked 5. It was the best kind of setup for an able young man with a future like Rony, who had probably had visitors of all kinds at all hours.

Upstairs it was the second key I tried that worked. Feeling that I was the host, in a way, I held the door open for Saul to precede me and then followed him in. We were at the center of a hall, not wide and not very long. Turning right, toward the street front, we stepped into a fairly large room with modern furniture that matched, bright-colored rugs that had been cleaned not long ago, splashy colored pictures on the walls, a good supply of books, and a fireplace.

"Pretty nice," Saul remarked, sending his eyes around. One difference between Saul and me is that I sometimes have to look twice at a thing to be sure I'll never lose it, but once will always do for him.

"Yeah," I agreed, putting my briefcase on a chair. "I understand the tenant has given it up, so maybe you could rent it." I got the rubber gloves from the briefcase and handed him a pair. He started putting them on.

"It's too bad," he said, "you didn't keep that membership card

Sunday night when you had your hands on it. It would have saved trouble. That's what we want, is it?"

"It's our favorite." I began on the second glove. "We would buy anything that looks interesting, but we'd love a souvenir of the American Communist party. The best bet is a safe of some kind, but we won't hop around." I motioned to the left. "You take that side."

It's a pleasure to work with Saul because I can concentrate completely on my part and pay no attention to him. We both like a searching job, when it's not the kind where you have to turn couches upside down or use a magnifying glass, because when you're through you've got a plain final answer, yes or no. For that room, on which we spent a good hour, it was no. Not only was there no membership certificate, there was nothing at all that was worth taking home to Wolfe. The only thing resembling a safe was a locked bond box, which one of the keys fitted, in a drawer of the desk, and all it contained was a bottle of fine liqueur Scotch, McCrae's, half full. Apparently that was the one item he didn't care to share with the cleaning woman. We left the most tedious part, flipping through the books, to the last, and did it together. There was nothing in any of them but pages.

"This bird trusted nobody," Saul complained.

In our next objective, the bedroom, which was about half the size of the front room, Saul darted a glance around and said, "Thank God, no books."

I agreed heartily. "We ought to always bring a boy along for it. Flipping through books is a hell of a way to earn a living for grownups."

The bedroom didn't take as long, but it produced as little. The further we went the more convinced I got that Rony had either never had a secret of any kind, or had had so many dangerous ones that no cut and dried precautions would do, and in view of what had happened to the plant rooms the choice was easy. By the time we finished with the kitchenette, which was about the size of Wolfe's elevator, and the bathroom, which was much larger and spick-and-span, the bottle of Scotch locked in the bond box, hidden from the cleaning woman, struck me as pathetic—the one secret innocent enough to let into his home.

Thinking that that notion showed how broad-minded I was, having that kind of a feeling even for a grade A bastard like Rony, I thought I should tell Saul about it. The gloves were back in the briefcase and the briefcase under my arm, and we were in the hall, headed for the door, ready to leave. I never got the notion fully explained to Saul on account of an interruption. I was just reaching for the doorknob, using my handkerchief, when the sound of the elevator came, stopping at that floor, and then its door opening. There was no question as to which apartment someone was headed for because there was only one to a floor. There were steps outside, and the sound of a key being inserted in the lock, but by the time it was turned and the door opened Saul and I were in the bathroom, with its door closed to leave no crack, but unlatched.

A voice said, not too loud, "Anybody here?" It was Jimmy Sperling.

Another voice said, lower but with no sign of a tremble in it, "Are you sure this is it?" It was Jimmy's mother.

"Of course it is," Jimmy said rudely. It was the rudeness of a guy scared absolutely stiff. "It's the fifth floor. Come on, we can't just stand here."

Steps went to the front, to the living room. I whispered to Saul to tell him who they were, and added, "If they came after something they're welcome to anything they find."

I opened the door to a half-inch crack, and we stood and listened. They were talking and, judging from other sounds, they weren't anything like as methodical and efficient as Saul and I had been. One of them dropped a drawer on the floor, and a little later something else hit that sounded more like a picture. Still later it must have been a book, and that was too much for me. If Saul and I hadn't been so thorough it might have been worth while to wait it out, on the chance that they might find what they were after and we could ask them to show us before they left; but to stand there and let them waste their time going through those books when we had just flipped every one of them—it was too damn silly. So I opened the bathroom door, walked down the hall into the living room, and greeted them.

"Hello there!"

Some day I'll learn. I thought I had Jimmy pretty well tagged. I have a rule never to travel around on homicide business without a shoulder holster, but my opinion of Jimmy was such that I didn't bother to transfer the gun to my pocket or hand. However, I have read about mothers protecting their young, and have also run across it now and then, and I might at least have been more alert. Not that a gun in my hand would have helped any unless I had been willing to slam it against her skull. Happening to be near the arch when I entered, she had only a couple of yards to come, just what she needed to get momentum.

She came at me like a hurricane, her hands straight for my face, screeching at the top of her voice, "Run run run!"

It didn't make any sense, but a woman in that condition never does. Even if I had been alone, and she had been able to keep me busy enough long enough for her son to make a getaway, what of it? Since I was neither a killer nor a cop, my only threat was the discovery that Jimmy was there, and since I had already seen him she couldn't peel that off of me no matter how long her fingernails were. However, she tried, and her first wild rush got her in so close that she actually reached my face. Feeling the stinging little streak of one of her nails, I stiff-armed her out of range, and would merely have kept her off that way if it hadn't been for Jimmy, who had been at the other side of the room when I entered. Instead of dashing in to support Mom's attack, he was standing there by the table pointing a gun. At the sight of the gun, Saul, following me in, had stopped just inside the arch to think it over, and I didn't blame him, for Jimmy's right hand, which held the gun, was anything but steady, which meant there was no way of telling what might happen next.

I lunged at Mom, and before she knew it she was hugged tight against me. She couldn't even wriggle, though she tried. With my chin dug into her shoulder, I spoke to Jimmy.

"I can snap her in two, and don't think I won't. Do you want to hear her spine crack? Drop it. Just open your fingers and let it fall."

"Run run run!" Mom was screeching as well as she could with me squeezing the breath out of her.

"Here we go," I said. "It'll hurt but it won't last long."

Saul walked over and tapped Jimmy's wrist underneath, and the gun fell to the floor. Saul picked it up and backed off. Jimmy started for me. When the distance was right I threw his mother at him. Then she was in his arms instead of mine, and for the first time she saw Saul. The damn fool actually hadn't known I wasn't alone until then.

"Go look at your face," Saul told me.

I went to the bathroom and looked in the mirror, and was sorry I had let her off so easy. It started just below my left eye and went straight down a good three inches. I dabbed cold water on it, looked for a styptic and found none, and took a damp towel back to the living room with me. Jimmy and Mom were at bay over by the table, and Saul, with Jimmy's gun, was at ease near the arch.

I complained. "What for?" I demanded. "All I said was hello. Why the scratching and shooting?"

"He didn't shoot," Mrs. Sperling said indignantly.

I waved it aside. "Well, you sure scratched. Now we've got a problem. We can search your son all right, that's easy, but how are we going to search you?"

"Try searching me," Jimmy said. His voice was mean and his face was mean. I had tagged him as the one member of the family who didn't count one way or another, but now I wasn't so sure.

"Nuts," I told him. "You're sore because you didn't have the guts to shoot, which shows how thick you are. Sit down on that couch, both of you." I used the damp towel on my face. They didn't move. "Will I have to come and sit you?"

Mom pulled at his arm and they went to the couch, sidewise, and sat. Saul dropped the gun in his pocket and took a chair.

"You startled us, Andy," Mom said. "That was all. I was so startled I didn't recognize you."

It was a nice little touch that no man would ever have thought of. She was putting us back on our original basis, when I had been merely a welcome guest at her home.

I refused to revert. "My name's Archie now, remember? And you've fixed me so that no one will recognize me. You certainly react strong to being startled." I moved a chair and sat. "How did you get in here?"

"Why, with a key!"

"Where did you get it?"

"Why, we—we had one—"

"How did *you* get in?" Jimmy demanded.

I shook my head at him. "That won't get you anywhere. I suppose you know that your father fired Mr. Wolfe. We now have another client, one of Rony's associates. Do you want to make a point of this? Like calling a cop? I thought not. Where did you get the key?"

"None of your damn business!"

"I just told you," Mom said reproachfully, "we had one."

Having quit using logic on women the day I graduated from high school, I skipped that. "We have a choice," I informed them. "I can phone the precinct and get a pair of city detectives here, a male and a female, to go over you and see what you came after, which would take time and make a stink, or you can tell us—by the way, I believe you haven't met my friend and colleague, Mr. Saul Panzer. That's him on the chair. Also by the way, don't you ever go to the movies? Why don't you wear gloves? You've left ten thousand prints all over the place. Or you can tell us where you got the key and what you came for—only it will have to be good. One reason you might prefer us is that we don't really have to search you, because you were still looking, so you haven't found it."

They looked at each other.

"May I make a suggestion?" Saul inquired.

"Yes indeed."

"Maybe they'd rather have us phone Mr. Sperling, to ask—"

"No!" Mom cried.

"Much obliged," I thanked Saul. "You remind me of Mr. Wolfe." I returned to them. "Now it will have to be even better. Where did you get the key?"

"From Rony," Jimmy muttered sullenly.

"When did he give it to you?"

"A long while ago. I've had it—"

"That's a swell start," I said encouragingly. "He had something here, or you thought he had, which you wanted so much that you two came here to get it the first possible chance after he died, but he gave you a key long ago so you could drop in for it someday while he was at his office. Mr. Panzer and I don't care for that. Try another one."

They exchanged glances.

"Why don't you try this?" I suggested. "That you borrowed it from your younger sister, and—"

"You sonofabitch," Jimmy growled, rising and taking a step. "No, I didn't shoot, but by God—"

"You shouldn't get nasty, Andy," Mom protested.

"Then give us something better." I had drawn my feet back for leverage in case Jimmy kept coming, but he didn't. "Whatever it is, remember we can always check it with Mr. Sperling."

"No you can't!"

"Why not?"

"Because he knows nothing about it! I'm just going to tell you the truth! We persuaded the janitor to lend us a key."

"How much did it take to persuade him?"

"I offered—I gave him a hundred dollars. He'll be downstairs in the hall when we go out, to see that we don't take anything."

"You got a bargain," I declared, "unless he intends to frisk you. Don't you think we ought to meet him, Saul?"

"Yes."

"Then get him. Bring him up here."

Saul went. As the three of us sat and waited Mom suddenly asked, "Does your face hurt, Andy?"

I thought of three replies, all good, but settled for a fourth because it was shortest.

"Yes," I said.

When the outside door opened again I stood up, thinking that the janitor's arrival would make it two to two, even not counting Mom, and he might be an athlete. But as soon as I saw him I sat down again. He was a welterweight, his expansion would have been not more than half of Madeline's, and his eyes refused to lift higher than a man's knees.

"His name's Tom Fenner," Saul informed me. "I had to take hold of him."

I eyed him. He eyed my ankles. "Look," I told him, "this can be short and simple. I represent an associate of Mr. Rony. As far as I know these people have done no harm here, and I'll see that they don't. I don't like to get people into trouble if I don't have to. Just show me the hundred bucks they gave you."

"Jeez, I never saw a hundred bucks," Fenner squeaked. "Why would they give me a hundred bucks?"

"To get a key to this apartment. Come on, let's see it."

"They never got a key from me. I'm in charge here. I'm responsible."

"Quit lying," Jimmy snapped.

"Here's the key," Mom said, displaying it. "You see, that proves it!"

"Give it here." Fenner took a step. "Let me take a look at it."

I reached for his arm and swiveled him. "Why drag it out? No matter how brave and strong you are, three of us could probably hold you while the lady goes through your pockets. Save time and energy, Mac. Maybe they planted it on you when you weren't looking."

He was so stubborn and game that his eyes got nearly as high as my knees before he surrendered. Then they dropped again, and

his hand went into his pants pocket and emerged with a tight little
roll between his fingers. I took it and unrolled it enough to see a
fifty, two twenties, and a ten, and offered it back. That was the only
time his eyes got higher; they came clear up to mine, wildly astonished.

"Take it and beat it," I told him. "I just wanted a look. Wait a
minute." I went to get the key from Mom and handed that to him
too. "Don't lend it again without phoning me first. I'll lock up when
I leave."

He was speechless. The poor goof didn't have enough wits left
even to ask my name.

When he had gone Saul and I sat down again. "You see," I said
genially, "we're easily satisfied as long as we get the truth. Now we
know how you got in. What did you come for?"

Mom had it ready and waiting, having been warned it was going
to be required. "You remember," she said, "that my husband thought
Louis was a Communist?"

I said I did.

"Well, we still thought so—I mean, after what Mr. Wolfe told us
Monday afternoon. We still thought so."

"Who is we?"

"My son and I. We talked it over and we still thought so. Today
when my husband told us that Mr. Wolfe didn't believe what Webster said in his statement and it might mean more trouble about it,
we thought if we came here and found something to prove that
Louis was a Communist and showed it to Mr. Wolfe, then it would
be all right."

"It would be all right," I asked, "because if he was a Communist
Mr. Wolfe wouldn't care who or what killed him? Is that it?"

"Of course, don't you see?"

I asked Saul, "Do you want it?"

"Not even as a gift," he said emphatically.

I nodded. I switched to Jimmy. "Why don't you take a stab at
it? The way your mother's mind works makes it hard for her. What
have you got to offer?"

Jimmy's eyes still looked mean. They were straight at mine. "I
think," he said glumly, "that I was a boob to stumble in here like
this."

"Okay. And?"

"I think you've got us, damn you."

"And?"

"I think we've got to tell you the truth. If we don't—"

"Jimmy!" Mom gripped his arm. "*Jimmy!*"

He ignored her. "If we don't you'll only think it's something worse. You brought my sister's name into this, insinuating she had a key to this apartment. I'd like to push that down your throat, and maybe I will some day, but I think we've got to tell you the truth, and I can't help it if it concerns her. She wrote him some letters—not the kind you might think—but anyhow my mother and I knew about them and we didn't want them around. So we came here to get them."

Mom let go of his arm and beamed at me. "That was it!" she said eagerly. "They weren't really bad letters, but they were—personal. You know?"

If I had been Jimmy I would have strangled her. The way he had told it, at least it wasn't incredible, but her gasping at him when he said he was going to tell the truth, and then reacting that way when he went on to tell it, was enough to make you wonder how she ever got across a street. However, I met her beam with a deadpan. From the expression of Jimmy's eyes I doubted if another squeeze would produce more juice, and if not, it ought to be left that their truth was mine. So my deadpan was replaced with a sympathetic grin.

"About how many letters?" I asked Jimmy, just curious.

"I don't know exactly. About a dozen."

I nodded. "I can see why you wouldn't want them kicking around, no matter how innocent they were. But either he destroyed them or they're some place else. You won't find them here. Mr. Panzer and I have been looking for some papers—nothing to do with your sister or you—and we know how to look. We had just finished when you arrived, and you can take it from me that there's no letter from your sister here—let alone a dozen. If you want me to sign a statement on that I'd be glad to."

"You might have missed them," Jimmy objected.

"*You* might," I corrected him. "Not us."

"The papers you were looking for—did you find them?"

"No."

"What are they?"

"Oh, just something needed for settling his affairs."

"You say they don't concern—my family?"

"Nothing to do with your family as far as I know." I stood up. "So

I guess that ends it. You leave empty-handed and so do we. I might add that there will be no point in my reporting this to Mr. Sperling, since he's no longer our client and since you seem to think it might disturb him."

"That's very nice of you, Andy," Mom said appreciatively. She arose to come to inspect me. "I'm so sorry about your face!"

"Don't mention it," I told her. "I shouldn't have startled you. It'll be okay in a couple of months." I turned. "You don't want that gun, do you, Saul?"

Saul took it from his pocket, shook the cartridges into his palm, and went to Jimmy and returned his property.

"I don't see," Mom said, "why we can't stay and look around some more, just to make sure about those letters."

"Oh, come on," Jimmy said rudely.

They went.

Saul and I followed soon after. On our way down in the elevator he asked, "Did any of that stick at all?"

"Not on me. You?"

"Nope. It was hard to keep my face straight."

"Do you think I should have kept on trying?"

He shook his head. "There was nothing to pry him loose with. You saw his eyes and his jaw."

Before leaving I had gone to the bathroom for another look at my face, and it was a sight. But the blood had stopped coming, and I don't mind people staring at me if they're female, attractive, and between eighteen and thirty; and I had another errand in that part of town. Saul went with me because there was a bare possibility that he could help. It's always fun to be on a sidewalk with him because you know you are among those present at a remarkable performance. Look at him and all you see is just a guy walking along, but I honestly believe that if you had shown him any one of those people a month later and asked him if he had ever seen that man before, it would have taken him not more than five seconds to reply, "Yes, just once, on Wednesday, June twenty-second, on Madison Avenue between Thirty-ninth and Fortieth Streets." He has got me beat a mile.

As it turned out he wasn't needed for the errand. The building directory on the wall of the marble lobby told us that the offices of Murphy, Kearfot and Rony were on the twenty-eighth floor, and we took the express elevator. It was the suite overlooking the ave-

nue, and everything was up to beehive standard. After one glance
I had to reconsider my approach because I hadn't expected that
kind of a setup. I told the receptionist, who was past my age limit
and looked good and tough, that I wanted to see a member of the
firm, and gave my name, and went to sit beside Saul on a leather
couch that had known a million fannies. Before long another one, a
good match for the receptionist only older, appeared to escort me
down a hall and into a corner room with four big double windows.

A big broad-shouldered guy with white hair and deep-set blue
eyes, seated at a desk even bigger than Wolfe's, got up to shake
hands with me.

"Archie Goodwin?" he rumbled cordially, as if he had been waiting for this for years. "From Nero Wolfe's office? A pleasure. Sit
down. I'm Aloysius Murphy. What can I do for you?"

Not having mentioned any name but mine to the receptionist, I
felt famous. "I don't know," I told him, sitting. "I guess you can't
do anything."

"I could try." He opened a drawer. "Have a cigar?"

"No, thanks. Mr. Wolfe has been interested in the death of your
junior partner, Louis Rony."

"So I understand." His face switched instantly from smiling welcome to solemn sorrow. "A brilliant career brutally snipped as it was
bursting into flower."

That sounded to me like Confucius, but I skipped it. "A damn
shame," I agreed. "Mr. Wolfe has a theory that the truth may be
holding out on us."

"I know he has. A very interesting theory."

"Yeah, he's looking into it a little. I guess I might as well be frank.
He thought there might be something around Rony's office—some
papers, anything—that might give us a hint. The idea was for me to
go and look. For instance, if there were two rooms and a stenographer in one of them, I could fold her up—probably gag her and
tie her—if there was a safe I could stick pins under her nails
until she gave me the combination—and really do a job. I brought
a man along to help, but even with two of us I don't see how we
can—"

I stopped because he was laughing so hard he couldn't hear
me. You might have thought I was Bob Hope and had finally
found a new one. When I thought it would reach him I protested
modestly, "I don't deserve all that."

He tapered off to a chuckle. "I should have met you long ago," he declared. "I've been missing something. I want to tell you, Archie, and you can tell Wolfe, you can count on us here—all of us—for anything you want." He waved a hand. "The place is yours. You won't have to stick pins in us. Louis's secretary will show you anything, tell you anything—all of us will. We'll do everything we can to help you get at the truth. For a high-minded man truth is everything. Who scratched your face?"

He was getting on my nerves. He was so glad to have met me at last, and was so anxious to help, that it took me a full five minutes to break loose and get out of the room, but I finally made it.

I marched back to the reception room, beckoned to Saul, and, as soon as we were outside the suite, told him, "The wrong member of the firm got killed. Compared to Aloysius Murphy, Rony was the flower of truth."

16

The pictures came out pretty well, considering. Since Wolfe had told me to order four prints of each, there was about half a bushel. That evening after dinner, as Saul and I sat in the office inspecting and assorting them, it seemed to me there were more of Madeline than I remembered taking, and I left most of them out of the pile we were putting to one side for Wolfe. There were three good ones of Rony—one full-face, one three-quarters, and one profile—and one of the shots of the membership card was something to be proud of. That alone should have got me a job on *Life*. Webster Kane wasn't photogenic, but Paul Emerson was. I remarked on that fact to Wolfe as I went to put his collection on his desk. He grunted. I asked if he was ready for my report for the afternoon, and he said he would go through the pictures first.

Paul Emerson was one of the causes for the delay on my report. Saul and I had got back to the office shortly after six, but Wolfe's schedule had been shattered by the emergency on the roof, and he didn't come down until 6:28. At that minute he strode in, turned the radio on and dialed to WPIT, went to his chair behind the desk, and sat with his lips tightened.

The commercial came, and the introduction, and then Emerson's acid baritone:

> This fine June afternoon it is no pleasure to have to report that the professors are at it again—but then they always are—oh, yes, you can count on the professors. One of them made a speech last night at Boston, and if you have anything left from last week's pay you'd better hide it under the mattress. He wants us not only to feed and clothe everybody on earth, but educate them also. . . .

Part of my education was watching Wolfe's face while Emerson was broadcasting. His lips, starting fairly tight, kept getting tighter and tighter until there was only a thin straight hairline and his cheeks were puffed and folded like a contour map. When the tension got to a certain point his mouth would pop open, and in a moment close, and it would start over again. I used it to test my powers of observation, trying to spot the split second for the pop.

Minutes later Emerson was taking a crack at another of his pet targets:

> . . . they call themselves World Federalists, this bunch of amateur statesmen, and they want us to give up the one thing we've got left—the right to make our own decisions about our own affairs. They think it would be fine if we had to ask permission of all the world's runts and funny looking dimwits every time we wanted to move our furniture around a little, or even to leave it where it is. . . .

I anticipated the pop of Wolfe's mouth by three seconds, which was par. I couldn't expect to hit it right on the nose. Emerson developed that theme a while and then swung into his finale. He always closed with a snappy swat at some personality whose head was temporarily sticking up from the mob.

> Well, friends and fellow citizens, a certain so-called genius has busted loose again right here in New York, where I live only because I have to. You may have heard of this fat fantastic creature who goes by the good old American name of Nero Wolfe. Just before I went on the air we received here at the studio a press release from a firm of midtown lawyers—a firm which is now minus a partner because one of them, a man named Louis Rony, got killed in an automobile accident Monday night. The authorities have investigated thoroughly and

properly, and there is no question about its being an accident or about who was responsible. The authorities know all about it, and so does the public, which means you.

But this so-called genius knows more than everybody else put together—as usual. Since the regrettable accident took place on the property of a prominent citizen—a man whom I have the honor to know as a friend and as a great American—it was too good a chance for the genius to miss, to get some cheap publicity. The press release from the firm of lawyers states that Nero Wolfe intends to pursue his investigation of Rony's death until he learns the truth. How do you like that? What do you think of this insolent abuse of the machinery of justice in a free country like ours? If I may be permitted to express an opinion, I think we could get along very well without that kind of a genius in our America.

Among four-legged brutes there is a certain animal which neither works for its food nor fights for it. A squirrel earns its acorns, and a beast of prey earns its hard-won meal. But this animal skulks among the trees and rocks and tall grass, looking for misfortune and suffering. What a way to live! What a diet that is, to eat misfortune! How lucky we are that it is only among four-legged brutes that we may find such a scavenger as that!

Perhaps I should apologize, my friends and fellow citizens, for this digression into the field of natural history. Good-by for another ten days. Tomorrow, and for the remainder of my vacation, Robert Burr will be with you again in my place. I had to come to town today, and the temptation to come to the studio and talk to you was too much for me. Here is Mr. Griswold for my sponsor.

Another voice, as cordial and sunny as Emerson's was acid, began telling us of the part played by Continental Mines Corporation in the greatness of America. I got up and crossed to the radio to turn it off.

"I hope he spelled your name right," I remarked to Wolfe. "What do you know? He went to all that trouble right in the middle of his vacation just to give you a plug. Shall we write and thank him?"

No reply. Obviously that was no time to ask if he wanted our report for the afternoon, so I didn't. And later, after dinner, as I have said, he decided to do a survey of the pictures first.

He liked them so much that he practically suggested I should quit detective work and take up photography. There were thirty-eight different shots in the collection I put on his desk. He rejected nine of them, put six in his top drawer, and asked for all four prints of the other twenty-three. As Saul and I got them together I noticed that he had no outstanding favorites. All the family and guests were well represented, and of course the membership card was included. Then they all had to be labeled on the back and placed in separate envelopes, also labeled. He put a rubber band around them and put them in his top drawer.

Again the report got postponed, this time by the arrival of Doc Vollmer. He accepted Wolfe's offer of a bottle of beer, as he always did when he called in the evening, and after it had been brought by Fritz and his throat was wet he told his story. His reception at White Plains had been neither warm nor cold, he said, just business-like, and after a phone call to Wolfe an Assistant DA had escorted him to the morgue. As for what he had found, the best he could do was a guess. The center of the impact of the car's wheels had been the fifth rib, and the only sign of injury higher on Rony than that was a bruise on the right side of his head, above the ear. Things that had happened to his hips and legs showed that they had been under the car, so his head and shoulders must have been projecting beyond the wheels. It was possible that the head bruise had been caused by contact with the gravel of the drive, but it was also possible that he had been struck on the head with something and knocked out before the car ran over him. If the latter, the instrument had not been something with a sharp edge, or with a limited area of impact like the head of a hammer or wrench, but neither had it had a smooth surface like a baseball bat. It had been blunt and rough and heavy.

Wolfe was frowning. "A golf club?"

"I shouldn't think so."

"A tennis racket?"

"Not heavy enough."

"A piece of iron pipe?"

"No. Too smooth."

"A piece of a branch from a tree with stubs of twigs on it?"

"That would be perfect if it were heavy enough." Vollmer swallowed some beer. "Of course all I had was a hand glass. With the hair and scalp under a microscope some evidence might be found. I suggested that to the Assistant District Attorney, but he showed no enthusiasm. If there had been an opportunity to snip off a piece

I would have brought it home with me, but he didn't take his eyes off of me. Now it's too late because they were ready to prepare the body for burial."

"Was the skull cracked?"

"No. Intact. Apparently the medical examiner had been curious too. The scalp had been peeled back and replaced."

"You couldn't swear that he had probably been knocked down before the car struck him?"

"Not 'probably.' I could swear he had been hit on the head, and that the blow might have been struck while he was still erect—as far as my examination went."

"Confound it," Wolfe grumbled. "I hoped to simplify matters by forcing those people up there to do some work. You did all you could, Doctor, and I'm grateful." He turned his head. "Saul, I understand that Archie gave you some money for safekeeping the other evening?"

"Yes, sir."

"Have you got it with you?"

"Yes, sir."

"Please give it to Doctor Vollmer."

Saul got an envelope from his pocket, took some folded bills from it, and stepped to Vollmer to hand them over.

Doc was puzzled. "What's this for?" he asked Wolfe.

"For this afternoon, sir. I hope it's enough?"

"But—I'll send a bill. As usual."

"If you prefer it, certainly. But if you don't mind I wish you'd take my word for it that it is peculiarly fitting to pay you with that money for examining Mr. Rony's head in an effort to learn the truth about his death. It pleases my fancy if it doesn't offend yours. Is it enough?"

Doc unfolded the bills and took a look. "It's too much."

"Keep it. It should be that money, and all of it."

Doc stuck it in his pocket. "Thanks. Anything to be mysterious." He picked up his beer glass. "As soon as I finish this, Archie, I'll take a look at your face. I knew you'd try to close in too fast some day."

I replied suitably.

After he had gone I finally reported for Saul and me. Wolfe leaned back and listened to the end without interrupting. In the middle of it Fred Durkin and Orrie Cather arrived, admitted by Fritz, and I waved them to seats and resumed. When I explained why I hadn't insisted on something better than Jimmy's corny tale about letters Gwenn had written Rony, in spite of the way Mom had scrambled it for him, Wolfe nodded in approval, and when I explained why I had walked out of the law office of Murphy, Kearfot and Rony without even trying to look in a wastebasket, he nodded again. One reason I like to work for him is that he never rides me for not acting the way he would act. He knows what I can do and that's all he ever expects; but he sure expects that.

When I got to the end I added, "If I may make a suggestion, why not have one of the boys find out where Aloysius Murphy was at nine-thirty Monday evening? I'd be glad to volunteer. I bet he's a D and a Commie both, and if he didn't kill Rony he ought to be framed for it. You ought to meet him."

Wolfe grunted. "At least the afternoon wasn't wasted. You didn't find the membership card."

"Yeah, I thought that was how you'd take it."

"And you met Mrs. Sperling and her son. How sure are you that he invented those letters?"

I shrugged. "You heard me describe it."

"You, Saul?"

"Yes, sir. I agree with Archie."

"Then that settles it." Wolfe sighed. "This is a devil of a mess." He looked at Fred and Orrie. "Come up closer, will you? I've got to say something."

Fred and Orrie moved together, but not alike. Fred was some bigger than Orrie. When he did anything at all, walk or talk or reach for something, you always expected him to trip or fumble, but he never did, and he could tail better than anybody I knew except Saul, which I would never understand. Fred moved like a bear, but Orrie like a cat. Orrie's strong point was getting people to tell him things. It wasn't so much the questions he asked. As a matter of fact, he wasn't very good at questions; it was just the way he looked at them. Something about him made people feel that he ought to be told things.

Wolfe's eyes took in the four of us. He spoke.

"As I said, we're in a mess. The man we were investigating has been killed, and I think he was murdered. He was an outlaw and a blackguard, and I owe him nothing. But I am committed, by circumstances I prefer not to disclose, to find out who killed him and why, and, if it was murder, to get satisfactory evidence. We may find that the murderer is one who, by the accepted standards, deserves to live as richly as Mr. Rony deserved to die. I can't help that; he must be found. Whether he must also be exposed I don't know. I'll answer that question when I am faced by it, and that will come only when I am also facing the murderer."

Wolfe turned a hand over. "Why am I giving you this lecture? Because I need your help and will take it only on my own terms. If you work with me on this and we find what we're looking for, a murderer, with the required evidence, any one or all of you may know all that I know, or at least enough to give you a right to share in the decision: what to do about it. That's what I won't accept. I reserve that right solely to myself. I alone shall decide whether to expose him, and if I decide not to, I shall expect you to concur; and if you concur you will be obliged to say or do nothing that will conflict with my decision. You'll have to keep your mouths shut, and that is a burden not to be lightly assumed. So before we get too far I'm giving you this chance to stay out of it."

He pressed a button on his desk. "I'll drink some beer while you think it over. Will you have some?"

Since it was the first group conference we had had for a long time, all five of us, I thought it should be done right, so I went to the kitchen, and Fritz and I collaborated. It was nothing fancy—a bourbon and soda for Saul, and gin fizzes for Orrie and me, and beer for Fred Durkin and Wolfe. Straight rye with no chaser was Fred's drink, but I had never been able to talk him out of the notion that he would offend Wolfe if he didn't take beer when invited. So while the rest of us sat and enjoyed what we liked, Fred sipped away at what I had heard him call slop.

Since they were supposed to be thinking something over, they tried to look thoughtful, and I tactfully filled in by giving Wolfe a few sidelights on the afternoon, such as the bottle of Scotch Rony had kept in the bond box. But it was too much for Saul, who hated to mark time. When his highball was half gone he lifted the glass, drained it, put it down, and spoke to Wolfe.

"What you were saying. If you want me to work on this, all I expect is to get paid. If I get anything for you, then it's yours. My mouth doesn't need any special arrangement to keep it shut."

Wolfe nodded. "I know you're discreet, Saul. All of you are. But this time what you'll get for me may be evidence that would convict a murderer if it were used, and there's a possibility that it may not be used. That would be a strain."

"Yes, sir. I'll make out all right. If you can stand it I can."

"What the hell," Fred blurted. "I don't get it. What do you think we'd do, play pattycake with the cops?"

"It's not that," Orrie told him impatiently. "He knows how we like cops. Maybe you never heard about having a conscience."

"Never did. Describe it to me."

"I can't. I'm too sophisticated to have one and you're too primitive."

"Then there's no problem."

"There certainly isn't." Orrie raised his glass. "Here's to crime, Mr. Wolfe. There's no problem." He drank.

Wolfe poured beer. "Well," he said, "now you know what this is like. The contingency I have described may never arise, but it had to be foreseen. With that understood we can proceed. Unless we have some luck this could drag on for weeks. Mr. Sperling's adroit stroke in persuading a man of standing to sign that confounded statement, not merely a chauffeur or other domestic employee, has made it excessively difficult. There is one possibility which I shall have explored by a specialist—none of you is equipped for it—but meanwhile we must see what we can find. Archie, tell Fred about the people who work there. All of them."

I did so, typing the names for him. If my week end at Stony Acres had been purely social I wouldn't have been able to give him a complete list, from the butler to the third assistant gardener, but during the examinations Monday night and Tuesday morning I had got well informed. As I briefed Fred on them he made notes on the typed list.

"Anyone special?" Fred asked Wolfe.

"No. Don't go to the house. Start at Chappaqua, in the village, wherever you can pick up a connection. We know that someone in that house drugged a drink intended for Mr. Rony on Saturday evening, and we are assuming that someone wanted him to die enough to help it along. When an emotion as violent as that is loose in a group of people there are often indications of it that are heard or seen by servants. That's all I can tell you."

"What will I be in Chappaqua for?"

"Whatever you like. Have something break on your car, something that takes time, and have it towed to the local garage. Is there a garage in Chappaqua, Archie?"

"Yes, sir."

"That will do." Wolfe drank the last of his beer and used his handkerchief on his lips. "Now Saul. You met young Sperling to-day."

"Yes, sir. Archie introduced us."

"We want to know what he and his mother were looking for at Mr. Rony's apartment. It was almost certainly a paper, since they were looking in books, and probably one which had supported a threat held by Mr. Rony over young Sperling or his mother. That conjecture is obvious and even trite, but things get trite by occurring frequently. There is a clear pattern. A month ago Mrs. Sperling reversed herself and readmitted Mr. Rony to her home as a friend of her daughter, and the son's attitude changed at the same time. A threat could have been responsible for that, especially since the main objection to Mr. Rony was then based on a mere surmise by Mr. Sperling. But Monday afternoon they were told something which so blackened Mr. Rony as to make him quite unacceptable. Yet the threat still existed. You see where that points."

"What blackened him?" Saul asked.

Wolfe shook his head. "I doubt if you need that, at least not now. We want to know what the threat was, if one existed. That's for you and Orrie, with you in charge. The place to look is here in New York, and the son is far more likely than the mother, so try him first —his associates, his habits—but for that you need no suggestions from me. It's as routine as Fred's job, but perhaps more promising. Report as usual."

That finished the conference. Fred got the rest of his beer down, not wanting to offend Wolfe by leaving some. I got money for them from the safe, from the cash drawer, not disturbing the contribution from our latest client. Fred had a couple of questions and got them answered, and I went to the front door to let them out.

Back in the office, Fritz had entered to remove glasses and bottles. I stood and stretched and yawned.

"Sit down," Wolfe said peevishly.

"You don't have to take it out on me," I complained, obeying. "I can't help it if you're a genius, as Paul Emerson says, but the best you can do is to sick Fred on the hired help and start Saul and Orrie hunting ratholes. God knows I have no bright suggestions, but then I'm not a genius. Who is my meat? Aloysius Murphy? Emerson?"

He grunted. "The others replied to the question I put. You didn't."

"Nuts. My worry about this murderer, if there is one, is not what you'll do with him after you get him, but whether you're going to get him." I gestured. "If you do, he's yours. Get him two thousand volts or a DSO—as you please. Will you need my help?"

"Yes. But you may be disqualified. I told you last week to establish a personal relationship."

"So you did. So I did."

"But not with the right person. I would like to take advantage of your acquaintance with the elder Miss Sperling, but you may balk. You may have scruples."

"Much obliged. It would depend on the kind of advantage. If all I'm after is facts, scruples are out. She knows I'm a detective and she knows where we stand, so it's up to her. If it turns out that she killed Rony I'll help you pin the medal on her. What is it you want?"

"I want you to go up there tomorrow morning."

"Glad to. What for?"

He told me.

17

Like all good drivers, I don't need my mind for country driving, just my eyes and ears and reflexes. So when we're on a case and I'm at the wheel of the car in the open, I'm usually gnawing away at the knots. But as I rolled north on the parkways that fine sunny June morning I had to find something else to gnaw on, because in that case I couldn't tell a knot from a doughnut. There was no puzzle to it; it was merely a grab bag. So I let my mind skip around as it pleased, now and then concentrating on the only puzzle in sight, which was this: had Wolfe sent me up here because he thought I might really get something, or merely to get me out of the way while he consulted his specialist? I didn't know. I took it for granted that the specialist was Mr. Jones, whom I had never been permitted to meet, though Wolfe had made use of him on two occasions that I knew of. Mr. Jones was merely the name he had given me offhand when I had had to make an entry in the expense book.

On the phone I had suggested to Madeline that it might be more tactful for me to park outside the entrance and meet her somewhere on the grounds, and she replied that when it got to where she had to sneak me in she would rather I stayed out. I didn't insist, because my errand would take me near the house anyway, and Sperling would be away, at his office in New York, and I doubted if Jimmy or Mom would care to raise a howl at sight of me since we were now better acquainted. So I turned in at the entrance and drove on up to the house, and parked on the plaza behind the shrubbery, at the exact spot I had chosen before.

The sun was shining and birds were twittering and leaves and flowers were everywhere in their places, and Madeline, on the west terrace, had on a cotton print with big yellow butterflies on it. She came to meet me, but stopped ten feet off to stare.

"My Lord," she exclaimed, "that's exactly what I wanted to do! Who got ahead of me?"

"That's a swell attitude," I said bitterly. "It hurts."

"Certainly it does, that's why we do it." She had advanced and was inspecting my cheek at close range. "It was a darned good job. You look simply awful. Hadn't you better go and come back in a week or two?"

"No, ma'am."

"Who did it?"

"You'd be surprised." I tilted my head to whisper in her ear. "Your mother."

She laughed a nice little laugh. "She might do the other side, at that, if you get near her. You should have seen her face when I told her you were coming. How about a drink? Some coffee?"

"No, thanks. I've got work to do."

"So you said. What's this about a wallet?"

"It's not really a wallet, it's a card case. In summer clothes, without enough pockets, it's a problem. You told me it hadn't been found in the house, so it must be outdoors somewhere. When we were out looking for your sister Monday night it was in my hip pocket, or it was when we started, and in all the excitement I didn't miss it until yesterday. I've got to have it because my license is in it."

"Your driving license?"

I shook my head. "Detective license."

"That's right, you're a detective, aren't you? All right, come on." She moved. "We'll take the same route. What does it look like?"

Having her along wasn't part of my plan. "You're an angel," I told her. "You're a little cabbage. In that dress you remind me of a girl I knew in the fifth grade. I'm not going to let you ruin it scrambling around hunting that damn card case. Leave me but don't forget me. If and when I find it I'll let you know."

"Not a chance." She was smiling with a corner of her mouth up. "I've always wanted to help a detective find something, especially you. Come on!"

She was either onto me or she wasn't, but in any case it was plain that she had decided to stay with me. I might as well pretend that nothing would please me better, so I did.

"What does it look like?" she asked as we circled the house and started to cross the lawn toward the border.

Since the card case was at that moment in my breast pocket, the simplest way would have been to show it to her, but under the circumstances I preferred to describe it. I told her it was pigskin, darkened by age, and four inches by six. It wasn't to be seen on the lawn. We argued about where we had gone through the shrubbery, and I let her win. It wasn't there either, and a twig whipped my wounded cheek as I searched beneath the branches. After we had passed through the gate into the field we had to go slower because the grass was tall enough to hide a small object like a card case. Naturally I felt foolish, kicking around three or four blocks away from where I wanted to be, but I had told my story and was stuck with it.

We finally finished with the field, including the route around the back of the outbuildings, and the inside of the barn. As we neared the vicinity of the house from the other direction, the southwest, I kept bearing left, and Madeline objected that we hadn't gone that way. I replied that I had been outdoors on other occasions than our joint night expedition, and went still further left. At last I was in bounds. Thirty paces off was a clump of trees, and just the other side of it was the graveled plaza where my car was parked. If someone had batted Rony on the head, for instance with a piece of a branch of a tree with stubs of twigs on it, before running the car over him, and if he had then put the branch in the car and it was still there when he drove back to the house to park, and if he had been in a hurry and the best he could do was give the branch a toss, it might have landed in the clump of trees or near by. That cluster of ifs will indicate the kind of errand Wolfe had picked for me. Searching the grounds for a likely weapon was a perfectly sound routine idea, but it needed ten trained men with no inhibitions, not a pretty girl in a cotton print looking for a card case and a born hero pretending he was doing likewise.

Somebody growled something that resembled "Good morning."

It was Paul Emerson. I was nearing the edge of the clump of trees, with Madeline not far off. When I looked up I could see only the top half of Emerson because he was standing on the other side of my car and the hood hid the rest of him. I told him hello, not expansively.

"This isn't the same car," he stated.

"That's right," I agreed. "The other one was a sedan. That's a convertible. You have a sharp eye. Why, did you like the sedan better?"

"I suppose," he said cuttingly, "you have Mr. Sperling's permission to wander around here?"

"I'm here, Paul," Madeline said sweetly. "Maybe you couldn't see me for the trees. My name's Sperling."

"I'm not wandering," I told him. "I'm looking for something."

"What?"

"You. Mr. Wolfe sent me to congratulate you on your broadcast yesterday. His phone's been busy ever since, people wanting to hire him. Would you mind lying down so I can run the car over you?"

He had stepped around the front of the hood and advanced, and I had emerged from the clump of trees. Within arm's reach he stood, his nose and a corner of his mouth twitching, and his eyes boring into me.

"There are restrictions on the air," he said, "that don't apply here. The animal I had in mind was the hyena. The ones with four legs are never fat, but those with two legs sometimes are. Your boss is. You're not."

"I'll count three," I said. "One, two, three." With an open palm I slapped him on the right cheek, and as he rocked I straightened him up with one on the left. The second one was a little harder, but not at all vicious. I turned and moved, not in haste, back among the trees. When I got to the other edge of the clump Madeline was beside me.

"That didn't impress me much," she declared, in a voice that wanted to tremble but didn't. "He's not exactly Joe Louis."

I kept moving. "These things are relative," I explained. "When your sister called Mr. Wolfe a cheap filthy little worm I didn't even shake a finger at her, let alone slap her. But the impulse to wipe his sneer off would have been irresistible even if he hadn't said a word and even if he had been only half the size. Anyway, it didn't leave a mark on him. Look what your mother did to me, and I wasn't sneering."

She wasn't convinced. "Next time do it when I'm not there. Who did scratch you?"

"Paul Emerson. I was just getting even. We'll never find that card case if you don't help me look."

An hour later we were side by side on the grass at the edge of the brook, a little below the bridge, discussing lunch. Her polite position was that there was no reason why I shouldn't go to the house for it, and I was opposed. Lunching with Mrs. Sperling and Jimmy, whom I had caught technically breaking and entering, with Webster Kane, whom Wolfe had called a liar, and with Emerson, whom I had just smacked on both cheeks, didn't appeal to me on the whole. Besides, my errand now looked hopeless. I had covered, as well as I could with company along, all the territory from the house to the bridge, and some of it beyond the bridge, and I could take a look at the rest of it on the way out.

Madeline was manipulating a blade of grass with her teeth, which were even and white but not ostentatious. "I'm tired and hungry," she stated. "You'll have to carry me home."

"Okay." I got to my feet. "If it starts me breathing fast and deep don't misunderstand."

"I will." She tilted her head back to look up at me. "But first why don't you tell me what you've been looking for? Do you think for one minute I'd have kept panting around with you all morning if I had thought it was only a card case?"

"You haven't panted once. What's wrong with a card case?"

"Nothing." She spat out the blade of grass. "There's nothing wrong with my eyes, either. Haven't I seen you? Half the time you've been darting into places where you couldn't possibly have lost a card case or anything else. When we came down the bank to the brook I expected you to start looking under stones." She waved a hand. "There's thousands of 'em. Go to it." She sprang to her feet and shook out her skirt. "But carry me home first. And on the way you'll tell me what you've been looking for or I'll tear your picture out of my scrapbook."

"Maybe we can make a deal," I offered. "I'll tell you what I've been looking for if you'll tell me what your idea was Tuesday afternoon. You may remember that you might have seen or heard something Monday evening that could have given you a notion about someone using my car, but you wouldn't tell me because you wanted to save your father some dough. That reason no longer holds, so why not tell me now?"

She smiled down at me. "You never let go, do you? Certainly I'll tell you. I saw Webster Kane on the terrace about that time, and if he hadn't used the car himself I thought he might have seen someone going to it or coming back."

"No sale. Try again."

"But that was it!"

"Oh, sure it was." I got to my feet. "It's lucky it happened to be Kane who signed that statement. You're a very lucky girl. I think I'll have to choke you. I'll count three. One, two—"

She sprinted up the bank and waited for me at the top. Going back up the drive, she got fairly caustic because I insisted that all I had come for was the card case, but when we reached the parking plaza and I had the door of the car open, she gave that up to end on the note she had greeted me with. She came close, ran a fingertip gently down the line of my scratch, and demanded, "Tell me who did that, Archie. I'm jealous!"

"Some day," I said, climbing in and pushing the starter button, "I'll tell you everything from the cradle on."

"Honest?"

"Yes, ma'am." I rolled away.

As I steered the curves down the drive my mind was on several things at once. One was a record just set by a woman. I had been with Madeline three hours and she hadn't tried to pump me with a single question about what Wolfe was up to. For that she deserved some kind of a mark, and I filed it under unfinished business. Another was a check on a point that Wolfe had raised. The brook made a good deal of noise. It wasn't the kind you noticed unless you listened, but it was loud enough so that if you were only twenty feet from the bridge, walking up the drive, and it was nearly dark, you might not hear a car coming down the drive until it was right on you. That was a point in support of Webster Kane's confession, and therefore a step backward instead of forward, but it would have to be reported to Wolfe.

However, the thing in the front of my mind was Madeline's remark that she had expected me to start looking under stones. It should have occurred to me before, but anyway it had now, and, not being prejudiced like Wolfe, I don't resent getting a tip from a woman. So I went on through the entrance onto the public highway, parked the car at the roadside, got a magnifying glass from the medicine case, walked back up the drive to the bridge, and stepped down the bank to the edge of the brook.

There certainly were thousands of stones, all shapes and sizes, some partly under water, more along the edge and on the bank. I shook my head. It was a perfectly good idea, but there was only one of me and I was no expert. I moved to a new position and looked some more. The stones that were in the water all had smooth surfaces, and the high ones were dry and light-colored, and the low ones were dark and wet and slippery. Those on the bank, beyond the water, were also smooth and dry and light-colored until they got up to a certain level, where there was an abrupt change and they were rough and much darker—a greenish gray. Of course the dividing line was the level of the water in the spring when the brook was up.

Good for you, I thought, you've made one hell of a discovery and now you're a geologist. All you have to do now is put every damn rock under the glass, and along about Labor Day you'll be ready to report. Ignoring my sarcasm, I went on looking. I moved along the edge of the brook, stepping on stones, until I was underneath the bridge, stood there a while, and moved again, upstream from the bridge. By that time my eyes had caught onto the idea and I didn't have to keep reminding them.

It was there, ten feet up from the bridge, that I found it. It was only a few inches from the water's edge, and was cuddled in a nest of larger stones, half hidden, but when I had once spotted it it was as conspicuous as a scratched cheek. About the size of a coconut, and something like one in shape, it was rough and greenish gray, whereas all its neighbors were smooth and light-colored. I was so excited I stood and gawked at it for ten seconds, and when I moved, with my eyes glued on it for fear it would take a hop, I stepped on a wiggler and nearly took a header into the brook.

One thing sure, that rock hadn't been there long.

I bent over double so as to use both hands to pick it up, touching it only with the tips of four fingers, and straightened to take a look. The best bet would of course be prints, but one glance showed that to be an outside chance. It was rough all over, hundreds of little indentations, with not a smooth spot anywhere. But I still held it with my fingertips, because while prints had been the best bet they were by no means the only one. I was starting to turn, to move away from the brook to better footing, when a voice came from right behind me.

"Looking for hellgrammites?"

I swiveled my head. It was Connie Emerson. She was close enough to reach me with a stretched arm, which would have meant that she was an expert at the silent approach, if it hadn't been for the noise of the brook.

I grinned at the clear strong blue of her eyes. "No, I'm after gold."

"Really? Let me see—"

She took a step, lit on a stone with a bad angle, gave a little squeal, and toppled into me. Not being firmly based, over I went, and I went clear down because I spent the first tenth of a second trying to keep my fingertip hold on my prize, but I lost it anyway. When I bounced up to a sitting position Connie was sprawled flat, but her head was up and she was stretching an arm in a long reach for something, and she was getting it. My greenish gray stone had landed less than a foot from the water, and her fingers were ready to close on it. I hate to suspect a blue-eyed blonde of guile, but if she had it in mind to toss that stone in the water to see it splash all she needed was another two seconds, so I did a headlong slide over the rocks and brought the side of my hand down on her forearm. She let out a yell and jerked the arm back. I scrambled up and got erect, with my left foot planted firmly in front of my stone.

She sat up, gripping her forearm with her other hand, glaring at me. "You big ape, are you crazy?" she demanded.

"Getting there," I told her. "Gold does it to you. Did you see that movie, *Treasure of Sierra Madre?*"

"Damn you." She clamped her jaw, held it a moment, and released it. "Damn you, I think you broke my arm."

"Then your bones must be chalk. I barely tapped it. Anyway, you nearly broke my back." I made my voice reasonable. "There's too much suspicion in this world. I'll agree not to suspect you of meaning to bump me if you'll agree not to suspect me of meaning to tap your arm. Why don't we move off of these rocks and sit on the grass and talk it over? Your eyes are simply beautiful. We could start from there."

She pulled her feet in, put a hand—not the one that had reached for my stone—on a rock for leverage, got to her feet, stepped carefully across the rocks to the grass, climbed the bank, and was gone.

My right elbow hurt, and my left hip. I didn't care for that, but there were other aspects of the situation that I liked even less. Counting the help, there were six or seven men in and around the house, and if Connie told them a tale that brought them all down to the brook it might get embarrassing. She had done enough harm as it was, making me drop my stone. I stooped and lifted it with my fingertips again, got clear of the rocks and negotiated the bank, walked down the drive and on out to the car, and made room for the stone in the medicine case, wedged so it wouldn't roll around.

I didn't stop for lunch in Westchester County, either. I took to the parkways and kept going. I didn't feel really elated, since I might have got merely a stray hunk of granite, not Exhibit A at all, and I didn't intend to start crowing unless and until. So when I left the West Side Highway at Forty-sixth Street, as usual, I drove first to an old brick building in the upper Thirties near Ninth Avenue. There I delivered the stone to Mr. Weinbach, who promised they would do their best. Then I drove home, went in and found Fritz in the kitchen, ate four sandwiches—two sturgeon and two home-baked ham—and drank a quart of milk.

18

When I swallowed the last of the milk it wasn't five o'clock yet, and it would be more than an hour before Wolfe came down from the plant rooms, which was just as well since I needed to take time out for an overhaul. In my room up on the third floor I stripped. There was a long scrape on my left knee and a promising bruise on my left hip, and a square inch of skin was missing from my right elbow. The scratch on my cheek was developing nicely, getting new ideas about color every hour. Of course it might have been worse, at least nobody had run a car over me; but I was beginning to feel that it would be a welcome change to take on an enemy my own sex and size. I certainly wasn't doing so well with women. In addition to the damage to my hide, my best Palm Beach suit was ruined, with a big tear in the sleeve of the coat. I showered, iodined, bandaged, dressed, and went down to the office.

A look in the safe told me that if I was right in supposing that the specialist to be hired was Mr. Jones, he hadn't been hired yet, for the fifty grand was still all there. That was a deduction from a limited experience. I had never seen the guy, but I knew two things about him: that it was through him that Wolfe had got the dope on a couple of Commies that had sent them up the river, and that when you bought from him you paid in advance. So either it wasn't to be him or Wolfe hadn't been able to reach him yet.

I had been hoping for a phone call from Weinbach before Wolfe descended at six o'clock, but it didn't come. When Wolfe entered, got seated behind his desk, and said "Well?" I thought I was still undecided about including the stone in my report before hearing from Weinbach, but he had to know about Connie, so I kept on to the end. I did not, however, tell him that it was a remark of Madeline's that made me think of stones, thinking it might irritate him to know that a woman had helped out.

He sat frowning.

"I was a little surprised," I said smugly, "that you didn't think of a stone yourself. Doc Volmer said something rough and heavy."

"Pfui. Certainly I thought of a stone. But if he used a stone all he had to do was walk ten paces to the bridge and toss it into the water."

"That's what he thought. But he missed the water. Lucky I didn't take the attitude you did. If I hadn't—"

The phone rang. A voice that hissed its esses was in my ear. Weinbach of the Fisher Laboratories hissed his esses. Not only that, he told me who he was. As I motioned to Wolfe to get on, I was holding my breath.

"That stone you left with me," Weinbach said. "Do you wish the technical terms?"

"I do not. I only want what I asked for. Is there anything on it to show it was used, or might have been used, to slam a man on the head?"

"There is."

"What!" I hadn't really expected it. "There is?"

"Yes. Everything is dried up, but there are four specks that are bloodstains, five more that may be bloodstains, one minute piece of skin, and two slightly larger pieces of skin. One of the larger pieces has an entire follicle. This is a preliminary report and none of it can be guaranteed. It will take forty-eight hours to complete all the tests."

"Go to it, brother! If I was there I'd kiss you."

"I beg your pardon?"

"Forget it. I'll get you a Nobel Prize. Write the report in red ink."

I hung up and turned to Wolfe. "Okay. He was murdered. Connie did it or knows who did. She knew about the stone. She stalked me. I should have established a personal relationship with her and brought her down here. Do you want her? I'll bet I can get her."

"Good heavens, no." His brows had gone up. "I must say, Archie, satisfactory."

"Don't strain yourself."

"I won't. But though you used your time well, to the purpose you were sent for, all you got was corroboration. The stone proves that Mr. Kane's statement was false, that Mr. Rony was killed deliberately, and that one of those people killed him, but there's nothing new in that for us."

"Excuse me," I said coldly, "for bringing in something that doesn't help."

"I don't say it doesn't help. If and when this gets to a courtroom, it will unquestionably help there. Tell me again what Mrs. Emerson said."

I did so, in a restrained manner. Looking back now, I can see that he was right, but at the time I was damn proud of that stone.

Since it gives the place an unpleasant atmosphere for one of us to be carrying a grudge, I thought it would be better if I got even immediately, and I did so by not eating dinner with him, giving as a reason my recent consumption of sandwiches. He loves to talk when he's eating, business being taboo, so as I sat alone in the office, catching up with the chores, my humor kept getting better, and by the time he rejoined me I was perfectly willing to speak to him—in fact, I had thought up a few comments about the importance of evidence in criminal cases which would have been timely and appropriate.

I had to put off making them because he was still getting himself arranged to his after-dinner position in his chair when the doorbell rang and, Fritz being busy with the dishes, I went to answer it. It was Saul Panzer and Orrie Cather. I ushered them into the office. Orrie got comfortable, with his legs crossed, and took out a pipe and filled it, while Saul sat erect on the front half of the big red leather chair.

"I could have phoned," Saul said, "but it's a little complicated and we need instructions. We may have something and we may not."

"The son or the mother?" Wolfe asked.

"The son. You said to take him first." Saul took out a notebook and glanced at a page. "He knows a lot of people. How do you want it, dates and details?"

"Sketch it first."

"Yes, sir." Saul closed the notebook. "He spends about half his time in New York and the rest all over. Owns his own airplane, a Mecklin, and keeps it in New Jersey. Belongs to only one club, the Harvard. Has been arrested for speeding twice in the past three years, once—"

"Not a biography," Wolfe protested. "Just items that might help."

"Yes, sir. You might possibly want this: he has a half interest in a restaurant in Boston called the New Frontier. It was started in nineteen forty-six by a college classmate, and young Sperling furnished the capital, around forty thousand, probably from his father, but that's not—"

"A night club?"

"No, sir. High-class, specializing in sea food."

"A failure?"

"No, sir. Successful. Not spectacular, but going ahead and showed a good profit in nineteen forty-eight."

Wolfe grunted. "Hardly a good basis for blackmail. What else?"

Saul looked at Orrie. "You tell him about the Manhattan Ballet."

"Well," Orrie said, "it's a bunch of dancers that started two years ago. Jimmy Sperling and two other guys put up the dough, and I haven't found out how much Jimmy's share was, but I can. They do modern stuff. The first season they quit town after three weeks in a dump on Forty-eighth Street, and tried it in the sticks, but that wasn't so good either. This last season they opened in November at the Herald Theater and kept going until the end of April. Everybody thinks the three angels got all their ante back and then some, but that will take checking. Anyhow they did all right."

It was beginning to sound to me as if we were up against a new one. I had heard of threats to tell a rich man how much his son had sunk, but not to tell how much his son was piling up. My opinion of Jimmy needed some shuffling.

"Of course," Orrie went on, "when you think of ballet you think of girls with legs. This ballet has got 'em all right; that's been checked. Jimmy is interested in ballet or why would he kick in? He goes twice a week when he's in New York. He also is personally interested in seeing that the girls get enough to eat. When I got that far I naturally thought I was on the way to something, and maybe I am but not yet. He likes the girls and they like him, but if that has led to anything he wouldn't want put in the paper it'll have to wait for another installment because I haven't caught up to it yet. Shall I keep trying?"

"You might as well." Wolfe went to Saul. "Is that all you have?"

"No, we've got plenty," Saul told him, "but nothing you might want except maybe the item I wanted to ask about. Last fall he contributed twenty thousand dollars to the CPBM."

"What's that?"

"Committee of Progressive Business Men. One of the funny fronts. It was for Henry A. Wallace for President."

"Indeed." Wolfe's eyes, which had been nearly closed, had opened a little. "Tell me about it."

"I can't tell you much, because it was afternoon when I scared it up. Apparently nobody was supposed to know about the contribution, but several people do, and I think I can get onto them if you say so. That's what I wanted to ask about. I had a break and got a line on a man in the furniture business who was pro-Wallace at first but later broke loose. He claims to know all about Sperling's contribution. He says Sperling made it in a personal check for twenty thousand, which he gave to a man named Caldecott one Thursday evening, and the next morning Sperling came to the CPBM office and wanted his check back. He wanted to give it in cash instead of a check. But he was too late because the check had already been deposited. And here's what I thought made it interesting: this man says that since the first of the year photostats of three different checks—contributions from three other people—have turned up in peculiar circumstances. One of them was his own check, for two thousand dollars, but he wouldn't give me the names of the other two."

Wolfe's brow was wrinkled. "Does he say that the people run-ning the organization had the photostats made for later use—in peculiar circumstances?"

"No, sir. He thinks some clerk did it, either for personal use or as a Republican or Democratic spy. This man says he is now a political hermit. He doesn't like Wallace, but he doesn't like Republicans or Democrats either. He says he's going to vote the Vegetarian ticket next time but go on eating meat. I let him talk. I wanted to get all I could because if there was a photostat of young Sperling's check—"

"Certainly. Satisfactory."

"Shall I follow up?"

"By all means. Get all you can. The clerk who had the photostats made would be a find." Wolfe turned to me. "Archie. You know that young man better than we do. Is he a ninny?"

"If I thought so," I said emphatically, "I don't now. Not if he's raking in profits on a Boston restaurant and a Manhattan ballet. I misjudged him. Three to one I know where the photostat of Jimmy's check is. In a safe at the office of Murphy, Kearfot and Rony."

"I suppose so. Anything else, Saul?"

I wouldn't have been surprised if the next item had been that Jimmy had cleaned up a million playing the ponies or running a chicken farm, but evidently he hadn't tried them yet. Saul and Orrie stayed a while, long enough to have a drink and discuss ways and means of laying hands on the Republican or Democratic spy, and then left. When I returned to the office after letting them out I con-sidered whether to get rid of the comments I had prepared regard-ing the importance of evidence in criminal cases, and decided to skip it.

I would just as soon have gone up to bed to give my bruises a rest, but it was only half past nine and my middle drawer was stuffed with memos and invoices connected with the repairs on the roof. I piled them on the desk and tackled them. It had begun to look as if Wolfe's estimate of the amount of the damage wasn't far off, and maybe too low if you included replacement of some of the rarer hybrids that had got rough treatment. Wolfe, seeing what I was at, offered to help, and I moved the papers over to his desk. But, as I had often discovered before, a man shouldn't try to run a detective business and an orchid factory at the same time. They're always tripping over each other. We hadn't been at the papers five minutes when the doorbell rang. I usually go when it's after nine o'clock, the hour when Fritz changes to his old slippers, so I went.

I switched on the stoop light, looked through the one-way glass panel, opened the door, said, "Hello, come in," and Gwenn Sperling crossed the threshold.

I closed the door and turned to her. "Want to see the worm?" I gestured. "That way."

"You don't seem surprised!" she blurted.

"It's my training. I hide it to impress you. Actually I'm overcome. That way?"

She moved and I followed. She entered the office, advanced three steps, and stopped, and I detoured around her.

"Good evening, Miss Sperling," Wolfe said pointedly. He indicated the red leather chair. "That's the best chair."

"Did I phone you I was coming?" she demanded.

"I don't think so. Did she, Archie?"

"No, sir. She's just surprised that we're not surprised."

"I see. Won't you sit down?"

For a second I thought she was going to turn and march out, as she had that afternoon in the library, but if the motion had been made she voted it down. Her eyes left Wolfe for a look at me, and I saw them stop at my scratched cheek, but she wasn't enough interested to ask who did it. She dropped her fur neckpiece onto a yellow chair, went to the red leather one and sat, and spoke.

"I came because I couldn't persuade myself not to. I want to confess something."

My God, I thought, I hope she hasn't already signed a statement. She looked harassed but not haggard, and her freckles showed hardly at all in that light.

"Confessions often help," Wolfe said, "but it's important to make them to the right person. Am I the one?"

"You're just being nice because I called you a worm!"

"That would be a strange reason for being nice. Anyhow, I'm not. I'm only trying to help you get started."

"You don't need to." Gwenn's hands were clasped tight. "I've decided. I'm a conceited nosy little fool!"

"You use too many adjectives," Wolfe said dryly. "For me it was cheap filthy little worm. Now, for you, it is conceited nosy little fool. Let's just say fool. Why? What about?"

"About everything. About Louis Rony. I knew darned well I wasn't really in love with him, but I thought I'd teach my father something. If I hadn't had him there he wouldn't have thought he could pique me by playing with Connie Emerson, and she wouldn't have played with him, and he wouldn't have got killed. Even if everything you said about him is true, it's my fault he got killed, and what am I going to do?"

Wolfe grunted. "I'm afraid I don't follow you. How was it your fault that Mr. Kane went to mail some letters and accidentally ran over Mr. Rony?"

She stared. "But you know that's not true!"

"Yes, but you don't—or do you?"

"Of course I do!" Her hands came unclasped. "I may be a fool, I guess I can't go back on that, but I've known Webster a long time and I know he couldn't possibly do such a thing!"

"Anyone can have an accident."

"I know they can; I don't mean that. But if he had run a car over Louis and saw he was dead, he would have gone back to the house, straight to a phone, and called a doctor and the police. You've met him. Couldn't you see he was like that?"

This was a new development, a Sperling trying to persuade Wolfe that Kane's statement was a phony.

"Yes," Wolfe said mildly, "I thought I saw he was like that. Does your father know you're here?"

"No. I—I didn't want to quarrel with him."

"It won't be easy to avoid it when he finds out. What made you decide to come?"

"I wanted to yesterday, and I didn't. I'm a coward."

"A fool and a coward." Wolfe shook his head. "Don't rub it in. And today?"

"I heard someone say something. Now I'm an eavesdropper too. I used to be when I was a child, but I thought I was completely over it. Today I heard Connie saying something to Paul, and I stayed outside the door and listened."

"What did she say?"

Gwenn's face drew together. I thought she was going to cry, and so did she. That would have been bad, because Wolfe's wits leave him when a woman cries.

I snapped at her, "What did you drive down here for?"

She pulled out of it and appealed to Wolfe. "Do I have to tell you?"

"No," he said curtly.

Naturally that settled it. She proceeded to tell. She looked as if she would rather eat soap, but she didn't stammer any.

"They were in their room and I was going by. But I didn't just happen to overhear it; I stopped and listened deliberately. She hit him or he hit her, I don't know which—with them you don't know who is doing the hitting unless you see it. But she was doing the talking. She told him that she saw Goodwin—" Gwenn looked at me. "That was you."

"My name's Goodwin," I admitted.

"She said she saw Goodwin finding a stone by the brook and she tried to get it and throw it in the water, but Goodwin knocked her down. She said Goodwin had the stone and would take it to Nero Wolfe, and she wanted to know what Paul was going to do, and he said he wasn't going to do anything. She said she didn't care what happened to him but she wasn't going to have her reputation ruined if she could help it, and then he hit her, or maybe she hit him. I thought one of them was coming to the door and I ran down the hall."

"When did this happen?" Wolfe growled.

"Just before dinner. Dad had just come home, and I was going to tell him about it, but I decided not to because I knew he must have got Webster to sign that statement, and he's so stubborn—I knew what he would say. But I couldn't just not do anything. I knew it was my fault Louis got killed, and after what you told us about him it didn't matter about him but it did about me. I guess that sounds selfish, but I've decided that from now on I'm going to be perfectly honest. I'm going to be honest to everyone about everything. I'm going to quit being a fake. Take the way I acted the day you came. I should have just phoned Louis and told him I didn't want to see him any more, that would have been the honest thing and that was what I really wanted to do; but no, I didn't do that, I had to phone him to come and meet me so I could tell him face to face—and what happened? I honestly believe I was hoping that someone would listen in on one of the extensions so they would know how fine and noble I was! I knew Connie did that all the time, and maybe others did too. Anyhow someone did, and you know what happened. It was just as if I had phoned him to come and get killed!"

She stopped for breath. Wolfe suggested, "You may be taking too much credit, Miss Sperling."

"That's a nasty crack." She wasn't through. "I couldn't say all this to my father or mother, not even to my sister, because—well, I couldn't. But I wasn't going to start being honest by hiding the worst thing I ever did. I thought it over very carefully, and I decided you were the one person who would know exactly what I meant. You knew I was afraid of you that afternoon, and you told me so. I think it was the first time anyone really understood me."

I had to keep back a snort. A fine freckled girl saying that to Wolfe with me present was approaching the limit. If there was anything on earth he didn't understand and I did, it was young women.

"So," Gwenn went on, "I had to come and tell you. I know you can't do anything about it, because Dad got Webster to sign that statement, and that ends it, but I felt I had to tell someone, and then when I heard what Paul and Connie said I knew I had to. But you've got to understand that I'm being absolutely honest. If this was me the way I was a year ago or a week ago I'd be pretending that I only came because I think I owe it to Louis to help to bring out the truth about how he died, but if he was the kind of man you said he was I don't really believe I owe him anything. It's only that if I'm going to be a genuine straightforward person I have to start now or I never will. I don't want ever to be afraid of anyone again, not even you."

Wolfe shook his head. "You're expecting a good deal of yourself. I'm more than twice your age, and up with you in self-esteem, but I'm afraid of someone. Don't overdo it. There are numerous layers of honesty, and the deepest should not have a monopoly. What else was said by Mr. and Mrs. Emerson?"

"Just what I told you."

"Nothing more—uh, informative?"

"I told you everything I heard. I don't—" She stopped, frowning. "Didn't I? About his calling her an idiot?"

"No."

"He did. When she said that about her reputation. He said, 'You idiot, you might as well have told Goodwin you killed him, or that you knew I did.' Then she hit him—or he hit her."

"Anything else?"

"No. I ran."

"Had you already suspected that Mr. Emerson had murdered Mr. Rony?"

"Why, I—" Gwenn was shocked. "I don't suspect that now. Do I?"

"Certainly you do. You merely hadn't put it so baldly. You may have got to honesty, Miss Sperling, but there is still sagacity. If I understand you, and you say I do, you think that Mr. Emerson killed Mr. Rony because he was philandering with Mrs. Emerson. I don't believe it. I've heard some of Mr. Emerson's broadcasts, and met him at your home, and I consider him incapable of an emotion so warm and direct and explosive. You said I can do nothing about Mr. Rony's death. I think I can, and I intend to try, but if I find myself reduced to so desperate an assumption as that Mr. Emerson was driven to kill by jealousy of his wife, I'll quit."

"Then—" Gwenn was frowning at him. "Then what?"

"I don't know. Yet." Wolfe put his hands on the edge of his desk, pushed his chair back, and arose. "Are you going to drive back home tonight?"

"Yes. But—"

"Then you'd better get started. It's late. Your newborn passion for honesty is admirable, but in that, as in everything, moderation is often best. It would have been honest to tell your father you were coming here; it would be honest to tell him where you have been when you get home; but if you do so he will think that you have helped me to discredit Mr. Kane's statement, and that would be false. So a better honesty would be to lie and tell him you went to see a friend."

"I did," Gwenn declared. "You *are* a friend. I want to stay and talk."

"Not tonight." Wolfe was emphatic. "I'm expecting a caller. Some other time." He added hastily, "By appointment, of course."

She didn't want to go, but what could the poor girl do? After I handed her her neckpiece she stood and prolonged it a little, with questions that got answers in one syllable, but finally made the best of it.

When she had gone I proceeded immediately to tell Wolfe what I thought of him. "You couldn't possibly ask for a better chance," I protested hotly. "She may not be Miss America 1949, but she's anything but an eyesore, and she'll inherit millions, and she's nuts about you. You could quit work and eat and drink all day. Evenings you could explain how well you understand her, which is apparently all she asks for. You're hooked at last, and it was about time." I extended a paw. "Congratulations!"

"Shut up." He glanced at the clock.

"In a minute. I approve of your lie about expecting a caller. That's the way to handle it, tease her on with the hard to get—"

"Go to bed. I *am* expecting a caller."

I eyed him. "Another one?"

"A man. I'll let him in. Put this stuff away and go to bed. At once."

That had happened not more than twice in five years. Once in a while I get sent out of the room, and frequently I am flagged to get off of my phone, when something is supposed to be too profound for me, but practically never am I actually chased upstairs to keep me from even catching a glimpse of a visitor.

"Mr. Jones?" I asked.

"Put this stuff away."

I gathered up the papers from his desk and returned them to my drawer before telling him, "I don't like it, and you know I don't. One of my functions is keeping you alive." I started for the safe. "What if I come down in the morning and find you?"

"Some morning you may. Not this one. Don't lock the safe."

"There's fifty grand in it."

"I know. Don't lock it."

"Okay, I heard you. The guns are in my second drawer but not loaded."

I told him good night and left him.

19

In the morning three-tenths of the fifty grand was no longer there. Fifteen thousand bucks. I told myself that before I died I must manage at least a look from a distance at Mr. Jones. A guy who could demand that kind of dough for piecework, and collect in advance, was something not to be missed.

When I arose at seven I had had only five hours' sleep. I had not imitated Gwenn and taken to eavesdropping, but I certainly didn't intend to snooze peacefully while Wolfe was down in the office with a character so mysterious I couldn't be allowed to see him or hear him. Therefore, not undressing, I got the gun I keep on my bed table and went to the hall and sat at the top of the stairs. From there, two flights up, I heard his arrival, and voices in the hall—Wolfe's and one other—and the office door closing, and then, for nearly three hours, a faint mumble that I had to strain my ears to catch at all. For the last hour of it I had to resort to measures to keep myself awake. Finally the office door opened and the voices were louder, and in half a minute he had gone and I heard Wolfe's elevator. I beat it to my room. After my head touched the pillow I tossed and turned for nearly three seconds.

In the morning my custom is not to enter the office until after my half an hour in the kitchen with Fritz and food and the morning paper, but that Friday I went there first and opened the safe. Wolfe is not the man to dish out fifteen grand of anybody's money without having a clear idea of what for, so it seemed likely that something might need attention at any moment, and when, a little after eight, Fritz came down from taking Wolfe's breakfast tray up to him, I fully expected to be told that I was wanted on the second floor. Nothing doing. According to Fritz, my name hadn't been mentioned. At the regular time, three minutes to nine, then at my desk in the office, I heard the sound of the elevator ascending. Apparently his sacred schedule, nine to eleven in the plant rooms, was not to be interrupted. He and Theodore were now handling the situation, no more outside help being needed.

There was one little cheep from him. Shortly after nine the house phone buzzed. He asked if any of the boys had called and I said no, and he said that when they did I was to call them off. I asked if that included Fred, and he said yes, all of them. I asked if there were fresh instructions, and he said no, just tell them to quit.

That was all for then. I spent two hours with the morning mail and the accumulation in my drawer. At 11:02 he entered, told me good morning as he always did no matter how much we had talked on the phone, got installed behind his desk, and inquired grumpily, "Is there anything you must ask me?"

"Nothing I can't hold, no, sir."

"Then I don't want to be interrupted. By anyone."

"Yes, sir. Are you in pain?"

"Yes. I know who killed Mr. Rony, and how and why."

"You do. Does it hurt?"

"Yes." He sighed deep. "It's the very devil. When you know all you need to know about a murderer, what is ordinarily the easiest thing to prove?"

"That's a cinch. Motive."

He nodded. "But not here. I doubt if it can be done. You have known me, in the past, to devise a stratagem that entailed a hazard. Haven't you?"

"That's understating it. I have known you to take chances that have given me nightmares."

"They were nothing to this. I have devised a stratagem and spent fifteen thousand dollars on it. But if I can think of a better way I'm not going to risk it." He sighed again, leaned back, closed his eyes, and muttered, "I don't want to be disturbed."

That was the last of him for more than nine hours. I don't think he uttered more than eighty words between 11:09 in the morning and 8:20 in the evening. While he was in the office he sat with his eyes closed, his lips pushing out and in from time to time, and his chest expanding every now and then, I would say five inches, with a deep sigh. At the table, during lunch and dinner, there was nothing wrong with his appetite, but he had nothing to offer in the way of conversation. At four o'clock he went up to the plant rooms for his customary two hours, but when I had occasion to ascend to check on a few items with Theodore, Wolfe was planted in his chair in the potting room, and Theodore spoke to me only in a whisper. I have never been able to get it into Theodore's head that when Wolfe is concentrating on a business problem he wouldn't hear us yelling right across his nose, so long as we don't try to drag him into it.

Of the eighty words he used during those nine hours, only nine of them—one to an hour—had to do with the stratagem he was working on. Shortly before dinner he muttered at me, "What time is Mr. Cohen free in the evening?"

I told him a little before midnight.

When, in the office after dinner, he once more settled back and shut his eyes, I thought my God, this is going to be Nero Wolfe's last case. He's going to spend the rest of his life at it. I had myself done a good day's work and saw no sense in sitting on my fanny all evening listening to him breathe. Considering alternatives, and deciding for Phil's and a few games of pool, I was just opening my mouth to announce my intention when Wolfe opened his.

"Archie. Get Mr. Cohen down here as soon as possible. Ask him to bring a *Gazette* letterhead and envelope."

"Yes, sir. Is the ironing done?"

"I don't know. We'll see. Get him."

At last, I thought, we're off. I dialed the number, and after some waiting because that was a busy hour for a morning paper, got him. His voice came. "Archie? Buy me a drink?"

"No," I said firmly. "Tonight you stay sober. What time can you get here?"

"Where is here?"

"Nero Wolfe's office. He thinks he wants to tell you something."

"Too late." Lon was crisp. "If it will rate the Late City, tell me now."

"It's not that kind. It hasn't come to a boil. But it's good enough so that instead of sending an errand boy, meaning me, he wants to see you himself, so when can you get here?"

"I can send a man."

"No. You."

"Is it worth it?"

"Yes. Possibly."

"In about three hours. Not less, maybe more."

"Okay. Don't stop for a drink, I'll have one ready, and a sandwich. Oh yes, bring along a *Gazette* letterhead and envelope. We've run out of stationery."

"What is it, a gag?"

"No, sir. Far from. It may even get you a raise."

I hung up and turned to Wolfe. "May I make a suggestion? If you want him tender and it's worth a steak, I'll tell Fritz to take one from the freezer and start it thawing."

He said to do so and I went to the kitchen and had a conference with Fritz. Then, back in the office, I sat and listened to Wolfe breathe some more. It went on for minutes that added up to an hour. Finally he opened his eyes, straightened up, and took from his pocket some folded papers which I recognized as sheets torn from his memo pad.

"Your notebook, Archie," he said like a man who has made up his mind.

I got it from the drawer and uncapped my pen.

"If this doesn't work," he growled at me, as if it were all my fault, "there will be no other recourse. I have tried to twist it so as to leave an alternative if it fails, but it can't be done. We'll either get him with this or not at all. On plain paper, double-spaced, two carbons."

"Heading or date?"

"None." He gazed, frowning, at the sheets he had taken from his pocket. "First paragraph:

> "At eight o'clock in the evening of August 19, 1948, twenty men were gathered in a living room on the ninth floor of an apartment house on East 84th Street, Manhattan. All of them were high in the councils of the American Communist party, and this meeting was one of a series to decide strategy and tactics for controlling the election campaign of the Progressive party and its candidate for President of the United States, Henry Wallace. One of them, a tall lanky man with a clipped brown mustache, was saying:
>
> " 'We must never forget that we can't trust Wallace. We can't trust either his character or his intelligence. We can count on his vanity, that's all right, but while we're playing him up we must remember that any minute he might pull something that will bring an order from Policy to let go of him.'
>
> " 'Policy' is the word the top American Communists use when they mean Moscow or the Kremlin. It may be a precaution, though it's hard to see why they need one when they are in secret session, or it may be merely their habit of calling nothing by its right name.
>
> "Another of them, a beefy man with a bald head and a pudgy face, spoke up:"

Wolfe, referring frequently to the sheets he had taken from his pocket, kept on until I had filled thirty-two pages of my notebook, then stopped, sat a while with his lips puckered, and told me to type it. I did so, double spacing as instructed. As I finished a page I handed it over to him and he went to work on it with a pencil. He rarely made changes in anything he had dictated and I had typed, but apparently he regarded this as something extra special. I fully agreed with him. That stuff, getting warmer as it went along, contained dozens of details that nobody lower than a Deputy Commissar had any right to know about—provided they were true. That was a point I would have liked to ask Wolfe about, but if the job was supposed to be finished when Lon Cohen arrived there was no time to spare, so I postponed it.

I had the last page out of the typewriter, but Wolfe was still fussing with it, when the bell rang and I went to the front and let Lon in.

Lon had been rank and file, or maybe only rank, when I first met him, but was now second in command at the *Gazette*'s city desk. As far as I knew his elevation had gone to his head only in one little way: he kept a hairbrush in his desk, and every night when he was through, before making a dash for the refreshment counter he favored, he brushed his hair good. Except for that there wasn't a thing wrong with him.

He shook hands with Wolfe and turned on me.

"You crook, you told me if I didn't stop—oh, here it is. Hello, Fritz. You're the only one here I can trust." He lifted the highball from the tray, nodded at Wolfe, swallowed a third of it, and sat in the red leather chair.

"I brought the stationery," he announced. "Three sheets. You can have it and welcome if you'll give me a first on how someone named Sperling willfully and deliberately did one Louis Rony to death."

"That," Wolfe said, "is precisely what I have to offer."

Lon's head jerked up. "Someone named Sperling?" he snapped.

"No. I shouldn't have said 'precisely.' The name will have to wait. But the rest of it, yes."

"Damn it, it's midnight! You can't expect—"

"Not tonight. Nor tomorrow. But if and when I have it, you'll get it first."

Lon looked at him. He had entered the room loose and carefree and thirsty, but now he was back at work again. An exclusive on the murder of Louis Rony was nothing to relax about.

"For that," he said, "you'd want more than three letterheads, even with envelopes. What if I throw in postage stamps?"

Wolfe nodded. "That would be generous. But I have something else to offer. How would you like to have, for your paper only, a series of articles, authenticated for you, describing secret meetings of the group that controls the American Communist party, giving the details of discussions and decisions?"

Lon cocked his head to one side. "All you need," he declared, "is long white whiskers and a red suit."

"No, I'm too fat. Would that interest you?"

"It ought to. Who would do the authenticating?"

"I would."

"You mean with your by-line?"

"Good heavens, no. The articles would be anonymous. But I would give my warranty, in writing if desired, that the source of information is competent and reliable."

"Who would have to be paid and how much?"

"No one. Nothing."

"Hell, you don't even need whiskers. What would the details be like?"

Wolfe turned. "Let him read it, Archie."

I took Lon the original copy of what I had typed, and he put his glass down on the table at his elbow, to have two hands. There were seven pages. He started reading fast, then went slower, and when he reached the end returned to the first page and reread it. Meanwhile I refilled his glass and, knowing that Fritz was busy, went to the kitchen for beer for Wolfe. Also I thought I could stand a highball myself, and supplied one.

Lon put the sheets on the table, saw that his glass had been attended to, and helped himself.

"It's hot," he admitted.

"Fit to print, I think," Wolfe said modestly.

"Sure it is. How about libel?"

"There is none. There will be none. No names or addresses are used."

"Yeah, I know, but an action might be brought anyhow. Your source would have to be available for testimony."

"No, sir." Wolfe was emphatic. "My source is covered and will stay covered. You may have my warranty, and a bond for libel damages if you want it, but that's all."

"Well—" Lon drank. "I love it. But I've got bosses, and on a thing like this they would have to decide. Tomorrow is Friday, and they —good God, what's this? Don't tell me—Archie, come and look!"

I had to go anyway, to remove the papers so Fritz could put the tray on the table. It was really a handsome platter. The steak was thick and brown with charcoal braid, the grilled slices of sweet potato and sautéed mushrooms were just right, the watercress was high at one end out of danger, and the over-all smell made me wish I had asked Fritz to make a carbon.

"Now I know," Lon said, "it's all a dream. Archie, I would have sworn you phoned me to come down here. Okay, I'll dream on." He sliced through the steak, letting the juice come, cut off a bite, and opened wide for it. Next came a bite of sweet potato, followed by a mushroom. I watched him the way I have seen dogs watch when they're allowed near the table. It was too much. I went to the kitchen, came back with two slices of bread on a plate, and thrust it at him.

"Come on, brother, divvy. You can't eat three pounds of steak."

"It's under two pounds."

"Like hell it is. Fix me up."

After all he was a guest, so he had to give in.

When he left a while later the platter was clean except for the bone, the level in the bottle of Scotch was down another three inches, the letterheads and envelopes were in my desk drawer, and the arrangement was all set, pending an okay by the *Gazette* high brass. Since the week end was nearly on us, getting the okay might hold it up, but Lon thought there was a fair chance for Saturday and a good one for Sunday. The big drawback, in his opinion, was the fact that Wolfe would give no guarantee of the life of the series. He gave a firm promise for two articles, and said a third was likely, but that was as far as he would commit himself. Lon tried to get him to sign up for a minimum of six, but nothing doing.

Alone with Wolfe again, I gave him a look.

"Quit staring," he said gruffly.

"I beg your pardon. I was figuring something. Two pieces of two thousand words each, four thousand words. Fifteen thousand—that comes to three seventy-five a word. And he doesn't even write the pieces. If you're going to ghost—"

"It's bedtime."

"Yes, sir. Besides writing the second piece, what comes next?"

"Nothing. We sit and wait. Confound it, if this doesn't work . . ."

He told me good night and marched out to the elevator.

20

The next day, Friday, two more articles got dictated, typed, and revised. The second one was delivered to Lon Cohen and the third one was locked in our safe. They carried the story through Election Day up to the end of the year, and while they had no names or addresses they had about everything else. I even got interested in them myself, and was wondering what was going to come next.

Lon's bosses were glad to get them on Wolfe's terms, including the surety protection against libel suits, but decided not to start them until Sunday. They gave them a three-column play on the front page:

HOW THE AMERICAN COMMUNISTS PLAY IT
THE RED ARMY IN THE COLD WAR
THEIR GHQ IN THE USA

There was a preface in italics:

The Gazette *presents herewith the first of a series of articles showing how American Communists help Russia fight the cold war and get ready for the hot one if and when it comes. This is the real thing. For obvious reasons the name of the author of the articles cannot be given, but the* Gazette *has a satisfactory guaranty of their authenticity. We hope to continue the series up to the most recent activities of the Reds, including their secret meetings before, during, and after the famous trial in New York. The second article will appear tomorrow. Don't miss it!*

Then it started off just as Wolfe had dictated it.

I am perfectly willing to hold out on you so as to tell it in a way that will give Wolfe's stratagem the best possible buildup, as you may know by this time, but I am now giving you everything I myself had at the time. That goes for Friday, Saturday, Sunday, and Monday up to 8:30 P.M. You know all that I knew, or you will when I add that the third article was revised Sunday and delivered to Lon Monday noon for Tuesday's paper, that Weinbach's final report on the stone verified the first one, that nothing else was accomplished or even attempted, and that during those four days Wolfe was touchier than I had ever known him to be for so long a period. I had no idea what he expected to gain by becoming a ghost writer for Mr. Jones and telling the Commies' family secrets.

I admit I tried to catch up. For instance, when he was up in the plant rooms Friday morning I did a thorough check of the photographs in his desk drawer, but they were all there. Not one gone. I made a couple of other well-intentioned efforts to get a line on his script, and not a glimmer. By Monday I was grabbing the mail each time a delivery came for a quick look, and hoping it was a telegram whenever the doorbell rang, and answering the phone in a hurry, because I had decided that the articles were just a gob of bait on a hook and we were merely sitting on the bank, hoping against hope for a bite. But if the bite was expected in the form of a letter or telegram or phone call, no fish.

Then Monday evening, in the office right after dinner, Wolfe handed me a sheet from his memo pad covered with his handwriting, and asked, "Can you read that, Archie?"

The question was rhetorical, since his writing is almost as easy to read as print. I read it and told him, "Yes, sir, I can make it out."

"Type it on a *Gazette* letterhead, including the signature as indicated. Then I want to look at it. Address a *Gazette* envelope to Mr. Albert Enright, Communist Party of the USA, Thirty-five East Twelfth Street. One carbon, single-space."

"With a mistake or two, maybe?"

"Not necessarily. You are not the only one in New York who can type well."

I pulled the machine around, got the paper out and put it in, and hit the keys. When I took it out I read it over:

June 27, 1949.

Dear Mr. Enright:

  I send this to you because I met you once and have heard you speak at meetings twice. You wouldn't know me if you saw me, and you wouldn't know my name.

  I work at the *Gazette*. Of course you have seen the series that started on Sunday. I am not a Communist, but I approve of many things they stand for and I think they are getting a raw deal, and anyway I don't like traitors, and the man who is giving the *Gazette* the material for those articles is certainly a traitor. I think you have a right to know who he is. I have never seen him and I don't think he has ever come to the office, but I know the man here who is working with him on the articles, and I had a chance to get something which I believe will help you, and I am enclosing it in this letter. I have reason to know that it was in the folder that was sent to one of the executives to show him that the articles are authentic. If I told you more than that it might give you a hint of my identity, and I don't want you to know who I am.

  More power to you in your fight with the imperialists and monopolists and warmakers.

A Friend.

I got up to hand it to Wolfe and returned to the typewriter to address the envelope. And, though I had done the whole letter without an error, on the envelope I fumbled and spelled Communist "Counimmst," and had to take another one. It didn't irritate me because I knew why: I was excited. In a moment I would know which photograph was going to be enclosed in that letter, unless the big bum dealt me out.

He didn't, but he might as well have. He opened his drawer and dug, held one out to me, and said, "That's the enclosure. Mail it where it will be collected tonight."

It was the picture, the best one, of the Communist party membership card of William Reynolds, Number 128-394. I withered him with a look, put the letter and picture in the envelope, sealed it and put a stamp on it, and left the house. In my frame of mind I thought a little air wouldn't hurt me any, so I walked to the Times Square Station.

I expected nothing more from Wolfe that evening, and that was what I got. We went to bed fairly early. Up in my room undressing, I was still trying to map it, having been unable to sketch one I would settle for. The main stratagem was now plain enough, but what was the follow up? Were we going to start sitting and waiting again? In that case, how was William Reynolds going to be given another name, and when and why and by whom? Under the sheet, I chased it out of my mind in order to get some sleep.

The next day, Tuesday, until noon and a little after, it looked like more sitting and waiting. It wasn't too dull, on account of the phone. The third article was in that morning's *Gazette*, and they were wild for more. My instructions were to stall. Lon called twice before ten o'clock, and after that it was practically chain phoning: city editor, managing editor, executive editor, publisher, everybody. They wanted it so bad that I had a notion to write one myself and peddle it for fifteen thousand bucks flat. By noon there would have been nothing to it.

When the phone rang again a little before lunchtime I took it for granted it was one of them, so instead of using my formula I merely said, "Yep?"

"Is this Nero Wolfe's office?" It was a voice I had never heard, a sort of an artificial squeak.

"Yes. Archie Goodwin speaking."

"Is Mr. Wolfe there?"

"Yes. He's engaged. Who is it, please?"

"Just tell him rectangle."

"Spell it, please?"

"R-e-c-t-a-n-g-l-e, rectangle. Tell him immediately. He'll want to know."

The connection went. I hung up and turned to Wolfe.

"Rectangle."

"What?"

"That's what he said, or rather squeaked. Just to tell you rectangle."

"Ah." Wolfe sat up and his eyes came clear open. "Get the national office of the Communist party, Algonquin four two two one five. I want Mr. Harvey or Mr. Stevens. Either one."

I swiveled and dialed. In a moment a pleasant feminine voice was in my ear. Its being pleasant was a shock, and also I was a little self-conscious, conversing for the first time with a female Commie, so I said, "My name's Goodwin, comrade. Is Mr. Harvey there? Mr. Nero Wolfe would like to speak to him."

"You say Nero Wolfe?"

"Yes. A detective."

"I've heard the name. I'll see. Hold the wire."

I waited. Accustomed to holding the wire while a switchboard girl or secretary saw, I leaned back and got comfortable, but it wasn't long before a man told me he was Harvey. I signaled to Wolfe and stayed on myself.

"How do you do, sir," Wolfe said politely. "I'm in a hole and you can help me if you want to. Will you call at my office at six o'clock today with one of your associates? Perhaps Mr. Stevens or Mr. Enright, if one of them is available."

"What makes you think we can help you out of a hole?" Harvey asked, not rudely. He had a middle bass, a little gruff.

"I'm pretty sure you can. At least I would like to ask your advice. It concerns a man whom you know by the name of William Reynolds. He is involved in a case I'm working on, and the matter has become urgent. That's why I would like to see you as soon as possible. There isn't much time."

"What makes you think I know a man named William Reynolds?"

"Oh, come, Mr. Harvey. After you hear what I have to say you may of course deny that you know him if that's the way you want it. This can't be done on the telephone, or shouldn't be."

"Hold the wire."

That wait was longer. Wolfe sat patiently with the receiver at his ear, and I did likewise. In three or four minutes he started to frown, and by the time Harvey's voice came again he was tapping the arm of his chair with a forefinger.

"If we come," Harvey asked, "who will be there?"

"You will, of course, and I will. And Mr. Goodwin, my assistant."

"Nobody else?"

"No, sir."

"All right. We'll be there at six o'clock."

I hung up and asked Wolfe, "Does Mr. Jones always talk with that funny squeak? And did 'rectangle' mean merely that the letter from a friend had been received? Or something more, such as which commissars had read it?"

21

I never got to see the Albert Enright I had typed a letter to, because the associate that Mr. Harvey brought along was Mr. Stevens.

Having seen one or two high-ranking Commies in the flesh, and many published pictures of more than a dozen of them, I didn't expect our callers to look like wart hogs or puff adders, but even so they surprised me a little, especially Stevens. He was middle-aged, skinny, and pale, with thin brown hair that should have been trimmed a week ago, and he wore rimless spectacles. If I had had a daughter in high school, Stevens was the guy I would have wanted her to ask for directions in a strange neighborhood after dark. I wouldn't have gone so far with Harvey, who was younger and much huskier, with sharp greenish-brown eyes and a well-assembled face, but I certainly wouldn't have singled him out as the Menace of the Month.

They didn't want cocktails or any other liquid, and they didn't sit back in their chairs and get comfortable. Harvey announced in his gruff bass, but still not rude, that they had an engagement for a quarter to seven.

"I'll make it as brief as I can," Wolfe assured them. He reached in the drawer and got one of the pictures and extended his hand. "Will you glance at this?"

They arose, and Harvey took the picture, and they looked at it. I thought that was carrying things a little too far. What was I, a worm? So when Harvey dropped it on the desk I stepped over and got an eye on it, and then handed it to Wolfe. Some day he'll get so damn frolicsome that I'll cramp his style sure as hell. I was now caught up.

Harvey and Stevens sat down again, without exchanging a glance. That struck me as being overcautious, but I suppose Commies, especially on the upper levels, get the habit early and it becomes automatic.

Wolfe asked pleasantly, "It's an interesting face, isn't it?"

Stevens stayed deadpan and didn't speak.

"If you like that kind," Harvey said. "Who is it?"

"That will only prolong it." Wolfe was a little less pleasant. "If I had any doubt that you knew him, none was left after the mention of his name brought you here. Certainly you didn't come because you were grieved to learn that I'm in a hole. If you deny that you know that man as William Reynolds you will have had your trip for nothing, and we can't go on."

"Let's put it this way," Stevens said softly. "Proceed hypothetically. If we say we do know him as William Reynolds, then what?"

Wolfe nodded approvingly. "That will do, I think. Then I talk. I tell you that when I met this man recently, for the first time, his name was not Reynolds. I assume you know his other name too, but since in his association with you and your colleagues he has been Reynolds, we'll use that. When I met him, a little more than a week ago, I didn't know he was a Communist; I learned that only yesterday."

"How?" Harvey snapped.

Wolfe shook his head. "I'm afraid I'll have to leave that out. In my years of work as a private detective I have formed many connections—the police, the press, all kinds of people. I will say this: I think Reynolds made a mistake. It's only a conjecture, but a good one I think, that he became frightened. He apprehended a mortal peril—I was responsible for that—and he did something foolish. The peril was a charge of murder. He knew the charge could be brought only if it could be shown that he was a Communist, and he thought I knew it too, and he decided to guard against that by making it appear that while pretending to be a Communist he was actually an enemy of communism and wanted to help destroy it. As I say, that is only a conjecture. But—"

"Wait a minute." Apparently Stevens never raised his voice, even when he was cutting in. "It hasn't quite got to where you can prove a man committed murder just by proving he's a Communist." Stevens smiled, and, seeing what he regarded as a smile, I decided to have my daughter ask someone else for directions. "Has it?"

"No," Wolfe conceded. "Rather the contrary. Communists are well advised to disapprove of private murders for private motives. But in this case that's how it stood. Since we're proceeding hypothetically, I may include in the hypothesis that you know about the death of a man named Louis Rony, run over by a car on the country estate of James U. Sperling, and that you know that William Reynolds was present. May I not?"

"Go on," Harvey rumbled.

"So we don't need to waste time on the facts that have been made public. The situation is this: I know that Mr. Reynolds murdered Mr. Rony. I want to have him arrested and charged. But to get him convicted it is essential to show that he is a member of the Communist party, because only if that is done can his motive be established. You'll have to accept that statement as I give it; I'm not going to show you all my cards, for if I do so and you choose to support Mr. Reynolds I'll be in a deeper hole than I am now."

"We don't support murderers," Harvey declared virtuously.

Wolfe nodded. "I thought not. It would be not only blameworthy, but futile, to try to support this one. You understand that what I must prove is not that William Reynolds is a member of the Communist party; that can be done without much difficulty; but that this man who was at the scene of Mr. Rony's death is that William Reynolds—whatever else he may be. I know of only two ways to accomplish that. One would be to arrest and charge Mr. Reynolds and put him on trial, lay the ground by showing that membership in the Communist party is relevant to his guilt, subpoena you and your associates—fifty of them, a hundred—as witnesses for the State, and put the question to you. 'Is the defendant, or was he, a member of the Communist party?' Those of you who know him, and who answer no, will be committing perjury. Will all of you risk it—not most of you, but all of you? Would it be worth such a risk, to protect a man who murdered as a private enterprise? I doubt it. If you do risk it, I think we can catch you up. I shall certainly try, and my heart will be in it."

"We don't scare easy," Harvey stated.

"What's the other way?" Stevens asked.

"Much simpler for everybody." Wolfe picked up the photograph. "You write your names across this. I paste it on a sheet of paper. Below it you write, 'The man in the above photograph, on which we have written our names, is William Reynolds, whom we know to be a member of the Communist Party of the USA.' You both sign it. That's all."

For the first time they swapped glances.

"It's still a hypothesis," Stevens said. "As such, we'll be glad to think it over."

"For how long?"

"I don't know. Tomorrow or next day."

"I don't like it."

"The hell you don't." Harvey's manners were showing. "Do you have to?"

"I suppose not." Wolfe was regretful. "But I don't like to leave a man around loose when I know he's a murderer. If we do it the simple way, and do it now, we'll have him locked up before midnight. If we postpone it—" Wolfe shrugged. "I don't know what he'll be doing—possibly nothing that will block us—"

I had to keep a grin back. He might as well have asked them if they wanted to give Reynolds a day or two to do some more articles for the *Gazette*, because of course that was where he had them. Knowing that was in their minds, I tried to find some sign of it, any sign at all, in their faces, but they were old hands. They might have been merely a couple of guys looking over a hypothesis and not liking it much.

Stevens spoke, in the same soft voice. "Go ahead and arrest him. If you don't get it the simple way you can try the other one."

"No, sir," Wolfe said emphatically. "Without your statement it won't be easy to get him charged. It can be done, but not just by snapping my fingers."

"You said," Harvey objected, "that if we sign that thing that will be all, but it won't. We'd have to testify at the trial."

"Probably," Wolfe conceded. "But only you two, as friendly witnesses for the prosecution, helping to get a murderer punished. The other way it will be you two and many more, and, if you answer in the negative, you will be shielding a murderer merely because he is a fellow Communist, which will not raise you in public esteem—in addition to risking perjury."

Stevens stood up. "We'll let you know in half an hour, maybe less."

"Good. The front room is soundproofed, or you can go upstairs."

"There's more room outdoors. Come on, Jerry."

Stevens led the way. I went to the front to let them out and then returned to the office. What I saw, re-entering, gave me an excuse to use the grin I had squelched. Wolfe had opened a drawer and got out a sheet of paper and the tube of paste.

"Before they're hatched?" I inquired.

"Bah. The screw is down hard."

"Taking candy from a baby," I admitted. "Though I must say they're no babies, especially Stevens."

Wolfe grunted. "He's third from the top in the American Communist hierarchy."

"He doesn't look it but he acts it. I noticed they didn't even ask what evidence you've got that Reynolds did the killing, because they don't give a damn. All they want is to get the articles stopped and him burned. What I don't get, why did they just swallow the letter from a friend? Why didn't they give Reynolds a chance to answer a question?"

"They don't give chances." Wolfe was scornful. "Could he have proved the letter was a lie? How? Could he have explained the photograph of his membership card? He could only have denied it, and they wouldn't have believed him. They trust no one, especially not one another, and I don't blame them. I suppose I shouldn't put paste on this thing until they have written their names on it."

I wasn't quite as cocksure as he seemed to be. I thought they might have to take it to a meeting, and that couldn't be done in half an hour. But apparently he knew more than I did about Stevens' rank and authority. I had let them out at 6:34, and at 6:52 the bell rang and I went to let them in again. Only eighteen minutes, but the nearest phone booth was only half a block away.

They didn't sit. Harvey stood gazing at me as if there were something about me he didn't like, and Stevens advanced to the end of Wolfe's desk and announced, "We don't like the wording. We want it to read this way:

"As loyal American citizens, devoted to the public welfare and the ideals of true democracy, we believe that all lawbreakers should be punished, regardless of their political affiliations. Therefore, in the interest of justice, we have written our names on the above photograph, and we hereby attest that the man in that photograph is known to us as William Reynolds, and that to our knowledge he has been for eight years, until today, a member of the Communist Party of the USA. Upon learning that he was to be charged with murder, the Communist Party's Executive Committee immediately expelled him."

My opinion of Stevens went up a notch, technically. With nothing to refer to, not even a cuff, he rattled that off as if he had known it by heart for years.

Wolfe lifted his shoulders and dropped them. "If you like it better with all that folderol. Do you want Mr. Goodwin to type it, or will you write it by hand?"

I was just as well pleased that he preferred to use his pen. It would have been an honor to type such a patriotic paragraph, but I wouldn't put anything beneath a Commie, and what if one of them happened to take a notion to pull the letter from a friend out of his pocket and compare the typing? Even with the naked eye it would have been easy to spot the n slightly off line and the faint defect in the w. So I gladly let Stevens sit at my desk to write it. He did so, and signed it, and wrote his name on the picture. Then Harvey did likewise. Wolfe and I signed as witnesses, after Wolfe had read it over. Having the tube of paste at hand, as I have said, he proceeded to attach the photograph to the top of the sheet.

"May I see it a moment?" Stevens asked.

Wolfe handed it to him.

"There's a point," Stevens said. "We can't let you have this without some kind of guarantee that Reynolds will be locked up tonight. You said before midnight."

"That's right. He will be."

"You can have this as soon as he is."

I knew damn well they'd have a monkey wrench. If it had been something not tearable, a stone for instance, I would simply have liberated it, and Harvey could have joined in if he felt like it.

"Then he won't be," Wolfe said, not upset.

"Why not?"

"Because that's the key I'm going to lock him in with. Otherwise, would I have gone to all this trouble to get it? Nonsense. I'm about to invite some people to come here this evening, but not unless I have that document. Please don't crumple it."

"Will Reynolds be here?"

"Yes."

"Then we'll come and bring this with us."

Wolfe shook his head. "You don't seem to listen to me. That paper stays here, or you're out of it until you get a subpoena. Give it to me, and I'll be glad to have you and Mr. Harvey come this evening. That's an excellent idea. You will be excluded from part of it, but you can be comfortable in the front room. Why don't you do that?"

That was the way it was finally compromised. They were plenty stubborn but, as Wolfe had said, the screw was down hard. They didn't know what Reynolds might spill in the next article, and they wanted him nailed quick, and Wolfe stood pat that he wouldn't move without the document. So he got it. It was arranged that they would return around ten o'clock and would stay put in the front room until invited to join the party.

When they had gone Wolfe put the document in his middle drawer.

"We're overstocked on photographs," I remarked. "So that's why Mr. Jones didn't need to load up. He knew him and one look was all he needed. Huh?"

"Dinner's waiting."

"Yes, sir. It would be a funny coincidence if Harvey or Stevens happened to be Mr. Jones. Wouldn't it?"

"No. You can find coincidence in the dictionary. Get Mr. Archer on the phone."

"Now? Dinner's waiting."

"Get him."

That wasn't so simple. At my first try, the District Attorney's office in White Plains, someone answered but couldn't help me any. I then got Archer's home and was told that he was out for the evening, but I wasn't to know where, and I had to press even to sell the idea that he should be informed immediately that Nero Wolfe wanted him to call. I hung up and settled back to wait for anything from five minutes to an hour. Wolfe was sitting up straight, frowning, with his lips tight; a meal was spoiling. After a while the sight of him was getting on my nerves, and I was about to suggest that we move to the dining room and start, when the phone rang. It was Archer.

"What is it?" He was crisp and indignant.

Wolfe said he needed his advice.

"What about? I'm dining with friends. Can't it wait until morning?"

"No, sir. I've got the murderer of Louis Rony, with evidence to convict, and I want to get rid of him."

"The murderer—" A short silence. Then, "I don't believe it!"

"Of course you don't, but it's true. He'll be at my office this evening. I want your advice on how to handle it. I can ask Inspector Cramer of the New York Police to send men to take him into custody, or I can—"

"No! Now listen, Wolfe—"

"No, listen to me. If your dinner is waiting, so is mine. I would prefer that you take him, for two reasons. First, he belongs to you. Second, I would like to clean it up this evening, and in order to do that the matter of Mr. Kane's statement will have to be disposed of. That will require the presence not only of Mr. Sperling and Mr. Kane, but also of the others who were there the evening Mr. Rony was killed. If you come or send someone, they'll have to come too. All of them, if possible; under the circumstances I don't think they'll be reluctant. Can you have them here by ten o'clock?"

"But my God, this is incredible! I need a minute to think—"

"You've had a week to think but preferred to let me do it for you. I have, and acted. Can you have them here by ten o'clock?"

"I don't know, damn it! You fire this at me point-blank!"

"Would you rather have had me hold it a day or two? I'll expect you at ten, or as close to that as you can make it. If you don't bring them along you won't get in; after all, in this jurisdiction you're merely visitors. If ends have to be left dangling I'll let the New York Police have him."

Wolfe and I hung up. He pushed his chair back and arose.

"You can't dawdle over your dinner, Archie. If we're to keep our promise to Mr. Cohen, and we must, you'll have to go to see him."

22

As I understand it, the Commies think that they get too little and capitalists get too much of the good things in life. They sure played hell with that theory that Tuesday evening. A table in the office was loaded with liquids, cheese, nuts, homemade pâté, and crackers, and not a drop or a crumb was taken by any of the thirteen people there, including Wolfe and me. On a table in the front room there was a similar assortment in smaller quantities, and Harvey and Stevens, just two of them, practically cleaned it up. If I had noticed it before the Commies left I would have called it to their attention. I admit they had more time, having arrived first, at ten sharp, and also they had nothing to do most of the evening but sit and wait.

I don't think I have ever seen the office more crowded, unless it was at the meeting of the League of Frightened Men. Either Archer had thought pressure was called for or Wolfe had been correct in assuming that none of the Stony Acres bunch would be reluctant about coming, for they were all there. I had let them choose seats as they pleased, and the three Sperling women—Mom, Madeline, and Gwenn—were on the big yellow couch in the corner, which meant that my back was to them when I faced Wolfe. Paul and Connie Emerson were on chairs side by side over by the globe, and Jimmy Sperling was seated near them. Webster Kane and Sperling were closer to Wolfe's desk. District Attorney Archer was in the red leather chair; I had put him there because I thought he rated it. What made it thirteen was the fact that two dicks were present: Ben Dykes, brought by Archer, and Sergeant Purley Stebbins of Manhattan Homicide, who had informed me that Westchester had invited him. Purley, my old friend and even older enemy, sat over by the door.

It started off with a bang. When they were all in and greetings, such as they were, had been attended to, and everyone was seated, Wolfe began his preamble. He had got only four words out when Archer blurted, "You said the man that murdered Rony would be here!"

"He is."

"Where?"

"You brought him."

After that beginning it was only natural that no one felt like having a slice of cheese or a handful of nuts. I didn't blame any of them, least of all William Reynolds. Several of them made noises, and Sperling and Paul Emerson both said something, but I didn't catch either of them because Gwenn's voice, clear and strong but with a tremble under it, came from behind my back.

"I told my father what I told you that evening!"

Wolfe ignored her. "This will go faster," he told Archer, "if you let me do it."

"The perfect mountebank!" Emerson sneered.

Sperling and Archer spoke together. A growl from the side made their heads turn. It was Sergeant Stebbins, raising his voice from his seat near the door. He got all eyes.

"If you take my advice," he told them, "you'll let him tell it. I'm from the New York Police, and this is New York. I've heard him before. If you pester him he'll string it out just to show you."

"I have no desire to string it out," Wolfe said crossly. His eyes went from left to right and back. "This shouldn't take long if you'll let me get on. I wanted you all here because of what I said to you up there in my bedroom eight days ago, the evening Mr. Rony was killed. I thereby assumed an obligation, and I want you to know that I have fulfilled it."

He took the audience in again. "First I'll tell you why I assumed that Mr. Rony was killed not accidentally but deliberately. While it was credible that the driver of the car might not have seen him until too late, it was hard to believe that Mr. Rony had not been aware of the car's approach, even in the twilight, and even if the noise of the brook had covered the noise of the car, which could not have been going fast. Nor was there any mark on the front of the car. If it had hit him when he was upright there would probably, though not certainly, have been a mark or marks."

"You said all this before," Archer cut in impatiently.

"Yes, sir. The repetition will take less time if you don't interrupt. Another point, better than either of those, why was the body dragged more than fifty feet to be concealed behind a shrub? If it had been an accident, and the driver decided not to disclose his part in it, what would he have done? Drag the body off the road, yes, but surely not fifty feet to find a hiding place."

"You said that before too," Ben Dykes objected. "And I said the same argument would apply just as well to a murderer."

"Yes," Wolfe agreed, "but you were wrong. The murderer had a sound reason for moving the body where it couldn't be seen from the drive if someone happened to pass."

"What?"

"To search the body. We are now coming to things I *haven't* said before. You preferred not to show me the list of articles found on the body, so I preferred not to tell you that I knew something had been taken from it. The way I knew it was that Mr. Goodwin had himself made an inventory when he found the body."

"The hell he had!"

"It would have been better," Archer said in a nasty voice for him, "to tell us that. What had been taken?"

"A membership card, in the name of William Reynolds, in the American Communist party."

"By God!" Sperling cried, and left his chair. There were exclamations from others. Sperling was following his up, but Archer's voice cut through.

"How did you know he had one?"

"Mr. Goodwin had seen it, and I had seen a photograph of it." Wolfe pointed a finger. "Please let me tell this without yanking me around with questions. I have to go back to Saturday evening a week ago. Mr. Goodwin was there ostensibly as a guest, but actually representing me in behalf of my client, Mr. Sperling. He had reason to believe that Mr. Rony was carefully guarding some small object, not letting it leave his person. There were refreshments in the living room. Mr. Goodwin drugged his own drink and exchanged it for Mr. Rony's. He drank Mr. Rony's. But it had been drugged by someone else, as he found to his sorrow."

"Oh!" A little cry came from behind me, in the voice of the little cabbage. Wolfe frowned past my shoulder.

"Mr. Goodwin had intended to enter Mr. Rony's room that night to learn what the object was, but didn't, because he was himself drugged and Mr. Rony was not. Instead of swallowing his drink, Mr. Rony had poured it into the ice bucket. I am still giving reasons why I assumed that he was not killed by accident, and that's one of them: his drink had been drugged and he either knew it or suspected it. Mr. Goodwin was mortified, and he is not one to take mortification lightly; also he wanted to see the object. The next day, Sunday, he arranged to have Mr. Rony return to New York in his car, and he also arranged for a man and woman—both of them have often worked for me—to waylay them and blackjack Mr. Rony."

That got a reaction from practically everybody. The loudest, from Purley Stebbins, reached me through the others from twenty feet off. "Jesus! Can you beat him?"

Wolfe sat and let them react. In a moment he put up a hand.

"That's a felony, I know, Mr. Archer. You can decide what to do about it at your leisure, when it's all over. Your decision may be influenced by the fact that if it hadn't been committed the killer of Mr. Rony wouldn't have been caught."

He took in the audience, now quiet again. "All they took from him was the money in his wallet. That was necessary in order to validate it as a holdup—and by the way, the money has been spent in my investigation of his death, which I think he would regard as fitting. But Mr. Goodwin did something else. He found on Mr. Rony the object he had been guarding, and took some photographs of it, not taking the object itself. It was a membership card, in the name of William Reynolds, in the American Communist party."

"Then I was right!" Sperling was so excited and triumphant that he yelled it. "I was right all the time!" He glared indignantly, sputtering, "Why didn't you tell me? Why didn't—"

"You were as wrong," Wolfe said rudely, "as a man can get. You may be a good businessman, Mr. Sperling, but you had better leave the exposure of disguised Communists to competent persons. It's a task for which you are disqualified by mental astigmatism."

"But," Sperling insisted, "you admit he had a membership card—"

"I don't admit it, I announce it. But it would have been witless to assume that William Reynolds was necessarily Louis Rony. In fact, I had knowledge of Rony that made it unlikely. Anyway, we have the testimony of three persons that the card was in his possession— you'll find that a help in the courtroom, Mr. Archer. So at that time the identity of William Reynolds—whether it was Mr. Rony or another person—was an open question."

Wolfe turned a hand up. "But twenty-four hours later it was no longer open. Whoever William Reynolds was, almost certainly he wasn't Louis Rony. Not only that, it was a workable assumption that he had murdered Rony, since it was better than a conjecture that he had dragged the body behind a bush in order to search it, had found the membership card, and had taken it. I made that assumption, tentatively. Then the next day, Tuesday, I was carried a step further by the news that it was my car that had killed Rony. So if William Reynolds had murdered Rony and taken the card, he was one of the people there present. One of those now in this room."

A murmur went around, but only a murmur.

"You've skipped something," Ben Dykes protested. "Why did it have to be Reynolds who murdered and took the card?"

"It didn't," Wolfe admitted. "These were assumptions, not conclusions. But they were a whole; if one was good, all were; if one was not, none. If the murderer had killed and searched the body to get that card, surely it was to prevent the disclosure that he had joined the Communist party under the name of William Reynolds, a disclosure threatened by Rony—who was by no means above such threats. That's where I stood Tuesday noon. But I was under an obligation to my client, Mr. Sperling, which would be ill met if I gave all this to the police—at least without trying my own hand at it first. That was what I had decided to do"—Wolfe's eyes went straight at Sperling—"when you jumped in with that confounded statement you had coerced Mr. Kane to sign. And satisfied Mr. Archer, and fired me."

His eyes darted at Kane. "I wanted you here for this, to repudiate that statement. Will you? Now?"

"Don't be a fool, Web," Sperling snapped. And to Wolfe, "I didn't coerce him!"

Poor Kane, not knowing what to say, said nothing. In spite of all the trouble he had caused us, I nearly felt sorry for him.

Wolfe shrugged. "So I came home. I had to get my assumptions either established or discredited. It was possible that Mr. Rony had not had the membership card on his person when he was killed. On Wednesday Mr. Goodwin went to his apartment and made a thorough search—not breaking and entering, Mr. Stebbins."

"You say," Purley muttered.

"He had a key," Wolfe asserted, which was quite true. "The card wasn't there; if it had been, Mr. Goodwin would have found it. But he did find evidence, no matter how or what, that Mr. Rony had had in his possession one or more objects, probably a paper or papers, which he had used as a tool of coercion on one or more persons here present. It doesn't matter what his demands were, but in passing let me say that I doubt that they were for money; I think what he required, and was getting, was support for his courtship of the younger Miss Sperling—or at least neutrality. Another—"

"What was the evidence?" Archer demanded.

Wolfe shook his head. "You may not need it; if you do, you may have it when the time comes. Another assumption, that Mr. Rony was not upright when the car hit him, also got confirmed. Although the car had not struck his head, there was a severe bruise above his right ear; a doctor hired by me saw it, and it is recorded on the official report. That helped to acquit the murderer of so slapdash a method as trying to kill a lively and vigorous young man by hitting him with a car. Obviously it would have been more workmanlike to ambush him as he walked up the drive, knock him out, and then run the car over him. If that—"

"You can't ambush a man," Ben Dykes objected, "unless you know he'll be there to ambush."

"No," Wolfe agreed, "nor can you expect me ever to finish if you take no probabilities along with facts. Besides the private telephone lines in Mr. Sperling's library there are twelve extensions in that house, and Miss Sperling's talk with Mr. Rony, arranging for his arrival at a certain hour for a rendezvous on the grounds, could have been listened to by anyone. William Reynolds could certainly have heard it; let him prove he didn't. Anyhow, the ambush itself is no longer a mere probability. By a brilliant stroke of Mr. Goodwin's, it was established as a fact. On Thursday he searched the grounds for the instrument used for laying Mr. Rony out, and he found it, in the presence of a witness."

"He didn't!" It was Madeline's voice from behind me. "I was with him every minute and he didn't find anything!"

"But he did," Wolfe said dryly. "On his way out he stopped at the brook and found a stone. The question of the witness, and of the evidence that the stone had been in contact with a man's head, can wait, but I assure you there's no doubt about it. Even if the witness prefers to risk perjury we'll manage quite well without her."

His eyes made an arc to take them in. "For while such details as the head bruise and the stone will be most helpful and Mr. Archer will be glad to have them, what clinches the matter is a detail of a different sort. I have hinted at it before and I now declare it: William Reynolds, the owner of that card, the Communist, is in this room. You won't mind, I hope, if I don't tell you how I learned it, so long as I tell you how I can prove it, but before I do so I would like if possible to get rid of a serious embarrassment. Mr. Kane. You're an intelligent man and you see my predicament. If the man who murdered Mr. Rony is charged and put on trial, and if that statement you signed is put in evidence by the defense, and you refuse to repudiate it, there can be no conviction. I appeal to you: do you want to furnish that shield to a Communist and a murderer?

No matter who he is. If you are reluctant to credit my assertion that he is a Communist, consider that unless that can be proven to the satisfaction of a judge and jury he will not be in jeopardy, for that is essential to the case against him. But as long as your statement stands it would be foolhardy even to arrest him; Mr. Archer wouldn't dare to move for an indictment."

Wolfe got a paper from a desk drawer. "I wish you would sign this. It was typed by Mr. Goodwin this evening before you came. It is dated today and reads, 'I, Webster Kane, hereby declare that the statement signed by me on June twenty-first, nineteen forty-nine, to the effect that I had killed Louis Rony accidentally by driving an automobile over him, was false. I signed it at the suggestion of James U. Sperling, Senior, and I hereby retract it.' Archie?"

I got up to reach for the paper and offer it to Kane, but he didn't move a hand to take it. The outstanding economist was in a hole, and his face showed that he realized it.

"Take out the last sentence," Sperling demanded. "It isn't necessary." He didn't look happy either.

Wolfe shook his head. "Naturally you don't like to face it, but you'll have to. On the witness stand you can't possibly evade it, so why evade it now?"

"Good God." Sperling was grim. "The witness stand. Damn it, if this isn't just an act, who is Reynolds?"

"I'll tell you when Mr. Kane has signed that, not before—and you have witnessed it."

"I won't witness it."

"Yes, sir, you will. This thing started with your desire to expose a Communist. Now's your chance. You won't take it?"

Sperling glowered at Wolfe, then at me, then at Kane. I thought to myself how different this was from smiling like an angel. Mrs. Sperling murmured something, but no one paid any attention.

"Sign it, Web," Sperling growled.

Kane's hand came out for it, not wanting to. With it I gave him a magazine to firm it, and my pen. He signed, big and sprawly, and I passed it along to the Chairman of the Board. His signature, as witness, was something to see. It could have been James U. Sperling, or it could have been Lawson N. Spiffshill. I accepted it without prejudice and handed it to Wolfe, who gave it a glance and put it under a paperweight.

He sighed. "Bring them in, Archie."

I crossed to the door to the front room and called out, "Come in, gentlemen!"

I would have given a nickel to know how much time and effort they had wasted trying to hear something through the soundproofed door. It couldn't be done. They entered in character. Harvey, self-conscious and aggressive in the presence of so much capitalism, strolled across nearly to Wolfe's desk, turned, and gave each of them in turn a hard straight eye. Stevens was interested in only one of them, the man he knew as William Reynolds; as far as he was concerned the others were dummies, including even the District Attorney. His eyes too were hard and straight, but they had only one target. They both ignored the chairs I had reserved for them.

"I think," Wolfe said, "we needn't bother with introductions. One of you knows these gentlemen well; the others won't care to, nor will they care to know you. They are avowed members of the American Communist party, and prominent ones. I have here a document"—he fluttered it—"which they signed early this evening, with a photograph of a man pasted on it. The writing on it, in Mr. Stevens' hand, states that for eight years the man in the photograph has been a fellow Communist under the name of William Reynolds. The document is itself conclusive, but these gentlemen and I agreed that it would be helpful for them to appear and identify Reynolds in person. You're looking at him, are you, Mr. Stevens?"

"I am," said Stevens, gazing at Webster Kane with cold hate.

"You goddam rat," rumbled Harvey, also at Kane.

The economist was returning their gaze, now at Stevens, now at Harvey, stunned and incredulous. His first confession had required words, written down and signed, but this one didn't. That stunned look was his second confession, and everybody there, looking at him, could see it was the real thing.

He wasn't the only stunned one.

"Web!" roared Sperling. "For God's sake—*Web!*"

"You're in for it, Mr. Kane," Wolfe said icily. "You've got no one left. You're done as Kane, with the Communist brand showing at last. You're done as Reynolds, with your comrades spitting you out as only they can spit. You're done even as a two-legged animal, with a murder to answer for. The last was my job—the rest was only incidental—and thank heaven it's over, for it wasn't easy. He's yours, Mr. Archer."

I wasn't needed to watch a possible outburst, since both Ben

Dykes and Purley Stebbins were there and had closed in, and I had an errand to attend to. I pulled my phone over to me and dialed the *Gazette,* and got Lon Cohen.

"Archie?" He sounded desperate. "Twelve minutes to go! Well?"

"Okay, son," I said patronizingly. "Shoot it."

"As is? Webster Kane? Pinched?"

"As specified. We guarantee materials and workmanship. If you're a leading economist I know where there's a vacancy."

23

Later, long after midnight, after everyone else had gone, James U. Sperling was still there. He sat in the red leather chair, eating nuts, drinking Scotch, and getting things clear.

What kept him, of course, was the need to get his self-respect back in condition before he went home and to bed, and after the terrific jolt of learning that he had nurtured a Commie in his bosom for years it wasn't so simple. The detail that seemed to hurt most of all was the first confession—the one he had got Kane to sign. He had drafted it himself—he admitted it; he had thought it was a masterpiece that even a Chairman of the Board could be proud of; and now it turned out that, except for the minor item that Rony had been flat instead of erect when the car hit him, it had been the truth! No wonder he had trouble getting it down.

He insisted on going back over everything. He even wanted answers to questions such as whether Kane had seen Rony pour his doped drink in the ice bucket, which of course we couldn't give him. Wolfe generously supplied answers when he had them. For instance, why had Kane signed the repudiation of his statement that he had killed Rony accidentally? Because, Wolfe explained, Sperling had told him to, and Kane's only hope had been to stick to the role of Webster Kane in spite of hell. True, within ten breaths he was going to be torn loose from it by the cold malign stares of his former comrades, but he didn't know that when he took the pen to sign his name.

When Sperling finally left he was more himself again, but I suspected he would need more than one night's sleep before anyone would see him smiling like an angel.

That was all except the tail. Every murder case, like a kite, has a tail. The tail to this one had three sections, the first one public and the other two private.

Section One became public the first week in July, when it was announced that Paul Emerson's contract was not being renewed. I happened to know about it in advance because I was in the office when, one day the preceding week, James U. Sperling phoned Wolfe to say that the Continental Mines Corporation was grateful to him for removing a Communist tumor from its internal organs and would be glad to pay a bill if he sent one. Wolfe said he would like to send a bill but didn't know how to word it, and Sperling asked him why. Because, Wolfe said, the bill would ask for payment not in dollars but in kind. Sperling wanted to know what he meant.

"As you put it," Wolfe explained, "I removed a tumor from your staff. What I would want in return is the removal of a tumor from my radio. Six-thirty is a convenient time for me to listen to the radio, and even if I don't turn it to that station I know that Paul Emerson is there, only a few notches away, and it annoys me. Remove him. He might get another sponsor, but I doubt it. Stop paying him for that malicious gibberish."

"He has a high rating," Sperling objected.

"So had Goebbels," Wolfe snapped. "And Mussolini."

A short silence.

"I admit," Sperling conceded, "that he irritates me. I think it's chiefly his ulcers."

"Then find someone without them. You'll be saving money, too. If I sent you a bill in dollars it wouldn't be modest, in view of the difficulties you made."

"His contract expires next week."

"Good. Let it."

"Well—I'll see. We'll talk it over here."

That was how it happened.

The tail's second section, private, was also in the form of a phone call, some weeks later. Just yesterday, the day after Webster Kane, alias William Reynolds, was sentenced on his conviction for the first degree murder of Louis Rony, I put the receiver to my ear and once more heard a hard cold precise voice that used only the best grammar. I told Wolfe who it was and he got on.

"How are you, Mr. Wolfe?"

"Well, thank you."

"I'm glad to hear it. I'm calling to congratulate you. I have ways of learning things, so I know how superbly you handled it. I am highly gratified that the killer of that fine young man will be properly punished, thanks to you."

"My purpose was not to gratify you."

"Of course not. All the same, I warmly appreciate it, and my admiration of your talents has increased. I wanted to tell you that, and also that you will receive another package tomorrow morning. In view of the turn events took the damage your property suffered is all the more regrettable."

The connection went. I turned to Wolfe.

"He sure likes to keep a call down to a nickel. By the way, do you mind if I call him Whosis instead of X? It reminds me of algebra and I was rotten at it."

"I sincerely hope," Wolfe muttered, "that there will never be another occasion to refer to him."

But one came the very next day, this morning, when the package arrived, and its contents raised a question that has not been answered and probably never will be. Did X have so many ways of learning things that he knew how much had been shelled out to Mr. Jones, or was it just a coincidence that the package contained exactly fifteen grand? Anyhow, tomorrow I'll make my second trip to a certain city in New Jersey, and then the total in the safe deposit box will be a nice round figure. The name I go by there need not be told, but I can say that it is not William Reynolds.

The tail's third section is not only private but strictly personal, and it goes beyond phone calls, though there are those too. This coming week end at Stony Acres I expect no complications like dope in the drinks, and I won't have to bother with a camera. Recently I quit calling her ma'am.

in the best families

1

It was nothing out of the ordinary that Mrs. Barry Rackham had made the appointment with her finger pressed to her lips. That is by no means an unusual gesture for people who find themselves in a situation where the best thing they can think of is to make arrangements to see Nero Wolfe.

With Mrs. Barry Rackham the shushing finger was only figurative, since she made the date speaking to me on the phone. It was in her voice, low and jerky, and also in the way she kept telling me how confidential it was, even after I solemnly assured her that we rarely notified the press when someone requested an appointment on business. At the end she told me once more that she would have preferred to speak to Mr. Wolfe himself, and I hung up and decided it rated a discreet routine check on a prospective client, starting with Mr. Mitchell at the bank and Lon Cohen at the *Gazette*. On the main point of interest, could she and did she pay her bills, the news was favorable: she was worth a good four million and maybe five. Calling it four, and assuming that Wolfe's bill for services rendered would come to only half of it, that would be enough to pay my current salary—as Wolfe's secretary, trusted assistant and official gnat—for a hundred and sixty-seven years; and in addition to that, living as I did there in Wolfe's house, I also got food and shelter. So I was fixed for life if it turned out that she needed two million bucks' worth of detective work.

She might have at that, judging from the way she looked and acted at 11:05 the next morning, Friday, when the doorbell rang and I went to let her in. There was a man on the stoop with her, and after glancing quickly east and then west she brushed past him and darted inside, grabbed my sleeve, and told me in a loud whisper, "You're not Nero Wolfe!"

Instantly she released me, seized the elbow of her companion to
hurry him across the sill, and whispered at him explosively, "Come
in and shut the door!" You might have thought she was a duchess
diving into a hock shop.

Not that she was my idea of a duchess physically. As I attended
to the door and got the man's hat and topcoat hung on the rack, I
took them in. She was a paradox—bony from the neck up and ample
from the neck down. On her chin and jawbone and cheekbone the
skin was stretched tight, but alongside her mouth and nose were
tangles of wrinkles.

As I helped her off with her fur coat I told her, "Look, Mrs. Rackham. You came to consult Nero Wolfe, huh?"

"Yes," she whispered. She nodded and said right out loud, "Of
course."

"Then you ought to stop trembling if you can. It makes Mr. Wolfe
uneasy when a woman trembles because he thinks she's going to
be hysterical, and he might not listen to you. Take a deep breath
and try to stop."

"You were trembling all the way down here in the car," the man
said in a mild baritone.

"I was not!" she snapped. That settled, she turned to me. "This is
my cousin, Calvin Leeds. He didn't want me to come here, but I
brought him along anyhow. Where's Mr. Wolfe?"

I indicated the door to the office, went and opened it, and
ushered them in.

I have never figured out Wolfe's grounds for deciding whether or
not to get to his feet when a woman enters his office. If they're objective they're too complicated for me, and if they're subjective I
wouldn't know where to start. This time he kept his seat behind his
desk in the corner near a window, merely nodding and murmuring
when I pronounced names. I thought for a second that Mrs. Rackham was standing gazing at him in reproach for his bad manners,
but then I saw it was just surprised disbelief that he could be that
big and fat. I'm so used to the quantity of him that I'm apt to forget
how he must impress people seeing him for the first time.

He aimed a thumb at the red leather chair beyond the end of
his desk and muttered at her, "Sit down, madam."

She went and sat. I then did likewise, at my own desk, not far
from Wolfe's and at right angles to it. Calvin Leeds, the cousin, had
sat twice, first on the couch toward the rear and then on a chair

which I moved up for him. I would have guessed that both he and Mrs. Rackham had first seen the light about the same time as the twentieth century, but he could have been a little older. He had a lot of weather in his face with its tough-looking hide, his hair had been brown but was now more gray, and with his medium size and weight he looked and moved as if all his inside springs were still sound and lively. He had taken Wolfe in, and the surroundings too, and now his eyes were on his cousin.

Mrs. Rackham spoke to Wolfe. "You couldn't very well go around finding out things. Could you?"

"I don't know," he said politely. "I haven't tried for years, and I don't intend to. Others go around for me." He gestured at me. "Mr. Goodwin, of course, and others as required. You need someone to go around?"

"Yes." She paused. Her mouth worked. "I think I do. Provided it can be done safely—I mean, without anyone knowing about it." Her mouth worked some more. "I am bitterly ashamed—having at my age, for the first time in my life—having to go to a private detective with my personal affairs."

"Then you shouldn't have come," Leeds said mildly.

"Then you have come too soon," Wolfe told her.

"Too soon? Why?"

"You should have waited until it became so urgent or so intolerable that it would cause you no shame to ask for help, especially from one as expensive as me." He shook his head. "Too soon. Come back if and when you must."

"Hear that, Sarah?" Leeds asked, but not rubbing it in.

Ignoring him, she leaned forward and blurted at Wolfe, "No, I'm here now. I have to know! I have to know about my husband!"

Wolfe's head jerked around to me, to give me a look intended to scorch. But I met his eyes and told him emphatically, "No, sir. If it is, she fibbed. I told her we wouldn't touch divorce or separation evidence, and she said it wasn't."

He left me and demanded, "Do you want your husband followed?"

"I—I don't know. I don't think so—"

"Do you suspect him of infidelity?"

"No! I don't!"

Wolfe grunted, leaned back in his chair, squirmed to get comfortable, and muttered, "Tell me about it."

Mrs. Rackham's jaw started to quiver. She looked at Leeds. His brows went up, and he shook his head, not as a negative apparently, but merely leaving it to her. Wolfe let out a grunt. She moved her eyes to him and said plaintively, "I'm neurotic."

"I am not," Wolfe snapped, "a psychiatrist. I doubt if—"

She cut him off. "I've been neurotic as long as I can remember. I had no brother or sister and my mother died when I was three, and my father didn't enjoy my company because I was ugly. When he died—I was twenty then—I cried all during the funeral service, not because he was dead but because I knew he wouldn't have wanted me so close to him all that time—in the church and driving to the cemetery and there at the grave."

Her jaw started to quiver again, but she clamped it and got control. "I'm telling you this because it's no secret anyway, and I want you to understand why I must have help. I have never been sure exactly why my first husband married me, because he had money of his own and didn't really need mine, but it wasn't long until he hated looking at me just as my father had. So I—"

"That isn't true, Sarah," Calvin Leeds objected. "You imagined—"

"Bosh!" she quashed him. "I'm not that neurotic! So I got a divorce with his consent and gratitude, I think, though he was too polite to say so, and I hurried it through because I didn't want him to know I was pregnant. Soon after the divorce my son was born, and that made complications, but I kept him—I kept him and he was mine until he went to war. He never showed the slightest sign of feeling about my looks the way my father and my husband had. He was never embarrassed about me. He liked being with me. Didn't he, Calvin?"

"Of course he did," Leeds assured her, apparently meaning it.

She nodded and looked thoughtful, looking into space and seeing something not there. She jerked herself impatiently back to Wolfe. "I admit that before he went away, to war, he got married, and he married a very beautiful girl. It is not true that I wished he had taken one who resembled me, even a little bit, but naturally I couldn't help but see that he had gone to the other extreme. Annabel is very beautiful. It made me proud for my son to have her—it seemed to even my score with all the beautiful women I had known and seen. She thinks I hate her, but that is not true. People as neurotic as I am should not be judged by normal standards. Not that I blame Annabel, for I know perfectly well that when the news came that he had been killed in Germany her loss was greater than mine. He wasn't mine any longer then, he was hers."

"Excuse me," Wolfe put in politely but firmly. "You wanted to consult me about your husband. You say you're divorced?"

"Certainly not! I—" She caught herself up. "Oh. This is my second husband. I only wanted you to understand."

"I'll try. Let's have him now."

"Barry Rackham," she said, pronouncing the name as if she held the copyright on it, or at least a lease on subsidiary rights. "He played football at Yale and then had a job in Wall Street until the war came. At the end of the war he was a major, which wasn't very far to get in nearly four years. We were married in 1946—three years and seven months ago. He is ten years younger than I am."

Mrs. Barry Rackham paused, her eyes fixed on Wolfe's face as if challenging it for comment, but the challenge was declined. Wolfe merely prodded her with a murmur.

"And?"

"I suppose," she said as if conceding a point, "there is no one in New York who does not take it for granted that he married me simply for my money. They all know more about it than I do, because I have never asked him, and he is the only one that knows for sure. I know one thing: it does not make him uncomfortable to look at me. I know that for sure because I'm very sensitive about it, I'm neurotic about it, and I would know it the first second he felt that way. Of course he knows what I look like, he knows how ugly I am, he can't help that, but it doesn't annoy him a particle, not even—"

She stopped and was blushing. Calvin Leeds coughed and shifted in his chair. Wolfe closed his eyes and after a moment opened them again. I didn't look away from her because when she blushed I began to feel a little uncomfortable myself, and I wanted to see if I could keep her from knowing it.

But she wasn't interested in me. "Anyway," she went on as the color began to leave, "I have kept things in my own hands. We live in my house, of course, town and country, and I pay everything, and there are the cars and so on, but I made no settlement and arranged no allowance for him. That didn't seem to me to be the way to handle it. When he needed cash for anything he asked for it and I gave it to him freely, without asking questions." She made a little gesture, a flip of a hand. "Not always, but nearly always. The second year it was more than the first, and the third year more again, and

I felt he was getting unreasonable. Three times I gave him less than he asked for, quite a lot less, and once I refused altogether—I still asked no questions, but he told me why he needed it and tried to persuade me; he was very nice about it, and I refused. I felt that I must draw the line somewhere. Do you want to know the amounts?"

"Not urgently," Wolfe muttered.

"The last time, the time I refused, it was fifteen thousand dollars." She leaned forward. "And that *was* the last time. It was seven months ago, October second, and he has not asked for money since, not once! But he spends a great deal, more than formerly. For all sorts of things—just last week he gave a dinner, quite expensive, for thirty-eight men at the University Club. I have to know where he gets it. I decided that some time ago—two months ago—and I didn't know what to do. I didn't want to speak to my lawyer or banker about a thing like this, or in fact anybody, and I couldn't do it myself, so I asked my cousin, Calvin Leeds." She sent him a glance. "He said he would try to find out something, but he hasn't."

We looked at Leeds. He upturned a palm.

"Well," he said, half apology and half protest, "I'm no trained detective. I asked him straight, and he just laughed at me. You didn't want anyone else to get a hint of it, that you were curious about money he wasn't getting from you, so I was pretty limited in my asking around. I did my best, Sarah, you know I did."

"It seems to me," Wolfe told her, "that Mr. Leeds had one good idea—asking him. Have you tried that yourself?"

"Certainly. Long ago. He told me that an investment he had made was doing well."

"Maybe it was. Why not?"

"Not with my husband." She was positive. "I know how he is with money. It isn't in him to make an investment. Another thing: he is away more now. I don't know where he is as much as I used to. I don't mean weeks or even days, just an afternoon or evening—and several times he has had an appointment that he couldn't break when I wanted him to—"

Wolfe grunted, and she was at him. "I know! You think I feel that I've bought him and I own him! That's not it at all! All I really want is to be like a wife, just any wife—not beautiful and not ugly, not rich and not poor—just a wife! And hasn't a wife a right to know the source of her husband's income—isn't it her *duty* to know? If you had a wife wouldn't you *want* her to know?"

Wolfe made a face. "I can tell you, madam, what I *don't* want. I don't want this job. I think you're gulling me. You suspect that your husband is swindling you, either emotionally or financially, and you want me to catch him at it." He turned to me. "Archie. You'll have to change that formula. Hereafter, when a request comes for an appointment, do not say merely that we will not undertake to get divorce or separation evidence. Make it clear that we will not engage to expose a husband for a wife, or a wife for a husband, under any camouflage. May I ask what you are doing, Mrs. Rackham?"

She had opened her brown leather handbag and taken out a checkfold and a little gold fountain pen. Resting the checkfold on the bag, she was writing in it with the pen. Wolfe's question got no reply until she had finished writing, torn out the check, returned the fold and pen to the bag, and snapped the bag shut. Then she looked at him.

"I don't want you to expose my husband, Mr. Wolfe." She was holding the check with her thumb and fingertip. "God knows I don't! I just want to know. You're not ugly and afraid and neurotic like me, you're big and handsome and successful and not afraid of anything. When I knew I had to have help and my cousin couldn't do it, and I wouldn't go to anyone I knew, I went about it very carefully. I found out all about you, and no one knows I did, or at least why I did. If my husband is doing something that will hurt me that will be the end; but I don't want to expose him, I just have to know. You are the greatest detective on earth, and you're an honest man. I just want to pay you for finding out where and how my husband is getting money, that's all. You can't possibly say you won't do it. Not possibly!"

She left her chair and went to put the check on his desk in front of him. "It's for ten thousand dollars, but that doesn't mean I think that's enough. Whatever you say. But don't you dare say I want to expose him! My God—expose him?"

She had my sympathy up to a point, but what stuck out was her basic assumption that rich people can always get anything they want just by putting up the dough. That's enough to give an honest workingman, like a private detective for instance, a pain in three places. The assumption is of course sound in some cases, but what rich people are apt not to understand is that there are important exceptions.

This, however, was not one of them, and I hoped Wolfe would see that it wasn't. He did. He didn't want to, but the bank account had by no means fully recovered from the awful blow of March fifteenth, only three weeks back, and he knew it. He came forward in his chair for a glance at the check, caught my eye and saw how I felt about it, heaved a sigh, and spoke.

"Your notebook, Archie. Confound it."

2

The following morning, Saturday, I was in the office typing the final report on a case which I will not identify by name because it was never allowed to get within a mile of a newspaper or a microphone. We were committed on Mrs. Rackham's job, since I had deposited her check Friday afternoon, but no move had been made yet, not even a phone call to any of the names she had given us, because it was Wolfe's idea that first of all we must have a look at him. With Wolfe's settled policy of never leaving his house on business, and with no plausible excuse for getting Barry Rackham to the office, I would have to do the looking, and that had been arranged for.

Mrs. Rackham had insisted that her husband must positively not know or even suspect that he was being investigated, and neither must anyone else, so the arrangements for the look were a little complicated. She vetoed my suggestion that I should be invited to join a small weekend gathering at her country home in Westchester, on the ground that someone would probably recognize the Archie Goodwin who worked for Nero Wolfe. It was Calvin Leeds who offered an amendment that was adopted. He had a little place of his own at the edge of her estate, where he raised dogs, called Hillside Kennels. A month ago one of his valuable dogs had been poisoned, and I was to go there Saturday afternoon as myself, a detective named Archie Goodwin, to investigate the poisoning. His cousin would invite him to her place, Birchvale, for dinner, and I would go along.

It was a quiet Saturday morning in the office, with Wolfe up in the plant rooms as usual from nine to eleven, and I finished typing the report of a certain case with no interruptions except a couple of phone calls which I handled myself, and one for which I had to give Wolfe a buzz—from somebody at Mummiani's on Fulton Street to say that they had just got eight pounds of fresh sausage from Bill Darst at Hackettstown, and Wolfe could have half of it. Since Wolfe regards Darst as the best sausage maker west of Cherbourg, he asked that it be sent immediately by messenger, and for heaven's sake not with dry ice.

When, at 11:01, the sound of Wolfe's elevator came, I got the big dictionary in front of me on my desk, opened to H, and was bent over it as he entered the office, crossed to his oversized custom-built chair, and sat. He didn't bite at once because his mind was elsewhere. Even before he rang for beer he asked, "Has the sausage come?"

Without looking up I told him no.

He pressed the button twice—the beer signal—leaned back, and frowned at me. I didn't see the frown, absorbed as I was in the dictionary, but it was in his tone of voice.

"What are you looking up?" he demanded.

"Oh, just a word," I said casually. "Checking up on our client. I thought she was illiterate, her calling you handsome—remember? But, by gum, it was merely an understatement. Here it is, absolutely kosher: 'Handsome: moderately large.' For an example it gives 'a handsome sum of money.' So she was dead right, you're a handsome detective, meaning a moderately large detective." I closed the dictionary and returned it to its place, remarking cheerfully, "Live and learn!"

It was a dud. Ordinarily that would have started him tossing phrases and adjectives, but he was occupied. Maybe he didn't even hear me. When Fritz came from the kitchen with the beer, Wolfe, taking from a drawer the gold bottle opener that a pleased client had given him, spoke.

"Fritz, good news. We're getting some of Mr. Darst's sausage—four pounds."

Fritz let his eyes gleam. "Ha! Today?"

"Any moment." Wolfe poured beer. "That raises the question of cloves again. What do you think?"

"I'm against it," Fritz said firmly.

Wolfe nodded. "I think I agree. I *think* I do. You may remember what Marko Vukcic said last year—and by the way, he must be invited for a taste of this. For Monday luncheon?"

"That would be possible," Fritz conceded, "but we have arranged for shad with roe—"

"Of course." Wolfe lifted his glass and drank, put it down empty, and used his handkerchief on his lips. That, he thought, was the only way for a man to scent a handkerchief. "We'll have Marko for the sausage at Monday dinner, followed by duck Mondor." He leaned forward and wiggled a finger. "Now about the shallots and fresh thyme: there's no use depending on Mr. Colson. We might get diddled again. Archie will have to go—"

At that point Archie had to go answer the doorbell, which I was glad to do. I fully appreciate, mostly anyhow, the results of Wolfe's and Fritz's powwows on grub when it arrives at the table, but the gab often strikes me as overdone. So I didn't mind the call to the hall and the front door. There I found a young man with a pug nose and a package, wearing a cap that said "Fleet Messenger Service." I signed the slip, shut the door, started back down the hall, and was met not only by Fritz but by Wolfe too, who can move well enough when there's something he thinks is worth moving for. He took the package from me and headed for the kitchen, followed by Fritz and me.

The small carton was sealed with tape. In the kitchen Wolfe put it on the long table, reached to the rack for a knife, cut the tape, and pulled the flaps up. My reflexes are quick, and the instant the hissing noise started I grabbed Wolfe's arm to haul him back, yelling at Fritz, "Watch out! Drop!"

Wolfe can move all right, considering what he has to move. He and I were through the open door into the hall before the explosion came, and Fritz came bounding after, pulling the door with him. We all kept going, along the short stretch of hall to the office door, and into the office. There we stopped dead. No explosion yet.

"It's still hissing," I said, and moved.

"Come back here!" Wolfe commanded.

"Be quiet," I commanded back, and dropped to my hands and knees and made it into the hall. There I stopped to sniff, crawled to within a yard of the crack under the kitchen door, and sniffed again.

I arose, returned to the office on my feet, and told them, "Gas. Tear gas, I think. The hissing has stopped."

Wolfe snorted.

"No sausage," Fritz said grimly.

"If it had been a trigger job on a grenade," I told him, "there would have been plenty of sausage. Not for us, of us. Now it's merely a damn nuisance. You'd better sit here and chat a while."

I marched to the hall and shut the door behind me, went and opened the front door wide, came back and stood at the kitchen door and took a full breath, opened the door, raced through and opened the back door into the courtyard, and ran back again to the front. Even there the air current was too gassy for comfort, so I moved out to the stoop. I had been there only a moment when I heard my name called.

"Archie!"

I turned. Wolfe's head with its big oblong face was protruding from a window of the front room.

"Yes, sir," I said brightly.

"Who brought that package?"

I told him Fleet Messenger Service.

When the breeze through the hall had cleared the air I returned to the kitchen and Fritz joined me. We gave the package a look and found it was quite simple: a metal cylinder with a valve, with a brass rod that had been adjusted so that when the package was opened so was the valve. There was still a strong smell, close up, and Fritz took it to the basement. I went to the office and found Wolfe behind his desk, busy at the phone.

I dropped into my chair and dabbed at my runny eyes with my handkerchief. When he hung up I asked, "Any luck?"

"I didn't expect any," he growled.

"Right. Shall I call a cop?"

"No."

I nodded. "The question was rhetorical." I dabbed at my eyes some more, and blew my nose. "Nero Wolfe does not call cops. Nero Wolfe opens his own packages of sausage and makes his own enemies bite the dust." I blew my nose again. "Nero Wolfe is a man who will go far if he opens one package too many. Nero Wolfe has never—"

"The question was not rhetorical," Wolfe said rudely. "That is not what rhetorical means."

"No? I asked it. I meant it to be rhetorical. Can you prove that I don't know what rhetorical means?" I blew my nose. "When you ask me a question, which God knows is often, do I assume—"

The phone rang. One of the million things I do to earn my salary is to answer it, so I did. And then a funny thing happened. There is

absolutely no question that it was a shock to me to hear that voice,
I know that, because I felt it in my stomach. But partly what makes
a shock a shock is that it is unexpected, and I do not think the sound
of that voice in my ear was unexpected. I think that Wolfe and I
had been sitting there talking just to hear ourselves because we both
expected, after what had happened, to hear that voice sooner or
later—and probably sooner.

What it said was only, "May I speak to Mr. Wolfe, please?"

I felt it in my stomach, sharp and strong, but damned if I was
going to let him know it. I said, but not cordially, "Oh, hello there.
If I get you. Was your name Duncan once?"

"Yes. Mr. Wolfe, please."

"Hold the wire." I covered the transmitter and told Wolfe,
"Whosis."

"Who?" he demanded.

"You know who from my face. Mr. X. Mr. Z. Him."

With his lips pressed tight, Wolfe reached for his phone. "This is
Nero Wolfe."

"How do you do, Mr. Wolfe." I was staying on, and the hard,
cold, precise voice sounded exactly as it had the four previous times
I had heard it, over a period of three years. It pronounced all its
syllables clearly and smoothly. "Do you know who I am?"

"Yes." Wolfe was curt. "What do you want?"

"I want to call your attention to my forbearance. That little package could have been something really destructive, but I preferred
only to give you notice. As I told you about a year ago, it's a more
interesting world with you in it."

"I find it so," Wolfe said dryly.

"No doubt. Besides, I haven't forgotten your brilliant exposure of
the murderer of Louis Rony. It happened then that your interest
ran with mine. But it doesn't now, with Mrs. Barry Rackham, and
that won't do. Because of my regard for you, I don't want you to
lose a fee. Return her money and withdraw, and two months from
today I shall send you ten thousand dollars in cash. Twice previously
you have disregarded similar requests from me, and circumstances
saved you. I advise strongly against a repetition. You will have to
understand—"

Wolfe took the phone from his ear and placed it on the cradle.
Since the effect of that would be lost if my line stayed open, I did
likewise, practically simultaneously.

"By God, we're off again," I began. "Of all the rotten—"

"Shut up," Wolfe growled.

I obeyed. He rested his elbows on his chair arms, interlaced his fingers in front of where he was roundest, and gazed at a corner of his desk blotter. I did not, as a matter of fact, have anything to say except that it was a lousy break, and that didn't need saying. Wolfe had once ordered me to forget that I had ever heard the name Arnold Zeck, but whether I called him Zeck or Whosis or X, he was still the man who, some ten months ago, had arranged for two guys with an SM and a tommy gun to open up on Wolfe's plant rooms from a roof across the street, thereby ruining ten thousand dollars' worth of glass and equipment and turning eight thousand valuable orchid plants into a good start on a compost heap. That had been intended just for a warning.

Now he was telling us to lay off of Barry Rackham. That probably meant that without turning a finger we had found the answer to Mrs. Rackham's question—where was her husband getting his pocket money? He had got inside the circle of Arnold Zeck's operations, about which Wolfe had once remarked that all of them were illegal and some of them were morally repulsive. And Zeck didn't want any snooping around one of his men. That was almost certainly the sketch, but whether it was or not, the fact remained that we had run smack into Zeck again, which was fully as bad as having a gob of Darst sausage turn into a cylinder of tear gas.

"He likes to time things right, damn him," I complained. "He likes to make things dramatic. He had someone within range of this house to see the package being delivered, and when I left the front door open and then went and stood on the stoop that showed that the package had been opened, and as soon as he got the word he phoned. Hell, he might even—"

I stopped because I saw that I was talking to myself. Wolfe wasn't hearing me. He still sat gazing at the corner of the blotter. I shut my trap and sat and gazed at him. It was a good five minutes before he spoke.

"Archie," he said, looking at me.

"Yes, sir."

"How many cases have we handled since last July?"

"All kinds? Everything? Oh, forty."

"I would have thought more. Very well, say forty. We crossed this man's path inadvertently two years ago, and again last year.

He and I both deal with crime, and his net is spread wide, so that may be taken as a reasonable expectation for the future: once a year, or in one out of every forty cases that come to us, we will run into him. This episode will be repeated." He aimed a thumb at the phone. "That thing will ring, and that confounded voice will presume to dictate to us. If we obey the dictate we will be maintaining this office and our means of livelihood only by his sufferance. If we defy it we shall be constantly in a state of trepidant vigilance, and one or both of us will probably get killed. Well?"

I shook my head. "It couldn't be made plainer. I don't care much for either one."

"Neither do I."

"If you got killed I'd be out of a job, and if I got killed you might as well retire." I glanced at my wristwatch. "The hell of it is we haven't got a week to decide. It's twelve-twenty, and I'm expected at the Hillside Kennels at three o'clock, and I have to eat lunch and shave and change my clothes. That is, if I go. If I go?"

"Precisely." Wolfe sighed. "That's the point. Two years ago, in the Orchard case, I took to myself the responsibility of ignoring this man's threat. Last year, in the Kane case, I did the same. This time I don't want to and I won't. Basic policy is my affair, I know that, but I am not going to tell you that in order to earn your pay you must go up there today and look at Mr. Rackham. If you prefer, you may phone and postpone it, and we'll consider the matter at greater length."

I had my brows raised at him. "I'll be damned. Put it on me, huh?"

"Yes. My nerve is gone. If public servants and other respected citizens take orders from this man, why shouldn't I?"

"You damn faker," I said indulgently. "You know perfectly well that I would rather eat soap than have you think I would knuckle under to that son of a bitch, and I know that you would rather put horseradish on oysters than have me think you would. I might if you didn't know about it, and you might if I didn't know about it, but as it is we're stuck."

Wolfe sighed again, deeper. "I take it that you're going?"

"I am. But under one condition, that the trepidant vigilance begins as of now. That you call Fritz in, and Theodore down from the plant rooms, and tell them what we're up against, and the chain bolts are to be kept constantly on both doors, and you keep away from windows, and nothing and no one is to be allowed to enter when I'm not here."

"Good heavens," he objected sourly, "that's no way to live."

"You can't tell till you try it. In ten years you may like it fine." I buzzed the plant rooms on the house phone to get Theodore.

Wolfe sat scowling at me.

3

When, swinging the car off Taconic State Parkway to hit Route 100, my dash clock said only 2:40, I decided to make a little detour. It would be only a couple of miles out of my way. So at Pines Bridge I turned right, instead of left across the bridge. It wouldn't serve my purpose to make for the entrance to the estate where EASTCREST was carved on the great stone pillar, since all I would see there was a driveway curving up through the woods, and I turned off a mile short of that to climb a bumpy road up a hill. At the top the road went straight for a stretch between meadows, and I eased the car off onto the grass, stopped, and took the binoculars and aimed them at the summit of the next hill, somewhat higher than the one I was on, where the roof and upper walls of a stone mansion showed above the trees. Now, in early April, with no leaves yet, and with the binoculars, I could see most of the mansion and even something of the surrounding grounds, and a couple of men moving about.

That was Eastcrest, the legal residence of the illegal Arnold Zeck —but of course there are many ways of being illegal. One is to drive through a red light. Another is to break laws by proxy only, for money only, get your cut so it can't be traced, and never try to buy a man too cheap. That was what Zeck had been doing for more than twenty years—and there was Eastcrest.

All I was after was to take a look, just case it from a hilltop. I had never seen Zeck, and as far as I knew Wolfe hadn't either. Now that we were headed at him for the third time, and this time it might be for keeps, I thought I should at least see his roof and count his chimneys. That was all. He had been too damn remote and mysterious. Now I knew he had four chimneys, and that the one on the south wing had two loose bricks.

I turned the car around and headed down the hill, and, if you

348

TRIPLE ZECK

care to believe it, I kept glancing in the mirror to see if something showed up behind. That was how far gone I was on Zeck. It was not healthy for my self-respect, it was bad for my nerves, and I was good and tired of it.

Mrs. Rackham's place, Birchvale, was only five miles from there, the other side of Mount Kisco, but I made a wrong turn and didn't arrive until a quarter past three. The entrance to her estate was adequate but not imposing. I went on by, and before I knew it there was a neat little sign on the left:

HILLSIDE KENNELS
Doberman Pinschers

The gate opening was narrow and so was the drive, and I kept going on past the house to a bare rectangle in the rear, not very well graveled, and maneuvered into a corner close to a wooden building. As I climbed out a voice came from somewhere, and then a ferocious wild beast leaped from behind a bush and started for me like a streak of lightning. I froze except for my right arm, which sent my hand to my shoulder holster automatically.

A female voice sounded sharp in command. "Back!"

The beast, ten paces from me, whirled on a dime, trotted swiftly to the woman who had appeared at the edge of the rectangle, whirled again and stood facing me, concentrating with all its might on looking beautiful and dangerous. I could have plugged it with pleasure. I do not like dogs that assume you're guilty until you prove you're innocent. I like democratic dogs.

A man had appeared beside the woman. They advanced.

She spoke. "Mr. Goodwin? Mr. Leeds had to go on an errand, but he'll be back soon. I'm Annabel Frey." She came to me and offered a hand, and I took it.

This was my first check on an item of information furnished us by Mrs. Rackham, and I gave her an A for accuracy. She had said that her daughter-in-law was very beautiful. Some might have been inclined to argue it, for instance those who don't like eyes so far apart or those who prefer pink skin to dark, but I'm not so finicky about details. The man stepped up, and she pronounced his name, Hammond, and we shook. He was a stocky middle-aged specimen in a bright blue shirt, a tan jacket, and gray slacks—a hell of a combination. I was wearing a mixed tweed made by Fradick, with an off-white shirt and a maroon tie.

"I'll sit in my car," I told them, "to wait for Mr. Leeds. With the livestock around loose like that."

She laughed. "Duke isn't loose, he's with me. He wouldn't have touched you. He would have stopped three paces off, springing distance, and waited for me. Don't you like dogs?"

"It depends on the dog. You might as well ask if I like lemon pie. With a dog who thinks of space between him and me only in terms of springing distance, my attitude is strictly one of trepidant vigilance."

"My Lord." She blinked long lashes over dark blue eyes. "Do you always talk like that?" The eyes went to Hammond. "Did you get that, Dana?"

"I quite agree with him," Hammond declared, "as you know. I'm not afraid to say so, either, because it shows the lengths I'll go to, to be with you. When you opened his kennel and he leaped out I could feel my hair standing up."

"I know," Annabel Frey said scornfully. "Duke knows too. I guess I'd better put him in." She left us, speaking to the dog, who abandoned his pose and trotted to her, and they disappeared around a corner of the building. There was a similarity in the movements of the two, muscular and sure and quick, but sort of nervous and dainty.

"Now we can relax," I told Hammond.

"I just can't help it," he said, irritated. "I'm not strong for dogs anyhow, and with these . . ." He shrugged. "I'd just as soon go for a walk with a tiger."

Soon Annabel rejoined us, with a crack about Hammond's hair. I suggested that if they had something to do I could wait for Leeds without any help, but she said no.

"We only came to see you," she stated impersonally. "That is, I did, and Mr. Hammond went to the length of coming along. Just to see you, even if you are Archie Goodwin, I wouldn't cross the street; but I want to watch you work. So many things fall short of the build-up, I want to see if a famous detective does. I'm skeptical already. You look younger than you should, and you dress too well, and if you really thought that dog might jump you, you should have done something to—where did that come from? Hey!"

Sometimes I fumble a little drawing from my armpit, but that time it had been slick and clean. I had the barrel pointed straight up. Hammond had made a noise and an involuntary backward jerk.

I grinned at her. "Showing off. Okay? Want to try it? Get him and send him out from behind that same bush, with orders to take me, and any amount up to two bits, even, that he won't reach me." I returned the gun to the holster. "Ready?"

She blinked. "You mean you *would?*"

Hammond giggled. He was a full-sized middle-aged man and he looked like a banker, and I want to be fair to him, but he giggled. "Look out, Annabel," he said warningly. "He might."

"Of course," I told her, "you would be in the line of fire, and I've never shot a fast-moving dog, so we would both be taking a risk. Only I don't like you being skeptical. Stick around and you'll see."

That was a mistake, caused by my temperament. It is natural and wholesome for a man of my age to enjoy association with a woman of her age, maid, wife, or widow, but I should have had sense enough to stop to realize what I was getting in for. She had said that she had come to watch me work, and there I was asking for it. As a result, I had to spend a solid hour pretending that I was hell bent to find out who had poisoned one of Leeds' dogs when I didn't care a hang. Not that I love dog poisoners, but that wasn't what was on my mind.

When Calvin Leeds showed up, as he did soon in an old station wagon with its rear taken up with a big wire cage, the four of us made a tour of the kennels and the runs, with Leeds briefing me, and me asking questions and making notes, and then we went in the house and extended the inquiry to aspects such as the poison used, the method employed, the known suspects, and so on. It was a strain. I had to make it good, because that was what I was supposed to be there for, and also because Annabel was too good-looking to let her be skeptical about me. And the dog hadn't even died! He was alive and well. But I went to it as if it were the biggest case of the year for Nero Wolfe and me, and Leeds got a good fifty bucks' worth of detection for nothing. Of course nobody got detected, but I asked damn good questions.

After Annabel and Hammond left to return to Birchvale next door, I asked Leeds about Hammond, and sure enough he was a banker. He was a vice-president of the Metropolitan Trust Company, who handled affairs for Mrs. Rackham—had done so ever since the death of her first husband. When I remarked that Hammond seemed to have it in mind to handle Mrs. Rackham's daughter-in-law also, Leeds said he hadn't noticed. I asked who else would be there at dinner.

"You and me," Leeds said. He was sipping a highball, taking his time with it. We were in the little living room of his little house, about which there was nothing remarkable except the dozens of pictures of dogs on the walls. Moving around outside, there had been more spring to him than to lots of guys half his age; now he was sprawled on a couch, all loose. I was reminded of one of the dogs we had come upon during our tour, lying in the sun at the door of its kennel.

"You and me," he said, "and my cousin and her husband, and Mrs. Frey, whom you have met, and Hammond, and the statesman, that's seven—"

"Who's the statesman?"

"Oliver A. Pierce."

"I'm intimate with lots of statesmen, but I never heard of him."

"Don't let him know it." Leeds chuckled. "It's true that at thirty-four he has only got as far as state assemblyman, but the war made a gap for him the same as for other young men. Give him a chance. One will be enough."

"What is he, a friend of the family?"

"No, and that's one on him." He chuckled again. "When he was first seen here, last summer, he came as a guest of Mrs. Frey—that is, invited by her—but before long either she had seen enough of him or he had seen enough of her. Meanwhile, however, he had seen Lina Darrow, and he was caught anyhow."

"Who's Lina Darrow?"

"My cousin's secretary—by the way, she'll be at dinner too, that'll make eight. I don't know who invited him—my cousin perhaps—but it's Miss Darrow that gets him here, a busy statesman." Leeds snorted. "At his age he might know better."

"You don't think much of women, huh?"

"I don't think of them at all. Much or little." Leeds finished his drink. "Look at it. Which would you rather live with, those wonderful animals out there, or a woman?"

"A woman," I said firmly. "I haven't run across her yet, there are so many, but even if she does turn out to be a dog I hope to God it won't be one of yours. I want the kind I can let run loose." I waved a hand. "Forget it. You like 'em, you can have 'em. Mrs. Frey is a member of the household, is she?"

"Yes," he said shortly.

"Mrs. Rackham keeping her around as a souvenir of her dead son? Being neurotic about it?"

"I don't know. Ask her." Leeds straightened up and got to his feet. "You know, of course, that I didn't approve of her going to Nero Wolfe. I went with her only because she insisted on it. I don't see how any good can come of it, but I think harm might. I don't think you ought to be here, but you are, and we might as well go on over and drink their liquor instead of mine. I'll go and wash up."

He left me.

4

Having been given by Leeds my choice of driving over—three minutes—or taking a trail through the woods, I voted for walking. The edge of the woods was only a hundred yards to the rear of the kennels. It had been a warm day for early April, but now, with the sun gone over the hill, the sharp air made me want to step it up, which was just as well because I had to, to keep up with Leeds. He walked as if he meant it. When I commented on the fact that we ran into no fence anywhere, neither in the woods nor in the clear, he said that his place was merely a little corner of Mrs. Rackham's property which she had let him build on some years ago.

The last stretch of our walk was along a curving gravel path that wound through lawns, shrubs, trees, and different-shaped patches of bare earth. Living in the country would be more convenient if they would repeal the law against paths that go straight from one place to another place. The bigger and showier the grounds are, the more the paths have to curve, and the main reason for having lots of bushes and things is to compel the paths to curve in order to get through the mess. Anyhow, Leeds and I finally got to the house, and entered without ringing or knocking, so apparently he was more or less a member of the household too.

All six of them were gathered in a room that was longer and wider than Leeds' whole house, with twenty rugs to slide on and at least forty different things to sit on, but it didn't seem as if they had worked up much gaiety, in spite of the full stock of the portable bar, because Leeds and I were greeted as though nothing so nice had happened in years. Leeds introduced me, since I wasn't supposed to have met Mrs. Rackham, and after I had been supplied with liquid Annabel Frey gave a lecture on how I worked. Then Oliver A. Pierce, the statesman, wanted me to demonstrate by grilling each of them as suspected dog poisoners. When I tried to beg off they insisted, so I obliged. I was only so-so.

Pierce was a smooth article. His manner was of course based on the law of nature regulating the attitude of an elected person toward everybody old enough to vote, but his timing and variations were so good that it was hard to recognize it, although he was only about my age. He was also about my size, with broad shoulders and a homely honest face, and a draw on his smile as swift as a flash bulb. I made a note to look up whether I lived in his assembly district. If he got the breaks the only question about him was how far and how soon.

If in addition to his own equipment and talents he acquired Lina Darrow as a partner, it would probably be farther and sooner. She was, I would have guessed, slightly younger than Annabel Frey—twenty-six maybe—and I never saw a finer pair of eyes. She was obviously underplaying them, or rather what was back of them. When I was questioning her she pretended I had her in a corner, while her eyes gave it away that she could have waltzed all around me if she wanted to. I didn't know whether she thought she was kidding somebody, or was just practicing, or had some serious reason for passing herself off as a flub.

Barry Rackham had me stumped and also annoyed. Either I was dumber than Nero Wolfe thought I was, and twice as dumb as I thought I was, or he was smarter than he looked. New York was full of him, and he was full of New York. Go into any Madison Avenue bar between five and six-thirty and there would be six or eight of him there: not quite young but miles from being old; masculine all over except the fingernails; some tired and some fresh and ready, depending on the current status; and all slightly puffy below the eyes. I knew him from A to Z, or thought I did, but I couldn't make up my mind whether he knew what I was there for, and that was the one concrete thing I had hoped to get done. If he knew, the question whether he was on Zeck's payroll was answered; if he didn't, that question was still open.

And I still hadn't been able to decide when, at the dinner table, we had finished the dessert and got up to go elsewhere for coffee.

At first I had thought he couldn't possibly be wise, when I had him sized up for a dummy who had had the good luck to catch Mrs. Rackham's eye somewhere and then had happened to take the only line she would fall for, but further observation had made me reconsider. His handling of his wife had character in it; it wasn't just yes or no. At the dinner table he had an exchange with Pierce about rent control, and without seeming to try he got the statesman so tangled up he couldn't wiggle loose. Then he had a good laugh, took the other side of the argument, and made a monkey out of Dana Hammond.

I decided I'd better start all over.

On the way back to the living room for coffee, Lina Darrow joined me. "Why did you take it out on me?" she demanded.

I said I didn't know I had.

"Certainly you did. Trying to indict me for dog poisoning. You went after me much harder than you did the others." Her fingers were on the inside of my arm, lightly.

"Certainly," I conceded. "Nothing new to you, was it? A man going after you harder than the others?"

"Thanks. But I mean it. Of course you know I'm just a working girl."

"Sure. That's why I was tougher with you. That, and because I wondered why you were playing dumb."

The statesman Pierce broke us up then, as we entered the living room, and I didn't fight for her. We collected in the neighborhood of the fireplace for coffee, and there was a good deal of talk about nothing, and after a while somebody suggested television, and Barry Rackham went and turned it on. He and Annabel turned out lights. As the rest of us got settled in favorably placed seats, Mrs. Rackham left us. A little later, as I sat in the semi-darkness scowling at a cosmetic commercial, some obscure sense told me that danger was approaching and I jerked my head around. It was right there at my elbow: a Doberman pinscher, looking larger than normal in that light, staring intently past me at the screen.

Mrs. Rackham, just behind it, apparently misinterpreting my quick movement, spoke hastily and loudly above the noise of the broadcast. "Don't try to pat him!"

"I won't," I said emphatically.

"He'll behave," she assured me. "He loves television." She went on with him, farther forward. As they passed Calvin Leeds the af-

fectionate pet halted for a brief sniff, and got a stroke on the head
in response. No one else was honored.

Ninety minutes of video got us to half-past ten, and got us nothing
else, especially me. I was still on the fence about Barry Rackham.
Television is raising hell with the detective business. It used to be
that a social evening at someone's house or apartment was a fine
opportunity for picking up lines and angles, moving around, watching and talking and listening; but with a television session you might
as well be home in bed. You can't see faces, and if someone does
make a remark you can't hear it unless it's a scream, and you can't
even start a private inquiry, such as finding out where a young
widow stands now on skepticism. In a movie theater at least you
can hold hands.

However, I did finally get what might have been a nibble. The
screen had been turned off, and we had all got up to stretch, and
Annabel had offered to drive Leeds and me home, and Leeds had
told her that we would rather walk, when Barry Rackham moseyed
over to me and said he hoped the television hadn't bored me too
much. I said no, just enough.

"Think you'll get anywhere on your job for Leeds?" he asked,
jiggling his highball glass to make the ice tinkle.

I lifted my shoulders and let them drop. "I don't know. A month's
gone by."

He nodded. "That's what makes it hard to believe."

"Yeah, why?"

"That he would wait a month and then decide to blow himself
to a fee for Nero Wolfe. Everybody knows that Wolfe comes high.
I wouldn't have thought Leeds could afford it." Rackham smiled
at me. "Driving back tonight?"

"No, I'm staying over."

"That's sensible. Night driving is dangerous, I think. The Sunday
traffic won't be bad this time of year if you leave early." He touched
my chest with a forefinger. "That's it, leave early." He moved off.

Annabel was yawning, and Dana Hammond was looking at
her as if that was exactly what he had come to Birchvale for, to see
her yawn. Lina Darrow was looking from Barry Rackham to me
and back again, and pretending she wasn't looking anywhere with
those eyes. The Doberman pinscher was standing tense, and Pierce,
from a safe ten feet—one more than springing distance—was regard-

ing it with an expression that gave me a more sympathetic feeling
for him than I ever expected to have for a statesman.

Calvin Leeds and Mrs. Rackham were also looking at the dog,
with a quite different expression.

"At least two pounds overweight," Leeds was saying. "You feed
him too much."

Mrs. Rackham protested that she didn't.

"Then you don't run him enough."

"I know it," she admitted. "I will from now on, I'll be here more.
I was busy today. I'll take him out now. It's a perfect night for a
good walk—Barry, do you feel like walking?"

He didn't. He was nice about it, but he didn't. She broadened the
invitation to take in the group, but there were no takers. She offered
to walk Leeds and me home, but Leeds said she would go too slow,
and he should have been in bed long ago since his rising time was
six o'clock. He moved, and told me to come on if I was coming.

We said good night and left.

The outdoor air was sharper now. There were a few stars but
no moon, and alone with no flashlight I would never have been able
to keep that trail through the woods and might have made the Hillside Kennels clearing by dawn. For Leeds a flashlight would have
been only a nuisance. He strode along at the same gait as in the
daytime, and I stumbled at his heels, catching my toes on things,
teetering on roots and pebbles, and once going clear down. I am
not a deerstalker and don't want to be. As we approached the kennels Leeds called out, and the sound came of many movements, but
not a bark. Who wants a dog, let alone thirty or forty, not even human enough to bark when you come home?

Leeds said that since the poisoning he always took a look around
before going to bed, and I went on in the house and up to the
little room where I had put my bag. I was sitting on the bed in pajamas, scratching the side of my neck and considering Barry Rackham's last-minute remarks, when Leeds entered downstairs and
came up to ask if I was comfortable. I told him I soon would be,
and he said good night and went down the short hall to his room.

I opened a window, turned out the light, and got into bed; but
in three minutes I saw it wasn't working. My practice is to empty
my head simultaneously with dropping it on the pillow. If something
sticks and doesn't want to come out I'll give it up to three minutes
but no more. Then I act. This time, of course, it was Barry Rackham

that stuck. I had to decide that he knew what I was there for or that he didn't, or, as an alternative, decide definitely that I wouldn't try to decide until tomorrow. I got out of bed and went and sat on a chair.

It may have taken five minutes, or it could have been fifteen; I don't know. Anyhow it didn't accomplish anything except getting Rackham unstuck from my head for the night, for the best I could do was decide for postponement. If he had his guard up, so far I had not got past it. With that settled, I got under the covers again, took ten seconds to get into position on a strange mattress, and was off this time. . . .

Nearly, but not quite. A shutter or something began to squeak. Calling it a shutter jerked me back part way, because there were no shutters on the windows, so it couldn't be that. I was now enough awake to argue. The sound continued, at brief intervals. It not only wasn't a shutter, it wasn't a squeak. Then it was a baby whining; but it wasn't, because it came from the open window, and there were no babies out there. To hell with it. I turned over, putting my back to the window, but the sound still came, and I had been wrong. It was more of a whimper than a whine. Oh, nuts.

I rolled out of bed, switched on a light, went down the hall to Leeds' door, knocked on it, and opened it.

"Well?" he asked, full voice.

"Have you got a dog that whimpers at night?"

"Whimpers? No."

"Then shall I go see what it is? I hear it through my window."

"It's probably—turn on the light, will you?"

I found the wall switch and flipped it. His pajamas were green with thin white stripes. Giving me a look which implied that here was one more reason for disapproving of my being there, he padded past me into the hall and on into my room, me following. He stood a moment to listen, crossed and stuck his head out the window, pulled it in again, and this time went by me with no look at all and moving fast. I followed him downstairs and to the side door, where he pushed a light switch with one hand while he opened the door with the other, and stepped across the sill.

"By God," he said. "All right, Nobby, all right."

He squatted.

I take back none of my remarks about Doberman pinschers, but I admit that that was no time to expand on them, nor did I feel like

it. The dog lay on its side on the slab of stone with its legs twitching, trying to lift its head enough to look at Leeds; and from its side
that was up, toward the belly and midway between the front and
hind legs, protruded the chased silver handle of a knife. The hair
around was matted with blood.

The dog had stopped whimpering. Now suddenly it bared its
teeth and snarled, but weakly.

"All right, Nobby," Leeds said. He had his palm against the
side, forward, over the heart.

"He's about gone," he said.

I discovered that I was shivering, decided to stop, and did.

"Pull the knife out of him?" I suggested. "Maybe—"

"No. That would finish him. I think he's finished anyhow."

He was. The dog died as Leeds squatted there and I stood not
permitting myself to shiver in the cold night breeze. I could see
the slender muscular legs stretch tight and then go loose, and after
another minute Leeds took his hand away and stood up.

"Will you please hold the door open?" he asked. "It's off plumb
and swings shut."

I obliged, holding it wide and standing aside to let him through.
With the dog's body in his arms, he crossed to a wooden bench at
one side of the little square hall and put the burden down. Then
he turned to me. "I'm going to put something on and go out and
look around. Come or stay, suit yourself."

"I'll come. Is it one of your dogs? Or—"

He had started for the stairs, but halted. "No. Sarah's—my cousin's. He was there tonight, you saw him." His face twitched. "By
God, look at him! Getting here with that knife in him! I gave him
to her two years ago; he's been her dog for two years, but when it
came to this it was me he came to. By God!"

He went for the stairs and up, and I followed. Over the years
there had been several occasions when I needed to get some clothes
on without delay, and I thought I was fast, but I was still in my room
with a shoe to lace when Leeds' steps were in the hall again and he
called in to me, "Wait downstairs. I'll be back in a minute."

I called that I was coming, but he didn't halt. By the time I got
down to the little square hall he was gone, and the outside door
was shut. I opened it and stepped out and yelled, "Hey, Leeds!"

His voice came from somewhere in the darkness. "I said wait!"

Even if he had decided not to bother with me there was no use trying to dash after him, with my handicap, so I settled for making my way around the corner of the house and across the graveled rectangle to where my car was parked. Getting the door unlocked, I climbed in and got the flashlight from the dash compartment. That put me, if not even with Leeds for a night outdoors in the country, at least a lot closer to him. Relocking the car door, I sent the beam of the flash around and then switched it off and went back to the side door of the house.

I could hear steps, faint, then louder, and soon Leeds appeared within the area of light from the hall window. He wasn't alone. With him was a dog, a length ahead of him, on a leash. As they approached I courteously stepped aside, but the dog ignored me completely. Leeds opened the door and they entered the hall, and I joined them.

"Get in front of her," Leeds said, "a yard off, and stand still."

I obeyed, circling.

"See, Hebe."

For the first time the beast admitted I was there. She lifted her head at me, then stepped forward and smelled my pants legs, not in haste. When she had finished Leeds crossed to where the dead dog lay on the bench, made a sign, and Hebe went to him.

Leeds passed his fingertips along the dead dog's belly, touching lightly the smooth short hair. "Take it, Hebe."

She stretched her sinewy neck, sniffed along the course his fingertips had taken, backed up a step, and looked up at him.

"Don't be so damn sure," Leeds told her. He pointed a finger. "Take it again."

She did so, taking more time for it, and again looked up at him.

"I didn't know they were hounds," I remarked.

"They're everything they ought to be." I suppose Leeds made some signal, though I didn't see it, and the dog started toward the door, with her master at the other end of the leash. "They have excellent scent, and this one's extraordinary. She's Nobby's mother."

Outside, on the slab of stone where we had found Nobby, Leeds said, "Take it, Hebe," and when she made a low noise in her throat as she tightened the leash, he added, "Quiet, now. I'll do the talking."

She took him, with me at their heels, around the corner of the house to the graveled space, across that, along the wall of the main outbuilding, and to a corner of the enclosed run. There she stopped and lifted her head.

Leeds waited half a minute before he spoke. "Bah. Can't you tell dogs apart? Take it!"

I switched the flashlight on, got a reprimand, and switched it off. Hebe made her throat noise again, got her nose down, and started off. We crossed the meadow on the trail to the edge of the woods and kept going. The pace was steady but not fast; for me it was an easy stroll, nothing like the race Leeds had led me previously. Even with no leaves on the trees it was a lot darker there, but unless my sense of direction was completely cockeyed we were sticking to the trail I had been over twice before.

"We're heading straight for the house, aren't we?" I asked.

For reply I got only a grunt.

For the first two hundred yards or so after entering the woods it was a steady climb, not steep, and then a leveling off for another couple of hundred yards to the start of the easy long descent to the edge of the Birchvale manicured grounds. It was at about the middle of the level stretch that Hebe suddenly went crazy. She dashed abruptly to one side, off the trail, jerking Leeds so that he had to dance to keep his feet, then whirled and came back into him, with a high thin quavering noise not at all like what she had said before.

Leeds spoke to her sharply, but I don't know what he said. By then my eyes had got pretty well accommodated to the circumstances. However, I am not saying that there in the dark among the trees, at a distance of twenty feet, I recognized the blob on the ground. I do assert that at the instant I pressed the button of the flashlight, before the light came, I knew already that it was the body of Mrs. Barry Rackham.

This time I got no reprimand. Leeds was with me as I stepped off the trail and covered the twenty feet. She was lying on her side, as Nobby had been, but her neck was twisted so that her face was nearly upturned to the sky, and I thought for a second it was a broken neck until I saw the blood on the front of her white sweater. I stooped and got my fingers on her wrist. Leeds picked up a dead leaf, laid it on her mouth and nostrils, and asked me to kneel to help him keep the breeze away.

When we had gazed at the motionless leaf for twenty seconds he said, "She's dead."

"Yeah." I stood up. "Even if she weren't, she would be by the time we got her to the house. I'll go—"

"She is dead, isn't she?"

"Certainly. I'll—"

"By God." He got erect, coming up straight in one movement. "Nobby and now her. You stay here—" He took a quick step, but I caught his arm. He jerked loose, violently.

I said fast, "Take it easy." I got his arm again, and he was trembling. "You bust in there and there's no telling what you'll do. Stay here and I'll go—"

He pulled free and started off.

"Wait!" I commanded, and he halted. "But first get a doctor and call the police. Do that first. I'm going to your place. We left that knife in the dog, and someone might want it. Can't you put Hebe on guard here?"

He spoke, not to me but to Hebe. She came to him, a darting shadow, close to him. He leaned over to touch the shoulder of the body of Mrs. Barry Rackham and said, "Watch it, Hebe." The dog moved alongside the body, and Leeds, with nothing to say to me, went. He didn't leap or run, but he sure was gone. I called after him, "Phone the police before you kill anybody!" stepped to the trail, and headed for Hillside Kennels.

With the flashlight I had no trouble finding my way. This time, as I approached, the livestock barked plenty, and, hoping the kennel doors were all closed tight, I had my gun out as I passed the runs and the buildings. Nothing attacked me but noise, and that stopped when I had entered the house and closed the door. Apparently if an enemy once got inside it was then up to the master.

Nobby was still there on the bench, and the knife was still in him. With only a glance at him in passing, I made for the little living room, where I had previously seen a phone on a table, turned on a light, went to the phone, and got the operator and gave her a number. As I waited a look at my wristwatch showed me five minutes past midnight. I hoped Wolfe hadn't forgotten to plug in the line to his room when he went up to bed. He hadn't. After the ring signal had come five times I had his voice.

"Nero Wolfe speaking."

"Archie. Sorry to wake you up, but I need orders. We're minus a client. Mrs. Rackham. This is a quick guess, but it looks as if someone stabbed her with a knife and then stuck the knife in a dog. Anyhow, she's dead. I've just—"

"What is this?" It was almost a bellow. "Flummery?"

"No, sir. I've just come from where she's lying in the woods. Leeds and I found her. The dog's dead too, here on a bench. I don't—"

"Archie!"

"Yes, sir."

"This is insupportable. In the circumstances."

"Yes, sir, all of that."

"Is Mr. Rackham out of it?"

"Not as far as I know. I told you we just found her."

"Where are you?"

"At Leeds' place, alone. I'm here guarding the knife in the dog. Leeds went to Birchvale to get a doctor and the cops and maybe to kill somebody. I can't help it. I've got all the time in the world. How much do you want?"

"Anything that might help."

"Okay, but in case I get interrupted here's a question first. On two counts, because I'm here working for you and because I helped find the body, they're going to be damn curious. How much do I spill? There's no one on this line unless the operator's listening in."

A grunt and a pause. "On what I know now, everything about Mrs. Rackham's talk with me and the purpose of your trip there. About Mrs. Rackham and Mr. Leeds and what you have seen and heard there, everything. But you will of course confine yourself strictly to that."

"Nothing about sausage?"

"Absolutely nothing. The question is idiotic."

"Yeah, I just asked. Okay. Well, I got here and met dogs and people. Leeds' place is on a corner of Mrs. Rackham's property, and we walked through the woods for dinner at Birchvale. There were eight of us at dinner. . . ."

I'm fairly good with a billiard cue, and only Saul Panzer can beat me at tailing a man or woman in New York, but what I am best at is reporting a complicated event to Nero Wolfe. With, I figured, a probable maximum of ten minutes for it, I covered all the essentials in eight, leaving him two for questions. He had some, of course. But I think he had the picture well enough to sleep on when I saw the light of a car through the window, told him good-by, and hung up. I stepped from the living room into the little hall, opened the outside door, and was standing on the stone slab as a car with STATE POLICE painted on it came down the narrow drive and stopped. Two uniformed public servants piled out and made for me. I only hoped neither of them was my pet Westchester hate, Lieutenant Con Noonan, and had my hope granted. They were both rank-and-file.

One of them spoke. "Your name Goodwin?"

I conceded it. Dogs had started to bark.

"After finding a dead body you went off and came here to rest your feet?"

"I didn't find the body. A dog did. As for my feet, do you mind stepping inside?"

I held the door open, and they crossed the threshold. With a thumb I called their attention to Nobby, on the bench.

"That's another dog. It had just crawled here to die, there on the doorstep. It struck me that Mrs. Rackham might have been killed with that knife before it was used on the dog, and that you guys would be interested in the knife as is, before somebody took it to slice bread with, for instance. So when Leeds went to the house to phone I came here. I have no corns."

One of them had stepped to the bench to look down at Nobby. He asked, "Have you touched the knife?"

"No."

"Was Leeds here with you?"

"Yes."

"Did he touch the knife?"

"I don't think so. If he did I didn't see him."

The cop turned to his colleague. "We won't move it, not now. You'd better stick here. Right?"

"Right."

"You'll be getting word. Come along, Goodwin."

He marched to the door and opened it and let me pass through first. Outdoors he crossed to his car, got in behind the wheel, and told me, "Hop in."

I stood. "Where to?"

"Where I'm going."

"I'm sorry," I said regretfully, "but I like to know where. If it's White Plains or a barracks, I would need a different kind of invitation. Either that or physical help."

"Oh, you're a lawyer."

"No, but I know a lawyer."

"Congratulations." He leaned toward me and spoke through his nose. "Mr. Goodwin, I'm driving to Mrs. Rackham's house, Birchvale. Would you care to join me?"

"I'd love to, thanks so much," I said warmly, and climbed in.

5

The rest of that night, more than six hours, from half-past midnight until well after sunrise, I might as well have been in bed asleep for all I got out of it. I learned only one thing, that the sun rises on April ninth at 5:39, and even that wasn't reliable because I didn't know whether it was a true horizon.

Lieutenant Con Noonan was at Birchvale, among others, but his style was cramped.

Even after the arrival of District Attorney Cleveland Archer himself, the atmosphere was not one of single-minded devotion to the service of justice. Not that they weren't all for justice, but they had to keep it in perspective, and that's not so easy when a prominent wealthy taxpayer like Mrs. Barry Rackham has been murdered and your brief list of suspects includes (a) her husband, now a widower, who may himself now be a prominent wealthy taxpayer, (b) an able young politician who has been elected to the state assembly, (c) the dead woman's daughter-in-law, who may possibly be more of a prominent wealthy taxpayer than the widower, and (d) a vice-president of a billion-dollar New York bank. They're all part of the perspective, though you wish to God they weren't so you could concentrate on the other three suspects: (e) the dead woman's cousin, a breeder of dogs which don't make friends, (f) her secretary, a mere employee, and (g) a private dick from New York whose tongue has needed bobbing for some time. With a setup like that you can't just take them all down to White Plains and tell the boys to start chipping and save the pieces.

Except for fifteen minutes alone with Con Noonan, I spent the first two hours in the big living room where we had looked at television, having for company the members of the family, the guests, five members of the domestic staff, and two or more officers of the law. It wasn't a bit jolly. Two of the female servants wept intermittently. Barry Rackham walked up and down, sitting occasionally and then starting up again, speaking to no one. Oliver Pierce and

Lina Darrow sat on a couch conversing in undertones, spasmodically, with him doing most of the talking. Dana Hammond, the banker, was jumpy. Mostly he sat slumped, with his chin down and his eyes closed, but now and then he would arise slowly as if something hurt and go to say something to one of the others, usually Annabel or Leeds. Leeds had been getting a blaze started in the fireplace when I was ushered in, and it continued to be his chief concern. He got the fire so hot that Annabel moved away, to the other side of the room. She was the quietest of them, but from the way she kept her jaw clamped I guessed that it wasn't because she was the least moved.

One by one they were escorted from the room for a private talk and brought back again. It was when my turn came, not long after I had arrived, that I found Lieutenant Noonan was around. He was in a smaller room down the hall, seated at a table, looking harassed. No doubt life was hard for him—born with the instincts of a Hitler or Stalin in a country where people are determined to do their own voting. The dick who took me in motioned me to a chair across the table.

"You again," Noonan said.

I nodded. "That's exactly what I was thinking. I haven't seen you since the time I didn't run my car over Louis Rony."

I didn't expect him to wince, and he didn't. "You're here investigating that dog poisoning at Hillside Kennels."

I had no comment.

"Weren't you?" he snapped. "If you're answering questions."

"Oh, I beg your pardon. I didn't know it was a question. It sounded more like a statement."

"You are investigating the dog poisoning?"

"I started to. I spent an hour at it there with Leeds, before we came here to dinner."

"So he said. Make any progress?"

"Nothing remarkable. For one thing, I had kibitzers, which is no help. Mrs. Frey and Mr. Hammond."

"Did you all come over here together?"

"No. Leeds and I came about an hour after Mrs. Frey and Mr. Hammond left."

"Did you drive?"

"Walked. He walked and I ran."

"You ran? Why?"

"To keep up with him."

Noonan smiled. He has the meanest smile I know of except maybe Boris Karloff. "You get your comedy from the comics, don't you, Goodwin?"

"Yes, sir."

"Tell me about the dinner here and afterwards. Make it as funny as you can."

I took ten minutes for it, as much as I had had for Wolfe, but getting interrupted with questions. I stuck to facts and gave them to him straight. When we came to the end he went back and concentrated on whether all of them had heard Mrs. Rackham say she was going for a walk with the dog, as of course they had since she had issued a blanket invitation for company. Then I was sent back to the living room, and it was Lina Darrow's turn in the preliminaries. I wondered if she would play dumb with him as she had with me.

It was as empty a stretch of hours as I have ever spent. I might as well have been a housebroken dog; no one seemed to think I mattered, and I was not in a position to tell them how wrong they were. At one point I made a serious effort to get into a conversation, making the rounds and offering remarks, but got nowhere. Dana Hammond merely gave me a look, without opening his trap. Oliver Pierce didn't even look at me. Lina Darrow mumbled something and turned away. Calvin Leeds asked me what they had done with Nobby's remains, nodded and frowned at my answer, and went to put another log on the fire. Annabel Frey asked me if I wanted more coffee, and when I said yes apparently didn't hear me. Barry Rackham, whom I tackled at the far end of the room, was the most talkative. He wanted to know whether anyone had come from the District Attorney's office. I said I didn't know. He wanted to know the name of the cop in the other room who was asking questions, and I told him Lieutenant Con Noonan. That was my longest conversation, two whole questions and answers.

I did get in one piece of detection, somewhat later, when finally District Attorney Cleveland Archer made an appearance. As he came into the room and made himself known and everybody moved to approach him, I took a look at his shoes and saw that he had undoubtedly been in the woods to inspect the spot where Mrs. Rackham's body was found. Likewise Ben Dykes, the dean of the Westchester County dicks, who was with him. That made me feel slightly better. It would have been a shame to stick there the whole night without detecting a single damn thing.

After a few preliminary words to individuals Archer spoke to them collectively. "This is a terrible thing, an awful thing. It is established that Mrs. Rackham was stabbed to death out there in the woods—and the dog that was with her. We have the knife that was used, as you know—it has been shown to you—one of the steak knives that are kept in a drawer here in the dining room—they were used by you at dinner last evening. We have statements from all of you, but of course I'll have to talk further with you. I won't try to do that now. It's after three o'clock, and I'll come back in the morning. I want to ask whether any of you has anything to say to me now, anything that shouldn't wait until then." His eyes went over them. "Anyone?"

No sound and no movement from any quarter. They sure were a chatty bunch. They just stood and stared at him, including me. I would have liked to relieve the tension with a remark or question, but didn't want to remind him that I was present.

However, he didn't need a reminder. After all the others, including the servants, had cleared out, Leeds and I were moving toward the door when Ben Dykes's voice came. "Goodwin!"

Leeds kept going. I turned.

Dykes came to me. "We want to ask you something."

"Shoot."

District Attorney Archer joined us, saying, "In there with Noonan, Ben."

"Him and Noonan bring sparks," Dykes objected. "Remember last year at Sperling's?"

"I'll do the talking," Archer stated, and led the way to the hall and along to the smaller room where Noonan was still seated at the table, conferring with a colleague—the one who had brought me from Hillside Kennels. The colleague moved to stand against the wall. Noonan arose, but sat down again when Archer and Dykes and I had pulled chairs up.

Archer, slightly plumper than he had been a year ago, with his round red face saggy and careworn by the stress of an extremely bad night for him, put his forearms on the table and leaned at me.

"Goodwin," he said earnestly but not offensively, "I want to put something up to you."

"Suits me, Mr. Archer," I assured him. "I've never been ignored more."

"We've been busy. Lieutenant Noonan has of course reported what you told him. Frankly, I find it hard to believe. Almost impossible to believe. It is well known that Nero Wolfe refuses dozens of jobs every month, that he confines himself to cases that interest him, and that the easiest and quickest way to interest him is to offer him a large fee. Now I—"

"Not the only way," I objected.

"I didn't say it was. I know he has standards—even scruples. Now I can't believe that he found anything interesting in the poisoning of a dog—certainly not interesting enough for him to send you up here over a weekend. And I doubt very much if Calvin Leeds, from what I know of him, is in a position to offer Wolfe a fee that would attract him. His cousin, Mrs. Rackham, might have, but she did not have the reputation of throwing money around carelessly—rather the contrary. We're going to ask Wolfe about this, naturally, but I thought I might save time by putting it up to you. I appeal to you to cooperate with us in solving this dastardly and cowardly murder. As you know, I have a right to insist on it; knowing you and Wolfe as I do, I prefer to appeal to you as to a responsible citizen and a man who carries a license to work in this state as a private detective. I simply do not believe that you were sent up here merely to investigate the poisoning of a dog."

They were all glaring at me.

"I wasn't," I said mildly.

"Ha, you weren't!"

"Hell no. As you say, Mr. Wolfe wouldn't be interested."

"So you lied, you punk," Noonan gloated.

"Wrong, as usual." I grinned at him. "You didn't ask me what I was sent here for or even hint that you would like to know. You asked if I was investigating the dog poisoning, and I told you I spent an hour at it, which I did. You asked if I had made any progress, and I told you nothing remarkable. Then you wanted to know what I had seen and heard here, and I told you, in full. It was one of the bummest and dumbest jobs of questioning I have ever run across, but you may learn in time. The first—"

Noonan blurted, "Why, you goddam—"

"I'll handle it," Archer snapped at him. Back to me: "You might have supplied it, Goodwin."

"Not to him," I said firmly. "I tried supplying him once and he was displeased. Anyway, I doubt if he would have understood it."

"See if I can understand it."

"Yes, sir. Mrs. Rackham phoned Thursday afternoon and made an appointment to see Mr. Wolfe. She came yesterday morning—Friday—at eleven o'clock, and had Leeds with her. She said that it had been her custom, since marrying Rackham three years and seven months ago, to give him money for his personal use when he asked for it, but that he kept asking for bigger amounts, and she began giving him less than he asked for, and last October second he wanted fifteen grand, and she refused. Gave him zero. Since then, the past seven months, he had asked for none and got none, but in spite of that he had gone on spending plenty, and that was what was biting her. She hired Mr. Wolfe to find out where and how he was getting dough, and I was sent up here to look him over and possibly get hold of an idea. I needed an excuse for coming here, and the dog poisoning was better than average." I fluttered a hand. "That's all."

"You say Leeds was with her?" Noonan demanded.

"That's partly what I mean," I told Ben Dykes, "about Noonan's notion of how to ask questions. He must have heard me say she had Leeds along."

"Yeah," Dykes said dryly. "But don't be so damn cute. This is not exactly a picnic." He spoke to Noonan. "Leeds didn't make any mention of this?"

"He did not. Of course I didn't ask him."

Dykes stood up and asked Archer, "Hadn't I better send for him? He went home."

Archer nodded, and Dykes went. "Good God," Archer said with feeling, not to Noonan or me, so probably to the People of the State of New York. He sat biting his lip a while and then asked me, "Was that all Mrs. Rackham wanted?"

"That's all she asked for."

"Had she quarreled with her husband? Had he threatened her?"

"She didn't say so."

"Exactly what did she say?"

That took half an hour. For me it was simple, since all I had to use was my memory, in view of the instructions from Wolfe to give them everything but the sausage. Archer didn't know what my memory is capable of, so I didn't repeat any of Mrs. Rackham's speeches verbatim, though I could have, because he would have thought I was dressing it up. But when I was through he had it all.

Then I was permitted to stay for the session with Leeds, who had arrived early in my recital but had been held outside until I was done. At last I was one of the party, but too late to hear anything that I didn't already know. With Leeds, who was practically one of the family, they had to cover not only his visit with his cousin to Wolfe's office, but also the preliminaries to it, so he took another half-hour and more. He himself had no idea, he said, where Rackham had been getting money. He had learned nothing from the personal inquiry he had undertaken at his cousin's request. He had never heard, or heard of, any serious quarrel between his cousin and her husband. And so on. As for his failure to tell Noonan of the visit to Wolfe's office and the real reason for my presence at Birchvale, he merely said calmly that Noonan hadn't asked and he preferred to wait until he was asked.

District Attorney Archer finally called it a night, got up and stretched, rubbed his eyes with his fingertips, asked Dykes and Noonan some questions and issued some orders, and addressed me. "You're staying at Leeds' place?"

I said I hadn't stayed there much so far, but my bag was there.

"All right. I'll want you tomorrow—today."

I said of course and went out with Leeds. Ben Dykes offered to give us a lift, but we declined.

Together, without conversation, Leeds and I made for the head of the trail at the edge of the woods, giving the curving paths a miss. Dawn had come and was going; it was getting close to sunrise. The breeze was down and the birds were up, telling about it. The pace Leeds set, up the long easy slope and down the level stretch, was not quite up to his previous performances, which suited me fine. I was not in a racing mood, even to get to a bed.

Suddenly Leeds halted, and I came abreast of him. In the trail, thirty paces ahead, a man was getting up from his hands and knees to face us. He called, "Hold it! Who are you?"

We told him.

"Well," he said, "you'll have to keep off this section of trail. Go around. We're just starting on it. Bright and early!"

We asked how far, and he said about three hundred yards, to where a man had started at the other end. We stepped off the trail, to the right into the rough, and got slowed down, though the woods were fairly clean. After a couple of minutes of that I asked Leeds if he would know the spot, and he said he would.

Soon he stopped, and I joined him. I would have known it my-self, with the help of a rope they had stretched from tree to tree, making a large semicircle. We went up to the rope and stood looking.

"Where's Hebe?" I asked.

"They had to come for me to get her. She's in Nobby's kennel. He won't be needing it. They took him away."

We agreed, without putting it in words, that there was nothing there we wanted, and resumed our way through the woods, keeping off the trail until we reached the scientist at the far end of the forbidden section, who not only challenged us but had to be per-suaded that we weren't a pair of bloodthirsty liars. Finally he was bighearted enough to let us go on.

I was glad they had taken Nobby away, not caring much for another view of the little hall with that canine corpse on the bench. Otherwise the house was as before. Leeds had stopped at the ken-nels. I went up to my room and was peeling off the pants I had pulled on over my pajamas when I was startled by a sudden dazzling blaze at the window. I crossed to it and stuck my head out: it was the sun showing off, trying to scare somebody. I glanced at my wrist and saw 5:39, but as I said, maybe it wasn't a true horizon. Not lowering the window shade, I went and stretched out on the bed and yawned as far down as it could go.

The door downstairs opened and shut, and there were steps on the stairs. Leeds appeared at my open door, stepped inside, and said, "I'll have to be up and around in an hour, so I'll close your door."

I thanked him. He didn't move.

"My cousin paid Mr. Wolfe ten thousand dollars. What will he do now?"

"I don't know, I haven't asked him. Why?"

"It occurred to me that he might want to spend it, or part of it, in her interest. In case the police don't make any headway."

"He might," I agreed. "I'll suggest it to him."

He still stood, as if there was something else on his mind. There was, and he unloaded it.

"It happens in the best families," he stated distinctly and backed out, taking the door with him.

I closed my eyes but made no effort to empty my head. If I went to sleep there was no telling when I would wake up, and I intended to phone Wolfe at eight, fifteen minutes before the scheduled hour for Fritz to get to his room with his breakfast tray. Meanwhile I would think of something brilliant to do or to suggest. The trouble with that, I discovered after some poking around, was that I had no in. Nobody would speak to me except Leeds, and he was far from loquacious.

I have a way of realizing all of a sudden, as I suppose a lot of people do, that I made a decision some time back without knowing it. It happened that morning at 6:25. Looking at my watch and seeing that that was where it had got to, I was suddenly aware that I was staying awake, not so I could phone Wolfe at eight o'clock, but so I could beat it the hell out of there as soon as I was sure Leeds was asleep; and I was now as sure as I would ever be.

I got up and shed my pajamas and dressed, not trying to set a record but wasting no time, and, with my bag in one hand and my shoes in the other, tiptoed to the hall, down the stairs, and out to the stone slab. While it wasn't Calvin Leeds I was escaping from, I thought it desirable to get out of Westchester County before anyone knew I wasn't upstairs asleep. Not a chance. I was seated on the stone slab tying the lace of the second shoe when a dog barked, and that was a signal for all the others. I scrambled up, grabbed the bag, ran to the car and unlocked it and climbed in, started the engine, swung around the graveled space, and passed the house on my way out just as Leeds emerged through the side door. I stepped on the brake, stuck my head through the window, yelled at him, "Got an errand to do, see you later!" and rolled on through the gate and into the highway.

At that hour Sunday morning the roads were all mine, the bright new sun was at my left out of the way, and it would have been a pleasant drive if I had been in a mood to feel pleased. Which I wasn't. This was a totally different situation from the other two occasions when we had crossed Arnold Zeck's path and someone had got killed. Then the corpses had been Zeck's men, and Zeck, Wolfe, and the public interest had all been on the same side. This time Zeck's man, Barry Rackham, was the number one suspect, and Wolfe had either to return his dead client's ten grand, keep it without doing anything to earn it, or meet Zeck head on. Knowing Wolfe as I did, I hit eighty-five that morning rolling south on the Sawmill River Parkway.

The dash clock said 7:18 as I left the West Side Highway at Forty-sixth Street. I had to cross to Ninth Avenue to turn south. It was as empty as the country roads had been. Turning right on Thirty-fifth Street, I went on across Tenth Avenue, on nearly to Eleventh, and pulled to the curb in front of Wolfe's old brownstone house.

Even before I killed the engine I saw something that made me goggle—a sight that had never greeted me before in the thousands of times I had braked a car to a stop there.

The front door was standing wide open.

6

My heart came up. I swallowed it down, jumped out, ran across the sidewalk and up the seven steps to the stoop and on in. Fritz and Theodore were there in the hall, coming to me. Their faces were enough to make a guy's heart pop right out of his mouth.

"Airing the house?" I demanded.

"He's gone," Fritz said.

"Gone where?"

"I don't know. During the night. When I saw the door was open—"

"What's that in your hand?"

"He left them on the table in his room—for Theodore and me, and one for you—"

I snatched the pieces of paper from his trembling hand and looked at the one on top. The writing on it was Wolfe's.

> Dear Fritz:
>   Marko Vukcic will want your services. He should pay you at least $2000 a month.
>   My best regards. . . .
>   Nero Wolfe

I looked at the next one.

> Dear Theodore:
>   Mr. Hewitt will take the plants and will need your help with them. He should pay you around $200 weekly.
>   My regards. . . .
>   Nero Wolfe

I looked at the third one.

AG:
   Do not look for me.
   My very best regards and wishes. . . .
                                                NW

I went through them again, watching each word, told Fritz and
Theodore, "Come and sit down," went to the office, and sat at my
desk. They moved chairs to face me.

"He's gone," Fritz said, trying to convince himself.

"So it seems," I said aggressively.

"You know where he is," Theodore told me accusingly. "It won't
be easy to move some of the plants without damage. I don't like
working on Long Island, not for two hundred dollars a week.
When is he coming back?"

"Look, Theodore," I said, "I don't give a good goddam what you
like or don't like. Mr. Wolfe has always pampered you because
you're the best orchid nurse alive. This is as good a time as any to
tell you that you remind me of sour milk. I do not know where Mr.
Wolfe is nor if or when he's coming back. To you he sent his regards. To me he sent his very best regards and wishes. Now shut
up."

I shifted to Fritz. "He thinks Marko Vukcic should pay you twice
as much as he does. That's like him, huh? You can see I'm sore as hell,
his doing it like this, but I'm not surprised. To show you how well
I know him, this is what happened: not long after I phoned him last
night he simply wrote these notes to us and walked out of the house,
leaving the door open—you said you found it open—to show anyone
who might be curious that there was no longer anyone or anything
of any importance inside. You got up at your usual time, six-thirty,
saw the open door, went up to his room, found his bed empty and
the notes on the table. After going up to the plant rooms to call Theodore, you returned to his room, looked around, and discovered
that he had taken nothing with him. Then you and Theodore stared
at each other until I arrived. Have you anything to add to that?"

"I don't want to work on Long Island," Theodore stated.

Fritz only said, "Find him, Archie."

"He told me not to."

"Yes—but find him! Where will he sleep? What will he eat?"

I got up and went to the safe and opened it, and looked in the
cash drawer, where we always kept a supply for emergency expenses. There should have been a little over four thousand bucks;

there was a little over a thousand. I closed the safe door and twirled the knob, and told Fritz, "He'll sleep and eat. Was my report accurate?"

"Not quite. One of his bags is gone, and pajamas, toothbrush, razor, three shirts, and ten pairs of socks."

"Did he take a walking stick?"

"No. The old gray topcoat and the old gray hat."

"Were there any visitors?"

"No."

"Any phone calls besides mine?"

"I don't know about yours. His extension and mine were both plugged in, but you know I don't answer when you're out unless he tells me to. It rang only once, at eight minutes after twelve."

"Your clock's wrong. That was me. It was five after." I went and gave him a pat on the shoulder. "Okay. I hope you like your new job. How's chances for some breakfast?"

"But Archie! His breakfast . . ."

"I could eat that too. I drove forty miles on an empty stomach." I patted him again. "Look, Fritz. Right now I'm sore at him, damn sore. After some griddle cakes and a broiled ham and eight or ten eggs in black butter and a quart of coffee, we'll see. I think I'll be even sorer than I am now, but we'll see. Is there any of his favorite honey left that you haven't been giving me lately? The thyme honey?"

"Yes—some. Four jars."

"Good. I'll finish off with that on a couple of hot cakes. Then we'll see how I feel."

"I would never have thought—" Fritz's voice had a quaver, and he stopped and started over again. "I would never have thought this could happen. What is it, Archie?" He was practically wailing. "What is it? His appetite has been good."

"We were going to repot some Miltonias today," Theodore said dismally.

I snorted. "Go ahead and pot 'em. He was no help anyhow. Beat it and let me alone. I've got to think. Also I'm hungry. Beat it!"

Theodore, mumbling, shuffled out. Fritz, following him, turned at the door. "That's it, Archie. Think. Think where he is while I get your breakfast."

He left me, and I sat down at my desk to do the thinking, but the cogs wouldn't catch. I was too mad to think. "Don't look for me."

That was him to a T. He knew damn well that if I should ever come home to find he had vanished, the one activity that would make any sense at all would be to start looking for him, and here I was stopped cold at the take-off. Not that I had no notion at all. That was why I had left Leeds' place without notice and stepped it up to eighty-five getting back: I did have a notion. Two years had passed since Wolfe had told me, "Archie, you are to forget that you know that man's name. If ever, in the course of my business, I find that I am committed against him and must destroy him, I shall leave this house, find a place where I can work—and sleep and eat if there is time for it—and stay there until I have finished."

So that part was okay, but what about me? On another occasion, a year later, he had said to five members of a family named Sperling, in my presence, "In that event he will know it is a mortal encounter, and so will I, and I shall move to a base of operations which will be known only to Mr. Goodwin and perhaps two others." Okay. There was no argument about the mortal encounter or about the move. But I was the Mr. Goodwin referred to, and here I was star-ing at it—"Don't look for me." Where did that leave me? Certainly the two others he had had in mind were Saul Panzer and Marko Vukcic, and I didn't even dare to phone Saul and ask a couple of discreet questions; and besides, if he had let Saul in and left me out, to hell with him. And what was I supposed to say to people—for instance, people like the District Attorney of Westchester County?

That particular question got answered, partly at least, from an unexpected quarter. When I had finished with the griddle cakes, ham, eggs, thyme honey, and coffee, I went back to the office to see if I was ready to quit feeling and settle down to thinking, and was working at it when I became aware that I was sitting in Wolfe's chair behind his desk. That brought me up with a jerk. No one else, including me, ever sat in that chair, but there I was. I didn't ap-prove of it. It seemed to imply that Wolfe was through with that chair for good, and that was a hell of an attitude to take, no matter how sore I was. I opened a drawer of his desk to check its con-tents, pretending that was what I had sat there for, and was start-ing a careful survey when the doorbell rang.

Going to answer it, I took my time because I had done no thinking yet and therefore didn't know my lines. Seeing through the one-way glass panel in the front door that the man on the stoop was a civilian stranger, my first impulse was to let him ring until he got tired, but curiosity chased it away and I opened the door. He was just a citizen with big ears and an old topcoat, and he asked to see Mr. Nero Wolfe. I told him Mr. Wolfe wasn't available on Sundays, and I was his confidential assistant, and could I help. He thought maybe I could, took an envelope from a pocket, extracted a sheet of paper, and unfolded it.

"I'm from the *Gazette*," he stated. "This copy for an ad we got in the mail this morning—we want to be sure it's authentic."

I took the paper and gave it a look. It was one of our large-sized letterheads, and the writing and printing on it were Wolfe's. At the top was written:

> Display advertisement for Monday's *Gazette*, first section, two columns wide, depth as required. In thin type, not blatant. Send bill to above address.

Below the copy was printed by hand:

MR. NERO WOLFE
ANNOUNCES HIS RETIREMENT
FROM THE DETECTIVE BUSINESS
TODAY, APRIL 10, 1950

> Mr. Wolf will not hereafter be available. Inquiries from clients on unfinished matters may be made of Mr. Archie Goodwin. Inquiries from others than clients will not receive attention.

Beneath that was Wolfe's signature. It was authentic all right.

Having learned it by heart, I handed it back. "Yeah, that's okay. Sure. Give it a good spot."

"It's authentic?"

"Absolutely."

"Listen, I want to see him. Give me a break! Good spot hell; it's page one if I can get a story on it!"

"Don't you believe your own ads? It says that Mr. Wolfe will not hereafter be available." I had the door swung to a narrow gap. "I never saw you before, but Lon Cohen is an old friend of mine. He gets to work at noon, doesn't he?"

"Yes, but—"

"Tell him not to bother to phone about this. Mr. Wolfe is not available, and I'm reserved for clients, as the ad says. Watch your foot, here comes the door."

I shut it and put the chain bolt on. As I went back down the hall Fritz emerged from the kitchen and demanded, "Who was that?"

I eyed him. "You know damn well," I said, "that when Mr. Wolfe was here you would never have dreamed of asking who was that, either of him or of me. Don't dream of it now, anyway not when I'm in the humor I'm in at present."

"I only wanted—"

"Skip it. I advise you to steer clear of me until I've had a chance to think."

I went to the office and this time took my own chair. At least I had got some instructions from Wolfe, though his method of sending them was certainly roundabout. The ad meant, of course, that I wasn't to try to cover his absence; on the contrary. More important, it told me to lay off of the Rackham thing. I was to handle inquiries from clients on unfinished matter, but only from clients; and since Mrs. Rackham, being dead, couldn't inquire, that settled that. Another thing—apparently I still had my job, unlike Fritz and Theodore. But I couldn't sign checks, I couldn't—suddenly I remembered something. The fact that I hadn't thought of it before indicates the state I was in. I have told, in my account of another case of Wolfe's, how, in anticipation of the possibility that some day a collision with Arnold Zeck would drive him into a foxhole, he had instructed me to put fifty thousand dollars in cash in a safe deposit box over in Jersey, and how I obeyed instructions. The idea was to have a source of supply for the foxhole; but anyway, there it was, fifty grand, in the box rented by me under the name I had selected for the purpose. I was sitting thinking how upset I must have been not to have thought of that before when the phone rang and I reached for it.

"Nero Wolfe's office, Archie Goodwin speaking."

I thought it proper to use that, the familiar routine, since according to Wolfe's ad he wouldn't retire until the next day.

"Archie?" A voice I knew sounded surprised. "Is that you, Archie?"

"Right. Hello, Marko. So early on Sunday?"

"But I thought you were away! I was going to give Fritz a message for you. From Nero."

Marko Vukcic, owner and operator of Rusterman's Restaurant, the only place where Wolfe really liked to eat except at home, was the only man in New York who called Wolfe by his first name. I told him I would be glad to take a message for myself.

"Not from Nero actually," he said. "From me. I must see you as soon as possible. Could you come here?"

I said I could. There was no need to ask where, since the only place he could ever be found was the restaurant premises, either on one of the two floors for the public, in the kitchen, or up in his private quarters.

I told Fritz I was going out and would be back when he saw me.

As I drove crosstown and up to Fifty-fourth Street, I was around eighty per cent sure that within a few minutes I would be talking with Wolfe. For him it would be hard to beat that for a foxhole—the place that cooked and served the best food in America, with the living quarters of his best and oldest friend above it. Even after I had entered at the side door, as arranged, ascended the two flights of stairs, seen the look on Marko's face as he welcomed me, felt the tight clasp of his fingers as he took my hands in his, and heard his murmured "My friend, my poor young friend!"—even then I thought he was only preparing dramatically to lead me to Wolfe in an inner room.

But he wasn't. All he led me to was a chair by a window. He took another one, facing me, and sat with his palms on his knees, his head cocked a little to one side as usual.

"My friend Archie," he said sympathetically. "It is my part to tell you exactly certain things. But before I do that I wish to tell you a thing of my own. I wish to remind you that I have known Nero a much longer time than you have. We knew each other as boys in another country—much younger than you were that day many years ago when you first saw him and went to work for him. He is my old and dear friend, and I am his. So it was natural that he should come to me last night."

"Sure," I agreed. "Why not?"

"You must feel no pique. No *courroux*."

"Okay. I'll fight it down. What time did he come?"

"At two o'clock in the night. He was here an hour, and then left. That I am to tell you, and these things. Do you want to write them down?"

"I can remember them if you can. Shoot."

Marko nodded. "I know of your great memory. Nero has often spoken of it." He shut his eyes and in a moment opened them again.

"There are these five things. First, the plants. He telephoned Mr. Hewitt last night, and tomorrow Mr. Hewitt will arrange for the plants to be moved to his place, and also for Theodore to go there to work. Second—"

"Am I to list the plants? Do the records go too?"

"I don't know. I can say only what I was told to say. That's all about the plants. Perhaps Mr. Hewitt can tell you. Second, that is Fritz. He will work here, and I will pay him well. I will see him today and arrange the details. Of course he is unhappy?"

"He thinks Mr. Wolfe will starve to death."

"But naturally. If not that, something else. I have always thought it a folly for him to be a detective. Third—I am third. I have a power of attorney. Do you want to see it?"

"No, thanks, I'll take your word for it."

"It is in there locked up. Nero said it is legal, and he knows. I can sign checks for you. I can sign anything. I can do anything he could do."

"Within certain limits. You can't—" I waved a hand. "Forget it. Fourth?"

"Fourth is the house. I am to offer the house and its contents for sale. On that I have confidential instructions."

I goggled at him. "Sell the house *and* contents?"

"Yes. I have private instructions regarding price and terms."

"I don't believe it."

His shoulders went up and down. "I told Nero you would think I was lying."

"I don't think you're lying. I just don't believe it. Also the bed and other articles in my room are my property. Must I move them out today or can I wait until tomorrow?"

Marko made a noise that I think was meant for sympathy. "My poor young friend," he said apologetically, "there is no hurry at all. Selling a house is not like selling a lamb chop. You will, I suppose, continue to live there for the present."

"Did he say I should?"

"No. But why shouldn't you? That is my own thought, and it brings us to the fifth and last thing: the instructions Nero gave me for you."

"Oh, he did. That was thoughtful. Such as?"

"You are to act in the light of experience as guided by intelligence."

He stopped. I nodded. "That's a cinch, I always do. And specifically?"

"That's all. Those are your instructions." Marko upturned his palms. "That's all about everything."

"You call that instructions, do you?"

"I don't. He did." He leaned to me. "I told him, Archie, that his conduct was inexcusable. He was standing ready to leave, after telling me those five things and no more. Having no reply, he turned and went. Beyond that I know nothing, but nothing."

"Where he went? Where he is? No word for me at all?"

"Nothing. Only what I have told you."

"Hell, he's gone batty, like lots of geniuses," I declared, and got up to go.

7

I drove around for two solid hours, mostly in the park. Now and then, for a change of scene, I left the park for a patrol of the avenues.

I hadn't been able to start thinking in the house, and it might work better on the move. Moreover, I didn't want any more just then of Fritz or Theodore, or in fact of anybody but me. So, in the light of experience and guided by intelligence, I drove around. Somewhere along the way I saw clearly what my trouble was: I was completely out of errands for the first time in years. How could I decide what to do when I had nothing to do? I now believe that the reason I never drove farther north than One Hundred and Tenth Street, nor farther south than Fourteenth Street during those two hours, was that I thought Wolfe was probably somewhere within those limits and I didn't want to leave them.

When I did leave them it wasn't voluntary. Rolling down Second Avenue in the Seventies, I had stopped for a red light abreast of a police car on my left. Just as the light was changing, the cop on my side stuck his head out and called, "Pull over to the curb."

Flattered at the attention as any motorist would be, not, I obeyed. The police car came alongside, and the cop got out and invented another new phrase. "Let me see your license."

I got it out and handed it to him, and he took a look.

"Yeah, I thought I recognized you." He handed the license back, walked around the front of my car to the other side, got in beside me, and suggested, "Let's go to the Nineteenth Precinct. Sixty-seventh east of Lexington."

"That's one idea," I admitted. "Or what's wrong with the Brooklyn Botanical Garden, especially on Easter? I'll toss you for it."

He was unmoved. "Come on, Goodwin, come on. I know you're a card, I've heard all about you. Let's go."

"Give me one reason, good or bad. If you don't mind?"

"I don't know the reason. All I know is the word that came an hour ago, to pick you up and take you in. Maybe you shouldn't have left the infant on the church steps on Easter Day."

"Of course not," I agreed. "We'll go get it."

I eased away from the curb into traffic, with the police car trailing behind. Our destination, the Nineteenth Precinct Station, was not new to me. That was where I had once spent most of a night, conversing with Lieutenant Rowcliff, the Con Noonan of the New York Police Department.

After escorting me in to the desk and telling the sergeant about it, my captor had a point to make. His name was not John F. O'Brien, it was John R. O'Brien. He explained to the sergeant that he had to insist on it because last year one of his heroic acts had been credited to John F., and once was enough, and he damn well wanted credit for spotting a wanted man on the street. That attended to, he bade me a pleasant good-by and left. Meanwhile the sergeant was making a phone call. When he hung up he looked at me with a more active interest.

"Westchester wants you," he announced. "Leaving the scene of a crime and leaving jurisdiction. Want to drag it out?"

"It might be fun, but I doubt it. What happens if I don't?"

"There's a Westchester man downtown. He's on his way up here to take you."

I shook my head. "I'll fight like a cornered rat. I know fourteen lawyers all told. Ten to one he has no papers. This is one of those brotherly acts which I do not like. You're on a spot, Sergeant."

"Don't scare me to death. If he has no papers I'll send you downtown and let them handle it."

"Yeah," I admitted, "that would let you out. But we can make it simpler for both of us if you care to. Get the Westchester DA on the phone and let me talk to him. I'll even pay for the call."

At first he didn't like the idea and then he did. I think what changed his mind was the chance of picking up a piece of hot gossip on the murder of the month. He had to be persuaded, but when I told him the DA would be at the Rackham place and gave him the number, that settled it. He put the call in. However, he covered. When he got the number he made it clear that he merely wanted to offer the DA an opportunity to speak to Archie Goodwin if he wished to. He did. I circled the railing to get to the desk and took the phone.

"Mr. Archer?"

"Yes! This is—"

"Just a minute!" I said emphatically. "Whatever you were going to say this is, I double it. It's an outrage. It—"

"You were told to stay here, and you sneaked away! You left—"

"I was not told to stay there. You asked me if I was staying at Leeds' place, and I said my bag was there, and you said you would want me today, and I said of course. If I had stayed at Leeds' place I might have been permitted seven hours' sleep. I decided to do something else with the seven hours, and they're not up yet. But you see fit to ring a bell on me. I'll do one of two things. I'll have a bite of lunch and then drive up there, unaccompanied, or I'll make it as hard as I possibly can for this man you sent to get me outside the city limits—whichever you prefer. Here he comes now."

"Here who comes?"

"Your man. Coming in the door. If you decide you want to see me today, tell him not to trail along behind me. It makes me self-conscious."

A silence. Then, "You were told not to leave the county."

"I was not. By no one."

"Neither you nor Wolfe was at home at eleven o'clock—or if you were you wouldn't see my man."

"I was in the Easter parade."

Another silence, longer. "What time will you be here? At Birchvale."

"I can make it by two o'clock."

"My man is there?"

"Yes."

"Let me talk to him."

That was satisfactory. I liked that all right, except for one thing. After the Westchester dick was finished on the phone and it was settled that I would roll my own, and the sergeant had generously said that the Police Department would contribute the phone call, I asked the dick if he understood that I didn't care to be tailed, and he replied that I needn't worry because he was going back to Thirty-fifth Street to see Nero Wolfe. I didn't care much for that, but said nothing because I hadn't yet decided exactly what to say. So when I found a place on Lexington Avenue for a sandwich and a malted, I went first to a phone booth, called the house, and told Fritz to leave the chain bolt on, tell callers that Wolfe was out of the city and no more, and admit no one.

Being on the move did help. Having decided, while touring the park and avenues, what my immediate trouble was, I now, on my way to Birchvale, got the whole thing into focus. Considering the entire picture, including the detail of putting the house up for sale and the lack of even one little hint for me, let alone a blueprint, it was by no means a bet that Wolfe had merely dived into a foxhole. Look how free Marko had been with his poor-young-friending. It was not inconceivable that Wolfe had decided to chuck it for good. A hundred times and more, when things or people—frequently me— didn't suit him, he had told me about the house he owned in Egypt and how pleasant it would be to live there. I had always brushed it off. I now realized that a man who is eccentric enough to threaten to go and live in Egypt is eccentric enough to do it, especially when it gets to the point where he opens a package of sausage and has to run for his life.

Therefore I would be a dimwit to assume that this was merely time out to gather ammunition and make plans. Nor could I assume that it wasn't. I couldn't assume anything. Was he gone for good, or was he putting on a charade that would make all his other performances look like piker stuff in comparison? Presumably I was to answer that question, along with others, by the light of experience guided by intelligence, and I did not appreciate the compliment. If I was finally and permanently on my own, very well; I would make out. But apparently I was still drawing pay, so what? The result of my getting the whole picture into focus was that as I turned in at the entrance to Birchvale I was sorer than ever.

I was stopped at the entrance by one of Noonan's colleagues, there on guard, and was allowed to proceed up the curving drive only after I had shown him four documents. Parking in a space at the side of the house that was bordered by evergreens, I walked around to the front door and was admitted by a maid who looked pale and puffy. She didn't say anything, just held the door open, but a man was there too, one of the county boys whom I knew by sight but not by name. He said, "This way," and led me to the right, to the same small room I had seen before.

Ben Dykes, sitting there at the table with a stack of papers, grunted at me, "So you finally got here."

"I told Archer two o'clock. It's one-fifty-eight."

"Uh-huh. Sit down."

I sat. The door was standing open, but no sound of any kind came to my ears except the rustling of the papers Dykes was going through.

"Is the case solved?" I inquired courteously. "It's so damn quiet. In New York they make more noise. If you—"

I stopped because I was being answered. A typewriter started clicking somewhere. It was faint, from a distance, but unmistakably a typewriter, with a professional at it.

"I suppose Archer knows I'm here," I stated.

"Don't work up a lather," Dykes advised me without looking up.

I shrugged, stretched my legs and crossed my ankles, and tried to see what his papers were. I was too far away to get any words, but from various aspects I finally concluded that they were type-written signed statements of the family, guests, and servants. Not being otherwise engaged at the moment, I would have been glad to help Dykes with them, but I doubted if it was worth the breath to make an offer. After the strain of trying to identify the papers, my eyes went shut, and for the first time I was aware how sleepy I was. I thought I had better open my eyes, and then decided it would show more strength of will if I kept awake with them shut. . . .

Someone was using my head for a cocktail shaker. Resenting it, I jerked away and made a gesture of protest with my fist closed, following up by opening my eyes and jumping to my feet. Backing away from me was a skinny guy with a long neck. He looked both startled and angry.

"Sorry," I told him. "I guess I dozed off a second."

"You dozed off forty minutes," Dykes declared. He was still at the table with the papers, and standing beside him was District Attorney Archer.

"That leaves me," I said, "still behind seven hours and more."

"We want a statement," Archer said impatiently.

"The sooner the better," I agreed, and pulled my chair up. Archer sat at the end of the table at my left, Dykes across from me, and the skinny guy, with a notebook and pen, at the other end.

"First," Archer said, "repeat what you told us last night about Mrs. Rackham's visit to Wolfe's office with Leeds."

"But," I objected, "that'll take half an hour, and you're busy. That's routine. I assure you it won't vary."

"Go ahead. I want to hear it, and I have questions."

I yawned thoroughly, rubbed my eyes with the heels of my palms, and started. At first it was fuzzy, but it flowed easy after a minute or two, and it would have been a pleasure to have them compare it with a record from the previous recital if there had been one.

Archer had some questions, and Dykes one or two. At the end Archer asked me, "Will you swear to that, Goodwin?"

"Sure, glad to. If you'll pay the notary fee."

"Go and type it, Cheney."

The skinny guy got up, with his notebook, and left. After the door was closed Archer spoke.

"You might as well know it, Goodwin; you've been contradicted. Mr. Rackham says you're lying about his wife's conversation with Wolfe."

"Yeah? How does he know? He wasn't there."

"He says that she couldn't possibly have said what you report because it wasn't true. He says that there was no question or misunderstanding about money between them. He also says that she told him that she suspected her financial affairs were being mishandled by Mr. Hammond of the Metropolitan Trust Company, and that she was going to consult Nero Wolfe about it."

"Well." I yawned. "That's interesting. Leeds is on my side. Who's on his?"

"No one so far."

"Have you tried it out on Leeds?"

"Yes. As you say, he's on your side. He has signed a statement. So has Mr. Rackham."

"What does Hammond say?"

"I haven't—" Archer paused, regarding me. "Perhaps I shouldn't have told you that. You will keep it to yourself. It's a delicate matter, to approach a responsible officer of a reputable bank on a thing like that."

"Right," I agreed. "It's also a delicate matter to call a millionaire a damn liar—that is, delicate for you. Not for me. I hereby call him a damn liar. I suppose he is a millionaire? Now?"

Archer and Dykes exchanged glances.

"Save it if you want to," I said understandingly. "Leeds will tell me. If he knows. Does he?"

"Yes. The will was read to the family today. I was present. There are a number of bequests to servants and distant relatives. Mrs. Frey gets this place and a million dollars. Leeds gets half a million. Lina Darrow gets two hundred thousand. The rest goes to Mr. Rackham."

"I see. Then he's a millionaire, so it's delicate. Even so, he's a damn liar and it's two to one. I'll sign that statement in triplicate if you want it. Beyond that what can I say?"

"I want to make it three to one." Archer leaned to me. "Listen, Goodwin. I have great respect for Nero Wolfe's talents. I have reason to, as you know. But I do not intend to let his whims interfere with the functions of my office. I want a statement from him supporting yours and Leeds', and I mean to have it without delay. I sent a man to get it. This morning at eleven o'clock he was told that Wolfe wasn't available and that you weren't there and your whereabouts were not known. That was when an alarm was spread for you. I had a phone call from my man an hour ago. He had gone back to Wolfe's house and had been told that Wolfe was out of the city, and that was all he could get."

Archer made a hand into a fist, resting on the table. "I won't stand for it, Goodwin. This is the toughest one I've had in my county since I took office, and I won't stand for it. Whatever else he is, he's a fat conceited peacock and it's time somebody called him. There's a phone you can use. Two hours from now, unless he's here and talking to me, there'll be a warrant for his arrest as a material witness. There's the phone."

"I doubt if you could paste material witness on him. He hasn't been anywhere near here."

"Nuts," Ben Dykes growled. "Don't be a sap. She takes troubles to him Friday and gets murdered Saturday."

I decided to take the plunge. The way I felt, it would have been a pleasure to let them go ahead with a warrant, but if I tried to stall I would need a very fancy excuse tomorrow when they saw the ad in the *Gazette*. So I thought what the hell, now is as good a time as any, and told them.

388 TRIPLE ZECKTRIPLE ZECK

"I can't phone him because I don't know where he is."

"Ha ha," Dykes said. "Ha ha ha."

"Yes," I admitted, "it could be a gag. But it isn't. I don't know whether he's out of the city or not. All I know is that he left the house last night, while I was up here, and he hasn't come back—no, that isn't true. I also know that he called on a friend of his named Vukcic and arranged for his plants to be moved out and his cook to take another job. And he gave Vukcic a power of attorney. And he sent an ad to the *Gazette* announcing his retirement from the detective business."

Dykes did not ha-ha again. He merely sat and frowned at me. Archer, his lips puckered, had his eyes focused on me, but as if he was trying to see not me but through me. That went on for seconds, and I got uncomfortable. I can meet a pair of eyes all right, but not two pairs at once, one in front and one off to the left.

Finally Dykes turned his head to tell Archer, "This makes it nice."

Archer nodded, not taking his regard from me. "It's hard to believe, Goodwin."

"I'll say it is. For him to—"

"No, no. It's hard to believe that Wolfe and you would try anything as fantastic as this. Obviously he was absolutely compelled to. You phoned him from Leeds' place last night, as soon as you could get to a phone after Mrs. Rackham was murdered. That was—"

"Excuse me," I said firmly. "Not as soon as I could get to a phone after Mrs. Rackham was murdered. As soon as I could get to a phone after I found out she had been murdered."

"Very well. We're not in court." He was leaning at me. "That was shortly after midnight. What did you say to him?"

"I told him what had happened. I reported, as fully as I could in the time I had, everything from my arrival here up to then. If the operator listened in you can check with her. I asked if I should limit my talk with the cops to events here and leave the rest for him to tell, and he said no, I should withhold nothing, including all details of Mrs. Rackham's talk with him. That was all. As you know, I followed instructions."

"Jesus," Dykes said. "Son, it looks like your turn to sweat has come."

Archer ignored him. "And after telling you to withhold nothing from the police, Wolfe suddenly decides, in the middle of the night, that he has had enough of detective work, sends an ad to a newspaper announcing his retirement, calls on a friend to arrange for the care of his orchids—and what did he do then? I was so engrossed I may have missed something."

"I don't know what he did. He walked out. He disappeared."

I was aware, of course, of how it sounded. It was completely cuckoo. It was all rayon and a yard wide. I damn near made it even worse by telling them about the sausage and the tear gas, of course without letting on that we knew who had sent it, but realized in time how that would go over in the circumstances. That *would* have made a hit. But I had to say or do something, and decided to produce evidence, so I reached to my pocket for it.

"He left notes on the table in his bedroom," I said, "for Fritz and Theodore and me. Here's mine."

I handed it to Archer. He read it and passed it to Dykes. Dykes read it twice and returned it to Archer, who stuck it in his pocket.

"Jesus," Dykes said again, looking at me in a way I didn't like. "This is really something. I've always thought Nero Wolfe had a lot on the ball, and you too in a way, but this is about the worst I ever saw. Really." He turned to Archer. "It's plain what happened."

"It certainly is." Archer made a fist. "Goodwin, I don't ask you to tell me. I'll tell you. When you found Mrs. Rackham there dead, you and Leeds agreed on a tale about the visit to Nero Wolfe. Leeds came here to break the news. You went to his place to phone Wolfe and report, both the murder and the tale you and Leeds had agreed on—or maybe Wolfe knew that already, since you had pretended to investigate the dog poisoning. In any case, Wolfe knew something that he didn't dare to try to cover and that, equally, he didn't dare to reveal. What made it unbearably hot was the murder. So he arranged to disappear, and we haven't got him, and it may take a day or a week to find him. But we've got you."

The fist hit the table, not hard. "You know where Wolfe is. You know what he knows that he had to run away from. It is vital information required by me in my investigation of a murder. Surely you must see that your position is untenable, you can't possibly get away with it. Twenty Nero Wolfes couldn't bring you out of this with a whole skin. Even if he's cooking up one of his flashy surprises, even if he walks into my office tomorrow with the murderer and the evidence to convict him, I will not stand for this. There is no written record of what you said last night. I'll get the stenographer back in here and we'll tear up his notebook and what he has typed, and you can start from scratch."

"Better grab it, son," Dykes said, perfectly friendly. "Loyalty to your employer is a fine thing, but not when he's got a screw loose."

I yawned. "My God, I'm sleepy. I wouldn't mind this so much if I was helping out with a fix, good or bad, but it's a shame to get stuck with the truth. Ask me tomorrow, ask me all summer, I refuse to tell a lie. And I do not know where Mr. Wolfe is."

Archer stood up. "Get a material witness warrant and lock him up," he said, almost squeaking, and marched out.

8

The jail at White Plains uses a gallon of strong disinfectant, diluting it, of course, every day including Sunday. I can back that statement up with two pieces of evidence: the word of the turnkey on the second-floor cell block, whose name is Wilkes, given to me personally, and my sense of smell, which is above average.

I had no opportunity to make a tour of inspection during the twenty hours I was there, that Easter Sunday and the day following, but except for the smell I found nothing to write to the newspapers about, once you grant that society must protect itself against characters like me. My cell—or rather, our cell, since I had a mate—was as clean as they come. There was something about the blankets that made you keep them away from your chin, but that could have been just prejudice. The light was nothing wonderful, but good enough to read by for thirty days.

I didn't really get acquainted with my surroundings or my mate until Monday, I was so darned sleepy when they finally finished with me down below and showed me up to my room. They had been insistent but not ferocious. I had been allowed to phone Fritz that I wouldn't be home, which was a good thing, as there was no telling what he would have done with no word from me coming on top of Wolfe's fadeout, and also to try to call Nathaniel Parker, the only lawyer Wolfe has ever been willing to invite to dinner; but that was no go because he was away for the weekend. When at last I stretched out on the cot, I was dead to the world ten seconds after my head hit the pillow, consisting of my pants wrapped in my shirt.

It was the pants, or rather the coat and vest that went with them, that made my stay pleasanter than it might have been right from the start. I had had perhaps half as much sleep as I could have used when a hell of a noise banged at me and I lifted my head and opened my eyes. Across the cell on another cot, so far away that I would have had to stretch my arm its full length to touch him, was my cell-mate—a broad-shouldered guy about my age, maybe a little older, with a mop of tousled black hair. He was sitting up, yawning.

"What's all the racket?" I asked. "Jail break?"

"Breakfast and check-up in ten minutes," he replied, getting his feet, with socks on, to the floor. "Stupid custom."

"Boneheads," I agreed, twisting up to sit on the edge of the cot.

Going to the chair where his wardrobe was, his eye fell on my chair, and he stepped to it for a look at the coat and vest. He fingered the lapel, looked inside at the lining, and inspected a buttonhole. Then, without comment, he returned to his side, two whole steps, and started to dress. I followed suit.

"Where do we wash?" I inquired.

"After breakfast," he replied, "if you insist."

A man in uniform appeared on the other side of the bars and used his hands, and the cell door swung open.

"Wait a minute, Wilkes," my mate told him, and then asked me, "You cleaned out?"

"Naturally. This is a modern jail."

"Would bacon and eggs suit you?"

"Just right."

"Toast white or rye?"

"White."

"Our tastes are similar. Make it two, Wilkes. Two of everything."

"As you say," the turnkey said distinctly, and went. My mate, getting his necktie under his shirt collar, told me, "They won't allow exceptions to the turnout and check-up, but you can pass up the garbage. We'll eat here in privacy."

"This," I said earnestly, "is the brotherhood of man. I would like this breakfast to be on me when I get my wallet back."

He waved it away. "Forget it."

The turnout and check-up, I discovered, were not to be taken as opportunities for conversation. There were around forty of us, all shapes and sizes, and on the whole we were frankly not a blue-ribbon outfit. The smell of the breakfast added to the disinfectant was enough to account for the expressions on the faces, not counting whatever it was that had got them there, and it was a relief to get back to my cozy cell with my mate.

We had our hands and faces washed, and he had his teeth brushed, when the breakfast came on a big clean aluminum tray. The eats were barely usable if you took Fritz's productions as a standard, but compared with the community meal which I had seen and smelled they were a handsome feast. My mate having ordered two of everything, there were two morning *Gazettes*, and before he even touched his orange juice he took his paper and, with no glance at the front page, turned to sports. Finishing his survey of the day's prospects, he drank some orange juice and inquired, "Are you interested in the rapidity of horses?"

"In a way." I added earnestly, "I like the way you talk. I enjoy being with cultured people."

He gave me a suspicious look, saw my honest candid countenance, and relaxed. "That's natural. Look at your clothes."

We were on the chairs, with the little wooden table between us. It was comfortable enough except that there was no room to prop up our morning papers. He flattened his out, still open at sports, on the end of the cot, and turned to it while disposing of a bite of food. I arranged mine, front page, on my knee. In the picture of Mrs. Rackham the poor woman looked homelier than she had actually been, which was a darned shame even though she wasn't alive to see it. Wolfe's name and mine both appeared in the subheads under the three-column spread about the murder. I glanced at the bottom, followed the instruction to turn to page four, and there saw more pictures. The one of Wolfe was only fair, making him look almost bloated, but the one of me was excellent. There was one of a Doberman pinscher standing at attention. It was captioned Hebe, which I doubted. The play in the text on Wolfe and me was on his sudden retirement from business and absence from the city, and on my presence at the scene of the murder and arrest as a material witness. There was also a report of an interview with Marko Vukcic, a *Gazette* exclusive, with Lon Cohen's by-line. I would have given at least ten to one that Lon had used my name in getting to Marko.

With the breakfast all down, including the coffee, which was pretty good, I was so interested in my reading that I didn't notice that my mate had finished with sports and proceeded to other current events. What got my attention was the feeling that I was being scrutinized, and sure enough I was. He was looking at me, and then at his page four, and back at me again.

I grinned at him. "Pretty good likeness, huh? But I don't think that's the right dog. I'm no expert, but Hebe isn't quite as slim as that."

He was regarding me with a new expression, not particularly matey. "So you're Nero Wolfe's little Archie."

"I was." I gestured. "Read the paper. Apparently I am now my own little Archie."

"So I bought a meal for a shamus."

"Not at all. Didn't I say it was on me when I get my wallet back?"

He shook his head. "I wouldn't have believed it. With them clothes? I supposed you had got snagged in the raid on the Covered Porch. It gets worse all the time, the dicks. Look at this, even here in the can I meet a guy with a suit of clothes like that, and he's a dick!"

"I am not a dick, strictly speaking." I was hurt. "I am a private eye. I said I liked the way you talk, but you're getting careless. I also noticed you were cultured, and that should have put me on my guard. Cultured people are not often found in the coop. But nowadays dicks are frequently cultured. They tossed me in here because they think I'm holding out on a murder, which I'm not, and the fact that it has been tried before doesn't mean they wouldn't try it again. Putting you in here with me wasn't so dumb, but you overplayed it, buying me a breakfast first pop. That started me wondering."

He was on his feet, glaring down at me. "Watch it, looselip. I'm going to clip you."

"What for?"

"You need a lesson. I'm a plant, am I?"

"Nuts. Who's insulted now?" I gestured. "You call me a name, I call you a name. I take it, you take it. Let's start over."

But he was too sensitive to make up as quick as all that. He undid his fist, glared at me some more, sidled between his chair and his cot, and got comfortable on the cot with his *Gazette*. With his head toward the corridor he was getting as good light as there was, and I followed his example, folding one of the blankets for a pillow and spreading my handkerchief on it. Two hours and ten minutes passed without a word from either cot. I happen to know because as I stretched out I glanced at my watch, wondering how soon I could reasonably expect Parker to show up with a crowbar to pry me loose, and it was twenty past nine; and, after giving that *Gazette* as good a play as a newspaper ever got, I had just looked at my watch for the twentieth time and seen 11:30 when he suddenly spoke.

"Look, Goodwin, what are you going to do now?"

I let the paper slide to the floor. "I don't know, take a nap, I guess."

"I don't mean now, this minute. Is anyone looking after you?"

"If he isn't he'd better be. A high-priced lawyer named Parker."

"Then what?"

"I'll go home and take a bath."

"Then what?"

"I'll brush my teeth and shave."

"Then what?"

I swiveled my head to glance at him. "You're pretty damn persistent. Where do you want us to get to?"

"Nowhere in particular." He stayed supine, and I noticed that in profile he looked a little like John L. Lewis, only a lot younger. He went on, "I was just thinking, with Nero Wolfe gone I suppose your job's gone. Can't I think?"

"Sure. If it doesn't hurt."

A brief silence. He spoke again. "I've heard about you a little. What kind of a guy are you?"

"Oh—I'm a thinker too, and I'm cultured. I got good marks in algebra. I sleep well. I'm honest and ambitious, with a good personality."

"You know your way around."

"In certain circles, yes. It would be hard to lose me within ten miles of Times Square unless I was blindfolded. What are the requirements of the position you are about to offer?"

He ignored that and took another angle. "My name is Christy— Max Christy. Ever hear of me?"

If I had it was vague, but I saw no point in hurting his feelings. "Max Christy?" I snorted. "Don't be silly."

"I thought you might have. I've only been around the big town a couple of years, and I don't toot a horn, but some people get talked about. How much has Wolfe been paying you?"

"That's asking," I objected mildly. "I wouldn't want it to get in the papers. I've been eating all right and I've got a government bond. Anything over—"

Footsteps in the corridor stopped at our door, and the turnkey's voice came. "Mr. Christy! They want you down in the office."

My mate stayed flat. "Come back in ten minutes, Wilkes," he called. "I'm busy."

I confirmed it. "We're in conference, Wilkes," I snapped.

"But I think it's your out."

"I suppose so. Come back in ten minutes."

Wilkes, mumbling something, went away. Christy resumed. "You were saying . . ."

"Yeah. That anything over fifty grand a year would find me a good listener."

"I'm being serious, Goodwin."

"So am I."

"You are not. You never got within a mile of fifty grand a year." His head was turned to face me now. "Anyway, it's not a question of so many grand a year—not in this business."

"In what business?"

"The business I'm in. What did I say my name is?"

"Max Christy."

"Then what more do you want? Take my being here now, for example. I got raked in at the Covered Porch yesterday by mistake, but I would have been loose in an hour if it hadn't been Sunday—and Easter too. Here it is"—he looked at his wrist—"not quite noon, and I'm walking out. There has never been an organization to compare with it. For a man like you there would be special jobs and special opportunities if you once got taken in. With your record, which is bad as far as I know it, that would take a while. You would have to show, and show good. Your idea about so many grand a year just isn't realistic, certainly not while you're being tried, but after that it would depend on you. If you've got it in you there's practically no limit. Another thing is income tax."

"Yeah, what about income tax?"

"You simply use your judgment. Say Wolfe paid you thirty grand a year, which he didn't, nothing like it, what did you have to say about income tax? Nothing. It was taken out before you got paid. You never even saw it. In this business you make your own decisions about it. You want to be fair, and you want to be in the clear, but you don't want to get gypped, and on that basis you use your judgment."

Christy raised his torso and sat on the edge of the cot. "You know,

Goodwin, I'm just tossing this at you on the spur of the moment. I laid here reading about you, and I thought to myself, here's a man the right age and experience, not married, the right personality, he knows people, he knows lots of cops, he has been a private eye for years and so he would be open to anything that sounds good enough; he is just out of a job, he's got himself tangled in a hot homicide here in Westchester, and he may need help right now. That's what I was thinking, and I thought why not ask him? I can't guarantee anything, especially if you're headed for a murder rap, but if you need help now and then later on you would like a chance at something, I'm Max Christy and I could pass the word along. If you—"

He paused at the sound of footsteps. Wilkes's voice came from the door. "They want you down there, Mr. Christy. I told them you was busy personally, but they're sending up."

"All right, Wilkes. Coming." My mate stood up. "What about it, Goodwin?"

"I appreciate it," I said warmly. Wilkes, having unlocked the door, was standing there, and, using my judgment, I kept it discreet. "When I get out and look around a little I'll know better how things stand." I had got to my feet. "How do I get in touch with you?"

"Phone is best. Churchill five, three two three two. I'm not there much, but a message will reach me promptly. Better write it down."

"I'll remember it." I took his offered hand and we shook. "It's been a pleasure. Where can I mail a check for the breakfast?"

"Forget it. It was a privilege. Be seeing you, I hope." He strode out like an executive going to greet a welcome caller, Wilkes holding the door for him.

I sat down on the cot, thinking it was a hell of a note for a Max Christy to get sprung before an Archie Goodwin. What was keeping Parker? In jail a man gets impatient.

9

It was seven o'clock that evening, just getting dark, when I left the car at the curb on West Thirty-fifth Street in front of Wolfe's house and climbed the seven steps to the stoop. Parker, armed with papers which stated, among other things, that my continued availability to the People of the State of New York was worth ten thousand dollars, had arrived at the jail shortly after two, and in another ten minutes I had been unleashed on society again, but District Attorney Archer had requested another session with me in the presence of my attorney, and Parker and I had obliged. It had dragged on and on, and was really a bore, because there was nothing for me to try to be witty about. Unlike some other occasions when I had been in conference with the law, there was nothing to stimulate me because all I had to do was tell the truth, and all of it—except the sausage part and the phone call from Arnold Zeck.

When they had finally called it a day and Parker and I were standing on the sidewalk in front of the courthouse, he asked me, "Am I to know where Wolfe is?"

"I doubt it. He told me not to look for him."

"I see."

His tone of voice irritated me. "Every word you heard me say in there," I asserted, "was the truth. I haven't the thinnest idea where he is or what he's doing."

He shrugged. "I'm not complaining. I only hope he hasn't tumbled in where it's too deep this time—and you too."

"Go to hell," I advised him, and marched off. I couldn't really blame the Westchester bunch, but Parker should have known me well enough to tell which side of my mouth I was talking out of. It's damn discouraging, when you do tell the truth, not to have it recognized.

Also discouraging was the welcome I got on entering Wolfe's house that evening. It was in the form of a note stuck in the corner of my desk blotter, unfolded.

Dear Archie—
  I am sorry you are in jail and hope it will not last long. Mr. Vukcic has been to see me and I am leaving now to go to work for him $1500. There has been no word from Mr. Wolfe. God grant he is safe and well and I think you should find him no matter what he wrote. I threw out the jar of sardines and stopped the milk. My very best regards and wishes,
                                        Fritz
                                        1:35 PM

I was pleased to observe that he stuck to routine to the end, putting the time down. Also it was nice of him to end his note to me the same as Wolfe had ended his. Nevertheless, it was a discouraging welcome home after a night in the hoosegow. And there had been a period of more than five hours when any phone calls that might have come would not have been answered, something that had never happened before in all the years I had worked and lived there. Unless Theodore . . .

I beat it to the stairs and up the three flights, and entered the plant rooms. One step inside the first room, the warm one, I stopped and surveyed. It was more of a shock, somehow, than it had been a year ago when it had been used as a target for tommy guns from across the street. Then they had at least left a mess; now there was nothing but the benches and stands. It really got me for a minute. I moved on through: medium room, cool room, potting room, spray chamber, Theodore's room—all empty. Hewitt must have sent an army to clean all that out in one day, I thought, heading back downstairs.

In the kitchen was another longer note from Fritz, reporting phone calls that had come before he left and various minor matters. I opened the refrigerator and poked around, and settled for a jar of home-made paté, a hunk of Italian bread, Vermont cheese, and milk. As I sat working at it with an evening paper propped up before me, I kept listening for something—nothing in particular, just something. That had never been a noisy house, but I had never known it anything like that quiet. Almost no cars went by, and the few that did must have been coasting in neutral.

My meal finished and things put away, I wandered into the dining room, office, front room, down to the basement to Fritz's room, up one flight to Wolfe's room, up another to my room. As I undressed for my post-jail bath, I thought that the hell of it wasn't how I felt, but that I didn't know how to feel. If I had actually seen the last of Nero Wolfe, it was a damn sad day for me, there were no two ways about that, and if I got a lump in my throat and somebody walked in I would just as soon show him the lump as not. But what if it was Wolfe himself who walked in? That was the trouble. Damned if I was going to work up a fancy lump and then have him suddenly appear and start crabbing about something.

After I had bathed and shaved and got into clean pajamas, and answered a couple of phone calls from journalists, and moseyed down to the office and fooled around a while, someone did walk in. When I heard the front door open I made for the hall as if I had been expecting another package of sausage, and there was Fritz. He turned from closing the door, saw me, and beamed.

"Ah! Archie! You escaped?"

"I'm out on bail." He seemed to want to shake hands, and I was willing. "Thanks for your note. How's the new job?"

"Terrible. I'm played up. Mr. Wolfe?"

"I know nothing about Mr. Wolfe. I ate half a jar of paté."

He stopped beaming. "Mr. Vukcic is going to sell this house."

"He's going to offer it for sale, which is not the same thing."

"Perhaps not." He sighed. "I'm tired. Mr. Vukcic said there is no reason why I should not sleep here but I should ask you. It would be good for me—I am so used to that room . . ."

"Certainly. I'm used to mine too. I'm going to sleep here until further notice."

"Good." He started for the kitchen, stopped, and turned. "Are you going to look for him?"

"No!" Hearing myself shout, it seemed a relief and I did it again. "I am not!" I went to the stairs and started up. "Good night."

"Good night, Archie."

I was on the first landing when his voice came. "I'll get your breakfast! I don't have to leave until ten!"

"Swell!" I called back. "We'll never miss him!"

The next day, Tuesday, I had no time to raise a lump. There were dozens of phone calls, from newspapers, former clients, friends, and miscellaneous. One was from Calvin Leeds, asking me to go up there to see him, and I told him I had had enough of Westchester for a while. When he insisted, I agreed to receive him at the office at two o'clock. I took advantage of another call, from Lon Cohen at the *Gazette*, to ask about my recent cellmate, Max Christy. Lon asked why I wanted to know. Lon is a good guy, but no newspaperman on earth can answer the simplest question without asking you one first, and more if possible.

"Just curious," I told him. "I met him in jail over the weekend, and thought he was charming. I don't want a biography, just a line or two."

"For quotation?"

"No."

"Right. He's comparatively new to this section, but he's a fast mover. Not really big yet. As far as I know, the only thing he's close to right in town is a string of rooms for transients. He seems to be specializing on little weekend roundups in the suburbs."

"Just games, or women, or what?"

"Anything men risk money for. Or pay it for. I have heard that he is seen around sometimes with Brownie Costigan. How curious are you? Is it worth a steak? Or is it worth a phone number or address where I can reach Nero Wolfe?"

By that time I had abandoned the idea of selling anyone, even Lon Cohen, the idea that I ever told the truth, so I thanked him and hung up.

A couple of checks in the morning mail, one from a man who was paying in installments for having a blackmailer removed from his throat, were no problem, since there was a rubber stamp for endorsing them, but in order to pay three bills that came in I had to make a trip to Fifty-fourth Street to see if the formalities about Marko's power of attorney had been attended to. They had, by Parker, and I was glad to see that Marko signed the checks on my say-so, without looking at the bills. If he had started auditing on me I swear to God I would have moved out and got a hotel room.

There were other chores, such as phoning Hewitt's place on Long Island to ask if the plants and Theodore had arrived safely, making arrangements with a phone-answering service, handling a report from Fred Durkin on a poison-letter job that was the main item of unfinished business, and so on, but I managed to have them all under control when two o'clock came and brought Calvin Leeds.

When I went to let him in and took him to the office, there was a problem. Should I sit at my desk or at Wolfe's? On the one hand, I was not Wolfe and had no intention of trying to be. On the other hand, when a pinch-hitter is called on he stands at the plate to bat, not off to one side. Also it would be interesting to see, from Wolfe's position, what the light was like on the face of a man sitting in the red leather chair. So again, this time intentionally, I sat behind Wolfe's desk.

"I came here to get an explanation," Leeds said, "and I'm going to get it."

He looked as if he could stand a dose of something—if not an explanation, then maybe castor oil. The hide of his face still looked tough and weathered, or rather as if it had been but someone had soaked it in something to make it stretch and get saggy. His eyes looked determined, but not clear and alert as before. No one would

have guessed that he had just inherited half a million bucks, and
not from a dearly beloved wife or sister but merely a cousin.

Something like a million times I had seen Wolfe, faced with a
belligerent statement from a caller, lean back and close his eyes. I
thought I might as well try it, and did so. But the springs which let
the chair's back slant to the rear were carefully adjusted to the pressure of Wolfe's poundage, not mine, and I had to keep pushing to
maintain the damn thing in the leaning position.

"A man who comes forty miles for an explanation," I said, with
my eyes closed, "is entitled to one. What needs explaining?"

"Nero Wolfe's behavior does."

"That's nothing new." It was too much of a strain keeping the
chair back in a leaning position, and I straightened up. "It often
has. But that's not my department."

"I want to see him."

"So do I."

"You're a liar, Goodwin."

I shook my head, my lips tight. "You know," I said, "I have probably told as many lies as any man my age except psychos. But I have
never been called a liar as frequently as in the past twenty-four
hours, and I have never stuck so close to the truth. To hell with it.
Mr. Wolfe has gone south to train with the Dodgers. He will play
shortstop."

"That won't help any," Leeds said, patient but determined, "that
kind of talk. If you don't like being called a liar, neither do I, and
the difference is that I'm not. The district attorney says I'm lying,
because Nero Wolfe has suddenly disappeared, and he disappeared
because he doesn't dare answer questions about my cousin Sarah's
visit to him here, and that proves that your report of that visit is
false, and since my report is the same as yours mine is false too. Now
that sounds logical, but there's a flaw in it. The flaw is their assumption that his disappearance was connected with my cousin's
visit. I know it couldn't have been, because there was nothing about
our talk that day that could possibly have had such a result. I have
told them that, and they think I'm lying. As long as they think I'm
lying, and you too, they'll have their minds on that and they won't
find out who killed my cousin and why—and anyway, I don't want
to be suspected of lying when I'm not, especially not in connection
with the murder of my cousin."

Leeds paused for breath and went on, "There's only one way out that I can see, and that's for you to tell them the real reason for Wolfe's disappearance—or, better still, he ought to tell them himself. I want you to put this up to him. Even if his own safety is involved, he ought to manage somehow. If it was something about some client that made him disappear, in the interest of some client, then you can tell him from me that I saw him take a check from my cousin for ten thousand dollars and it seems to me he's under obligation to her as much as any other client, to protect her interests, and it surely isn't in her interest to have suspicion centered in the wrong place about who killed her—and killed her dog too." His jaw quivered a little, and he clamped it tight.

"Do you mean," I inquired, "that suspicion is centered on you? How come?"

"Not on me as—as a murderer, I don't suppose so, but on me as a liar, and you and Wolfe. Even though she left me a great deal of money—I'm not thinking about being arrested for murder."

"Who do you think ought to be?"

"I don't know." He gestured. "You're trying to change the subject. It's not a question of me and what I think, it's you and what you're going to do. From what I've heard of Wolfe, I doubt if it would help for you to tell him what I've said; I've got to see him and tell him myself. If he has really got to hide from somebody or something, do it however you want to. Blindfold me and put me face down in your car. I've got to see him. My cousin would have wanted me to, and he took her money."

I was half glad there for a moment that I did not know where Wolfe was. I had no admiration for Leeds' preference in pets, since I would put a woman ahead of a Doberman pinscher any day, and there was room for improvement in him in a few other respects, but I couldn't help but admit he had a point and was not being at all unreasonable. So if I had known where Wolfe was I would have had to harden my heart, and as it was all I had to harden was my voice. It struck me then, for the first time, that maybe I shouldn't be so sore at Wolfe after all.

Leeds hung on for another quarter of an hour, and I prolonged it a little myself by trying to get something out of him about the progress the cops had made, without success. He went away mad, still calling me a liar, which kept it unanimous. What he got from me was nothing. What I got from him was that Mrs. Rackham's

funeral would be the next morning, Wednesday. Not a profitable
way to spend most of an hour, for either of us.

I spent what was left of the afternoon looking into the matter of
sausage. Within ten minutes after the package had been opened
that day, Wolfe had phoned both Mummiani and the Fleet Messenger Service and got a blank as expected; but on the outside
chance that I might at least get a bone for my curiosity to gnaw on
I made a trip to Fulton Street and one uptown. At Mummiani's
no one knew anything. Since Wolfe had been getting Darst's sausage
from them for years, and in that time their personnel had come and
gone, any number of outsiders could know about it. At the Fleet
Messenger Service they were willing to help but couldn't. They remembered the package because Wolfe had phoned about it, but all
I learned was that it had been left there by a youth who might have
been playing hookey from the eighth grade, and I didn't even bother
to listen to the description, such as it was.

Fed up with an empty house and the phone ringing and being
called a liar, I put in a call myself from a drugstore booth, and made
personal arrangements for dinner and a show.

Wednesday morning a visitor came that I let in. I had formed
the habit, since returning from jail, of hearing the doorbell ring,
going to the hall, observing through the one-way glass panel who
it was out on the stoop, making a face, and returning to the office. If
the bell kept ringing long enough to be a nuisance I flipped the
switch that turned it off. This time, around eleven Wednesday morning, instead of making a face I went and opened the door and said,
"Well, hello! Coming in?"

A chunky specimen about my height, with wrinkled pink skin
and gray hair and sharp gray-blue eyes, grunted a greeting and
stepped over the sill. I said it was cold for April, and he agreed. As
I hung his topcoat on the rack I told myself that I must be more restrained. The fact that I was alone in the house was no reason to
give Inspector Cramer of Manhattan Homicide the impression that
I was glad to see him. Wolfe or no Wolfe, I could keep up appearances.

I let him lead the way to the office. This time I sat at my own
desk. I was tempted to take Wolfe's chair again just to see how he
would react, but it would have put me at a disadvantage, I was so
used to dealing with him, in the red leather chair, from my own
angle.

He eyed me. "So you're holding the fort," he growled.

"Not exactly," I objected. "I'm only the caretaker. Or maybe I'm going down with the ship. Not that those who have left are rats."

"Where's Wolfe?"

"I don't know. Next, you call me a liar. Then I say I have been, but not now. Then you—"

"Nuts. Where is he, Archie?"

That cleared the atmosphere. Over the years he had called me Goodwin fifty times to one Archie. He called me Archie only when he wanted something awful bad or when he had something wrapped up that Wolfe had given him and his humanity overcame him. So we were to be mellow.

"Listen," I said, friendly but firm. "That routine is all right for people like district attorneys and state cops and the representatives of the press, but you're above it. Either I don't know where he is, or I do know but I'm sitting on it. What's the difference? Next question."

He took a cigar from his pocket, inspected it, rubbed it between his palms, and inspected it again. "It must be quite a thing," he remarked, not growling. "That ad in the paper. The plants gone. Fritz and Theodore gone. Vukcic listing the house for sale. I'm going to miss it, I am, never dropping in to see him sitting there thinking he's smarter than God and all His angels. Quite a thing, it must be. What is it?"

I said slowly and wearily, "Either I don't know what it is, or I do know but—"

"What about the sausage that turned into tear gas? Any connection?"

I am always ready for Inspector Cramer, in the light of experience guided by intelligence, and therefore didn't bat an eye. I merely cocked my head a little, met his gaze, and considered the matter until I was satisfied. "I doubt if it was Fritz," I stated. "Mr. Wolfe has him too well trained. But in the excitement Sunday morning, Mr. Wolfe being gone, Fritz told Theodore, and you got it out of Theodore." I nodded. "That must be it."

"Did the tear gas scare him out of his skin? Or out of his house, which is the same thing. Was that it?"

"It might have, mightn't it? A coward like him?"

"No." Cramer put the cigar between his teeth, tilted up. "No, there are plenty of things about Wolfe I can and do object to, but he's not a coward. There might have been something about that tear gas that would have scared anybody. Was there?"

"As far as I know, it was just plain tear gas, nothing fancy." I decided to shove a little. "You know, it's nice to have you here any time, just for company, but aren't you spreading out some? Your job is homicide, and the tear gas didn't even make us sick, let alone kill us. Also your job is in the County of New York, and Mrs. Rackham died in Westchester. I enjoy talking with you, but have you got credentials?"

He made a noise that could have been a chuckle. "That's more like it," he said, not sarcastically. "You're beginning to sound natural. I'll tell you. I'm here at the request of Ben Dykes, who would give all his teeth and one ear to clear up the Rackham case ahead of the state boys. He thinks that Archer, the DA, may have swallowed the idea that you and Leeds are lying too deep, and he came to me as an expert on Nero Wolfe, which God knows I am. He laid it all out for me and wanted my opinion."

He shifted the cigar to a new angle. "The way it looked to me, there were three possibilities. First, the one that Archer has sold himself on, that you and Leeds are lying, and that what Mrs. Rackham really told Wolfe when she came here, together with her getting murdered the next day, somehow put Wolfe on a spot that was too hot for him, and he scooted, after fixing with you to cover as well as you could. I told Dykes I would rule that out, for various reasons—chiefly because neither you nor Wolfe would risk that much on a setup that depended on a stranger like Leeds sticking to a lie. Shall I analyze it more?"

"No, thanks, that'll do."

"I thought so. Next, the possibility that when you phoned Wolfe right after the body was found you told him something that gave him a line on the murderer, but it's tricky and he had to go outdoors to get his evidence, preparing to grandstand it for the front page. I told Dykes I would rule that out too. Wolfe is quite capable of a play like that, sure he is, but if that's all it amounted to, why move the plants out and put Fritz to work in a restaurant and list the house for sale? He's colorful, but not that colorful. Mrs. Rackham only paid him ten thousand, about what I make a year. Why should he spend it having his orchids carted around?"

Cramer shook his head. "Not for my money. That leaves the third possibility: that something really did scare him. That there was something about Mrs. Rackham's murder, or anyhow connected with it, that he knew he couldn't handle sitting there in that chair, but for some reason he had to handle it. So he scooted. As you say, you either don't know where he is or you know and won't tell—and that's no help either way. Now I've got a lot to say about this possibility. You got time to listen?"

"I've got all day, but Fritz isn't here to get our lunch."

"We'll go without." He clasped his hands behind his head and shifted his center of gravity. "You know, Archie, sometimes I'm not as far behind as you think I am."

"Also sometimes I don't think you're as far behind as you think I do."

"That's possible. Anyhow, I can add. I think he got word direct from Arnold Zeck. Did he?"

"Huh? Who's Arnold Zeck? Did you just make it up?"

I knew that was a mistake the instant it was out of my mouth. Then I had to try to keep it from showing on my face, the realization that I had fumbled it, but whether that was a success or not— and I couldn't very well look in a mirror to find out—it was too late.

Cramer looked pleased. "So you've been around all these years, a working detective, meeting the people you do, and you've never heard of Arnold Zeck. Either I've got to believe that, or I touched a tender spot."

"Sure I've heard of him. It just didn't click for a second."

"Oh, for God's sake. It's affecting you already, having Wolfe gone. That wasn't just a shot in the dark. One day two years ago I sat here in this chair. Wolfe sat there." He nodded at Wolfe's chair. "You were where you are now. A man named Orchard had been murdered, and so had a woman named Poole. In the course of our long talk Wolfe explained in detail how an ingenious and ruthless man could operate a blackmail scheme, good for at least a million a year, without sticking his neck out. Not only could; it was being done. Wolfe refused to name him, and since he wasn't behind the murders it was out of my territory, but a thing or two I heard and a couple of things that happened gave me a pretty clear idea. Not only me—it was whispered around: Arnold Zeck. You may perhaps remember it."

"I remember the Orchard case, certainly," I conceded. "I didn't hear the whispering."

"I did. You may also remember that a year later, last summer, Wolfe's plant rooms got shot up from a roof across the street."

"Yep. I was sitting right here and heard it."

"So I understand. Since no one was killed that never got to me officially, but naturally I heard things. Wolfe had started to investigate a man named Rony, and Rony's activities were the kind that might lead a first-class investigator like Wolfe in the direction of Arnold Zeck, maybe up close to Zeck, possibly even clear to him. I thought then that Wolfe had got warned off, by Zeck himself or someone near him, and he had disregarded it, and for a second warning they messed up his orchids. Then Rony got killed, and that was a break for Wolfe because it put him and Zeck on the same side."

"Gosh," I remarked, "it sounds awful complicated to me."

"I'll bet it does." Cramer moved the cigar—getting shorter now, although he never lit one—to the other side of his mouth. "All I'm doing is showing you that I'm not just hoping for a bite, and I don't want to string it out. It was a good guess that Wolfe had jostled up against Arnold Zeck in both the Orchard case and the Rony case, and now what happens? Not long after Mrs. Rackham calls on him and hires him to check on her husband's income, someone sends him a cylinder of tear gas—not a bomb to blow out his guts, which it could have been, just tear gas, so of course it was for a warning. And that night Mrs. Rackham gets murdered. You tell him about it on the phone, and when you get home he's gone."

Cramer took the cigar from his mouth and pointed it at me. "I'll tell you what I believe, Archie. I believe that if Wolfe had stayed and helped, the murderer of Mrs. Rackham would be locked up by now. I believe that he had reason to think that if he did that, helped to catch the murderer, he would have to spend the rest of his life trying to keep Arnold Zeck from getting him. I believe that he decided that the only way out was for him to get Zeck. How's that?"

"No comment," I said politely. "If you're right you're right, and if you're wrong I wouldn't want to hurt your feelings."

"Much obliged. But he did get a warning from Zeck—the tear gas."

"No comment."

"I wouldn't expect any. Now here's what I came for. I want you to give Wolfe a personal message from me, not as a police officer but as a friend. This is between you and me—and him. Zeck is out of his reach. He is out of anybody's reach. It's a goddam crime for an officer of the law to have to say a thing like that, even privately, but it's true. Here's a murder case, and thank God it's not mine. I'm not pointing at Ben Dykes or the DA up there, I'm not pointing at any person or persons, but if the setup is that Barry Rackham is tied in with one or more of Zeck's operations, and if Rackham killed his wife, I say he will never burn. I don't say at what point Zeck will get his hand in, or who or what he will use, but Rackham will never burn."

Cramer hurled his cigar at my wastebasket and missed it a foot. Since it wasn't lit I ignored it. "Hooray for justice," I cheered.

He snarled, but apparently not at me. "I want you to tell Wolfe that. Zeck is out of his reach. He can't get him."

"But," I objected, "granting that you've got it all straight, which I haven't, that's a hell of a message. Look at it from the other end. He is not out of Zeck's reach, not if he comes home. I know he doesn't go out much, but even if he never did people have to come in—and things, like packages of sausage. Not to mention that the damage they did to the plants and equipment last year came to thirty-eight thousand bucks. I get the idea that he is to lay off of Zeck, but that's only what he doesn't do. What does he do?"

Cramer nodded. "I know. That's it. He's so damn bullheaded. I want you to understand, Archie, why I came here. Wolfe is too cocky to live. He has enough brass and bluster to outfit a thousand sergeants. Sure, I know him; I ought to. I would love to bloody his nose for him, I've tried to often enough, and some day I will and enjoy it. But I would hate to see him break his neck on a deal like this where he hasn't got a chance. It's a good guess that in the past ten years there have been over a hundred homicides in this town that were connected in one way or another with one of the operations Arnold Zeck has a hand in. But not in a single case was there the remotest hope of tying Zeck up with it. We couldn't possibly have touched him."

"You're back where you started," I complained. "He can't be reached. So what?"

"So Wolfe should come back where he belongs, return what Mrs. Rackham paid him to her estate, let the Westchester people take care of the murder, which is their job anyhow, and go on as before. You can tell him I said that, but by God don't quote me around. I'm not responsible for a man like Zeck being out of reach."

"But you never strained a muscle stretching for him."

"Nuts. Facts are facts."

"Yeah, like sausage is tear gas." I stood up so as to look down my nose at him. "There are two reasons why your message will not get to Mr. Wolfe. First, he is to me as Zeck is to him. He's out of my reach. I don't know where he is."

"Oh, keep it up."

"I will. Second, I don't like the message. I admit that I have known Mr. Wolfe to discuss Arnold Zeck. I once heard him tell a whole family about him, only he was calling him X. He was describing the difficulties he would be in if he ever found himself tangled with X for a showdown, and he told them that he was acquainted, more or less, with some three thousand people living or working in New York, and there weren't more than five of them of whom he could say with certainty that they were in no way involved in X's activities. He said that none might be or that any might be. On another occasion I happened to be inquiring about Zeck of a newspaperman, and he had extravagant notions about Zeck's payroll. He mentioned, not by name, politicians, barflies, cops, chambermaids, lawyers, private ops, crooks of all types, including gunmen—maybe housewives, I forget. He did not specifically mention police inspectors."

"Just forgot, perhaps."

"I suppose so. Another thing, those five exceptions that Mr. Wolfe made out of his three thousand acquaintances, he didn't say who they were, but I was pretty sure I could name three of them. I thought probably one of the other two was you, but I could have been wrong. You have made a point of how you would hate to see him break his neck where he hasn't got a chance. You took the trouble to come here with a personal message but don't want to be quoted, which means that if I mention this conversation to anyone but Mr. Wolfe you'll call me a liar. And what's the message? That he should lay off of Zeck, that's what it amounts to. If in earning the fee Mrs. Rackham paid him he is liable to hurt somebody Zeck doesn't want hurt, he should return the fee. The way it looks from here, sending a message like that to the best and toughest detective on earth is exactly the kind of service Zeck would pay good money for. I wouldn't say—"

I didn't get to say what I wouldn't say. Cramer, out of his chair and coming, had a look on his face that I had never seen before.

Time and again I had seen him mad at Wolfe, and me too, but never to the point where the pink left his cheeks completely and his eyes looked absolutely mean.

He swung with his right. I ducked. He came up from beneath with his left, and I stopped it with my forearm. He tried with the right again, and I jerked back, stepped aside, and dived around the corner of Wolfe's desk.

I spoke. "You couldn't hit me in a year and I'm not going to plug you. I'm twenty years younger, and you're an inspector. If I'm wrong, some day I'll apologize. If I'm wrong."

He turned and marched out. I didn't go to the hall to help him on with his coat and open the door.

10

Three weeks went by.

At first, that first night, I was thinking that word might come from Wolfe in the next hour. Then I started thinking it might come the next day. As the days kept creeping along they changed my whole attitude, and before the end of April I was thinking it might come next week. By the time May had passed, and most of June, and the calendar and the heat both said summer, I was beginning to think it might never come.

But first to finish with April. The Rackham case followed the routine of spectacular murders when they never quite get to the point of a first-degree charge against anyone. For a week, the front page by unanimous consent; then, for a week or ten days, the front page only by cooking up an angle; and then back to the minors. None of the papers happened to feel like using it to start a crusade in the name of justice, so it took a normal course. It did not roll over and die, not with that all-star cast, including Nobby and Hebe; even months later a really new development would have got a three-column spread; but the development didn't come.

I made three more trips, by official request, to White Plains, with no profit to anyone, including me. All I could do was repeat myself, and all they could do was think up new ways to ask the same questions. For mental exercise I tried to get a line on whether Cramer's

notions about Arnold Zeck had been passed on to Archer and Ben
Dykes, but if so they never let on.

All I knew was what I read in the papers, until one evening I
ran into Sergeant Purley Stebbins at Jake's and bought him a lobster.
From him I got two little unpublished items: two FBI men had
been called in to settle an argument about the legibility of fingerprints on the crinkly silver handle of the knife, and had voted no;
and at one point Barry Rackham had been held at White Plains for
twenty straight hours while the battle raged over whether they had
enough to charge him. The noes won that time too.

The passing days got very little help from me. I had decided not
to start pawing the ground or rearing up until Wolfe had been gone
a full month, which would be May ninth, and I caught up on a lot
of personal things, including baseball games, which don't need to
be itemized. Also, with Fred Durkin, I finished up the poison-pen
case and other loose ends that Wolfe had left dangling—nothing
important—drove out to Long Island to see if Theodore and the
plants had got settled in their new home, and put one of the cars,
the big sedan, in dead storage.

One afternoon when I went to Rusterman's Restaurant to see
Marko Vukcic he signed the checks I had brought, for telephone
and electricity bills and my weekly salary, and then asked me what
the bank balance was. I told him a little over twenty-nine thousand
dollars, but I sort of regarded Mrs. Rackham's ten grand as being
in escrow, so I would rather call it nineteen.

"Could you bring me a check for five thousand tomorrow? Drawn
to cash."

"Glad to. But speaking as the bookkeeper, what do I charge it to?"

"Why—expense."

"Speaking as a man who may some day have to answer questions
from an internal revenue snoop, whose expense and what kind?"

"Call it travel expense."

"Travel by whom and to where?"

Marko made some kind of a French noise, or foreign at least, in-
dicating impatience, I think. "Listen, Archie, I have a power of
attorney without limit. Bring me a check for five thousand dollars at
your convenience. I am stealing it from my old friend Nero to spend
on beautiful women or olive oil."

So I was not entirely correct when I said that I got no word at all
from Wolfe during those weeks and months, but you must admit it

was pretty vague. How far a man gets on five grand, and where he goes, depends on so many things.

When I returned to the office from a morning walk on the third day of May, a Wednesday, and called the phone-answering service as usual, I was told there had been three calls but only one message —to ring a Mount Kisco number and ask for Mrs. Frey. I considered the situation, told myself the thing to do was skip it, and decided that I must be hard of hearing when I became aware that I had dialed the operator and asked for the number. Then, after I had got it and spelled my name and waited a minute, Annabel Frey's voice was in my ear. At least the voice said it was her, but I wouldn't have recognized it. It was sort of tired and hopeless.

"You don't sound like you," I told her.

"I suppose not," she conceded. "It seems like a million years since you came that day and we watched you being a detective. You never found out who poisoned the dog, did you?"

"No, but don't hold it against me. I wasn't expected to. You may have heard that that was just a blind."

"Yes, of course. I don't suppose Nero Wolfe is back?"

"Nope."

"You're running his office for him?"

"Well, I wouldn't call it running. I'm here."

"I want to see you."

"Excuse me for staring, but do you mean on business?"

"Yes." A pause, then her voice got more energetic. "I want you to come up here and talk with us. I don't want to go on like this, and I'm not going to. When people look at me I can see it in their eyes—was it me that killed my mother-in-law?—or in some of them I can see it, and that makes me think it's there with all of them. It's been nearly a month now, and all the police are doing—but you read the papers. She left me this place and a lot of money, and I wish I could hire Nero Wolfe. You must know where he is."

"Sorry. I don't."

"Then I want to hire you. You're a good detective, aren't you?"

"Opinions vary. I rate myself close to the top, but you have to discount that for my bias."

"Could you come up here today? This evening?"

"I couldn't make it today." My brain was having some exercise for the first time in weeks. "Look, Mrs. Frey, I wouldn't be in a hurry about this. There's—"

"A hurry?" She sounded bitter. "It's been nearly a month!"

"I know, and that's why another few days won't matter. There's nothing fresh about it, to get stale. Why don't you do this, let me do a little looking around, just on my own, and then you'll hear from me. After that you can decide whether you want to hire me or not."

"I've already decided."

"I haven't. I don't want your dough if there's no chance of earning it."

Since her mind had been made up before she called me, she didn't like it my way but finally settled for it.

I discovered when I hung up that my mind was made up too. It had made itself up while I was talking to her. I couldn't go on like this forever, nothing but a damn caretaker with no telling from day to day how long it might last. Nor could I, while drawing pay as Wolfe's assistant, take a boat for Europe or run for Mayor of New York or buy an island and build up a harem, or any of the other things on my deferred list; and certainly, while taking his pay, I couldn't personally butt into a case that he had run away from.

But there was nothing to prevent me from taking advantage of the gratitude that was still felt, even after paying the fee, by certain former clients of ours, and I took up the phone again and got the president of one of the big realty outfits, and was glad to learn that I hadn't overestimated his gratitude. When I had explained my problem he said he would do all he could to help, starting right then.

So I spent the afternoon looking at offices in the midtown section. All I wanted was one little room with a light that worked, but the man that the realty president sent to go around with me was more particular than I was, and he turned his nose up at two or three that I would have bought. We finally got to one on Madison Avenue, tenth floor, in the forties, which he admitted might do. It wouldn't be vacated until the next day, but that didn't matter much because I still had to buy furniture. I was allowed to sign for it on a month-to-month basis.

The next couple of days I had to keep myself under control. I had never been aware of any secret longing to have my own agency, but I had to choke off an impulse to drop in at Macgruder's Thursday morning and blow a couple of thousand of my own jack on office equipment. Instead, I went to Second Avenue and found bargains. Having decided not to take anything from Thirty-fifth

Street, I made up a shopping list of about forty items, from ash trays to a Moorhead's Directory, and shot the works.

Late Saturday afternoon, with a package under my arm, I emerged from the elevator, went down the hall to the door of 1019, and backed off to give it a look.

ARCHIE GOODWIN
Private Detective

Not bad at all, I thought, unlocking the door and entering. I had considered having the painter put beneath it "By Appointment Only," to keep the crowd down, but decided to save the extra three bucks. I put my package on the desk, unwrapped it, and inspected my new letterheads and envelopes. The type of my name was a little too bold, maybe, but otherwise it was pretty neat. I uncovered the typewriter, a rebuilt Underwood that had set me back $62.75, inserted one of the letterheads, and wrote:

> Dear Mrs. Frey:
>
> If you still feel as you did when you phoned me on Wednesday, I would be glad to call on you to discuss the situation, with the understanding that I shall be representing no one but myself.
>
> My new business address and phone number are above. Ring me or write if you wish me to come.
>
> Sincerely,
>
> AG:hs

I read it over and signed it. It looked businesslike, I thought, with the regulation initialing at the bottom, the "hs" being for "himself." When I left, after putting the stationery in a drawer and getting things in order for the rush of business on Monday morning, I dropped the envelope in the mail chute. I was doing it that way, instead of phoning her, for three reasons: if she had changed her mind she could just ignore it; I had a date, purely personal, for the weekend; and I had drawn myself a salary check, the last one, for that week. On my way home I made a detour to Fifty-fourth Street, to tell Marko Vukcic what I had done, because I thought he should be the first to know.

He made it not only plain but emphatic that he disapproved. I told him, "Experience tells me that pants wear out quicker sitting down than moving around. Intelligence tells me that it's better to

wait till you die to start to rot. I would appreciate it if you will convey that to him next time you write him or phone him."

"You know perfectly good, Archie, that—"

"Not perfectly good. Perfectly well."

"You know that I have said nothing, but nothing, that might make
you think I can write him or phone him."

"You didn't need to. I know it's not your fault, but where does it
leave me? Let me know any time you get a buyer for the house,
and I'll move out."

I left him still wanting to argue.

I was not kidding myself that I had really cut loose, since I hadn't
moved my bed out, but the way I figured it a caretaker who is
drawing no pay has a right to a room; and besides, Fritz was still
sleeping there and we were splitting on the groceries for breakfast,
and I didn't want to insult either him or my stomach by breaking
that up.

I shall now have to specify when I say office—or, better, I'll say
office when I mean Wolfe's office, and when I mean my Madison
Avenue suite I'll say 1019. Monday morning, arriving at 1019 a little
after ten, I rang the phone-answering service and was told that there
had been no calls, and then dug into the morning mail, which consisted of a folder from a window-cleaning outfit. After giving it full
consideration, I typed notes on my new stationery to some personal
friends, and an official letter to the City of New York giving notice
of my change of address as a licensed detective. I was sitting trying
to think who else I might write to when the phone rang—my first
incoming call.

I picked it up and told the transmitter plainly, "Archie Goodwin's office."

"May I speak to Mr. Goodwin, please?"

"I'll see if he's in. Who is calling, please?"

"Mrs. Frey."

"Yes, he's in. This is me. You got my note?"

"It came this morning. I don't know what you mean about representing no one but yourself."

"I guess I didn't make it very clear. I only meant I wouldn't be
acting as Nero Wolfe's assistant. I'm just myself now."

"Oh. Well—naturally, if you don't even know where he is. Can
you come this evening?"

"To Birchvale?"

"Yes."

"What time?"

"Say eight-thirty."

"I'll be there."

You can't beat that, I thought to myself as I hung up, for the first incoming call to a new office—making a deal with a client who has just inherited a country estate and a million monetary units. Then, fearing that if it kept up like that I might get swamped, I closed the office for the day and headed for Sulka's to buy a tie.

11

On my previous visit to Birchvale I had got the impression that Annabel Frey had her head on right side up, and her conduct that Monday evening strengthened it. For one thing, she had had sense enough not to gather that bunch around a dining table but invite them for half-past eight. With the kind of attitudes and emotions that were crisscrossing among those six people, an attempt to feed them at the same trough would have resulted in an acidosis epidemic.

In her first phone call, Wednesday, she had indicated that it was not a tête-à-tête she had in mind, so I was expecting to find company, probably the widower and the cousin, but to my surprise it was a full house. They were all there when I was shown into the big living room. Annabel Frey, as hostess there now, came to meet me and gave me her hand. The other five gave me nothing but dirty looks. I saw right off that my popularity index was way down, so I merely stood, gave them a cool collective greeting, and lifted a brow at my hostess.

"It's not you, Goodwin," the politician Pierce assured me, but in a raspy tone. "It's simply the strain of this unbearable situation. We haven't been all together like this since that terrible night." He glared at Annabel. "It was a mistake to get us here."

"Then why did you come?" Barry Rackham demanded, really nasty. "Because you were afraid not to, like the rest of us. We all hated to come, but we were all afraid to stay away. A bunch of cowards—except one, of course. You can't blame *that* one for coming."

"Nonsense," said Dana Hammond, the banker. The look he was

giving Rackham was just the opposite of the kind of look a banker is supposed to give a millionaire. "It has nothing to do with coward-ice. Not with me. By circumstances beyond my control I am forced into an association that is hateful to me."

"Have they," Lina Darrow asked him sweetly, "finished with the audit of your department?"

"They haven't finished anything," Calvin Leeds growled, and I didn't know he was aiming at her until he went on. "Not even with wondering what you see in Barry Rackham all of a sudden—if it is sudden."

Rackham was out of his chair, moving toward Leeds, snarling, "You can eat that, Cal, or—"

"Oh, stop it!" Annabel stepped to head Rackham off. She whirled, taking them in. "My God, isn't it bad enough without this?" She ap-pealed to me. "I didn't know this was how it would be!" To Rack-ham, "Sit down, Barry!"

Rackham backed up and sat. Lina Darrow, who had been stand-ing, went and stretched out on a couch, detaching herself. The others stayed put, with Annabel and me on our feet. I have had plenty of contacts with groups of people, all kinds, who have sud-denly had a murder explode among them, but I don't think I have ever seen a bunch blown quite so high.

Annabel said, "I didn't want to have Mr. Goodwin come and discuss it just with me. I didn't want any of you to think—I mean, all I wanted was to find out, for all of us. I thought it would be best for all of us to be here."

"All of us?" Pierce asked pointedly. "Or all but one?"

"It was a mistake, Annabel," Hammond told her. "You can see it was."

"Exactly what," Rackham inquired, "was your idea in sending for Goodwin?"

"I want him to work for us. We can't let it go on this way, you all know we can't. I'll pay him, but he'll be working for all of us."

"All but one," Pierce insisted.

"Very well, all but one! As it is now, it isn't all but one, it's all of us!"

Lina Darrow sang out from the couch, "Is Mr. Goodwin giving a guarantee?"

I had taken a chair. Annabel dropped into one facing me and put it to me. "What about it? Can you do anything?"

"I can't give a guarantee," I told her.

"Of course not. Can you do anything?"

"I don't know. I don't know how it stands. Shall I try sketching it?"

"Yes."

"Stop me if I go wrong. It's true I was here when it happened, but that's no help except what I actually saw and heard. Does everyone know what I was here for?"

"Yes."

"Then they understand why I wasn't much interested in anyone but Rackham. And you and Miss Darrow, of course, but that interest wasn't professional. It looks to me like a case that will probably never be solved by exhibits or testimony on facts. The cops have had plenty of good men on it, and if they had got anything usable on footprints or fingerprints, or getting the steak knife from the drawer, or alibis or timetables, or something like shoes that had been worn in the woods, someone would have been arrested long ago. And they've had it for a month, so no kind of routine would be any good now, and that's all most detective work amounts to. Motive is no help, with four of you inheriting piles from two hundred grand up, and the other two possibly counting on marrying one of the piles. Only I must say, in the atmosphere here tonight, courtship doesn't seem to be on the program."

"It isn't," Annabel asserted.

I glanced at Hammond and Pierce, but neither of them seemed to want the floor.

"So," I continued, "unless the cops have got a trap set that you don't know about, it's one of those things. You never can tell. It would be a waste of money to pay me to go over the ground the cops have covered—or any other detective except Nero Wolfe, and he's not around. There's only one way to use me, or anyhow only one way to start, and stand a chance of getting your money's worth, and that would be to give me a good eight or ten hours with each of you six people, each one separately. I have watched and listened to Nero Wolfe a good many years and I can now do a fair imitation. It might possibly turn out to be worth it to all of you—except one, as Mr. Pierce would say."

I flipped a hand. "That's the best suggestion I can offer. With nothing like a guarantee."

Annabel said, "No one would tell you everything you asked. I haven't myself, to the police."

"Sure. I understand that. That's part of it."

"You would be working for me—for us. It would be confidential."

"Things that weren't used would be confidential. Nothing that was evidence would be."

Annabel sat and regarded me. She had had her fingers twisted tight together, and now she loosened them and then they twisted again. "I want to ask you something, Mr. Goodwin. Do you think one of us killed Mrs. Rackham?"

"I do now. I don't know what I would think after I had worked at it."

"Do you think you know which one?"

"Nope. I'm impartial."

"All right. You can start with me." She turned her head. "Unless one of you would rather first?"

No one moved or spoke. Then Calvin Leeds: "Count me out, Annabel. Not with Goodwin. Let him tell us first where Nero Wolfe is and why."

"But Cal—you won't?"

"Not with him I won't."

"Dana?"

Hammond looked unhappy. He got up and went to her. "Annabel, this was a mistake. The whole idea was no good. What can Goodwin do that the police couldn't do? I doubt if you have any conception of how a private detective works."

"He can try. Will you help, Dana?"

"No. I hate to refuse, but I must."

"Oliver? Will you?"

"Well." The statesman was frowning, not at her, at me. "This seems to me to be a case of all or none. I don't see how anything could be accomplished—"

"Then you refuse me too?"

"Under the circumstances I have no other course."

"I see. You won't even give me a straight no. Barry?"

"Certainly not. Goodwin has lied to the police about my wife's visit to Wolfe. I wouldn't give him eight seconds, let alone eight hours."

Annabel left her chair and went toward the couch. "Lina, I guess it's up to the women. You and me. She was darned good to us, Lina —both of us. What about it?"

"Darling," Lina Darrow said. She sat up. "Darling Annabel. You know you don't like me."

"That isn't true," Annabel protested. "Just because—"

"Of course it's true. You thought I was trying to squeeze you out. You thought I was making a play for Barry merely because I was willing to admit he might be human, so wait and see. You thought I was trying to snatch Ollie from you, when as a matter of fact—"

"Lina, for God's sake," Pierce implored her.

Her fine dark eyes flashed at him. "She did, Ollie! When as a matter of fact she got bored with you, and I happened to be near." The eyes darted right to left, sweeping them. "And look at you now, all of you, and listen to you! You all think Barry killed her—all except one, you would say, Ollie. But you haven't got the guts to say so. And this Mr. Goodwin of yours, darling Annabel, have you told him that what you really want him for is to find some kind of proof that Barry did it? No, I suppose you're saving that for later."

Lina arose, in no hurry, and confronted Annabel from springing distance. "I thought it would be something like this," she said, and left us, detouring around Leeds' chair and heading for the door to the reception hall. Eyes followed her, but no one said anything; then, as she passed out of sight, Barry Rackham got up and, without a glance for any of us, including his hostess, tramped from the room.

The remaining three guests exchanged looks. Leeds and Pierce left their chairs.

"I'm sorry, Annabel," Leeds said gruffly. "But didn't I tell you about Goodwin?"

She didn't reply. She only stood and breathed. Leeds went, with not as much spring to his step as I had seen, and Pierce, mumbling a good night, followed. Dana Hammond went to Annabel, had a hand out to touch her arm, and then let it drop.

"My dear," he said, appealing to her, "it was no good. It couldn't be. If you had consulted me—"

"I'll remember next time, Dana. Good night."

"I want to talk with you, Annabel. I want to—"

"For God's sake, let me alone! Go!"

He backed up a step and scowled at me, as if I were to blame for everything. I lifted my right brow at him. It's one of my few outstanding talents, lifting one brow, and I save it for occasions when nothing else would quite serve the purpose.

He walked out of the room without another word.

Annabel dropped onto the nearest chair, put her elbows on her knees, and buried her face in her hands.

I stood looking down at her. "It was not," I told her sympathetically, "what I would call a success, but anyhow you tried. Not to try to make you feel better, but for future guidance, it might have been wiser, instead of calling a convention, to tackle them one at a time. And it was too bad you picked Leeds to sell first, since he has a grudge against me. But the truth is you were licked before you started. The shape their nerves are in, touching them with a feather wouldn't tickle them, it would give them a stroke. Thanks all the same for asking me."

I left her. By the time I got out to the parking space the cars of the other guests were gone. Rolling down the curving driveway, I was thinking that my first incoming phone call hadn't been so damned magnificent after all.

12

One or two of my friends have tried to tell me that some of my experiences that summer are worth telling about, but even taking them at their word, I'm not going to drag it in here. However, it is true that after I ran an ad in the *Gazette* and word got around I soon quit keeping count of the incoming calls. All I'll do here is summarize it by months:

May. Woman with pet cat stolen. Got it back; fifty dollars and expenses. Guy who got rolled in a joint on Eighth Avenue and didn't want to call the cops. Found her and scared most of it out of her. Two Cs for me. Man who wanted his son pried loose from a blond sharpie. Shouldn't have tried it; fell on my nose; took a C above expenses anyhow. Restaurant with a dumb cashier with sticky fingers; took only one afternoon to hook her; client beefed about my request for sixty-five dollars but paid it.

June. Spent two full weeks handling a hot insurance case for Del Bascom and damn near got my skull cracked for good. Cleaned it up. Del had the nerve to offer me three Cs; demanded a grand and got it. My idea was to net more per week than I had been getting from Wolfe, not that I cared for the money, but as a matter of principle. Found a crooked bookie for a man from Meadville, Pa. A hundred and fifty dollars. Man wanted me to find his vanished wife, but it looked dim and he could pay only twenty bucks a day, so I passed it. Girl unjustly accused, she said, of giving secret business dope to a rival firm, and fired from her job, pestered me into tackling it. Proved she was right and got her job back, doing five hundred dollars' worth of work for a measly hundred and twenty, paid in installments. Her face wasn't much, but she had a nice voice and good legs. Got an offer of a job from the FBI, my ninth offer from various sources in six weeks, and turned it down.

July. Took a whirl at supervising ten men for a bunch of concessionaires at Coney Island; caught one of them taking a cut from doobey stands; he jumped me with a cooler and I broke his arm. Got tired of looking at a thousand acres of bare skin, mostly peeling, practically all nonseductive, and quit. Eight fifty for seventeen days. Had passed up at least two thousand worth of little chores. Screwball woman on Long Island had had jewelry stolen, uninsured, thought cops were in on it and stalling. Two things happened: I got some breaks, and I did a damn good piece of work. It took me into August. I got all the jewelry back, hung it on an interior decorator's assistant with proof, billed her for thirty-five hundred gross, and collected.

August. I had drawn no pay from Wolfe's checkbook since May sixth, I had not gone near my personal safe deposit box, and my personal bank balance had not only not sunk, it had lifted. I decided I had a vacation coming. The most I had ever been able to talk Wolfe out of was two weeks, and I thought I should double that at least. A friend of mine, whose name has appeared in print in connection with one of Wolfe's cases, had the idea that we should take a look at Norway, and her point of view seemed sound.

Slow but sure, I was working myself around to an attitude toward life without Nero Wolfe on a permanent basis. One thing that kept it slow was the fact that early in July Marko Vukcic had asked me to bring him another check for five grand drawn to cash. Since if you wanted to eat in his restaurant you had to reserve a table a day in advance, and then pay six bucks for one helping of guinea hen, I knew he wasn't using it himself, so who was? Another thing, the house hadn't been sold, and, doing a little snooping on my own account, I had learned that the asking price was a hundred and twenty thousand, which was plain silly. On the other hand, if Marko was getting money to Wolfe, that didn't prove that I was ever going to

see him again, and there was no hurry about selling the house until
the bank balance began to sag; and also there was Wolfe's safe deposit box. Visiting his safe deposit box was one item on the select
list of purposes for which Wolfe had been willing to leave his house.

I did not really want to leave New York, especially to go as far as
Norway. I had a feeling that I would about be passing Sandy Hook
when word would come somehow, wire or phone or letter or messenger, to Thirty-fifth Street or 1019, in a code that I would understand—if I was there to get it. And if it did come I wanted to be
there, or I might be left out of the biggest charade Wolfe had ever
staged. But it hadn't been days or weeks, it had been months, and
my friend was pretty good at several things, including riding me
about hanging on forever to the short end of the stick, so we had
reservations on a ship that sailed August twenty-sixth.

Four days before that, August twenty-second, a Tuesday afternoon, I was sitting at my desk at 1019, to keep an appointment
with a man who had phoned. I had told him I was soon leaving for
a month's vacation, and he hadn't felt like giving a name, but I
thought I recognized the voice and had agreed to see him. When
he walked in on the dot, at 3:15, I was glad to know that my memory
for voices was holding up. It was my old cellmate, Max Christy.

I got up and we shook. He put his panama on the desk and
glanced around. His black mop was cut a little shorter than it had
been in April, but the jungle of his eyebrows hadn't been touched,
and his shoulders looked just as broad in gray tropical worsted. I
invited him to sit and he did.

"I must apologize," I said, "for never settling for that breakfast.
It was a life-saver."

He waved it away. "The pleasure was mine. How's it going?"

"Oh—no complaints. You?"

"I've been extremely busy." He got out a handkerchief and
dabbed at his face and neck. "I certainly sweat. Sometimes I think
it's stupid, this constant back and forth, push and shove."

"I hear you mentioned around."

"Yes, I suppose so. You never phoned me. Did you?"

"The number," I said, "is Churchill five, three two three two."

"But you never called it."

"No, sir," I admitted, "I didn't. One thing and another kept coming up, and then I didn't care much for your line about if I got taken

in and my being given a trial. I am by no means a punk, and the ink on my license dried long ago. Here, look behind my ears."

He threw back his head and haw-hawed, then shut it off and told me soberly, "You got me wrong, Goodwin. I only meant we'd have to go slow on account of your record." He used the handkerchief on his forehead. "I certainly do sweat. Since then your name has been discussed a little, and I assure you, you are not regarded as a punk. We have noticed that you seem to have plenty of jobs since you opened this office, but so trivial for a man like you. Why did you turn down the offer from the Feds?"

"Oh, they keep such long hours."

He nodded. "And you don't like harness, do you?"

"I've never tried it and don't intend to."

"What have you got on hand now? Anything important?"

"Nothing whatever, important or otherwise. I told you on the phone, I'm taking a vacation. Sailing Saturday."

He regarded me disapprovingly. "You don't need a vacation. If anybody needs a vacation it's me, but I don't get one. I've got a job for you."

I shook my head. "Not right now. When I get back maybe."

"It won't wait till you get back. There's a man we want tailed and we're short of personnel, and he's tough. We had two good men on him, and he spotted both of them. You would need at least two helpers; three would be better. You use men you know, handle that yourself, and pay them and expenses out of the five hundred a day you'll get."

I whistled. "What's so hot about it?"

"Nothing. It's not hot."

"Then who's the subject, the Mayor?"

"I'm not naming him. Perhaps I don't even know. It's merely a straight tailing job, but it has to be watertight and no leaks. You can net three hundred a day easy."

"Not without a hint who he is or what he looks like." I waved it away. "Forget it. I'd like to oblige an old cellmate, but my vacation starts Saturday."

"Your vacation can wait. This can't. At ten o'clock tonight you'll be walking west on Sixty-seventh Street halfway between First and Second Avenues. A car will pick you up, with a man in it that wants to ask you some questions. If your answers suit him he'll tell you about the job—and it's your big chance, Goodwin. It's your chance for your first dip into the biggest river of fast dough that ever flowed."

"What the hell," I protested, "you're not offering me a job, you're just giving me a chance to apply for one I don't want."

It was perfectly true at that point, and it was still true ten minutes later, when Max Christy left, that I didn't want the job, but I did want to apply for it. It wasn't that I had a hunch that the man in the car who wanted to ask me some questions would be Arnold Zeck, but the way it had been staged gave me the notion that it was just barely possible; and the opportunity, slim as it was, was too good to miss. It would be interesting to have a chat with Zeck; besides, he might give me an excuse to take a poke at him and I might happen to inadvertently break his neck. So I told Christy that I would be walking on Sixty-seventh Street at ten that evening as suggested. I had to break a date to do it, but even if the chance was only one in a million I wanted it.

To get that point settled and out of the way, the man who wanted to quiz me was not Arnold Zeck. It was not even a long black Cadillac; it was only a '48 Chevvy two-door sedan.

It was a hot August night, and as I walked along that block I was sweating a little myself, especially my left armpit under the holster. There was a solid string of parked cars at the curb, and when the Chevvy stopped and its door opened and my name was called, not loud, I had to squeeze between bumpers to get to it. As I climbed in and pulled the door shut the man in the front seat, behind the wheel, swiveled his head for a look at me and then, with no greeting, went back to his chauffeuring, and the car started forward.

My companion on the back seat muttered at me, "Maybe you ought to show me something."

I got out my display case and handed it to him with the license—detective, not driver's—uppermost. When we stopped for a light at Second Avenue he inspected it with the help of a street lamp, and returned it. I was already sorry I had wasted an evening. Not only was he not Zeck; he was no one I had ever seen or heard of, though I was fairly well acquainted, at least by sight, with the high brass in the circles that Max Christy moved in. This bird was a complete stranger. With more skin supplied for his face than was needed, it had taken up the slack in pleats and wrinkles, and that may have accounted for his sporting a pointed brown beard, since it must be hard to shave pleats.

As the car crossed the avenue and continued west, I told him, "I came to oblige Max Christy—if suggestions might help any. I'll only be around till Saturday."

He said, "My name's Roeder," and spelled it.

I thanked him for the confidence. He broadened it. "I'm from the West Coast, in case you wonder how I rate. I followed something here and found it was tied in with certain operations. I'd just as soon leave it to local talent and go back home, but I'm hooked and I have to stick." Either he preferred talking through his nose or that was the only way he knew. "Christy told you we want a man tailed?"

"Yes. I explained that I'm not available."

"You have got to be available. There's too much involved." He was twisted around to face me. "It'll be harder than ever now, because he's on guard. It's been messed up. They say if anyone can do it you can, especially with the help of a couple of men that Nero Wolfe used. You can get them, can't you?"

"Yeah, I can get them, but I can't get me. I won't be here."

"You're here now. You can start tomorrow. As Christy told you, five Cs a day. It's a straight tailing job, where you're working for a man named Roeder from Los Angeles. The cops might not like it too well if you tied in with a local like Wilts or Brownie Costigan, but what's wrong with me? You never heard of me before. You're in business as a private detective. I want to hire you, at a good price, to keep a tail on a man named Rackham and report to me on his movements. That's all, a perfectly legitimate job."

We had crossed Park Avenue. The light was dim enough that I didn't have to be concerned about my face showing a reaction to the name Rackham. The reaction inside me was my affair.

"How long would it last?" I inquired.

"I don't know. A day, a week, possibly two."

"What if something hot develops? A detective doesn't take a tailing job sight unseen. You must have told me why you were curious about Rackham. What did you tell me?"

Roeder smiled. I could just see the pleats tightening. "That I suspected my business partner had come east to make a deal with him, freezing me out."

"That could be all right if you'll fill it in. But why all the mystery? Why didn't you come to my office instead of fixing it to pick me off the street at night?"

"I don't want to show in the daytime. I don't want my partner to know I'm here." Roeder smiled again. "Incidentally, that's quite true, that I don't want to show in the daytime—not any more than I can help."

"That I believe. Skipping the comedy, there aren't many Rackhams. There are none in the Manhattan phone book. Is this the Barry Rackham whose wife got killed last spring?"

"Yes."

I grunted. "Quite a coincidence. I was there when she was murdered, and now I'm offered the job of tailing him. If he gets murdered too that *would* be a coincidence. I wouldn't like it. I had a hell of a time getting out from under a bond as a material witness so I could take a vacation. If he got killed while I was on his tail—"

"Why should he?"

"I don't know. I didn't know why she should either. But it was Max Christy who arranged this date, and while he is not himself a marksman as far as I know, he moves in circles that like direct action." I waved a hand. "Forget it. If that's the kind of interest you've got in Rackham you wouldn't tell me anyhow. But another thing: Rackham knows me. It's twice as hard to tail a guy that knows you. Why hire a man that's handicapped to begin with? Why not—"

I held it because we had stopped for a red light, on Fifth Avenue in the Seventies, and our windows were open, and the open window of a car alongside was only arm's distance away.

When the light changed and we rolled again Roeder spoke. "I'll tell you, Goodwin, this thing's touchy. There'll be some people scattered around that are in on things together, and they trust each other up to a point. As long as their interests all run the same way they can trust each other pretty well. But when something comes up that might help some and hurt others, then it gets touchy. Then each man looks out for himself, or he decides where the strength is and lines up there. That's where I am, where the strength is. But I'm not trying to line you up; we wouldn't want to even if we could; how could we trust you? You're an outsider. All we want you for is an expert tailing job, and you report to me and me only. Where are you going, Bill?"

The driver half-turned his head to answer, "Here in the park it might be cooler."

"It's no cooler anywhere. I like straight streets. Get out again, will you?"

The driver said he would, in a hurt tone. Roeder returned to me. "There are three men named Panzer, Cather, and Durkin who worked for Nero Wolfe off and on. That right?"

I said it was.

"They'll work for you, won't they?"

I said I thought they would.

"Then you can use them, and you won't have to show much. I'm told they're exceptionally good men."

"Saul Panzer is the best man alive. Cather and Durkin are way above average."

"That's all you'll need. Now I want to ask you something, but first here's a remark. It's a bad thing to mislead a client, I'm sure you realize that, but in this case it would be worse than bad. I don't have to go into details, do I?"

"No, but you're going too fast. I haven't got a client."

"Oh, yes, you have." Roeder smiled. "Would I waste my time like this? You were there when Mrs. Rackham was killed, you phoned Nero Wolfe and in six hours he was gone, and you were held as a material witness. Now here I want to hire you to tail Rackham, and you don't know why. Can you say no? Impossible."

"It could be," I suggested, "that I've had all I want."

"Not you, from what I've heard. That's all right, not being able to let go is a good thing in a man, but it brings up this question I mentioned. You're on your own now apparently, but you were with Nero Wolfe a long time. You're still living in his house. Of course you're in touch with him—don't bother to deny it—but that's no concern of ours as long as he doesn't get in the way. Only on this job it has to be extra plain that you're working for the man who pays you. If you get facts about Rackham and peddle them elsewhere, to Nero Wolfe for example, you would be in a very bad situation. Perhaps you know how bad?"

"Sure, I know. If I were standing up my knees would give. Just for the record, I don't know where Mr. Wolfe is, I'm not in touch with him, and I'm in no frame of mind to peddle him anything. If I take this on, tailing Rackham, it will be chiefly because I've got my share of monkey in me. I doubt if Mr. Wolfe, wherever he is, would recognize the name Rackham if he heard it."

The brown pointed beard waggled as Roeder shook his head. "Don't overplay it, Goodwin."

"I'm not. I won't."

"You are still attached to Wolfe."

"Like hell I am."

"I couldn't pay you enough to tell me where he is—assuming you know."

"Maybe not," I conceded. "But not selling him is one thing, and carrying his picture around is another. I freely admit he had his good points, I have often mentioned them and appreciated them, but as the months go by one fact about him stands out clearer than anything else. He was a pain in the ass."

The driver's head jerked around for a darting glance at me. We had left the park and were back on Fifth Avenue, headed uptown in the Eighties. My remarks about Wolfe were merely casual, because my mind was on something else. Who was after Rackham and why? If it was Zeck, or someone in one of Zeck's lines of command, then something drastic had happened since the April day when Zeck had sent Wolfe a package of sausage and phoned him to let Rackham alone. If it wasn't Zeck, then Max Christy and this Roeder were lined up against Zeck, which made them about as safe to play with as an atomic stockpile. Either way, how could I resist it? Besides, I liked the logic of it. Nearly five months ago Mrs. Rackham had hired us to do a survey on her husband, and paid in advance, and we had let it slide. Now I could take up where we had left off. If Roeder and his colleagues, whoever they were, wanted to pay me for it, there was no use offending them by refusing.

So, rolling north on the avenue, Roeder and I agreed that we agreed in principle and got down to brass tacks. Since Rackham was on guard it couldn't be an around-the-clock operation with less than a dozen men, and I had three at the most. Or did I? Saul and Fred and Orrie might not be immediately available. There was no use discussing an operation until I found out if I had any operators. Having their phone numbers in my head, I suggested that we stop at a drugstore and use a booth, but Roeder didn't like that. He thought it would be better to go to my office and phone from there, and I had no objection, so he told the driver to go over to Madison and downtown.

At that hour, getting on toward eleven, Madison Avenue was wide open, and so was the curb in front of the office building. Roeder told the driver we would be an hour or more, and we left him parked there. In the brighter light of the elevator the pleats of Roeder's face were less noticeable, and he didn't look as old as I would have guessed him in the car, but I could see there was a little gray in his beard. He stood propped in a corner with his shoulders slumped and his eyes closed until the door opened for the tenth floor, and then came to and followed me down the hall to 1019. I unlocked the door and let us in, switched on the light, motioned him to a chair, sat at the desk, pulled the phone to me, and started dialing.

"Wait a minute," he said gruffly.

I put it back on the cradle, looked at him, got a straight clear view of his eyes for the first time, and felt a tingle in the small of my back. But I didn't know why.

"This must not be heard," he said. "I mean you and me. How sure are you?"

"You mean a mike?"

"Yes."

"Oh, pretty sure."

"Better take a look."

I left my chair and did so. The room being small and the walls mostly bare, it wasn't much of a job, and I made it thorough, even pulling the desk out to inspect behind it. As I straightened up from retrieving a pencil that had rolled off the desk when I pushed it back in place, he spoke to my back.

"I see you have my dictionary here."

Not through his nose. I whirled and went rigid, gaping at him. The eyes again—and now other items too, especially the forehead and ears. I had every right to stare, but I also had a right to my own opinion of the fitness of things. So while staring at him I got myself under control, and then circled the end of my desk, sat down and leaned back, and told him, "I knew you all—"

"Don't talk so loud."

"Very well. I knew you all the time, but with that damn driver there I had to—"

"Pfui. You hadn't the slightest inkling."

I shrugged. "That's one we'll never settle. As for the dictionary, it's the one from my room which you gave me for Christmas nineteen thirty-nine. How much do you weigh?"

"I've lost a hundred and seventeen pounds."

"Do you know what you look like?"

He made a face. With the pleats and whiskers, he didn't really have to make one, but of course it was an old habit which had probably been suppressed for months.

"Yes," he said, "I do. I look like a sixteenth-century prince of Savoy named Philibert." He flipped a hand impatiently. "This can wait, surely, until we're home again?"

"I should think so," I conceded. "What's the difference, another year or two? It won't be as much fun, though, because now I'll know what I'm waiting for. What I really enjoyed was the suspense. Were you dead or alive or what? A perfect picnic."

He grunted. "I expected this, of course. It is you, and since I decided long ago to put up with you, I even welcome it. But you, also long ago, decided to put up with me. Are we going to shake hands or not?"

I got up and went halfway. He got up and came halfway. As we shook, our eyes met, and I deliberately focused on his eyes, because otherwise I would have been shaking with a stranger, and one hell of a specimen to boot. We returned to our chairs.

As I sat down I told him courteously, "You'll have to excuse me if I shut my eyes or look away from time to time. It'll take a while to get adjusted."

13

"No other course," Wolfe said, "was possible. I had accepted money from Mrs. Rackham and she had been murdered. I was committed in her interest, and therefore against Arnold Zeck, and I was no match for him. I had to ambush him. With me gone, how should you act? You should act as if I had disappeared and you knew nothing. Under what circumstances would you do that most convincingly? You are capable of dissimulation, but why try you so severely? Why not merely—"

"Skip it," I told him. "Save it for later. Where do we stand now, and what chance have we got? Any at all?"

"I think so, yes. If the purpose were merely to expose one or more of Zeck's operations, it could be done like that." He snapped his fingers. "But since he must himself be destroyed—all I can say is that I have reached the point where you can help. I have talked with him three times."

"Exactly who and what are you?"

"I come from Los Angeles. When I left here, on April ninth, I went to southern Texas, on the Gulf, and spent there the most painful month of my life—except one, long ago. At its end I was not recognizable." He shuddered. "I then went to Los Angeles, because a man of importance there considers himself more deeply in my debt even than he is. He is important but not reputable. The terms are not interchangeable."

"I never said they were."

"Through him I met people and I engaged in certain activities. In appearance I was monstrous, but in the circles I frequented my stubble was accepted as a masquerade, which indeed it was, and I displayed myself publicly as little as possible. With my two invaluable assets, my brains and my important debtor, and with a temporary abandonment of scruple, I made a substantial impression in the shortest possible time, especially with a device which I conceived for getting considerable sums of money from ten different people simultaneously, with a minimum of risk. Luck had a hand in it too, but without luck no man can keep himself alive, let alone prevail over an Arnold Zeck."

"So then Los Angeles was too hot for you."

"It was not. But I was ready to return east, both physically and psychologically, and knowing that inquiries sent to Los Angeles would get a satisfactory response. I arrived on July twelfth. You remember that I once spoke of Arnold Zeck, calling him X, to the Sperling family?"

"I do."

"And I described briefly the echelons of crime. First, the criminal himself—or gang. In the problem of disposal of the loot, or of protection against discovery and prosecution, he can seldom avoid dealing with others. He will need a fence, a lawyer, witnesses for an alibi, a channel to police or political influence—no matter what, he nearly always needs someone or something. He goes to one he knows, or knows about, one named A. A, finding a little difficulty, consults B. B may be able to handle it; if not, he takes it on to C. C is usually able to oblige, but when he isn't he communicates with D. Here we are getting close. D has access to Arnold Zeck, not only for the purpose described, but also in connection with one or more of the enterprises which Zeck controls."

Wolfe tapped his chest with a forefinger, a gesture I had never before seen him use, acquired evidently along with his pleats and whiskers. "I am a D, Archie."

"Congratulations."

"Thank you. Having earned them, I accept them. Look at me."

"Yeah, I am. Wait till Fritz sees you."

"If he ever does," Wolfe said grimly. "We have a chance, and that's all. If all we needed were evidence of Zeck's complicity in felonies, there would be no problem; I know where it is and I could get it. But his defenses are everywhere, making him next to invulnerable. It would be fatuous to suppose that he could ever be convicted, and even if he were, he would still be living, so that wouldn't help any. Now that I am committed against him, and he knows it, there are only two possible outcomes—"

"How does he know it?"

"He knows me. Knowing me, he knows that I intend to get the murderer of Mrs. Rackham. He intends to prevent me. Neither—"

"Wait a minute. Admitting he knows that about Nero Wolfe, what about you as Roeder? You say you're a D. Then you're on Zeck's payroll."

"Not on his payroll. I have been placed in charge of the operation here of the device which I conceived and used in Los Angeles. My handling of it has so impressed him that I am being trusted with other responsibilities."

"And Max Christy and that driver downstairs—they're Zeck men?"

"Yes—at a distance."

"Then how come salting Barry Rackham? Wasn't it Zeck money that Rackham was getting?"

Wolfe sighed. "Archie, if we had more time I would let you go on and on. I could shut my eyes and pretend I'm back home." He shook his head vigorously. "But we must get down to business. I said that driver is a Zeck man at a distance, but that is mere surmise. Being new and by no means firmly established in confidence, I am certainly being watched, and that driver might even report to Zeck himself. That was why I prolonged our talk in the car before suggesting that we come here. We shouldn't be more than an hour, so you'd better let me—"

He stopped as I grasped the knob and pulled the door open. I had tiptoed across to it as he talked. Seeing an empty hall in both directions, I closed the door and went back to my chair.

"I was only asking," I protested, "why the play on Rackham?"

"How long," Wolfe asked, "have you and I spent, there in the office, discussing some simple affair such as the forging of a check?"

"Oh, anywhere from four minutes to four hours."

"Then what should we take for this? By the way, you will resume drawing your pay check this week. How much have you taken from the safe deposit box in New Jersey?"

"Nothing. Not a cent."

"You should have. That was put there for the express purpose of financing this eventuality if it arose. You have been using your personal savings?"

"Only to buy these little items." I waved a hand. "Put it back long ago. I've been taking it easy, so my income from detective work has only been a little more than double what you were paying me."

"I don't believe it."

"I didn't expect you to, so I'll have an audit—" I stopped. "What the hell! My vacation!"

Wolfe grunted. "If we get Zeck you may have a month. If he gets me—" He grunted again. "He will, confound it, if we don't get to work. You asked about Rackham; yes, the source of his income, which his wife asked us to discover, was Zeck. He met him through Calvin Leeds."

I raised the brows. "Leeds?"

"Don't jump to conclusions. Leeds sold dogs to Zeck, two of them, to protect his house, and spent a week there, training them for their job. Zeck does not miss an opportunity. He used Rackham in one of his less offensive activities, gambling arrangements for people with too much money. Then when Rackham inherited more than half of his wife's wealth a new situation developed; it was already developing when I arrived six weeks ago. I managed to get informed about it. Of course I had to be extremely careful, new as I was, but on the other hand my being a newcomer was an advantage. In preparing a list of prospects for the device I had conceived, a man in Rackham's position was an eminently suitable candidate, and naturally I had to know all about him. That placed me favorably for starting, with the greatest caution, certain speculations and suspicions, and I got it to the point where it seemed desirable to put him under surveillance. Luckily I didn't have to introduce your name; your enlistment had previously been considered, on a suggestion by Max Christy. I was ready for you anyhow—I had gone as far as I could without you—and that made it easier. I wouldn't have dared to risk naming you myself, and was planning accordingly, but it's vastly better this way."

"Am I to proceed? Get Saul and Orrie and Fred? Tail Rackham?"

Wolfe looked at his wrist. His charade was certainly teaching him new tricks. In all my years with him he had never sported a watch, and here he was glancing at his wrist as if born to it. The way that wrist had been, normal, it would have required a custom-made strap.

"I told that man an hour or more," he said, "but we shouldn't be that long. A minimum of cause for suspicion and I'm through. Nothing is too fantastic for them; they could even learn if we've been using the phone. Confound it, I must have hours with you."

"Ditch him and we'll meet somewhere."

"Impossible. No place would be safe—except one. There is only one circumstance under which any man is granted the right to an extended period of undisturbed privacy, either by deliberation or on impulse. We need a woman. You know all kinds."

"Not all kinds," I objected. "I do draw the line. What kind do we need?"

"Fairly young, attractive, a little wanton in appearance, utterly devoted to you and utterly trustworthy, and not a fool."

"My God, if I knew where to find one like that I'd have been married long ago. Also I would be bragging—"

"Archie," he snapped. "If after all your promiscuous philandering you can't produce a woman to those specifications, I've misjudged you. It's risky to trust anyone at all, but any other way would be still riskier."

I had my lips puckered. "Ruth Brady?"

"No. She's an operative, and known. Out of the question."

"There's one who might take this as a substitute for a trip to Norway, which is now out. I could ask her."

"What's her name?"

"You know. Lily Rowan."

He made a face. "She is rich, intemperate, and notorious."

"Nuts. She is well-heeled and playful. You remember the time she helped out with an upstate murderer. I have no further suggestions. Do I phone her?"

"Yes."

"And tell her what?"

He explained in some detail. When he had answered my three or
four questions, and filed my objection by asking if I had something
better to offer, I pulled the phone to me and dialed a number. No
answer. I tried the Troubadour Room of the Churchill; she wasn't
there. Next in order of priority was the Flamingo Club. That found
her. Asked my name, I said to tell her it was Escamillo, though she
hadn't called me that for quite a while.

After a wait her voice came. "Archie? Really?"

"I prefer Escamillo," I said firmly. "It's a question of security. How
high are you?"

"Come and find out. I'm tired of the people I'm with anyhow.
Listen, I'll wander out and meet you in front and we'll go—"

"We will not. I'm working, and I'm on a spot, and I need help.
You're just the type for it, and I pay a dollar an hour if you give
satisfaction. I'm offering you a brand new thrill. You have never
earned a nickel in your life, and here's your chance. What mood
are you in?"

"I'm bored as the devil, but all I need is six dances with you and—"

"Not tonight, my colleen donn. Damn it, I'm working. Will you
help?"

"When?"

"Now."

"Is it any fun?"

"So-so. Nothing to brag of."

"Are you coming here for me?"

"No. I'm going—you must get this straight. Now listen."

"That's exactly what I had in mind. I was just telling myself, Lily,
my precious, if he starts talking you must listen, because he is very
shy and sensitive and therefore—did you say something?"

"I said shut up. I'm at my office. A man is here with me. We'll
leave as soon as I hang up. I'll go alone to your place and wait for
you outside your door. The man—"

"You won't have to wait. I can make it—"

"Shut up, please. Your first hour has started, so this is on my time.
The man with me has a car with a driver parked down in front.
He will be driven to the Flamingo Club and stop at the curb, and
you will be waiting there in front, and when he opens the door you
will climb in, *not* waiting for him to get out like a gentleman, because he won't. You will not speak to the driver, who, when you're

inside, will proceed to your address, where you and the man will find me waiting at your door."

"Unless I get in the wrong car, and—"

"I'm telling you. It's a dark gray forty-eight Chevvy two-door sedan, New York license OA six, seven, one, one, three. Got that?"

"Yes."

"I'll make it a dollar ten an hour. The man will call you Lily, and you will call him Pete. Joining him in the car and riding up to your place, you need not go to extremes, but it is important for the driver to get the idea that you are mighty glad to see Pete and that you are looking forward with pleasure to the next several hours with him. But—"

"Is it a reunion after a long absence?"

"I'll make it a dollar twenty an hour. I was about to say, you can leave it vague whether you last saw Pete a week ago or two months ago. You're just glad to be with him because you're so fond of him, but don't get thinking you're Paulette Goddard and ham it. Do it right. Pretend it's me. Which brings me to the crux. It's going to be an ordeal for you. Wait till you see Pete."

"What's the matter with him?"

"Everything. He's old enough to be your father and then some. He has whiskers, turning gray. His face is pleated. You will have to fight down the feeling that you're having a nightmare, and—"

"Archie! It's Nero Wolfe!"

Goddam a woman anyhow. There was absolutely no sense or reason for it. My brain buzzed.

"Sure," I said admiringly. "You do it with mirrors. If it was him, the way I feel about him, the first thing I would do would be to get him a date with you, huh? Okay, then don't call him Pete, call him Nero."

"Then who is it?"

"It's a man named Pete Roeder, and I've got to have a long talk with him that won't get in the papers."

"We could take him to Norway."

"Maybe. We have to discuss Norway. Give me a ring later in the week and tell me how you feel about this proposition."

"I'll be out on the sidewalk in ten minutes, less than that, waiting for my Pete."

"No public announcement."

"Certainly not."

"I'm very pleased with your work so far. We'll have to get you a social security number. I'll be waiting anxiously at your door."

I hung up and told Wolfe, "All set."

Out of his chair, he grunted. "You overdid it a little, perhaps? Nightmare, for instance?"

"Yes, sir," I agreed. "I get too enthusiastic."

I glared at him, and he glared back.

14

Since I do not intend to use up paper reporting the five-hour conference I had with Wolfe that night in Lily Rowan's living room, I could just as well go on to Wednesday morning, except for one thing. I have got to tell about their arrival at the door of Lily's penthouse apartment on East Sixty-third Street. Wolfe didn't speak and wouldn't look at me. Lily shook hands with me, a form of greeting we hadn't used for I don't know how long, then unlocked the door, and we entered. When her wrap and Wolfe's hat had been disposed of and we passed to the living room, she tossed her firecracker.

"Archie," she said, "I knew darned well that something would happen some day to make up for all the time I've wasted on you. I just felt it would."

I nodded. "Certainly. You'll show a profit on the night even if you feed us sandwiches, especially since Pete is a light eater. He's on a diet."

"Oh," she said, "I didn't mean money, and you can go the limit on sandwiches. I meant the distinction you've brought me. I'm the only woman in America who has necked with Nero Wolfe. Nightmare, my eye. He has a flair."

Wolfe, who had seated himself, cocked his head to frown at her —a first-rate performance.

I smiled at her. "I told Pete what you said on the phone, and he was flattered. Okay, woman of distinction."

She shook her head. "Turn loose, my brave fellow. I've got hold of it." She moved to Wolfe, looking down at him. "Don't be upset, Pete. I wouldn't have known you from Adam, no one would; that wasn't it. It's my hero here. Archie's an awful prude. He has been up against some tough ones, lots of them, and not once has he ever called on me to help. Never! A proud prude. Suddenly he calls me away from revelry—I might have been reveling for all he knew—to get into a car and be intimate with a stranger. There's only one person on earth he would do that for: you. So if I was pretty ardent in the car, I knew what I was doing. And don't worry about me—whatever you're up to, my lips are sealed. Anyway, to me you will always be Pete. The only woman in America who has necked with Nero Wolfe—my God, I'll treasure it forever. Now I'll go make some sandwiches. What kind of a diet are you on?"

Wolfe said through his teeth, "I care for nothing."

"That can't be. A peach? Grapes? A leaf of lettuce?"

"No!"

"A glass of water?"

"Yes!"

She left the room, leering at me as she went by. In a moment the sound of her movements in the kitchen came faintly.

I told Wolfe offensively, "It was you who said we needed a woman."

"It was you who selected her."

"You okayed her."

"It's done," he said bitterly. "So are we. She'll blab, of course."

"There's one hope," I suggested. "Marry her. She wouldn't betray her own husband. And apparently in that one short ride uptown with her—"

I stopped abruptly. The face as a whole was no longer his, but the eyes alone were enough to tell me when I had gone far enough.

"I'll tell you what I'll do," I offered. "I know her quite well. Two things that could conceivably happen: first, you might go to Zeck tomorrow and tell him who you are, and second, Lily might spill it either thoughtfully or thoughtlessly. I'll bet you ten bucks the first happens as soon as the second."

He growled. "She's a woman."

"All right, bet me."

The bet didn't get made. Not that Wolfe came to my point of view about Lily Rowan, but what could the poor son of a gun do? He couldn't even take to the bushes again and start all over. From that point on, though, up to the end, the strain was ten times worse for him than for me. It cramped his style some all that night, after Lily had gone off to bed and we talked in the living room until long after dawn. At six o'clock he went. Probably it would then have

been safe for me to go too, since if they were enough interested in
him to have posted a sentry outside the building he would almost
certainly leave when Roeder did, but probabilities weren't good
enough now, not after the picture Wolfe had given me and the program he had drawn up, so I took a good two-hour nap before leaving for Thirty-fifth Street and a bath and breakfast.

At ten o'clock I was at 1019, starting at the phone to get hold
of Saul and Orrie and Fred.

I did not like it at all. The way Wolfe was getting set to play it, it
looked to me as if we had one chance in a thousand, and while that
may be good enough to go ahead on when what you're after is to
nail a guy on a charge, and if you muff it the worst you get is a new
start under a handicap, it's a little different when a muff means curtains. I had of couse told Wolfe all I knew, including Inspector
Cramer's visit and advice, but that only made him stubborner. With
Zeck on Rackham's tail, through me, it seemed likely that the murderer of Mrs. Rackham might get his proper voltage with Zeck's
blessing, and since that was all that Wolfe was committed to, why
not settle for it? For now anyway, and then take a good breath. As
for commitments, I had one of my own. I had promised myself to
see Norway before I died.

So I didn't like it, and I either had to lump it or bow out. I tossed
a coin: heads I stick, tails I quit. It landed tails, but I had to veto it
because I had already talked to Orrie Cather and he was coming
at noon, and I had left messages for Fred Durkin and Saul Panzer.
I tossed again, tails again. I tossed once more and it was heads,
which settled it. I had to stick.

The tailing of Barry Rackham was a classic, especially after the
first week. It was a shame to waste the talents of Saul Panzer on
what was actually a burlesque, but it was good to have him around
anyhow. I briefed them all together at 1019, Wednesday evening,
with Saul perched on a corner of the desk because there were only
three chairs. Saul was undersized, inconspicuous all but his nose,
and the best all-round man alive. Fred Durkin was big and clumsy,
with a big red face, with no Doberman pinscher in him but plenty
of bulldog. Orrie Cather was slender and muscular and handsome,
just the man to mingle with the guests at a swell dinner party when
circumstances called for it. After I had explained the job, with details as required, I supplied a little background.

"As far as you know," I told them, "I'm only doing this for practice. Your only contact is me. There is no client."

"Jesus," Fred remarked, "a hundred bucks a day and more with expenses? I guess you ought to pay in advance."

"Take it up with the NLRB," I said stiffly. "As an employer, I do not invite familiarities from the help."

"Of course," Orrie stated with an understanding smile, "it's just a coincidence that this Rackham was with you once at the scene of a murder. When you got tossed in the coop."

"That's irrelevant. Let us stick to the point, gentlemen. I want to make it clear that I do not actually care a damn where Rackham goes or what he does or who he sees. You are to hang on and report in full, since that's the proper way to handle a dry run, but I don't want anyone to get hurt. If he turns on you and starts throwing rocks, dodge and run. If you lose him, as of course you will, don't bark your shins trying to hurdle."

"You ought to have workmen's compensation insurance," Fred advised. "Then we could be serious about it."

"Do you mean," Saul Panzer asked, "that the purpose is to get on his nerves?"

"No. Play it straight. I only mean it's not life and death—until further notice." I pushed my chair back and got up. "And now I wish to prove that being an employer hasn't changed me any. You may continue to call me Archie. You may come with me to Thirty-fifth Street, where we will find a poker deck, and Fritz will make five, and when we have finished I'll lend you carfare home."

For the record, I lost twelve dollars. Saul was the big winner. One hand, I had three nines and—but I'd better get on.

Rackham was living at the Churchill, in an air-conditioned suite in the tower. During the first week we compiled quite a biography of him. He never stuck his nose outside before one o'clock, and once not until four. His ports of call included two banks, a law office, nine bars, two clubs, a barber shop, seven other shops and stores, three restaurants, three theaters, two night spots, and miscellaneous. He usually ate lunch with a man or men, and dinner with a woman. Not the same woman; three different ones during the week. As described by my operatives, they were a credit to their sex, to the American way of life, and to the International Ladies' Garment Workers' Union.

I took on a little of it myself, but mostly I left it to the help. Not

that I loafed. There were quite a few hours with Lily Rowan, off
and on, both as a substitute for the trip to Norway, indefinitely postponed, and as a check on the soundness of the estimate of her I had
given Wolfe. She caused me no qualms. Once when we were dancing she sighed for Pete, and once at her apartment she said she
would love to help some more with my work, but when I tactfully
made it plain that the detective business was not on our agenda she
took it nicely and let it lay.

There were other things, including the reports on Rackham to be
typed. Late every afternoon Max Christy called at my office to get
the report of the day before, and he would sit and read it and ask
questions. When he got critical, I would explain patiently that I
couldn't very well post a man at the door of Rackham's suite to
take pictures of all the comers and goers, and that we were scoring
better than eighty per cent on all his hours outside, which was exceptional for New York tailing.

I had the advantage, of course, of having had the situation described to me by their Pete Roeder. They were worried a little about
Westchester, but more about the city. Shortly after he had become
a millionaire by way of a steak knife, whoever had used it, Rackham had got word to Zeck that he was no longer available for contacts. Brownie Costigan had got to Rackham, thinking to put the bee
on him, and had been tossed out on his ear. The stink being raised
in Washington on gambling and rackets, and the resulting enthusiasm in the office of the New York County District Attorney, had
started an epidemic of jitters, and it was quite possible that if one
of my typed reports had told of a visit by Rackham to the DA's office, or of one by an assistant DA to Rackham's suite, Rackham
would have had a bad accident, like getting run over or falling
into the river with lead in him. That was why Wolfe had given me
careful and explicit instructions about what I should report and what
I shouldn't.

I had no sight or sound of Wolfe. He was to let me know if and
when there was something stirring, and I had been told how to reach
him if I had to.

Meanwhile I had my schedule, and on the ninth day, a Friday,
the first of September, it called for a move. Things looked right for
it. Saul, on instructions, had let himself get spotted once, and Orrie
twice, and Fred, without instructions, at least three times. I too had
cooperated by letting myself be seen at the entrance of the Crooked

Circle one night as Rackham emerged with companions. So Friday at five o'clock, when Saul phoned that the subject had entered the Romance Bar on Forty-ninth Street, I went for a walk, found Saul window-shopping, told him to go home to his wife and children, moseyed along to the Romance Bar entrance, and went on in.

Business was rushing, with as many as five at a table the size of a dishpan. Making no survey, I found a place at the long bar where two customers were carelessly leaving enough room for a guy to get an elbow through, and took the opening. After a while the bartender admitted I was there and let me buy a highball. I took a casual look around, saw Rackham at a table with a pair of males, turned my back that way, and got his range in the mirror.

I did not really expect a bite at the very first try; I thought it might take two or three exposures. But evidently he was ripe. I was in the middle of my second highball when my mirror view showed me the trio getting up and squeezing through the mob to the clear. I dropped my chin and looked at my thumb. They went on by, toward the door, and I turned to watch their manly backs. As soon as they were out I followed, and, on the sidewalk, immediately turned right, thinking to reconnoiter from the shop entrance next door. But I was still two paces from it when there was a voice at my elbow.

"Here I am, Goodwin."

I turned to face him, looking mildly startled. "Oh, hello."

"What's the idea?" he demanded.

"Which one?" I asked politely. "There's so many around."

"There are indeed. You and three others that I know of. Who wants to know so much about me?"

"Search me." I was sympathetic. "Why, are you being harassed?"

Color had started to show in his face, and the muscles of his jaw were called upon. His right shoulder twitched.

"Not here on the street," I suggested. "A crowd will collect, especially after I react. See that man turning to look? You're standing like Jack Dempsey."

He relaxed a little. "I think I know," he said.

"Good for you. Then I'm not needed."

"I want to have a talk with you."

"Go ahead."

"Not here. At my place—the Churchill."

"I think I have a free hour next Tuesday."

"Now. We'll go there now."

I shrugged. "Not together. You lead the way, and I'll tag along."

He turned and marched. I gave him twenty paces and then followed. It takes the strain off of tailing a man to have a date with him, and since we had only a few blocks to go it would have been merely a pleasant little stroll if he hadn't been in such a hurry. I had to use my full stride to keep my distance. As we neared the Churchill I closed in a little, and when he entered an elevator I was there ready for the next one.

He had a corner suite at the setback, which gave him a terrace and also a soundbreak for the street noises. It was cool and quiet in his big sitting room, with light blue summer rugs and pretty pictures and light blue slipcovers on the furniture. While he adjusted venetian blinds I glanced around, and when he was through I told him, "Very nice. A good place for a heart-to-heart talk."

"What will you have to drink?"

"Nothing, thanks. I had my share at the bar, and anyway I don't drink with people I'm tailing."

I was in a comfortable chair, and he pulled a smaller one around to face me. "You've got your own office now," he stated.

I nodded. "Doing pretty well. Of course, summer's the slack season. After Labor Day they'll start coming back and bringing their troubles along."

"You didn't take on that job for Mrs. Frey."

"How could I?" I upturned a palm. "No one would speak to me."

"You can't blame them." He got out a cigarette and lit it, and his hands were almost steady but not quite. "Look, Goodwin. There on the street I nearly lost my head for a second. You're merely doing what you're paid for."

"Right," I said approvingly. "People resent detectives more than they do doctors or plumbers, I don't see why. We're all trying to make it a better world."

"Certainly. Who are you working for?"

"Me."

"Who pays you to work for you?"

I shook my head. "Better start over. Show a gun or a steak knife or something. Even if I'm not hard to persuade, I must keep up appearances."

He licked his lips. Apparently that was his substitute for counting ten, but if so it didn't work, for he sprang up, towering over me, making fists. I moved nothing but my head, jerking it back to focus on his face.

"It's a bad angle," I assured him. "If you swing from up there I'll duck and hit your knees, and you'll lose your balance."

He held it a second, then his fists became hands, and he stooped to use one of them to recover the cigarette he had dropped on the rug. He sat down, took a drag, inhaled, and let it out.

"You talk too much, Goodwin."

"No," I disagreed, "not too much, but too frankly, maybe. Perhaps I shouldn't have mentioned a steak knife, but I was irritated. I might name my client if you stuck needles under my nails or showed me a dollar bill, but your being so damn casual annoyed me."

"I didn't kill my wife."

I smiled at him. "That's a straightforward categorical statement, and I appreciate it very much. What else didn't you do?"

He ignored it. "I know Annabel Frey thinks I did, and she would spend all the money my wife left her—well, say half of it—to prove it. I don't mind your taking her money, that's your business, but I hate to see her waste it, and I don't like having someone always behind me. There ought to be some way I can satisfy you and her that I didn't do it. Can't you figure one out? If it's arranged so you won't lose anything by it?"

"No," I said flatly.

"Why not? I said satisfy you."

"Because I'm getting irritated again. You don't care a damn what Mrs. Frey thinks. What's eating you is that you don't know who is curious enough about you to spend money on it, and you're trying to catch a fish without bait, which is unsportsmanlike. I'll bet you a finif you can't worm it out of me."

He sat regarding me half a minute, then got up and crossed to a portable bar over by the wall and began assembling a drink. He called to me, "Sure you won't have one?"

I declined with thanks. Soon he returned with a tall one, sat, took a couple of swallows, put the glass down, burped, and spoke. "A thousand dollars for the name."

"Just the name, cold?"

"Yes."

"It's a sale." I extended a hand. "Gimme."

"I like to get what I pay for, Goodwin."

"Absolutely. Guaranteed against defects."

He arose and left the room through a door toward the far end. I decided I was thirsty and went to the bar for a glass of soda and ice, and was back in my chair when he re-entered and came to me. I took his offering and counted it by flipping the edges: ten crackly new hundreds.

He picked up his glass, drank, and eyed me. "Well?"

"Arnold Zeck," I said.

He made a little squeaking noise, went stiff for a short count, and hurled the tall glass against the wall, where it smacked into the middle of the glass of a picture, which improved the effect both for the ear and for the eye.

15

I admit I was on my feet when it hit. He was so slapdash that there was no certainty about his target, and a well-thrown heavy glass can make a bruise.

"Now look what you've done," I said reproachfully, and sat down again. He glared at me a second, then went to the bar, and with slow precise movements of his hands mixed another long one. I was pleased to note that the proportion of whisky was the same as before. He returned to his chair and put the glass down without drinking.

"I thought so, by God," he said.

I merely nodded.

"Who hired you? Zeck himself?"

"Not in the contract," I objected firmly. "You bought the name, and you've got it."

"I'm in the market for more. I'll take it all."

I frowned at him. "Now I guess I'll have to do some talking. You comfortable?"

"No."

"Listen anyway. I'm taking Zeck's money and I'm crossing him. How do you know I won't cross you?"

"I don't. But I'll top him."

"That's the point exactly; you don't. Who is Zeck and who are you? You know the answer to that. You were taking his money too, up to five months ago, and you know for what. When your wife hired Nero Wolfe to take the lid off of you for a look, you yapped to Zeck and he took aim at Wolfe, and when your wife got it with that steak knife Wolfe took a powder, and for all I know he is now in Egypt, where he owns a house, talking it over with the Sphinx. It was Zeck and you, between you, that broke up our happy home on Thirty-fifth Street, and you can have three guesses how I feel about it. I may like it fine this way, with my own office and my time my own. I may figure to work close to Zeck and get in the big dough, which would mean I'm poison to you, or I may be loving a chance to stick one between Zeck's ribs and incidentally get a nice helping from your pile, or I may even be kidding both of you along with the loony idea of trying to earn the ten grand your wife paid Nero Wolfe. Zeck can guess and you can guess. Do I make myself clear?"

"I don't know. Are you just warning me not to trust you? Is that it?"

"Well, yes."

"Then save your breath. I've never trusted anybody since I started shaving. As for a nice helping from my pile, that depends. How do you earn it?"

I shrugged. "Maybe I don't want it. Guess. I got the impression that I have something you want."

"I think you have. Who hired you and what were you told to do?"

"I told you, Zeck."

"Zeck himself?"

"I would be risking my neck and you know it. Five grand now, and beyond that we can decide as we go along."

It was a mistake, though not fatal. He was surprised. I should have made it ten. He said, "I haven't got that much here."

"Tut. Send downstairs for it."

He hesitated a moment, regarding me, then got up and went to a phone on a side table. It occurred to me that it would be of no advantage for a clerk or assistant manager to see whose presence in Rackham's suite required the delivery of so much cash, so I asked where the bathroom was and went there. After a sufficient interval I returned, and the delivery had been made.

"I said I don't trust anybody," Rackham told me, handing me the engravings. "But I don't like to be gypped."

It was used bills this time, Cs and five-hundreds, which didn't seem up to the Churchill's standard of elegance. To show Rackham how vulgar it was not to trust people, I stowed it away without counting it.

"What do you want?" I asked, sitting. "Words and pictures?"

"I can ask questions, can't I?"

"Sure, that's included. I have not yet seen Zeck himself, but expect to. I was first approached by Max Christy. He—"

"That son of a bitch."

"Yeah? Of course you're prejudiced now. He was merely scouting. He didn't name Zeck and he didn't name you, but offered good pay for an expert tailing job. I was interested enough to make a date to get picked up on the street that night by a man in a car. He gave—"

"Not Zeck. He wouldn't show like that."

"I said I haven't seen Zeck. He gave me the layout. He said his name was Roeder—around fifty—"

"Roeder?" Rackham frowned.

"So he said. He spelled it—R-o-e-d-e-r. Around fifty, brown hair slicked back, face wrinkled and folded, sharp dark eyes, brown pointed beard with gray in it."

"I don't know him."

"He may be in a different department from the one you were in. He did name Zeck. He said—"

"He actually named Zeck?"

"Yes."

"To you? That's remarkable. Why?"

"I don't know, but I can guess. I had previously been tapped by Max Christy, some time ago, and I think they've got an idea that I may have it in me to work up to an executive job—now that Nero Wolfe is gone. And they figure I must know that Christy plays with Brownie Costigan, and that Costigan is close to the top, so why not mention Zeck to me to make it glamorous? Anyhow, Roeder did. He said that what they wanted was a tail on you. They wanted it good and tight. They offered extra good pay. I was to use as many men as necessary. I took the job, got the men, and we started a week ago yesterday. Christy comes to my office every day for the reports. You know what's been in them; you know where you've been and what you've done."

Rackham was still frowning. "That's all there is to it?"

"That's the job as I took it and as I've handled it."

"You weren't told why?"

"In a way I was. I gathered that they think you might be a bad influence on the District Attorney, and they want to be sure you don't start associating with him. If you do they would probably make a complaint. I suppose you know what their idea is of making a complaint."

The frown was going. "You say you gathered that?"

"I didn't put it right. I was told that in so many words."

"By Roeder?"

"Yes."

The frown was gone. "If this is straight, Goodwin, I've made a good buy."

"It's straight all right, but don't trust me. I warned you. Those are the facts, but you can have a guess without any additional charge if you want it."

"A guess about what?"

"About them and you. This guess is why I'm here. This guess is why I went into that bar so you would see me, and followed you out like a halfwit to give you a chance to flag me."

"Oh. So you staged this."

"Certainly. I wanted to tell you about this guess, and if you were in a mood to buy something first, why not?"

He looked aloof. "Let's have the guess."

"Well—" I considered. "It really is a guess, but with a background. Do you want the background first?"

"No, the guess."

"Right. That Zeck is getting set to frame you for the murder of your wife."

I think Rackham would have thrown another glass if he had happened to have it in his hand, possibly at me this time. His blood moved fast. The color came up in his neck and face, and he sort of swelled all over; then his jaw clamped.

"Go on," he mumbled.

"That's all the guess amounts to. Do you want the background?"

He didn't answer. I went on. "It won't cost you a cent. Take the way I was approached. If it's a plain tailing job with no frills, why all the folderol? Why couldn't Christy just put it to me? And why pay me double the market of the highest-priced agencies? Item. If Zeck has his friends at White Plains, which is far from incredible, and if the current furor is upsetting their stomachs, there's nothing they would appreciate more than having their toughest unsolved murder case wrapped up for them. Item. Hiring me is purely defensive, and Zeck and his staff don't function that way, especially not when the enemy is a former colleague and they've got a grudge."

I shook my head. "I can't see it with that background. But listen to this. Roeder came up to my office and stayed an hour, and do you know what he spent most of it doing? Asking me questions about the evening of April eighth! What has that got to do with my handling a tailing job? Nothing! Why should they be interested in April eighth at all? I think they brought me this job, at double pay, just to start a conversation with me and soften me up. It has already been hinted that Zeck might like to meet me. I think that to frame you for murder they've got to have first-hand dope from someone who was there, and I'm elected. I think they're probably sizing me up, to decide whether I'm qualified to be asked to remember something that happened that night which has slipped my mind up to now, at a nice juicy price."

I turned my palms up. "It's just a guess."

He still had nothing to say. His blood had apparently eased up a little. He was staring at my face, but I doubted if he was seeing it.

"If you care to know why I wanted you to hear it," I went on, "you can have that too. I have my weak spots, and one of them is my professional pride. It got a hard blow when Nero Wolfe scooted instead of staying to fight it out, with your wife's check for ten grand deposited barely in time to get through before she was croaked. If the ten grand is returned to her estate, who gets it? You. And it could be that you killed her. I prefer to leave it where it is and earn it. Among other things, she was killed while I was there, and I helped find the body. That's a fine goddam mess for a good detective, and I was thinking I was one."

He found his tongue. "I didn't kill her. I swear to you, Goodwin, I didn't kill her."

"Oh, skip it. Whether you did or didn't, not only do I not want to help frame you, I don't want anyone to frame anybody, not on this one. I've got a personal interest in it. I intend to earn that ten grand, and I don't want Zeck to bitch it up by getting you burned, even if you're the right one, on a fix. Therefore I wanted you to know about this. As I told you, I haven't got it spelled out, it's only a guess with background, and I admit it may be a bum one. What do you think? Am I hearing noises?"

Rackham picked up his drink, which hadn't been touched, took a little sip, about enough for a sparrow, and put it down again. He sat a while, licking his lips. "I don't get you," he said wistfully.

"Then forget it. You're all paid up. I've been known to guess wrong before."

"I don't mean that, I mean you. Why? What's your play?"

"I told you, professional pride. If that's too fancy for you, consider how I was getting boxed in, with Zeck on my right and you on my left. I wanted a window open. If you don't like that either, just cross me off as screwy. You don't trust me anyhow. I merely thought that if my guess is good, and if I get approached with an offer of a leading part, and maybe even asked to help with the script, and if I decided I would like to consult you about it, it would be nice if we'd already met and got a little acquainted." I flipped a hand. "If you don't get me, what the hell, I'm ahead six thousand bucks."

I stood up. "One way to settle it, you could phone Zeck and ask him. That would be hard on me, but what can a double-crosser expect? So I'll trot along." I moved toward the door and was navigating a course through the scattered fragments of glass in the path when he decided to speak.

"Wait a minute," he said, still wistful. "You mentioned when you get approached."

"*If* I get approached."

"You will. That's the way they work. Whatever they offer, I'll top it. Come straight to me and I'll top it. I want to see you anyhow, every day—wait a minute. Come back and sit down. We can make a deal right now, for you to—"

"No," I said, kind but firm. "You're so damn scared it would be a temptation to bargain you out of your last pair of pants. Wait till you cool off a little and get some spunk back. Ring me any time. You understand, of course, we're still tailing you."

I left him.

Several times, walking downtown, I had to rein myself in. I would slow down to a normal gait, and in another block or so there I would be again, pounding along as fast as I could swing it, though all I had ahead was an open evening. I grinned at myself indulgently. I was excited, that was all. The game was on, I had pitched the first ball, and it had cut the inside corner above his knees. Not only that, it was a game with no rules. It was hard to believe that Rackham could possibly go to Zeck or any of his men with it, but if he did I was on a spot hot enough to fry an egg, and Wolfe was as good as gone. That was why I had tried to talk Wolfe out of it. But now that I had started it rolling and there was no more argument, I was merely so excited that I couldn't walk slow if you paid me.

I had had it in mind to drop in at Rusterman's Restaurant for dinner and say hello to Marko that evening, but now I didn't feel like sitting through all the motions, so I kept going to Eleventh Avenue, to Mart's Diner, and perched on a stool while I cleaned up a plate of beef stew, three ripe tomatoes sliced by me, and two pieces of blueberry pie. Even with a full stomach I was still excited. It must have shown, I suppose in my eyes, for Mart asked me what the glow was about, and though I had never had any tendency to discuss my business with him, I had to resist an impulse to remark casually that Wolfe and I had finally mixed it up with the most dangerous baby on two legs, one so tough that even Inspector Cramer had said he was out of reach.

I went home and sat in the office all evening, holding magazines open as if I were reading them. All I really did was listen for the phone or doorbell. When the phone rang at ten o'clock and it was only Fred Durkin wanting to know where Saul and the subject were, I was so rude that I hurt his feelings and had to apologize. I told him to cover the Churchill as usual, which was one of the factors that made it a burlesque, since that would have required four men at least. What I wanted to do so bad I could taste it was call the number Wolfe had given me, but that had been for emergency only. I looked emergency up in the dictionary, and got "an unforeseen combination of circumstances which calls for immediate action." Since this was just the opposite, a foreseen combination of circumstances which called for getting a good night's sleep, I didn't dial the number. I did get the good night's sleep.

Saturday morning at 1019 I had to pitch another ball, but not to the same batter. The typing of Friday's reports required only the customary summarizing of facts as far as Saul and Fred and Orrie were concerned, but my own share took time and thought. I had to account for the full time I had spent in Rackham's suite, since there was a double risk in it: the chance that I was being checked and had been seen entering and leaving, and the chance that Rack-

ham had himself split a seam. So it was quite a literary effort and
I spent three hours on it. That afternoon, when Max Christy called
to get the report as usual, and sat to look it over, I had papers on
my desk which kept me so busy that I wasn't even aware if he sent
me a glance when he got to the middle of the second page, where
my personal contribution began. I looked up only when he finally
spoke.

"So you had a talk with him, huh?"

I nodded. "Have you read it?"

"Yes." Christy was scowling at me.

"He seemed so anxious that I thought it would be a shame not
to oblige him. It's my tender heart."

"You took his money."

"Certainly. He was wild to spend it."

"You told him you're working for Mrs. Frey. What if he takes a
notion to ask her?"

"He won't. If he does, who will know who to believe or what?
I warned him about me. By the way, have I ever warned you?"

"Why did you play him?"

"It's all there in the report. He knew he had a tail, how could he
help it, already on guard, after eight days of it? I thought I might
as well chat with him and see what was on his mind. He could have
said something interesting, and maybe he did, I don't know, because I don't know what you and your friends would call interesting. Anyway, there it is. As for his money, he practically stuffed it
in my ear, and if I had refused to take it he would have lost all respect for me."

Christy put the report in his pocket, got up, rested his fingertips
on the desk, and leaned over at me. "Goodwin," he asked, "do you
know who you're dealing with?"

"Oh, for God's sake," I said impatiently. "Have I impressed you
as the sort of boob who would jump off a building just to hear his
spine crack? Yes, brother, I know who I'm dealing with, and I expect to live to ninety at least."

He straightened up. "Your chief trouble," he said, not offensively,
"is that you think you've got a sense of humor. It confuses people,
and you ought to get over it. Things strike you as funny. You thought
it would be funny to have a talk with Rackham, and it may be all
right this time, but some day something that you think is funny will
blow your goddam head right off your shoulders."

Only after he had gone did it occur to me that that wouldn't prove it wasn't funny.

I had a date that Saturday evening with Lily Rowan, but decided to call it off. Evidently I wasn't tactful enough about it, for she took on. I calmed her down by promising to drown myself as soon as the present crisis was past, went home and got my dinner out of the refrigerator, and settled down in the office for another evening of not reading magazines. A little after nine the minutes were beginning to get too damn long entirely when the phone rang. It was Lily.

"All right," she said briskly, "come on up here."

"I told you—"

"I know, but now I'm telling you. I'm going to have company around eleven, and as I understand it you're supposed to get here first. Get started."

"Phooey. I'm flattered that you bothered to try it, but—"

"I wouldn't have dreamed of trying it. The company just phoned, and I'm following instructions. My God, are you conceited!"

"I'll be there in twenty minutes."

It took twenty-two, to her door. She was vindictive enough to insist that there were three television programs she wouldn't miss for anything, which was just as well, considering my disposition. I suppose I might have adjusted to it in time, say ten years, but I was so used to having Wolfe right at hand any minute of the day or night when difficulties were being met that this business of having to sit it out until word came, and then rushing up to a friend's penthouse and waiting another hour and a half, was too much of a strain.

He finally arrived. I must admit that when the bell rang Lily, having promised to behave like a lady, did so. She insisted on opening the door for him, but having got him into the living room, she excused herself and left us.

He sat. I stood and looked at him. Eleven days had passed since our reunion, and I hadn't properly remembered how grotesque he was. Except for the eyes, he was no one I had ever seen or cared to see.

"What's the matter?" I asked peevishly. "You look as if you hadn't slept for a week."

"I'm a little tired, that's all," he growled. "I have too much to watch, and I'm starving to death. So far as I know everything at my end is satisfactory. What about Miss Rowan?"

"She's all right. As you may remember, every week or so I used to send her a couple of orchids of a kind that couldn't be bought. I have told her that the custom may be resumed some day provided we get this difficulty ironed out, and that it depends on her. Women like to have things depend on them."

He grunted. "I don't like to have things depend on them." He sighed. "It can't be helped. I can only stay an hour. Bring me some of Miss Rowan's perfume."

I went and tapped on a door, got no answer, opened it and crossed a room to another door, tapped again, was told to enter, and did so. Lily was on a divan with a book. I told her what I wanted.

"Take the Houri de Perse," she advised. "Pete likes it. I had it on that night."

I got it from the dressing table, returned to the living room, aimed it at him from the proper distance, and squeezed the bulb. He shut his eyes and tightened his lips to a thin line.

"Now the other side," I said gently. "What's worth doing—"

But he opened his eyes, and their expression was enough. I put the sprayer on a table and went to a chair.

He looked at his wristwatch. "I read the report of your talk with Rackham. How did it go?"

"Fine. You might have thought he had rehearsed it with us."

"Tell me about it."

I obeyed. It felt good, giving him a communiqué again, and since it needed no apologies I enjoyed it. What I always tried for was to present it so that few or no questions were required, and though I was a little out of practice I did well enough.

When I was through he muttered, "Satisfactory. Confound this smell."

"It'll go away in time. Sixty dollars an ounce."

"Speaking of dollars, you didn't deposit what you took from Rackham?"

"No. It's in the safe."

"Leave it there for the present. It's Mrs. Rackham's money, and we may decide we've earned it. Heaven knows no imaginable sum could repay me for these months. I was thinking—"

He cut it off, tilted his head a little, and regarded me with eyes narrowed to slits.

"Well?" I said aggressively. "More bright ideas?"

"I was thinking, Archie. August is gone. The risk would be negligible. Get Mr. Haskins on the phone tomorrow and tell him to start a dozen chicks on blueberries. Uh—two dozen. You can tell him they are for gifts to your friends."

"No, sir."

"Yes. Tomorrow."

"I say no. He would know damn well who they were for. My God, is your stomach more important than your neck? Not to mention mine. You can't help it if you were born greedy, but you can try to control—"

"Archie." His voice was thin and cold with fury. "Nearly five months now. Look at me."

"Yes, sir." He had me. "You're right. I beg your pardon. But I am not going to phone Haskins. You just had a moment of weakness. Let's change the subject. Does Rackham's biting on the first try change the schedule any?"

"You could tell Mr. Haskins—"

"No."

He gave up. After sitting a while with his eyes closed, he sighed so deep it made him shudder, and then came back to black reality. Only a quarter of his hour was left, and we used it to review the situation and program. The strategy was unchanged. At midnight he arose.

"Please thank Miss Rowan for me?"

"Sure. She thinks you ought to call her Lily."

"You shouldn't leave on my heels."

"I won't. She's sore and wants to have a scene."

I went ahead to open the door for him. As I did so he asked, "What is this stuff called?"

"Houri de Perse."

"Great heavens," he muttered, and went.

16

Having my own office was giving me a new slant on some of the advantages of the setup I had long enjoyed at Wolfe's place. With a tailing job on, Sunday was like any other day, and I had to be at 1019 at the usual hour, both to type the report and to take calls from the man on the job in case he needed advice or help. It was no longer just burlesque, at least not for me. Even though Rackham knew we were on him, those were three good men, particularly Saul, and I stood a fair chance of being informed if he strayed anywhere out of bounds to keep an appointment. To some extent the tail now served a purpose: to warn me if the subject and the client made a contact, which was somewhat bassackwards but convenient for me.

After a leisurely Sunday dinner at Rusterman's Restaurant, where I couldn't make up my mind whether Marko Vukcic knew that I had my old job back, I returned to 1019 to find Max Christy waiting at the door. He seemed a little upset. I glanced at my wrist and told him he was early.

"This one-man business is no good," he complained. "You ought to have someone here. I tried to get you on the phone nearly two hours ago."

Unlocking the door and entering, I explained that I had dawdled over tournedos à la Béarnaise, which I thought would impress him. He didn't seem to hear me. When I unlocked a desk drawer to get the report, and handed it to him, he stuffed it in his pocket without glancing at it.

I raised the brows. "Don't you want to read it?"

"I'll read it in the car. You're coming along."

"Yeah? Where to?"

"Pete Roeder wants to see you."

"Well, here I am. As you say, this is a one-man business. I've got to stick here, damn it."

Christy was glaring at me under his brow thickets. "Listen, Goodwin, I'm supposed to have you somewhere at four o'clock, and it's five to three now. I waited for you nearly half an hour. Let's go. You can argue on the way."

I had done my arguing, double-quick, while he was speaking. To balk was out of the question. To stall and try to get an idea what the program really was would have been sappy. I got my keys out again, unlocked the bottom drawer, took off my jacket, got out the shoulder holster, slipped it on, and twisted my torso to reach for the buckle.

"What's that for, woodchucks?" Christy asked.

"Just force of habit. Once I forgot to wear it and a guy in an elevator stepped on my toe. I had to cut his throat. If we're in a hurry, come on."

We went. Down at the curb, as I had noticed on my way in, force of habit again, was a dark blue Olds sedan, a fifty, with a cheerful-looking young man with a wide mouth, no hat, behind the wheel. He gave me an interested look as Christy and I got in the back seat, but no words passed. The second the door slammed the engine started and the car went forward.

The Olds fifty is the only stock car that will top a hundred and ten, but we never reached half of that—up the West Side Highway, Saw Mill River, and Taconic State. The young man was a careful, competent, and considerate driver. There was not much conversation. When Christy took the report from his pocket and started reading it my first reaction was mild relief, on the ground that if I were about to die they wouldn't give a damn what my last words were, but on second thought it seemed reasonable that he might be looking for more evidence for the prosecution, and I left the matter open.

It was a fine sunny day, not too hot, and everything looked very attractive. I hoped I would see many more days like it, in either town or country, I didn't care which, though ordinarily I much prefer the city. But that day the country looked swell, and therefore I resented it when, as we were rolling along the Taconic State Parkway a few miles north of Hawthorne Circle, Christy suddenly commanded me, "Get down on the floor, face down."

"Have a heart," I protested. "I'm enjoying the scenery."

"I'll describe it to you. Shall we park for a talk?"

"How much time have we?"

"None to waste."

"Okay, pull your feet back."

The truth was, I was glad to oblige. Logic had stepped in. If that was intended for my last ride I wouldn't ever be traveling that road again, and in that case what difference did it make if I saw where we turned off and which direction we went? There must have been some chance that I would ride another day, and without a chaperon, or this stunt was pointless. So as I got myself into position, wriggling and adjusting to keep my face downward without an elbow or knee taking my weight, the worst I felt was undignified. I heard the driver saying something, in a soft quiet voice, and Christy answering him, but I didn't catch the words.

There was no law against looking at my watch. I had been playing hide and seek, with me it, a little more than sixteen minutes, with the car going now slower and now faster, now straight and now turning left and now right, when finally it slowed down to a full stop. I heard a strange voice and then Christy's, and the sound of a heavy door closing. I shifted my weight.

"Hold it," Christy snapped at me. He was still right above me. "We're a little early."

"I'm tired of breathing dust," I complained.

"It's better than not breathing at all," the strange voice said and laughed, not attractively.

"He's got a gun," Christy stated. "Left armpit."

"Why not? He's a licensed eye. We'll take care of it."

I looked at my watch, but it was too dark to see the hands, so of course we were in out of the sun. The driver had got out, shut the car door, and walked away, if I was any good at reading sounds. I heard voices indistinctly, not near me, and didn't get the words. My left leg, from the knee down, got bored and decided to go to sleep. I moved it.

"Hold it," Christy commanded.

"Nuts. Tape my eyes and let me get up and stretch."

"I said hold it."

I held it, for what I would put at another seven minutes. Then there were noises—a door opening, not loud, footsteps and voices, a door closing, again not loud, still steps and voices, a car's doors opening and shutting, an engine starting, a car moving, and in a minute the closing of the heavy door that had closed after we had stopped. Then the door which my head was touching opened.

"All right," a voice said. "Come on out."

It took acrobatics, but I made it. I was standing, slightly wobbly, on concrete, near a concrete wall of a room sixty feet square with no windows and not too many lights. My darting glance caught cars scattered around, seven or eight of them. It also caught four men: Christy, coming around the rear end of the Olds, and three serious-looking strangers, older than our driver, who wasn't there.

Without a word two of them put their hands on me. First they took the gun from my armpit and then went over me. The circumstances didn't seem favorable for an argument, so I simply stood at attention. It was a fast and expert job, with no waste motion and no intent to offend.

"It's all a matter of practice," I said courteously.

"Yeah," the taller one agreed, in a tenor that was almost a falsetto. "Follow me."

He moved to the wall, with me behind. The cars had been

stopped short of the wall to leave an alley, and we went down it a few paces to a door where a man was standing. He opened the door for us—it was the one that made little noise—and we passed through into a small vestibule, also with no windows in its concrete walls. Across it, only three paces, steps down began, and we descended—fourteen shallow steps to a wide metal door. My conductor pushed a button in the metal jamb. I heard no sound within, but in a moment the door opened and a pasty-faced bird with a pointed chin was looking at us.

"Archie Goodwin," my conductor said.

"Step in."

I waited politely to be preceded, but my conductor moved aside, and the other one said impatiently, "Step in, Goodwin."

I crossed the sill, and the sentinel closed the door. I was in a room bigger than the vestibule above: bare concrete walls, well-lighted, with a table, three chairs, a water-cooler, and a rack of magazines and newspapers. A second sentinel, seated at the table, writing in a book like a ledger, sent me a sharp glance and then forgot me. The first one crossed to another big metal door directly opposite to the one I had entered by, and when he pulled it open I saw that it was a good five inches thick. He jerked his head and told me, "On in."

I stepped across and passed through, with him at my heels.

This was quite a chamber. The walls were paneled in a light gray wood with pink in it, from the tiled floor to the ceiling, and the rugs were the same light gray with pink borders. Light came from a concealed trough continuous around the ceiling. The six or seven chairs and the couch were covered in pinkish gray leather, and the same leather had been used for the frames of the pictures, a couple of big ones on each wall. All that, collected in my first swift survey, made a real impression.

"Archie Goodwin," the sentinel said.

The man at the desk said, "Sit down, Goodwin. All right, Schwartz," and the sentinel left us and closed the door.

I would have been surprised to find that Pete Roeder rated all this splash so soon after hitting this territory, and he didn't. The man at the desk was not Roeder. I had never seen this bozo, but no introduction was needed. Much as he disliked publicity, his picture had been in the paper a few times, as for instance the occasion of his presenting his yacht to the United States Coast Guard during the war. Also I had heard him described.

I had a good view of him at ten feet when I sat in one of the pink-ish gray leather chairs near his desk. Actually there was nothing to him but his forehead and eyes. It wasn't a forehead, it was a dome, sloping up and up to the line of his faded thin hair. The eyes were the result of an error on the assembly line. They had been intended for a shark and someone got careless. They did not now look the same as shark eyes because Arnold Zeck's brain had been using them to see with for fifty years, and that had had an effect.

"I've spoken with you on the phone," he said.

I nodded. "When I was with Nero Wolfe. Three times altogether—no, I guess it was four."

"Four. Where is he? What has happened to him?"

"I'm not sure, but I suspect he's in Florida, training with an air hose, preparing to lay for you in your swimming pool and get you when you dive."

There was no flicker of response, of any kind, in the shark eyes. "I have been told of your habits of speech, Goodwin," he said. "I make no objection. I take men for what they are or not at all. It pleases me that, impressed as you must be by this meeting, you insist on being yourself. But it does waste time and words. Do you know where Wolfe is?"

"No."

"Have you a surmise?"

"Yeah, I just told you." I got irritated. "Say I tell you he's in Egypt, where he owns a house. I don't, but say I do. Then what? You send a punk to Cairo to drill him? Why? Why can't you let him alone? I know he had his faults—God knows how I stood them as long as I did—but he taught me a lot, and wherever he is he's my favorite fatty. Just because he happened to queer your deal with Rackham, you want to track him down. What will that get you, now that he's faded out?"

"I don't wish or intend to track him down."

"No? Then what made me so interesting? Your Max Christy and your bearded wonder offering me schoolboy jobs at triple pay. Get me sucked in, get me branded, and when the time comes use me to get at Wolfe so you can pay him. No." I shook my head. "I draw the line somewhere, and all of you together won't get me across that one."

I'm not up enough on fish to know whether sharks blink, but Zeck was showing me. He blinked perhaps one-tenth his share. He asked, "Why did you take the job?"

"Because it was Rackham. I'm interested in him. I was glad to know someone else was. I would like to have a hand in his future."

No blink. "You think you know, I suppose, the nature of my own interests and activities."

"I know what is said around. I know that a New York police inspector told me that you're out of reach."

"Name him."

"Cramer. Manhattan Homicide."

"Oh, him." Zeck made his first gesture: a forefinger straightened and curved again. "What was the occasion?"

"He wouldn't believe me when I said I didn't know where Wolfe was. He thought Wolfe and I were fixing to try to bring you down, and he was just telling me. I told him that maybe he would like to pull us off because he was personally interested, but that since Wolfe had scooted he was wasting it."

"That was injudicious, wasn't it?"

"All of that. I was in a bad humor."

Zeck blinked; I saw him. "I wanted to meet you, Goodwin. I've allowed some time for this because I want to look at you and hear you talk. Your idea of my interests and activities probably has some relation to the facts, and if so you may know that my chief problem is men. I could use ten times as many good men as I can find. I judge men partly by their record and partly by report, but mainly by my first-hand appraisal. You have disappointed me in one respect. Your conclusion that I want to use you to find Nero Wolfe is not intelligent. I do not pursue an opponent who has fled the field; it would not be profitable. If he reappears and gets in my path again, I'll crush him. I do want to suck you in, as you put it. I need good men now more than ever. Many people get money from me, indirectly, whom I never see and have no wish to see; but there must be some whom I do see and work through. You might be one. I would like to try. You must know one thing: if you once say yes it becomes impractical to change your mind. It can't be done."

"You said," I objected, "you would like to try. How about my liking to try?"

"I've answered that. It can't be done."

"It's already being done. I'm tailing Rackham for you. When he approached me I took it on myself to chat with him and report it.

Did you like that or not? If not, I'm not your type. If so, let's go on with that until you know me better. Hell, we never saw each other before. You can let me know a day in advance when I'm to lose the right to change my mind, and we'll see. Regarding my notion that you want to use me to find Nero Wolfe, skip it. You couldn't anyway, since I don't know whether he went north, east, south, or west."

I had once remarked to Wolfe, when X (our name then for Zeck) had brought a phone call to a sudden end, that he was an abrupt bastard. He now abruptly turned the shark eyes from me, which was a relief, to reach for the switch on an intercom box on his desk, flip it, and speak to it. "Send Roeder in."

"Tell him to shave first," I suggested, thinking that if I had a reputation for a habit of speech I might as well live up to it. Zeck did not react. I was beginning to believe that he never had reacted to anything and never would. I turned my head enough for the newcomer to have my profile when he entered, not to postpone his pleasure at seeing me.

It was a short wait till the door opened and Roeder appeared. The sentinel did not come in. Roeder crossed to us, stepping flat on the rugs so as not to slide. His glance at me was fleeting and casual.

"Sit down," Zeck said. "You know Goodwin."

Roeder nodded and favored me with a look. Sitting, he told me, "Your reports haven't been worth what they cost."

It gave me a slight shock, but I don't think I let it show. I had forgotten that Roeder talked through his nose.

"Sorry," I said condescendingly. "I've been sticking to facts. If you want them dressed up, let me know what color you like."

"You've been losing him."

I flared up quietly. "I used to think," I said, "that Nero Wolfe expected too much. But even he had brains enough to know that hotels have more than one exit."

"You're being paid enough to cover the exits to the Yankee Stadium."

Zeck said, in his hard, cold, precise voice that never went up or down, "These are trivialities. I've had a talk with Goodwin, Roeder, and I sent for you because we got to Rackham. We have to decide how it is to be handled and what part Goodwin is to play. I want your opinion on the effect of Goodwin's telling Rackham that he is working for Mrs. Frey."

Roeder shrugged. "I think it's unimportant. Goodwin's main purpose now is to get Rackham scared. We've got to have him scared good before we can expect him to go along with us. If he killed his wife—"

"He did, of course. Unquestionably."

"Then he might be more afraid of Mrs. Frey than of you. We can see. If not, it will be simple for Goodwin to give him a new line." Roeder looked at me. "It's all open for you to Rackham now?"

"I guess so. He told me he wanted to see me every day, but that was day before yesterday. What are we scaring him for? To see him throw glasses?"

Zeck and Roeder exchanged glances. Zeck spoke to me. "I believe Roeder told you that he came here recently from the West Coast. He had a very successful operation there, a brilliant and profitable operation which he devised. It has some novel features and requires precise timing and expert handling. With one improvement it could be enormously profitable here in New York, and that one improvement is the cooperation of a wealthy and well-placed man. Rackham is ideal for it. We intend to use him. If you help materially in lining him up, as I think you can, your share of the net will be five per cent. The net is expected to exceed half a million, and should be double that."

I was frowning skeptically. "You mean if I help scare him into it."

"Yes."

"And help with the operation too?"

"No."

"What have I got to scare him with?"

"His sense of guilt first. He escaped arrest and trial for the murder of his wife only because the police couldn't get enough evidence for a case. He is under the constant threat of the discovery of additional evidence, which for a murderer is a severe strain. If he believes we have such evidence he will be open to persuasion."

"Have we got it?"

Zeck damn near smiled. "I shouldn't think it will be needed. If it is needed we'll have it."

"Then why drag him in on a complicated operation? He's worth what, three million? Ask him for half of it, or even a third."

"No. You have much to learn, Goodwin. People must not be deprived of hope. If we take a large share of Rackham's fortune he will be convinced that we intend to wring him dry. People must be allowed to feel that if our demands are met the outlook is not intolerable. A basic requirement for continued success in illicit enterprises is a sympathetic understanding of the limitations of the human nervous system. Getting Rackham's help in Roeder's operation will leave plenty of room for future requests."

I was keeping my frown. "Which I may or may not have a hand in. Don't think I'm playing hard to get, but this is quite a step to take. Using a threat of a murder rap to put the screws on a millionaire is a little too drastic without pretty good assurance that I get more than peanuts. You said five per cent of a probable half a million, but you're used to talking big figures. Could I have that filled in a little?"

Roeder reached for a battered old leather briefcase which he had brought in with him and deposited on the floor. Getting it on his lap, he had it opened when Zeck asked him, "What are you after, the estimates?"

"Yes, if you want them."

"You may show them to him, but no names." Zeck turned to me. "I think you may do, Goodwin. You're brash, but that is a quality that may be made use of. You used it when you talked with Rackham. He must be led into this with tact or he may lose his head and force our hand, and all we want is his cooperation. His conviction for murder wouldn't help us any; quite the contrary. Properly handled, he should be of value to us for years."

The shark eyes left me. "What's your opinion of Goodwin, Roeder? Can you work with him?"

Roeder had closed the briefcase and kept it on his lap. "I can try," he said, not enthusiastically. "The general level here is no higher than on the coast. But we can't get started until we know whether we have Rackham or not, and the approach through Goodwin does seem the best way. He's so damned cocky I don't know whether he'll take direction."

"Would you care to have my opinion of Roeder?" I inquired.

Zeck ignored it. "Goodwin," he said, "this is the most invulnerable organization on earth. There are good men in it, but it all comes to me. I am the organization. I have no prejudices and no emotions. You will get what you deserve. If you deserve well, there is no limit to the support you will get, and none to the reward. If you deserve ill, there is no limit to that either. You understand that?"

"Sure." His eyes were the hardest to meet in my memory. "Provided you understand that I don't like you."

"No one likes me. No one likes the authority of superior intellect. There was one man who matched me in intellect—the man you worked for, Nero Wolfe—but his will failed him. His vanity wouldn't let him yield, and he cleared out."

"He was a little handicapped," I protested, "by his respect for law."

"Every man is handicapped by his own weaknesses. If you communicate with him give him my regards. I have great admiration for him."

Zeck glanced at a clock on the wall and then at Roeder. "I'm keeping a caller waiting. Goodwin is under your direction, but he is on trial. Consult me as necessary within the routine."

He must have had floor buttons for foot-signaling, for he touched nothing with his hands, but the door opened and the sentinel appeared.

Zeck said, "Put Goodwin on the B list, Schwartz."

Roeder and I arose and headed for the door, him with his briefcase under his arm.

Remembering how he had told me, tapping his chest, "I am a D, Archie," I would have given a lot if I could have tapped my own bosom and announced, "I am a B, Mr. Wolfe."

17

There was one chore Wolfe had given me which I haven't mentioned, because I didn't care to reveal the details—and still don't. But the time will come when you will want to know where the gun at the bottom of the briefcase came from, so I may as well say now that you aren't going to know.

Since filing the number from a gun has been made obsolete by the progress of science, the process of getting one that can't be traced has got more complicated and requires a little specialized knowledge. One has to be acquainted with the right people. I am. But there is no reason why you should be, so I won't give their names and addresses. I couldn't quite meet Wolfe's specifications—the size and weight of a .22 and the punch of a .45—but I did pretty well: a Carson Snub Thirty, an ugly little devil, but straight and powerful. I tried it out one evening in the basement at Thirty-fifth Street. When I was through I collected the bullets and dumped them in the river. We were taking enough chances without adding another, however slim.

The next evening after our conference with Zeck, a Monday, Wolfe and I collaborated on the false bottom for the briefcase. We did the job at 1019. Since I was now a B and Roeder's lieutenant on his big operation, and he was supposed to keep in touch with me, there was no reason why he shouldn't come to Thirty-fifth Street for an evening visit, but when I suggested it he compressed his lips and scowled at me with such ferocity that I quickly changed the subject. We made the false bottom out of an old piece of leather that I picked up at a shoe hospital, and it wasn't bad at all. Even if a sentinel removed all the papers for a close inspection, which wasn't likely with the status Roeder had reached, there was little chance of his suspecting the bottom; yet if you knew just where and how to pry you could have the Carson out before you could say Jackie Robinson.

However, something had happened before that: my second talk with Barry Rackham. When I got home late Sunday night the phone-answering service reported that he had been trying to reach me, both at 1019 and at the office, and I gave him a ring and made a date for Monday at three o'clock.

Usually I am on the dot for an appointment, but that day an errand took less time than I had allowed, and it was only twelve to three when I left the Churchill tower elevator at Rackham's floor and walked to his door. I was lifting my hand to push the button, when the door opened and I had to step back so a woman wouldn't walk into me. When she saw me she stopped, and we both stared. It was Lina Darrow. Her fine eyes were as fine as ever.

"Well, hello," I said appreciatively.

"You're early, Goodwin," Barry Rackham said. He was standing in the doorway.

Lina's expression was not appreciative. It didn't look like embarrassment, more like some kind of suspicion, though I had no notion what she could suspect me of so spontaneously.

"How are you?" she asked, and then, to make it perfectly clear that she didn't give a damn, went by me toward the elevator. Rackham moved aside, giving me enough space to enter, and I did so and kept going to the living room. In a moment I heard the door close, and in another moment he joined me.

"You're early," he repeated, not reproachfully.

He looked as if, during the seventy hours since I had last seen him, he had had at least seventy drinks. His face was mottled, his eyes were bloodshot, and his left cheek was twitching. Also his tie had a dot of egg yolk on it, and he needed a shave.

"A week ago Saturday," I said, "I think it was, one of my men described a girl you were out with, and it sounded like Miss Darrow, but I wasn't sure. I'm not leading up to something, I'm just gossiping."

He wasn't interested one way or the other. He asked what I would have to drink, and when I said nothing thank you he went to the bar and got himself a straight one, and then came and moved a chair around to sit facing me.

"Hell," I said, "you look even more scared than you did the other day. And according to my men, either you've started sneaking out side doors or you've become a homebody. Who said boo?"

Nothing I had to say interested him. "I said I wanted to see you every day," he stated. His voice was hoarse.

"I know, but I've been busy. Among other things, I spent an hour yesterday afternoon with Arnold Zeck."

That did interest him. "I think you're a goddam liar, Goodwin."

"Then I must have dreamed it. Driving into the garage, and being frisked, and the little vestibule, and fourteen steps down, and the two sentinels, and the soundproof door five inches thick, and the pinkish gray walls and chairs and rugs, and him sitting there drilling holes in things, including me, with his eyes, and—"

"When was this? Yesterday?"

"Yeah. I was driven up, but now I know how to get there myself. I haven't got the password yet, but wait."

With an unsteady hand he put his glass down on a little table. "I told you before, Goodwin, I did not kill my wife."

"Sure, that's out of the way."

"How did it happen? Your going to see him."

"He sent Max Christy for me."

"That son of a bitch." Suddenly his mottled face got redder and he yelled at me, "Well, go on! What did he say?"

"He said I may have a big career ahead of me."

"What did he say about me?"

I shook my head. "I'll tell you, Rackham. I think it's about time I let my better judgment in on this. I had never seen Zeck before, and he made quite an impression on me." I reached to my breast pocket. "Here's your six thousand dollars. I hate to let go of it, but—"

"Put that back in your pocket."

"No, really, I—"

"Put it back." He wasn't yelling now. "I don't blame you for being impressed by Zeck—God knows you're not the first. But you're wrong if you think he can't ever miss and I'm all done. There's one thing you ought to realize: I can't throw in my hand on this one; I've got to play it out, and I'm going to. You've got me hooked, because I can't play it without you since you were there that night. All right, name it. How much?"

I put the six grand on the little table. "My real worry," I said, "is not Zeck. He is nothing to sneer at and he does make a strong impression, but I have been impressed before and got over it. What called my better judgment in was the New York statutes relating to accessories to murder. Apparently Zeck has got evidence that will convict you. If you—"

"He has not. That's a lie."

"He seems to think he has. If you want to take dough from a murderer for helping him beat the rap you must be admitted to the bar, and I haven't been. So with my sincere regret at my inability to assist you in your difficulty, there's your dough."

"I'm not a murderer, Goodwin."

"I didn't mean an actual murderer. I meant a man against whom evidence has been produced in court to convince a jury. He and his accessory get it just the same."

Rackham's bloodshot eyes were straight and steady at me. "I'm not asking you to help me beat a rap. I'm asking you not to help frame me—and to help me keep Zeck from framing me."

"I know," I said sympathetically. "That's the way you tell it, but not him. I don't intend to get caught in a backwash. I came here chiefly to return your money and to tell you that it's got beyond the point where I name a figure and you pay it and then we're all hunky-dory, but I do have a suggestion to make if you care to hear it—strictly on my own."

Rackham started doing calisthenics. His hands, resting on his thighs, tightened into fists and then opened again, and repeated it several times. It made me impatient watching him, because it seemed so inadequate to the situation. By now the picture was pretty clear, and I thought that a guy who had had enough initiative to venture into the woods at night to stalk his wife, armed only with a steak knife, when she had her Doberman pinscher with her, should now, finding himself backed into a corner, respond with something more forceful than sitting there doing and undoing his fists.

He spoke. "Look, Goodwin, I'm not myself, I know damn well I'm not. It's been nearly five months now. The first week it wasn't so bad—there was the excitement, all of us suspected and being questioned; if they had arrested me then I wouldn't have skipped a pulse beat. I would have met it fair and square and fought it out. But as it stretched out it got tougher. I had broken off with Zeck without thinking it through—the way it looked then, I ought to get clean and keep clean, especially after the hearings in Washington, those first ones, and after the New York District Attorney took a hand. But what happened, every time the phone rang or the doorbell, it hit me in the stomach. It was murder. If they came and took me or sent for me and kept me, I could be damn sure it had been fixed so they thought it would stick. A man can stand that for a day or a week, or a month perhaps, but with me it went on and on, and by God, I've had about all I can take."

He had ended his calisthenics with the fists closed tight, the knobs of the knuckles the color of boils. "I made a mistake with Zeck," he said fretfully. "When I broke it off he sent for me and as good as told me that the only thing between me and the electric chair was his influence. I lost my temper. When I do that I can never remember what I said, but I don't think I actually told him that I had evidence of blackmailing against him personally. Anyhow, I said too much." He opened his fists and spread his fingers wide, his palms flat on his thighs. "Then this started, this stretching into months. Did you say you have a suggestion?"

"Yeah. And brother, you need one."

"What is it?"

"On my own, I said."

"What is it?"

"For you and Zeck to have a talk."

"What for? No matter what he said I couldn't trust him."

"Then you'd be meeting on even terms. Look straight at it. Could your wife trust you? Could your friends trust you—the ones you helped Zeck get at? Could I trust you? I warned you not to trust me, didn't I? There are only two ways for people to work together: when everybody trusts everyone or nobody trusts no one. When you mix them up it's a mess. You and Zeck ought to get along fine."

"Get along with Zeck?"

"Certainly." I turned a palm up. "Listen, you're in a hole. I never saw a man in a deeper one. You're even willing and eager to shell out to me, a double-crosser you can't trust, to give you a lift. You can't possibly expect to get out in the clear with no ropes tied to you—what the hell, who is? Your main worry is getting framed for murder, so your main object is to see that you don't. That ought to be a cinch. Zeck has a new man, a guy named Roeder, came here recently from the coast, who has started to line up an operation that's a beaut. I've been assigned to help on it, and I think I'm going to. It's as tight as a drum and as slick as a Doberman pinscher's coat. With the help of a man placed as you are, there would be absolutely nothing to it, without the slightest risk of any noise or a comeback."

"No. That's what got—"

"Wait a minute. As I said, this is on my own. I'm not going to tell you what Zeck said to me yesterday, but I advise you to take my suggestion. Let me arrange for you to see him. You don't have to take up where you left off, a lot of dirty little errands; you're a man of wealth now and can act accordingly. But also you're a man who is suspected by thirty million people of killing his wife, and that calls for concessions. Come with me to see Zeck, let him know you're willing to discuss things, and if he mentions Roeder's operation let him describe it and then decide what you want to do. I told you why I don't want to see you or anyone else framed for that murder, and I don't think Zeck will either if it looks as though you might be useful."

"I hate him," Rackham said hoarsely. "I'm afraid of him and I hate him!"

"I don't like him myself. I told him so. What about tomorrow? Say four o'clock tomorrow, call for you here at a quarter to three?"

"I don't—not tomorrow—"

"Get it over with! Would you rather keep on listening for the phone and the doorbell? Get it over with!"

He reached for his straight drink, which he hadn't touched, swallowed it at a gulp, shuddered all over, and wiped his mouth with the back of his hand.

"I'll ring you around noon to confirm it," I said, and stood up to
go. He didn't come with me to the door, but under the circumstances
I didn't hold it against him.

So that evening when Wolfe came to 1019 it appeared to be high
time for getting the false bottom in the briefcase ready, and we
went on until midnight, discussing the program from every angle
and trying to cover every contingency. It's always worth trying,
though it can never be done, especially not with a layout as tricky
as that one.

Then the next morning, Tuesday, a monkey wrench, thrown all
the way from White Plains, flew into the machinery and stopped
it. I had just finished breakfast, with Fritz, when the phone rang
and I went to the office to get it. It was the Westchester DA's office.

The talk was brief. When I had hung up I sat a while, glaring at
the phone, then with an exasperated finger dialed the Churchill's
number. That talk was brief too. Finished with it, I held the button
down for a moment and dialed another number.

There had been only two buzzes when a voice came through a
nose to me. "Yes?"

"I'd like to speak to Mr. Roeder."

"Talking."

"This is Goodwin. I've just had a call from White Plains to come
to the DA's office at once. I asked if I could count on keeping a two
o'clock appointment and was told no. I phoned the Churchill and
left a message that I had been called out of town for the day. I hope
it can be tomorrow. I'll let you know as soon as I can."

Silence.

"Did you hear me?"

"Yes. Good luck, Goodwin."

The connection went.

18

I had once sat and cooled my heels for three hours on one of the
wooden benches in the big anteroom of the DA's office in the White
Plains courthouse, but this time I didn't sit at all. I didn't even give
my name. I entered and was crossing to the table in the fenced-off

corner when a man with a limp intercepted me and said, "Come with me, Mr. Goodwin."

He took me down a long corridor, past rows of doors on either side, and into a room that I was acquainted with. I had been entertained there for an hour or so the evening of Sunday, April ninth. No one was in it. It had two big windows for the morning sun, and I sat and watched the dust dance. I was blowing at it, seeing what patterns I could make, when the door opened and Cleveland Archer, the DA himself, appeared, followed by Ben Dykes. I have never glanced at faces with a deeper interest. If they had looked pleased and cocky it would probably have meant that they had cracked the case, and in that event all our nifty plans for taking care of Arnold Zeck were up the flue and God help us.

I was so glad to see that they were far from cocky that I had to see to it that my face didn't beam. I responded to their curt greeting in kind, and when they arranged the seating with me across a table from them I said grumpily as I sat, "I hope this is going to get somebody something. I had a full day ahead, and now look at it."

Dykes grunted, not with sympathy and not with enmity, just a grunt. Archer opened a folder he had brought, selected from its contents some sheets of paper stapled in a corner, glanced at the top sheet, and gave me his eyes, which had swollen lids.

"This is that statement you made, Goodwin."

"About what? Oh, the Rackham case?"

"For God's sake," Dykes said gloomily, "forget to try to be cute just once. I've been up all night."

"It was so long ago," I said apologetically, "and I've been pretty busy."

Archer slid the statement across the table to me. "I think you had better read it over. I want to ask some questions about it."

I couldn't have asked for a better chance to get my mind arranged, but I didn't see that that would help matters any, since I hadn't the vaguest notion from which direction the blow was coming.

"May I save it for later?" I inquired. "If you get me up a tree and I need time out for study, I can pretend I want to check with what I said here." I tapped the statement with a forefinger.

"I would prefer that you read it."

"I don't need to, really. I know what I said and what I signed." I slid it back to him. "Test me on any part of it."

Archer closed the folder and rested his clasped hands on it. "I'm not as interested in what is in that statement as I am in what isn't in it. I think you ought to read it because I want to ask you what you left out—of the happenings of that day, Saturday, April eighth."

"I can answer that without reading it. I left nothing out that was connected with Mrs. Rackham."

"I want you to read what you said and signed and then repeat that statement."

"I don't need to read it. I left out nothing."

Archer and Dykes exchanged looks, and then Dykes spoke. "Look, Goodwin, we're not trying to sneak up on you. We've got something, that's all. Someone has loosened up. It looks like this is the day for it."

"Not for me." I was firm. "I loosened up long ago."

Archer told Dykes, "Bring her in." Dykes arose and left the room. Archer took the statement and returned it to the folder and pushed the folder to one side, then pressed the heels of his palms to his eyes and took a couple of deep breaths. The door opened and Dykes escorted Lina Darrow in. He pulled a chair up to the end of the table for her, to my left and Archer's right, so that the window was at her back. She looked as if she might have spent the night in jail, with red eyes and a general air of being pooped, but judging from the clamp she had on her jaw, she was darned determined about something. I got a glance from her but nothing more, not even a nod, as she took the chair Dykes pulled up.

"Miss Darrow," Archer told her, gently but firmly, "you understand that there is probably no chance of getting your story corroborated except through Mr. Goodwin. You haven't been brought in here to face him for the purpose of disconcerting or discrediting him, but merely so he can be informed first-hand." Archer turned to me. "Miss Darrow came to us last evening of her own accord. No pressure of any kind has been used with her. Is that correct, Miss Darrow? I wish you would confirm that to Mr. Goodwin."

"Yes." She lifted her eyes to me, and though they had obviously had a hard night, I still insist they were fine. She went on, "I came voluntarily. I came because—the way Barry Rackham treated me. He refused to marry me. He treated me very badly. Finally—yesterday it was too much."

Archer and Dykes were both gazing at her fixedly. Archer prodded her. "Go on, please, Miss Darrow. Tell him the main facts."

She was trying the clamp on her jaw to make sure it was working right. Satisfied, she released it. "Barry and I had been friendly, a little, before Mrs. Rackham's death. Nothing but just a little friendly. That's all it meant to me, or I thought it was, and I thought it was the same with him. That's how it was when we went to the country for the Easter weekend. She had told me we wouldn't do any work there, answer any mail or anything, but Saturday at noon she sent for me to come to her room. She was crying and was so distressed she could hardly talk."

Lina paused. She was keeping her eyes straight at mine. "I can rattle this off now, Mr. Goodwin. I've already told it now."

"That always makes it easier," I agreed. "Go right ahead."

She did. "Mrs. Rackham said she had to talk about it with someone, and she wanted to with her daughter-in-law, Mrs. Frey, but she just couldn't, so there was only me. She said she had gone to see Nero Wolfe the day before, to ask him to find out where her husband was getting money from, and he had agreed to do it. Mr. Wolfe had phoned her that evening, Friday evening, and told her that he had already partly succeeded. He had learned that her husband was connected with something that was criminal. He was helping somebody with things that were against the law, and he was getting well paid for it. Mr. Wolfe advised her to keep it to herself until he had more details. He said his assistant, Mr. Goodwin, would come up Saturday afternoon, and might have more to report then."

"And that Goodwin knew all about it?" Archer asked.

"Well, naturally she took that for granted. She didn't say that Mr. Wolfe told her in so many words that Mr. Goodwin knew all about it, but if he was his assistant and helping with it, naturally she would think so. Anyway that didn't seem to be important then, because she had told it all to her husband. They used the same bedroom at Birchvale, and she said that after they had gone to bed she simply couldn't help it. She didn't tell me their conversation, what they said to each other, but they had had a violent quarrel. She had told him they would have to separate, she was through with him, and she would have Mr. Wolfe go on with his investigation and get proof of what he had done. Mrs. Rackham had a very strong character, and she hated to be deceived. But the next day she wasn't sure she really meant it, that she really wanted to part from him. That was why she wanted to talk about it with someone. I think the reason she didn't want to talk with Mrs. Frey—"

"If you don't mind, Miss Darrow," Archer suggested gently, "just the facts now."

"Yes, of course." She sent him a glance and returned to me. "I told her I thought she was completely wrong. I said that if her husband had been untrue to her, or anything like that, that would be different, but after all he hadn't done wrong to her, only to other people and himself, and that she should try to help him instead of destroying him. At the very least, I said, she should wait until she knew all the details of what he had done. I think that was what she wanted to hear, but she didn't say so. She was very stubborn. Then, that afternoon, I did something that I will regret all my life. I went to Barry and told him she had told me about it, and said I was sure it would come out all right if he would meet her halfway—tell her the whole thing, tell her he was sorry, as he certainly should be—and no more foolishness in the future. And Barry said he loved me."

She weakened a little there for the first time. She dropped her eyes. I had been boring at her with as steady and sharp a gaze as I had in me, but up to that point she had met it full and fair.

"So then?" I asked.

Her eyes lifted and she marched on. "He said he didn't want it to come out all right because he loved me. Shall I try to tell you what I—how I felt?"

"Not now. Just what happened."

"Nothing happened then. That was in the middle of the afternoon. I didn't tell Barry I loved him—I didn't even know I loved him then. I got away from him. Later we gathered in the living room for cocktails, and you and Mr. Leeds came, and we played that game —you remember."

"Yep, I do."

"And dinner, and television afterward, and—"

"Excuse me. That is common knowledge. Skip to later, when the cops had come. Did you tell them all this?"

"No."

"Why not?"

"Because I didn't think it would be fair to Barry. I didn't think he had killed her, and I didn't know what criminal things he had helped with, and I thought it wouldn't be fair to tell that about him when all I knew was what Mrs. Rackham had told me." The fine eyes flashed for the first time. "Oh, I know the next part. Then why am I telling it now? Because I know more about him now—a great deal more! I don't know that he killed Mrs. Rackham, but I know he could have; he is cruel and selfish and unscrupulous—there is nothing he wouldn't do. I suppose you think I'm vindictive, and maybe I am, but it doesn't matter what you think about me as long as I'm telling the truth. What the criminal things were that he did, and whether he killed his wife—I don't know anything about it; that's your part."

"Not mine, sister. I'm not a cop."

She turned to the others. "Yours, then!"

This would have been a good moment for me to take time out to read my signed statement, since I could have used a few minutes for some good healthy thinking. Here was a situation that was new to me. About all that Barry Rackham's ticket to the electric chair needed was my endorsement, and I thought he had it coming to him. All I had to do was tell the truth. I could say that I had no knowledge whatever of the phone call Nero Wolfe was purported to have made to Mrs. Rackham, but that it was conceivable that he had made such a call without mentioning it to me, since he had often withheld information from me regarding his actions and intentions. You couldn't beat that for truth. On various occasions I had used all my wits to help pin it on a murderer, and here it would take no wit at all, merely tossing in a couple of facts.

But if I let it go at that, it was a cinch that before the sun went down Rackham would be locked up, and that would ruin everything. The program sunk, the months all wasted, the one chance gone, Zeck sailing on with the authority of his superior intellect, and Wolfe and me high and dry. My wits had a new job, and quick. I liked to think that they had done their share once or twice in getting a murderer corraled; now it was up to them to do more than their share in keeping a murderer running loose and free to keep appointments. Truth was not enough.

There was no time to draw a sketch and see how I liked it. All three of them were looking at me, and Archer was saying, "You can see, Goodwin, why I wanted you to read your statement and see if you left anything out."

"Yeah." I was regretful. "I can also see you holding your breath, and I don't blame you. If I now say that's right, I forgot, Wolfe did phone Mrs. Rackham that Friday evening and tell her that, you've got all you need and hallelujah. I would love to help out, but I like to stick to the truth as far as practical."

"The truth is all I'm asking for. Did you call on Rackham at his apartment yesterday afternoon?"

That punch had of course been telegraphed. "Yes," I said.

"What for?"

"On a job for a client. At first it was a tailing job, and then when Rackham spotted me my client thought I might learn something by chatting with him."

"Why is your client interested in Rackham?"

"He didn't say."

"Who's the client?"

I shook my head. "I don't think that would help you any. He's a man who came here recently from the West Coast, and I suspect he's connected with gambling or rackets or both, but my suspicions are no good at the bank. Let's table it for now."

"I want the name, Goodwin."

"And I want to protect my client within reason. You can't connect him up with the murder you're investigating. Go ahead and start the rigmarole. Charge me again as a material witness and I get released on bail. Meanwhile I'll be wanting my lawyer present and all that runaround. What will it get you in the long run?"

Ben Dykes said in a nasty voice, "We don't want to be arbitrary about it. We wouldn't expect you to name a client if you haven't got one. West Coast, huh?"

"Is Rackham your client?" Archer asked.

"No."

"Have you done any work for him?"

"No."

"Has he given you or paid you any money in the past week?"

That was enough and to spare. I was hooked good, and if the best I could do was flop around trying to wriggle off, the outlook was damn thin. "Oh," I said, "so that's it." I gave Lina Darrow an appreciative look and then transferred it to Archer. "This narrows it down. I've collected for withholding evidence against a murderer. That's bad, isn't it?"

No one answered. They just looked at me.

So I went on. "First, I hereby state that I have no money from Rackham, and that's all on that for now. Second, I'm a little handicapped because although I know what Miss Darrow has in her mind, I don't know how it got there. She's framing Rackham for murder, or trying to, but I'm not sure whether it's her own idea or whether she has been nudged. I would have to find out about that first before I could decide how I stand. I know you've got to give me the works, and that's all right, it's your job, you've got all day and all night for it, but you can take your pick. Either I clam up as of now, and I mean clam, and you start prying at me, or first I am allowed to have a talk with Miss Darrow—with you here, of course. Then you can have the rest of the week with me. Well?"

"No," Archer said emphatically.

"Okay. May I borrow some adhesive tape?"

"We know everything Miss Darrow has to say."

"Sure you do. I want to catch up. I said with you here. You can always stop it if you get bored."

Archer looked at Dykes. I don't know whether he would have rather had Dykes nod his head or shake it, but he got neither. All Dykes did was concentrate.

"You gentlemen," I said, "want only one thing, to crack the case. It certainly won't help if I shut my trap and breathe through my nose. It certainly won't hurt if I converse with Miss Darrow in your presence."

"Let him," Lina said belligerently. "I knew he would deny it."

"What do you want to ask her?" Archer demanded.

"The best way to find that out is to listen." I turned to Lina. "When I saw you yesterday afternoon, coming out of his apartment, I thought something was stirring. It was rude the way you went right by me."

She met my gaze but had no comment.

"Was it yesterday," I asked, "that he treated you badly?"

"Not only yesterday," she said evenly. "But yesterday he refused definitely and finally to marry me."

"Is that so bad? I mean, a guy can't marry everyone."

"He has said he would—many times."

"But hadn't you been keeping your fingers crossed? After all, it was a kind of a special situation. He knew that you knew something that would get him arrested for murder if you spilled it—not to mention other criminal things, whatever they were. Didn't it occur to you that he might be kidding you along for security reasons?"

"Yes, I—yes, it did, but I didn't want to believe it. He said he loved me. He made love to me—and I wanted him for my husband." She decided that wasn't adequate and improved on it. "I wanted him so much!" she exclaimed.

"I'll bet you did." I tried not to sound sarcastic. "How do you feel about it now? Do you think he ever loved you?"

"No, I don't! I think he was heartless and cruel. I think he was afraid of me. He just wanted me not to tell what I knew. And I began to suspect—the way he acted—and yesterday I insisted that we must be married immediately, this week, and when I insisted he lost his temper and he was—he was hateful."

"I know he's got a temper. Was there any urgent reason for wanting to get married quick, like expecting a visitor from heaven, for instance a baby?"

She flushed and appealed to Archer. "Do I have to let him insult me?"

"I beg your pardon," I said stiffly, "but you seem to be pretty sensitive for a woman who was hell-bent to marry a murderer. Did—"

"I didn't know he was a murderer! I only knew if I told about what Mrs. Rackham told me and what he told me—I knew he would be suspected even more than he was."

"Uh-huh. When the blowup came yesterday, did you threaten to tell what you knew?"

"Yes."

I goggled at her. "You know, sister," I declared, "you should have spent more time thinking this through. You are unquestionably the bummest liar I have ever run across. I thought maybe—"

Dykes broke in. "She says Rackham probably figured he wasn't in much danger, so many months had passed."

"Yeah? That's partly what I mean. Whatever she says, what about Rackham? He's not boob enough to figure like that. He would know damn well that five months is nothing in the life of a murder. He has his choice between marrying this attractive specimen or having her run to you with the ink for his death warrant, and not only does he act heartless and cruel, he actually opens the door for her to go! This guy who had it in him to sneak into the woods at night with a knife to stab his wife to death *and* a fighting dog—he just opens the door for this poor pretty creature to tell the world about it! My God, you would buy that?"

"You can't tell about people," Archer said. "And she has details. Take the detail of the phone call Wolfe made to Mrs. Rackham and what he told her about her husband. Not even a good liar would have that detail, let alone a bum one."

"Nuts." I was disgusted. "No such phone call was made, and Mrs. Rackham never said it was. As for Rackham's having been in with crooks, either he wasn't and sister here invented it, in which case you'd better watch your step, or he was, and sister here got his tongue loosened enough for him to tell her about it. I'm perfectly willing to believe she is capable of that, however bum a liar she may be."

"You say Wolfe didn't make that call to Mrs. Rackham?"

"Yes."

"And he didn't learn that Rackham's income came from a connection with criminal activities?"

"My God, Mrs. Rackham didn't leave our office until after noon that Friday. And he called her that evening to tell her? When he hadn't moved a finger to start an inquiry, and I hadn't either? He was good, but not that good." I turned to Lina. "I thought maybe you had had a coach for this, possibly got in with some professionals yourself, but not now, the way you tell it. Obviously this is your own baby—I beg your pardon if you don't want babies mentioned—say your own script—and it is indeed a lulu. Framing a man for murder is no job for an amateur. Aside from the idea of Rackham's preferring a jury trial to you, which if I may get personal is plain loco, look at other features. If it had been the way you say, what would Wolfe and I have done after I phoned him that night and told him Mrs. Rackham had got it? Our only interest was the fee she had paid us. Why didn't we just hand it all to the cops? Another little feature, do you remember that gathering that evening? Did either Rackham or his wife act like people who were riding the kind of storm you describe? Don't ask me, I could be prejudiced; ask all the others."

I left her for Archer. "I could go on for an hour, but don't tell me you need it. I don't wonder you grabbed at it, it looked as if it might possibly be the break you had been hoping for, and besides, she had fixed it up with some trimmings that might be very juicy, like the crap about me working for Rackham. I have not and am not, and I have none of his dough. Must I punch more holes in it?"

Archer was studying me. "Is it your contention that Miss Darrow invented all this?"

"It is."

"Why?"

I shrugged. "I don't know. Do you want me to guess?"

"Yes."

"Well—my best one first. Have you noticed her eyes—the deep light in them? I think she's trying to take over for you. She liked Mrs. Rackham, and when she got left that two hundred grand it went to her head. She thought Rackham had killed her—I don't know whether it was a hunch or what—and when time passed and it looked as if he wasn't going to get tagged for it, she decided it was her duty or mission, or whatever word she uses for it, to step in. Having the two hundred grand, she could afford a hobby for a while. That was when she started to put the eyes on Rackham. I expect she thought she could get him into a state where he would dump it all out for her, and then she would not only know she was right but would also be able to complete her mission. But the months went by and he never dumped, and it probably got a little embarrassing, and she got fanatic about it, and she must even have got desperate, judging by the performance she finally ended up with. She decided Rackham was guilty, that part was all right, and the only thing lacking was evidence, so it was up to her to furnish it."

I leaned forward at her. "It's not enough to want to do a good deed, you damn fool. Wanting is fine, but you also need some slight idea of how to go about it. It didn't bother you that one by-product was making me out a cheap crook, did it? Many thanks sincerely yours."

She dropped her head into her hands to cover her face, and convulsions began.

They sat and looked at her. I looked at them. Archer was pulling jerkily at his lower lip. Dykes was shaking his head, his lips compressed.

"I suggest," I said modestly, raising my voice to carry over the noise Lina Darrow was making, "that when she quiets down it might pay to find out if Rackham has told her anything that might help. That item about his getting dough from gambling or rackets could be true, if they actually got intimate enough for him to tell her the story of his life."

They kept their eyes on her. She was crying away what had looked like a swell chance to wrap up a tough one, and I wouldn't have been surprised if they had burst into tears too. I pushed back my chair and stood up.

"If you get anything that I can be of any help on, give me a ring. I'll have a crowded afternoon, but word will reach me."

I walked out.

19

As I hit the sidewalk in front of the courthouse my watch said 11:17. It was sunny and warm, and people looked as if they felt pleased with the way things were going. I did not. In another few minutes they would have Lina Darrow talking again, and whether she gave it to them straight this time or tried her hand on a revised version, they might decide any minute that they wanted to talk with Barry Rackham, and that could lead to anything. The least it could lead to was delay, and my nerves were in no condition for it.

I dived across the street to a drugstore, found a booth, and dialed Roeder's number. No answer. I went to where my car was parked, got in, and headed for the parkway.

On my way back to Manhattan I stopped four times to find a phone and dial Roeder's number, and the fourth try, at a Hundred and Sixteenth Street, I got him. I told him where I was. He asked what they had wanted at White Plains.

"Nothing much, just to ask some questions about a lead they had got. I'm going to the Churchill to fix it to go ahead with that date today."

"You can't. It has been postponed until tomorrow at the other end. Arrange it for tomorrow."

"Can't you switch it back to today at your end?"

"It would be difficult and therefore inadvisable."

I considered how to put it, in view of the fact that there was no telling who or how many might hear me. "There is a possibility," I said, "that the Churchill will have a vacant suite tomorrow. So my opinion is that it would be even more inadvisable to postpone it. I don't know, but I have an idea that it may be today or never."

A silence. Then, "How long will it take you to get to your office?"

"Fifteen minutes, maybe twenty."

"Go there and wait."

I returned to the car, drove to a parking lot on Third Avenue in the upper Forties, left the car there, and made steps to Madison

Avenue and up to 1019. I sat down, stood at the window, sat down, and stood at the window. I wouldn't ring the phone-answering service because I wanted my line free, but after a few minutes I began thinking I better had, in case Roeder had tried for me before I arrived. The debate on that was getting hot when the ring came and I jumped for it.

It was Roeder. He asked me through his nose, "Have you phoned the Churchill?"

"No, I was waiting to hear from you."

"I hope you will have no trouble. It has been arranged for today at four o'clock."

I felt a tingle in my spine. My throat wanted to tighten, but I wouldn't let it. "I'll do my best. In my car?"

"No. I'll have a car. I'll stop in front of your office building precisely at two forty-five."

"It might be better to make it the Churchill."

"No. Your building. If you have to reach me I'll be here until two-thirty. I hope you won't have to."

"I do too."

I pressed the button down, held it for three breaths, and dialed the Churchill's number. It was only ten to one, so surely I would get him.

I did. As soon as he heard my name he started yapping about the message I had sent him, but I didn't want to try to fix it on the phone, so I merely said I had managed to call off the trip out of town and was coming to see him. He said he didn't want to see me. I said I didn't want to see him either, but we were both stuck with this and I would be there at one-thirty.

At a fountain service down on a side street I ate three corned-beef sandwiches and three glasses of milk without knowing how they tasted, burned my tongue on hot coffee, and then walked to the Churchill and took the elevator to the tower.

Rackham was eating lunch, and it was pitiful. Apparently he had done all right with a big glass of clam juice, since the glass was empty and I couldn't see where the contents had been thrown at anything, but all he did in my presence was peck at things—some wonderful broiled ham, hashed brown potatoes, an artichoke with anchovy sauce, and half a melon. He swallowed perhaps five bites altogether, while I sat at a distance with a magazine, not wanting to disturb his meal. When, arriving, I had told him that the ap-

pointment with Zeck was set for four o'clock, he had just glared at
me with no comment. Now, as he sat staring at his coffee without
lifting the cup, I got up and crossed to a chair near him and remarked that we would ride up to Westchester with Roeder.

I don't think I handled it very well, that talk with Barry Rackham,
as he sat and let his coffee get cold and tried to pretend to himself
that he still intended to eat the melon. It happened that he had
already decided that his only way out was to come to some kind of
an understanding with Arnold Zeck, but if he had been balky I
doubt if I would have been able to manage it. I was so damned
edgy that it was all I could do to sit still. It had been a long spring
and summer, those five months, and here was the day that would
give us the answer. So there are two reasons why I don't report in
detail what Rackham and I said there that afternoon: first, I doubt
if it affected the outcome any, one way or another; and second, I
don't remember a word of it. Except that I finally said it was time
to go, and he got himself a man-sized straight bourbon and poured
it down.

We walked the few blocks to my building. As we waited at the
curb I kept my eyes peeled for a Chevvy sedan, but apparently
Roeder had been promoted, either that or the Chevvy wasn't used
for important guests, for when a car nosed in to us it was a shiny
black Cadillac. I got in front with the driver and Rackham joined
Roeder in the rear. They didn't shake hands when I pronounced
names. The driver was new to me—a stocky middle-aged number
with black hair and squinty black eyes. He had nothing whatever
to say to anyone, and for that matter neither did anybody else, all
the way to our destination. Once on the Taconic State Parkway a
car passed and cut in ahead of us so short that it damn near grazed
our bumper, and the driver muttered something, and I went so far
as to glance at him but ventured no words. Anyway my mind was
occupied.

Evidently Rackham had been there before with his eyes open,
for there was no suggestion that he should take to the floor, and of
course I was now a B. We left the parkway a couple of miles south
of Millwood, to the right, followed a curving secondary road a while,
turned onto another main route, soon left it for another secondary
road, and after some more curves hit concrete again. The garage was
at a four-corners a little out of Mount Kisco, and I never did know
what the idea was of that roundabout way of getting there. In front

it looked like any other garage, with gas-pumps and a graveled plaza, and cars and miscellaneous objects around, except that it seemed a little large for its location. Two men were there in front, one dressed like a mechanic and the other in a summer suit, even a necktie, and they exchanged nods with our driver as we headed in.

The big room we drove into was normal too, like a thousand others anywhere, but a variation was coming. Our car rolled across, past pillars, to the far end, and stopped just in front of a big closed door, and our driver stuck his head out, but said nothing. Nothing happened for thirty seconds; then the big door slowly opened, rising; the driver pulled his head in, and the car went forward. As we cleared the entrance the door started back down, and by the time we had eased across to a stop the door was shut again, and our reception committee was right there—two on one side and one on the other. I had seen two of them before, but one was a stranger. The stranger was in shirt sleeves, with his gun in a belt holster.

Stepping out, I announced, "I've got that same gun under my armpit."

"Okay, Goodwin," the tenor said. "We'll take care of it."

They did. I may have been a B, but there was no discernible difference between inspection of a B and of an unknown. In fact, it seemed to me that they were slightly more thorough than they had been on Sunday, which may have been because there were three of us. They did us one at a time, with me first, then Rackham, then Roeder. With Roeder they were a little more superficial. They went over him, but not so enthusiastically, and all they did with the brief-case was open it and glance inside and let Roeder himself shut it again.

One change from Sunday was that two of them, not one, accompanied us to the door in the rear wall, and through, across the vesti-bule, and down the fourteen steps to the first metal door. The sentinel who opened and let us in was the same pasty-faced bird with a pointed chin—Schwartz. This time the other sentinel did not stay at the table with his book work. He was right there with Schwartz, and interested in the callers, especially Rackham.

"We're a little early," Roeder said, "but they sent us on in."

"That's all right," Schwartz rumbled. "He's ahead of schedule today. One didn't come."

He went to the big metal door at the other end, pulled it open, and jerked his head. "On in."

Entering, Roeder took the lead, then Rackham, then me. Schwartz brought up the rear. He came in three paces and stood. Arnold Zeck, from behind his desk, told him, in the cold precise tone that he used for everything, "All right, Schwartz."

Schwartz left us. As the door closed I hoped to heaven it was as soundproof as it was supposed to be.

Zeck spoke. "The last time you were here, Rackham, you lost control of yourself and you know what happened."

Rackham did not reply. He stood with his hands behind him like a man ready to begin a speech, but his trap stayed shut, and from the expression of his face it was a good guess that his hands, out of sight, were making a tight knot.

"Sit down," Zeck told him.

Since the seating was an important item of the staging, I had stepped up ahead after we entered and made for the chair farthest front, a little to the left of Zeck's desk and about even with it, and Roeder had taken the one nearest me, to my right. That left, for Rackham, of the chairs near the desk, the one on the other side, and he went to it. He was about twelve feet from Zeck, Roeder about the same, and I was slightly closer.

Zeck asked Roeder, "Have you had a talk?"

Roeder shook his head. "Since Mr. Rackham had never met me before, I thought it might be better for you to explain the proposal to him. Naturally he will want to know exactly how it is to be handled before deciding whether to help with it." He reached to get his briefcase from the floor, put it on his lap, and opened it.

"I think," Zeck said, "that you should describe the operation, since you conceived it and will manage it. But you were right to wait." He turned to Rackham. "You remember our last talk some time ago."

Rackham said nothing.

"You remember it?" Zeck demanded. He made it a demand by the faintest possible sharpening of his tone.

"I remember it," Rackham stated, not much above a whisper.

"You know the position you took. Ordinarily that course is not permitted to any man who has been given a place in my organization, and I made an exception of you only because the death of your wife had changed your circumstances. I thought it better to await an opportunity to take advantage of that change, and now it has come—through Roeder here. We want your help and we are prepared to insist on getting it. How do you feel about it?"

"I don't know." Rackham licked his lips. "I'd have to know more about what you want."

Zeck nodded. "But first your attitude. You will need to recognize the existence of mutual interests—yours and mine."

Rackham said nothing.

"Well?" The faint sharpening.

"Damn it, of course I recognize them!"

"Good. Go ahead, Roeder."

Roeder had got some papers from his briefcase. One of them fluttered away from him, and I left my chair to retrieve it for him. I believe he did that on purpose. I believe he knew that now that the moment had come every nerve and muscle in me was on a hair trigger, and he was giving me an excuse to loosen them up.

"As I understand it," he said, "we're going to give Rackham a cut, and before I tell him about it I wish you'd take a look at this revised list of percentages. Yours is of course fixed, and I don't like to reduce mine unless it's absolutely unavoidable . . ."

He had a sheet of paper in his hand. With his briefcase on his lap, and loose papers, it was awkward for him to get up, so I obliged. I reached, and he handed me the paper, and I had to leave my chair to get it to Zeck. On my way I took a glance at the paper because I thought it was in character to do that, and if I ever needed my character to stay put for another four seconds I did right then. When I extended my hand to Zeck I released the paper an instant too soon and it started to drop. I grabbed at it and missed, and that made me take another step and bend over, which put me in exactly the right position to take him away from there before he could possibly get a toe on one of the buttons under his desk.

Not wanting to knock his chair over, I used my left knee to push him back, chair and all, my right knee to land on his thighs and keep him there, and my hands for his throat. There was only one thing in my mind at that precise instant, the instant I had him away from the desk, and that was the fear that I would break his neck. Since I was in front of him I had to make absolutely sure, not only that he didn't yap, but also that he was too uncomfortable to try things like jabbing his thumbs in my eyes, but God knows I didn't want to overdo it, and bones and tendons are by no means all alike.

What will be merely an inconvenience for one man will finish another one for good.

His mouth was open wide and his shark eyes were popping. With my knee on him he couldn't kick, and his arms were just flopping around. And Roeder was there by me, with a wadded handkerchief in one hand and a piece of cord in the other. As soon as he had the handkerchief stuffed tight in the open mouth he moved to the rear of the chair, taking Zeck's right hand with him, and reached around for the left hand. It tried to elude him, and I increased the pressure of my fingers a little, and then he got it.

"Hurry up," I growled, "or I'll kill him sure as hell."

It took him a year. It took him forever. But finally he straightened up, came around to take another look at the handkerchief and poke it in a little tighter, backed up, and muttered, "All right, Archie."

When I took my hands away my fingers ached like the devil, but that was nerves, not muscles. I leaned over to get my ear an inch away from his nose; there was no question about his breathing.

"His pulse is all right," Roeder said, not through his nose.

"You're crazy," Rackham said hoarsely. "Good God! You're crazy!"

He was out of his chair, standing there in front of it, trembling all over. Roeder's hand went to his side pocket for the Carson Snub Thirty, which he had got from the briefcase along with the piece of cord. I took it and aimed it at Rackham.

"Sit down," I said, "and stay."

He sank down into the chair. I moved to the end of the desk so as to have him in a corner of my eye while looking at Zeck. Roeder, at my left elbow, spoke rapidly but distinctly.

"Mr. Zeck," he said, "you told me on the telephone two years ago that you had great admiration for me. I hope that what has just happened here has increased it. I'm Nero Wolfe, of course. There are many things it would give me satisfaction to say to you, and perhaps I shall some day, but not now. It is true that if one of your men suddenly opened the door Mr. Goodwin would kill you first, but I'm afraid you'd have company. So I'll get on. Having by your admission matched you in intellect, it's a question of will, and mine has not failed me, as you thought. Confound it, I wish you could speak."

The expression of Zeck's eyes, no longer popping, indicated that Wolfe had nothing on him there.

"Here's the situation," Wolfe went on. "During the two months I've been here in this outlandish guise I have collected enough evidence to get you charged on thirty counts under Federal law. I assure you that the evidence is sound and sufficient, and is in the hands of a man whom you cannot stop or deflect. You'll have to take my word for it that if that evidence is produced and used you are done for, and that it will be immediately produced and used if anything untoward happens to Mr. Goodwin or me. I fancy you will take my word since you admit that I match you in intellect, and to climax these five frightful months with such a bluff as this, if it were one, would be witless. However, if you think I'm bluffing there's no point in going on. If you think I'm bluffing, please shake your head no, meaning you don't believe me."

No shake.

"If you think I have the evidence as described, please nod your head."

No nod.

"I warn you," Wolfe said sharply, "that Mr. Goodwin and I are both ready for anything whatever."

Zeck nodded. Nothing violent, but a nod.

"You assume my possession of the evidence?"

Zeck nodded again.

"Good. Then we can bargain. While I have great respect for the Federal laws, I am under no obligation to catch violators of them. Without compunction I can leave that to others. But I am under an obligation to a certain individual which I feel strongly and which I must discharge. Mrs. Rackham paid me a large sum to serve her interest, and the next day she was murdered. It was clearly my duty to expose her murderer—not only my duty to her but to my own self-respect—and I have failed. With an obligation of that nature I have never accepted failure and do not intend to. Mr. Goodwin, working in my behalf, has been a party to that failure, and he too will not accept it."

Zeck nodded again, or I thought he did, probably to signify approval of our high moral standards.

"So we can bargain," Wolfe told him. "You said day before yesterday that you have evidence, or can easily get it, that will convict Rackham of the murder of his wife. Was that true?"

Zeck nodded. The shark eyes were intent on Wolfe.

"Very well. I believe you because I know what you are capable of. I offer a trade. I'll trade you the evidence I have collected against you for the evidence that will convict Rackham. Will you make the trade?"

Zeck nodded.

"It will have to be more or less on my terms. I can be trusted; you cannot. You will have to deliver first. But I realize that the details of anything as vital as this is to you cannot be settled without discussion, and it must be discussed and settled now. We are going to release your hands and take that handkerchief from your mouth, but before we do so, one more warning. You are to stay where you are until we're finished. If you move toward the floor signals under your desk, or try to summon your men in any other manner, you will die before anyone else does. Also, of course, there is the evidence that exists against you. You understand the situation?"

Zeck nodded.

"Are you ready to discuss the matter?"

Zeck nodded.

"Release him, Archie," Wolfe snapped.

Needing two hands to untie the cord, I put the Carson Snub Thirty down on the polished top of Zeck's desk. I would have given a year's pay for a glance at Rackham, to see what the chances were, but that might have ruined it. So I put the gun there, stepped around to the rear of Zeck's chair, knelt, and started untying the knot. My heart was pounding my ribs like a sledgehammer.

So I didn't see it happen; I could only hear it. I did see one thing there behind Zeck's chair: a sudden convulsive jerk of his arms, which must have been his reaction to the sight of Rackham jumping for the gun I had left on the desk. More even than a sight of Rackham, to see if he was rising to it, I wanted a sight of Wolfe, to see if he was keeping his promise to duck for cover the instant Rackham started for the gun, but I couldn't afford it. My one desperate job now was to get that cord off of Zeck's wrists in time, and while Wolfe had used the trick knot we had practiced with, he had made it damn tight. I barely had it free and was unwinding the cord from the wrists when the sound of the shot came, followed immediately by another.

As I got the cord off and jammed it in my pocket, Zeck's torso slumped sideways and then forward. Flat on the floor, I slewed around, saw Zeck's contorted face right above my eyes, pulled the handkerchief out of his mouth and stuffed it in my pocket with the cord, slid forward under the desk, and reached for one of the signal buttons.

I didn't know, and don't know yet, whether the noise of the shots had got through the soundproof door or whether it was my push on the button that brought them. I didn't hear the door open, but the next shots I heard were a fusillade that came from no Carson, so I came back out from under the desk and on up to my feet. Schwartz and his buddy were standing just inside the door, one with two guns and one with one. Rackham was stretched out on the floor, flat on his face. Wolfe was standing at the end of the desk, facing the door, scowling as I had never seen him scowl before.

"The dirty bastard," I said bitterly, and I admit my voice might have trembled even if I hadn't told it to.

"Reach up," Schwartz said, advancing.

Neither Wolfe nor I moved a muscle. But Wolfe spoke. "What for?" He was even bitterer than me, and contemptuous. "They let him in armed, not us."

"Watch 'em, Harry," Schwartz said, and came forward and on around behind the desk where I was. Ignoring me, he bent over Zeck's collapsed body, spent half a minute with it, and then straightened and turned.

"He's gone," he said.

Harry, from near the door, squealed incredulously. "He's gone?"

"He's gone," Schwartz said.

Harry wheeled, pushed the door open, and was gone too.

Schwartz stared after him three seconds, not more than that, then jumped as if I had pinched him, made for the door, and on through.

I went and took a look at Rackham, found he was even deader than Zeck, and turned to Wolfe. "Okay, that's enough. Come on."

"No." He was grim. "It will be safer when they've all skedaddled. Phone the police."

"From here?"

"Yes."

I went to Zeck's desk and pulled one of the phones to me.

"Wait." I had never heard him so grim. "First get Marko's number. I want to speak to Fritz."

"Now? For God's sake, now?"

"Yes. Now. A man has a right to have his satisfactions match his pains. I wish to use Mr. Zeck's phone to tell Fritz to go home and get dinner ready."

I dialed the operator.

20

Three days later, Friday afternoon, I said to Wolfe, "Anyway, it's all over now, isn't it?"

"No, confound it," he said peevishly. "I still have to earn that fee."

It was six o'clock, and he had come down from the plant rooms with some more pointed remarks about the treatment the plants had got at Hewitt's place. The remarks were completely uncalled for. Considering the two journeys they had taken, out to Long Island and then back again, the plants were in splendid shape, especially those hard to handle like the Miltonias and Phalaenopsis. Wolfe was merely trying to sell the idea, at least to himself, that the orchids had missed him.

Fritz might have been a mother whose lost little boy has been brought home after wandering in the desert for days, living on cactus pulp and lizards' tails. Wolfe had gained not an ounce less than ten pounds in seventy-two hours, in spite of all the activity of getting resettled, and at the rate he was going he would be back to normal long before Thanksgiving. The pleats in his face were already showing a tendency to spread out, and of course the beard was gone, and the slick had been shampooed out of his hair. I had tried to persuade him to stay in training, but he wouldn't even bother to put up an argument. He just spent more time than ever with Fritz, arranging about meals.

He had not got home for dinner Tuesday evening after all, in spite of the satisfaction he had got by putting in a call to Fritz on Zeck's phone. We were now cleaned up with Westchester, but it had not been simple. The death of Arnold Zeck had of course started a chain reaction that went both deep and wide, and naturally there had been an earnest desire to make goats out of Wolfe and me, but they didn't have a damn thing on us, and when word came from somewhere that Wolfe, during his association with Zeck, might have collected some facts that could be embarrassing to people who shouldn't be embarrassed, the attitude toward us changed for the better right away.

As for the scene that ended with the death of Zeck and Rackham, we were clean as a whistle. The papers in Roeder's briefcase, which of course the cops took, proved nothing on anybody. By the time the cops arrived, there had been no one on the premises but Wolfe and me and the two corpses. A hot search was on, especially for Schwartz and Harry, but so far no take. No elaborate lying was required; our basic story was that Wolfe, in his disguise as Roeder, had got in with Zeck in order to solve the murder of Mrs. Rackham, and the climax had come that afternoon when Zeck had put the screws on Rackham by saying that he had evidence that would convict him for killing his wife, and Rackham had pulled a gun, smuggled somehow past the sentinels, and had shot Zeck, and Schwartz and Harry had rushed in and drilled Rackham. It was surprising and gratifying to note how much of it was strictly true.

So by Friday afternoon we were cleaned up with Westchester, as I thought, and therefore it was a minor shock when Wolfe said, "No, confound it, I still have to earn that fee."

I was opening my mouth to ask him how come, when the phone rang. I got it. It was Annabel Frey. She wanted to speak to Wolfe. I told him so. He frowned and reached for his phone, and I stayed on.

"Yes, Mrs. Frey? This is Nero Wolfe."

"I want to ask you a favor, Mr. Wolfe. That is, I expect to pay for it of course, but still it's a favor. Could you and Mr. Goodwin come up here this evening? To my home, Birchvale?"

"I'm sorry, Mrs. Frey, but it's out of the question. I transact business only in my office. I never leave it."

That was a little thick, I thought, from a guy who had just spent five months the way he had. And if she read newspapers she knew all about it—or anyhow some.

"I'm sorry," she said, "because we must see you. Mr. Archer is here, the District Attorney, and I'm calling at his suggestion. We have a problem—two problems, really."

"By 'we' do you mean you and Mr. Archer?"

"No, I mean all of us—all of us who inherited property from Mrs. Rackham, and all of us who were here the night she was killed. Our problem is about evidence that her husband killed her. Mr. Archer says he has none, none that is conclusive—and perhaps you know what people are saying, and the newspapers. That's what we want to consult you about—the evidence."

"Well." A pause. "I'm trying to get a little rest after a long period of overexertion. But—very well. Who is there?"

"We all are. We met to discuss this. You'll come? Wonderful! If you—"

"I didn't say I'll come. All five of you are there?"

"Yes—and Mr. Archer—"

"Be at my office, all of you, at nine o'clock this evening. Including Mr. Archer."

"But I don't know if he will—"

"I think he will. Tell him I'll be ready then to produce the evidence."

"Oh, you will? Then you can tell me now—"

"Not on the phone, Mrs. Frey. I'll be expecting you at nine."

When we had hung up I lifted the brows at him. "So that's what you meant about earning that fee? Maybe?"

He grunted, irritated that he had to interrupt his convalescence for a job of work, sat a moment, reached for a bottle of the beer Fritz had brought, grunted again, this time with satisfaction, and poured a glass with plenty of foam.

I got up to go to the kitchen, to tell Fritz we were having company and that refreshments might be required.

21

I was mildly interested when the six guests arrived—a little early, five to nine—in such minor issues as the present state of relations between Annabel Frey and the banker, Dana Hammond, and between Lina Darrow and the statesman, Oliver Pierce, and whether Calvin Leeds would see fit to apologize for his unjust suspicions about Wolfe and me.

To take the last first, Leeds was all out of apologies. The spring was in his step all right, but not in his manners. First to enter the office, he plumped himself down in the red leather chair, but I figured that Archer rated it ex officio and asked him to move, which he did without grace. As for the others, there was too much atmosphere to get any clear idea. They were all on speaking terms, but the problem that brought them there was in the front of their minds, so much so that no one was interested in the array of liquids and accessories that Fritz and I had arranged on the table over by the big globe. Annabel was in the most comfortable of the yellow chairs, to Archer's left; then, working toward me at my desk, Leeds and Lina Darrow; and Hammond and Pierce closest to me.

Wolfe's eyes swept the arc.

"This," he said, "is a little awkward for me. I have met none of you before except Mr. Leeds. I must be sure I have you straight." His eyes went along the line again. "I think I have. Now if you'll tell me what you want—you, Mrs. Frey, it was you who phoned me."

Annabel looked at the DA. "Shouldn't you, Mr. Archer?"

He shook his head. "No, you tell him."

She concentrated, at Wolfe. "Well, as I said, there are two problems. One is that it seems to be supposed that Barry Rackham killed his wife, but it hasn't been proven, and now that he is dead how can it be proven so that everyone will know it and the rest of us will be entirely free of any suspicion? Mr. Archer says there is no official suspicion of us, but that isn't enough."

"It is gratifying, though," Wolfe murmured.

"Yes, but it isn't gratifying to have some of the people who say they are your friends looking at you as they do." Annabel was earnest about it. "Then the second problem is this. The law will not allow a man who commits a murder to profit by it. If Barry Rackham killed his wife he can't inherit property from her, no matter what her will said. But it has to be legally proven that he killed her, and unless that is done her will stands, and what she left to him will go to his heirs."

She made a gesture. "It isn't that we want it—the rest of us. It can go to the state or to charity—we don't care. But we think it's wrong and a shame for it to go to his people, whoever will inherit from him. It's not only immoral, it's illegal. It can't be stopped by convicting him of murder, because he's dead and can't be tried. My lawyer and Mr. Archer both say we can bring action and get it before a court, but then we'll have to have evidence that he killed her, and Mr. Archer says he hasn't been able to get it from you, and he hasn't got it. But surely you can get it, or anyhow you can try. You see, that would solve both problems, to have a court rule that his heirs can't inherit because he murdered her."

"You have stated it admirably," Archer declared.

"We don't want any of it," Lina blurted.

"My interest," Pierce put in, "is only to have the truth fully and universally known and acknowledged."

"That," Wolfe said, "will take more than me. I am by no means up to that. And not only my capacities, but the circumstances themselves, restrict me to a much more modest ambition. I can get you one of the things you want, removal of all suspicion from the innocent, but the other, having Mrs. Rackham's bequest to her husband set aside, is beyond me."

They all frowned at him, in their various fashions. Hammond, the banker, protested, "That doesn't seem to make sense. What accomplishes one accomplishes the other. If you prove that Rackham killed his wife—"

"But I can't prove that." Wolfe shook his head. "I'm sorry, but it can't be done. It is true that Rackham deserved to die, and as a murderer. He killed a woman here in New York three years ago, a woman named Delia Montrose—one of Mr. Cramer's unsolved cases; Rackham ran his car over her. That was how Zeck originally got a noose on Rackham, by threatening to expose him for the murder he did commit. As you know, Mr. Archer, I penetrated some distance —not very far, but far enough—into Zeck's confidence, and I learned a good deal about his methods. I doubt if he ever had conclusive evidence that Rackham had killed Delia Montrose, but Rackham, conscious of his guilt, hadn't the spine to demand a showdown. Murderers seldom have. Then Rackham got a spine, suddenly and fortuitously, by becoming a millionaire; he thought then he could fight it; he defied Zeck; and Zeck, taking his time, retorted by threatening to expose Rackham for the murder of his wife. The threat was dangerous and effective even without authentic evidence to support it; there could of course be no authentic evidence that Rackham killed his wife, because he didn't."

They all froze, still wearing the frowns. Knowing Wolfe as I did, I had suspected that was coming, so I was taking them all in to get the impact, but there wasn't much to choose. After the first shock they all began to make noises, then words came, and then, as the full beauty of it hit them, the words petered out.

All but Archer's. "You have signed a statement," he told Wolfe, "to the effect that Zeck told Rackham he could produce evidence that would convict him of murder, and that Rackham thereupon shot Zeck. Now you say, in contradiction—"

"There is no contradiction," Wolfe declared. "The fact of Rackham's innocence would have been no defense against evidence manufactured by Zeck, and Rackham knew it. Innocent as he was—of this murder, that is—he knew what Zeck was capable of."

"You have said that you think Rackham killed his wife, but that you have no proof."

"I have not," Wolfe snapped. "Read your transcripts."

"I shall. And you now say that you think Rackham did not kill his wife?"

"Not that I think he didn't. I know he didn't, because I know who did." Wolfe flipped a hand. "I've known that from the beginning. That night in April, when Mr. Goodwin phoned me that Mrs. Rackham had been murdered, I knew who had murdered her. But I also knew that the interests of Arnold Zeck were involved and I dared not move openly. So I—but you know all about that." Wolfe turned to me. "Archie. Precautions may not be required, but you might as well take them."

I opened a desk drawer and got out the Grisson .38. My favorite Colt, taken from me in Zeck's garage antechamber, was gone forever. After a glance at the cylinder I dropped the Grisson in my side pocket and as I did so lifted my head to the audience. As if they had all been on one circuit, the six pairs of eyes left me and went to Wolfe.

"I don't like this," Archer said in a tight voice. "I am here officially, and I don't like it. I want to speak to you privately."

Wolfe shook his head. "It's much better this way, Mr. Archer, believe me. We're not in your county, and you're free to leave if it gets too much for you, but—"

"I don't want to leave. I want a talk with you. If you knew, that night, who had killed Mrs. Rackham, I intend to—"

"It is," Wolfe said cuttingly, "of no importance what you intend. You have had five months to implement your intentions, and where are you? I admit that up to three days ago I had one big advantage over you, but not since then—not since I told you of the package I got with a cylinder of tear gas in it, and of the phone call from Mr. Zeck. That brought you even with me. It was after noon on a Friday that Mrs. Rackham left here after hiring me. It was the next morning, Saturday, that I received that package and the phone call from Zeck. How had he learned about it? Apparently he even knew the amount of the check she had given me. How? From whom?"

I was not really itching to shoot anybody. So I got up and unobtrusively moved around back of them, to the rear of the chair that was occupied by Calvin Leeds. Wolfe was proceeding.

"It was not inconceivable that Mrs. Rackham had told someone else about it, her daughter-in-law or her secretary, or even her husband, but it was most unlikely, in view of her insistence on secrecy. She said she had confided in no one except her cousin, Calvin Leeds." Wolfe's head jerked right and he snapped, "That's correct, Mr. Leeds?"

Being back of Leeds, I couldn't see his face, but there was no difficulty about hearing him, since he spoke much too loud.

"Certainly," he said. "Up to then—before she came to see you—certainly."

"Good," Wolfe said approvingly. "You're already drawing up your lines of defense. You'll need them."

"What you're doing," Leeds said, still too loud, "if I understand you—you're intimating that I told Zeck about my cousin's coming here and hiring you. You're intimating that in front of witnesses."

"That's right," Wolfe agreed. "But it's not vital to me; I mention it chiefly to explain why I suspected you of duplicity, and of being involved in some way with Arnold Zeck even before Mr. Goodwin left here that day to go up there. It draws attention to you, no doubt of that; but it is not primary evidence that you murdered your cousin. The proof that it was you who killed her was given to me on the phone that night by Mr. Goodwin."

There were stirrings and little noises. Leeds ignored them.

"So," he said, not so loud now, "you're actually accusing me before witnesses of murdering my cousin?"

"I'm accusing you of that, yes, sir, but also I'm accusing you of something much worse than that." Wolfe spat it at him. "I'm accusing you of deliberately and ruthlessly, to protect yourself from the consequences of your murder of your cousin for the money you would inherit from her, thrusting that knife into the belly of a dog that loved you and trusted you!"

Leeds started up, but hadn't got far when my hands were on his shoulders, and with plenty of pressure. He let down. I moved my hands to the back of his chair.

Wolfe's voice was cold and cutting. "No one could have done that but you, Mr. Leeds. In the woods at night, that trained dog would not have gone far from its mistress. Someone else might possibly have killed the dog first and then her, but it wasn't done that way, because the knife was left in the dog. And if someone else, permitted to get close to her, had succeeded in killing her with a sudden savage thrust and then defended himself against the dog's attack, it is not believable that he could have stopped so ferocious a beast by burying the knife in its side without himself getting a single toothmark on him. You know those dogs; you wouldn't be-lieve it; neither will I.

"No, Mr. Leeds, it could have been only you. When Mr. Goodwin went on to your house and you stayed out at the kennels, you joined your cousin on her walk in the woods. I doubt if the dog would have permitted even you to stab her to death in its presence; I don't know; but you didn't have to. You sent the dog away momentarily, and, when the knife had done its work on your cousin, you with-drew it, stood there in the dark with the knife in your hand, and called the dog to come. It came, and despite the smell of fresh blood, it behaved itself because it loved and trusted you. You could have spared it; you could have taken it home with you; but no. That would have put you in danger. It had to die for you, and by your hand."

Wolfe took a breath. "To this point I know I am right; now con-jecture enters. You stabbed the dog, of course, burying the blade in its belly, but did you leave the knife there intentionally, to prevent a gush of blood on you, or did the animal convulsively leap from you at the feel of the prick, jerking the knife from your grasp? How-ever that may be, all you could do was make for home, losing no time, for you must show yourself to Mr. Goodwin as soon as pos-sible. So you did that. You said good night and went to bed. I don't think you slept; you may even have heard the dog's whimpering outside the door, after it had dragged itself there; but maybe not, since it was beneath Mr. Goodwin's window, not yours. You pre-tended sleep, of course, when he came for you."

Leeds was keeping his head up, but I could see his hands gripping his legs just above the knees.

"You used that dog," Wolfe went on, his voice as icy as Arnold Zeck's had ever been, "even after it died. You were remorseless to your dead friend. To impress Mr. Goodwin, you were overcome with emotion at the thought that, though you had given the dog to your cousin two years ago, it had come to your doorstep to die. It had not come to your doorstep to die, Mr. Leeds, and you knew it; it had come there to try to get at you. It wanted to sink its teeth in you just once. I say you knew it, because when you squatted beside the dog and put your hand on it, it snarled. It would not have snarled if it had felt your hand as the soothing and sympathetic touch of a trusted friend in its last agony; indeed not; it snarled because it knew you, at the end, to be unworthy of its love and trust, and it scorned and hated you. That snarl alone is enough to convict you. Do you remember that snarl, Mr. Leeds? Will you ever forget it? Your old friend Nobby, his last words for you—"

Leeds' head went forward, dropping, and his hands came up to cover his face.

He made no sound, and no one else did either. The silence darted around us and into us, coming out from Leeds. Then Lina Darrow took in a breath with a sighing, sobbing sound, and Annabel got up and went to her.

"Take him, Mr. Archer," Wolfe said grimly. "I'm through with him, and it's about time."

22

I'm sitting at a window overlooking a fiord, typing this on a new portable I bought for the trip. In here it's pleasant. It's late in the season for outdoors in Norway, but if you run hard to keep your blood going you can stand it.

I got a letter yesterday which read as follows:

Dear Archie:

The chickens came from Mr. Haskins Friday, four of them, and they were satisfactory. Marko came to dinner. He misses Fritz, he says. I have given Fritz a raise.

Mr. Cramer dropped in for a talk one day last week. He made some rather pointed comments about you, but on the whole behaved himself tolerably.

I am writing this longhand because I do not like the way the man sent by the agency types.

Vanda peetersiana has a raceme 29 in. long. Its longest last year was 22 in. We have found three snails in the warm room. I thought of mailing them to Mr. Hewitt but didn't.

Mr. Leeds hanged himself in the jail at White Plains yesterday and was dead when discovered. That of course cancels your

promise to Mr. Archer to return in time for the trial, but I trust
you will not use it as an excuse to prolong your stay.

We have received your letters and they were most welcome.
I have received an offer of $315 for the furniture in your office
but am insisting on $350. Fritz says he has written you. I am
beginning to feel more like myself.

My best regards,
NW

I let Lily read it. "Darn him anyhow," she said. "No message, not
a mention of me. My Pete! Huh. Fickle Fatty."

"You'd be the last," I told her, "that he'd ever send a message to.
You're the only woman that ever got close enough to him, at least
in my time, to make him smell of perfume."